THE BEST OF KATHLEEN NORRIS

KATHLEEN NORRIS

THE BEST OF
Kathleen Norris

HANOVER HOUSE
Garden City, New York

CONTENTS

DEDICATORY
BY KATHLEEN NORRIS

"Here they are, my fifty men and women," wrote Browning, in presenting to his adored wife a collection of his poems. And with a faint and faraway echo of Browning's phrase I introduce this new collection that includes some fifty men and women of my own creating, gathered because I especially like them, or someone else has especially liked them, or because they fill out a cross section of the work that has given me so much pleasure since MOTHER, my first book, was published in 1912.

Three essays are here, two of them love letters, MY CALIFORNIA and MY SAN FRANCISCO, which present their own reason for being, their own apologia, coming from my hand. The third is BEAUTY IN LETTERS which was written to order for a magazine that was handling a series of "Beauties in the Arts," but that has pleased me by getting itself into more than one college course.

MOTHER is of course here. It was Arthur Guitterman, I think, who suggested that President Theodore Roosevelt should institute the "Order of the Stork" in its honor; he never did. But Mr. Roosevelt did climb the three flights to my 92nd Street apartment one day, to tell me he liked it. And what value that liking was to a beginner only that beginner knows! Once more it is gratefully acknowledged.

The Irish-in-New York stories became a regular series and gave me real delight, for my mail took on the delicate flavor of a brogue, and more than one woman wrote me that I must have known her "Auntie Mag" or the "Cahills' Cousin Dan." Writing these stories a wind from my lost country blew beside me, and I was again a small girl, safe in the warm kitchen atmosphere of Old Country gossip and the sound of kindly laughter, and the scent of tea.

Two or three of the other short stories won mild distinctions here and there, and there was a letter about "The Mother of Angela Hogan" that came from a remote Irish parish, to fill my eyes with tears whenever I read it. THE AMERICAN FLAGGS would be in the first five, if I listed my own favorites among some eighty published novels, exactly why I don't know. The name was selected as a pun, but it brought me a flood of letters from patriotic Flaggs all over the country, boasting Revere bowls, samplers, old blue bedspreads and old blue china, and Pembroke chests. I was offered spinning wheels and warming pans at moderate prices, and threatened with one lawsuit because of a coincidence in given names. "Thomas Jefferson Flagg is my husband's name, and my son's," one woman wrote haughtily. "You have taken a liberty, and frankly, I don't like it."

Finally, here is my first play. It has not before seen the light of day. I had hoped for the footlights, but playwriting evidently has its own sinister requisites, and my Remington never studied them. Anyway, I'm very pleased to see it in print.

Dickens' own name for himself was the "Inimitable," and the hundred years that have passed since he said it have underscored it afresh with every generation. There were "sets" of books on the shelves of the old country house where I grew up,—Scott and Bulwer-Lytton, Thackeray and Wilkie Collins, Kingsley and Trollope. But it was the Dickens books that were first worn to thumbed pages and loose covers. We dragged them on picnics, we read them by early dawn and late firelight. They became part of us, and we who were children in the last decades of the old century felt ourselves part of them.

Charles Dickens, I dedicate this book to you, in the wonderful words Bret Harte wrote from a mining camp in California, when the news went forth that your chair and your desk were empty, at Gad's Hill, in London:

> ". . . and on that grave where English oak and holly
> With laurel leaves entwine,
> Oh, deem it not a too presumptive folly,
> This spray of western pine."

THE BEST OF KATHLEEN NORRIS

Mother

CHAPTER I

"Well, we couldn't have much worse weather than this for the last week of
school, could we?" Margaret Paget said in discouragement. She stood at
one of the school windows, her hands thrust deep in her coat pockets for
warmth, her eyes following the whirling course of the storm that howled
outside. The day had commenced with snow, but now, at twelve o'clock,
the rain was falling in sheets, and the barren schoolhouse yard and the
playshed roof ran muddy streams of water.

Margaret had taught in this schoolroom for nearly four years now, ever
since her seventeenth birthday, and she knew every feature of the big
bare room by heart, and every detail of the length of village street that
the high, uncurtained windows commanded. She had stood at this window
in all weathers: when locust and lilac made even ugly little Weston enchanting, and all the windows were open to floods of sweet spring air;
when the dry heat of autumn burned over the world; when the common
little houses and barns, and the bare trees, lay dazzling and transfigured
under the first snowfall, and the wood crackled in the schoolroom stove;
and when, as to-day, mid-winter rains swept drearily past the windows,
and the children must have the lights lighted for their writing lesson. She
was tired of it all, with an utter and hopeless weariness. Tired of the bells,
and the whispering, and the shuffling feet, of the books that smelled of
pencil-dust and ink and little dusty fingers; tired of the blackboards,
cleaned in great irregular scallops by small and zealous arms; of the clear-
ticking big clock; of little girls who sulked, and little girls who cried after
hours in the hall because they had lost their lunch baskets or their overshoes, and little girls who had colds in their heads, and no handkerchiefs.
Looking out into the gray day and the rain, Margaret said to herself that
she was *sick* of it all!

There were no little girls in the schoolroom now. They were for the most part downstairs in the big playroom, discussing cold lunches, and planning, presumably, the joys of the closely approaching holidays. One or two windows had been partially opened to air the room in their absence, and Margaret's only companion was another teacher, Emily Porter, a cheerful little widow, whose plain rosy face was in marked contrast to the younger woman's unusual beauty.

Mrs. Porter loved Margaret and admired her very much, but she herself loved teaching. She had had a hard fight to secure this position a few years ago; it meant comfort to her and her children, and it still seemed to her a miracle of God's working, after her years of struggle and worry. She could not understand why Margaret wanted anything better; what better thing indeed could life hold! Sometimes, looking admiringly at her associate's crown of tawny braids, at the dark eyes and the exquisite lines of mouth and forehead, Mrs. Porter would find herself sympathetic with the girl's vague discontent and longings, to the extent of wishing that some larger social circle than that of Weston might have a chance to appreciate Margaret Paget's beauty. But, after all, sensible little Mrs. Porter would say to herself, Weston was a "nice" town, only four hours from New York, absolutely up-to-date; and Weston's best people were all "nice," and the Paget girls were very popular, and "went everywhere,"—young people were just discontented and exacting, that was all!

She came to Margaret's side now, buttoned snugly into her own storm coat, and they looked out at the rain together. Nothing alive was in sight. The bare trees tossed in the wind, and a garden gate halfway down the row of little shabby cottages banged and banged.

"Shame—this is the worst yet!" Mrs. Porter said. "You aren't going home to lunch in all this, Margaret?"

"Oh, I don't know," Margaret said despondently. "I'm so dead that I'd make a cup of tea here if I didn't think Mother would worry and send Julie over with lunch."

"I brought some bread and butter—but not much. I hoped it would hold up. I hate to leave Tom and Sister alone all day," Mrs. Porter said dubiously. "There's tea and some of those bouillon cubes and some crackers left. But you're so tired, I don't know but what you ought to have a hearty lunch."

"Oh, I'm not hungry." Margaret dropped into a desk, put her elbows on it, pushed her hair off her forehead. The other woman saw a tear slip by the lowered, long lashes.

"You're exhausted, aren't you, Margaret?" she said suddenly.

The little tenderness was too much. Margaret's lip shook.

"Dead!" she said unsteadily. Presently she added, with an effort at cheerfulness, "I'm just cross, I guess, Emily; don't mind me! I'm tired out with examinations and"—her eyes filled again—"and I'm sick of wet cold weather and rain and snow," she added childishly. "Our house is full of muddy rubbers and wet clothes! Other people go places and do pleasant things," said Margaret, her breast rising and falling stormily; "but nothing ever happens to us except broken arms, and bills, and boilers bursting, and chicken-pox! It's drudge, drudge, drudge, from morning until night!"

With a sudden little gesture of abandonment she found a handkerchief in her belt, and pressed it, still folded, against her eyes. Mrs. Porter watched her solicitously but silently. Outside the schoolroom windows the wind battered furiously, and rain slapped steadily against the panes.

"Well!" the girl said resolutely and suddenly. And after a moment she added frankly, "I think the real trouble to-day, Emily, is that we just heard of Betty Forsythe's engagement—she was my brother's girl, you know; he's admired her ever since she got into High School, and of course Bruce is going to feel awfully bad."

"Betty engaged? Who to?" Mrs. Porter was interested.

"To that man—boy, rather, he's only twenty-one—who's been visiting the Redmans," Margaret said. "She's only known him two weeks."

"Gracious! And she's only eighteen——"

"Not quite eighteen. She and my sister, Julie, were in my first class four years ago; they're the same age," Margaret said. "She came fluttering over to tell us last night, wearing a diamond the size of a marble! Of course"— Margaret was loyal—"I don't think there's a jealous bone in Julie's body; still, it's pretty hard! Here's Julie plugging away to get through the Normal School, so that she can teach all the rest of her life, and Betty's been to California, and been to Europe, and now is going to marry a rich New York man! Betty's the only child, you know, so, of course, she has everything. It seems so unfair, for Mr. Forsythe's salary is exactly what Dad's is; yet they can travel, and keep two maids, and entertain all the time! And as for family, why, Mother's family is one of the finest in the country, and Dad's had two uncles who were judges—and what were the Forsythes! However"—Margaret dried her eyes and put away her handkerchief— "however, it's for Bruce I mind most!"

"Bruce is only three years older than you are, twenty-three or four," Mrs. Porter smiled.

"Yes, but he's not the kind that forgets!" Margaret's flush was a little resentful. "Oh, of course, you can laugh, Emily. I know that there are plenty of people who don't mind dragging along day after day, working and eating and sleeping—but I'm not that kind!" she went on moodily. "I used to hope that things would be different; it makes me sick to think how brave I was; but now here's Ju coming along and Ted growing up, and Bruce's girl throwing him over—it's all so *unfair!* I look at the Cutter girls, nearly fifty, and running the post office for thirty years, and Mary Page in the Library, and the Norberrys painting pillows—and I could scream!"

"Things will take a turn for the better some day, Margaret," said the other woman, soothingly; "and as time goes on you'll find yourself getting more and more pleasure out of your work, as I do. Why, I've never been so securely happy in my life as I am now. You'll feel differently some day."

"Maybe," Margaret assented unenthusiastically. There was a pause. Perhaps the girl was thinking that to teach school, live in a plain little cottage on the unfashionable Bridge Road, take two roomers, and cook and sew and plan for Tom and little Emily, as Mrs. Porter did, was not quite an ideal existence.

"You're an angel, anyway, Emily," said she, affectionately, a little shamefacedly. "Don't mind my growling. I don't do it very often. But I look about at other people, and then realize how my mother's slaved for twenty years and how my father's been tied down, and I've come to the conclusion that while there may have been a time when a woman could keep a house, tend a garden, sew and spin and raise twelve children, things are different now; life is more complicated. You owe your husband something, you owe yourself something. I want to get on, to study and travel, to be a companion to my husband. I don't want to be a mere upper servant!"

"No, of course not," assented Mrs. Porter, vaguely, soothingly.

"Well, if we are going to stay here, I'll light the stove," Margaret said after a pause. "B-r-r-r! this room gets cold with the windows open! I wonder why Kelly doesn't bring us more wood?"

"I guess—I'll stay!" Mrs. Porter said uncertainly, following her to the big book closet off the schoolroom, where a little gas stove and a small china closet occupied one wide shelf. The water for the tea and bouillon was put over the flame in a tiny enamelled saucepan; they set forth on a fringed napkin crackers and sugar and spoons.

At this point a small girl of eleven with a brilliant, tawny head, and a wide and toothless smile, opened the door cautiously, and said, blinking rapidly with excitement—

"Mark, Mother theth pleath may thee come in?"

This was Rebecca, one of Margaret's five younger brothers and sisters, and a pupil of the school herself. Margaret smiled at the eager little face.

"Hello, darling! Is Mother here? Certainly she can! I believe"—she said, turning, suddenly radiant, to Mrs. Porter—"I'll just *bet you* she's brought us some lunch!"

"Thee brought uth our luncheth—eggth and thpith caketh and everything!" exulted Rebecca, vanishing, and a moment later Mrs. Paget appeared.

She was a tall woman, slender but large of build, and showing, under a shabby raincoat and well pinned-up skirt, the gracious generous lines of shoulders and hips, the deep-bosomed erect figure that is rarely seen except in old daguerreotypes, or the ideal of some artist two generations ago. The storm to-day had blown an unusual color into her thin cheeks, her bright, deep eyes were like Margaret's, but the hair that once had shown an equally golden lustre was dull and smooth now, and touched with gray. She came in smiling, and a little breathless.

"Mother, you didn't come out in all this rain just to bring us our lunches!" Margaret protested, kissing the cold, fresh face.

"Well, look at the lunch you silly girls were going to eat!" Mrs. Paget protested in turn, in a voice rich with amusement. "I love to walk in the rain, Mark; I used to love it when I was a girl. Tom and Sister are at our house, Mrs. Porter, playing with Duncan and Baby. I'll keep them until after school, then I'll send them over to walk home with you."

"Oh, you are an angel!" said the younger mother, gratefully. And "You *are* an angel, Mother!" Margaret echoed, as Mrs. Paget opened a shabby suitcase, and took from it a large jar of hot rich soup, a little blue bowl of stuffed eggs, half a fragrant whole-wheat loaf in a white napkin, a little glass full of sweet butter, and some of the spice cakes to which Rebecca had already enthusiastically alluded.

"There!" said she, pleased with their delight, "now take your time, you've got three-quarters of an hour. Julie devilled the eggs, and the sweet-butter man happened to come just as I was starting."

"Delicious! You've saved our lives," Margaret said, busy with cups and spoons. "You'll stay, Mother?" she broke off suddenly, as Mrs. Paget closed the suitcase.

"I can't, dear! I must go back to the children," her mother said cheerfully. No coaxing proving of any avail, Margaret went with her to the top of the hall stairs.

"What's my girl worrying about?" Mrs. Paget asked, with a keen glance at Margaret's face.

"Oh, nothing!" Margaret used both hands to button the top button of her mother's coat. "I was hungry and cold, and I didn't want to walk home in the rain!" she confessed, raising her eyes to the eyes so near her own.

"Well, go back to your lunch," Mrs. Paget urged, after a brief pause, not quite satisfied with the explanation. Margaret kissed her again, watched her descend the stairs, and leaning over the banister called down to her softly:

"Don't worry about *me*, Mother!"

"No—no—no!" her mother called back brightly. Indeed, Margaret reflected, going back to the much-cheered Emily, it was not in her nature to worry.

No, Mother never worried, or if she did, nobody ever knew it. Care, fatigue, responsibility, hard long years of busy days and broken nights had left their mark on her face; the old beauty that had been hers was chiselled to a mere pure outline now; but there was a contagious serenity in Mrs. Paget's smile, a clear steadiness in her calm eyes, and her forehead, beneath an unfashionably plain sweep of hair, was untroubled and smooth.

The children's mother was a simple woman; so absorbed in the hourly problems attendant upon the housing and feeding of her husband and family that her own personal ambitions, if she had any, were quite lost sight of, and the actual outlines of her character were forgotten by every one, herself included. If her busy day marched successfully to nightfall; if darkness found her husband reading in his big chair, the younger children sprawled safe and asleep in the shabby nursery, the older ones contented with books or games, the clothes sprinkled, the bread set, the kitchen dark and clean; Mrs. Paget asked no more of life. She would sit, her overflowing workbasket beside her, looking from one absorbed face to another, thinking perhaps of Julie's new school dress, of Ted's impending siege with the dentist, or of the old bureau up attic that might be mended for Bruce's room. "Thank God we have all warm beds," she would say, when they all went upstairs, yawning and chilly.

She had married, at twenty, the man she loved, and had found him better than her dreams in many ways, and perhaps disappointing in some few others, but "the best man in the world" for all that. That for more than twenty years he had been satisfied to stand for nine hours daily behind one dingy desk, and to carry home to her his unopened salary envelope twice a month, she found only admirable. Daddy was "steady," he was "so gentle with the children," he was "the easiest man in the world to cook for." "Bless his heart, no woman ever had less to worry over in her husband!" she would say, looking from her kitchen window to the garden where he trained the pea-vines, with the children's yellow heads bobbing about him. She never analyzed his character, much less criticised him. Good and bad, he was taken for granted; she was much more lenient to him than to any of the children. She welcomed the fast-coming babies as gifts from God, marvelled over their tiny perfectness, dreamed over the soft relaxed little forms with a heart almost too full for prayer. She was, in a word, old-fashioned, hopelessly out of the modern current of thoughts and events. She secretly regarded her children as marvellous, even while she laughed down their youthful conceit and punished their naughtiness.

Thinking a little of all these things, as a girl with her own wifehood and motherhood all before her does think, Margaret went back to her hot luncheon. One o'clock found her at her desk, refreshed in spirit by her little outburst, and much fortified in body. The room was well aired, and a reinforced fire roared in the little stove. One of the children had brought her a spray of pine, and the spicy fragrance of it reminded her that Christmas and the Christmas vacation were near; her mind was pleasantly busy with anticipation of the play that the Pagets always wrote and performed some time during the holidays, and with the New Year's costume dance at the Hall, and a dozen lesser festivities.

Suddenly, in the midst of a droning spelling lesson, there was a jarring interruption. From the world outside came a child's shrill screaming, which was instantly drowned in a chorus of frightened voices, and in the schoolroom below her own Margaret heard a thundering rush of feet, and answering screams. With a suffocating terror at her heart she ran to the window, followed by every child in the room.

The rain had stopped now, and the sky showed a pale, cold, yellow light low in the west. At the schoolhouse gate an immense limousine had come to a stop. The driver, his face alone visible between a great leather coat and visored leather cap, was talking unheard above the din. A tall woman, completely enveloped in sealskins, had evidently jumped from the limousine, and now held in her arms what made Margaret's heart turn sick and cold, the limp figure of a small girl.

About these central figures there surged the terrified crying small children of the just-dismissed primer class, and in the half moment that Margaret watched, Mrs. Porter, white and shaking, and another teacher, Ethel Elliot, an always excitable girl, who was now sobbing and chattering hysterically, ran out from the school, each followed by her own class of crowding and excited boys and girls.

With one horrified exclamation, Margaret ran downstairs, and out to the gate. Mrs. Porter caught at her arm as she passed her in the path.

"Oh, my God, Margaret! It's poor little Dorothy Scott!" she said. "They've killed her. The car went completely over her!"

"Oh, Margaret, don't go near, oh, how can you!" screamed Miss Elliot. "Oh, and she's all they have! Who'll tell her mother!"

With astonishing ease, for the children gladly recognized authority, Margaret pushed through the group to the motor-car.

"Stop screaming—stop that shouting at once—keep still, every one of you!" she said angrily, shaking various shoulders as she went with such good effect that the voice of the woman in sealskins could be heard by the time Margaret reached her.

"I don't think she's badly hurt!" said this woman, nervously and eagerly. She was evidently badly shaken, and was very white. "Do quiet them, can't you?" she said, with a sort of apprehensive impatience. "Can't we take her somewhere, and get a doctor? Can't we get out of this?"

Margaret took the child in her own arms. Little Dorothy roared afresh, but to Margaret's unspeakable relief she twisted about and locked her arms tightly about the loved teacher's neck. The other woman watched them anxiously.

"That blood on her frock's just nosebleed," she said; "but I think the car went over her! I assure you we were running very slowly. How it happened——! But I don't think she was struck."

"Nosebleed!" Margaret echoed, with a great breath. "No," she said quietly, over the agitated little head; "I don't think she's much hurt. We'll take her in. Now, look here, children," she added loudly to the assembled pupils of the Weston Grammar School, whom mere curiosity had somewhat quieted, "I want every one of you children to go back to your schoolrooms; do you understand? Dorothy's had a bad scare, but she's got no bones broken, and we're going to have a doctor see that she's all right. I want you to see how quiet you can be. Mrs. Porter, may my class go into your room a little while?"

"Certainly," said Mrs. Porter, eager to coöperate, and much relieved to have her share of the episode take this form. "Form lines, children," she added calmly.

"Ted," said Margaret to her own small brother, who was one of Mrs. Porter's pupils, and who had edged closer to her than any boy unprivileged by relationship dared, "will you go down the street, and ask old Doctor Potts to come here? And then go tell Dorothy's mother that Dorothy has had a little bump, and that Miss Paget says she's all right, but that she'd like her mother to come for her."

"Sure I will, Mark!" Theodore responded enthusiastically, departing on a run.

"Mama!" sobbed the little sufferer at this point, hearing a familiar word.

"Yes, darling, you want Mama, don't you?" Margaret said soothingly, as she started with her burden up the schoolhouse steps. "What were you doing, Dorothy," she went on pleasantly, "to get under that big car?"

"I dropped my ball!" wailed the small girl, her tears beginning afresh, "and it rolled and rolled. And I didn't see the automobile, and I *didn't* see it! And I fell down and b-b-bumped my nose!"

"Well, I should think you did!" Margaret said, laughing. "Mother won't know you at all with such a muddy face and such a muddy dress!"

Dorothy laughed shakily at this, and several other little girls, passing in orderly file, laughed heartily. Margaret crossed the lines of children to the room where they played and ate their lunches on wet days. She shut herself in with the child and the fur-clad lady.

"Now you're all right!" said Margaret, gayly. And Dorothy was presently comfortable in a big chair, wrapped in a blanket, with her face washed, and her head dropped languidly back against her chair, as became an interesting invalid. The Irish janitor was facetious as he replenished the fire, and made her laugh again. Margaret gave her a numerical chart to play with, and saw with satisfaction that the little head was bent interestedly over it.

Quiet fell upon the school; the muffled sound of lessons recited in concert presently reached them. Theodore returned, reporting that the doctor would come as soon as he could and that Dorothy's mother was away at a card-party, but that Dorothy's "girl" would come for her as soon as the bread was out of the oven. There was nothing to do but wait.

"It seems a miracle," said the strange lady, in a low tone, when she and Margaret were alone again with the child. "But I don't believe she was scratched!"

"I don't think so," Margaret agreed. "Mother says no child who can cry is very badly hurt."

"They made such a horrible noise," said the other, sighing wearily. She passed a white hand, with one or two blazing great stones upon it, across her forehead. Margaret had leisure now to notice that by all signs this was a very great lady indeed. The quality of her furs, the glimpse of her gown that the loosened coat showed, her rings, and most of all the tones of her voice, the authority of her manner, the well-groomed hair and skin and hands, all marked the thoroughbred.

"Do you know that you managed that situation very cleverly just now?" said the lady, with a keen glance that made Margaret color. "One has such a dread of the crowd, just public sentiment, you know. Some officious bystander calls the police, they crowd against your driver, perhaps a brick gets thrown. We had an experience in England once——" She paused, then interrupted herself. "But I don't know your name?" she said brightly.

Margaret supplied it, was led to talk a little of her own people.

"Seven of you, eh? Seven's too many," said the visitor, with the assurance that Margaret was to learn characterized her. "I've two myself, two girls," she went on. "I wanted a boy, but they're nice girls. And you've six brothers and sisters? Are they all as handsome as you and this Teddy of yours? And why do you like teaching?"

"Why do I like it?" Margaret said, enjoying these confidences and the unusual experience of sitting idle in mid-afternoon. "I don't, I hate it."

"I see. But then why don't you come down to New York, and do something else?" the other woman asked.

"I'm needed at home, and I don't know any one there," Margaret said simply.

"I see," the lady said again thoughtfully. There was a pause. Then the same speaker said reminiscently, "I taught school once for three months when I was a girl, to show my father I could support myself."

"I've taught for four years," Margaret said.

"Well, if you ever want to try something else—there are such lots of fascinating things a girl can do now—be sure you come and see me about it," the stranger said. "I am Mrs. Carr-Boldt, of New York."

Margaret's amazed eyes flashed to Mrs. Carr-Boldt's face; her cheeks crimsoned.

"Mrs. Carr-Boldt!" she echoed blankly.

"Why not?" smiled the lady, not at all displeased.

"Why," stammered Margaret, laughing and rosy, "why, nothing—only I never dreamed who you were!" she finished, a little confused.

And indeed it never afterward seemed to her anything short of a miracle that brought the New York society woman—famed on two continents and from ocean to ocean for her jewels, her entertainments, her gowns, her establishments—into a Weston schoolroom, and into Margaret Paget's life.

"I was on my way to New York now," said Mrs. Carr-Boldt.

"I don't see why you should be delayed," Margaret said, glad to be able to speak normally, with such a fast-beating and pleasantly excited heart. "I'm sure Dorothy's all right."

"Oh, I'd rather wait. I like my company," said the other. And Margaret decided in that instant that there never was a more deservedly admired and copied and quoted woman.

Presently their chat was interrupted by the tramp of the departing school children; the other teachers peeped in, were reassured, and went their ways. Then came the doctor, to pronounce the entirely cheerful Dorothy unhurt, and to bestow upon her some hoarhound drops. Mrs. Carr-Boldt settled at once with the doctor, and when Margaret saw the size of the bill that was pressed into his hand, she realized that she had done her old friend a good turn.

"Use it up on your poor people," said Mrs. Carr-Boldt, to his protestations; and when he had gone, and Dorothy's "girl" appeared, she tipped that worthy and amazed Teuton, and after promising Dorothy a big doll from a New York shop, sent the child and maid home in the car.

"I hope this hasn't upset your plans," Margaret said, as they stood waiting in the doorway. It was nearly five o'clock, the school was empty and silent.

"No, not exactly. I had hoped to get home for dinner. But I think I'll get Woolcock to take me back to Dayton; I've some very dear friends there who'll give me a cup of tea. Then I'll come back this way and get home, by ten, I should think, for a late supper." Then, as the limousine appeared, Mrs. Carr-Boldt took both Margaret's hands in hers, and said, "And now good-bye, my dear girl. I've got your address, and I'm going to send you something pretty to remember me by. You saved me from I don't know what annoyance and publicity. And don't forget that when you come to New York I'm going to help you meet the people you want to, and give you a start if I can. You're far too clever and good-looking to waste your life down here. Good-bye!"

"Good-bye!" Margaret said, her cheeks brilliant, her head awhirl.

She stood unmindful of the chilly evening air, watching the car wheel and slip into the gloom. The rain was over; a dying wind moaned mysteriously through the dusk. Margaret went slowly upstairs, pinned on her hat, buttoned her long coat snugly about her. She locked the schoolroom door, and, turning the corner, plunged her hands into her pockets, and faced the wind bravely. Deepening darkness and coldness were about her, but she felt surrounded by the warmth and brightness of her dreams. She saw the brilliant streets of a big city, the carriages and motor-cars coming and going, the idle, lovely women in their sumptuous gowns and hats. These things were real, near—almost attainable—to-night.

"Mrs. Carr-Boldt!" Margaret said, "the darling! I wonder if I'll ever see her again!"

CHAPTER II

Life in the shabby, commonplace house that sheltered the Paget family sometimes really did seem to proceed, as Margaret had suggested, in a long chain of violent shocks, narrow escapes, and closely averted catastrophes. No sooner was Duncan's rash pronounced not to be scarlet fever than Robert swallowed a penny, or Beck set fire to the dining-room wastebasket, or Dad foresaw the immediate failure of the Weston Home Savings Bank, and the inevitable loss of his position there. Sometimes there was a paternal explosion because Bruce liked to murmur vaguely of "dandy chances in Manila," or because Julie, pretty, excitable, and sixteen, had an occasional dose of stage fever, and would stammer desperately between convulsive sobs that she wasn't half as much afraid of "the terrible temptations of the life" as she was afraid of dying a poky old maid in Weston. In short, the home was crowded, the Pagets were poor, and every one of the seven possessed a spirited and distinct entity. All the mother's effort could not keep them always contented. Growing ambitions made the Weston horizon seem narrow and mean, and the young eyes that could not see beyond to-morrow were often wet with rebellious tears.

Through it all they loved each other; sometimes whole weeks went by in utter harmony; the children contented over "Parches" on the hearthrug in the winter evenings, Julie singing in the morning sunlight, as she filled the vases from the shabby marguerite bushes on the lawn. But there were other times when to the dreamy studious Margaret the home circle seemed all discord, all ugly dinginess and threadbareness; the struggle for ease and beauty and refinement seemed hopeless and overwhelming. In these times she would find herself staring thoughtfully at her mother's face, bent over the mending basket, or her eyes would leave the chessboard that held her father's attention so closely, and move from his bald spot, with its encircling crown of fluffy gray, to his rosy face, with its kind, intent blue eyes and the little lines about his mouth that his moustache didn't hide—with a half-formed question in her heart. What hadn't they done, these dearest people, to be always struggling, always tired, always "behind the game?" Why should they be eternally harassed by plumbers' bills, and dentists' bills, and shoes that would wear out, and school-books that must be bought? Why weren't they holding their place in Weston society, the place to which they were entitled by right of the Quincy grandfather, and the uncles who were judges?

And in answer Margaret came despondently to the decision, "If you have children, you never have anything else!" How could Mother keep up with her friends, when for some fifteen years she had been far too busy to put on a dainty gown in the afternoon, and serve a hospitable cup of tea on the east porch? Mother was buttering bread for supper, then; opening little beds and laying out little nightgowns, starting Ted off for the milk, washing small hands and faces, soothing bumps and binding cuts, admonishing, praising, directing. Mother was only too glad to sink wearily into her rocker after dinner, and, after a few spirited visits to the rampant nursery upstairs, express the hope that nobody would come in to-night. Gradually the friends dropped away, and the social life of Weston flowed smoothly on without the Pagets.

But when Margaret began to grow up, she grasped the situation with all the keenness of a restless and ambitious nature. Weston, detested Weston, it must apparently be. Very well, she would make the best of Weston. Margaret called on her mother's old friends; she was tireless in charming little attentions. Her own first dances had not been successful; she and Bruce were not good dancers, Margaret had not been satisfied with her gowns, they both felt out of place. When Julie's dancing days came along, Margaret saw to it that everything was made much easier. She planned social evenings at home, and exhausted herself preparing for them, that Julie might know the "right people." To her mother all people were alike, if they were kind and not vulgar; Margaret felt very differently. It was a matter of the greatest satisfaction to her when Julie blossomed into a fluffy-haired butterfly, tremendously in demand, in spite of much-cleaned slippers and often-pressed frocks. Margaret arranged Christmas theatricals, May picnics, Fourth of July gatherings. She never failed Bruce when this dearest brother wanted her company; she was, as Mrs. Paget told her over and over, "the sweetest daughter any woman ever had." But deep in her heart she knew moods of bitter distaste and restlessness. The struggle did not seem worth the making; the odds against her seemed too great.

Still dreaming in the winter dark, she went through the home gate, and up the porch steps of a roomy, cheap house that had been built in the era of scalloped and pointed shingles, of colored glass embellishments around the window-panes, of perforated scroll work and wooden railings in Grecian designs. A mass of wet overshoes lay on the porch, and two or three of the weather-stained porch rockers swayed under the weight of spread wet raincoats. Two opened umbrellas wheeled in the current of air that came around the house; the porch ran water. While Margaret was adding her own rainy-day equipment to the others', a golden-brown setter, one ecstatic wriggle from nose to tail, flashed into view, and came fawning to her feet.

"Hello, Bran!" Margaret said, propping herself against the house with one hand, while she pulled at a tight overshoe. "Hello, old fellow! Well, did they lock him out?"

She let herself and a freezing gust of air into the dark hall, groping to the hat-rack for matches. While she was lighting the gas, a very pretty girl of sixteen, with crimson cheeks and tumbled soft dark hair, came to the dining-room door. This was her sister Julie, Margaret's roommate and warmest admirer, and for the last year or two her inseparable companion. Julie had her finger in a book, but now she closed it, and said affectionately between her yawns: "Come in here, darling! You must be dead."

"Don't let Bran in," cried some one from upstairs.

"He *is* in, Mother!" Margaret called back, and Rebecca and the three small boys—Theodore, the four-year-old baby, Robert, and Duncan, a grave little lad of seven—all rushed out of the dining-room together, shouting, as they fell on the delighted dog:

"Aw, leave him in! Aw, leave the poor little feller in! *Come* on, Bran, come on, old feller! Leave him in, Mark, can't we?"

Kissing and hugging the dog, and stumbling over each other and over him, they went back to the dining-room, which was warm and stuffy. A coal fire was burning low in the grate, the window-panes were beaded, and the little boys had marked their initials in the steam. They had also pushed the fringed table-cover almost off, and scattered the contents of a box of "Lotto" over the scarred walnut top. The room was shabby, ugly, comfortable. Julie and Margaret had established a tea-table in the bay window, had embroidered a cover for the wide couch, had burned the big wooden bowl that was supposedly always full of nuts or grapes or red apples. But these touches were lost in the mass of less pleasing detail. The "body Brussels" carpet was worn, the wall paper depressing, the woodwork was painted dark brown, with an imitation burl smeared in by the painter's thumb. The chairs were of several different woods and patterns, the old black walnut sideboard clumsy and battered. About the fire stood some comfortable worn chairs. Margaret dropped wearily into one of these, and the dark-eyed Julie hung over her with little affectionate attentions. The children returned to their game.

"Well, what a time you had with little Dolly Scott!" said Julie, sympathetically. "Ted's been getting it all mixed up! Tell us about it. Poor old Mark, you're all in, aren't you? Mark, would you like a cup of tea?"

"Love it!" Margaret said, a little surprised, for this luxury was not common.

"And toast—we'll toast it!" said Theodore, enthusiastically.

"No, no—no tea!" said Mrs. Paget, coming in at this point with some sewing in her hands. "Don't spoil your dinner, now, Mark dear; tea doesn't do you any good. And I think Blanche is saving the cream for an apple tapioca. Theodore, Mother wants you to go right downstairs for some coal, dear. And, Julie, you'd better start your table; it's close to six. Put up the game, Rebecca!"

[13]

There was general protest. Duncan, it seemed, needed only "two more" to win. Little Robert, who was benevolently allowed by the other children to play the game exactly as he pleased, screamed delightedly that he needed only *one* more, and showed a card upon which even the blank spaces were lavishly covered with glass. He was generously conceded the victory, and kissed by Rebecca and Julie as he made his way to his mother's lap.

"Why, this can't be Robert Paget!" said Mrs. Paget, putting aside her sewing to gather him in her arms. "Not this great, big boy!"

"Yes, I *am!*" the little fellow asserted joyously, dodging her kisses.

"Good to get home!" Margaret said luxuriously.

"You must sleep late in the morning," her mother commanded affectionately.

"Yes, because you have to be fresh for the party Monday!" exulted Julie. She had flung a white cloth over the long table, and was putting the ringed napkins down with rapid bangs. "And New Year's Eve's the dance!" she went on buoyantly. "I just love Christmas, anyway!"

"Rebecca, ask Blanche if she needs me," that was Mother.

"You'd go perfectly crazy about her, Ju, she's the most fascinating, and the most *unaffected* woman!" Margaret was full of the day's real event.

"And Mother theth that Ted and Dunc and I can have our friendth in on the day after Chrithmath to thee the Chrithmath tree!" That was Rebecca, who added, "Blanche theth no, Mother, unleth you want to make thom cream gravy for the chopth!"

"And, Mark, Eleanor asked if Bruce and you and I weren't going as Pierrot and Pierettes; she's simply *crazy* to find out!" This was Julie again; and then Margaret, coaxingly, "Do make cream gravy for Bruce, Mother. Give Baby to me!" and little Robert's elated "I know *three* things Becky's going to get for Christmas, Mark!"

"Well, I think I will, there's milk," Mrs. Paget conceded, rising. "Put Bran out, Teddy; or put him in the laundry if you want to, while we have dinner." Margaret presently followed her mother into the kitchen, stopping in a crowded passageway to tie an apron over her school gown.

"Bruce come in yet?" she said in a low voice.

Her mother flashed her a sympathetic look.

"I don't believe he's coming, Mark."

"*Isn't!* Oh, Mother! Oh, Mother, does he feel so badly about Betty?"

"I suppose so!" Mrs. Paget went on with her bread cutting.

"But, Mother, surely he didn't expect to *marry* Betty Forsythe?"

"I don't know why not, Mark. She's a sweet little thing."

"But, Mother——" Margaret was a little at a loss. "We don't seem old enough to really be getting married!" she said, a little lamely.

"Brucie came in about half-past five, and said he was going over to Richie's," Mrs. Paget said, with a sigh.

"In all this rain—that long walk!" Margaret ejaculated, as she filled a long wicker basket with sliced bread.

"I think an evening of work with Richie will do him a world of good," said his mother. There was a pause. "There's Dad. I'll go in," she said, suddenly ending it, as the front door slammed.

Margaret went in, too, to kiss her father, a tired-looking, gray-haired man close to fifty, who had taken her chair by the fire. Mrs. Paget was anxious to be assured that his shoulders and shoes were not damp.

"But your hands are icy, Daddy," said she, as she sat down behind a smoking tureen at the head of the table. "Come, have your nice hot soup, dear. Pass that to Dad, Becky, and light the other gas. What sort of a day?"

"A hard day," said Mr. Paget, heavily. "Here, one of you girls put Baby into his chair. Let go, Bob—I'm too tired to-night for monkey-shines!" He sat down stiffly. "Where's Bruce? Can't that boy remember what time we have dinner?"

"Bruce is going to have supper with Richie Williams, Dad," said Mrs. Paget, serenely. "They'll get out their blue prints afterward and have a good evening's work. Fill the glasses before you sit down, Ju. Come, Ted— put that back on the mantel. Come, Becky! Tell Daddy about what happened to-day, Mark——"

They all drew up their chairs. Robert, recently graduated from a high chair, was propped upon "The Officers of the Civil War" and "The Household Book of Verse." Julie tied on his bib, and kissed the back of his fat little neck before she slipped into her own seat. The mother sat between Ted and Duncan, for reasons that immediately became obvious. Margaret sat by her father, and attended to his needs, telling him all about the day, and laying her pretty slim hand over his as it rested beside his plate. The chops and cream gravy, as well as a mountain of baked potatoes, and various vegetables, were under discussion, when every one stopped short in surprise at hearing the doorbell ring.

"Who——?" said Margaret, turning puzzled brows to her mother, and "I'm sure I——" her mother answered, shaking her head. Ted was heard to mutter uneasily that, gee, maybe it was old Pembroke, mad because the fellers had soaked his old skate with snowballs; Julie dimpled and said, "Maybe it's flowers!" Robert shouted "Bakeryman!" more because he had recently acquired the word than because of any conviction on the subject. In the end Julie went to the door, with the four children in her wake. When she came back, she looked bewildered, and the children a little alarmed.

"It's—it's Mrs. Carr-Boldt, Mother," said Julie.

"Well, don't leave her standing there in the cold, dear!" Mrs. Paget said, rising quickly, to go into the hall. Margaret, her heart thumping with an unanalyzed premonition of something pleasant, and nervous, too, for the hospitality of the Pagets, followed her. So they were all presently crowded into the hall, Mrs. Paget all hospitality, Margaret full of a fear she would have denied that her mother would not be equal to the occasion, the children curious, Julie a little embarrassed.

The visitor, fur-clad, rain-spattered—for it was raining again—and beaming, stretched a hand to Mrs. Paget.

"You're Mrs. Paget, of course—this is an awful hour to interrupt you," she said in her big, easy way, "and there's my Miss Paget—how do you do? But you see I must get up to town to-night—in this door? I can see perfectly, thank you—and I did want a little talk with you first. Now, what a shame!"—for the gas, lighted by Theodore at this point, revealed Duncan's bib, and the napkins some of the others were still carrying. "I've interrupted your dinner! Won't you let me wait here until——"

"Perhaps—if you haven't had your supper—you will have some with us," said Mrs. Paget, a little uncertainly. Margaret inwardly shuddered, but Mrs. Carr-Boldt was gracious.

"Mrs. Paget, that's charming of you," she said. "But I had tea at Dayton, and mustn't lose another moment. I shan't dine until I get home. I'm the busiest woman in the world, you know. Now, it won't take me two minutes——"

She was seated now, her hands still deep in her muff, for the parlor was freezing cold. Mrs. Paget, with a rather bewildered look, sat down, too.

"You can run back to your dinners," said she to the children. "Take them, Julie. Mark, dear, will you help the pudding?" They all filed dutifully out of the room, and Margaret, excited and curious, continued a meal that might have been of sawdust and sand for all she knew. The strain did not last long; in about ten minutes Mrs. Paget looked into the room, with a rather worried expression, and said, a little breathlessly: "Daddy, can you come here a moment?—You're all right, dear," she added, as Mr. Paget indicated with an embarrassed gesture his well-worn housecoat. They went out together. The young people sat almost without speaking, listening to the indistinguishable murmur from the adjoining room, and smiling mysteriously at each other. Then Margaret was called, and went as far as the dining-room door, and came back to put her napkin uncertainly down at her place, hesitated, arranged her gown carefully, and finally went out again. They heard her voice with the others in the parlor . . . questioning . . . laughing . . .

Presently the low murmur broke into audible farewells; chairs were pushed back, feet scraped in the hall.

"Good-night, then!" said Mrs. Carr-Boldt's clear tones, "and so sorry to have—— Good-night, Mr. Paget!—Oh, thank you—but I'm well wrapped. Thank you! Good-night, dear! I'll see you again soon—I'll write."

And then came the honking of the car, and a great swish where it grazed a wet bush near the house. Somebody lowered the gas in the hall, and Mrs. Paget's voice said regretfully, "I wish we had had a fire in the parlor—just one of the times!—but there's no help for it." They all came in, Margaret flushed, starry-eyed; her father and mother a little serious. The three blinked at the brighter light, and fell upon the cooling chops as if eating were the important business of the moment.

"We waited the pudding," said Julie. "What *is* it?"

"Why——" Mrs. Paget began, hesitatingly. Mr. Paget briskly took the matter out of her hands.

"This lady," he said, with an air of making any further talk unnecessary, "needs a secretary, and she has offered your sister Margaret the position. That's the whole affair in a nutshell. I'm not at all sure that your mother and I think it a wise offer for Margaret to accept, and I want to say here and now that I don't want any child of mine to speak of this matter, or make it a matter of general gossip in the neighborhood. Mother, I'd like very much to have Blanche make me a fresh cup of tea."

"Wants Margaret!" gasped Julie, unaffected—so astonishing was the news—by her father's unusual sternness. "Oh, Mother! Oh, Mark! Oh, you lucky thing! When is she coming down here?"

"She isn't coming down here—she wants Mark to go to her—that's it," said her mother.

"Mark—in New York!" shrilled Theodore. Julie got up to rush around the table and kiss her sister; the younger children laughed and shouted.

"There is no occasion for all this," said Mr. Paget, but mildly, for the fresh tea had arrived. "Just quiet them down, will you, Mother? I see nothing very extraordinary in the matter. This Mrs.—Mrs. Carr-Boldt —is it?—needs a secretary and companion; and she offers the position to Mark."

"But—but she never even *saw* Mark until to-day!" marvelled Julie.

"I hardly see how that affects it, my dear!" her father observed unenthusiastically.

"Why, I think it makes it simply extraordinary!" exulted the generous little sister. "Oh, Mark, isn't this just the sort of thing you would have *wished* to happen! Secretary work—just what you love to do! And you, with your beautiful handwriting, you'll just be *invaluable* to her! And your German—and I'll bet you'll just have them all *adoring* you——!"

"Oh, Ju, if I only can do it!" burst from Margaret, with a little childish gasp. She was sitting back from the table, twisted about so that she sat sideways, her hands clasped about the top bar of her chair-back. Her tawny soft hair was loosened about her face, her dark eyes aflame. "New York she said," Margaret went on dazedly; "and Europe, and travelling everywhere! And a hundred dollars a month, and nothing to spend it on, so I can still help out here! Why, it—I can't believe it!"—she looked from one smiling interested face to another, and suddenly her radiance underwent a quick eclipse. Her lip trembled, and she tried to laugh as she pushed her chair back, and ran to the arms her mother opened. "Oh, Mother!" sobbed Margaret, clinging there, "do you want me to go—shall I go? I've always been so happy here, and I feel so ashamed of being

[17]

discontented—and I don't deserve a thing like this to happen to me!"

"Why, God bless her heart!" said Mrs. Paget, tenderly; "of course you'll go!"

"Oh, you silly! I'll never speak to you again if you don't!" laughed Julie, through sympathetic tears.

Theodore and Duncan immediately burst into a radiant reminiscence of their one brief visit to New York; Rebecca was heard to murmur that she would "vithet Mark thome day"; and the baby, tugging at his mother's elbow, asked sympathetically if Mark was naughty, and was caught between his sister's and his mother's arms and kissed by them both. Mr. Paget, picking his paper from the floor beside his chair, took an armchair by the fire, stirred the coals noisily, and while cleaning his glasses, observed rather huskily that the little girl always knew she could come back again if anything went wrong.

"But suppose I don't suit?" suggested Margaret, sitting back on her heels, refreshed by tears, and with her arms laid across her mother's lap.

"Oh, you'll *suit*," said Julie, confidently; and Mrs. Paget smoothed the girl's hair back and said affectionately, "I don't think she'll find many girls like you for the asking, Mark!"

"Reading English with the two little girls," said Margaret, dreamily, "and answering notes and invitations. And keeping books——"

"You can do that anyway," said her father, over his paper.

"And dinner lists, you know, Mother—doesn't it sound like an English story!" Margaret stopped in the middle of an ecstatic wriggle. "Mother, will you *pray* I succeed?" she said solemnly.

"Just be your own dear simple self, Mark," her mother advised. "January!" she added, with a great sigh. "It's the first break, isn't it, Dad? Think of trying to get along without our Mark!"

"January!" Julie was instantly alert. "Why, but you'll need all *sorts* of clothes!"

"Oh, she says there's a sewing woman always in the house," Margaret said, almost embarrassed by the still-unfolding advantages of the proposition. "I can have her do whatever's left over." Her father lowered his paper to give her a shrewd glance.

"I suppose somebody knows something about this Mrs. Carr-Boldt, Mother?" asked he. "She's all right, I suppose?"

"Oh, Dad, her name's *always* in the papers," Julie burst out; and the mother smiled as she said, "We'll be pretty sure of everything before we let our Mark go!" Later, when the children had been dismissed and he himself was going, rather stiffly, toward the stairs, Mr. Paget again voiced a mild doubt.

"There was a perfectly good reason for her hurry, I suppose? Old secretary deserted—got married——? She had good reason for wanting Mark in all this hurry?"

Mrs. Paget and her daughters had settled about the fire for an hour's delicious discussion, but she interrupted it to say soothingly, "It was her cousin, Dad, who's going to be married, and she's been trying to get hold of just the right person—she says she's fearfully behindhand——"

"Well, you know best," said Mr. Paget, departing a little discontentedly.

Left to the dying fire, the others talked, yawned, made a pretence of breaking up, talked and yawned again. The room grew chilly. Bruce— oldest of the children—dark, undemonstrative, weary—presently came in, and was given the news, and marvelled in his turn. Bruce and Margaret had talked of their ambitions a hundred times: of the day when he might enter college and when she might find the leisure and beauty in life for which her soul hungered. Now, as he sat with his arm about her, and her head on his shoulder, he said with generous satisfaction over and over:

"It was *coming* to you, Mark; you've earned it!"

At midnight, loitering upstairs, cold and yawning, Margaret kissed her mother and brother quietly, with whispered brief good-nights. But Julie, lying warm and snug in bed half an hour later, had a last word:

"You know, Mark, I think I'm as happy as you are—no, I'm not generous at all! It's just that it makes me feel that things do come your way finally, if you wait long enough, and that we aren't the only family in town that never has anything decent happen to it! . . . I'll miss you awfully, Mark, darling! . . . Mark, do you suppose Mother'd let me take this bed out, and just have a big couch in here? It would make the room seem so much bigger. And then I could have the girls come up here, don't you know—when they came over. . . . Think of you—you—going abroad! I'd simply die! I can't wait to tell Betty! . . . I hope to goodness Mother won't put Beck in here! . . . We've had this room a long time together, haven't we? Ever since Grandma died. Do you remember her canary, that Teddy hit with a plate? . . . I'm going to miss you terribly, Mark. But we'll write. . . ."

CHAPTER III

In the days that followed, the miracle came to be accepted by all Weston, which was much excited for a day or two over this honor done a favorite daughter, and by all the Pagets—except Margaret. Margaret went through the hours in her old, quiet manner, a little more tender and gentle perhaps than she had been; but her heart never beat normally, and she lay awake late at night, and early in the morning, thinking, thinking, thinking. She tried to realize that it was in her honor that a farewell tea was planned at the club, it was for her that her fellow-teachers were planning a good-bye luncheon; it was really she—Margaret Paget—whose voice said at the telephone a dozen times a day, "On the fourteenth.—Oh, do I? I don't *feel* calm! Can't you try to come in—I do want to see you before I go!" She dutifully repeated Bruce's careful directions; she was to give her check to an expressman, and her suitcase to a red-cap; the expressman would probably charge fifty cents, the red-cap was to have no more than fifteen. And she was to tell the latter to put her into a taxicab.

"I'll remember," Margaret assured him gratefully, but with a sense of unreality pressing almost painfully upon her. One of a million ordinary school teachers, in a million little towns—and this marvel had befallen her!

The night of the Pagets' Christmas play came, a night full of laughter and triumph; and marked for Margaret by the little parting gifts that were slipped into her hands, and by the warm good wishes that were murmured, not always steadily, by this old friend and that. When the time came to distribute plates and paper napkins, and great saucers of ice cream and sliced cake, Margaret was toasted in cold sweet lemonade; and drawing close together to "harmonize" more perfectly, the circle about her touched their glasses while they sang, "For she's a jolly good fellow." Later, when the little supper was almost over, Ethel Elliot, leaning over to lay her hand on Margaret's, began in her rich contralto:

"When other lips and other hearts . . ."

and as they all went seriously through the two verses, they stood up, one by one, and linked arms; the little circle, affectionate and admiring, that had bounded Margaret's friendships until now.

Then Christmas came, with a dark, freezing walk to the pine-spiced and candle-lighted early service in the little church, and a quicker walk home, chilled and happy and hungry, to a riotous Christmas breakfast and a littered breakfast table. The new year came, with a dance and revel, and the Pagets took one of their long tramps through the snowy afternoon, and came back hungry for a big dinner. Then there was dressmaking—Mrs. Schmidt in command, Mrs. Paget tireless at the machine, Julie all eager interest. Margaret, patiently standing to be fitted, conscious of the icy, wet touch of Mrs. Schmidt's red fingers on her bare arms, dreamily acquiescent as to buttons or hooks, was totally absent in spirit.

A trunk came, Mr. Paget very anxious that the keys should not be "fooled with" by the children. Margaret's mother packed this trunk scientifically. "No, now the shoes, Mark—now that heavy skirt," she would say. "Run get Mother some more tissue paper, Beck. You'll have to leave the big cape, dear, and you can send for it if you need it. Now the blue dress, Ju. I think that dyed so prettily, just the thing for mornings. And here's your prayer book in the tray, dear; if you go Saturday you'll want it the first thing in the morning. See, I'll put a fresh handkerchief in it——"

Margaret, relaxed and idle, in a rocker, with Duncan in her lap busily working at her locket, would say over and over:

"You're all such angels—I'll never forget it!" and wish that, knowing how sincerely she meant it, she could *feel* it a little more. Conversation languished in these days; mother and daughters feeling that time was too precious to waste speech on little things, and that their hearts were too full to touch upon the great change impending.

A night came when the Pagets went early upstairs, saying that, after all, it was not like people marrying and going to Russia; it was not like a real parting; it wasn't as if Mark couldn't come home again in four hours if anything went wrong at either end of the line. Margaret's heart was beating high and quick now; she tried to show some of the love and sorrow she knew she should have felt, she knew that she *did* feel under the hurry of her blood that made speech impossible. She went to her mother's door, slender and girlish in her white nightgown, to kiss her good-night again. Mrs. Paget's big arms went about her daughter. Margaret laid her head childishly on her mother's shoulder. Nothing of significance was said. Margaret whispered, "Mother, I love you!" Her mother said, "You were such a little thing, Mark, when I kissed you one day, without hugging you, and you said, 'Please don't love me just with your face, Mother, love me with your heart!'" Then she added, "Did you and Julie get that extra blanket down to-day, dear?—it's going to be very cold." Margaret nodded. "Good-night, little girl——" "Good-night, Mother——"

That was the real farewell, for the next morning was all confusion. They dressed hurriedly; clocks were compared, Rebecca's back buttoned; Duncan's overcoat jerked on; coffee drunk scalding hot as they stood about the kitchen table; bread barely tasted. They walked to the railway station on wet sidewalks, under a broken sky, Bruce, with Margaret's suitcase, in the lead. Weston was asleep in the gray morning, after the storm. Far and near belated cocks were crowing.

A score of old friends met Margaret at the train; there were gifts, promises, good wishes. There came a moment when it was generally felt that the Pagets should be left alone, now—the far whistle of the train beyond the bridge—the beginning of good-byes—a sudden filling of the mother's eyes that was belied by her smile.—"Good-bye, sweetest—don't knock my hat off, baby dear! Beck, darling—Oh, Ju, *do!* don't just *say* it— start me a letter to-night! ALL write to me! Good-bye, Dad, darling—all right, Bruce, I'll get right in!—good-bye! Good-bye!"

Then for the Pagets there was a walk back to the empty disorder of the house: Julie very talkative, at her father's side; Bruce walking far behind the others with his mother—and the day's familiar routine to be somehow gone through without Margaret.

But for Margaret, settling herself comfortably in the grateful warmth of the train, and watching the uncertain early sunshine brighten unfamiliar fields and farmhouses, every brilliant possibility in life seemed to be waiting. She tried to read, to think, to pray, to stare steadily out of the window; she could do nothing for more than a moment at a time. Her thoughts went backward and forward like a weaving shuttle: "How good they've all been to me! How grateful I am! Now if only, *only*, I can make good!"

"Look out for the servants!" Julie, from the depth of her sixteen-years-old wisdom had warned her sister. "The governess will hate you because she'll be afraid you'll cut her out, and Mrs. Carr-Boldt's maid will be a cat! They always are, in books."

Margaret had laughed at this advice, but in her heart she rather believed it. Her new work seemed so enchanting to her that it was not easy to believe that she did not stand in somebody's light. She was glad that by a last-moment arrangement she was to arrive at the Grand Central Station at almost the same moment as Mrs. Carr-Boldt herself, who was coming home from a three-weeks' visit in the Middle West. Margaret gave only half her attention to the flying country that was beginning to shape itself into streets and rows of houses; all the last half-hour of the trip was clouded by the nervous fear that she would somehow fail to find Mrs. Carr-Boldt in the confusion at the railroad terminal.

But happily enough the lady was found without trouble, or rather Margaret was found, felt an authoritative tap on her shoulder, caught a breath of fresh violets and a glimpse of her patron's clear-skinned, resolute face. They whirled through wet, deserted streets; Mrs. Carr-Boldt gracious and talkative, Margaret nervously interested and amused.

Their wheels presently grated against a curb, a man in livery opened the limousine door. Margaret saw an immense stone mansion facing the park, climbed a dazzling flight of wide steps, and was in a great hall that faced an interior court, where there were Florentine marble benches, and the great lifted leaves of palms. She was a little dazed by crowded impressions: impressions of height and spaciousness and richness, and opening vistas; a great marble stairway, and a landing where there was an immense designed window in clear leaded glass; rugs, tapestries, mirrors, polished wood and great chairs with brocaded seats and carved dark backs. Two little girls, heavy, well-groomed little girls—one spectacled and good-natured looking, the other rather pretty, with a mass of fair hair—were coming down the stairs with an eager little German woman. They kissed their mother, much diverted by the mad rushes and leaps of the two white poodles who accompanied them.

"These are my babies, Miss Paget," said Mrs. Carr-Boldt. "This is Victoria, who's eleven, and Harriet, who's six. And these are Monsieur——"

"Monsieur Patou and Monsieur Mouche," said Victoria, introducing the dogs with entire ease of manner. The German woman said something forcibly, and Margaret understood the child's reply in that tongue:

"Mamma won't blame you, Fräulein; Harriet and I wished them to come down!"

Presently they all went up in a luxuriously fitted little lift, Margaret being carried to the fourth floor to her own rooms, to which a little maid escorted her.

When the maid had gone Margaret walked to the door and tried it, for no reason whatever; it was shut. Her heart was beating violently. She walked into the middle of the room and looked at herself in the mirror, and laughed a little breathless laugh. Then she took off her hat carefully and went into the bedroom that was beyond her sitting-room, and hung her hat in a fragrant white closet that was entirely and delightfully empty, and put her coat on a hanger, and her gloves and bag in the empty big top drawer of a great mahogany bureau. Then she went back to the mirror and looked hard at her own beauty reflected in it; and laughed her little laugh again.

"It's too good—it's too much!" she whispered.

She investigated her domain, after quelling a wild desire to sit down at the beautiful desk and try the new pens, the crystal ink-well, and the heavy paper, with its severely engraved address, in a long letter to Mother.

There was a tiny upright piano in the sitting-room, and at the fireplace a deep thick rug, and an immense leather armchair. A clock in crystal and gold flanked by two crystal candlesticks had the centre of the mantelpiece. On the little round mahogany centre table was a lamp with a wonderful mosaic shade; a little bookcase was filled with books and magazines. Margaret went to one of the three windows, and looked down upon the bare trees and the snow in the park, and upon the rumbling green omnibuses, all bathed in bright chilly sunlight.

A mahogany door with a crystal knob opened into the bedroom, where there was a polished floor, and more rugs, and a gay rosy wall paper, and a great bed with a lace cover. Beyond was a bathroom, all enamel, marble, glass, and nickel-plate, with heavy monogrammed towels on the rack, three new little wash-cloths sealed in glazed paper, three new toothbrushes in paper cases, and a cake of famous English soap just out of its wrapper.

Over the whole little suite there brooded an exquisite order. Not a particle of dust broke the shining surfaces of the mahogany, not a fallen leaf lay under the great bowl of roses on the desk. Now and then the radiator clanked in the stillness; it was hard to believe in that warmth and silence that a cold winter wind was blowing outside, and that snow still lay on the ground.

Margaret, resting luxuriously in the big chair, became thoughtful; presently she went into the bedroom, and knelt down beside the bed.

"O Lord, let me stay here," she prayed, her face in her hands. "I want so to stay—make me a success!"

Never was a prayer more generously answered. Miss Paget was an instant success. In something less than two months she became indispensable to Mrs. Carr-Boldt, and was a favorite with every one, from the rather stolid, silent head of the house down to the least of the maids. She was so busy, so unaffected, so sympathetic, that her sudden rise in favor was resented by no one. The butler told her his troubles, the French maid darkly declared that but for Miss Paget she would not for one second r-r-remain! The children went cheerfully even to the dentist with their adored Miss Peggy; they soon preferred her escort to matinee or zoo to that of any other person. Margaret also escorted Mrs. Carr-Boldt's mother, a magnificent old lady, on shopping expeditions, and attended the meetings of charity boards for Mrs. Carr-Boldt. With notes and invitations, account books and check books, dinner lists, and interviews with caterers, decorators, and florists, Margaret's time was full, but she loved every moment of her work, and gloried in her increasing usefulness.

At first there were some dark days; notably the dreadful one upon which Margaret somehow—somewhere—dropped the box containing the new hat she was bringing home for Harriet, and kept the little girl out in the cold afternoon air while the car made a fruitless trip back to the milliner's. Harriet contracted a cold, and Harriet's mother for the first time spoke severely to Margaret. There was another bad day when Margaret artlessly admitted to Mrs. Pierre Polk at the telephone that Mrs. Carr-Boldt was not engaged for dinner that evening, thus obliging her employer to snub the lady, or accept a distasteful invitation to dine. And there was a most uncomfortable occasion when Mr. Carr-Boldt, not at all at his best, stumbled in upon his wife with some angry observations meant for her ear alone; and Margaret, busy with accounts in a window recess, was, unknown to them both, a distressed witness.

"Another time, Miss Paget," said Mrs. Carr-Boldt, coldly, upon Margaret's appearing scarlet-cheeked between the curtains, "don't oblige me to ascertain that you are not within hearing before feeling sure of privacy. Will you finish those bills upstairs, if you please?"

Margaret went upstairs with a burning heart, cast her bills haphazard on her own desk, and flung herself, dry-eyed and furious, on the bed. She was far too angry to think, but lay there for perhaps twenty minutes with her brain whirling. Finally rising, she brushed up her hair, straightened her collar, and, full of tremendous resolves, stepped into her little sitting-room, to find Mrs. Carr-Boldt in the big chair, serenely eying her.

"I'm so sorry I spoke so, Peggy," said her employer, generously. "But the truth is, I am not myself when—when Mr. Carr-Boldt——" The little hesitating appeal in her voice completely disarmed Margaret. In the end the little episode cemented the rapidly growing friendship between the two women, Mrs. Carr-Boldt seeming to enjoy the relief of speaking rather freely of what was the one real trial in her life.

"My husband has always had too much money," she said, in her positive way. "At one time we were afraid that he would absolutely ruin his health by this—habit of his. His physician and I took him around the world—I left Victoria, just a baby, with Mother—and for two years he was never out of my sight. It has never been so bad since. You know yourself how reliable he usually is," she finished cheerfully, "unless some of the other men get hold of him!"

As the months went on Margaret came to admire her employer more and more. There was not an indolent impulse in Mrs. Carr-Boldt's entire composition. Smooth-haired, fresh-skinned, in spotless linen, she began the day at eight o'clock, full of energy and interest. She had daily sessions with butler and housekeeper, shopped with Margaret and the children, walked about her greenhouse or her country garden with her skirts pinned up, and had tulips potted and stone work continued. She was prominent in several clubs, a famous dinner-giver, she took a personal interest in all her servants, loved to settle their quarrels and have three or four of them up on the carpet at once, tearful and explanatory. Margaret kept for her a list of some two hundred friends, whose birthdays were to be marked with carefully selected gifts. She pleased Mrs. Carr-Boldt by her open amazement at the latter's vitality. The girl observed that her employer could not visit any institution without making a few vigorous suggestions as she went about; she accompanied her checks to the organized charities—and her charity flowed only through absolutely reliable channels—with little friendly, advisory letters. She liked the democratic attitude for herself—even while promptly snubbing any such tendency in children or friends—and told Margaret that she only used her coat of arms on house linen, stationery, and livery, because her husband and mother liked it. "It's of course rather nice to realize that one comes from one of the oldest of the Colonial families," she would say. "The Carterets of Maryland, you know. —But it's all such bosh!"

And she urged Margaret to claim her own right to family honors: "You're a Quincy, my dear! Don't let that woman intimidate you—she didn't remember that her grandfather was a captain until her husband made his money. And where the family portraits came from I don't know, but I think there's a man on Fourth Avenue who does 'em!" she would say, or, "I know all about Lilly Reynolds, Peggy. Her father was as rich as she says, and I daresay the crest is theirs. But ask her what her maternal grandmother did for a living, if you want to shut her up!" Other people she would condemn with a mere whispered "Coal!" or "Patent bathtubs!" behind her fan, and it pleased her to tell people that her treasure of a secretary had the finest blood in the world in her veins. Margaret was much admired, and Margaret was her discovery, and she liked to emphasize her find.

Mrs. Carr-Boldt's mother, a tremulous, pompous old lady, unwittingly aided the impression by taking an immense fancy to Margaret, and by telling her few intimates and the older women among her daughter's friends that the girl was a perfect little thoroughbred. When the Carr-Boldts filled their house with the reckless and noisy company they occasionally affected, Mrs. Carteret would say majestically to Margaret:

"You and I have nothing in common with this riff-raff, my dear!"

Summer came, and Margaret headed a happy letter "Bar Harbor." Two months later all Weston knew that Margaret Paget was going abroad for a year with those rich people, and had written her mother from the *Lusitania*. Letters from London, from Germany, from Holland, from Russia, followed. "We are going to put the girls at school in Switzerland, and (ahem!) winter on the Riviera, and then Rome for Holy Week!" she wrote.

She was presently home again, chattering French and German to amuse her father, teaching Becky a little Italian song to match her little Italian costume.

"It's wonderful to me how you get along with all these rich people, Mark," said her mother, admiringly, during Margaret's home visit. Mrs. Paget was watering the dejected-looking side garden with a straggling length of hose; Margaret and Julie shelling peas on the side steps. Margaret laughed, coloring a little.

"Why, we're *just* as good as they are, Mother!"

Mrs. Paget drenched a dried little clump of carnations.

"We're as *good*," she admitted; "but we're not as rich or as, travelled—we haven't the same ideas; we belong to a different class."

"Oh, no, we don't, Mother," Margaret said quickly. "Who are the Carr-Boldts, except for their money? Why, Mrs. Carteret—for all her family!—isn't *half* the aristocrat Grandma was! And you—you could be a Daughter of The Officers of the Revolution, Mother!"

"Why, Mark, I never heard that!" her mother protested, cleaning the sprinkler with a hairpin.

"Mother!" Julie said eagerly, "Great-grandfather Quincy!"

"Oh, Grandpa," said Mrs. Paget. "Yes, Grandpa was a paymaster. He was on Governor Hancock's staff. They used to call him 'Major.' But Mark——" she turned off the water, holding her skirts away from the combination of mud and dust underfoot, "that's a very silly way to talk, dear! Money does make a difference; it does no good to go back into the past and say that this one was a judge and that one a major; we must live our lives where we *are!*"

Margaret had not lost a wholesome respect for her mother's opinion in the two years she had been away, but she had lived in a very different world, and was full of new ideas.

"Mother, do you mean to tell me that if you and Dad hadn't had a perfect pack of children, and moved so much, and if Dad—say—had been in that oil deal that he said he wished he had the money for, and we still lived in the brick house, that you wouldn't be in every way the equal of Mrs. Carr-Boldt?"

"If you mean as far as *money* goes, Mark—no. We might have been well-to-do as country people go, I suppose——"

"Exactly!" said Margaret; "and you would have been as well off as dozens of the people who are going about in society this minute! It's the merest chance that we aren't rich. Just for instance: Father's father had twelve children, didn't he?—and left them—how much was it?—about three thousand dollars apiece——"

"And a Godsend it was, too," said her mother, reflectively.

"But suppose Dad had been the only child, Mother," Margaret persisted, "he would have had——"

"He would have had the whole thirty-six thousand dollars, I suppose, Mark."

"Or more," said Margaret, "for Grandfather Paget was presumably spending money on them all the time."

"Well, but Mark," said Mrs. Paget, laughing as at the vagaries of a small child, "Father Paget *did* have twelve children—and Daddy and I eight—" she sighed, as always, at the thought of the little son who was gone—"and there you are! You can't get away from that, dear."

Margaret did not answer. But she thought to herself that very few people held Mother's views of this subject.

Mrs. Carr-Boldt's friends, for example, did not accept increasing cares in this resigned fashion; their lives were ideally pleasant and harmonious without the complicated responsibilities of large families. They drifted from season to season without care, always free, always gay, always irreproachably gowned. In winter there were daily meetings, for shopping, for luncheon, bridge, or tea; summer was filled with a score of country visits. There were trips for week-ends, dinners, theatre, and the opera to fill the evenings, German or singing lessons, manicure, masseuse, and dressmaker to crowd the morning hours all the year round. Margaret learned from these exquisite, fragrant creatures the art of being perpetually fresh and charming, learned their methods of caring for their own beauty, learned to love rare toilet waters and powders, fine embroidered linen and silk stockings. There was no particular strain upon her wardrobe now, nor upon her purse; she could be as dainty as she liked. She listened to the conversations that went on about her—sometimes critical or unconvinced; more often admiring; and as she listened she found slowly but certainly her own viewpoint. She was not mercenary. She would not marry a man *just* for his money, she decided, but just as certainly she would not marry a man who could not give her a comfortable establishment, a position in society.

The man seemed in no hurry to appear; as a matter of fact, the men whom Margaret met were openly anxious to evade marriage, even with the wealthy girls of their own set. Margaret was not concerned; she was too happy to miss the love-making element; the men she saw were not of a type to inspire a sensible, busy, happy girl with any very deep feeling. And it was with generous and perfect satisfaction that she presently had news of Julie's happy engagement. Julie was to marry a young and popular doctor, the only child of one of Weston's most prominent families. The little sister's letter bubbled joyously with news.

"Harry's father is going to build us a little house on the big place, the darling," wrote Julie; "and we will stay with them until it is done. But in five years Harry says we will have a real honeymoon, *in Europe!* Think of going to Europe *as a married woman.* Mark, I wish you could see my ring; it is a *beauty*, but don't tell Mother I was silly enough to write about it!"

Margaret delightedly selected a little collection of things for Julie's trousseau. A pair of silk stockings, a scarf she never had worn, a lace petticoat, pink silk for a blouse. Mrs. Carr-Boldt, coming in in the midst of these preparations, insisted upon adding so many other things, from trunks and closets, that Margaret was speechless with delight. Scarves, cobwebby silks in uncut lengths, lingerie still in the tissue paper of Paris shops, parasols, gloves, and lengths of lace—she piled all of them into Margaret's arms. Julie's trousseau was consequently quite the most beautiful Weston had ever seen; and the little sister's cloudless joy made the fortnight Margaret spent at home at the time of the wedding a very happy one. It was a time of rush and flurry, laughter and tears, of roses, and girls in white gowns. But some ten days before the wedding Julie and Margaret happened to be alone for a peaceful hour over their sewing, and fell to talking seriously.

"You see, our house will be small," said Julie; "but I don't care—we don't intend to stay in Weston all our lives. Don't breathe this to any one, Mark, but if Harry does as well as he's doing now for two years, we'll rent the little house, and we're going to Baltimore for a year for a special course. Then—you know he's devoted to Doctor McKim, he always calls him 'the chief'—then he thinks *maybe* McKim will work him into his practice—he's getting old, you know, and that means New York!"

"Oh, Ju—*really!*"

"I don't see why not," Julie said, dimpling. "Harry's crazy to do it. He says he doesn't propose to live and die in Weston. McKim could throw any amount of hospital practice his way, to begin with. And you know Harry'll have something—and the house will rent. I'm crazy," said Julie, enthusiastically, "to take one of those lovely old apartments on Washington Square, and meet a few nice people, you know, and really *make* something of my life!"

"Mrs. Carr-Boldt and I will spin down for you every few days," Margaret said, falling readily in with the plan. "I'm glad you're not going to simply get into a rut the way some of the other girls have, cooking and babies and nothing else!" she said.

"I think that's an awful mistake," Julie said placidly. "Starting in right is so important. I don't want to be a mere drudge like Ethel or Louise— they may like it. I don't! Of course, this isn't a matter to talk of," she went on, coloring a little. "I'd never breathe this to Mother! But it's perfectly absurd to pretend that girls don't discuss these things. I've talked to Betty and Louise—we all talk about it, you know. And Louise says they haven't had *one* free second since Buddy came. Some one's got to be with him every single second, even now, when he's four—to see that he doesn't fall off something or put things in his mouth. And as Louise says—it means no more week-end trips; you can't go visiting overnight, you can't even go for a day's drive or a day on the beach, without extra clothes for the baby, a mosquito-net and an umbrella for the baby—milk packed in ice for the baby—somebody trying to get the baby to take his nap—it's awful! It would *end* our Baltimore plan, and that means New York, and New York means everything to Harry and me!" finished Julie, contentedly, flattening a finished bit of embroidery on her knee, and regarding it complacently.

"Well, I think you're right," Margaret approved. "Things are different now from what they were in Mother's day."

"And look at Mother," Julie said. "One long slavery! Life's too short to wear yourself out that way!"

Mrs. Paget's sunny cheerfulness was sadly shaken when the actual moment of parting with Julie came; her face worked pitifully in its effort to smile; her tall figure, awkward in an ill-made, unbecoming new silk, seemed to droop tenderly over the little clinging wife. Margaret, stirred by the sight of tears on her mother's face, stood with an arm about her, when the bride and groom drove away in the afternoon sunshine.

"I'm going to stay with you until she gets back!" she reminded her mother.

"And you know you've always said you wanted the girls to marry, Mother," urged Mr. Paget. Rebecca felt this a felicitous moment to ask if she and the boys could have the rest of the ice cream.

"Divide it evenly," said Mrs. Paget, wiping her eyes and smiling. "Yes, I know, Daddy dear, I'm an ungrateful woman! I suppose your turn will come next, Mark, and then I don't know what I *will* do!"

CHAPTER IV

But Margaret's turn did not come for nearly a year. Then—in Germany again, and lingering at a great Berlin hotel because the spring was so beautiful, and the city so sweet with linden bloom, and especially because there were two Americans at the hotel whose game of bridge it pleased Mr. and Mrs. Carr-Boldt daily to hope they could match—then Margaret transformed within a few hours from a merely pretty, very dignified, perfectly contented secretary, entirely satisfied with what she wore as long as it was suitable and fresh, into a living woman whose cheeks paled and flushed at nothing but her thoughts, who laughed at herself in her mirror, loitered over her toilet trying one gown after another, and walked half-smiling through a succession of rosy dreams.

It all came about very simply. One of the aforementioned bridge players wondered if Mrs. Carr-Boldt and her niece—oh, wasn't it?—her secretary then—would like to hear a very interesting young American professor lecture this morning?—wondered, when they were fanning themselves in the airy lecture-room, if they would care to meet Professor Tenison?

Margaret looked into a pair of keen, humorous eyes, answered with her own smile Professor Tenison's sudden charming one, lost her small hand in his big firm one. Then she listened to him talk, as he strode about the platform, boyishly shaking back the hair that fell across his forehead. After that he walked to the hotel with them, through dazzling seas of perfume, and of flowers, under the enchanted shifting green of great trees—or so Margaret thought. There was a plunge from the hot street into the awninged cool gloom of the hotel, and then a luncheon, when the happy steady murmur from their own table seemed echoed by the murmurous clink and stir and laughter all about them, and accented by the not-too-close music from the band.

Doctor Tenison was everything charming, Margaret thought, instantly drawn by the unaffected, friendly manner, and watching the interested gleam of his blue eyes and the white flash of his teeth. He was a gentleman, to begin with; distinguished at thirty-two in his chosen work; big and well-built, without suggesting the athlete, of an old and honored American family, and the only son of a rich—and eccentric—old doctor whom Mrs. Carr-Boldt chanced to know.

He was frankly delighted at the chance that had brought him in contact with these charming people; and as Mrs. Carr-Boldt took an instant fancy to him, and as he was staying at their own hotel, they saw him after that every day, and several times a day. Margaret would come down the great sun-bathed stairway in the morning to find him patiently waiting in a porch chair. Her heart would give a great leap—half joy, half new strange pain, as she recognized him. There would be time for a chat over their fruit and eggs before Mr. Carr-Boldt came down, all ready for a motor-trip, or Mrs. Carr-Boldt, swathed in cream-colored coat and flying veils, joined them with an approving "Good-morning."

Margaret would remember these breakfasts all her life: the sun-splashed little table in a corner of the great dining-room, the rosy fatherly waiter who was so much delighted with her German, the busy picturesque traffic in the street just below the wide-open window. She would always re-member a certain filmy silk striped gown, a wide hat loaded with daisies; always love the odor of linden trees in the spring.

Sometimes the professor went with them on their morning drive, to be dropped at the lecture-hall with Margaret and Mrs. Carr-Boldt. The latter was pleased to take the course of lectures very seriously, and carried a hand-some Russian leather note-book, and a gold pencil. Sometimes after luncheon they all went on an expedition together, and now and then Margaret and Doctor Tenison went off alone on foot, to explore the city. They would end the afternoon with coffee and little cakes in some tea-room, and come home tired and merry in the long shadows of the spring sunset, with wilted flowers from the street markets in their hands.

There was one glorious tramp in the rain, when the professor's great laugh rang out like a boy's for sheer high spirits, and when Margaret was an enchanting vision with her cheeks glowing through the blown wet ten-drils of her hair. That day they had tea in the deserted charming little parlor of a tiny inn, and drank it toasting their feet over a glowing fire.

"Is Mrs. Carr-Boldt your mother's or your father's sister?" John Tenison asked, watching his companion with approval.

"Oh, good gracious!" said Margaret, laughing over her teacup. "Haven't I told you yet that I'm only her secretary? I never saw Mrs. Carr-Boldt until five years ago."

"Perhaps you did tell me. But I got it into my head, that first day, that you were aunt and niece——"

"People do, I think," Margaret said thoughtfully, "because we're both fair." She did not say that but for Mrs. Carr-Boldt's invaluable maid the likeness would have been less marked, on this score at least. "I taught school," she went on simply, "and Mrs. Carr-Boldt happened to come to my school, and she asked me to come to her."

"You're all alone in the world, Miss Paget?" The direct question came quite naturally.

"Oh, dear me, no! My father and mother are living"; and feeling, as she always did, a little claim on her loyalty, she added: "We are, or were, rather, Southern people—but my father settled in a very small New York town——"

"Mrs. Carr-Boldt told me that—I'd forgotten——" said Professor Tenison, and he carried the matter entirely out of Margaret's hands—much, much further indeed than she would have carried it, by continuing, "She tells me that Quincyport was named for your mother's grandfather, and that Judge Paget was your father's father."

"Father's uncle," Margaret corrected, although as a matter of fact Judge Paget had been no nearer than her father's second cousin. "But Father always called him uncle," Margaret assured herself inwardly. To the Quincyport claim she said nothing. Quincyport was in the county that Mother's people had come from; Quincy was a very unusual name, and the original Quincy had been a Charles, which certainly was one of Mother's family names. Margaret and Julie, browsing about among the colonial histories and genealogies of the Weston Public Library years before, had come to a jubilant certainty that Mother's grandfather *must* have been the same man. But she did not feel quite so positive now.

"Your people aren't still in the South, you said?"

"Oh, no!" Margaret cleared her throat. "They're in Weston—Weston, New York."

"*Weston!* Not near Dayton?"

"Why, yes! Do you know Dayton?"

"Do I know Dayton?" He was like an eager child. "Why, my aunt Pamela lives there; the only mother I ever knew! I knew Weston, too, a little. Lovely homes there, some of them—old colonial houses. And your mother lives there? Is she fond of flowers?"

"She loves them," Margaret said, vaguely uncomfortable.

"Well, she must know Aunt Pamela," said John Tenison, enthusiastically. "I expect they'd be great friends. And *you* must know Aunt Pam. She's like a dainty old piece of china, or a—I don't know, a tea rose! She's never married, and she lives in the most charming brick house, with brick walls and hollyhocks all about it, and such an atmosphere inside! She has an old maid and an old gardener, and—don't you know—she's the sort of woman who likes to sit down under a portrait of your great-grandfather, in a dim parlor full of mahogany and rose jars, with her black silk skirts spreading about her, and an Old Blue cup in her hand, and talk family— how cousin this married a man whose people aren't anybody, and cousin that is outraging precedent by naming her child for her husband's side of the house. She's a funny, dear old lady! You know, Miss Paget," the professor went on, with his eager, impersonal air, "when I met you, I *thought* you didn't quite seem like a New Yorker and a Bar Harborer—if that's the word! Aunt Pam—you know she's my only mother, I got all my early knowledge from her!—Aunt Pam detests the usual New York girl, and the minute I met you I knew she'd like you. You'd sort of fit into the Dayton picture, with your braids, and those ruffly things you wear!"

[32]

Margaret said simply, "I would love to meet her," and began slowly to draw on her gloves. It surely was not requisite that she should add, "But you must not confuse my home with any such exquisitely ordered existence as that. We are poor people, our house is crowded, our days a severe and endless struggle with the ugly things of life. We have good blood in our veins, but not more than hundreds of thousands of other American families. My mother would not understand one tenth of your aunt's conversation; your aunt would find very uninteresting the things that are vital to my mother."

No, she couldn't say that. She picked up her dashing little hat, and pinned it over her loosened soft mass of yellow hair, and buttoned her coat, and plunged her hands deep in her pockets. No, the professor would call on her at Bar Harbor, take a yachting trip with the Carr-Boldts perhaps, and then—and then, when they were really good friends, some day she would ask Mother to have a simple little luncheon, and Mrs. Carr-Boldt would let her bring Doctor Tenison down in the motor from New York. And meantime—no need to be too explicit.

For just two happy weeks Margaret lived in Wonderland. The fourteen days were a revelation to her. Life seemed to grow warmer, more rosy-colored. Little things became significant; every moment carried its freight of joy. Her beauty, always notable, became almost startling; there was a new glow in her cheeks and lips, new fire in the dark-lashed eyes that were so charming a contrast to her bright hair. Like a pair of joyous and irresponsible children she and John Tenison walked through the days, too happy ever to pause and ask themselves whither they were going.

Then abruptly it ended. Victoria, brought down from school in Switzerland with various indications of something wrong, was in a flash a sick child; a child who must be hurried home to the only surgeon in whom Mrs. Carr-Boldt placed the least trust. There was hurried packing, telephoning, wiring; it was only a few hours after the great German physician's diagnosis that they were all at the railway station, breathless, nervous, eager to get started.

Doctor Tenison accompanied them to the station, and in the five minutes' wait before their train left, a little incident occurred, the memory of which clouded Margaret's dreams for many a day to come. Arriving, as they were departing, were the St. George Allens, noisy, rich, arrogant New Yorkers, for whom Margaret had a special dislike. The Allens fell joyously upon the Carr-Boldt party, with a confusion of greetings. "And Jack Tenison!" shouted Lily Allen, delightedly. "Well, what *fun!* What are you doing here?"

"I'm feeling a little lonely," said the professor, smiling at Mrs. Carr-Boldt.

"Nothing like that; unsay them woyds," said Maude Allen, cheerfully. "Mamma, make him dine with us! Say you will."

"I assure you I was dreading the lonely evening," John Tenison said gratefully. Margaret's last glimpse of his face was between Lily's pink and cherry hat and Maude's astonishing headgear of yellow straw, gold braid, spangled quills, and calla lilies. She carried a secret heartache through the worried fortnight of Victoria's illness and the busy days that followed; for Mrs. Carr-Boldt had one of many nervous breakdowns, and took her turn at the hospital when Victoria came home. For the first time in five happy years Margaret drooped, and for the first time a longing for money and power of her own gnawed at the girl's heart. If she had but her share of these things, she could hold her own against a hundred Maude and Lily Allens.

As it was, she told herself a little bitterly, she was only a secretary, one of the hundred paid dependents of a rich woman. She was only, after all, a little middle-class country school teacher.

CHAPTER V

"So you're going home to your own people for the week-end, Peggy? And how many of you are there, I always forget?" said young Mrs. George Crawford, negligently. She tipped back in her chair, half shut her novel, half shut her eyes, and looked critically at her fingernails.

Outside the big country house summer sunshine flooded the smooth lawns, sparkled on the falling diamonds and still pool of the fountain, glowed over acres of matchless wood and garden. But deep awnings made a clear cool shade indoors, and the wide rooms were delightfully breezy.

Margaret, busy with a ledger and checkbook, smiled absently, finished a long column, made an orderly entry, and wiped her pen.

"Seven," said she, smiling.

"Seven!" echoed Mrs. Potter, lazily. "My heaven—seven children! How early Victorian!"

"Isn't it?" said a third woman, a very beautiful woman, Mrs. Watts Watson, who was also idling and reading in the white-and-gray morning-room. "Well," she added, dropping her magazine, and locking her hands about her head, "my grandmother had ten. Fancy trying to raise ten children!"

"Oh, everything's different now," the first speaker said indifferently. "Everything's more expensive, life is more complicated. People used to have roomier houses, aunts and cousins and grandmothers living with them; there was always some one at home with the children. Nowadays we don't do that."

"And thank the saints we don't!" said Mrs. Watson, piously. "If there's one thing I *can't* stand, it's a houseful of things-in-law!"

"Of course; but I mean it made the family problem simpler," Mrs. Crawford pursued. "Oh—and I don't know! Everything was so simple. All this business of sterilizing, and fumigating, and pasteurizing, and vaccinating, and boiling in boracic acid wasn't done in those days," she finished vaguely.

"Now there you are—now *there you are!*" said Mrs. Carr-Boldt, entering into the conversation with sudden force. Entirely recovered after her nervous collapse, as brisk as ever in her crisp linen gown, she was signing the checks that Margaret handed her, frowningly busy and absorbed with her accounts. Now she leaned back in her chair, glanced at the watch at her wrist, and relaxed the cramped muscles of her body. "That's exactly it, Rose," said she to Mrs. Crawford. "Life *is* more complicated. People— the very people who ought to have children—simply cannot afford it! And who's to blame? Can you blame a woman whose life is packed full of other things she simply cannot avoid, if she declines to complicate things any further? Our grandmothers didn't have telephones, or motor-cars, or week-end affairs, or even—for that matter—manicures and hair-dressers! A good heavy silk was full dress all the year 'round. They washed their own hair. The 'upstairs girl' answered the door-bell—why, they didn't even have talcum powder and nursery refrigerators, and sanitary rugs that have to be washed every day! Do you suppose my grandmother ever took a baby's temperature, or had its eyes and nose examined, or its adenoids cut? They had more children, and they lost more children—without any reason or logic whatever. Poor things, they never thought of doing anything else, I suppose! A fat old darky nurse brought up the whole crowd— it makes one shudder to think of it! Why, I had *always* a trained nurse, and the regular nurse used to take two baths a day. I insisted on *that*, and both nurseries were washed out every day with chloride of potash solution, and the iron beds washed every week! And even then Vic had this mastoid trouble, and Harriet got everything, almost."

"Exactly," said Mrs. Watson. "That's you, Hattie, with all the money in the world. Now do you wonder that some of the rest of us, who have to think of money—in short," she finished decidedly, "do you wonder that people are *not* having children? At first, naturally, one doesn't want them —for three or four years, I'm sure, the thought doesn't come into one's head. But then, afterward—you see, I've been married fifteen years now!— afterward, I think it would be awfully nice to have one or two little kiddies, if it was a possible thing. But it isn't."

"No, it isn't," Mrs. Crawford agreed. "You don't want to have them unless you're able to do everything in the world for them. If I were Hat here, I'd have a dozen."

"Oh, no, you wouldn't," Mrs. Carr-Boldt assured her promptly. "No, you wouldn't! You can't leave everything to servants—there are clothes to think of, and dentists, and special teachers, and it's frightfully hard to get a nursery governess. And then you've got to see that they know the right people—don't you know?—and give them parties—I tell you it's a *strain*."

"Well, I don't believe my mother with her seven ever worked any harder than you do!" said Margaret, with the admiration in her eyes that was so sweet to the older woman. "Look at this morning—did you sit down before you came in here twenty minutes ago?"

"I? Indeed I didn't!" Mrs. Carr-Boldt said. "I had my breakfast and letters at seven, bath at eight, straightened out that squabble between Swann and the cook—I think Paul is still simmering, but that's neither here nor there!—then I went down with the vet to see the mare. Joe'll never forgive me if I've really broken the creature's knees!—then I telephoned Mother, and saw Harriet's violin man, and—let's see——"

"Italian lesson," Margaret prompted.

"Italian lesson," the other echoed, "and then came in here to sign my checks."

"You're so executive, Harriet!" said Mrs. Crawford, languidly.

"Apropos of Swann," Margaret said, "he confided to me that *he* has seven children—on a little farm down on Long Island."

"The butler—oh, I dare say!" Mrs. Watson agreed. "They can, because they've no standard to maintain—seven, or seventeen—the only difference in expense is the actual amount of bread and butter consumed."

"It's too bad," said Mrs. Crawford. "But you've got to handle the question sanely and reasonably, like any other. Now, I love children," she went on. "I'm perfectly crazy about my sister's little girl. She's eleven now, and the cutest thing alive. But when I think of all Mabel's been through, since she was born—I realize that it's a little *too* much to expect of any woman. Now, look at us—there are thousands of people fixed as we are. We're in an apartment hotel, with one maid. There's no room for a second maid, no porch and no backyard. Well, the baby comes—one loses, before and after the event, just about six months of *everything*, and of course the expense is frightful, but no matter!—the baby comes. We take a house. That means three indoor maids, George's chauffeur, a man for lawn and furnace—that's five——"

"Doubling expenses," said Mrs. Carr-Boldt, thoughtfully.

"Doubling——! *Trebling*, or more. But that's not all. Baby must be out from eleven to three every day. So you've got to go sit by the carriage in the park while nurse goes home for her lunch. Or, if you're out for luncheon, or giving a luncheon, she brings baby home, bumps the carriage into the basement, carries the baby upstairs, eats her lunch in snatches—the maids don't like it, and I don't blame them! I know how it was with Mabel; she had to give up that wonderful old apartment of theirs on Gramercy Park. Sid had his studio on the top floor, and she had such a lovely flat on the next floor, but there was no lift, and no laundry, and the kitchen was small—a baby takes so much fussing! And then she lost that splendid cook of hers, Germaine. *She* wouldn't stand it. Up to that time she'd been cooking and waiting, too, but the baby ended that. Mabel took a house, and Sid paid studio rent besides, and they had two maids, and then three maids—and what with their fighting, and their days off, and eternally changing, Mabel was a *wreck*. I've seen her trying to play a bridge hand with Dorothy bobbing about on her arm—poor girl! Finally they went to a hotel, and of course the child got older, and was less trouble. But to this day Mabel doesn't dare leave her alone for one second. And when they go out to dinner, and leave her alone in the hotel, of course the child cries——!'"

"That's the worst of a kiddie," Mrs. Watson said. "You can't ever turn 'em off, as it were, or make it spades! They're always right on the job. I'll never forget Elsie Clay. She was the best friend I had—my bridesmaid, too. She married, and after a while they took a house in Jersey because of the baby. I went out there to lunch one day. There she was in a house perfectly buried in trees, with the rain sopping down outside, and smoke blowing out of the fireplace, and the drawing-room as dark as pitch at two o'clock. Elsie said she used to nearly die of loneliness, sitting there all afternoon long listening to the trains whistling, and the maid thumping irons in the kitchen, and picking up the baby's blocks. And they quarrelled, you know, she and her husband—that was the beginning of the trouble. Finally the boy went to his grandmother, and now I believe Elsie's married again, and living in California somewhere."

Margaret, hanging over the back of her chair, was an attentive listener.

"But people—people in town have children!" she said. "The Blankenships have one, and haven't the de Normandys?"

"The Blankenship boy is in college," said Mrs. Carr-Boldt; "and the little de Normandys lived with their grandmother until they were old enough for boarding-school."

"Well, the Deanes have three!" Margaret said triumphantly.

"Ah, well, my dear! Harry Deane's a rich man, and she was a Pell of Philadelphia," Mrs. Crawford supplied promptly. "Now the Eastmans have three, too, with a trained nurse apiece."

"I see," Margaret admitted slowly.

"Far wiser to have none at all," said Mrs. Carr-Boldt, in her decisive way, "than to handicap them from the start by letting them see other children enjoying pleasures and advantages they can't afford. And now, girls, let's stop wasting time. It's half-past eleven. Why can't we have a game of auction right here and now?"

Margaret returned to her checkbook with speed. The other two, glad to be aroused, heartily approved the idea.

"Well, what does this very businesslike aspect imply?" Mrs. Carr-Boldt asked her secretary.

"It means that I can't play cards, and you oughtn't," Margaret said, laughing.

"Oh? Why not?"

"Because you've *lots* of things to do, and I've got to finish these notes, and I have to sit with Harriet while she does her German——"

"Where's Fräulein?"

"Fräulein's going to drive Vic over to the Partridges' for luncheon, and I promised Swann I'd talk to him about favors and things for to-morrow night."

"Well—busy Lizzie! And what have I to do?"

Margaret reached for a well-filled date-book.

"You were to decide about those alterations, the porch and dining-room, you know," said she. "There are some architect's sketches around here; the man's going to be here early in the morning. You said you'd drive to the yacht club, to see about the stage for the children's play; you were to stop on the way back and see old Mrs. McNab a moment. You wanted to write Mrs. Polk a note, and luncheon's early because of the Kellogg bridge." She shut the book. "And call Mr. Carr-Boldt at the club at one," she added.

"All that, now fancy!" said her employer, admiringly.

She had swept some scattered magazines from a small table, and was now seated there, negligently shuffling a pack of cards in her fine white hands.

"Ring, will you, Peggy?" said she.

"And the boat races are to-day, and you dine at Oaks-in-the-Field," Margaret supplemented inflexibly.

"Yes? Well, come and beat the seven of clubs," said Mrs. Carr-Boldt, spreading the deck for the draw.

"Fräulein," she said sweetly, a moment later, when a maid had summoned that worthy and earnest governess, "tell Miss Harriet that Mother doesn't want her to do her German to-day, it's too warm. Tell her that she's to go with you and Miss Victoria for a drive. Thank you. And, Fräulein, will you telephone old Mrs. McNab, and say that Mrs. Carr-Boldt is lying down with a severe headache, and she won't be able to come in this morning? Thank you. And, Fräulein, telephone the yacht club, will you? And tell Mr. Mathews that Mrs. Carr-Boldt is indisposed and he'll have to come back this afternoon. I'll talk to him before the children's races. And—one thing more! Will you tell Swann Miss Paget will see him about to-morrow's dinner when she comes back from the yacht club to-day? And tell him to send us something cool to drink now. Thank you so much. No, shut it. Thank you. Have a nice drive!"

They all drew up their chairs to the table.

"You and I, Rose," said Mrs. Watson. "I'm so glad you suggested this, Hattie. I am dying to play."

"It really rests me more than anything else," said Mrs. Carr-Boldt. "Two spades."

CHAPTER VI

Archerton, a blur of flying trees and houses, bright in the late sunlight, Pottsville, with children wading and shouting, under the bridge, Hunt's Crossing, then the next would be Weston and home.

Margaret, beginning to gather wraps and small possessions together, sighed. She sighed partly because her head ached, partly because the hot trip had mussed her usual fresh trimness, largely because she was going home.

This was August; her last trip home had been between Christmas and the New Year. She had sent a box from Germany at Easter, ties for the boys, silk scarves for Rebecca, books for Dad; and she had written Mother for her birthday in June, and enclosed an exquisite bit of lace in the letter; but although Victoria's illness had brought her to America nearly three months ago, it had somehow been impossible, she wrote them, to come home until now. Margaret had paid a great deal for the lace, as a sort of salve for her conscience—not that Mother would ever wear it!

Here was Weston. Weston looking its very ugliest in the level pitiless rays of the afternoon sun. The town, like most of its inhabitants, was wilted and grimed after the burden and heat of the long summer day. Margaret carried her heavy suitcase slowly up Main Street. Shop windows were spotted and dusty, and shopkeepers, standing idle in their doorways, looked spotted and dusty, too. A cloud of flies fought and surged about the closely guarded door of the butcher shop; a delivery cart was at the curb, the discouraged horse switching an ineffectual tail.

As Margaret passed this cart, a tall boy of fourteen came out of the shop with a bang of the wire-netting door, and slid a basket into the back of the cart.

"Teddy!" said Margaret, irritation evident in her voice in spite of herself.

"Hello, Mark!" said her brother, delightedly. "Say, great to see you! Get in on the four-ten?"

"Ted," said Margaret, kissing him, as the Pagets always quite simply kissed each other when they met, "what are you driving Costello's cart for?"

"Like to," said Theodore, simply. "Mother doesn't care. Say, you look swell, Mark!"

"What makes you want to drive this horrid cart, Ted?" protested Margaret. "What does Costello pay you?"

"Pay me?" scowled her brother, gathering up the reins. "Oh, come out of it, Marg'ret! He doesn't pay me anything. Don't you make Mother stop me, either, will you?" he ended anxiously.

"Of course I won't!" Margaret said impatiently.

"Giddap, Ruth!" said Theodore; but departing, he pulled up to add cheerfully, "Say, Dad didn't get his raise."

"Did?" said Margaret, brightening.

"*Didn't!*" He grinned affectionately upon her as with a dislocating jerk the cart started a ricochetting career down the street with that abandon known only to butchers' carts. Margaret, changing her heavy suitcase to the rested arm, was still vexedly watching it, when two girls, laughing in the open doorway of the express company's office across the street, caught sight of her. One of them, a little vision of pink hat and ruffles, and dark eyes and hair, came running to join her.

Rebecca was now sixteen, and of all the handsome Pagets the best to look upon. She was dressed according to her youthful lights; every separate article of her apparel to-day, from her rowdyish little hat to her open-work hose, represented a battle with Mrs. Paget's preconceived ideas as to propriety in dress, with the honors largely for Rebecca. Rebecca had grown up, in eight months, her sister thought, confusedly; she was no longer the adorable, unself-conscious tomboy who fought and skated and tobogganed with the boys.

"Hello, darling dear!" said Rebecca. "Too bad no one met you! We all thought you were coming on the six. Crazy about your suit! Here's Maudie Pratt. You know Maudie, don't you, Mark?"

Margaret knew Maudie. Rebecca's infatuation for plain, heavy-featured, complacent Miss Pratt was a standing mystery in the Paget family. Margaret smiled, bowed.

"I think we stumbled upon a pretty little secret of yours to-day, Miss Margaret," said Maudie, with her best company manner, as they walked along. Margaret raised her eyebrows. "Rebel and I," Maudie went on—Rebecca was at the age that seeks a piquant substitute for an unpoetical family name—"Rebel and I are wondering if we may ask you who Mr. John Tenison is?"

John Tenison! Margaret's heart stood still with a shock almost sickening, then beat furiously. What—how—who on earth had told them anything of John Tenison? Coloring high, she looked sharply at Rebecca.

"Cheer up, angel," said Rebecca, "he's not dead. He sent a telegram to-day, and Mother opened it——"

"Naturally," said Margaret, concealing an agony of impatience, as Rebecca paused apologetically.

"He's with his aunt, at Dayton, up the road here," continued Rebecca; "and wants you to wire him if he may come down and spend to-morrow here."

Margaret drew a relieved breath. There was time to turn around, at least.

"Who is he, sis?" asked Rebecca.

"Why, he's an awfully clever professor, honey," Margaret answered serenely. "We heard him lecture in Germany this spring, and met him afterward. I liked him very much. He's tremendously interesting." She tried to keep out of her voice the thrill that shook her at the mere thought of him. Confused pain and pleasure stirred her to the very heart. He wanted to come to see her, he must have telephoned Mrs. Carr-Boldt and asked to call, or he would not have known that she was at home this week-end—surely that was significant, surely that meant something! The thought was all pleasure, so great a joy and pride indeed that Margaret was conscious of wanting to lay it aside, to think of, dream of, ponder over, when she was alone. But, on the other hand, there was instantly the miserable conviction that he mustn't be allowed to come to Weston, no—no—she couldn't have him see her home and her people on a crowded hot summer Sunday, when the town looked its ugliest, and the children were home from school, and when the scramble to get to church and to safely accomplish the one o'clock dinner exhausted the women of the family. And how could she keep him from coming, what excuse could she give?

"Don't you want him to come—is he old and fussy?" asked Rebecca, interestedly.

"I'll see," Margaret answered vaguely. "No, he's only thirty-two or four."

"*And* charming!" said Maudie archly. Margaret eyed her with a coolness worthy of Mrs. Carr-Boldt herself, and then turned rather pointedly to Rebecca.

"How's Mother, Becky?"

"Oh, she's fine!" Rebecca said, absently in her turn. When Maudie left them at the next corner, she said quickly:

"Mark, did you see where we were when I saw you?"

"At the express office——? Yes," Margaret said, surprised.

"Well, listen," said Rebecca, reddening. "Don't say anything to Mother about it, will you? She thinks those boys are fresh in there—she don't like me to go in!"

"Oh, Beck—then you oughtn't!" Margaret protested.

"Well, I wasn't!" Rebecca said uncomfortably. "We went to see if Maudie's racket had come. You won't—will you, Mark?"

"Tell Mother—no, I won't," Margaret said, with a long sigh. She looked sideways at Rebecca—the dainty, fast-forming little figure, the even ripple and curl of her plaited hair, the assured pose of the pretty head. Victoria

Carr-Boldt, just Rebecca's age, was a big schoolgirl still, self-conscious and inarticulate, her well-groomed hair in an unbecoming "club," her well-hung skirts unbecomingly short. Margaret had half expected to find Rebecca at the same stage of development.

Rebecca was cheerful now, the promise exacted, and cheerfully observed:

"Dad didn't get his raise—isn't that the limit?"

Margaret sighed again, shrugged wearily. They were in their own quiet side street now, a street lined with ugly, shabby houses and beautified by magnificent old elms and maples. The Pagets' own particular gate was weather-peeled, the lawn trampled and bare. A bulging wire-netting door gave on the shabby old hall Margaret knew so well; she went on into the familiar rooms, acutely conscious, as she always was for the first hour or two at home, of the bareness and ugliness everywhere—the old sofa that sagged in the seat, the scratched rockers, the bookcases overflowing with coverless magazines, and the old square piano half-buried under loose sheets of music.

Duncan sat on the piano bench. Robert—nine now, with all his pretty baby roundness gone, a lean little burned, peeling face, and big teeth missing when he smiled, stood in the bay window, twisting the already limp net curtains into a tight rope. Each boy gave Margaret a kiss that seemed curiously to taste of dust, sunburn, and freckles, before she followed a noise of hissing and voices to the kitchen to find Mother.

The kitchen, at five o'clock on Saturday afternoon, was in wild confusion, and insufferably hot. Margaret had a distinct impression that not a movable article therein was in place, and not an available inch of tables or chairs unused, before her eyes reached the tall figure of the woman in a gown of chocolate percale, who was frying cutlets at the big littered range. Her face was dark with heat and streaked with perspiration. She turned as Margaret entered, and gave a delighted cry.

"Well, there's my girl! Bless her heart! Look out for this spoon, lovey," she added immediately, giving the girl a guarded embrace. Tears of joy stood frankly in her fine eyes.

"I meant to have all of this out of the way, dear," apologized Mrs. Paget, with a gesture that included cakes in the process of frosting, salad vegetables in the process of cooling, soup in the process of getting strained, great loaves of bread that sent a delicious fragrance over all the other odors. "But we didn't look for you until six."

"Oh, no matter!" Margaret said bravely.

"Rebecca tell you Dad didn't get his raise?" called Mrs. Paget, in a voice that rose above the various noises of the kitchen. "Dad saw Redman himself; he'll tell you about it! Don't stay in the kitchen in that pretty dress, dear! I'm coming right upstairs."

It was very hot upstairs; the bedrooms smelled faintly of matting, the soap in the bathroom was shrivelled in its saucer. In Margaret's old room

[42]

the week's washing had been piled high on the bed. She took off her hat and linen coat, brushed her hair back from her face, flinging her head back and shutting her eyes the better to fight tears as she did so, and began to assort the collars and shirts and put them away. For Dad's bureau —for Bruce's bureau—for the boys' bureau, tablecloths to go downstairs, towels for the shelves in the bathroom. Two little shirtwaists for Rebecca with little holes torn through them where collar and belt pins belonged.

Her last journey took her to the big, third-story room where the three younger boys slept. The three narrow beds were still unmade, and the western sunlight poured over tumbled blankets and the scattered small possessions that seem to ooze from the pores of little boys. Margaret set her lips distastefully as she brought order out of chaos. It was all wrong, somehow, she thought, gathering handkerchiefs and matches and "Nick Carters" and the oiled paper that had wrapped caramels from under the pillows that would in a few hours harbor a fresh supply.

She went out on the porch in time to put her arms about her father's shabby shoulders when he came in. Mr. Paget was tired, and he told his wife and daughters that he thought he was a very sick man. Margaret's mother met this statement with an anxious solicitude that was very soothing to the sufferer. She made Mark get Daddy his slippers and loose coat, and suggested that Rebecca shake up the dining-room couch before she established him there, in a rampart of pillows. No outsider would have dreamed that Mrs. Paget had dealt with this exact emergency some hundreds of times in the past twenty years.

Mr. Paget, reclining, shut his eyes, remarked that he had had an "awful, awful day," and wondered faintly if it would be too much trouble to have "somebody" make him just a little milk toast for his dinner. He smiled at Margaret when she sat down beside him; all the children were dear, but the oldest daughter knew she came first with her father.

"Getting to be an old, old man!" he said wearily, and Margaret hated herself because she had to quell an impatient impulse to tell him he was merely tired and cross and hungry, before she could say, in the proper soothing tone, "Don't talk that way, Dad darling!" She had to listen to a long account of the "raise," wincing every time her father emphasized the difference between her own position and that of her employer. Dad was at least the equal of any one in Weston! Why, a man Dad's age oughtn't to be humbly asking a raise, he ought to be dictating now. It was just Dad's way of looking at things, and it was all wrong.

"Well, I'll tell you one thing!" said Rebecca, "Joe Redman gave a picnic last month, and he came here with his mother, in the car, to ask me. And I was the scornfullest thing you ever saw, wasn't I, Ted? Not much!"

"Oh, Beck, you oughtn't to mix social and business things that way!" Margaret said helplessly.

"Dinner!" screamed the nine-year-old Robert, breaking into the room at this point, and "Dinner!" said Mrs. Paget, wearily, cheerfully, from the chair into which she had dropped at the head of the table. Mr. Paget, revived by sympathy and Margaret's attentions, took his place at the foot, and Bruce the chair between Margaret and his mother. Like the younger boys, whose almost confluent freckles had been brought into unusual prominence by violently applied soap and water, and whose hair dripped on their collars, he had brushed up for dinner, but his negligee shirt and corduroy trousers were stained and spotted from machine oil. Margaret, comparing him secretly to the men she knew, as daintily groomed as women, in their spotless white, felt a little resentment that Bruce's tired face was so contented, and said to herself again that it was all wrong.

Dinner was the same old haphazard meal with which she was so familiar; Blanche supplying an occasional reproof to the boys, Ted ignoring his vegetables, and ready in an incredibly short time for a second cutlet, and Robert begging for corn syrup, immediately after the soup, and spilling it from his bread. Mrs. Paget was flushed, her disappearances kitchenward frequent. She wanted Margaret to tell her all about Mr. Tenison. Margaret laughed, and said there was nothing to tell.

"You might get a horse and buggy from Peterson's," suggested Mrs. Paget, interestedly, "and drive about after dinner."

"Oh, Mother, I don't think I had better let him come!" Margaret said. "There's so many of us, and such confusion, on Sunday! Ju and Harry are almost sure to come over."

"Yes, I guess they will," Mrs. Paget said, with her sudden radiant smile. "Ju is so dear in her little house, and Harry's so sweet with her," she went on with vivacity. "Daddy and I had dinner with them Tuesday. Bruce said Rebecca was lovely with the boys—we're going to Julie's again some time. I declare it's so long since we've been anywhere without the children that we both felt funny. It was a lovely evening."

"You're too much tied, Mother," Margaret said affectionately.

"Not now!" her mother protested radiantly. "With all my babies turning into men and women so fast. And I'll have you all together tomorrow—and your friend I hope, too, Mark," she added hospitably. "You had better let him come, dear. There's a big dinner, and I always freeze more cream than we need, anyway, because Daddy likes a plate of it about four o'clock, if there's any left."

"Well—but there's nothing to do," Margaret protested.

"No, but dinner takes quite a while," Mrs. Paget suggested a little doubtfully; "and we could have a nice talk on the porch, and then you could go driving or walking. I wish there *was* something cool and pleasant to do, Mark," she finished a little wistfully. "You do just as you think best about asking him to come."

"I think I'll wire him that another time would be better," said Margaret, slowly. "Some time we'll regularly arrange for it."

"Well, perhaps that would be best," her mother agreed. "Some other time we'll send the boys off before dinner, and have things all nice and quiet. In October, say, when the trees are so pretty. I don't know but what that's my favorite time of all the year!"

Margaret looked at her as if she found something new in the tired, bright face. She could not understand why her mother—still too heated to commence eating her dinner—should radiate so definite an atmosphere of content, as she sat back a little breathless, after the flurry of serving. She herself felt injured and sore, not at the mere disappointment it caused her to put off John Tenison's visit, but because she felt more acutely than ever to-night the difference between his position and her own.

"Something nice has happened, Mother?" she hazarded, entering with an effort into the older woman's mood.

"Nothing special." Her mother's happy eyes ranged about the circle of young faces. "But it's so lovely to have you here, and to have Ju coming to-morrow," she said. "I just wish Daddy could build a house for each one of you, as you marry and settle down, right around our house in a circle, as they say people do sometimes in the Old World. I think then I'd have nothing in life to wish for!"

"Oh, Mother—in Weston!" Margaret said hopelessly, but her mother did not catch it.

"Not, Mark," she went on hastily and earnestly, "that I'm not more than grateful to God for all His goodness, as it is! I look at other women, and I wonder, I wonder—what I have done to be so blessed! Mark—" her face suddenly glowed, she leaned a little toward her daughter, "dearie, I *must* tell you," she said; "it's about Ju——"

Their eyes met in the pause.

"Mother—really?" Margaret said slowly.

"She told me on Tuesday," Mrs. Paget said, with glistening eyes. "Now, not a word to any one, Mark—but she'll want you to know!"

"And is she glad?" Margaret said, unable to rejoice.

"Glad?" Mrs. Paget echoed, her face gladness itself.

"Well, Ju's so young—just twenty-one," Margaret submitted a little uncertainly; "and she's been so free—and they're *just* in the new house! And I thought they were going to Europe!"

"Oh, Europe!" Mrs. Paget dismissed it cheerfully. "Why, it's the happiest time in a woman's life, Mark! Or I don't know, though," she went on thoughtfully, "I don't know but what I was happiest when you were all tiny, tumbling about me, and climbing into my lap. . . . Why, you love children, dear," she finished, with a shade of reproach in her voice, as Margaret still looked sober.

"Yes, I know, Mother," Margaret said. "I hope to goodness Ju won't get herself all run down!"

Her mother laughed. "You remind me of Grandma Paget," said she, cheerfully; "she lived ten miles away when we were married, but she came in when Bruce was born. She was rather a proud, cold woman herself, but she was very sweet to me. Well, then little Charlie came, fourteen months later, and she took that very seriously. Mother was dead, you know, and she stayed with me again, and worried me half sick telling me that it wasn't fair to Bruce and it wasn't fair to Charlie to divide my time between them that way. Well, then when my third baby was coming, I didn't dare tell her. Dad kept telling me to, and I couldn't, because I knew what a calamity a third would seem to her! Finally she went to visit Aunt Rebecca out West, and it was the very day she got back that the baby came. She came upstairs—she'd come right up from the train, and not seen any one but Dad; and he wasn't very intelligible, I guess—and she sat down and took the baby in her arms, and says she, looking at me sort of patiently, yet as if she was exasperated, too: 'Well, this is a nice way to do, the minute my back's turned! What are you going to call him, Julia?' And I said, 'I'm going to call her Margaret, for my dear husband's mother, and she's going to be beautiful and good, and grow up to marry the President!'" Mrs. Paget's merry laugh rang out. "I never shall forget your grandmother's face.

"Just the same," Mrs. Paget added, with a sudden deep sigh, "when little Charlie left us, the next year, and Brucie and Dad were both so ill, she and I agreed that you—you were just talking and trying to walk—were the only comfort we had! I could wish my girls no greater happiness than my children have been to me," finished Mother, contentedly.

"I know," Margaret began, half angrily; "But what about the children?" she was going to add. But somehow the arguments she had used so plausibly did not utter themselves easily to Mother, whose children would carry into their own middle age a wholesome dread of her anger. Margaret faltered, and merely scowled.

"I don't like to see that expression on your face, dearie," her mother said, as she might have said it to an eight-year-old child. "Be my sweet girl! Why, marriage isn't marriage without children, Mark. I've been thinking all week of having a baby in my arms again—it's so long since Rob was a baby."

Margaret devoted herself, with a rather sullen face, to her dessert. Mother would never feel as she did about these things, and what was the use of arguing? In the silence she heard her father speak loudly and suddenly.

"I am not in a position to have my children squander money on concerts and candy," he said. Margaret forgot her own grievance, and looked up. The boys looked resentful and gloomy; Rebecca was flushed, her eyes dropped, her lips trembling with disappointment.

"I had promised to take them to the Elks' Concert and dance," Mrs. Paget interpreted hastily. "But now Dad says the Bakers are coming over to play whist."

"Is it going to be a good show, Ted?" Margaret asked.

"Oh," Rebecca flashed into instant glowing response. "It's going to be a *dandy!* Every one's going to be there! Ford Patterson is going to do a monologue—he's as good as a professional!—and George is going to send up a bunch of carrots and parsnips! And the Weston Male Quartette, Mark, and a playlet by the Hunt's Crossing Amateur Theatrical Society!"

"Oh—oh!"—Margaret mimicked the eager rush of words. "Let me take them, Dad," she pleaded, "if it's going to be as fine as all that! I'll stand treat for the crowd."

"Oh, Mark, you darling!" burst from the rapturous Rebecca.

"Say, gee, we've got to get there early!" Theodore warned them, finishing his pudding with one mammoth spoonful.

"If you take them, my dear," Mr. Paget said graciously, "of course Mother and I are quite satisfied."

"I'll hold Robert by one ear and Rebecca by another," Margaret promised; "and if she so much as dares to look at George or Ted or Jimmy Barr or Paul, I'll——"

"Oh, Jimmy belongs to Louise, now," said Rebecca, radiantly. There was a joyous shout of laughter from the light-hearted juniors, and Rebecca, seeing her artless admission too late, turned scarlet while she laughed. Dinner broke up in confusion, as dinner at home always did, and everybody straggled upstairs to dress.

Margaret, changing her dress in a room that was insufferably hot, because the shades must be down, and the gas-lights as high as possible, reflected that another forty-eight hours would see her speeding back to the world of cool, awninged interiors, uniformed maids, the clink of iced glasses, the flash of white sails on blue water. She could surely afford for that time to be patient and sweet. She lifted Rebecca's starched petticoat from the bed to give Mother a seat, when Mother came rather wearily in to watch them.

"Sweet girl to take them, Mark," said Mother, appreciatively. "I was going to ask Brucie. But he's gone to bed, poor fellow; he's worn out to-night."

"He had a letter from Ned Gunther this morning," said Rebecca, cheerfully—powdering the tip of her pretty nose, her eyes almost crossed with concentration—"and I think it made him blue all day."

"Ned Gunther?" said Margaret.

"Chum at college," Rebecca elucidated; "a lot of them are going to Honolulu, just for this month, and of course they wanted Bruce. Mark, does that show?"

Margaret's heart ached for the beloved brother's disappointment. There it was again, all wrong! Before she left the house with the rioting youngsters, she ran upstairs to his room. Bruce, surrounded by scientific magazines, a drop-light with a vivid green shade over his shoulder, looked up with a welcoming smile.

"Sit down and talk, Mark," said he.

Margaret explained her hurry.

"Bruce—this isn't much fun!" she said, looking about the room with its shabby dresser and worn carpet. "Why aren't you going to the concert?"

"Is there a concert?" he asked, surprised.

"Why, didn't you hear us talking at dinner? The Elks, you know."

"Well—sure! I meant to go to that. I forgot it was to-night," he said, with his lazy smile. "I came home all in, forgot everything."

"Oh, come!" Margaret urged, as eagerly as Rebecca ever did. "It's early, Bruce, come on! You don't have to shave! We'll hold a seat—come on!"

"Sure, I will!" he said, suddenly roused. The magazines rapped on the floor, and Margaret had barely shut the door behind her when she heard his bare feet follow them.

It was like old times to sit next to him through the hot merry evening, while Rebecca glowed like a little rose among her friends, and the smaller boys tickled her ear with their whispered comments. Margaret had sent a telegram to Professor Tenison, and felt relieved that at least that strain was spared her. She even danced with Bruce after the concert, and with one or two old friends.

Afterward they strolled back slowly through the inky summer dark, finding the house hot and close when they came in. Margaret went upstairs, hearing her mother's apologetic, "Oh, Dad, why didn't I give you back your club?" as she passed the dining-room door. She knew Mother hated whist, and wondered rather irritably why she played it. The Paget family was slow to settle down. Robert became tearful and whining before he was finally bumped protesting into bed. Theodore and Duncan prolonged their ablutions until the noise of shouting, splashing, and thumping in the bathroom brought Mother to the foot of the stairs. Rebecca was conversational. She lay with her slender arms locked behind her head on the pillow, and talked, as Julie had talked on that memorable night five years ago. Margaret, restless in the hot darkness, wondering whether the maddening little shaft of light from the hall gas was annoying enough to warrant the effort of getting up and extinguishing it, listened and listened.

Rebecca wanted to join the Stage Club, but Mother wouldn't let her unless Bruce did. Rebecca belonged to the Progressive Diners. Did Mark suppose Mother'd think she was crazy if she asked the family not to be in evidence when the crowd came to the house for the salad course? And Rebecca wanted to write to Bruce's chum, not regularly, you know, Mark, but just now and then, he was so nice! And Mother didn't like the idea. Margaret was obviously supposed to lend a hand with these interesting tangles.

". . . and I said, 'Certainly not! I won't unmask at all, if it comes to that!'

. . . And imagine that elegant fellow carrying my old books and my skates! So I wrote, and Maudie and I decided. . . . And Mark, if it wasn't a perfectly *gorgeous* box of roses! . . . That old, old dimity, but

Mother pressed and freshened it up. . . . Not that I want to marry him, or any one . . ."

Margaret wakened from uneasy drowsing with a start. The hall was dark now, the room cooler. Rebecca was asleep. Hands, hands she knew well, were drawing a light covering over her shoulders. She opened her eyes to see her mother.

"I've been wondering if you're disappointed about your friend not coming to-morrow, Mark?" said the tender voice.

"Oh, no-o!" said Margaret, hardily. "Mother—why are you up so late?"

"Just going to bed," said the other, soothingly. "Blanche forgot to put the oatmeal into the cooker, and I went downstairs again. I'll say my prayers in here."

Margaret went off to sleep again, as she had so many hundred times before, with her mother kneeling beside her.

CHAPTER VII

It seemed but a few moments before the blazing Sunday was precipitated upon them, and everybody was late for everything.

The kitchen was filled with the smoke from hot griddles blue in the sunshine when Margaret went downstairs; and in the dining-room the same merciless light fell upon the sticky syrup pitcher, and upon the stains on the tablecloth. Cream had been brought in in the bottle, the bread tray was heaped with orange skins, and the rolls piled on the tablecloth. Bruce, who had already been to church with Mother and was off for a day's sail, was dividing his attention between Robert and his watch. Rebecca, daintily busy with the special cup and plate that were one of her little affectations, was all ready for the day, except as to dress, wearing a thin little kimono over her blue ribbons and starched embroideries. Mother was putting up a little lunch for Bruce. Confusion reigned. The younger boys were urged to hurry, if they wanted to make the "nine." Rebecca was going to wait for the "half-past ten," because the "kids sang at nine, and it was fierce." Mr. Paget and his sons departed together, and the girls went upstairs for a hot, tiring tussle with beds and dusting before starting for church. They left their mother busy with the cream freezer in the kitchen. It was very hot even then.

But it was still hotter, walking home in the burning midday stillness. A group of young people waited lazily for letters, under the trees outside the post-office door. Otherwise the main street was deserted. A languid little breeze brought the far echoes of pianos and phonographs from this direction and that.

"Who's that on the porch?" said Rebecca, suddenly, as they neared home, instantly finding the stranger among her father and the boys. Margaret, glancing up sharply, saw, almost with a sensation of sickness, the big, ungainly figure, the beaming smile, and the shock of dark hair that belonged to nobody else in the world but John Tenison. A stony chill settled about her heart as she went up the steps and gave him her hand.

Oh, if he only couldn't stay to dinner, she prayed. Oh, if only he could spare them time for no more than a flying visit! With a sinking heart she smiled her greetings.

"Doctor Tenison—this is very nice of you!" Margaret said. "Have you met my father—my small brothers?"

"We have been having a great talk," said John Tenison, genially, "and this young man"—he indicated Robert—"has been showing me the colored supplement of the paper. I didn't have any word from you, Miss Paget," he went on, "so I took the chance of finding you. And your mother has assured me that I will not put her out by staying to have luncheon with you."

"Oh, that's nice!" Margaret said mechanically, trying to dislodge Robert from the most comfortable chair by a significant touch of her fingers on his small shoulder. Robert perfectly understood that she wanted the chair, but continued in absorbed study of the comic supplement, merely wriggling resentfully at Margaret's touch. Margaret, at the moment, would have been glad to use violence on the stubborn, serene little figure. When he was finally dislodged, she sat down, still flushed from her walk and the nervousness Doctor Tenison's arrival caused her, and tried to bring the conversation into a normal channel. But an interruption occurred in the arrival of Harry and Julie in the runabout; the little boys swarmed down to examine it. Julie, very pretty, with a perceptible little new air of dignity, went upstairs to freshen hair and gown, and Harry, pushing his hat back the better to mop his forehead, immediately engaged Doctor Tenison's attention with the details of what sounded to Margaret like a particularly uninteresting operation, which he had witnessed the day before.

Utterly discouraged, and acutely wretched, Margaret presently slipped away, and went into the kitchen, to lend a hand with the dinner preparations if help was needed. The room presented a scene if possible a little more confused than that of the day before, and was certainly hotter. Her mother, flushed and hurried, in a fresh but rather unbecoming gingham, was putting up a cold supper for the younger boys, who, having duly attended to their religious duties, were to take a long afternoon tramp, with a possible interval of fishing. She buttered each slice of the great loaf before she cut it, and lifted it carefully on the knife before beginning the next slice. An opened pot of jam stood at her elbow. A tin cup and the boys' fishing-gear lay on a chair. Theodore and Duncan themselves hung over these preparations; never apparently helping themselves to food, yet never with empty mouths. Blanche, moaning "The Palms" with the insistence of one who wishes to show her entire familiarity with a melody, was at the range.

Roast veal, instead of the smothered chickens her mother had so often, and cooked so deliciously, a mountain of mashed potato—corn on the cob, and an enormous heavy salad mantled with mayonnaise—Margaret could have wept over the hopelessly plebeian dinner!

"Mother, mayn't I get down the fingerbowls," she asked; "and mayn't we have black coffee in the silver pot, afterward?"

Mrs. Paget looked absently at her for a dubious second. "I don't like to ask Blanche to wash all that extra glass," she said, in an undertone, adding briskly to Theodore, "No, no, Ted! You can't have all that cake. Half that!" and to Blanche herself, "Don't leave the door open when you go in, Blanche; I just drove all the flies out of the dining-room." Then she returned to Margaret with a cordial: "Why, certainly, dear! Any one who wants coffee, after tea, can have it! Dad always wants his cup of tea."

"Nobody but us ever serves tea with dinner!" Margaret muttered; but her mother did not hear it. She buckled the strap of the lunch-box, straightened her back with an air of relief, and pushed down her rolled-up sleeves.

"Don't lose that napkin, Ted," said she, and receiving the boy's grateful kiss haphazard between her hair and forehead, she added affectionately: "You're more than welcome, dear! We're all ready, Mark—go and tell them, dear! All right, Blanche."

Ruffled and angry, Margaret went to summon the others to dinner. Maudie had joined them on the porch now, and had been urged to stay, and was already trying her youthful wiles on the professor.

"Well, he'll have to leave on the five o'clock!" Margaret reflected, steeled to bitter endurance until that time. For everything went wrong, and dinner was one long nightmare for her. Professor Tenison's napkin turned out to be a traycloth. Blanche, asked for another, disappeared for several minutes, and returned without it, to whisper in Mrs. Paget's ear. Mrs. Paget immediately sent her own fresh napkin to the guest. The incident, or something in their murmured conversation, gave Rebecca and Maudie "the giggles." There seemed an exhausting amount of passing and repassing of plates. The room was hot, the supply of ice insufficient. Mr. Paget dwelt on his favorite grievance—"The old man isn't needed, these days. They're getting all young fellows into the bank. They put young college fellows in there who are getting pretty near the money I am—after twenty-five years!" In any pause, Mrs. Paget could be heard, patiently dissuading little Robert from his fixed intention of accompanying the older boys on their walk, whether invited or uninvited.

John Tenison behaved charmingly, eating his dinner with enjoyment, looking interestedly from one face to the other, sympathetic, alert, and amused. But Margaret writhed in spirit at what he must be thinking.

Finally the ice cream, in a melting condition, and the chocolate cake, very sticky, made their appearance; and although these were regular Sunday treats, the boys felt called upon to cheer. Julie asked her mother in an audible undertone if she "ought" to eat cake. Doctor Tenison produced an enormous box of chocolates, and Margaret was disgusted with the frantic scramble her brothers made to secure them.

"If you're going for a walk, dear," her mother said, when the meal was over, "you'd better *go*. It's almost three now."

"I don't know whether we will, it's so hot," Margaret said, in an indifferent tone, but she could easily have broken into disheartened tears.

"Oh, go," Julie urged, "it's much cooler out." They were up in Margaret's old room, Mrs. Paget tying a big apron about Julie's ruffled frock, preparatory to an attack upon the demoralized kitchen. "We think he's lovely," the little matron went on approvingly. "Don't fall in love with him, Mark."

"Why not?" Margaret said carelessly, pinning on her hat.

"Well, I don't imagine he's a marrying man," said the young authority, wisely. Margaret flushed, and was angry at herself for flushing. But when Mrs. Paget had gone downstairs, Julie came very simply and charmingly over to her sister, and standing close beside her with embarrassed eyes on her own hand—very youthful in its plain ring—as she played with the bureau furnishing, she said:

"Mother tell you?"

Margaret looked down at the flushed face.

"Are you sorry, Ju?"

"Sorry!" The conscious eyes flashed into view. "*Sorry!*" Julie echoed in astonishment. "Why, Mark," she said dreamily—there was no affectation of maturity in her manner now, and it was all the more impressive for that. "Why, Mark," said she, "it's—it's the most wonderful thing that ever happened to me! I think and think"—her voice dropped very low—"of holding it in my arms—mine and Harry's, you know—and of its little face!"

Margaret, stirred, kissed the wet lashes.

"Ju, but you're so young—you're such a baby yourself!" she said.

"And, Mark," Julie said, unheeding, "you know what Harry and I are going to call her, if it's a girl? Not for Mother, for it's so confusing to have two Julias, but for you! Because," her arms went about her sister, "you've always been such a darling to me, Mark!"

Margaret went downstairs very thoughtfully, and out into the silent Sunday streets. Where they walked, or what they talked of, she did not know. She knew that her head ached, and that the village looked very commonplace, and that the day was very hot. She found it more painful than sweet to be strolling along beside the big, loose-jointed figure, and to send an occasional side glance to John Tenison's earnest face, which wore its pleasantest expression now. Ah, well, it would be all over at five o'clock, she said wearily to herself, and she could go home and lie down with her aching head in a darkened room, and try not to think what to-day *might* have been. Try not to think of the dainty little luncheon Annie would have given them at Mrs. Carr-Boldt's, of the luxurious choice of amusements afterward: motoring over the lovely country roads, rowing on the wide still water, watching the tennis courts, or simply resting in deep chairs on the sweep of velvet lawn above the river.

She came out of a reverie to find Doctor Tenison glancing calmly up from his watch.

"The train was five o'clock, was it?" he said. "I've missed it!"

"Missed it!" Margaret echoed blankly. Then, as the horrible possibility dawned upon her, "Oh, *no!*"

"Oh, yes—bad as that!" he said, laughing at her.

Poor Margaret, fighting despair, struggled to recover herself.

"Well, I thought it might have been important to you!" she said, laughing quite naturally. "There's a seven-six, but it stops everywhere, and a ten-thirty. The ten-thirty is best, because supper's apt to be a little late."

"The ten-thirty," Doctor Tenison echoed contentedly. Margaret's heart sank—five more hours of the struggle! "But perhaps that's an imposition," he said. "Isn't there a tea-room—isn't there an inn here where we could have a bite?"

"We aren't in Berlin," Margaret reminded him cheerfully. "There's a hotel—but Mother would never forgive me for leading any one *there!* No, we'll take that little walk I told you of, and Mother will give us something to eat later. Perhaps if we're late enough," she added to herself, "we can have just tea and bread and jam alone, after the others."

Suddenly, unreasonably, she felt philosophical and gay. The little episode of missing the train had given her the old dear feeling of adventure and comradeship again. Things couldn't be any worse than they had been at noon, anyway. The experience had been thoroughly disenchanting. What did a few hours, more or less, matter! Let him be disgusted if he wanted to, she couldn't help it!

It was cooler now, the level late shadows were making even Weston pretty. They went up a steep shady lane to the old graveyard, and wandered, peacefully, contentedly, among the old graves. Margaret gathered her thin gown from contact with the tangled, uncut grass; they had to disturb a flock of nibbling sheep to cross to the crumbling wall. Leaning on the uneven stones that formed it, they looked down at the roofs of the village, half lost in tree-tops; and listened to the barking of dogs, and the shrill voices of children. The sun sank, lower, lower. There was a feeling of dew in the air as they went slowly home.

When, at seven o'clock, they opened the gate, they found on the side porch only Rebecca, enchanting in something pink and dotted, Mother, and Dad.

[53]

"Lucky we waited!" said Rebecca, rising, and signalling some wordless message to Margaret that required dimples, widened eyes, compressed lips, and an expression of utter secrecy. "Supper's all ready," she added casually.

"Where are the others?" Margaret said, experiencing the most pleasant sensation she had had in twenty-four hours.

"Ju and Harry went home, Rob's at George's, boys walking," said Rebecca, briefly, still dimpling mysteriously with additional information. She gave Margaret an eloquent side glance as she led the way into the dining-room. At the doorway Margaret stopped, astounded.

The room was hardly recognizable now. It was cool and delightful, with the diminished table daintily set for five. The old silver candlesticks and silver teapot presided over blue bowls of berries and the choicest of Mother's preserved fruits. Some one had found time to put fresh parsley about the Canton platter of cold meats, some one had made a special trip to Mrs. O'Brien's for the cream that filled the Wedgwood pitcher. Margaret felt tears press suddenly against her eyes.

"Oh, Beck!" she could only stammer when the sisters went into the kitchen for hot water and tea biscuit.

"Mother did it," said Rebecca, returning her hug with fervor. "She gave us all an awful talking to after you left! She said here was dear old Mark, who always worked herself to death for us, trying to make a nice impression, and to have things go smoothly, and we were all acting like Indians, and everything so confused at dinner, and hot and noisy! So, later, when Paul and I and the others were walking, we saw you and Doctor Tenison going up toward the graveyard, and I tore home and told Mother he'd missed the five and would be back; it was after five then, and we just flew!"

It was all like a pleasant awakening after a troubled dream. As Margaret took her place at the little feast she felt an exquisite sensation of peace and content sink into her heart. Mother was so gracious and charming, behind the urn; Rebecca irresistible in her admiration of the famous professor. Her father was his sweetest self, delightfully reminiscent of his boyhood, and his visit to the White House in Lincoln's day, with "my uncle, the judge." But it was to her mother's face that Margaret's eyes returned most often; she wanted—she was vaguely conscious that she wanted—to get away from the voices and laughter, and think about Mother. How sweet she was, just sweet, and after all, how few people were that in this world! They were clever, and witty, and rich—plenty of them, but how little sweetness there was! How few faces, like her mother's, did not show a line that was not all tenderness and goodness.

They laughed over their teacups like old friends; the professor and Rebecca shouting joyously together, Mr. Paget one broad twinkle, Mrs. Paget radiantly reflecting, as she always did reflect, the others' mood. It was a memorably happy hour.

And after tea they sat on the porch, and the stars came out, and presently the moon sent silver shafts through the dark foliage of the trees. Little Rob came home, and climbed silently, contentedly, into his father's lap.

"Sing something, Mark," said Dad, then; and Margaret, sitting on the steps with her head against her mother's knee, found it very simple to begin in the darkness one of the old songs he loved:

> "Don't you cry, ma honey,
> Don't you weep no more."

Rebecca, sitting on the rail, one slender arm flung above her head about the pillar, joined her own young voice to Margaret's sweet and steady one. The others hummed a little. John Tenison, sitting watching them, his locked hands hanging between his knees, saw in the moonlight a sudden glitter on the mother's cheek.

Presently Bruce, tired and happy and sunburned, came through the splashed silver-and-black of the street to sit by Margaret, and put his arm about her; and the younger boys, returning full of the day's great deeds, spread themselves comfortably over the lower steps. Before long all their happy voices rose together, on "Believe me," and "Working on the Railroad," and "Seeing Nellie Home," and a dozen more of the old songs that young people have sung for half a century in the summer moonlight.

And then it was time to say good-night to Professor Tenison. "Come again, sir!" said Mr. Paget, heartily; the boys slid their hands, still faintly suggestive of fish, cordially into his; Rebecca promised to mail him a certain discussed variety of fern the very next day; Bruce's voice sounded all hearty good-will as he hoped that he wouldn't miss Doctor Tenison's next visit. Mrs. Paget, her hand in his, raised keen, almost anxious eyes to his face.

"But surely you'll be down our way again?" said she, unsmilingly.

"Oh, surely." The professor was unable to keep his eyes from moving toward Margaret, and the mother saw it.

"Good-bye for the present, then," she said, still very gravely.

"Good-bye, Mrs. Paget," said Doctor Tenison. "It's been an inestimable privilege to meet you all. I haven't ever had a happier day."

Margaret, used to the extravagant speeches of another world, thought this merely very charming politeness. But her heart sang as they walked away together. He liked them—he had had a nice time!

"Now I know what makes you so different from other women," said John Tenison, when he and Margaret were alone. "It's having that wonderful mother! She—she—well, she's one woman in a million; I don't have to tell you that! It's something to thank God for, a mother like that; it's a privilege to know her. I've been watching her all day, and I've been wondering what *she* gets out of it—that was what puzzled me; but now, just now, I've found out! This morning, thinking what her life is, I couldn't see what *repaid* her, do you see? What made up to her for the unending, unending effort, and sacrifice, the pouring out of love and sympathy and help—year after year after year. . . ."

He hesitated, but Margaret did not speak.

"You know," he went on musingly, "in these days, when women just serenely ignore the question of children, or at most, as a special concession, bring up one or two—just the one or two whose expenses can be comfortably met!—there's something magnificent in a woman like your mother, who begins eight destinies instead of one! She doesn't strain and chafe to express herself through the medium of poetry or music or the stage, but she puts her whole splendid philosophy into her nursery—launches sound little bodies and minds that have their first growth cleanly and purely about her knees. Responsibility—that's what these other women say they are afraid of! But it seems to me there's no responsibility like that of decreeing that young lives simply *shall not be.* Why, what good is learning, or elegance of manner, or painfully acquired fineness of speech, and taste and point of view, if you are not going to distil it into the growing plants, the only real hope we have in the world! You know, Miss Paget," his smile was very sweet in the half darkness, "there's a higher tribunal than the social tribunal of this world, after all; and it seems to me that a woman who stands there, as your mother will, with a forest of new lives about her, and a record like hers, will—will find she has a Friend at court!" he finished whimsically.

They were at a lonely corner, and a garden fence offering Margaret a convenient support, she laid her arms suddenly upon the rosevine that covered it, and her face upon her arms, and cried as if her heart was broken.

"Why, why—my dear girl!" the professor said, aghast. He laid his hand on the shaking shoulders, but Margaret shook it off.

"I'm not what you think I am!" she sobbed out, incoherently. "I'm not different from other women; I'm just as selfish and bad and mean as the worst of them! And I'm not worthy to t-tie my m-mother's *shoes!*"

"Margaret!" John Tenison said unsteadily. And in a flash her drooping bright head was close to his lips, and both his big arms were about her. "You know I love you, don't you, Margaret?" he said hoarsely, over and over, with a sort of fierce intensity. "You know that, don't you? *Don't* you, Margaret?"

Margaret could not speak. Emotion swept her like a rising tide from all her familiar moorings; her heart thundered, there was a roaring in her ears. She was conscious of a wild desire to answer him, to say one hundredth part of all she felt; but she could only rest, breathless, against him, her frightened eyes held by the eyes so near, his arms about her.

"You do, don't you, Margaret?" he said more gently. "You love me, don't you? Don't you?"

And after a long time, or what seemed a long time, while they stood motionless in the summer night, with the great branches of the trees moving a little overhead, and garden scents creeping out on the damp air, Margaret said, with a sort of breathless catch in her voice:

"You *know* I do!" And with the words the fright left her eyes, and happy tears filled them, and she raised her face to his.

Coming back from the train half an hour later, she walked between a new heaven and a new earth! The friendly stars seemed just overhead; a thousand delicious odors came from garden beds and recently watered lawns. She moved through the confusion that always attended the settling down of the Pagets for the night like one in a dream, and was glad to find herself at last lying in the darkness beside the sleeping Rebecca again. Now, now, she could think!

But it was all too wonderful for reasonable thought. Margaret clasped both her hands against her rising heart. He loved her. She could think of the very words he had used in telling her, over and over again. She need no longer wonder and dream and despair: he had *said* it. He loved her, had loved her from the very first. His old aunt suspected it, and his chum suspected it, and he had thought Margaret knew it. And beside him in that brilliant career that she had followed so wistfully in her dreams, Margaret saw herself, *his wife*. Young and clever and good to look upon—yes, she was free to-night to admit herself all these good things for his sake!— and his wife, mounting as he mounted beside the one man in the world she had elected to admire and love. "Doctor and Mrs. John Tenison"—so it would be written. "Doctor Tenison's wife"—"This is Mrs. Tenison"— she seemed already to hear the magical sound of it!

Love—what a wonderful thing it was! How good God was to send this best of all gifts to her! She thought how it belittled the other good things of the world. She asked no more of life, now; she was loved by a good man, and a great man, and she was to be his wife. Ah, the happy years together that would date from to-night—Margaret was thrilling already to their delights. "For better or worse," the old words came to her with a new meaning. There would be no worse, she said to herself with sudden conviction— how could there be? Poverty, privation, sickness might come—but to bear them with John—to comfort and sustain him, to be shut away with him from all the world but the world of their own four walls—why, that would be the greatest happiness of all! What hardship could be hard that knitted their two hearts closer together; what road too steep if they essayed it hand in hand?

And that—her confused thoughts ran on—that was what had changed all life for Julie. She had forgotten Europe, forgotten all the idle ambitions of her girlhood, because she loved her husband; and now the new miracle was to come to her—the miracle of a child, the little perfect promise of the days to come. How marvellous—how *marvellous* it was! The little imperative, helpless third person, bringing to radiant youth and irresponsibility the terrors of danger and anguish, and the great final joy, to share together. That was life. Julie was living; and although Margaret's own heart was not yet a wife's, and she could not yet find room for the love beyond that, still she was strangely, deeply stirred now by a longing for all the experiences that life held.

How she loved everything and everybody to-night—how she loved just being alive—just being Margaret Paget, lying here in the dark dreaming and thinking. There was no one in the world with whom she would change places to-night! Margaret found herself thinking of one woman of her acquaintance after another—and her own future, opening all color of rose before her, seemed to her the one enviable path through the world.

In just one day, she realized with vague wonder, her slowly formed theories had been set at naught, her whole philosophy turned upside down. Had these years of protest and rebellion done no more than lead her in a wide circle, past empty gain, and joyless mirth, and the dead sea fruit of riches and idleness, back to her mother's knees again? She had met brilliant women, rich women, courted women—but where among them was one whose face had ever shone as her mother's shone to-day? The overdressed, idle dowagers; the matrons, with their too-gay frocks, their too-full days, their too-rich food; the girls, all crudeness, artifice, all scheming openly for their own advantage—where among them all was happiness? Where among them was one whom Margaret had heard say—as she had heard her mother say so many, many times—"Children, this is a happy day,"—"Thank God for another lovely Sunday all together,"—"Isn't it lovely to get up and find the sun shining?"—"Isn't it good to come home hungry to such a nice dinner?"

And what a share of happiness her mother had given the world! How she had planned and worked for them all—Margaret let her arm fall across the sudden ache in her eyes as she thought of the Christmas mornings, and the stuffed stockings at the fireplace that proved every childish wish remembered, every little hidden hope guessed! Darling Mother—she hadn't had much money for those Christmas stockings, they must have been carefully planned, down to the last candy cane. And how her face would beam, as she sat at the breakfast-table, enjoying her belated coffee, after the cold walk to church, and responding warmly to the onslaught of kisses and hugs that added fresh color to her cold, rosy cheeks! What a mother she was—Margaret remembered her making them all help her clear up the Christmas disorder of tissue paper and ribbons; then came the inevitable bed making, then tippets and overshoes, for a long walk with Dad. They would come back to find the dining-room warm, the long table set, the house deliciously fragrant from the immense turkey that their mother, a fresh apron over her holiday gown, was basting at the oven. Then came the feast, and then games until twilight, and more table-setting; and the baby, whoever he was, was tucked away upstairs before tea, and the evening ended with singing, gathered about Mother at the piano.

"How happy we all were!" Margaret said; "and how she worked for us!"

And suddenly theories and speculation ended, and she *knew*. She knew that faithful, self-forgetting service, and the love that spends itself over and over, only to be renewed again and again, are the secret of happiness. For another world, perhaps leisure and beauty and luxury—but in this one, "Who loses his life shall gain it." Margaret knew now that her mother was not only the truest, the finest, the most generous woman she had ever known, but the happiest as well.

She thought of other women like her mother; she suddenly saw what made their lives beautiful. She could understand now why Emily Porter, her old brave little associate of school-teaching days, was always bright, why Mary Page, plodding home from the long day at the library desk to her little cottage and crippled sister, at night, always made one feel the better and happier for meeting her.

Mrs. Carr-Boldt's days were crowded to the last instant, it was true; but what a farce it was, after all, Margaret said to herself in all honesty, to humor her in her little favorite belief that she was a busy woman! Milliner, manicure, butler, chef, club, card-table, tea-table—these and a thousand things like them filled her day, and they might all be swept away in an hour, and leave no one the worse. Suppose her own summons came; there would be a little flurry throughout the great establishment, legal matters to settle, notes of thanks to be written for flowers. Margaret could imagine Victoria and Harriet, awed but otherwise unaffected, home from school in midweek, and to be sent back before the next Monday. Their lives would go on unchanged, their mother had never buttered bread for them, never schemed for their boots and hats, never watched their work and play, and called them to her knees for praise and blame. Mr. Carr-Boldt would have his club, his business, his yacht, his motor-cars—he was well accustomed to living in cheerful independence of family claims.

But life without Mother——! In a sick moment of revelation Margaret saw it. She saw them gathering in the horrible emptiness and silence of the house Mother had kept so warm and bright, she saw her father's stooped shoulders and trembling hands, she saw Julie and Beck, red-eyed, white-cheeked, in fresh black—she seemed to hear the low-toned voices that would break over and over again so cruelly into sobs. What could they do—who could take up the work she laid down—who would watch and plan and work for them all, now? Margaret thought of the empty place at the table, of the room that, after all these years, was no longer "Mother's room——"

Oh, no—no—no!—She began to cry bitterly in the dark. No, please God, they would hold her safe with them for many years. Mother should live to see some of the fruits of the long labor of love. She should know that with every fresh step in life, with every deepening experience, her children grew to love her better, turned to her more and more! There would be Christmases as sweet as the old ones, if not so gay; there would come a day—Margaret's whole being thrilled to the thought—when little forms would run ahead of John and herself up the worn path, and when their children would be gathered in Mother's experienced arms! Did life hold a more exquisite moment, she wondered, than that in which she would hear her mother praise them!

All her old castles in the air seemed cheap and tinselled to-night, beside these tender dreams that had their roots in the real truths of life. Travel and position, gowns and motor-cars, yachts and country houses, these things were to be bought in all their perfection by the highest bidder, and always would be. But love and character and service, home and the wonderful charge of little lives—the "pure religion breathing household laws" that guided and perfected the whole—these were not to be bought, they were only to be prayed for, worked for, bravely won.

"God has been very good to me," Margaret said to herself very seriously; and in her old childish fashion she made some new resolves. From now on, she thought, with a fervor that made it seem half accomplished, she would be a very different woman. If joy came, she would share it as far as she could; if sorrow, she would show her mother that her daughter was not all unworthy of her. To-morrow, she thought, she would go and see Julie. Dear old Ju, whose heart was so full of the little Margaret! Margaret had a sudden tender memory of the days when Theodore and Duncan and Rob were all babies in turn. Her mother would gather the little daily supply of fresh clothes from bureau and chest every morning, and carry the little bath-tub into the sunny nursery window, and sit there with only a bobbing downy head and waving pink fingers visible from the great warm bundle of bath apron. . . . Ju would be doing that now.

And she had sometimes wished, or half formed the wish, that she and Bruce had been the only ones! Yes, came the sudden thought, but it wouldn't have been Bruce and Margaret, after all, it would have been Bruce and Charlie.

Good God! That was what women did, then, when they denied the right of life to the distant, unwanted, possible little person! Calmly, constantly, in all placid philosophy and self-justification, they kept from the world— not only the troublesome new baby, with his tears and his illnesses, his merciless exactions, his endless claim on mind and body and spirit—but perhaps the glowing beauty of a Rebecca, the buoyant indomitable spirit of a Ted, the sturdy charm of a small Robert, whose grip on life, whose energy and ambition were as strong as Margaret's own!

Margaret stirred uneasily, frowned in the dark. It seemed perfectly incredible, it seemed perfectly *impossible* that if Mother had had only the two—and how many thousands of women didn't have that!—she, Margaret, a pronounced and separate entity, travelled, ambitious, and to be the wife of one of the world's great men, might not have been lying here in the summer night, rich in love and youth and beauty and her dreams!

It was all puzzling, all too big for her to understand. But she could do what Mother did, just take the nearest duty and fulfil it, and sleep well, and rise joyfully to fresh effort.

Margaret felt as if she would never sleep again. The summer night was cool, she was cramped and chilly; but still her thoughts raced on, and she could not shut her eyes. She turned and pressed her face resolutely into the pillow, and with a great sigh renounced the joys and sorrows, the lessons and the awakening that the long day had held.

A second later there was a gentle rustle at the door.

"Mark," a voice whispered. "Can't you sleep?"

Margaret locked her arms tight about her mother, as the older woman knelt beside her.

"Why, how cold you are, sweetheart!" her mother protested, tucking covers about her. "I *thought* I heard you sigh! I got up to lock the stairway door: Baby's gotten a trick of walking in his sleep when he's overtired. It's nearly one o'clock, Mark! What have you been doing?"

"Thinking." Margaret put her lips very close to her mother's ear. "Mother——" she stammered and stopped. Mrs. Paget kissed her.

"Daddy and I thought so," she said simply; and further announcement was not needed. "My darling little girl!" she added tenderly; and then, after a silence, "He is very fine, Mark, so unaffected, so gentle and nice with the boys. I—I think I'm glad, Mark. I lose my girl, but there's no happiness like a happy marriage, dear."

"No, you won't lose me, Mother," Margaret said, clinging very close. "We hadn't much time to talk, but this much we did decide. You see, John—John goes to Germany for a year, next July. So we thought—in June or July, Mother, just as Julie's was! Just a little wedding like Ju's. You see, that's better than interrupting the term, or trying to settle down, when we'd have to move in July. And, Mother, I'm going to write Mrs. Carr-Boldt—she can get a thousand girls to take my place, her niece is dying to do it!—and I'm going to take my old school here for the term. Mr. Forbes spoke to me about it after church this morning; they want me back. I want this year at home; I want to see more of Bruce and Ju, and sort of stand by darling little Beck! But it's for you, most of all, Mother," said Margaret, with difficulty. "I've always loved you, Mother, but you don't know how wonderful I think you are——" She broke off pitifully, "Ah, *Mother!*"

For her mother's arms had tightened convulsively about her, and the face against her own was wet.

"Are you talking?" said Rebecca, rearing herself up suddenly, with a web of bright hair falling over her shoulder. "You said your prayers on Mark last night," said she, reproachfully; "come over and say them on me to-night, Mother."

The American Flaggs

CHAPTER I

"Well, I'll see the Flagg place anyway," Penelope thought. "They can't kill me for coming in. They can't do anything more than throw me out!"

The spring morning was still and hot with that particular stillness and hotness that is essentially Californian. No breeze stirred the rich beauty of the Flagg gardens. They spread about in every direction like a royal park in beds of the blazing colors of tulips and primulas and pansies, in masses of rich low shrubs polished like enamel in every shade of green under the overhanging trees. Oaks and poplars and willows, birches and alders, and the perennial foliage of peppers and evergreens were all set out together, hiding the turn of the road, hiding the house. Houses, rather. Everyone knew—even Penelope Fitzpercy, who had never been within a mile of the place before this morning—that all summer long the Flaggs all lived together, an enormous clan, on this hundred-acre estate, and that rather than one house they occupied half a dozen different houses.

A charming young woman in a bright little convertible had given her a lift from the station. "The Flagg place?" she had said. "Oh, but that's a good mile up—toward the hills here. I'll take you to the gate anyway. I've never been inside."

Which she had most obligingly done. Otherwise, Penelope mused, as she toiled upward through the interminable rises of the gardens, otherwise it would have been an exhausting walk. The tremendous iron gates, wreathed this morning in creamy Banksia roses over their dark old ivy coats, were far behind and below her now, and still the parterres, the terraces, the dignity of stately lawns stretched on, and still there was no indication of a dwelling.

A small sign appeared: "LOOK OUT FOR CHILDREN PLAYING." That was something, at least. Penelope passed the sign, turned a wide bend, and saw a house at last, an old-fashioned wooden house, high on flowered brick terraces, with spiraled porch pillars and a cupola, white-painted to a dazzling cream, generously bay-windowed. It stood on a rising slope of emerald lawn, surrounded by exquisitely groomed flower beds blazing with glory.

Prim white net curtains were looped back at all the windows; there was a little bowed conservatory at one side; the front door, set in panels of glass, was wide open on this warm morning. Penelope went up the steps.

She was panting a little from her walk now and stood for a moment with her back turned to the doorway, her eyes moving over the scene below her. A footpath descended between the shrubberies straight ahead, ending at a glint of water. A swimming pool for the Flagg youngsters perhaps. On either side, more than half concealed in the magnificent trees, were suggestions of roofs, where houses were hidden away. No human being was in sight, yet there was somehow a sense of life and activity all about; in the fragrant stillness Penelope could hear voices; children's shrill piping laughter, some man's deep-pitched note.

She turned to face a maid. Could she see Mrs Flagg?

The maid looked dubious. Had she telephoned Mrs Lindenborg? They were announcing Miss Constance's engagement——

"Who's Mrs Lindenborg?"

"The housekeeper, miss." The maid was looking at Penelope's hair with great approval.

"Could I see her now?"

"She may have gone to see her son in San Francisco. She goes most Saturdays. If you'll wait just a minute, miss." There was something pleasant and simple about the little maid. She nodded encouragingly to a porch chair, and went tripping away in her gray moiré and lace bows, down the path between the shrubberies, toward the glint of water and the sound of voices.

Penelope waited; she looked at the flowers that were so richly gay in the sunshine, so richly dark in the shadows, looked at the great overhanging trees. The moments went by; delicious odors of something cooking in butter came from the big west wing of the house. The kitchen was there; they were going to have popovers or fritters or fried oysters for lunch. A clock struck the half-hour after twelve solemnly, and a sudden wave of uncertainty and embarrassment went over Penelope; this was an awkward hour to call on strangers; hers was a silly enough business here. A sampler —an old American sampler for sale. That was what it amounted to, when all was said and done! In a panic she thought that she would escape; hurry down that stretch of road between the terraced rose beds, be gone before any Flagg caught sight of her.

It was too late. The maid was returning from behind the shrubberies, mounting the wide terraced steps between them, a gray-headed man walking with her. Penelope was usually self-contained and calm enough, could even be arrogant upon occasion, but there was something about the ordered beauty and quiet of this place that affected her oddly, made her feel young and fluttered. She sat on, rooted to her porch chair, her eyes on the approaching couple.

They ascended the steps; the man—he was a handsome, middle-aged man, squarely built and not tall—greeted her with a pleasant expectant smile.

"You wanted to see my mother?"

"Well—anybody," Penelope altered it, haltingly.

"We're having a sort of family party," he said. "One of my nieces has just announced her engagement. There's to be a lunch down in the garden, and Mother's down there. We don't let her move about much. After all," he added, a little proud of it, "she's getting on for seventy-seven."

"Oh, you'll do!" Penelope said hastily, and laughed. The man laughed, too.

"What was it?" he said. He spoke agreeably enough, but guardedly, and Penelope knew why. He thought she was going to borrow money or try to sell him books. He was regretting that the housekeeper wasn't here to stave her off. "I'm Mark Flagg," he added, "and you're——?"

"Penelope Fitzpercy. I'm from Menlo Park," Penelope said. "My mother is Mrs Ellabeth Fitzpercy—she writes a weekly column—for papers, you know—under the name of 'Ariel Hunter.'"

"I see," the man said slowly, with a glance at the package Pen held wrapped in her hand. It looked like an unpublished book—a manuscript —the girl was peddling her mother's productions——

"This isn't one of Mother's books," Pen said, proud and amused and secretly hurt. "It's a sampler. It belonged to my grandfather, Philip Fitzpercy, of Baltimore, and we only found it when his things were sent out after he died. It was with a lot of other pictures."

The man sat down comfortably in a neighboring chair; at his gesture Pen sat down, too.

"Let's hear about it," he said patiently.

"Well, it's just an old sampler," the girl began. Young and flushed and lovely in her shabby white dress and old white hat, she bent forward, and the great coil of ashen-gold hair moved on her neck. "My grandfather was a sort of—collector," she explained. "He used to buy etchings and pictures—in lots, you know. That is, when he was young, he did. The family," Pen interpolated delicately, "hasn't had very much money since then."

"I see," the man said.

"So this sampler—it was among a lot of other things. And Mother read somewhere—everyone knows, I guess, that your mother has a wonderful collection of that sort of thing. And so Mother wondered—she doesn't know what it's worth. But we know it's valuable, and the letter, too. And

[65]

of course," the girl ended with a little uncomfortable laugh, "the Fitz-percys are always hard up!"

"But what my mother has is only family stuff," Mark Flagg said kindly, as Pen paused, a little at a loss. "She doesn't want things just because they're old—just because they are Americana. She's in no sense a collector. I'm sorry."

He added the last word gently. The girl was young and beautiful and obviously tired from her walk.

"I hope you'll let them give you a sandwich and a glass of milk. We're all down in the garden, but they'll take care of you at the house here," he said. "You've had a hot walk."

"This is a Flagg sampler," Pen persisted. She felt discouraged and flat, but at least she would not be beaten too easily.

("It ought to be worth a hundred at least to them," her mother had said, discussing the sale. "We came by it honestly; we've a right to sell it.")

"It's the sampler of a little girl of eight, Hannah Carter Flagg, and it was done for Colonel Washington—there's a letter from him with it," Penelope persisted. A hundred dollars was a lot of money.

There was a sudden change in the browned, intelligent face of the man watching her. His eyes grew keen; he shifted about in his chair to face her.

"You mean——?" he began and stopped. "I hardly imagine," he said, and there was a tenseness in his voice and manner that made Pen think he might actually be trembling, "I hardly imagine that you mean that it —a Washington letter——"

"The letter was bound in, at the back of the picture," Pen explained. "My brother Phil was fixing it for Mother, and he found it. The letter was to Mrs Bartlett Flagg—Mrs Thomas Bartlett Flagg, I think it was—for Hannah. But I have it here!"

She began to struggle with the string that tied the package she had carried; the man's hands were suddenly, expertly, helping her. They opened the tissue-paper wrappings; not very nice tissue paper, Pen had time to think ashamedly; it had the wrinkled limp look of a washwoman's hands, had been used many times before.

When the unframed sampler, loosely wrapped with the frame, glass and all, was revealed, Mark Flagg took it gently into his hands, holding it reverently, as a man might hold a jewel. He turned it to the light, studied it.

"The binding is ripped there—up at the top," Pen said. "And the letter's inside."

Mark Flagg looked up.

"I wonder if I might take this down and show it to my mother?" he asked, in an odd restrained tone that shook a little. "I'll not take it out of your sight, of course. You mean—I may tell my mother that you will part with it? You *will* sell it?"

The girl smiled, laughed indifferently.

"Certainly. It doesn't mean anything to me!" she assured him.

"A Washington letter doesn't?" he asked sharply.

"Well—*Washington*," Penelope murmured, with a deprecatory smile. "I mean—he was fine and all that!" she said.

The man had started down the steps; she went with him. They crossed the drive and descended the terrace levels between the shrubberies, as she had seen the maid do before. They had not gone far before a great amphitheater of green lawn, with a pool in its center, opened before them, and Penelope saw what seemed to be a formidable number of persons scattered about under the trees.

There were awnings, too, tiled spaces where small iron tables were set; there were many comfortable basket chairs; there was at least one rug, with two babies in sun suits and browned satiny skins tumbling about on it. There was one long table of polished brown wood, upon which luncheon arrangements had been laid.

Penelope had but a confused impression of all this and of much more as she followed her host down the green lengths. She was vaguely aware of brown-legged children screaming and plunging near the water, of maids moving about the table, of other persons—men and women, old and young, and almost all dressed in white—who were laughing and lounging and chattering like so many white-plumaged birds against the glorious background of the lawns and the trees.

In great wicker chairs that were set somewhat close together were several decidedly elderly figures; a pair of broadly built, gray-headed men in light summer clothes; a broadly built silver-headed woman with a skin as brown as the children's. To these three she was introduced.

"Mother, Dad," Mark Flagg said, "this is Miss Fitzpercy. My uncle, Judge Farmer, Miss Fitzpercy. My brother Teege. Yesterday was your birthday, Mother, but here's a rather late present for you!"

The fine gray eyes of the old woman—Pen had already learned that her years were moving through the late seventies—studied her with a sharp, even a somewhat unfriendly, smile. Pen could read her thoughts quickly enough: "What possesses Mark to bring this complete stranger right into our family luncheon group?"

"What's all this, Mark?" she demanded, in a voice that held the notes of a man's voice, and yet that was pleasant, too, and full of an easy assurance.

"This," Mark Flagg said simply, as he put the framed sampler into her hands. He had taken the letter from behind it, and now he laid on the glass the discolored yellow page.

"What's this, Mark?" she asked again. "Look here, Thomas!" The old men were leaning near to look now, and some of the other figures—white-clad, fluttering, interested—had gathered behind the chairs.

"Judge for yourself," the son said. Mrs Flagg bent over the poster; her

[67]

square old brown hand touched the letter. She looked up, speaking with a sort of stupefied directness:

"Who had 'em, Mark?"

"This isn't the Carter sampler, Mark?" the nearer of the old men asked, with an amazed crack in his voice.

"*Gram!*" a girl said, like a pistol shot.

"Mark, it can't be the Hannah Carter sampler come home!" the old woman said, in a voice almost a whisper. She bent over it in passionate attention.

"Looks like it, Mother," her old husband said.

"It's it," she pronounced finally. "I saw it when I was a girl, in Grand-mother Flagg's house." A silence had fallen as she very quietly and definitely spoke, and now she repeated once again: "This is it. This is the Washington letter, and this is the Hannah Carter sampler."

An exclamation of incredulous pleasure burst from the group as from one throat at this announcement, and they gathered about the framed discolored bit of fine old canvas and the yellowed old letter in an ecstasy of delight. Hannah Carter Flagg had commenced her work with a poem, done in careful cross-stitch in the center of the picture. Somebody reverently read it aloud:

> "*Jesus, my love, Thy name shall stand*
> *As the first work of Hannah's hand,*
> *And while her laboring fingers move,*
> *Incline her heart to seek Thy love.*"

Across the top two alphabets had been painstakingly stitched; one in German capitals, one in script. After these came the numerals, beginning with one and ending with zero. Underneath were trees and a green with geese on it, and tombstones set under willows before a rigid white church. And at the bottom was the cross-stitched inscription, with a date: "for Col. G. Washington from Hannah Carter, 1774. Eight years old."

"Congratulations, Gram," someone said solemnly, in a shaking voice.

"Congratulations to us all," the old woman said in a low tone that was shaken, too. She was having help in holding the sampler now. A tall, slender, dark grandson had singled himself out from among the others and had come to kneel beside her on the grass and support his grandmother's arm and the sampler with it. Pen did not know why, but there was something about his easy quiet manner, his authoritative voice, that made him seem the only person there for a moment, that seemed to affect the quality of the grass and the flowers and the trees, and enhance their colors and their fragrance and their significance.

The impression passed, and the values of the group flowed back, and she was Penelope Fitzpercy again, having a ridiculous experience with the Flaggs, and trying to remember all its features so that she might retail them to Mother and Phil and Persis later on. They were all gathered about the sampler and the letter; the exclamations had changed from awe and incredulity to ecstatic delight and triumph. Whatever their intrinsic value, this old sampler and this old letter were inestimable treasures to the Flaggs.

"We knew they were somewhere, at least if they hadn't been destroyed," a fine plain woman of perhaps forty-five, who had been introduced as another Mrs Flagg, and who was generally addressed as "Aunt Margaret," said enthusiastically. "But the family lost sight of them. . . . When did they go out of the family, Gram?"

The treasures were still being passed from hand to hand; all eyes following them, all eyes constantly upon them, but the group had settled somewhat. A score of persons of all ages were seated in a semicircle on the grass; all the chairs were filled; Penelope had a chair next to that of the old people.

"In the house of—well, she was my aunt, so she'd be your great-aunt," the oldest Mrs Flagg—there seemed to be innumerable Mrs Flaggs, but the others were all young or comparatively young—said judicially, after consideration. "She was from Augusta, Georgia. None of our people had ever come from there. It was a strange, a most unfortunate marriage. He died—Tom Flagg died—and this girl, his wife, disappeared. Nobody seemed to know where she was, for years and years. She remarried, and little Tom—she only had the one child—died. My mother-in-law, Lewis Flagg's wife, went down to get the letter and the emerald and the sampler. She'd sold them all, but we could trace the ring easily enough."

The speaker paused and looked at a great emerald that blazed in green fire on her brown hand.

"We got it back," she said, "and Mrs Lewis Flagg wore it until she gave it to me. But we never could find a trace of—these."

The last word was said almost reverently; the emerald sparkled afresh as it was moved across the yellowed surface of the old letter once more, with a touch that was a caress. For a moment there was silence. Then everyone looked at Penelope.

"Now, Miss——?" The old woman hesitated for the name. "You will let us buy these?"

"Fitzpercy," supplied the dark, quiet young man quickly. He did not look at Penelope; he had not seemed to listen especially to the talk, but he spoke before even she could speak.

"Miss Fitzpercy," old Mrs Flagg said. "This *is* for sale? I needn't tell you that it is of great value to us."

"Oh yes, it's for sale," Penelope answered smilingly. "And my mother will be only too pleased to hear that it means so much to you. When we found the letter it occurred to her that it might be valuable—to you, that is, for family reasons. And she said that if you wanted it she would sell it because it hasn't any especial value," she explained, smiling about the circle, "to us."

"Your mother bought it?"

"No, my father's father did. My grandfather Fitzpercy—Arthur Tripper Fitzpercy," Pen explained, with a touch of dignity. "He was English," she went on. "He collected things." ("Well," she thought, "he *did* collect things. He was an auctioneer, and if auctioneers don't collect things, who does?")

"This sort of thing?"

"Well, that and others. Books and rugs. They sent us boxes of things when he died."

Old Mrs Flagg looked up from the caressing touch her square old brown hands had never ceased to bestow on the glass that protected the sampler.

"We will be very glad to buy this at any price your mother places on it," she said simply.

"Penciled on the back of it is 'forty-five dollars,' Gram," a second young man, perhaps a year or two younger than the other, and looking extremely like him, as all these dark-skinned, black-headed folk looked alike, said animatedly. This boy was called "Jeff." "Turn the picture over," he added. "You'll see."

"And then there's the letter," Penelope said determinedly, but feeling a little scared. "My mother wrote to a collector in New York, and he said a Washington letter had sold for forty dollars some years ago, but that they were scarcer now. So my mother thought . . ."

Her words faltered for a barely perceptible second. She must say it now. A hundred dollars. It sounded like a million. "But they're rich," her flying thoughts said. "They can't say any more than 'no!'"

She managed it, aloud.

"My mother thought she'd want a hundred dollars for it," she said bravely.

There was a frightful moment while various Flagg eyes moved and met, moved and met again. Penelope felt a sick feeling inside. Their expressions weren't reassuring. Then the oldest woman spoke.

"My dear child, these are worth a *great deal* more than that!" she said amusedly, and everybody laughed. Penelope felt her heart rise on a rush of relief. More than a hundred dollars! Mother would be so pleased. Everything was all right now, and the hot walk and awkward interview well justified.

"How about lunch, Mother?" somebody asked, in the general stir and pleasant confusion. "Oh yes, lunch!" a dozen voices said.

"Lunch," the grandmother agreed, reaching for her cane. A young hand —it belonged to the serious-looking young man who had known Penelope's name, helped her to her feet. She led the way to the tables, speaking as she did so to the other dark Flagg man, the one called "Jeff." "Jeff," she said, "you take charge of Miss Fitzpercy, and see that she gets enough to eat and meets the others."

Jeff immediately attached himself to Penelope; she did not see where the older, quieter cousin went, for everyone was moving toward the long tables now; maids were passing trays of cups; there was cold chicken and ham and rolls and salads and dark, bubbling Spanishy-looking baked dishes in sight, and Penelope was frankly ravenous. The long table in the shade of the oaks had been set with every variety of food appropriate to a lawn luncheon, and the meal began at once without formality. Everybody passed everything and reached for everything; maids went about with pots of coffee and great glass pitchers of fruit punch; laughter and chatter went up and down the lines incessantly. Her heart rose on something like laughter. She was lunching with the Flaggs!

CHAPTER II

Penelope found her particular boy, the one they called "Jeff," to be an exceptionally charming young man. He was dark, like all the Flaggs, with an Indian-brown skin, black eyes, the heavy Flagg brows, and thick black hair. His mouth had the attractive Flagg peculiarity of being a little thrust forward by big teeth; his smile was particularly engaging. He wore comfortable flannels and a white shirt with the tiny monogram "T.J.F." on the left sleeve; he talked constantly and amusingly; he liked talking to Penelope. But most of the time the younger group in which she was placed talked all together, with shouts of laughter and much teasing.

Dazed, she made no effort to identify them or to keep their names straight. Not counting the small babies, who had been carried off early in the scene, there were more than thirty persons of all ages present; Flaggs, Beville-Atwoods, Townes, Clines, Farmers.

Six or seven of the number were still children who foregathered for giggling and undertones at one end of the table: Tommy, Mary Lucy, Farmer, Billy, Bunny. There were a sister and brother in the early twenties, Judson and Concy Forsythe; it was the engagement of Concy to a young French nobleman, Gilbert de Puy, that had been announced today. Penelope's neighbor, Jeff, had presented a younger brother Mark and two younger sisters, Lucy and Peggy, all four unmarried, as was their cousin Tom, the dark young man Pen had so particularly noticed. Tom's father was Teege, the fine keen invalid of the wheeled chair; the gentle middle-aged woman called "Aunt 'Lizabeth" was Tom's mother. Jeff's parents were "Aunt Margaret," a fine, talkative woman in strong eyeglasses, and that particular Flagg to whom Pen had first talked, up on the terrace, Mark senior. "Uncle Mark" was a silent man, shorter and squarer than the others; rather stern in his manner. He was interested in business and golf, Pen decided; Jeff told her that Dad was "the works" in the family law office in San Francisco; she heard the older Mark speak only twice or three times, and then it was of golf, of greens and drives and irons and the tenth hole.

She counted six Toms and at least three Lucys in the group; the oldest man of all, the great-grandfather of most of the youngsters, was a Tom; the very smallest boy, Mary Flagg Cline's year-old baby, was addressed as "Thomas."

The talk was general; good family talk going back and forth, but it always returned to the sampler and the Washington letter. It was evidently a great day in the Flagg annals when these treasures came home. After lunch a pleasant young woman named Hannah Beville-Atwood offered, at her grandmother's suggestion, to take Miss Fitzpercy to the gallery—wherever and whatever the "gallery" might be—and show her where the recovered trophies would presently be installed in state.

Luncheon was over by this time, and the group had scattered in all directions. Penelope had had a few minutes of talk with the older folk, telling them who she was and who her mother was.

"My mother is 'Ariel Hunter'—she writes poetry. We don't—exactly know," Penelope had said hesitantly, "where my father is. He went away when we were babies—to Arizona first, and afterward he simply—didn't write."

She had smiled about the circle; a small circle now. The handsome, quiet Tom had disappeared. Jeff had been still in attendance and had been commissioned to drive Miss Fitzpercy home whenever she wanted to go.

But first Hannah would show her the gallery. Penelope walked with Hannah back to the main house, the old-fashioned white-painted house with the bays and cupolas and porch pillars, and through a series of cool orderly rooms where there were old-fashioned chairs and table, fireplaces and books, a grand piano, and a chessboard with all the men set out, and went with her guide into a long, plain room that had perhaps been built onto the old building for the special purpose of housing the heirlooms that were arranged there. It was an enormous skylighted room with doors at the ends only, and deep leather chairs arranged in the center in little groups facing the walls.

On the walls were fine old portraits, and many not so fine, and some samplers not comparable to that of little Hannah Carter Flagg. But all the names were here again: Farmer, Babcock, Forsythe, Pierce, Flagg, Flagg, Flagg.

There were warming pans and spinning wheels in the room; there was one beautiful bed of carved black oak, complete with the paneling of the wall into which it had originally been built, and there were other beds; one small trundle bed was pushed into place under a tasseled four-poster.

There were beautiful old rugs, Pembroke and Hepplewhite chairs, high-boys and lowboys built in mellowed fruitwood with all the simple grace and sturdy practicability of a bygone day.

On the tables were innumerable specimens of old American china and silver, two-tined forks and long-handled spoons. There was glass: primitive, shadowy, brown-white glass, blue glass decanters, red cut glass that sparkled like rubies in pitchers and goblets. There were quilts and looms, exquisite old christening garments heavy with fine embroidery, lace mitts and mantles; there were taffeta gowns complete with fichus and pantalettes, and Quaker "calash" bonnets that opened and shut like the hoods of old-fashioned phaetons, and that were almost as large. A little collection of mille-fleurs paperweights made Penelope smile; her own grandmother had had one like these years and years ago; it had been long lost or destroyed. In one corner was a group of Indian relics and curios, but there was no time for them. Penelope could not assimilate all this at once, and Hannah did not attempt to display it. The two merely glanced at various outstanding items and were presently out in the sunshine again, to find Jeff and the car waiting on the drive.

Hannah, like all the Flaggs, was olive-skinned and black of hair. She was rather a puzzle to Penelope; she was a Beville-Atwood, her father was dead; she appeared to be "Aunt Hannah's" daughter; everyone seemed to like her and need her. What was puzzling was that she was all of thirty, and not married. . . .

Penelope was at the age when the question of marriage or not marriage was all-important; she looked at friendly, quick, kindly Hannah and wondered. One of the handsomest of the lot, in her canary-yellow plain tennis dress, with a pale yellow hat on her dark hair, alert and straight and full of humor, it seemed odd that Hannah was not already a Mrs Somebody with the usual Tom and Lucy and Farmer of her own.

Hannah suggested to Jeff that she drive with him and Miss Fitzpercy to Menlo Park, and then he would not have to drive back alone, and they all got into the front seat of the car, Penelope in the middle.

"We have to squeeze a little," said Hannah cheerfully, "but it's more sociable."

Talking and laughing eagerly, in the first pleasure of a new friendship, they were out on the highway in no time, they had rushed past San Carlos and Redwood City; they had turned west toward the hills. Penelope directed the driver carefully; here they turned left—here right. Up this lane and down the dirt road under the orchard trees.

"Am I crowding you?" Pen, slender and lovely, ivory of skin and gold of hair, said with an oblique glance at the driver.

"You are not," said Jeff Flagg, returning the look with accrued interest. Penelope laughed suddenly. "What's funny?" he asked.

"The—the way you looked!" Pen answered with a little stutter.

"I can't help the way I look," Jeff said reproachfully. "Before I was born my mother was thrown against a barbed-wire fence."

"Jeff, stop it," Hannah said, amused and maternal. "Here, I'll square about," she said, "and you'll have more elbow space."

"If you were a true friend to me, Hannah, you'd bump Miss Fitzpercy my way."

"Does he always talk like this, Miss Beville-Atwood?"

"No, he's a very sensible person as a rule," Hannah said, knowing that all this was joking, but not quite at ease. But the look that Penelope and Jeff exchanged left nothing misunderstood. Penelope's Irish lightheartedness was more than a match for the easy, leisurely, sophisticated nonsense of Thomas Jefferson Flagg. He was very sure of himself, she thought. He had a more comfortable manner with a strange girl than any she had ever encountered in a man before. He took his time; silent when he wanted to be silent, and quite unruffled when he wanted to be personal and flattering. She liked him. No woman born could help liking him.

"This is our house," she said. Hannah and Jeff were cordiality's self in good-byes, but they would not get out. Penelope knew why. Maddening old colored Mrs Peet had spread washing to dry all over the neglected bushes of the cottage's little front garden; Persis, seated on the porch steps, her head bowed and her gold mop dangling, was drying her hair; Kelly Quentin, looking completely disreputable in a baggy old sweater and dirty white shorts, was on the stepladder pruning the Crimson Rambler. At the moment that Jeff Flagg's car stopped, Kelly was swearing elaborately and furiously over a pricked thumb, and the inept Mrs Peet had sallied forth from the kitchen to tip a dishpan full of gray water upon the sweet peas.

The Fitzpercy house was shabby and humble at best; today it was at its worst. Penelope was not sensitive about it as a rule; home had always been like that, and it suited the Fitzpercys. But she had just come from a very different scene, and she felt a sudden hot shame in the contrast.

"Will you get out and meet my mother?" she asked, hating herself for conceding to these Flaggs, in spite of herself, an unwonted formality of manner of speech. Hannah said pleasantly and quickly no; there was to be a father-son croquet match this afternoon. "We have to be there to take sides," Hannah explained simply. She spoke with that sureness that was characteristic of all the Flaggs, and maddening somehow, and yet admirable, too, and all the more maddening for that.

"Some other time!" Hannah said. And then the car was gone, and Penelope was left to walk slowly toward the house and stop to tell Persis and Kelly of her adventure. Her face was unusually red, she did not know why; her skin burned, and she felt suddenly weary and dispirited. One usually felt so, getting home on a spring afternoon that was too warm for the season.

It would have been unfortunate to have the Flaggs come in, of course, to meet Persis with her hair sopping, Kelly looking a disgrace, and the parlor undergoing one of its rare cleansing upheavals under the hands of the tactless Mrs Peet. The Flaggs had grasped the situation with that quiet superb adequacy of theirs, and had been quite right to decline the invitation. They had gone back to their own atmosphere of cool old-fashioned rooms enhanced by flowers and books and shaded windows; to those clear rich voices that said "Gram darling," and "Aunt Margaret," and "Tom" so pleasantly.

At supper Penelope was eloquent on the subject of the Flaggs.

"They sound to me just about a hundred years behind the times," Philip said. "Do they know what's been going on in Russia and Germany and Italy?"

"Four-posters and warming pans," Pen's mother contributed. "I'd rather help one tenement child to health and sunshine than have rooms full of them!"

"Except that we never do," Penelope observed smoothly. She had been talking fast and furiously about the Flaggs, her face flushed, her manner a mixture of amusement and contempt and reluctant admiration. Now she suddenly felt dull and weary and chilled; she spoke idly, indifferently.

"Never do what, Pen?"

"Never treat tenement children to hours of health and sunshine." Penelope rose from the table, began to pile plates together.

"Well," said her mother, "we *would*, if we had the Flagg money, you may be very sure of that!"

"My people came over in the Mayflower, too," Kelly Quentin said, "but the poor souls were crushed to death in the mob!"

Penelope, in the kitchen doorway, felt her mouth twitch with a reluctant smile. The Flagg experience had left her with some feeling that was not comfortable. She was conscious of not wanting to think of them, and yet she thought of them a great deal; green lawns and scattered white figures, brown children splashing in a pool, mille-fleurs paperweights and Queen Anne spoons, and brown men in white flannels, interested, attentive, polite.

"They're nothing to me!" she would say restlessly, as the days went by and there was no word or message from them beyond the letter Mrs Flagg had written her mother warmly thanking her for the sampler, enclosing a check. To the Fitzpercys it seemed an enormous check, but old Mrs Flagg's letter made light of the actual money consideration. "*I have offered various sums at various times for either sampler or letter,*" she wrote. "*Their value to me is not to be estimated in dollars or cents.*" Mrs. Fitzpercy's first impulse was to decline the money, returning the check with a note as charmingly fine as Mrs Flagg's own. But Phil and Persis, Isolde and Grandy and Kelly talked her out of this preposterous notion. What did they care about impressing the Flaggs!

Penelope was silent. She *did* care about impressing the Flaggs. Not that it mattered; they were nothing to her! She put them resolutely out of her mind.

But the thought of them came back again and again. "I wish I had never met them!" Penelope would mutter, half aloud.

CHAPTER III

The commonplace white cottage under low apple trees that was the Fitzpercys' home was alive with sound and color on a May morning two weeks later. After heavy rains had come one of the golden days of the year. All doors and windows were open to fresh sweet airs, the scent of lilac and orange blossoms was heavy everywhere. Doves throbbed their eternal grief on the sloping porch roof; chickens murmured in shade; an old spotted horse at a farm gate occasionally whinnied wistfully. On the sill of the kitchen window a great gold Persian cat lay watchful; Penelope was playing with a stumbling puppy on the grass of the side yard, her laughter rising in wild trills into the chorus of other sounds. From the sitting room, a low apartment that seemed yearly to slip closer into the garden shrubs and trees that encircled it, came ripples of piano music; Chopin's études were being played rapidly and inaccurately by young swift fingers. A young man of twenty astride a sawhorse in the side yard worked with a shotgun, fired it into the air, fingered the gun again. In an arbor lighted through a dense-packed screen of new leaves with splotches and glints of sunshine, a slender untidy woman was busy with scattered sheets of paper and a pencil.

"Should you be firing that gun, Phil?" she presently said absently. The boy, only a few feet away from her, glanced at her amiably, but made no answer. Penelope on the grass, now lying flat on her back, with the squirming puppy elevated to the length of her arms, observed to nobody in particular: "This lad needs a bath."

"Don't wash him in the tub, then," the woman said. "I think Persis has some shirtwaists soaking there."

"Shirtwaists are blouses now, Mother," Penelope said.

"Philip, is there a rhyme for 'month'?" his mother asked.

"Which month, darling?"

"'Month' itself. Any month."

"There are plenty of rhymes for 'May' and 'June,'" the boy said. "'August'—'April'—not so good. 'October' you can always rhyme with 'sober,' and you could rhyme it with 'Rover' if you had a head cold. . . ."

[76]

"Nobody ever names dogs 'Rover' any more," Pen observed, as her brother's meditative voice dwindled away into silence, his attention returned to his bolts and barrels, and the other woman sank absorbed once more into composition. " 'Rover' and 'Dobbin'—who ever hears of them?" the girl continued. "Fido. 'Fido' ought to be pronounced 'Feedoe,' of course, but who ever does it? Let's name the horse 'Fido' and this little —old—fat—silly puppy 'Dobbin.' Cheerio, Dobbin!"

With one graceful movement of her long slender body she had rolled over, to rest on her elbows on the uncut fresh green of the lawn, and tousle and tumble the puppy between her long fine hands. Now she poked him gently with every emphasized word, and he squealed and scrambled in sheer ecstasy.

"June, of all months the perfumed flowers' month . . ." Mrs Fitzpercy murmured, biting her pencil, staring into space.

"I had a birthday party in you wunth," Penelope suggested.

"I don't believe there *is* a rhyme!" the older woman said.

"June, of all months the perfumed flowers' hour," the girl offered.

" 'Flowers' hour' sounds sort of jumbly." Mrs Fitzpercy put down her pencil, sighed. "Poetry has to be so *perfect*," she said. "June, of all months the month——"

"We love the best!" the boy put into the pause brilliantly.

"Phil, that sounds like a grammar-school pageant!"

" 'The March of the Flowers,' " Penelope said. " 'I represent the blushing rose that in old-fashioned gardens grows. And I the sunflower. You may laugh, but at my cup the birdies quaff——' "

She buried the rest of the jingle against the fluffy little puppy's head.

"No question about it, you could write poetry, Pen," her mother said fondly.

"No question about it, I could do anything," Penelope agreed, with just a hint of bitterness in her voice. "But I'm twenty-two, and I haven't done anything yet, except help at the Gifte Shoppe when Alice is rushed, and work last month in the bookstore. But there's plenty of time. I've only been out of school five years!"

"Now why does she act like that?" the boy demanded aggrievedly, as Penelope, her mood suddenly changed, and angry tears in her eyes, pushed the puppy aside, scrambled to her feet, and walked into the house. "What's been the matter with her lately?"

"I don't know, dear." Mrs Fitzpercy yawned, put her elbows on the table, and rested her untidy golden head in her hands. "May is moody weather," she said. "We all feel it. Did you practice, my darling?" she added, as another girl came out across the porch and the strip of lawn and threw herself down at the table, burying her head in her crossed arms wearily.

"Into blind staggers. Can we have lunch?" the girl demanded. Like all the others she was conspicuously blond; she wore a faded pair of cotton pajamas and a loose thin cotton Japanese coat patterned with dragons and chrysanthemums.

"Pen said something awhile back about it."

"Did anyone get butter?"

"I don't know. I hardly think so."

"How much would we have to pay to get the telephone put in again? Now that the car isn't working it's awful not to have a phone."

"If there's *one* word I hate *more* than another it's 'phone,'" Penelope, who had returned to the end of the table and was peeling tomatoes, said casually.

"You hate every word I use, lately," Persis aswered smoothly.

"I imagine we would have to pay the back bills, Phil," Mrs Fitzpercy said dreamily, of the telephone situation. "The bill is there in the house somewhere, on my desk, I think. In fact, the man came about it. He was very disagreeable; they always are. They seem to feel that if one had the money one wouldn't pay it. Good gracious, no woman in the world would like being rich more than I! A good cook gets a hundred a month, and my column only pays me eighteen a week! Ah, well! If it weren't for an occasional poor little poem selling . . . ! I suppose the world needs me, somehow!"

"The world needs common sense," said Philip, with twenty-year-old calm.

"Samplers and blue teapots! America seems to me the biggest flop of any country in the world," Penelope began morosely, cutting away the rotted sections of tomatoes, putting what could be saved into a bowl. "I mean it!" she added with feeling, although no one had challenged her. "I loathe American customs and I loathe American ways. I wish to goodness we weren't Americans! We aren't, really. We're Irish-Danish-English people who happen to live in America, that's what we are. Italian, Irish, Jewish, Russian, German, Italian, Chinese——"

"You said Italian twice," Persis said annoyingly.

"Double allowance of Italians," the boy said lazily.

"We're no nation at all, for all the fuss they make about the Mayflower," the girl summarized it disgustedly. "In China they wouldn't dare take out the telephone of people of quality—aristocrats——"

"Listen to this—does this sound cute to you? I'm not quite satisfied with it," Mrs Fitzpercy said, fluttered. And from her penciled pages she began to read:

> "May, you and I have a quarrel.
> You have taken April away.
> The dogwoods, the mountain laurel,
> Where are they vanished today?"

"Go on; it's cute," Penelope said politely. Mother was painfully sensitive about her poetry. She must always be encouraged.

"That's as far as I've gone."

"Oh?" the three listeners said together, possibly a little relieved. There was a silence in which Penelope peeled tomatoes, Philip sat idle, the gun beside him, and Persis played with the puppy. Far away, in the village, noon whistles sounded, then stillness swam over the gold-and-green world again. Splotches of light came softly green into the cheap little grape arbor; airs so soft that they did not stir the fresh leaves brought the scent of lilac and stock and hot noontime odors over the world. A cock somewhere unseen triumphantly announced his supremacy to the neighborhood.

"Are those the Madisons' tomatoes?" Persis presently asked.

"Yes, and it's a shame we didn't use them up! I forgot all about them; they were down in the cellar."

"We make a great fuss about a man's getting a college education," Philip presently said. "Well, I had it. At least I had two years of it, before I went round the world. What good did it do me? I've been trying for two years to get a job."

"That's America," Penelope said simply. "In England there'd be a job for you, because you're a gentleman, and Mother is a genius. Here you get a job as a deck hand or dining-room steward on a liner, and then lose that!"

"Give me Russia," Philip said. "They may not know where they're going, but at least they're on their way!"

"I wonder how it is in Italy," Persis murmured dreamily. "They seem happy enough."

"Well, at least they're all one nation," Penelope answered vigorously. "And so's Switzerland, and so's Holland! You never hear of any trouble from Switzerland and Holland. I'd like to belong to a nation that's a *nation*. I'd like to take a chance anywhere—I'd be an East Indian woman in Cairo —or is Cairo East India?"

"Darlings, we're all so frightfully ignorant!" the mother murmured fondly.

"I'm sure I don't care where it is!" Penelope said. She was silent a moment, and then added suddenly, from dark thought: "How utterly ridiculous it is for anyone to hoard American heirlooms—old chairs and portraits! Why, we're not a nation! We're just a mix-up of the scourings of every other nation in the world; the only things that matter to us are gum machines and movies and Amos 'n' Andy! Hot dogs and comic supplements and gas stations, and people talk about their ancestors and the Revolution as if they mattered!"

"Those Flaggs certainly got under your hide, Pen," Philip said amusedly.

"They wouldn't get under mine," Persis said with animation. She studied the fingertips of a soft dirty hand, from whose nails irregular splotches of red were wearing away. "I'd tell 'em that my Irish grandfather was a

[79]

drunken auctioneer and that my Danish grandfather had a fish stand in the old country!"

"You don't *know* that," Pen said stiffly. "You know he was in the fish business, and that's all you know. As for Grandfather Fitzpercy, if he hadn't bought up lots of old books and things they wouldn't have their precious sampler back."

"Tell 'em your brother was a Communist?" Philip asked.

"Don't be silly, Phil," Mrs Fitzpercy said.

"I'm a Communist," Kelly Quentin's voice said. He had come into the arbor from the rear door; he stopped, in passing, to brush the top of Penelope's untidy knot of gold hair with his cheek before he sank into a seat. "But let that pass," he added. "What I've come down from the studio to say is that you've got your wish, girls. Your prayers are answered. I'm here. I've come to lunch."

"Inasmuch as there is no lunch, you're heartily welcome!" Penelope said, dryly.

"Why no lunch?"

"Late breakfast," Persis answered briefly.

"Well, looka here, *you* may have had a late breakfast . . ." Kelly began on a high-pitched, aggrieved note. He looked about the circle.

"It's a day for iced tea and sandwiches," Mrs Fitzpercy said. "It's a day that makes one believe in summer!"

"What would you like, Kelly?" Persis asked, on a long yawn. "The more you sleep the more you want to sleep," she muttered.

"I'd like welcome, I'd like consideration, I'd like hospitality, that's what I'd like!" Kelly said sharply. "A neighbor, an orphan, one who deserves only kindly treatment at the hands of others—— Pen, you're so criminally beautiful! Why is anyone so beautiful?"

The last phrases were added especially for Pen; Kelly, who was sitting opposite her, stretched a painter's dirty oily fingers across the table, and she laid one of her fine long white-veined hands in his and smiled at him slowly from her long, heavy-lidded eyes.

It was no secret that he loved her, this red-headed artist who lived in an old barn half a mile up the road and came down to the Fitzpercys' house every day, or twice a day, for companionship and advice and food, or to extend an invitation, or run an errand. To the girls he was like another brother; they teased him, scolded him, imposed upon him and spoiled him by turns. Often he bored and annoyed them; often the girls muttered when his voice, raised in conversation somewhere about the place, announced that he had come for dinner. But if he did not appear for a day or two they always went after him, and when she was counting up the elements that made her life, Penelope put him in the list of assets.

Square and freckled and hirsute, he joined the group today with all the ease of old custom, dropping into a chair at the table, hardly taking the trouble to greet them individually even with a glance.

"Let's have sandwiches and iced tea," Philip said.

"No ice. The icebox is hot and smells of tin and sour milk," Penelope said.

"Go get ice, Phil, and look sharp about it, my lad!" Kelly said. Long, lean, redheaded, untidy, he stretched out his arms to their full length on the table and laid his head on them.

"Car off song," Philip remarked.

"Take mine." There was further argument before Philip finally dragged himself away from the group. Penelope and Persis began to wander to and fro, dawdling, gossiping, as they brought blue plates of strangely assorted foods out to the arbor. Presently Philip was cracking ice; it was after two o'clock now, and they were all hungry. Slopping, spilling, melting went on; Mrs Fitzpercy pushed her papers away from her tall brimming glass. "You fill these too full, darlings," she protested lovingly.

Seated between her two daughters, with the men lounging opposite, the bread being cut by whosoever wanted a slice of it, the butter still in the square block in which it had come from the grocery, the viands being pushed to and fro, the startling resemblance between mother and daughters was more than ordinarily noticeable. All three had gray-blue eyes thickly lashed in black, and creamy firm skin hardly touched with color. All three had sweet wide sensitive mouths, high cheekbones like those of Rossetti's women, clean-cut chins and long nervous hands. And all three had for a crown of glory straight soft slipping masses of pure gold hair, pale gold, like butter or buttercups—heavy, dense and soft.

About the older woman's eternally puzzled, pleasant eyes fine wrinkles had been drawn; there were strands of whitish silver in her hair; she was thinner than either daughter and slightly stooped, in gentle poetic fashion. Persis, at seventeen, was still gauche and undeveloped, a little gawky, a little heavy, in adolescent richness and beauty. But Penelope was at the flood tide of young perfection; her skin firm as magnolia petals, her rounded chin molded clean, her long mysterious Irish eyes lashed heavily in black. The brows, as fine and thick as paintbrushes, were black too, but the hair was the famous Fitzpercy taffy color—heavy, smooth, silken; it wrapped her proud young head like a folded golden banner. The eyes of every man, woman and child she had ever encountered in her twenty-two years had told Penelope that she was beautiful—not that it mattered very much. The Fitzpercys all took beauty for granted. Penelope's older sister, Isolde, had been, and indeed, at twenty-five, still was only something less lovely than Pen. Yet Isolde's destiny had not been particularly distinguished. She had married, more than a year ago, one Grandison Tasker, an idle, lovable, unsuccessful musician whose career closely paralleled that of Kelly Quentin. The two, in fact, had been chums, had worked together in the cabin Kelly now occupied alone, a mile up the road. For a year or two Grandy had played on the Fitzpercys' old square piano, had borrowed and loaned small sums from and to the family, had eaten countless meals and returned a few, had talked the queer mixture of young socialism and ambition characteristic of his type, and had finally persuaded Isolde to add her nothing to his nothing and face the world as his wife.

They had a studio now in San Francisco, where puny twin sons had recently joined them. They starved, laughed, prospered and rejoiced, and returned to first principles of starving as regularly as the tides that washed the Western city; they quarreled, despaired, were reconciled and laughed again.

Isolde had not loved Grandy Tasker; she never had made any pretensions in the matter. But Grandy was the Fitzpercy pattern; he was not a smug young stupid bank clerk or insurance agent; that was in his favor. He knew just what they liked and how they lived, and inevitably that was his choice, too. Their mother had made few social contacts for herself and none at all for her daughters; they depended for company upon such bohemian strays as found their way to their hillside; Grandy was one of the nicest, and Isolde was generous and inexacting, and so they had been married. Grandy had been madly infatuated with his glorious bride; Isolde had been receptive and good-natured. No thrills, no ecstasies for Isolde. She hadn't pretended to be in love; she had amusedly told her younger sister that the Fitzpercys didn't fall in love; men fell in love with them.

"You and I'll never be in love, Pen, not until after you're married anyway," Isolde had said.

"Can't there be marriages where both are in love?"

"There may be, but I doubt it. One or the other is kidding," Isolde had said. She had presently expanded her idea. "The trouble with us is our hair, Pen. The minute men see a woman with our sort of hair they get interested—it doesn't matter who they are or where they are. Their first thought is, 'Gosh, what hair!' and from that moment on you simply don't like them. You know what fools they are."

"I know," Pen had conceded despondently. "Being in love makes them *idiots*."

"Well, exactly! They change. They go affected and awkward and queer. I've seen men," Isolde had developed it mournfully, "I've seen men— other girls' brothers or cousins from the East or something—who really seemed to me tremendously attractive. But the moment I've met them I've seen that idiot look in their eyes—that 'I'm making a hit with this blond baby!' look. And of course that ruins everything."

"Oh, it does, it does!" Pen had agreed fervently.

"I really don't know why I'm marrying Grandison," Isolde had said. "He's as sweet as he can be, and it may be that after twenty years or so he'll be a concert pianist. Besides, I love San Francisco, and we'll live there. We do nothing here at home, and we never go away from home; I'm not sacrificing much. But I'd just as soon do something else, if you know what I mean."

"I know exactly what you mean!" Pen had said.

"Only, don't fool yourself about falling in love with anyone, Pen," the sister had concluded warningly. "Women of our type don't. Big, fair, good-natured women mother men; they don't go in for the grand passion. Little women are always falling madly in love with men; big women sit back and are fallen in love with."

And despite the colloquialisms and the false constructions, Pen had completely grasped the idea; it was one that added vaguely to her general disinclination toward marriage, her general dissatisfaction with her life. It had shocked her that Isolde could serenely marry handsome, penniless Grandison in this mood; Isolde's motherhood had given her additional food for serious thought. Isolde had sailed through the difficulties of child-bearing with casual calm; not ill, not worried, not self-conscious, not thrilled. Within five hours of the boys' birth Penelope had been admitted to Isolde's hospital room and had found her sister manicuring her long fine hands.

"Wouldn't you know I'd have two!" Isolde had demanded, amused and impatient at once. "I didn't even want *one*."

"They're cute."

"I think they're awfully cute."

"Did you have a rotten time, Isolde?"

"Rotten." Isolde had bitten at a hangnail, studied an index finger attentively. "Everyone messing about," she had said meditatively. Isolde had never been ill, and like the other Fitzpercys was somewhat inclined to despise sickness. "However, my trays are divine!" she had said, brightening.

Penelope could have followed in her footsteps, of course. As Mrs Kelly Quentin she could have gone to San Francisco to find a studio in the same steep little street with the Grandison Taskers. The routine of borrowing butter and arguing with landlords and sitting late over Italian dinners seasoned with red wine and garlic and peppers would have enveloped herself and Kelly as smoothly as it had Grandison and Isolde; Telegraph Hill was covered with gallant little shanties housing gallant little adventurers. But somehow, instinctively, deep in her soul, Penelope of late had wondered if she must not have a stronger feeling, going into all this, than any she had ever felt for Kelly Quentin or for any other man. The new hazard must shoot out at a sharpe-angle from the old days and ways.

CHAPTER IV

Thinking of these things today, thinking a thousand vague, unhappy thoughts, Penelope lingered with the others through the luncheon, sat long over the table in the spring heat, reluctantly attacked the inevitable clearing. Always dishes, she said in her heart disgustedly, always cooling dishwater and a crumb-littered kitchen, always smells of grease and coffee grounds and onions! Afternoon shadows were long on the world before the last traces of the noon meal were fairly out of the way; Penelope, emerging from casual ablutions lovelier than ever in a thin old white dress, found the faithful Kelly still in attendance. He was stretched on the grass, reading Shelley; Persis had practiced for another ten minutes listlessly, had disappeared. Mrs. Fitzpercy was in the hammock, half asleep. She opened her long gray eyes as her middle daughter came out to the garden.

"Darling," she said, "you have a completely worthless mother. But I am having the nicest time out here with Kelly!"

"Affairs of state seem to have lightened for you this afternoon," Penelope said, with significance, to Kelly.

"Yes," he answered, yawning elaborately. "I wired the President to try his own hand at things. It'll be good for the boy. He can't have me eternally at his elbow."

Penelope had sunk into a frayed basket chair; she was moodily studying her fingertips. She was thinking of the Flaggs.

"Which is the greatest country in the world?" she presently asked in an undertone, as if she spoke to herself.

"Russia, right now!" Kelly answered unhesitatingly.

"You know nothing of Russia," Mrs Fitzpercy said firmly.

"I know nothing of anything," Kelly conceded brilliantly. "I simply move through a jumble called life, cashing my uncle's checks hither and yon. He calls them 'chex,' by the way—c-h-e-x. 'Kindly be prompter in cashing your chex,' he writes me. And at the bottom it says 'Aff'ly, Jno. T. Maginnis, dict. but not signed.'"

"His name couldn't be Genno," Penelope said indifferently.

"Not Genno, but that's the way he spells 'John.'"

"Who ever started that?" the girl wondered. "Well, I don't care," she recommenced, out of a silence, half aloud. "I could live any sort of life,

[84]

I know it. I could do anything! I could be a leader. But I never get started."

"What are we all talking about?" demanded Kelly, from the grass.

"I'm sure I don't know," Penelope answered wearily.

"Why don't you get a book, darling? I thought you and Phil were going to read all of Dickens?"

Penelope looked into space with expressionless eyes; she spoke on a level note of patience.

"Yes," she said, "we must begin to read Dickens, of course."

Kelly had fallen into a doze, his face hidden against the grass. Mrs Fitzpercy moved placid eyes over the garden scene: the arbor, the neglected patches of grass and garden beds, the paths whose flags were set at all angles, the overturned dry flowerpots and abandoned bits of garden equipment; a broken watering can, a handleless trowel, a length of rotted hose. Above all spread the gnarled apple tree and the single aged pepper. This had once been an orchard; it had been divided years earlier into building lots; poor little cottages—brown-shingled, colonial white, Spanish plaster—had been set down under the prunes and apples.

The rising hills lifted the world toward the west; on the other side they swept away below the cottage toward the town in a jumble of dirt roads, trees of every variety, garden patches, roofs and gates. Beyond, to the east, the great valley of the Santa Clara opened between the far coast range and the lower line of the Santa Cruz mountains. Everywhere today were blossoms, color, sweetness; the meanest little bungalows were set in waves of buttercups, in blazing poppies, in delicate wild fleurs-de-lis and blue onion flowers. Among them the shaggy soft spears of the scarlet "Indian paintbrush" showed in sharp vermilion; wild lilac, up toward the canyons, smoked in royal pale blue plumes against the dark redwoods.

"Let's flock north," Kelly said, "and see if we can work Isolde for a dinner."

"Oh, not today," Pen protested. "They were down here last week; they only went home yesterday."

"Well, we'll have to do something!" Kelly mumbled. "I did a lot of work this morning. I scraped a lot of old canvases and cleaned up my place and everything. Do you love me, Pen?"

"Fondly," Pen said absently. "I wonder——" she began suddenly, and stopped.

"What do you wonder, my darling?" her mother asked, opening her eyes.

"I wonder sometimes——" Penelope recommenced, and again she stopped. "Nothing," she said. "Only—sometimes I wonder if the way we do things is the best way," she added, hesitatingly, as if she were merely thinking aloud.

"The Flaggs again," Kelly said annoyingly. He saw the color rush up under her clear skin, although she did her best to show no sign of irritation.

"You've had a hair on the brain ever since you were there!" he added.

Penelope paid no attention to this remark.

"How do we do things?" her mother asked, interested.

"Oh, I don't know," Penelope said, in a bored voice.

"No, but how, darling?"

"The way the Flaggs don't," Kelly supplied.

"It has nothing whatever to do with the Flaggs!" Penelope said, on a flash of anger.

"The Flaggs are undoubtedly respectable," Mrs Fitzpercy observed. Her daughter laughed briefly, mirthlessly. "But it has always seemed to me that their lives must be extraordinarily *dull*," the older woman went on. "They're always so—so decent. Always a judge and a congressman and someone in the diplomatic service, and engagements being announced, and then homes being brightened by a son or a daughter. I don't think I should like to live that way, and be so—so highly respectable!" she finished plaintively.

"One feels they change their underwear practically daily," Kelly contributed.

Penelope looked at him soberly. "Not very funny," she said.

"Oh, come, rather apt, I think!" the man said undaunted. Mrs Fitzpercy, dropping many papers en route, had gone into the house now; Kelly and Penelope were alone in the side garden. "Listen, what was there about those Flaggs that got your goat?" he demanded.

"I really don't know why you're so silly!" the girl said, displeased. "I saw them once. I hardly know them. 'Hardly know them!'" she repeated her own phrase scornfully. "I don't know them at all," she said.

"Were they shirty to you?"

"No, they weren't shirty at all. They're perfectly simple people, who have clean table napkins for every meal, and family customs, and a big flag over the lawn."

"So what?"

"Well, nothing. Only," Penelope said, in a bored voice that shook a little in spite of her, "only sometimes I think that I like clean table linen and family customs. It's a mere——" She tried to indicate a yawn. "It's a mere fancy," she said.

"As far as family customs go," Kelly began animately, "don't fool yourself that you Fitzpercys aren't strong on customs! Taking your mother her breakfast in bed, and leaving books about, and being late for everything and fighting about words! I never saw such a family!"

"Yes, those are our family customs, sure enough," Penelope said in a level, expressionless voice. Her eyes were far away.

"Absolutely the only difference between the Flaggs and everyone else is that they're lersy with money," Kelly observed. "In what other way have they got it on any of us?"

"I didn't hear you," Penelope said, still gazing dreamily into space.

"Look," Kelly said abruptly, after a pause in which he had studied her obliquely. "Listen here. Remember the talk we had out here in the garden Sunday night, Pen?"

He had changed his position; he was on an old wicker hassock at her knee and had taken possession of one of her hands. Quite suddenly his characteristic joking tone and light manner were abandoned, and he was in serious earnest. "Listen here, dear," he said, "d'you know what's the matter with you?"

Her mood was so desponding, so uncertain, that tears came into her eyes; his eager freckled face and red head were dazzled through them.

"What?" she asked, holding her voice low and steady.

"You want to marry me, Pen. That's what it is. 'Member what you said Sunday night? When we were up at my place? You said, 'I don't like anyone better than I do you, Kelly. And I do like you a lot.' Pen I walked around the hills for hours after I brought you home, thinking about you. I know I seem like a fool. But I'm not a fool! I'm going to do good stuff someday. You'll never be sorry. We can live in San Francisco winters, near Isolde, and summers come down here. I make a lot of fun of Uncle John. But, after all, he does send me these 'chex' of his—we could live on 'em, all right! You'd never have to worry as Isolde does. Why don't you make up your mind?"

Penelope's hand lay passive in his; her eyes were far away, fixed on some point in the valley, or the mountains beyond the valley.

"Isolde never worries," she temporized, with a brief laugh.

"No, but I mean—we'd have enough. Will you, Pen? Will you take a chance?"

"Look here, dear," the girl said, in a tone that was suddenly almost maternal in firmness. "I like you—terribly. I'd like—any change, more shame to me! I've tried to get work; I'm not trained for anything. I've never made any money except a dollar or two earned selling books or candlesticks. I'm restless. The way we live here isn't—well, it isn't my way. I'd like to write or go on the stage or into the movies, or do something—*something!*—but I don't know how to get started. We've no money for special courses or classes. You know how we are!

"Mother's completely shiftless," she presently resumed, as Kelly continued to look up at her intently, from the hassock, and did not speak. "Meals are at any hour; bills never get paid; Phil can coax her out of the grocer's money without half trying. She's a darling, we all adore her, but sometimes my mother's way of doing things makes me want to *scream.* As for my father—Persis and I were talking about Dad the other night, and we think we hate him. We despise him, anyway. He never made himself responsible for us or for anything; Mother doesn't know where he is, even. She doesn't know that he's alive. Someone wrote her and sent her his things, but that doesn't mean he's dead; he might have walked out without paying his rent.

"Phil's something the same, sweet as he is. If poor little Persis makes a few dollars in the camera shop, Christmas time, Phil will borrow it if he wants it. Kelly," Pen went on, looking into his eyes now, and with a touch of passion in her voice, "I'm afraid of the way we do things. I'm afraid of the way we live. I'm afraid of *me*. I might marry you——"

"Don't say that!" the man said quickly, flushing under his burned freckled skin. "Don't say it unless you mean it."

"I might marry you, Kelly, and then this awful restlessness might begin again. It'd be late meals and studio scrambling and sleeping on couches and lending Phil money and no clean towels——"

"It needn't!" he said quickly.

"No, I'd try not to have it that way. But you see, Kelly, I don't *know*. We'd have enough to do things a little better, but I couldn't help Persis or Isolde; I couldn't do anything for Mother——"

"You could as soon as I begin to sell pictures."

"Yes, I know," she said thoughtfully, abandoning argument. And for a while she stared away into space. "Somewhere," she presently began again, "there must be families who pay bills and make beds up fresh and have meals on time and plenty of money for what they need——"

Kelly rose abruptly, with an impatient exclamation, and walked to the end of the short path, his back toward her.

"God, I wish you could get those people out of your head!" he muttered. "You're not going to marry one of the Flaggs, if that's what you mean!"

"Those people!" Penelope echoed, mortally hurt. The man came back to her side. She would not meet his eyes.

"I'm sorry," he said quickly. "I'm jealous, I know it. But I'm in love with you, Pen, and on Sunday night it seemed as if you might perhaps someday come to care for me. Isolde said——"

"Oh, you told Isolde?"

"They all know it!" he said, with an unhappy jerk of his head. "Isolde said you were the kind that loved after marriage. Can't you just forget those Flaggs, Pen? They're nothing to us. Someday you'll just laugh at all this. Don't you believe that? If I had anything to say about these Flaggs——"

"Which you haven't," Penelope said with dignity. She rose and turned toward the house just in time to meet a young man who was coming toward her with an inquiring look on his dark face, and his cap in his hand. Her heart gave a great spring. It was Jeff Flagg.

CHAPTER V

Immediately the world was miraculously all right again. Spring afternoon light was soft on the garden and the arbor; the shadows were long and clear; the air was sweet. Bees were charging to and fro, angry audible buzzes through the stillness; the Millers' chickens were making the unmistakable sleepy sounds that meant they were ready to go to roost. Jeff sat down in the grape arbor, and Penelope sat opposite him across the old green iron table, where her mother's typewriter and pencils and odd drafts of verse were still littered about, and they smiled at each other.

Kelly had dragged his lazy length away; Penelope and Jeff were alone. Jeff, immaculately groomed, in flannels and blue coat, dark and handsome and compact, presented as striking a contrast to the loosely built Kelly as could be imagined. Pen noted every difference with a little jealous prick at her heart.

"I was going by," Jeff said, "and I thought I'd come in and pay my respects."

Inasmuch as the cottage was remote and inaccessible, Penelope knew that nobody ever chanced to be going by. But she did not question the statement; she carried the conversation at once to ground familiar to him.

"How is the big family?"

"Did it get you all mixed up?"

"I couldn't straighten you out at all. Uncle Tom and Cousin Tom, and little Tom."

"I'm a Tom," said Jeff. "The oldest son is always Thomas Jefferson. He was my great-grandfather's friend—a cousin, in fact."

"Well, Mark, then—there were Marks."

"My brother and my father. Mark's out from college this quarter on account of typhoid. He came home sick six weeks ago, but he's all right now. He would have graduated this June."

"Constance, then. The one who's just engaged."

"Connie Forsythe. That's Gram's brother's granddaughter. That's Gram's great-niece. She's an ace," Jeff said.

"And you're the oldest son's son?"

"No, that's Tommy. You saw him."

"I didn't identify him. Was he the one who knelt down and held the sampler for your grandmother?"

"I think he did. Handsome?"

"Good-looking. He's—whose son?"

"Uncle Teege's. The one in the invalid chair."

"Hopeless!" Pen laughed. "Then the one I first talked to is your father?" she resumed.

"Mark Flagg, you heard them calling him that. My mother's called Aunt Margaret. And Aunt Hannah's Mrs Beville-Atwood."

"It sounds English."

"It is. Or was. My cousin Hannah—you got her straight?"

"Hannah isn't married?"

"Hannah? The one who came with us. No. She's Hannah Beville-Atwood; Mrs Towne and Mrs Merry are her sisters. You met them. She's my cousin. Nothing confusing about that."

"Nothing confusing!" Pen said. "That's the funniest thing you've said yet. Was her mother a Flagg?"

"Aunt Hannah? Yep. My grandfather's oldest daughter."

"Why didn't your cousin—Hannah Flagg—marry?" Penelope didn't know why she asked it, but she had wondered about Hannah.

"Oh, she had an affair, years ago, but something went wrong. I never knew the man; I was just a kid. And after that she fell for someone she couldn't marry. Hannah's eight years older than I am—that makes her thirty-two, by George," Jeff said, struck by his own words. "She ought to marry," he added; "she's such a peach. Everyone in the family is crazy about her."

"She's beautiful, I think."

"Both her sisters are married. Ann is Mrs Merry and Lucy's Mrs Towne. They both have kids."

"I'll get a pencil and paper someday and work it all out. I suppose you know each other apart."

"Ha! There are others who weren't there that day," Jeff said. "My sister Lucy wasn't there; she's in school in New York. She's twenty."

"I'm almost ashamed to say that I have only two sisters and one brother," Pen said, "and that all my grandparents are dead."

After a while she said: "And the cousin you call Tommy, is he married?"

"Nope. And he's the head of the lot, too. I think it worries Gram."

"How do you mean 'the head of the lot'?"

"Well, Uncle Teege's oldest son. There's George, his brother, who comes next; but Uncle Peter hasn't any sons, so after George it'd be me."

"Eldest son's eldest son, like England? D'you mean to inherit anything, the estate—something like that?"

"No, not that. Just being head, you know. Running things like Uncle Teege and Grandfather."

"But suppose some of the others—some of the younger ones—were much the stronger characters?" Pen asked.

"Ha, don't worry about Tommy's strength of character!" Jeff said, laughing. "He's iron, that lad is, mixed with granite."

"I see," Penelope said. She was very happy sitting there with him in the arbor, listening to the pleasant hoarse Flagg voice, watching the expressions of his brown face and dark eyes, and feeling herself cool and lovely in her thin old white frock. The ache that had possessed her during these past days, the need to see or hear from the Flaggs again, was satisfied. Her long eyes smiled, and once or twice her laugh rang out as it had not done for a long time.

Jefferson Flagg watched her closely. Afternoon light filtered in through the young grape leaves; the day stood still at a perfect moment; not a leaf stirred, except where birds were hopping from bough to low bough, chirping good nights. Even the cheap neighborhood of Armitage Lane, the line of plain little houses, the cluttered back yards seemed to acquire a momentary grace. Something of the utter stillness and peace of the hour fell suddenly between the two who were sitting at the old green iron table; words were unnecessary. It was enough to be together. Penelope had only to look at her caller, to tip the rich pale gold braids of her head, to narrow the long eyes; she did not say very much. Jeff talked, but it was more and more confusedly, and finally he abandoned the general conversation and, moving quickly to sit close beside her and catching at her hand, he broke off in a sort of laughing desperation:

"Miss Fitzpercy—do you mind my saying this? Do you mind if I tell you? I've been like a crazy man since I met you. I went north with Mark and Tom—I left 'em at Vancouver; it was no use! I'm terribly—horribly in love with you."

Penelope looked at him without speaking. There seemed to be nothing to say.

"It sounds crazy," Jeff said. "But listen—you're so beautiful! You're so cool and lovely and different in every way!"

He was close beside her. He put an arm half about her; Penelope straightened herself and looked almost smilingly into his eyes. She was quite cool.

"I didn't know," she said, musingly.

"Of course you didn't know. I didn't know myself. But my mother did; she knew right away. And they all know now."

Penelope's voice was faint with surprise.

"Who knows now?"

"All of them. I told them."

"Told them? When?"

"Yesterday. You see, this Canadian trip was planned to get me away. Tom and Mark and I were to drive up as far as we could, and then pack in to the big woods. But when we got to Vancouver I couldn't stand it. I've never been this way before! I told Tom, and told him I couldn't stick it, and that I had to see you. I drove down," Jeff said. "I brought the little car back and surprised my mother last night. So we talked it all over—with Gram and Dad, I mean."

"You mean they didn't like it? They tried to send you away to forget it." She was still quiet, still detached.

Perhaps the boy saw that he had made a mistake. She saw the dark quick color rise under his clear olive skin.

"Well, they knew I'd only seen you once!" he countered.

"I know."

"They thought it was only kid stuff. That was why—that was the reason —that was why——" Jeff stammered eagerly.

"How old *are* you, Jeff?" the girl asked, in the pause.

"Twenty-four."

"And you're in the family law firm?"

"No; I've not taken my law-school finals yet. I flunked 'em. But I will, and then they want me to go in for diplomacy. My grandfather, James Ogilvie, was consul general somewhere or other some time or other, and it's more or less expected of me."

She knew, and she was deeply if vaguely offended to know, that he knew exactly where his Ogilvie grandfather had been consul general, and when. He was merely not hurting her, making the whole thing unimportant. He suspected perhaps, and she was angry that he should suspect, that she had but an indefinite idea of what a consulship was.

"We don't go in for diplomacy," he said. "Not smart enough, I guess. But there's usually one of us in the service abroad."

"But I thought this was the Ogilvie grandfather?"

"But his wife was a Farmer, you know, and his grandmother was the great Siamele."

"Who on earth was she?"

"Oh, she was a great-great-aunt or something," the boy said carelessly. "Someone was kidnaped by Indians, and brought up by them, and then came home with this kid. In Boston there are lots of girls named Siamele."

"For a second name, I hope!"

Jeff laughed in relief. Perhaps he had sensed something faintly chilled in her manner; she was like herself again now, and he was all earnestness once more.

"Penelope," he said, "I don't mean now. But sometime—sometime . . . ah, I love you so much!" He broke off, sudden color in his face.

"You don't know me," the girl protested. But her tone was kinder than her words. "You don't know anything about me. Our family isn't—like yours. We've only what my mother makes with her column, or if she sells a poem. Phil isn't working. I have jobs on and off with some of the gift shops and tearooms. We don't even own this house—we pay seventeen dollars a month for it. My father's probably living—did you know that? He deserted us. Walked out."

"Aw, what of it?" Jeff stammered, his face very red.

"Nothing. Except that I don't blame your family for not being enthusiastic."

"I know that you're the most wonderful girl I've ever seen," he said soberly.

"You're very kind!" She was angrily close to tears; she looked away. "But you don't really know that," she said, more gently.

"I know that if you're what you are, everything has to be all right."

"Your people hate me," Penelope said slowly.

"Hate you!" He laughed, a little too heartily. "They don't know you."

"They tried to get you out of my way."

"Oh well, they would have done that no matter who you'd been. Do you know," Jeff said, "that since the day you came to our place—the day Con's engagement was announced, remember?—I've thought of you—hours and hours? I've been—starving, for just this, to hear your voice and look at you! It's just music to me to hear you."

"Idiot," Pen said thoughtfully, with a smile.

"Oh yes, I am. I'm an idiot. I didn't know, the day Hannah and I brought you home, what was the matter. Only everything seemed—it *was* a nice day you know," Jeff rushed on, "but everything seemed to be just soaring and singing. I could hardly stay in the car. I wanted to fly. And that night, and all the next day, I had a half-awake sort of feeling—honest, I mean I really did. I kept remembering what you had said, and every time I'd remember a new word or two it would make me feel all trembly. I know," he said, soberly, holding her hand now, moving his brown thumb against it as he looked down at it, looked up seriously into her eyes, looked down again, "I know there's a raft of preliminaries—Mother asking you to our house, and meeting your mother and all that. But I—well, I'm here, and I've told you, and that's all that matters!"

"And now what?" Pen asked smiling.

"I don't know. I don't care."

Her world was slipping and sliding about her. It was all too amazing, too breath-taking to be true. And yet this brown hand that was holding hers had a human warmth and reality about it; this man was one of the famous Flaggs, here in the Fitzpercy grape arbor, in shabby, straggling Armitage Lane, among the gnarled apple trees and cheap new corrugated iron garages. Penelope had a youthful sensation that she did not want to let go of him until she knew whether she wanted him or not; to tell Isolde and Mother this—yes, and Kelly, too—would be enormously gratifying. Somehow it was good for one's pride to have had a Flagg fall in love at first sight, and come down like an honest man to offer his heart and hand in this forthright way.

"And your people don't like the idea?" she said, frowning a little.

"That wouldn't matter, would it?"

"I don't know that it would. Other things would, though."

"You mean our knowing each other better—being friends. Penelope," Jeff said, "I'll never change! But maybe you'll change."

"I'd have to change to like you, wouldn't I?" she suggested, with a significant unsmiling glance.

"No. You like me now," Jeff said stoutly. "Maybe you don't love me yet. But you *know* you like me!"

"I have to like you!" she confessed, laughing.

"But you think I'm funny. Well, maybe I am. But you'll let me come see you, and know your people, and soon—how soon?"

"How soon what?"

"How soon would you let me tell you—how soon would you feel sure?"

"Jeff!" she protested. And quite suddenly they were both laughing and holding each other's hands.

Mrs Fitzpercy chose this moment to announce, with a little cough, that she was approaching the arbor, and Jeff and Penelope came out of their dream somewhat dazedly and still laughing. Penelope introduced her mother. She saw her mother at once assume that somewhat mincing air of elegance that meant that she was trying to make a good impression. Even at this moment Penelope contrasted it to old Mrs Flagg's quiet simple sureness of manner, and hated herself for seeing it, and felt a wave of loyalty to her untidy, vague, pretentiously affected mother.

Almost immediately Jeff, tardily presenting an enormous box of chocolates, went away. The two women were left alone in the arbor.

"Well! We have made a conquest, have we?" Mrs. Fitzpercy said archly.

"Apparently," Penelope responded lazily, with an undisturbed smile.

"Which is he?"

"He's a Flagg. Thomas Jefferson Flagg. His father is Mark Flagg."

"I remember his mother's wedding. She was named Ogilvie, from the East somewhere. Well!" Mrs Fitzpercy was obviously pleased. "He's a nice fellow," she said.

"Yes, I think he's awfully nice," Penelope said slowly. What did she think of him? She did not know. He was just an attractive, dark, earnest young man who had sat opposite her, here in the collapsing old grape arbor, and stammered the things that every girl liked every man to say. He was only—well, only one more young man in the world. One did not know what to think about him.

But what lent the moment magic was that he came from the world of the Flaggs; he belonged to it. He had the right to enter that enchanted garden, where babies tumbled on the lawn, where brown-limbed slim children dived and splashed, where maids set out great platters of salad and fruit on long tables, and where the white-clad groups formed and dissolved harmoniously to the accompaniment of laughter and pleasant voices. Her one glimpse of that world had been haunting Penelope, had been a shadow between her and the sun ever since she had seen it.

She wandered into the house after a while. It was a commonplace little abode. It had been erected, with some dozen other "model bungalows," just before the Spanish colonial craze had swept the Western state. It had cheap round porch pillars painted white, a bay window sinking down into a neglected rose bed; it had a pink concrete path curving between dry weed-choked garden beds in a firm question mark from the sidewalk to the steps.

Inside, the five downstairs rooms followed the regular pattern: living room and dining room on the bay-window side, bedrooms on the flat side, bath between the bedrooms, and at the back the kitchen, small, square, unimaginative. There were hundreds like it in the county, and thousands like it in the state. They were no longer called bungalows; they were called "old cottages" now. Even the cheapest developments had departed from their type and had gone Andalusian, with brick-colored tiles, patios, grilles.

Penelope and Persis had the back bedroom; their mother had the front one. Philip slept upstairs in cold weather, and in summer on a cot shielded by shrubbery and set just outside the dining-room windows. The nearest house was but fifty feet away, but its blind side was toward the Fitzpercys, and in the general irregularity and disorder of the neighborhood no very critical standard was maintained. The rusty frame of Philip's bed, its discolored mattress and tumble of blankets were not visible except to one who had penetrated the thicket of pampas grass and come upon them. In foggy weather Philip moved in to the couch in the dining room rather than bother with the stairs. This room was rarely used for its original purpose, anyway. The family meals were always informal and eaten either in the garden or the kitchen.

This afternoon Persis was making fudge. The little kitchen smelled of hot chocolate; it was six o'clock, but no dinner preparations were afoot.

"Who was it?" Persis said.

"Who?"

"That man who was with you out there."

"Oh? His name is Jeff Flagg."

"One of *the* Flaggs?"

"Uh-huh." Penelope touched the tip of a finger to the fudge, put the finger in her mouth. "Vanilla?" she said.

"There was just about half a teaspoonful. Pen, what'd he come for?"

"I don't know." Pen was detached, vague. She opened the bread box.

"He came to see you," Persis decided. "Pen, is he nice?"

"*Awfully* nice."

"Is he the one who brought you home?"

"He and his cousin, Miss Beville-Atwood."

"He likes you!" Persis said electrically.

"Ha!" Pen murmured, as one absorbed in other thoughts. "Stew for dinner?"

[95]

"Pen, do you realize what it would *mean* to have one of the Flaggs— well, like you?" Persis demanded. "Is he coming again?"

"He said so."

"He said so! Pen, why aren't you excited? One of the Flaggs! Wouldn't it be perfectly marvelous!" Persis exclaimed. "Oh, Pen, do you like him? *Do* be decent to him! We'll all pull for you. It'd be so wonderful if one of us—one of us ever did anything—ever, I mean, really married a man of any position, and with money, and you say he's nice, too. If he *does* like you—if he *should* ask you——"

"Again, you mean," Pen said dryly, in the pause, scraping cold stiff stew from a bowl to a saucepan.

"Again! You mean——? He *didn't!*"

"He did." Penelope dragged a match across one of the spattered and grease-blackened jets of the rusted gas stove.

"Why, he only saw you once!"

"I know it. To say that I'm tired of this stew is to say nothing," Pen observed, at the stove with her back toward her sister.

"But, Pen, could he mean it?"

"I don't know."

"But then why should he say it?"

"Exactly. That's what I don't know."

"What'd you say? Oh, I love things like this to happen!" Persis exclaimed, on a burst.

"I couldn't say anything, of course. I told him he was an idiot. That is, I laughed at him."

"Didn't hurt his feelings?" Persis asked fearfully.

"Oh no."

"Tell me what he said. That he'd admired you and thought about you——?"

"You're terrible, Persis," Pen said, laughing and flushing. "It was something like that."

"It's the hair," Persis said with conviction.

"He had to mention that, of course."

"Mine, too," the younger sister observed with satisfaction. "Pen, this is exciting," she said. "Flagg, hey? A Flagg. Oh, I think this is fun!"

"I may never see him again," Penelope said cheerfully. She put the remainder of the peeled tomatoes into the stew. "These may take the curse off it," she said.

"Don't say that, Pen! A man of that type wouldn't come here this way, and say all that, unless he meant something."

"I don't know," Penelope said.

"Well, I say he wouldn't!" Persis said decidedly.

"Quand eations-nous?" Kelly said, in the doorway. He crossed the floor swiftly to snatch up a spoon and stir the stew, which gave a sudden dry smack. "Evidently your feeling for the Flaggs was reciprocated, Pen," he

[96]

said in her ear. A sudden wave of pity for him, kindliness toward him, went over Pen. He was so miserable with helplessness and jealousy! And she was unhappy, too, although on far vaguer and less reasonable grounds; she could feel for him, feel, too, that perhaps she had not been quite fair to Kelly. Only a few weeks ago she had been seriously considering marrying him.

She was gracious to him tonight, and she saw his spirits rise and his whole being basking in the joy of it. And yet, and yet—things weren't straightened out yet; even being kind to Kelly didn't ease the burning pain in her heart. Through every minute of it she knew that she couldn't accept life on these terms; she was sick of it all! She was sick of the grime and the smallness of the kitchen; of Phil's lazy length in the open-throated shirt and dirty cords, of his unshaven face, of the bills in the desk in the dining room and the broken step at the side door. She was sick of the smooth excuses, the easy evasions, the torn dish towels and the chipped china. Her heart yearned toward order and graciousness in living, wide lawns and cool rooms, polished surfaces and great crystal bowls of flowers. She hated this cheap little backwater of a neighborhood, men running for trains in the mornings or rattling away in muddy little cars, women pinning long rows of wet baby linens on the lines on Mondays, baking upside-down cakes on Saturday noons. Tonight it all seemed to be on top of her, the whole narrow pettiness of it, stifling her, holding her down like a weight.

The night was unwontedly close and warm. It was midnight when Penelope decided that it was useless to waste it further in tossing and sighing in the hot little bedroom. Persis was deeply, beautifully asleep. Penelope picked up a discarded blanket, put on her slippers and an old Japanese wrapper, and went quietly through the kitchen and into the side yard.

The world was flooded with white moonshine; the old rabbit hutch, the chicken shed, the gnarled apple trees were equally transformed into exciting beauty by the purity, the incalculable wealth and spread, of the white glory. Penelope walked into the Parsonses' yard; there were no intervening fences, and the Parsonses, she knew, were staying with Mr Parsons' people in Sunnyvale for the spring vacation. She climbed the stairs of the windmill, climbed still higher on the ladder, her rolled blanket under her arm.

It was glorious, up on the little mill balcony. Penelope wrapped herself well, seated herself with her feet dangling over the top of the ladder, her back braced against the great dark bulk of the tank. There was a refreshing breeze up here; there was a view of all the beautiful silver-drenched world. Distant villages, sleeping under the moony mist, showed only occasional flecks of light; oaks were rounded and furry in the magic wash of whiteness; the roofs near by were romantic between straight shafts of eucalyptus and poplar, bowed fountains of willow and pepper.

She had often climbed the old mill in wilder and younger days; she had once before done this on another moonlighted night, when the ache of life and the strangeness of young dreams had kept her waking. But she had never in her life felt as she felt now—felt the pain of a definite longing, a definite hope and fear. Surely this chance—this door into beauty and service and self-development and infinite satisfaction—had not been opened to her just to be closed again! The world of the Flaggs, that world so satisfying, so dazzling, and yet so simple and right, had been hers only for an hour. And yet that hour had changed her life for Penelope Fitzpercy, and she knew it.

"'Tis to disrelish all life's sober taste.'" The words came to her unsought, and she repeated them musingly, half aloud. "''Tis to have drunk too well the drink that is divine, maketh the kind earth waste, and breath intolerable.'"

But suppose herself to be given the chance, her somber thoughts ran. Suppose Jeff to be really in earnest, suppose him to come again Saturday, as he had said he would come, to take her away for lunch and polo, suppose the affair someday to develop duly into seriousness, and he and she to become engaged, married, attached as one more Flagg family among all the Flaggs; then what? What of Mother, with her gentle sloppiness of dressing, working, thinking? What of Philip, almost always idle now, but bound to be hopelessly irresponsible from the moment a rich brother-in-law entered the family? What of Isolde, disorderly of hair, hopelessly late and slovenly and unorganized in everything that she did and thought, scrambling somehow through debts and privations in the studio on Telegraph Hill? What would a family dinner be like, with these persons as guests of magnificent old Mrs Flagg, of quiet, aristocratic "Mrs Teege," of Jeff's mother, "Mrs Mark"?

Musing uncomfortably in the darkness of her high perch on the mill, her eyes on the moon-drenched trees below her, her forehead wrinkled, Penelope's heart rose on a moment of fear as she saw car lights cautiously threading the twisted little unpaved lane. Who could be coming back so late, and if it should by unlucky chance be Van Parsons, what would he think if he glanced upward and saw a figure on his mill ladder? Thinking this confusedly, Penelope silently and swiftly descended to the dry ungroomed grass about the mill, and dragging her blanket after her slipped between overgrown bushes toward the house. She stopped halfway for one look at the car, and saw it in the clear open moonlight; stopped, and with its lights out.

Left there in the center of the road? No, there was a man at the wheel. He was sitting there quietly, looking at the Fitzpercy house. Quite suddenly she knew, although she could not see his face, that it was Jeff.

Her heart began to hammer fast with fright and joy and amazement.

She went noiselessly on, between the high bushes, noiselessly entered the hot kitchen that smelled of wood and food and dishwater, noiselessly found her way to the bay window, and stood looking out between the parted limp dirty curtains. For fifteen minutes she stayed motionless, watching the motionless car, thinking in a strange tumult of broken thoughts.

Then the car lights came up, the ignition stirred, there was the sound of gears. Jeff wheeled it about; it went flashing away down the lane, its lamps picking up a gatepost here and a rose tree there, glinting on leaves, gone. Penelope stood looking out for another full minute; she saw a cat's bright eyes hang like blazing smaller lamps against the hedge for a few seconds; then they, too, disappeared, and the night was left to the white glory of the moon.

Creeping in beside Persis, chilled and sleepy, the girl had time only for a little laugh of excitement and triumph before waking dreams changed to sleeping dreams.

CHAPTER VI

Two days later Jeff Flagg's convertible was in Armitage Lane again; on the following Sunday he took Penelope away for luncheon and for the polo. For the latter occasion Penelope borrowed Persis' white coat and a picture hat that had seen long service; she polished her shoes, washed the family's one pair of long gloves. She looked beautiful—no denying that—but she also looked home made, countrified and poor.

"I wouldn't go, if I couldn't dress right for it," Persis said.

"It may mean going other places sometime when she *can* dress for it," Isolde suggested significantly. Penelope merely laughed at them both; she was a leaf on the current now, letting each day's events carry her where they would.

The Fitzpercys were not calculating folk, but they were a little dazzled by Pen's latest conquest. One man or another had been in love with Pen since her fifteenth year; that Pen would eventually choose one of them for a husband, as Isolde had, was a foregone conclusion. But that a Fitzpercy would ever improve the family fortunes by marriage had never been considered, even by Philip, who was the person most in need of money and oftenest in financial straits. To think of the wealth, position, power that were possessed even by the least considerable of the great Flaggs was to open a new door to speculation. The Fitzpercys were essentially adventurers; they watched the development—the approach of this new adventure—with something like mingled amusement, pride and awe.

Penelope, being the most concerned, was also the least concerned. Jeff Flagg was a matrimonial prize, of course, but Pen was not sure she wanted that exact prize. Impersonally considered, he was everything any girl wanted; he was handsome and friendly and rich and socially prominent. But naturally one could not impersonally consider a man who was violently in love with oneself, who was constantly maneuvering for moments alone, and in those moments wanted kisses and embraces and the murmur of vows and protestations. Penelope sometimes reflected ruefully that she liked the whole situation—except Jeff.

Yes, and she liked Jeff, too. It would have been impossible not to like a man who made so determined, so flattering an attack, who was so openly and so honestly devoted. "Of course I like him," Penelope said, when Isolde accused her of it, "but liking isn't loving."

"You'll never love any man that way until you marry him, Pen," the older sister said, as she had said before.

"But how do I know I will then, Isa? Do you? Do you love Grandy more now than you did when you married him? Remember how you cried that night before you were married, and how you said that you couldn't think whether you even liked him or not?"

"Ha, you forget all that!" Isolde said, with a reminiscent narrowing of eyes and a brief laugh. "You see, once you're a man's wife, you feel entirely different," she said. "Now take Grandy. We hadn't been married two days before his money gave out; I'd always thought he had plenty somehow, without thinking much about it. We'd gone to Del Monte, which was an idiotic thing for him to do to begin with, and he had exactly two shirts, a blue one and a striped one. I said that we could go over to Monterey and buy some more shirts, and he said he hadn't any money—none at all. He'd bought me orchids, and we'd bought a sort of fruit strainer; remember the fruit strainer? We saw it in a window in Carmel, and Grandy had to have it. We've never used it; I think it's to make jam in. Well, anyway, I washed his shirts in the hand basin, and we wired Mother for money—remember?—and came home here, and by that time I felt as if we'd been married ten years, and as if it was my job to manage Grandy."

"Somehow," Persis said, in her youthful bored voice, as she lay on her bed staring up at the ceiling, her arms locked behind her head, "somehow I imagine that if Jeff Flagg ever took Pen to Del Monte on a honeymoon, he'd have more than two shirts with him."

The three sisters laughed joyously; Pen with the others. But deep inside her, when she thought of a honeymoon with Jeff, at Del Monte or anywhere else, a certain shrinking went on in her soul and mind and body. She wanted to marry him and she did not want to marry him; it was confusing to think about. It was especially confusing when she was not with him and when her sisters and mother were enlarging upon the brilliance of the connection. At such times she felt strongly that she did not want to lose Jeff; she did not want to let him go. A girl would be a fool to let him go. This was a chance to enter a different sort of world, a world of dignity and beauty and pride; if she lost it, it might never come again.

But at the same time, neither Isolde nor Persis nor Mother was the person admired by Jeff. They did not know him as Pen did. They did not know, admiring and awed as they were by the Flagg name, that Jeff had an inflated opinion of it, too. Jeff calmly took it for granted that there was no family in the world as remarkable as the Flaggs. Jeff took it for granted that any girl would snap at such an opportunity as he was offering Pen; of *course* she'd marry him, her hesitation was all nonsense; girls did not decline marriage offers from the Flaggs!

Penelope had her pride, too. She was too proud to hint these things to her mother and sisters; she thought it extremely probable that she would marry Jeff, and to what purpose then would be any such revelations? She never told them that on the day of the polo game some of his relatives, the Merrys and the Forsythes and Jeff's own sister Lucy, had been in box seats a few rows below the seats where he and Pen had been sitting, and that he had made no effort, in any of the intervals between chukkers, to take her down to join them. He had bought her gardenias and peanuts and a pennant; he had lounged beside her in his impeccable flannels murmuring personalities, telling her that he loved her and assuring her that, whether she knew it or not, she loved him, but he had not taken her to his people. She knew very well, by this time, that the Flagg family was not enthusiastic on the subject of Jeff's new love.

She was gradually getting Jeff's family clear in her mind. His father was Mark Farmer Flagg, a senior partner in the family firm of lawyers; his mother was the stout handsome Mrs Flagg with the very dark eyes, the "Aunt Margaret" who wore glasses on a fine gold chain and argued brightly about politics and sociology. He had a younger brother, Mark junior, known as Bunny, and two younger sisters, Lucy and Peggy.

The dark, sunburned, lean, tall Flagg who had knelt beside his grandmother's chair on the occasion of Pen's one visit to the Flagg homestead was the older son's son. His mother, "Aunt 'Lizabeth" to the younger crew, was *the* Mrs Flagg, and rightly should someday wear Gram's emerald ring. But Jeff's mother was the one who hoped to wear it, and gentle Aunt 'Lizabeth didn't care. She cared for only one thing—the welfare of her invalided husband, "Uncle Teege."

Tom was not married, although he was twenty-eight years old; "and we're hell on early marriages!" Jeff said. Tom had a married brother whose wife had a baby daughter, "one of those kids that were on the lawn," and also had a married younger sister, Mary Flagg Cline, whose year-old son was still another Thomas Jefferson.

The subject of Tom Flagg persistently interested Pen, although she had seen him but once and had never exchanged a word with him. Brown and lean, with broad shoulders under a thin shirt and comfortable old white flannels belted about a thin waist, somehow she remembered him distinctly among all the others. He had been playing tennis that day; he had come up to his grandmother unrolling his sleeves, slipping into a dark blue coat. There had been something clear cut, definite, almost stern in his manner. He had not looked at Pen.

"Does your cousin Tom know you like me, Jeff?"

"You bet your life he does. They all do."

"And what does he advise?"

"I don't take any advice from old Tom."

"But he gives it, does he?"

"Oh, well, I think he feels I ought to graduate, and stop booming, before I get married."

"He doesn't boom?"

"Well, he had a lot of trouble when he was a kid, and I guess it kind of sobered him."

"How could anyone in your clan have trouble? There isn't any trouble except money trouble," Pen said, with a little laugh.

"Don't you believe it!" Jeff answered. "Uncle Teege, his father, has been sick for years. That's why Aunt 'Lizabeth is so quiet. About ten years ago Uncle Teege had a stroke—he was in a chair that day; you might have noticed that they had to wheel him to the table? He can't walk. Tom reads to him and plays chess with him—it's kind of made him older. He and Hannah are great pals, and that's all the girl he wants."

"That's Miss Beville-Atwood?"

"Hannah, yep."

"In love with each other? Isn't she older?"

"Cousins. No, not exactly in love with each other. But Tom thinks there's no one like Hannah. She's a swell girl, too."

"She's awfully attractive." Penelope thought of the dark young woman in the plain lemon-yellow tennis dress, her feet so squarely set on the green lawn, her eyes and voice and manner so frank and pleasant and sure of themselves. But all the Flaggs were that!

Once again her heart wavered between longing to enter that enchanted world and reluctance to enter it by means of Jeff. Wide lawns and big trees, neat little maids in gray moiré coming and going with platters of food; pleasant voices, "Aunt Margaret," "Tom dear," "Gram." And the cool, big, orderly rooms, and the old silver and old portraits, and the sense of dignity and security—oh, it would be a good place to be, a place where all the dreams of girlhood might come true! Why couldn't she—why didn't she love Jeff so madly, so blindly, that hope and excitement and passion would carry her over all the quicksands, as his feeling for her was indeed carrying him? Penelope had never loved any man that way; sometimes she thought that Isolde was right, and that tall blond women never did. They just let the men love them, and submitted to kisses and murmurs, and were gentle and generous and maternal in return.

The days went by and were weeks. Summer deepened in Armitage Lane and over all the world surrounding it. The fruit blossoms were gone; instead the old trees were thickly leaved, with the tiny green nubbles that would someday be apricots and prunes hidden among the leaves, and trim plats of shadow falling on dried heavy yellow grass when the sun was high. The Fitzpercy house was hot; the grape arbor, a rickety little affair built twenty years before by the Italian tenant of the old ranch this tract once had been, was hot. Isolde and her boys came down for a noisy restless period of baby washing, baby voices, sour baby bottles and sour baby linen. Mrs Fitzpercy distractedly wrote a poem for a prize offer, won two hundred and fifty dollars, paid a colored woman to come and restore order and peace to the exhausted household. Through it all Jeff Flagg came and came; nothing mattered to him except that Penelope was somewhere in the picture, his golden girl, with her hoarse Fitzpercy voice and her long Fitzpercy eyes, and the coil of pure gold at the nape of her white neck.

"Jeff dear," she said one day, when they had stopped the car for a while up on the cool Skyline, with the hills descending to the fresh salty ocean just below their eyes, "the catch is, I don't love you."

"How do you know you don't?"

"Any girl knows."

"Not if she hasn't ever loved anyone any better."

"I've never loved anyone any better," she said musingly.

"Well!" Jeff had his arm about her, and although she still sat erect, although there was no surrender in her attitude, yet their eyes were close together, and she felt the warmth of his shoulder pressed against her own. "Don't you see, darling," he said, "I'm going to do all that for two? I'm the crazy one. You don't have to do anything but be nice to me, belong to me. Tom—Tom and Hannah, you know, have been telling me that I ought to go back East, finish up my law work, show you that I'm in earnest. Bush-wah!" said Jeff, eloquently. "If I had you with me I'd straighten out in two seconds. I know it. I've never been so sure of anything in my life! George—that's Tom's brother—married Emily when he was twenty-three, and I'm twenty-four! That cousin of mine—Con Forsythe, 'member her engagement was announced the day you were there?—she's only twenty-one. It's all bush-wah."

"It's all awful!" Penelope thought. But she did not say it aloud. She had to think this thing out herself; she could get no help from anyone else.

CHAPTER VII

The Fitzpercys never were hurried in the morning. Winter mornings they slept late, like hibernating animals, everyone dreading the chilly first beginnings of the day; even in spring Penelope and Persis rarely stirred until the sun came in through the southern windows. Breakfast occupied the better part of two hours, what with their languid approach to it, their long lingering at the table, talking, musing, or working out the cross-word puzzles in the papers. There was usually a dog to feed, the cats to quiet; often the clock's hands stood at twelve before any move was made. Then one after another the Fitzpercys would start their day; beds were made in a desultory fashion, dishes were piled in the sink and crumbs shaken to the chickens, conversation rambling on all the while, and the young voices calling from one room to another. Persis would drag herself to the old square piano, Penelope perhaps carry her mother's papers and pens out to the arbor. One girl or the other usually had ironing to do, or must immerse her glorious thick waves of hair in hot suds.

When Isolde and the babies were with them it was the twin boys who had to adapt themselves to the strange system, or rather complete lack of system, in their grandmother's house. No concessions were made them. They fretted in their wet uncomfortable cribs, dozed, awakened to fret again. Sometimes their young Aunt Persis opened the door of the little back porch where they slept and said, "Oh, for heaven's sake, darlings, shut up!" Sometimes their golden Aunt Penelope appeared with brown teething crackers and silently distributed them, whispering "Hush!" The twins, in this first summer of their lives, reached their tenth month; they knew what "shut up" and "hush" meant. Almost always they obeyed, and fell off into light sleep again, the crackers drying in a mush on their thin little faces.

At about nine they would be carried into the kitchen and made dry, with wiped faces and hands, and given bottles.

"It's not the slightest use fussing with them before their ten o'clocks!" Isolde would say drowsily from between two intervals of carefree slumber, "for if you get them out in the garden it's nothing but more crying, and mosquitoes, and the neighbors slamming their windows down. Wait until nine and sleep through them, the way I do!"

Grandison Tasker, the small, dark, eager musician who was their father, was not disturbed. When they came to the Fitzpercys for a visit he invariably took up his old quarters, with Kelly Quentin, half a mile up the lane; he might spend the entire day there, rippling out old études and concertos on Kelly's aged square piano, thumbing mismated sheets of torn music in a dim corner of the studio. He took no visible pleasure in the possession of small sons, but he obeyed Isolde loyally even to the accomplishment of their laundry work, when she asked for his help. The Taskers, Penelope thought, watching them in these hot summer days, were not lovers any more. They were a man and a woman caught in a snare and handling the web gallantly, philosophically, in their young ignorance and bewilderment. Rent, and food, and a woman's health, and twin boys— gosh, Grandy's attitude seemed to say, a man didn't count on all that when he fell in love! But since all that was the logical sequence, he was sweet about it, and he and Isolde laughed a great deal, enjoyed their gypsy quarters and their gypsy meals, scolded and swore when things went wrong, dodged bill collectors and landlord as long as they could, borrowed money and pawned their possessions, and between times worried not at all.

That was the kind of life Pen knew. She could contrast it with any other only in her imagination, an imagination stimulated now by her hour with the Flaggs, in that heaven of emerald lawn and white-clad figures, splashing children, and babies safe and sun tanned on their garden rug. Her spirit burned with an incessant fierce jealousy of all the Flaggs; Jeff, whose pocketbook was always so filled with fives and tens and twenties; Hannah, cool and secure and lovely and beloved at an unmarried thirty-two; Tom, "the head of the line when Uncle Tom dies, of course," who had not spoken to Pen, but who had supplied her name so quickly to someone who was in doubt of it. She resented the Flaggs; she wished she never had known them. She wished she had kept their worthless old Hannah Carter sampler, burned it, and then told them that she had burned it. But she had to think of them now.

She was twenty-two, restless, bewildered, unhappy. Isolde and Persis could go on wasting the summer hours sleeping late, idling over meals, putting off the grocer and the telephone collector; Penelope was not satisfied to live that way any more. Yet how could she become one of the Flaggs when they so obviously did not want her, and when her own feeling toward Jeff was so puzzling a mixture of impatience and tolerance, liking and disliking, criticism and envy? Jeff had no right to be a Flagg, to come and go at his will among those lovely houses, among those important people. What had he done to be inside, while Penelope Fitzpercy was an outsider?

"They're trying to get me to go to Harvard and take my law-school finals," Jeff told her.

"In September?"

"And September is month after next, darling."

"Are you going?"

"Am I going? I am not. Too far away from my girl."

"Your girl thinks you ought to."

"She *does* not. She says she does. She's trying to make me mad."

"But if you don't finish your law, what then?"

"O-o-oh, I could finish it here! Fine law courses here. Get married and finish it here!"

"Not if They don't want you to." "They" meant the family. She always thought of it in terms of capital letters. To antagonize Them would be to start all wrong, and perhaps prejudice Them against her forever. Jeff defying them, and on her account! She could not have that. But even while she said it she felt a little prick that he did not deny the power of the family, did not laugh off their importance with a "What do they matter; you're not marrying them?"

It would be compromise, compromise all the way, marrying Jeff. The question was whether the end would be worth the means. The question was whether she could rise superior to all the difficulties she foresaw, and to a thousand others she could not foresee, and beat the Flaggs at their own game. There were moments when Penelope thought she could. There were others when she knew wretchedly that, handicapped as she was by her own family, handicapped as she was by her lack of background, of culture, of plain education, she could not.

The Taskers were to leave for their city studio on a certain blazing Sunday in August. Such heat was a sort of sensation in the smooth course of the Western summer. Newspapers commented upon it, the delivery boys panted and wiped their brows. The confusion in the Fitzpercy household rose to fever pitch, what with crowding, with the babies crying, with the usual disorder augmented a hundredfold in anticipation of the move back to town, and the usual impecuniousness not helped by Grandison's and Isolde's cheerful habit of borrowing. To all these was added the complication of the weather; the night was hot, and morning broke merciless and blinding in a buzzing of mosquitoes; Persis was wretched with an arm swollen and tingling with poison oak. At about eight o'clock Penelope gave up all idea of further rest and went to bring the crying babies from the sun porch to the kitchen.

The sun porch was drenched with sunshine and smelled of sweet rotting prunes. Flies banged angrily at its rusted wire screens. Both the little boys were tortured with sunburn and upset from the heat and the bright light and from the carelessly mixed bottles of the day before. Penelope, who really loved her small nephews in her young impatient way, brought them into the house; the air in the kitchen was not much of an improvement upon the sun porch, but at least there was shade in here, and Penelope, tying a faded old apron firmly about her slender waist, and bunching her fair hair sternly from her flushed wet face, tried to pacify them with drinks of water. They didn't want water; they wailed despairingly. She looked at the clock. Quarter to nine; they would have bottles at ten, but they were supposed to have baths first.

Surely, the girl thought, as Donny fell into wearied sleep in the basket, and little pale Davy grew quiet, his cheek against hers, surely there was some easier way of managing babies than this. Isolde's boys cried all the time, fretted through the daytime hours, awakened to sudden wailing in the night. Pen hunched herself on a chair, Davy like a watchful little monkey in her arms, and sat staring absently at the kitchen scene, yawning, closing her eyes, opening them sleepily again. She had not had her sleep out.

With so many persons in the house, two of them babies, the kitchen was never in order these days. Not that it mattered much; the Fitzpercy kitchen was a free-and-easy place, and it was nobody's business to keep it clean. There were unwashed pots and dishes in the sink; the window shade was awry; milk or some other fluid had been spilled on the stove, and streaked the oven door with caked white. Burnt matches, newspapers, a crusted sugar bowl, three rolls on a plate and two empty beer bottles were on the table; the saucepan in which cereal had been cooked was soaking on the stove. The windowpanes were smeared with fingerprints and speckled by flies.

Added to all these details were the worn linoleum, its pattern completely merged into brown dimness at the sink, and the sink itself, its woodwork grease-stained and worn, its zinc basin nicked and discolored. A faucet dripped and splashed into a full saucepan; an alarm clock ticked busily among the crowded objects on the narrow shelf above—cookbooks, spice cans, a can opener.

The girl rocked herself to and fro slowly; it was somehow touching to have Davy quiet while she held him. She looked at Don, lightly asleep, tears still wet on his cheeks, and wished that she dare lay Davy beside him and straighten them both out for a nap. It was entirely the wrong time for their sleep, but peace was sweet, after so many hours of half-waking, of restless worry and weary anticipation of the hot day.

Isolde came out, pale and disheveled.

"Weren't they awful last night?" she whispered.

"Poor kids."

"Is he asleep?"

"Donny? Yes. It was hot for them, I guess."

"It was Phil," Isolde said darkly, resentfully.

"Was he——?"

"Was he! I heard him talking to Mama in the night. Or trying to talk," Isolde said disgustedly. "He had some kind of a smash-up. He went out to phone and was gone the longest time! And he went off early this morning and took the car."

Pen still rocked automatically; her face paled a little.

"I didn't hear any of it. I was on the couch. He's gone?"

"Early this morning. Six, I guess. About the time the neighbors got started. It takes them five minutes to get that old car going; I never heard such a racket! Talk about city noises," Isolde said. She sighed. "Have any coffee, Pen?"

"No. The boys were crying, and I brought them in. They can have their bottles in half an hour."

"Well, it's up to me to make coffee, I guess. I don't see how we can get off this morning unless Phil brings the car back."

"Kelly'll drive you to the station, maybe take you all the way in. He said last night he'd go if I would."

"H'm!" Isolde had her fingers under the stream of water at the sink. "No hot water; that's delightful!" she said.

"Kelly said it was much cooler in the city, and that perhaps we could all go downtown somewhere for supper. It's going to be another scorcher."

"Probably foggy in town," Isolde said. "But I don't think you ought to come in."

"Don't think I ought to?" But Pen was not surprised. A slow flush stained the magnolia cream of her skin.

"No. You might miss—somebody. Isn't he here every Sunday?"

"If I did miss him, he'd come again."

"Pen," Isolde said seriously, "if you can get out of all this I think you ought to."

"Don't cry, little boy," Pen said, getting to her feet as Davy's bitter wailing started again. She did not answer her sister, nor did Isolde pursue the subject. In heat and disorder and confusion the morning hours dragged themselves along. Persis appeared clear-eyed and flushed at about eleven, and would say of last night's dance only that it had been lousy. She sat drinking coffee, her lipstick still smeared on her young fresh face, poison-oak paste drying white on her swollen arms.

"You knew you'd have a rotten time before you went," Pen said. Both babies were crying lustily, despairingly, when their grandmother appeared, her own hair and kimono as casual, as disorderly as were her daughters'.

"I suppose you heard about Phil. Sometimes I think he simply doesn't understand," she said, sitting down at one end of the table, pushing cups and plates restlessly about. "He was quite sober, poor fellow; he'd had two cocktails, he says, but he was as calm as I am now. The man was right out in the center of the road. Phil had to see someone named Leonard, and get a check cashed, and be in court this morning. It all seems too awful, after last—when was it? March. Is there any way we can keep these babies quiet?"

Noon, and no Phil. Heat, flies, confusion. The day was burning hot. The little boys refused to sleep, although their eyes were heavy and their crying little voices hoarse with fatigue.

"Isolde, isn't there some book, something, that tells you just how to run babies?"

"Oh, someone sent me one; it's round the studio somewhere! But there's no sense to it. You'd think they were machines! Babies aren't machines, to have their food measured and weighed. They'll be all right!" Isolde said easily.

When Phil came back at two o'clock he found the family gathered in the side yard in the shade. It was not cool there, but it was cooler than any other available spot. A casual lunch had attached itself to a casual breakfast; Mrs. Fitzpercy was at the open arbor table, buttering a bun; Persis, with much spilling and spattering, was serving a watermelon on paper plates. Penelope had Don on her lap now and was soothing him as she had earlier soothed his brother.

Philip looked tired and hot; he knew he was completely out of favor with his sisters and avoided their eyes. He slumped into a chair, and to his mother's anxious "Did you *fix* it, Phil?" answered only with a brief, "O.K."

Somewhere in the distracted morning hours Grandison Tasker had joined the group; he now extended a brother's sympathy to Phil and asked amiably: "What's the fuss about this time? Seems to me a lot of excitement about nothing."

"Oh, leave it to those state cops!" Philip grumbled, not eagerly, but with obvious relief in being drawn into any sort of talk. "Look, I'm coming along the Bayshore . . ." he began. The girls eyed him coldly; their glances occasionally meeting. Another smash, and perhaps talk of lawyers and damages again, and another uncomfortable day when Mother must go to court, pale and lovely and poetic . . .

"I hate everyone and everything," Penelope thought. Aloud she said: "There are so many things we can't afford I think we ought to go light on accidents."

"Well, but darling, you don't think Phil enjoys this sort of thing?" her mother demanded pathetically.

"Was the car much hurt, Phil?"

"Nope. He was walking, you know."

"Walking! Oh, heavens!"

"Yep. But he wasn't hurt. Just scared!"

"Shoo!" Mrs Fitzpercy said to one of the Millers' chickens.

"I wish," Persis said, lying back in a ragged old beach chair, her hands locked behind her head, "I wish I were in a deep forest, roofed over with green, green trees. I wish there was a pool a block square, fringed with ferns and black as ink. I wish I had nothing on——"

"As soon as they get started," Penelope said, pinning busily at Donny's garments, "we'll get everything into order."

"They'll never get started," the younger sister said darkly. Isolde and Grandy, now both out of hearing, were indeed dilatory in gathering up their babies and their belongings. A blanket, spread over a dry bush to dry, would not get dry.

"I looked at that chicken stew from Friday, Pen," Mrs Fitzpercy said. "I think it's spoiled. It sort of bubbled and frothed . . ."

Pen picked the baby from the table; he was ready to start now, bottled and dressed and for the moment quiet, but nobody else appeared to be prepared. She raised her eyes toward the gate; her heart jumped, turned to lead. Her warm face, already flushed, flushed deeper, and she was suddenly conscious of her faded apron, her slipping knot of disorderly hair, and of the utter squalor of the crowded scene. Phil needing a shave; Mother in her old housecoat; twins, blankets, flies, dishes, bottles in evidence on all sides; the hot sun of midafternoon streaming down upon the dry earth and the rickety arbor and the untended garden.

"I wish I were dead!" she said in her soul.

CHAPTER VIII

A man in white, his hat in his hand, was standing only a few feet away from her, smiling interrogatively. She had seen him but once before; she knew him instantly. It was Tom Flagg, the man who had known her name on that memorable day of the restoration of the Hannah Carter Flagg sampler.

"There you are, Miss Fitzpercy," he said easily, coming forward. Penelope could extend a hand beyond the bonneted twin. The scene would have been impossibly difficult except for the obvious fact that it existed. Nothing so terrible could happen; only it had happened.

Somehow introductions were managed, and a general exodus took place. Grandy and Kelly and Isolde and the babies melted away; Persis, dragging the puppy, was gone. Philip had disappeared first of all. Mrs Fitzpercy lingered for a few elegant words of greeting.

"You find us at a disadvantage," she said, gathering her wrapper about her. "Where there are babies there is always confusion, and last night my son had a most unfortunate motor accident. Not his fault at all, but of course that doesn't make it any better for the poor man who was hurt. Run into the house and jump into something decent, Pen dearest, and I'll talk to Mr Flagg."

And somehow her mother's gallant, pathetic efforts to carry off the situation hurt Pen more than any other feature of it. Tom Flagg was young, cool, handsome, correctly dressed, rich. Mother wasn't any of these things. Yet it was Mother who must be apologetic and explanatory.

Pen and Persis whispered fiercely to each other, upstairs in the disorderly cluttered bedroom, while Pen splashed her face and ran a comb through her hair, pulled a clean dress over her head and thrust her feet into Persis' white shoes. In three minutes she was down in the arbor again, and left alone by her tactful mother with the man who would someday be "*the* Flagg, the head of the line."

Every detail of the disorder about her was imprinted on her very soul. She seized upon a rag of tea toweling and brushed crumbs from the table, scattering flies. She tossed a score of small things into a basket and set it out of sight.

"My sister, Mrs Tasker, has been here from San Francisco for a month with the babies, and the confusion has been something beyond description!"

"I can imagine it. I would have telephoned you, but Jeff tells me you have no telephone."

"We're getting it back. It wasn't satisfactory . . ." This is what her mother always said of the things the Fitzpercys lacked. Servant, car, radio, private schools, luxuries of every sort were often dismissed by Mrs Fitzpercy in conversation as having been tried and found "not satisfactory." But even as she said it Pen despised herself for the transparent fiction.

"Well, I've found you. That's the main thing," Tom said. "Could we talk for a few minutes?"

"Surely." It was said in the pleasant hoarse Fitzpercy voice, with a flash of the big-toothed Fitzpercy smile. "But I know what you're going to say," Penelope thought, "and I hate you!"

They sat at the old tin-topped table in the grape arbor. The day was at its ugliest hour; no shadow anywhere. A radio in some neighboring house was talking loudly; a man's voice; a woman's voice. Someone called, "Harry! Harry!" Children, climbing the windmill, squawked happily to each other as the breeze caught their hot little faces.

"It's about Jeff," Tom Flagg said.

"Of course," Penelope agreed steadily.

"It's a funny kind of a situation," Tom said. "Jeff's father, my Uncle Mark, was coming to have a little talk with you, but he's been called East by business; he had to leave on Thursday night. I'm afraid he's struck some pretty hot weather."

"Awful," she said, her eyes not moving from his face, her voice low.

"Jeff," Tom began again, with a brief dubious smile as he thought of Jeff, "happens to be a great favorite with my grandmother . . ."

"And she doesn't want him to get married," Pen said, in the pause.

"No," he said quickly, with another little shred of laughter, shocked this time. "It isn't that at all. As a matter of fact I believe she'd be delighted to see him settle down. The trouble is that settling down seems to be the last thing Jeff wants to do."

Penelope said nothing. There seemed to be nothing to say. She continued to regard her companion steadily. A great velvet bumblebee buzzed noisily through the arbor, was gone. The dropped pale shadows of the grape leaves seemed as hot as the white blots of sunshine that pierced them.

"He tells me you know that he has twice flunked his law-school finals," Tom said. "And that last year he went off for three or four months, Panama and Cuba—we didn't know where he was. Well! Then he wrote us that he was going to be married to a nurse in the hospital in Havana."

"He told me that, too."

"He said he did. Jeff knows," Tom explained, raising his fine eyes from the little marks he was making with a closed fountain pen on the tin table, "I'm talking to you. The truth is," he added, with a sudden brilliant smile, "he's in Dutch with my grandmother at present, and there's been something like a family conference about it. He played roulette, I think at Agua Caliente, on his way home, two months ago. Last night, in an attempt to recover some of that loss—it was several thousand—he went to a gambling resort in Colma, just outside of San Francisco, and lost twice as much more. None of us knew anything about this.

"Two weeks ago my grandmother had a letter from this nurse in Havana. Jeff's written her quite honestly, and it can be straightened out, but it's awkward, of course. Now comes the news of these two gambling losses. My aunt Margaret, his mother, is crushed about it; we're keeping most of it from Uncle Mark, because he's away."

"I knew of the nurse. And he told me he never ought to gamble, so I supposed that he'd lost, because my brother did once," Penelope said simply.

"My grandmother and his mother," Tom said, "want to get him out of all this before he——"

"Before he gets into fresh trouble," Penelope supplied coldly. She felt her throat thicken a little and her nose tingle; whatever else disgraceful was inevitable today, she told her inner self angrily, she would not cry before this man!

"No, that's not it at all. But they do feel, Miss Fitzpercy, that Jeff ought to show that he's in earnest before—well, before anything. They think that Cuba affair ought to be given time to cool off, and that he ought to coach for the rest of the holidays—he'd live in the house with his coach, incidentally, in San Francisco, take his law-school examinations next Christmas, or at Easter anyway, and graduate. Then he can try for the bar, and he'd be in the office here, probably. He'd be—grown up, he'd be settled," Tom said, with an explanatory smile. "The trouble with him now is that he's—scatterbrained."

"And what of all these gambling debts?"

"My grandmother will settle those. Her bargain is that he leaves for the East tomorrow, gets down to work, gives her his word not to gamble again, and doesn't consider himself engaged to anyone until at least a few months have gone by. And my job here," Tom finished, looking up seriously, "is to assure you that this arrangement is made as much for your protection as for any good it may ever do him. My grandmother has very—well, exalted ideas of marriage, you know, and she can't bear the idea of any woman trying to do anything with Jeff as he is now—as he has been, rather. You know he's one of the finest kids in the world," Tom added, not very comfortable under Penelope's steady thoughtful stare, "but he's reckless, that's all; he's undeveloped. This—this plan, if you agree to it, might be the making of him. He loves you very much; he seems to be desperately in earnest this time. I believe it may stimulate him to make a real effort, if you will agree."

She had flushed and paled once or twice while he was talking. Now she said in a level voice:

"Agree to what?"

"To not seeing him, or writing him, for a year. For less than a year—only until he graduates. To not announcing any engagement."

A silence. Penelope spoke presently in a voice of biting scorn:

"There is no engagement, Mr. Flagg."

Tom, feeling sorry for her, took the opening eagerly:

"But there's an understanding. It's that—the hope of that, that we're building on!"

"I never had the slightest intention of becoming engaged to Jeff," Pen said.

"I hope you had," the man said quickly and seriously. "I know that my errand here seems odd to you, Miss Fitzpercy," he added, "but the chief thing I have to do is persuade you that my grandmother feels, and we all feel—I mean everyone Jeff's talked to—that it would be the best thing in the world for him to settle down."

"I can imagine, with me," Pen thought ironically. But she did not say it. She continued to regard him in silence.

"You don't believe that, do you?" he said, suddenly sighing in the heat and fatigue of this hard talk.

"Naturally not," Pen said. "It would be an odd thing," she added, "if my influence over him was so good that his mother wanted me not to write to him or see him for a year."

"You to be his reward, his inducement, can't you see?" Tom said. "They had—they had a pretty serious family talk about it," he went on. "With gambling, and with the claim of this woman—she's at least ten years his senior, by the way—and with the flunking, it's really serious. If he'll pull himself together and promise that this is the finish, the family'll stand back of him once more. And of course that's where *you* come in."

"Or go out," Penelope said simply. "We're not engaged. I like him tremendously. But I don't love him, and I've told him so. I've told him I'd never marry any man without caring for him. His being a Flagg is very important, to *you*. But it's not so important to me! I'm sorry you were all so worried about it. Jeff could have told you," Penelope said proudly and coolly, "that there was nothing to worry about!"

"If you mean that," Tom said, "then there *is* something to worry about."

Anger shook her, and she answered with her first show of feeling:

"You don't mean that! You're letting me down easily! You needn't. You can go back to them and say that I quite understand, that it's all right. I'll not see Jeff again, I promise you that, and I'll not write him. If he doesn't keep his end of the bargain it's not my responsibility."

"I've been extremely stupid about this," Tom said in distress. "You make me feel very badly. We wanted you on our side in this thing; we felt that if you cared for Jeff you'd see that he's got to show what he's made of before any of us can trust him."

"Well," she said in a low voice, hands locked on the table, eyes on space, "you were mistaken. I like Jeff, very much. If he wants to come and see us when he gets home again next June, he'll be welcome. But as for marrying him, it seems to me that his mother, and his grandmother," Pen went on, forming the names definitely with her lips, "have taken a good deal for granted!"

"You can't see that they were thinking of you, too, in the matter?"

"No, I confess I can't. And I'll say frankly," Pen said, "that if I loved Jeff I'd marry him, in spite of them all, and I'd go East with him, and get a job, before I'd ask help from them or from anyone! But I don't love Jeff, as it happens, no matter what he told you, and consequently it's all over. It's *finished*. And thank you very much!"

She stood up; the man also got to his feet.

"Perhaps," Penelope said stiffly, "Jeff was the one to explain this to me. But tell him I said good-bye and wish him a fine trip."

Tom put his fingers to his thick black forelock and rumpled his hair in a gesture of despair.

"I've done this very badly," he said regretfully. "We asked Jeff to talk to you before all this happened——"

"All this?"

"Before my grandmother knew just—just how deep in he was."

"With me?" Pen asked quickly.

"No, no, no! In all these other ways. But Jeff, today," Tom said, delicately, "couldn't come. He's all shaken up from last night. And he's to go tomorrow."

"If Jeff told you what is absolutely true," Penelope said, "he told you that no—no explanation of this sort was necessary, as far as I am concerned. As for your grandmother," she added, walking beside the man now, toward the car, "you don't have to tell me what her attitude would be."

"And yet my grandmother wanted you to know what we feel about Jeff," Tom said. "Wanted you to know what her plans for him are. She felt that no girl ought to—to get interested in him without knowing that he—in a sense, is on probation."

"Thank you," Penelope said perfunctorily. The man looked at her as if he would add something more, smiled irresolutely, and held out his hand. She touched it, unsmilingly, and without another word or glance turned away and walked back through the hot strip of garden.

She sat down in the arbor, her eyes narrowed, her jaw set, and put her elbows on the table and her chin in her hands. And for a long time she did not move.

After a while the Fitzpercys began to creep quietly back, like trout that have been disturbed in a pool. Penelope was noncommittal about the visitor. Jeff Flagg had been unable to come to see her, she explained, and his cousin had come instead. Brother? No, cousin. This was a Mr Tom Flagg.

"Well, it seems to me we are getting rather important to the great Flagg family," Pen's mother said, flattered. Pen echoed neither the words nor the sentiment; she was anything but complacent over the episode. Tom Flagg, however nice his manner, however ingenuous his attempt to make her feel that she was merely being consulted, had managed to say a very definite "Hands off." The burning truth of it smarted in her soul.

Saying little, seeming to be only tired, as they all were, by the events of the long scorching day, she moved through the ensuing hours. Kelly had taken the Taskers all the way into town, but he came back, wilted and weary, at seven, and the Fitzpercys walked with him up the lane and helped him get a supper in his studio cottage and shared it with him.

Penelope saw all the familiar surroundings, heard the familiar voices on the familiar phrases, like one newly awakened from a dream. The disorder and shabbiness of her life, the unnecessary ugliness of it, were spreading in her consciousness like the ripples of a stone fallen into a pond. Gradually her whole spirit became possessed, and she could see nothing that was not squalid and stupid, and feel nothing but shame.

The neglected dooryard, the frayed wicker chairs and the scattered rubbish, the bedrooms in which garments were scattered over heterogeneously assorted blankets and comforters, and in which shoes lay carelessly on the rumpled rugs, the window shades that were all cracks and seams, the kitchen-greasy splinters and battered tins, all these were a mountain upon her, and when she got into bed that night the mountain seemed to be upon her soul. The afternoon's bitter mood was a hundred times accentuated now. "I wish—I were—dead," Penelope breathed again into the hotness of the night. "I wish—I were dead."

She, and all the others, tired from the long day, had gone to bed early; it was not yet nine o'clock. The night stretched itself out endlessly. The little upstairs bedroom was low and hot.

Wherever her thoughts went they could find no rest, no dignity, no peace. The Flaggs, for no merit of their own, were one way; the Fitzpercys, through no fault of their own, were another. Penelope tossed and turned in her bed, trying to work it out, trying to make it all seem reasonable and right. She thought a long time of the way things were in the house; everything should be different, of course. But how? How would the situation be bettered if Persis and Penelope had jobs; Persis selling flowers in Ye Tulip Potte down in the village, for example; herself teaching in the primary grades?

The memory of her mother's gracious social manner with Tom Flagg today came back to her, and her face flushed, and she felt shame and loyalty and puzzlement again. She loved her mother's little finger more than all the Flaggs put together!

After a while she began to think of her own life in terms of alteration. The kitchen cleaned, white-enameled. The dooryard raked and scraped as the Peters' yard was; always in order. The bedrooms put in order scrupulously every day; towels washed and blued and ironed; regular hours set for regular tasks. . . .

No use! Even at its best the commonplace cottage in Armitage Lane would not be dainty, cool, dignified, satisfying. There was something fundamentally wrong in the way the Fitzpercys did things and did not do things. Persis and she were too good to be mere peasants, content to scrub pots and pans and rake weeds and tend chickens and settle down in white aprons to rest in the long afternoon, and yet, bafflingly enough, they did not seem to have the requisite qualities to lift themselves above the routine of peasants. They ought to be in movies now, or on the stage, she and Persis, with their slim bodies and heavily lashed eyes and mops of pure gold hair. They ought to be writing poems or short stories—registering their personalities upon the world, developing their gifts in these precious years. Instead they were playing with the puppy, and spilling iced tea on the kitchen floor, and putting off the telephone collector, the gas man, the grocer.

"Pen!" she heard a man's voice whisper from the garden below. In an instant she was at the porch rail; two minutes later she descended the stairs, and was out in the moon-washed world, and in the arms of Jeff Flagg.

"I parked 'way down the road there and walked up!" he said. "Pen, I had to see you! Isn't this the hell of a note?"

Laughing, she disengaged herself from his embrace, and stood close to him, a hand on his arm, a tall fragrant girl with her coil of hair loosened.

"You're crazy!" she said.

"Listen, Pen, Tom was here today, wasn't he? Tell you what a mess I got myself into?"

"You mean gambling?" Her tone was dispassionate; she saw him stoop to look anxiously to see the expression on her face.

"Uh-huh. Damn fool!" he said.

"Jeff, how can you do it? No sensible person does!"

"I know. But you see, I'd lost an awful lot at Agua Caliente, when I was down there with Lewis last month. I hadn't told anyone—but I had to ship them a check, somehow. So last night a couple of fellows and I went up to the Villa Fortuna, and I dropped seven grand."

"Seven *thousand!*"

"Yep. And the other was four. Fool," Jeff said simply.

"And flunked out of law school."

"Yep. I failed the exams last year. But this year was worse."

"Jeff!" she said sadly and affectionately. She had led him to the arbor where they had had their first long talk, and they were sitting there in the blotches of moonlight and inky shadow. The whole world lay under the enchantment of the moon. Pen knew the boy had been drinking. He was not intoxicated, but there was a quick feverish urgency in his manner, a certain thickness in his speech that betrayed him. She felt a sudden maternal fondness for him; she felt a sudden desire to make all this simpler, easier, if she could.

"So they want you to go away and get down to work," she said.

Jeff sighed profoundly, shrugged and nodded in the shadows.

"And I can't leave you," he began. Penelope laid a hand on his, and he took it quickly to his hot cheek in both of his, and pressed it there. "I love you!" he said under his breath.

"Your leaving me or your staying wouldn't matter, if you're going on this way," Pen said. "It's up to you, really. Whether you mean to—to stop all this sort of thing, or not. You're the only one that knows."

"You mean I could just as well take my coaching here!" he agreed, with a sort of heavy eagerness.

"Or anywhere, or do without it. *That's* not what matters," Pen said. "It's what you decide, what you feel about it. Isn't it?"

"That's what I told them. I told them I was in earnest; I told them I'm *through*," Jeff argued. "No more roulette, no more anything, except maybe a game of golf once a month. Plugging, knocking it cold. Fourteen hours' work a day."

"Now there you go, Jeff, being extreme. A game of golf once a month! Why can't you be reasonable? Six hours' work a day would do it. And then they'd all be so proud of you, they'd all be so glad to help."

"Yes, but not without you," he said jealously. "I don't go one step of the way to New York without you."

"I thought you had agreed to."

"Well, that was when I was woozy and tired and scared that I'd gotten myself in too deep. My mother and Gram lit into me, and they had Tom advising me all over the place, and finally Tom said, 'Look here, you're not up to going anywhere today. I'll go talk to Miss Fitzpercy, explain to her—you'll see that she'll think it's wise!'" Jeff rumpled his heavy black hair wearily. "I don't know what it's all about," he said. "But I know I don't go away without you!"

Penelope saw the whole picture in a moment: the spoiled, sweet, amusing boy and herself going to the City Hall—possibly in Redwood City—announcing the marriage to the family, being shipped East together as the best solution of a bad business, defying the family, defying convention, breaking pledges, and yet sure all the time that the family must stand by them, because there was nothing else to do, being sure all the time that all the Flaggs in their power could not do anything then except face the situation, pay the bills, and hope for the best.

"She may straighten him out; she seems like a nice quiet girl, in spite of that peculiar family," Gram might say. "She *can't* be nice," some other voice, perhaps the cool, beautiful Hannah's voice would protest. "No nice girl would do a thing like that! Marry a man against his family's wishes, knowing that his profession and his future depended on that family, persuading him to break his promises . . ."

"I didn't hear you, Jeff; I wasn't listening," she said aloud, "but I think, my dear, that you and I can't be married now."

"Why can't we? The family, hey?"

"Not entirely."

"Why, then?"

"Perhaps for the reason I told you the other day."

"Pshaw!" he said scornfully. "I'm not worried about that. I'll make you love me! I know you and I know myself. Listen, we could have a little place, back East there . . ."

She let him spin the dream for a few minutes unchecked. Then she said steadily: "No, now listen. This is really the best thing for you to do. A few months' hard work won't kill you, and you can show them in half that time that you're in earnest."

"Oh, gosh, you talk like Tom!" he said, boyishly angry. "They know now that I'm in earnest. I've promised my grandmother never to gamble again, and I told her and Mom that I'd go on the wagon until Christmas. I will, too. Pen, listen, if I work like hell from now until Christmas, will you marry me then? Will you announce the engagement now, and let us get married then?"

"That isn't the family's bargain, is it? They were to pay your debts and you were to work until graduation without seeing me or writing me. Can't you see, Jeff," Pen said proudly, "that I'm in this, too? They don't want you to marry anyone until you graduate, and especially they don't want you—ever—to marry me. I don't blame them; they don't know me. Your family's not like most families. It's like a club, and they like to know the people who come into it—the new members. They've probably got a fourth cousin picked out for you."

Jeff was gazing at her adoringly in the gloom, his hands stretched across the table to hold hers.

"Not a fourth cousin," he said, in a tone that expressed nothing but a sort of dreamy love, and with small cognizance of what the words would mean to her. Her heart gave a quick jealous jump, and she felt pride thicken in her throat.

"Someone, then."

"Amanda von Bagger. I told you that."

"I thought you said that that was years ago, in dancing-school days. Amanda, then."

"Mark can have her. He likes her."

A silence, then she said:

"You have to go back now, Jeff. This is breaking your promise. It isn't fair to them."

"You mean actually not to see you again or write you?"

"Well, what else?"

"But don't you see I *can't?* It isn't what I want to do, it's what I've got to do. You're the only thing I think about. I wanted to get out of this money scrape just for you. If I ever do pass the bar exams it'll be just for you."

"Perhaps," she said, "they'll soften, if you really do cut out all this nonsense and settle down. I *know* they will! Meanwhile, what else can you do?"

"But you'll be waiting for me at Christmas? You'll let me tell them that's why I'm doing it?"

It would have been so easy to say yes, so easy to say to herself that by Christmastime not only might his character have changed, but that her feeling toward him might have! It would have been so easy, out of the dullness and bewilderment and dissatisfaction of her days to say to herself that any chance was worth taking! And yet quite coolly, quite definitely, in the back of her mind, Penelope knew that she could not do that; stronger than any secondary considerations of the benefit of such a marriage, of the wealth that must inevitably be his someday, of the triumph it would be to prove to the Flaggs that their decisions were not law to Penelope Fitzpercy, no matter what they might be to the rest of the world, was that innate honesty that told her that she could not marry this man.

"At Christmas we can talk about it," she temporized.

"I may have to be digging at Christmas. I may not come home."

"Don't worry, the family'll want you at home!"

They were walking toward his car now; he put his arm about Penelope. He began to grumble against the whole scheme. Darn it, what right had anyone to say that he did or didn't mean his promises, that he could or couldn't display sufficient character to fulfill them? He wished he had back the ten grand that he had been given by his Ogilvie grandfather upon coming of age. He and Bruce Bannister had spent most of it touring Europe on bicycles. At first they had won sensationally at Monte Carlo; afterward it had all suddenly gone "sour."

"I wish he was different, I wish he was different, I wish he was different!" Pen kept thinking. But she let him kiss her good-bye and lingered for a few minutes, leaning against the car door, when he had taken the driver's seat.

"Not good-bye," he said. "For I'm going to talk to them in the morning! I'm not going to be crated and shipped off like a sheep. The train doesn't go until half past seven—my mother and Gram will have time to cool off! They may feel differently about it tomorrow."

"It won't help much, your having come down here tonight."

"Well," he said, "they can't do anything about it."

He started the car; she watched the red rear light dwindle away down the lane, and walked slowly back to the house.

For a while she lay wakeful on her balcony, thinking. But after an hour the moon waned, and the world turned darker. A cool breeze swept down from the hills, bringing with it a faint foggy tang from the ocean; Penelope flung away her pillow, flattened herself face down, and was instantly sound asleep.

CHAPTER IX

She was dressing the next morning, at about eight o'clock, when Persis came up the stairs in her pajamas, with her gold hair in a tousle, to announce Mr Flagg.

"Oh, he oughtn't do things like this!" Pen said. He probably hadn't gone home at all last night, and the family would be more than ever incensed against him.

"Not Jeff. The other one," Persis said.

Pen stood transfixed, staring at her sister.

"Tom Flagg!" she gasped.

"There was an accident," Persis said simply. "Jeff was hurt. Not dead—he said not dead. But hurt."

"Oh no!" Pen whispered.

"You'd better go down."

Penelope, descending the stairs a few minutes later, was principally conscious of a thrill not all unpleasant. It was startling to hear of any accident, of course, but under her sense of sympathy and shock was another sense of keen excitement, a satisfied feeling that something was happening and that she was in it. The Flaggs were conscious of her existence, at least. They had sent an envoy to tell her of Jeff's mischance; they had not left her uninformed, to learn of it in the papers.

Tom Flagg was alone in the morning sunshine of the sitting room

when she entered it; he got up from the chair in which he had been waiting, as she came in, and crossed the room to reach her. He looked very
grave.

"Your sister told you—Jeff's been badly smashed up," he said.

"Oh, not badly, I hope?"

"They don't know. They're afraid so."

"When was it?"

"This morning at about one."

"He was here at ten last night," Pen said honestly. "I was asleep on
a porch upstairs and he called me and I came down. He seemed excited
about going away. We talked for about half an hour and then he went."

"He probably stopped somewhere. He was unconscious when they
brought him home," Tom said. "The smash occurred not a mile below
our gates; one of my grandmother's gardeners was the first on the scene.
He's been unconscious ever since, Jeff has, until about half an hour ago.
He isn't out of it even now; he's doped—they gave him something. He
doesn't know his mother, or his brother, but he keeps asking for you.
Would you come back with me and see if he knows you? The doctor thinks
it would quiet him down. They have to X-ray him; they want to give him
a transfusion, if he can stand it."

She had pulled on a white hat, slipped her arms into Persis' white
coat while he was talking. A little pale, entirely silent, she went out with
him to the car.

"You'll tell your mother? You'll explain that it may be a matter of life
and death?" Tom said to Persis, in good-bye. Persis, somewhat bewildered
and immensely curious and excited, followed them out to the car and
nodded a head that blazed silver-bright in the rays of the sun.

"Is it really so bad?"

"They're afraid so," Tom said. He nodded good-bye to Persis; started
the car. "He's lost an enormous amount of blood," he told Pen. "Poor
fellow. His lips were cut; they've got his head bandaged—he looks—*awful*.
Dr Cox, the head man, said there was no fracture, only scalp cuts, and
they fixed them up. Now De Vecchio is on the job; he got there just as I
left; he says it's something inside. Jeff seemed a little brighter, but he
kept looking about and muttering about you," Tom said, with his sudden
serious smile and a swift oblique glance at the girl beside him. " 'Where's
Pen? Where's Pen?' Cox asked who you were, and my grandmother said,
'Go ask her to be kind enough to come. Tell her it may mean the boy's
life!' "

"I would do that much for anyone," Pen said simply. There was a silence. "He broke his word to you and his grandmother," she added then.

"You mean in going to see you last night?"

"Hadn't he promised?"

"I think he may have thought that that promise only began when he
left for the East."

"No," she said. "You told me yesterday that he was not to see me again, not to write."

"She was thoroughly out of patience with him yesterday. Gram has a hot temper, though we don't often see it," Tom said. "But she meant that for him; it had nothing to do with you."

"If he'd let me know he was coming last night I would have told him I wouldn't be here; I'd have gone to Isolde," Pen said soberly. "Poor Jeff! He was angry and excited, and I suppose he stopped somewhere, going home——"

"He did indeed."

"Now he may be seriously hurt. . . ." She said it musingly, thinking of the nearness of life to death.

"It's not his first bad smash-up. But he's never been injured himself, before. It was late and he was tired; he was probably driving crazily. Had you—nothing had happened to make him think—I mean, there wouldn't have been anything deliberate about it?"

"He was angry at his mother and grandmother," she said. "But I only told him what I had told him before—that I don't want to marry—well, anyone, really. I don't want to be engaged."

In the shock of the news, and in the quiet early morning, with the markets they passed opening for the day, and only the shabby little cars of workers on the highway, it seemed easy to be quite frank and simple about it. Everything was fresh and wet and untouched; in the gardens roses were heavy with dew; kitchen chimneys smoked into the still air of the summer morning.

Penelope remembered the entrance to the Flagg place, and her own weariness and heat when she had first walked up under the great trees and past the lawns and the massed flowers. The car moved swiftly onward; again she entered the old-fashioned white house with the colonnades and the bay windows, this time to follow a maid and Tom upstairs.

Space and comfort were everywhere, and that spotless delicate cleanness and order that is beauty in an old house. The wide halls were paneled in white, with white-frilled windows at either end. Penelope saw jars of flowers, open doors that gave glimpses of bedrooms, fireplaces, lamps.

A little breathless and nervous now, she was suddenly in a bedroom in which three or four other women were standing in a group. They turned, and she saw that one of them was the oldest Mrs Flagg, that mighty, rather formidable "Gram" whose opinions were the law of the clan. Another was Jeff's mother; a third, Hannah. They all smiled at her, but their faces were white and strained, and Jeff's mother, the firm, dictatorial "Aunt Margaret" of the glasses and the political opinion, seemed wilted and quiet enough now, and had been crying.

"You remember Miss Fitzpercy, Gram. How is he? Are they to operate?" Tom said, in a low voice.

Hannah's eye caught Penelope's, and she very slightly shook her head. She drew Penelope aside.

"Your hat and coat," she said, taking charge of them. "You were so good to come."

"What else could I do!" Penelope said, shocked. "Is he so bad?" she added in an undertone. Hannah smiled, shaking her head, her eyes suddenly brimming with tears.

"They're not going to let him suffer, anyway. Shall we go in, Aunt Margaret?"

Jeff's mother was in a chair now, leaning back with closed eyes. She touched her cheeks with a folded handkerchief.

"Is that Jeff's girl?" Pen heard a child ask in the hall as she followed Hannah to Jeff's room. Two or three children had come to the top of the stairs and were sitting there, awed and curious. "If he didn't know Aunt Margaret or Mark, how's he going to know her?"

Then Pen was in Jeff's room, a big room, with tennis rackets and photographs and trophies on the mantel and bookcases, with deep couches and big windows, with a desk and textbooks; shades were drawn against the bright light. She had of all this only a general impression; she saw only the figure on the bed. She sensed rather than saw that there were other persons in the room; a doctor sitting on the far side of the bed with Jeff's limp bandaged hand in his; a nurse with a basin in her hands; another nurse. A pretty girl younger than Jeff, whom she was presently to identify as his sister Peggy, was kneeling with her elbows close to the mound made by his still feet, and crying quietly, and drying her eyes, and looking at his face only to cry again.

Jeff's head was so bandaged that only the brown oval of his face was visible. His mouth had been cut and was swollen; he was muttering incessantly. Pen had heard the sound in the hall; now she heard the words.

"I wonder if you will be so good——" Jeff said. He gritted his teeth on the last word. "Good," he said loudly. "Will you please be a good fellow, Doc, and send for my girl? She'll take this accursed thing off my shoulder. . . . Will you please be a good sport . . . will you please be a good sport . . ."

His words came with emphasis as fresh pains twisted and bit at him. In between them he murmured in a lower voice:

"Pen . . . Pen. Hands . . . such cool hands. You wouldn't let me kiss you—damn it, I know you don't love me! I know you don't love me!" he shouted, writhing against the hands and bandages that held him. "Where is she? I don't know who you are. I don't know who you are," he said feverishly to Hannah, who was standing looking down at him pityingly. "Go away, will you, please? Will you *please* go away until I get control of this car . . ."

Pen quietly took Hannah's place. Jeff lay very still, looking at her. She began to speak.

"You're all right, Jeff. Just keep quiet, dear. You're in your own bed—everything's all right."

"You're Pen," the swollen, bloody mouth said slowly.

"I've come here to look out for you," the girl said, in what was only a deep soft shadow of her usual voice.

"I knew you would. You're so sweet," he said, tears of weakness running down his face. "You're so wonderful!" He shut his eyes, his waxen face glittering. "I love you so," he whispered, his lips trembling.

After a while Pen was back in the other room, feeling tired. It was Tom who remembered that she had had no breakfast; when a maid presently brought up a tray, Hannah sat with her while she ate. Pen merely crumbled the rolls, but she drank the hot coffee gratefully; everything seemed like a dream now, and herself a figure in a dream. These men and women about her were all tense under great strain; they were quiet, serious, swift in what they did and said. But they were gentle and polite, too; it was Jeff's white-faced mother who presently came after a while to sit with the two girls, and who, watching Pen finish her second heartening cup, said simply:

"Dr de Vecchio said that he was quieter after you were with him, Miss Fitzpercy. If he lives—if he lives——"

"He'll pull through, Aunt Margaret," Hannah said quickly, as the other woman faltered and was still. "He's as strong as an ox."

"How badly is he hurt?" Pen asked. "They all seem to feel that it is very bad. But do they know?"

"You've finished. Would you go back to him?" the boy's mother pleaded. Pen, shocked, got to her feet.

"You were waiting for me! Why didn't you tell me?"

"I don't believe they know how bad it is," Hannah said, answering Pen's question.

"Then maybe it isn't so terrible," Pen said. She went back to the sickroom and took a low chair someone placed beside the bed. She took Jeff's hand into her own hand. He opened sunken eyes.

"Funny way to have it end, Pen?" he whispered.

"This isn't the end," she said, smiling at him.

"Oh yes, it is! They don't fool me. And now that the pain's better, I don't care. They're giving me all the dope I want, and they're not going to operate, are they, Doc? That means something. That means I'm washed up."

"We do not operate now, no," said the handsome old Italian doctor from the foot of the bed. Jeff moved his eyes, with a weak laugh of triumph, to Pen's look.

"See?" he said. He closed his eyes. After a while she gave the doctor a quick frightened look; the old man shook his head again. Things were bad —bad, but the end was not yet.

CHAPTER X

The day dragged on. Penelope was presently taken out to a lofty sleeping porch, where there was an awning, and where the stately old matriarch of the family occupied a deep basket chair. Mrs Flagg's fine eagle eyes went to the doctors' faces, as they talked; she anxiously attended the reports of the nurses; she had little to say. Once her voice was quick and definite:

"Tom, you got in touch with Miss Fitzpercy's people? They know what is detaining her?"

"I didn't," Tom said apologetically. "I will, right away."

Cups of hot chocolate, sandwiches appeared; the strange hours dragged by. Pen, curiously exhausted, leaned back in her chair and shut her eyes. Jeff, they said, was weaker. They must get ready for surgery.

Mark Flagg was with them again, bringing the older Mark from the flying field he had reached an hour earlier. He had dined in New York the night before, had been roused from sleep in his hotel at three o'clock; the three thousand miles between the great city buildings and the roses and oaks of his mother's estate had streamed by him like a dream; he was at his boy's side. He came out to the porch haggard, wiping his eyes.

"Didn't know me. Didn't open his eyes," he said, kissing his mother, taking a chair from which he could take his wife's hand and hold it.

"All in God's hands, Mark," the older Mrs Flagg said steadily.

"Yes. Well, well, well! We didn't see this coming, twenty-four years ago, when our first boy was born, did we, Mag?"

Margaret Flagg wiped her eyes again; she smiled, but she did not trust herself to speak.

The old doctor came to the white-frilled french door that opened upon the porch. Everyone—there were ten or a dozen persons in the group— looked at him quickly, fearfully. He raised a reassuring hand.

"Now!" he said, coming out to sit down amongst them. "We must spik of these thing. It is to you I would spik."

He indicated Penelope, and Tom, glancing at her, saw the rich color rush into her face.

"The boy is very wik," the old doctor said. "We do not try the blood infusion; it is too much to reesk. He does not slip. He watch. He watch for the young woman to come in. Now!"

Putting away with a flourish the silk handkerchief with which he had wiped his glasses, he put them on and looked about the circle. He laid an aristocratic old hand upon Pen's knee.

"You are to marry these boy?" he said.

"No, we are not engaged!" Pen said quickly. She dared not look about. Her eyes were fixed on the physician's face.

"But he love you!" De Vecchio exclaimed, disappointed.

Pen could find no ready answer. She was silent, not moving her eyes.

"He go to see you last night?"

Still she was silent, but this time she nodded slowly.

"He wish to marry you," De Vecchio said flatly. He looked about the circle. "He die, poor child," he added, and Pen heard one of the women catch a quick sobbing breath. "He die today," De Vecchio went on, "but he wish to marry his girl first."

Pen's look about the group was quick and anxious.

"Couldn't we let him think we were to be married?" she asked, forgetting everything else but the immediate tragedy of his going. "If it would help him—you wouldn't mind—now that he's so ill? If we told him that tomorrow—whenever he was well enough—we would be married, that you'd agree to it, that he didn't have to go away——?"

Quite suddenly she was conscious of a change in the atmosphere. Jeff's mother, Margaret Flagg, was looking at her steadily, but it was with a strangely softened look. Little Mrs George Flagg was crying, her head awkwardly on her husband's shoulder; Mark Flagg's lip was shaking; he seemed bewildered by this new development, but he was smiling at Pen. Tom, who had just come onto the sleeping porch, came over to Pen and held out his hand to help her to rise, something wonderfully kind, wonderfully friendly, even admiring, in his eyes.

"You're a sport, Pen," he said. He had never called her by her name before. "Jeff wants you. He roused up a moment ago and asked for you. I don't think it's going to be long now."

Obediently she went back with him to the sickroom. Jeff looked lifeless; his skin shone whitely; his face was more sunken than ever, his voice only a whisper.

"Pen," he panted, "I've not got long. I want you to be my widow, not just my girl. Tom's going to ask them—he said he would. Tell them—to rush it—will you?"

Stirred to the deeps of her being, forgetting that he had ever disappointed her, if he ever had, remembering only that this was generous, eager, boyish Jeff Flagg, who had poured his young admiration and love at her feet in spite of everything that his family could do to discourage him, Pen slipped to her knees beside the bed and put an arm under the bandaged head. Jeff closed his eyes.

"Tom said he'd fix it with Gram," he breathed. "Kiss me, Pen."

She knelt, perfectly still, for a long while. Minutes ticked by; it was late afternoon now. This time yesterday, Pen thought, Tom had been talking to her in the grape arbor; it seemed weeks ago. It was a dream, and this big airy room, with the shades drawn at the windows and the green tops of great trees moving outside in a breath of summer air, the quiet figures coming and going, was only a dream too.

Someone propped her up with pillows; a nurse, on the other side of the bed, reached for Jeff's limp hand, held it, her eyes on the watch that was in her free hand.

"Get up, Pen," Tom said, his strong hands at her cramped elbows. Staggering, stumbling against him, she was on her feet. He steadied her.

"He's still breathing," she said to him, without sound.

"I know it. We have to speak to you."

Jeff opened his eyes, spoke naturally, if very weakly.

"Fixed everything, Tom?"

"All fixed. Half a sec, old boy."

Tom guided her to the hallway; Jeff's mother and grandmother were there, with the doctor, and some other persons Pen hardly saw. Margaret Flagg was clinging to her big square husband; it was he who spoke.

"Miss Fitzpercy, will you do this for the boy?"

"What?" Pen asked bewildered.

"They think it may be his one chance. He's fretted about it. It was the last thing on his mind before his accident; you can see how he's thinking of it. Uncle George can marry you right away. Will you do it?"

"I'll do anything," Pen said. Margaret Flagg burst into tears and kissed her.

Old Mrs Flagg spoke in her deep voice.

"We can't wait for your mother, your sisters. We dare not."

"I understand," Pen said, very white. The mention of her mother had sent her thoughts in a great wave of homesickness to the cottage in Armitage Lane. If only one of them were here—Isolde, Persis, above all Mother—to tell her that this was the right thing to do!

She looked at all their faces: Margaret's swollen with tears, colorless, middle-aged; her husband's anxious and grave; Tom's watchful, concerned, kind. Hannah was close beside her; Hannah had whispered, "Oh, you will," but instinctively, she did not know why, Penelope spoke to Jeff's grandmother, her young eyes fixed on her face, her young voice trembling with a sudden excitement. Jeff's grandmother should tell her to do this.

"You—you tell me. Shall I?"

The two women looked steadily at each other, in a dead silence, and it was as if the older measured the younger, and the younger threw down her challenge.

"An upstart and a commoner, the girl who trapped Jeff," Pen's eyes said.

"You will be Mrs Thomas Jefferson Flagg in spite of me," Jeff's grandmother's eyes answered. Or did they? Was it only Penelope's imagination?

The exchange of glances lasted but a second; then Mrs Flagg said, in appeal to someone else in the group: "Doctors can be wrong, can't they?"

"You mean that he may live?" Penelope whispered. Her manner was quiet, but her whole being trembled with hurt and anger. "Then suppose," she said trembling, "suppose we wait and see?"

A new voice spoke. Penelope had not heard this voice before. It came from Jeff's grandfather, the fine, broad, quiet old man who had been a part of the general scene throughout this whole hard hot day, without having, to her knowledge, spoken before. A silver fringe about his bald, venerable head, he had somehow given Penelope an impression of kindness and gentleness.

Now he came forward with a certain old-fashioned stateliness and gave her his arm.

"I think I'll take this bride to her husband," he said. Tears stood in his eyes, and suddenly Pen felt weak and broken, felt her own eyes brimming. She hesitated at the sickroom door, and he gave her his big soft handkerchief; her face white and tired and tear stained, her eyes reddened, her splendid pale gold hair in disorder, she knelt down again beside Jeff, and as he opened his eyes and smiled at her she whispered, "We're being married, dear."

"Oh, Pen, I love you so!" he whispered back. "My wife, darling, my wife after all!"

"I think we can begin," old Judge Farmer, ready to officiate, said quietly.

"Go ahead, Uncle George!" Jeff said faintly.

After the promises were made he spoke only once, his lips trembling with weakness.

"And I have to leave you!"

She laid her face against his. She did not know who had been in the room, who had witnessed the ceremony; she did not know or care whether Jeff's grandmother had been there. Everything else was a blank, except that Jeff had managed to make audible his feeble "I do!" and that on her hand was a borrowed wedding ring of heavy gold. The day died, sunset bombarded the window shades with shafts of gold; the light died, and dusk was in the room. But Jeff lived on.

After a while a nurse lighted a soft lamp somewhere behind her. Pen was half asleep with weariness now, her gold head resting against Jeff's pillow; her fingers, holding his own bandaged fingers, were in exquisite agonies of cramp.

"When he dies," she thought, "I'll go home. I'll beat her at her own game. I'll never use the name of Flagg; I'll ignore them—all of them! They think they'll have to give me money as Jeff's wife. They won't. Not a cent of it! I'll learn something—library work or post-office work, and I'll get a job."

Tom was beside her again.

"You'll have to move," he said, in a low voice that was not a whisper. "You'll be ill."

Jeff had been only semiconscious for perhaps an hour; now he stirred a little, as if to free her.

"He heard you!" she said amazedly to Tom, in the voiceless lip movement she had used before. Tom leaned over the bed.

"Pen's got to have a rest, Jeff," he said. "I'm taking her off for a bath and a rest. She'll be back."

Penelope stooped to put her lips to Jeff's forehead, where the white bandage met the burned brown skin. She went with Tom from the room. Hannah, who had evidently been waiting in the hall, came forward, smiling and a little tearful, and kissed Penelope.

"Miss Fitzpercy's mother is here," an elderly maid said, coming from the top of the stairway and addressing Hannah.

"You mean Mrs Flagg's mother?" Tom corrected it sharply. The old servant flushed.

"Yes, sir. I meant Mrs Flagg's mother, of course."

"Suppose we ask her to come upstairs, Pen," Hannah suggested, "and you come and lie down?"

"Tell me, first of all, how is the poor dear boy?" Mrs Fitzpercy said, coming into the big comfortable bedroom where Pen was awaiting her, a moment later. Her lace hat, her rather soiled dress, her fluttered poetic voice smote sharply on Pen's senses, even while she went into her mother's arms for a full minute of tears and kisses.

"Mommy!" she said.

"My dear, what a dreadful day! Is he—am I—is it too late?"

"He's living," Pen said dully. Rumpled and pale, she sat down next to her mother, holding her mother's hand.

"I'm running you a bath and getting you some things," Hannah said, disappearing into the bathroom. Stout and square and pathetically draggled and dowdy, Jeff's mother came in at the half-opened hall door.

"Mrs Flagg, this is my mother."

"I think you will have to call me Aunt Margaret, as the other children do, now," Margaret Flagg said wearily to her, with a strained shadow of a smile.

"This is my mother."

"How do you do." There was no life in the voice of Jeff's mother. "You will have heard that we've been having a terrible day here," she said. "They give us—Penelope told you?—no hope."

"The only son!?" Penelope's mother said, dramatically resigned.

"We have a younger boy, two girls. But Jeff——" His mother could go no further. She was silent for a moment, controlling her lips, then she said in resolute kindness: "Tom, or someone, Mark perhaps, asked them to bring you up some supper. Perhaps your mother would have some, too? I can easily—I'll get hold of Lucy or Hannah——"

"Now I won't put you out at this time of all times!" Mrs Fitzpercy protested, not to be outdone in politeness. Mrs Flagg looked vaguely at her for a moment, as if she did not hear her.

"Pen, what a magnificent place!" her mother murmured, when the other woman had gone away.

"Hot bath all ready, and I've got you some of my things!" Hannah said, coming back.

"Miss Beville-Atwood, Mother."

"Your mother!" Hannah gave her a welcoming smile. "Well, you get a kiss from your bride, after all!" she said cheerfully.

"From——?" Pen's mother said dazedly.

"We were married at about four, Mother, Jeff and I. He wanted it so. It had been fretting him all day."

"You were married, Pen?" The voice was completely incredulous.

"We thought he was dying—he was very bad."

"But my dear!" Mrs Fitzpercy said, with a glance at Hannah, "without your mother, and your little veil and wedding dress, what will all these new relatives of yours think of you!"

"We didn't have time for any preparations," Hannah said sensibly and pleasantly, and it angered and hurt Pen to note that Hannah was making allowances for her mother, and it hurt her pride afresh that when Hannah went out of the room her mother should let a certain satisfaction, a certain triumph, appear in her tones.

"Well, my dearest! My little-big girl married, and Mrs Flagg! We didn't expect that, did we, dear? And what a beautiful place, darling! I had Phil borrow the Rogerses' car," Mrs Fitzpercy said, "for I simply couldn't wait for news any longer. I thought poor Jeff might have gone. Poor fellow, poor fellow. Pen, if he *does* go, there is a silver lining in that you *are* married, you *are* his wife—you have your rights—they can't take that away from you."

It was all said lightly, cautiously, with elaborate care that no listening ear in the hallways could catch it. Pen secretly writhed under it; she was relieved when the supper trays came in. She had had a hot, luxurious bath by this time, her mother following her step by step, sitting on the edge of the tub; she was dressed in silk pajamas and a heavy silk robe belonging to Hannah. Pen knotted the cord firmly about her waist, brushed her thick hair and braided it into a coronet about her head.

"Shall you go into his room—shall you see him again, dear?"

"Oh yes. I'll wait. They'll all be up. The doctor says his heart may go on this way for hours, and then simply—stop. That's what we expect."

"He's unconscious?"

"Not always. Most of the time. When he does rouse up he wants me."

"It seems to me very beautiful," Mrs Fitzpercy said sentimentally. "Eat something, Pen."

"I am eating. But I seem more thirsty than hungry."

"Mr Flagg was asking for you," a nurse said, from the doorway.

"I'll go right in. Mother, do stay and finish your supper. I never thought of Phil," Pen said distractedly. "I imagine they gave him something downstairs."

"My dear," her fussy, romantic, insistent mother, obviously reveling in the novelty and thrill of all this, said solicitously, "just tell me this: Shall Phil and I stay? If we would be the slightest comfort to you——"

"I'd so much rather you wouldn't!" Pen said quickly, nervously. "I'd really rather. I'll be—in there, and if I do come out they're all waiting. His mother is always there . . ."

She kissed her own mother hurriedly, absently, went with the nurse to the hall. She heard her mother's quick apologetic "We'll just slip away, then!" It came back to her in the still watches of the night with a home-sick pang of compunction. Her mother had hurried to her, and she had let her go. . . .

Jeff breathed; seemed to stop breathing for incredibly long intervals; breathed again. Now and then he moaned or sighed, but he asked no longer for Pen; he seemed to know that the hand holding his was hers; she sat drowsily in her chair, propped in pillows, smiling now and then at the family as they noiselessly came and went in the eerie soft gloom of the room. Jeff's mother was kneeling at the foot of the bed, her locked hands motionless on the stretched sheet that covered him so trimly. Pen's heart ached for her; she wished that she cared for Jeff one half as much as his mother did.

She thought dreamily of his death; of the sorrow in all these houses. Anxious though he often made them, they loved him dearly; his mother had told her today of his boyhood, recounting sadly a hundred joyous examples of his fun and his mischief. The grandmother was evidently sick with grief. "How she hates me!" Pen thought. "His mother doesn't—she's gentler. And that pale one they call 'Aunt 'Lizabeth' is nice. That must be Tom's mother," she decided, surprised to get the relationship straight. "Of course it is, for his brother George called her 'Mom.' And Emily, the haughty younger one with the baby whose uncle is a senator, is George's wife.

"When Jeff dies they'll be awkward and kind about my claim on him. And that's where I'll fool her—fool their grandmother. I'll tell them I only did it to help him, and that I don't intend to use the name. I'll be Penelope Fitzpercy again, and I'll—I'll . . ."

Just what she would do was indefinite; her musings trailed away into vagueness at this point. But for some reason she could not define, some reason of which she was perhaps not even conscious, the events of the past two days—Tom's visit, Jeff's visit, the accident, her quick coming to Jeff's side, her strange vigils with all the different members of the family—had had an effect already. Penelope was no longer the girl who had played and idled and slept away the first twenty-two years of her life; excitement and anger, pity and nervousness and shame had all combined to force her into a new groove. She felt new potentialities within her; she would go out of the lives of these Flaggs within a few hours' time, but it would not be to go back to the old ways.

It was midnight, and she was having soup in Hannah's room. . . . It was two o'clock, and the doctors were there, and old De Vecchio was saying that he would not go home, he would stay for a while. Pen, heavy with the agonies of refused sleep, Jeff's white-faced mother, tense and silent, the quiet nurses all knew what that meant. . . .

But four o'clock came, with dawn fingering the wet garden and bringing color to the rose bushes. Birds hopped about in the dew; there was a fragrance of coffee somewhere. Penelope was being tucked down under blankets by Tom's kindly faded little mother; she was falling off into deep and blessed sleep. And still Jeff breathed.

CHAPTER XI

She was one of the Flaggs; she was inside the magic circle; she had somehow found the key to the door, but it was different from what Pen had supposed it would be, and she found that she needed all her courage and all her dignity to meet the new life with self-respect. They were so complete, so busily self-absorbed, they needed her so little! Even Jeff, contentedly invalided for pleasant summer weeks, needed her not at all! Penelope had few moments when she did not feel the tall awkward outsider that she knew herself to be; even the kindliest of the Flaggs—and Tom's mother, "Aunt 'Lizabeth," and Hannah, were always kind—could not pretend that the situation was altogether a natural and pleasant one. They did not know Jeff's wife at all; they did know each other intimately, affectionately, confidentially. It was a quite obvious effort for everyone to make room for another Mrs Flagg.

"Grandfather" and "Gram" were the head of the clan; they lived in the old-fashioned white house to which the big museum room had been added, with four or five elderly servants, among whom an elderly housekeeper was manager of all the houses. With them just now were the oldest son and his wife, "Uncle Teege" and "Aunt 'Lizabeth," Tom's parents. Tom lived in San Francisco, dividing his time between the homes of his brother George, whose wife was Emily, and his sister Mary Farmer, whose husband was John Brewster Cline. George and Emily had a baby daughter, and Mary had a baby son; these were the babies Pen had seen rolling on the lawn.

Next to Uncle Teege in years, just one more of the dark, definite Flagg women, came widowed Aunt Hannah, Mrs Dana Beville-Atwood, nearing sixty, strong and vital, and mother of young Hannah and of two older daughters, Ann, wife of Benjamin Franklin Merry, and Lucy Farmer, wife of James Eliot Towne. The Townes and the Merrys had children, brown girls and boys with gold bands on their teeth, and freckles spattered over their dark Flagg faces. Frank, Billy, Tommy, Mary. Penelope was familiar with their shouted names long before she could identify or segregate them.

The third member of the older generation was the first Flagg she had met, Uncle Mark, Jeff's father, a quiet, businesslike man rather like his own mild old silver-headed father in type; Jeff's mother was Aunt Margaret, the spectacled, plain-haired, aristocratic woman who was just now slowly recovering from the fright and shock of Jeff's accident. Aunt Margaret had been an Ogilvie of Boston; she and her old mother-in-law spent whole contented days in puttering over the family museum, comparing spindle-legged chairs and faded canvases to lists in catalogs. Aunt Margaret's children were Jeff and Mark, and the two young girls, Lucy Farmer and Margaret Ogilvie.

Fourth and last child of the old couple was Uncle Peter, a rubicund gray-headed man of fifty, with a wife, Amy, fully twenty years younger than he, and an engaging redheaded sprite of a child named Sally. Sally was the unpopular cousin, in the hardy Flagg group, and Penelope frequently saw Hannah's white gown and dark head swoop over the lawn like a flying gull to rescue Sally from persecution. The Peter Flaggs lived in San Francisco ten months a year, and were only at the old home for occasions.

Beside these, living in the immediate group, was old Mrs Flagg's brother, Judge Farmer, who had retired from practice in Macon, Georgia, some years before, and was occupying a place called "the old theater" close to the big house, his widowed daughter, Constance Forsythe, and Aunt Con's two children, Jud and Concy.

The old theater had been given its name in the long-ago days of children's theatricals; it had been transformed into a comfortable brown-shingled cottage now, the nearest to the house. Even nearer were the garage, the corral that rose steeply uphill to the stable, and to sheds and chicken runs and barns always in a scrupulous condition of fresh white-wash, fresh raking, fresh dampening down with the ever-active sprinklers.

Off toward the west, in a very jungle of natural oaks and planted poplars and peppers and a hundred other trees, was a little group of cottages designed for summer and week-end use, comfortable, airy, bedded in plots of bright flowers. Aunt Hannah's cottage was informally colonial in type, painted white, with a red roof and green window sills; its brick garden walk and white picket fencing made it look like a stage set. Aunt Hannah lived alone here, for Hannah junior was at the big house, being a sort of secretary to her doting grandmother, and in constant conference with Mrs Lindenborg, the Danish housekeeper. Hannah had an office, a typewriter, a salary. "She knows more about the Flagg business than anyone but Gram," Jeff told Pen.

The house the Mark Flaggs used was the oldest building on the place or in the country. "The Adobe" had been erected by Spanish settlers perhaps a hundred years earlier, and occupied by rancheros as a dwelling house, stable, grain storehouse, a community kitchen. At the end of the low, irregular living room the plastered bake oven still stood next to the enormous blackened fireplace. Aunt Margaret set her luncheon table out under the patio oaks where once men had bargained for cattle and women had worked at their lace cushions.

The Peter Flaggs, when they came down, had a two room lodge just back of "The Adobe," with a big sleeping porch nosing up into a canyon. A few hundred feet further into the trees stood a guest house—cool, impersonal, chintzy, with a little wood fire always laid, and fat towels always ready in the tiled bathroom. Half of the guest house was to be made ready for the Jeffs. It would be weeks before Jeff could move into it, but as soon as his doctors announced the miracle of his eventual recovery, his grandmother set about vigorous plans for its alteration.

The guest house stood so close to the rise of the hill that it boasted a ground entrance at the front and another ground entrance at the back above. Pen would enter her domain from the hillside path; her four rooms would boast a view down the hill to strips of blazing garden, the roofs of the Flagg homestead, and the faraway stone walls beyond the furthest lawn.

She would have a long sitting room dainty in dotted swiss, a bedroom that opened upon a sleeping porch twice its size, a smaller room to be used for an emergency guest room, and a little kitchen complete in detail: cabinet, refrigerator, electric stove, nests of blue bowls, nests of spice and sugar tins.

But this would not be until winter. The house was being reinforced throughout for cold weather.

Meanwhile Pen occupied alone the pleasant big bedroom to which Hannah had taken her on her first night in the house, and Jeff lay convalescent in an adjoining chamber. She came and went in the sickroom at her own will, sometimes finding Hannah or his grandmother with the invalid, sometimes his young sisters, oftenest finding his mother there. The one weak spot in Margaret Flagg's strong character was her feeling for her older son; sensible, calculating, self-controlled upon every other point in the world, she was not sane on the subject of Jeff. Penelope had not long been a member of the family before she perceived exactly how Jeff had been spoiled, and knew who was responsible.

But this discovery was so much a part of other uncomfortable feelings that it had no special significance. What was significant was that Jeff was spoiled, not who had happened to spoil him. What was significant was that she was to have no opportunity to show the Flaggs just how haughty, how independent she could be as Jeff's widowed bride, for Jeff would live. Bewildered, ignorant, strange, she moved through these days; not seeming to know as Jeff the invalid who lay bandaged in a wide flat bed, hardly knowing as herself the girl who looked back at her from the mirror in the Flagg spare room.

Just a week after the accident she drove down to see her mother. Her shining, long blue car was a present from her husband's old grandfather. Jeff's car had been smashed to kindling wood; Jeff would not drive a car for a long, long time; old Tom Flagg presented the new car to the family's youngest bride with a kindly little speech.

"Your grandmother and I aren't calling this a wedding present, Penelope. We're none of us in the mood for wedding presents, with the poor fellow just out of the woods! But it's yours, and we all feel that you mustn't stick quite so close to the sickroom; get out in the air a little more, go see your own people."

On the day when Penelope first tried the new car Hannah had come into her room with an armful of summer clothing.

"Here," she had said, with a too perfect carelessness and cheerfulness, "you've got neither the time nor inclination to go buy clothes. I've gathered these from everyone—Concy, Peg, Mary. See if any of them fit!"

They all fitted, of course. Trust Hannah to guess sizes and lengths correctly. Penelope was but twenty-two, after all; it was exciting to her to find herself beautiful in dark blue linen, with a white collar standing off at daring angles from her throat, and a white hat shading her gold hair and gray-blue eyes.

"Hannah, I can't take these!"

"I assure you that it's you or the rummage sale. You've no idea how those girls of Aunt Margaret's buy clothes! That pink belonged to my sister Lucy—she never could stand it, and it looked awful on her; she's much too dark. That's a darling with the dots—it's only a little too long for you; that was Concy's. It's all trousseau for her now; she and Aunt Con are in New York buying things, and Concy left me a whole closetful to give away. Lindenborg will fix it for you; do ask her to, or for anything else, for she's nothing to do in the afternoons."

Hannah had rattled away pleasantly, hanging things on Penelope's hangers. Penelope, all in blue, had gone in to show herself to Jeff before descending to the blue car. Jeff had been enthusiastic.

"Gosh, you do look swell!" His mother had been reading to him, some sort of detective story, for Penelope heard mention of the redoubtable McCann from the central office as she went away. He loved his mother's voice droning along in the pleasant quiet of the afternoon; Penelope read spasmodically and unevenly and had seen herself that her one and only attempt to amuse him in this way was not successful. Yet she felt a little baffled as she went downstairs. Between his nurses and his mother Jeff's time was pretty well filled.

She drove along slowly, enjoying the perfect movement of the beautiful new toy. A radio had been installed in it, and presently Pen dared to touch the dials, and organ music began to flow out into the warm green sweetness of the tree-bordered road. Her car, her radio, her new platinum ring on the steering wheel. Mrs Flagg going down to see her mother. These were the facts. Only they did not seem to have the value they had always had in her imaginings of them, her anticipations of them.

The car found Armitage Lane, was stopped close to the rank dry hollyhocks; Pen jumped out, and for a little while there was great rejoicing and kissing in the arbor. Mrs Fitzpercy beamed with satisfaction; Persis hung over her sister in adoring awe.

"Pen, Mom says it's a perfect palace!"

"Well, it's really not. It's just an old-fashioned white house, but the place is beautiful!"

"And are they nice to you, Pen? They're not mad because you married him?"

"I asked Gram—that's Mrs Thomas Jefferson Flagg, you know, the old one—what she would advise. I was *that* smart!" Pen said.

"With him dying, and all of them around, I don't see how you had the nerve to think of anything!" Persis exulted. "If I were in love with a man and he was all mashed to custard——"

"Persis!" said her mother faintly.

"Well, he was. How Pen could do anything but bawl and carry on is more than I see," Persis persisted. Penelope laughed a little constrainedly. It was strange to be back in the slipshod atmosphere of home again. The words gave her a little twinge. The answer was of course that she did not—or had not—loved Jeff to an extent that robbed her of her reasoning faculties. The situation had been between his grandmother and herself at that moment; they had met for their first encounter.

"Mom, want to go for a drive in your 'darter's' new car? Is there something we need downtown, butter or something?"

"If there was," Mrs Fitzpercy said fondly, "I don't think I'd let Mrs Jefferson Flagg go for it! Oh, Pen," she said, inspired as always with an idea, "I wonder if we could go and see Isolde?"

"Isolde? Is she down here?"

"Oh no, she's at home. But she would so love to see you! How long would it take, darling?"

"Well . . ." This was a little more than Pen had anticipated. She considered it reluctantly. San Francisco was thirty miles away. Kelly and Phil made the trip in an hour; with Pen it would take a little longer; it was twenty minutes past three now. Say that they would get there at half past four, have half an hour with Isolde, and start home again at

[136]

five. It could be done. But the undertaking seemed formidable none the less.

"We wouldn't be back here until six, Mom, and then I'd have half an hour's drive to get back to Flaggwood. Maybe some other time——"

"Oh, you wouldn't have to bring us home, darling. Phil's in town; he has the car. He took in some of the children's clothes."

"Were they down—Isolde and the boys?"

"Last week, you know."

"Oh, heavens, it seems a year! They went home just a week ago, that's so. Time at the Flaggs goes slowly," Pen said, with a little grimace. "It'll be different when Jeff's well; it'll be different even when the nurses go," she hastened to say. "But just now I'm getting through a good deal of reading. Well, you decide, Mother, shall we go in?"

"Pen, it would be so lovely! And if we're going to drive anyway?"

"Phil will be there surely, I suppose?"

"If he isn't," Persis said, in the hoarse, sweet Fitzpercy voice, "we'll come back on the train."

"Then let's," Pen said, suddenly sad. A sense of complete desolation enveloped her. She had come home, and they not only had not helped her; they had not perceived at all that anything was wrong. They had not seen any need for help. It was all roses, to them—Pen's marrying Jeff, and his not dying after all, and her coming down to see them in her new car, with her new clothes, and the new platinum ring. Now to see Isolde, and impress her with this new change that had come to the fortunes of the Fitzpercys!

Penelope had thought that if she found her mother alone she would try to explain it. She had imagined herself saying: "You see, Mother, I don't really belong! It isn't really marriage, to have old Judge Farmer mumbling things over a man who's almost completely unconscious, who can barely move his lips to say yes and no. I don't feel married. I don't want them to think I'd hold Jeff to that sort of marriage. . . ."

But there seemed to be no right moment to say this. To them the occasion was one full of innocent pleasure and novelty; to drive in and share it with Isolde was the entirely natural thing. Penelope had been away for an entire week, devoting herself to her injured husband, the means indeed of saving his life. Now let her have a little change and see her own people!

The slight delay while Persis and her mother put on their wraps fretted Penelope a little; when at last the bright shining car was on its way she drove steadily, swiftly, determined to be at Isolde's by quarter of five anyway, determined to be on her way home again not one moment later than quarter past five. That would mean that she'd reach the Flagg house at a little after six—not that there was anything that she could do when she got there, except go up and smile at Jeff, and perhaps sit with him for a few minutes, and linger to chat with the nurse before going to her own room to change for dinner.

For the few days when his life hung in the balance there had been neither regularity nor formality at meals; Pen and Jeff's mother and the other members of the family had had trays; odd cups of soup and coffee, anxious breakfasts when any interruption might be the one they dreaded. But that was over now, and the household was resuming its normal order. Breakfast was at half past eight; luncheon at one; dinner at half past seven; promptness was an essential always. Pen somehow knew. No one had told her so in words; everyone had managed to convey a definite impression to that effect.

The car moved like a cloud. They were in the city, going down Columbus Avenue; they were turning off to the right, mounting the steep street between the cheap wooden houses and tenements; they were on a great ramp protected by a pipe railing on the bank side. Here was Isolde's dwelling, a rickety structure that seemed about to coast down the sharp, grassy cliff to the waterfront far below, and yet that seemed substantial enough once one was inside it, and unconventional enough to please even the erratic Taskers.

Grandy was at home; Isolde was very much at home, not dressed yet, but casually clad in pajamas, fur slippers and an old coat; the babies were at home; they had caught colds on the drive home, and looked more pinched than ever. But Isolde had seen a doctor and a good nurse, and reported that they were much happier on the new diet. She and Grandy had been to a dance the night before and were very sleepy, but they were delighted to welcome the family and eager to hear all they could of Penelope's marriage.

"But he is going to live?"

"Oh, yes, he's round the corner. There were two or three days—but he's all right now. He'll have to be very careful for months, Dr de Vecchio says, but he's all right. Bandaged, of course, and in plaster——"

"They've a nurse?"

"They've three nurses. And for forty-eight hours Dr Cox didn't leave the house."

"Imagine," said Isolde, enthralled. "How much do you stay in there, in his room, I mean?"

"Almost always, until today. This is the first time I've been away. Jeff's grandfather gave me a car——"

"I wish you could see the car!" Mrs Fitzpercy said, in the pause.

"Imagine!" Isolde repeated, her eyes dancing. "Are they all nice to you, Pen? I'll bet they didn't want you to marry him, at that. Don't you care how they treat you! Once he's well it'll all be different. Are you going to Cambridge with him?"

"Nobody's made plans that far ahead." Pen was seated among her own people again; they were talking her own language. Her own old language, that is. Already it sounded unfamiliar in her ears, the old lazy talk, the yawning over obligations, the procrastinations and evasions. "It'll be weeks before Jeff can open a book," she said.

"Whose swell car outside?" Phil asked, coming in. He kissed Penelope affectionately, and she thought that it was nice to have a big brother; nice to feel so comfortably free from strain. "Any time you feel an overpowering inclination to lend that car to anyone," Phil said, "telephone me, reversing the charges."

"I'll remember!" she laughed. That was sheer fun, but it was not quite so amusing when Phil added:

"Say, why wouldn't those people like some Regal Heaters? I get seven-seventeen for every one I sell. They've got a lot of houses down there, haven't they?"

"You may be pretty sure they're not waiting for heaters until this late date," Pen said, with a laugh that hid a slight uneasiness. "You never saw anything so complete! Paths raked, porches brushed twice a day, Lindenborg going around with fresh sheets; it all works like a clock!"

"Who's Lindenborg, Pen?"

"Housekeeper."

"For heaven's *sake*," Isolde said, in an admiring undertone.

"And we're so *American*," Pen said. "It seems so odd! To be continually talking *country*."

"Well, we're all Americans, dear!" her mother said. "Your father's father was Irish, but he was born in Rochester. Or was it Baltimore? It was Baltimore or Buffalo, for he was an auctioneer, and that's how he got that ridiculous old sampler!"

"I thought we called him a 'collector,'" Penelope said.

"It's the same thing."

"If it's all the same to you, I don't consider myself an American, nor will my sons be brought up in America," Grandison Tasker said firmly but pleasantly, over the gripped stem of his pipe. "The moment Isolde and I can get out . . ."

"I'm an American," Phil admitted, after a while, when Grandison had held forth with some eloquence upon the imperfections of the democratic theory, "but I don't see that it's anything to get chesty about. I'd rather be almost anything else."

Penelope listened, smiling absently. Her whole world was changed, but that hadn't changed them; they were arguing, ranting; they were listening to their own voices with the same old gusto.

"How d'you mean American? All you mean is hoarding up a lot of old junk," Grandison presently said to her, in a general attack upon the whole Flagg theory. "Patchwork quilts and spoons. That hasn't anything to do with the country! America has gone into dry rot, and everyone knows it!"

"It does seem to have something to do with the country," Penelope protested mildly. "They—they're tremendously proud of American history. They believe that America's still the best of all countries—they believe in America's future—they speak of it all the time. 'Ah, that's the American way! That's the time America acted so magnificently. There isn't any other country in the world that does this for its children, or this for its people.' That's the way they talk. Old Mrs Flagg will show you American blankets and American china, and boast about them; she makes it a point to buy American things. They—they're delighted to be Americans."

"Then they don't know much about what's going on, and they've been asleep for a hundred years!" Grandison summarized it. "Indian reservations, colored districts, Jewish ghettos, Italian quarters—it's a swell country!"

Penelope felt the beginnings of loyalty, just acquired, after a week in the Flagg environment, shaken beneath her. She shrugged, declining the argument to which she might have been unequal, and glanced at the clock.

"What's the time, someone? That's stopped."

"That's going," said Isolde. "It's about ten minutes fast. I'm always going to set it, and I never do."

"Then—but good heavens, it isn't five minutes of six!"

"It's about quarter of."

"Oh, dear!" Pen exclaimed in sudden quiet despair. It was such a stupid thing to do, to drive off in the new car and be late for dinner on the very first occasion of her absence from Jeff's side. No use telling anyone; no one of her family would understand. "Let 'em go roll their hoops!" they would say of the Flaggs generally. "I have to fly!" she said, already kissing the top of her mother's head in farewell, seizing gloves and bag, nodding general good-byes.

"You do not," said Isolde. "It's bright day yet. Stay and help me put the boys to bed."

"Oh, I can't. You've the car, Phil? You'll get Mom and Persis home?"

"I've the car, but no gas," Phil said cheerfully. "I stopped at the station, over here on Montgomery, and told him to fill her up. I thought he'd charge it. But no, he said he remembered me perfectly, but that his orders were not to charge. I said he might as well take a good look at me, then, for he'd never see me within a hundred feet of his cheap joint again. Can't speak English, but he can tell me he's not permitted to charge three dollars' worth of gas!"

"That's America for you," Grandison said dryly.

"I came off without a cent," Mrs Fitzpercy said, as one who had large sums in reserve, by chance forgotten.

"I've got a dollar, and I don't propose to spend it for gas," Persis said firmly.

Penelope laughed hopelessly, with no mirth in her soul, and opened her purse.

[140]

"Here, Phil," she said, "take this, and give Mother the change. Good-bye, everyone! I'll come in next week and have lunch with you, Isolde, and see the boys. Good-bye!"

CHAPTER XII

She had come away in a light dress and thin coat; a cold, foggy wind was blowing when she got down to the street; it tore at her hair, blew loose gold strands about her face. On the slope of the ramp above the waterfront other cars had been parked in the time that she had been upstairs; the new blue car was tightly wedged in between two smaller cars. Penelope stood for a moment looking at it in dismay.

"Here, Pen," Kelly Quentin said quietly, beside her. She turned and, seeing the look in his eyes, matched it with as unsmiling a glance from her own. "Hello, Pen," he added.

"Kelly, how are you? I've just been upstairs seeing Isolde. Mother and Persis are there."

"Still good news from Mr Flagg?"

"If you can call it good news when two ribs are broken, and his leg smashed, and terrible things done inside!" Pen said, trying for lightness.

"You look tired, Pen." He was studying her gravely.

"I'm tired *now*, for I drove my new car down to see Mother, and then we foolishly decided to come in to town—which was a little too much! So now I'm late, which is stupid, for it's the first time I've left Jeff."

"They say you saved his life, Pen."

"Well, he was feverish, and it quieted him to have me there."

They stood in the windy twilight of the steep street looking at each other, Pen holding her white hat in place with one hand.

"Nothing for me to do but hope you'll be happy, Pen."

Kelly said it very simply, looking big and boyish and troubled as he smiled at her.

"No, not now," she agreed, smiling nervously.

He was so strong and quiet, with his homely good face and freckles and red hair, she knew him so well, it was so comfortable to be with Kelly again, that Pen was conscious of a longing to rest her head on his shoulder and cry. Instead she stood smiling uncertainly at him in the cool city twilight, and for a moment there was an awkward little silence between them.

"That's what I want to ask you, I suppose, Pen."

"What?" But of course she knew.

"You *are* happy?"

"Well, with Jeff so ill . . ." Her words halted, and he saw her color rise. She was more beautiful than ever in the dusk; somehow she seemed older tonight, not young restless Pen any more, but a woman, dignified and subdued, and so disquietingly beautiful.

"You married him because you loved him, didn't you?"

"I don't know that I thought of that, then," she said, very low and with a troubled swift glance.

"But, I mean—all those days he came to see you, took you places? You loved him then?"

A silence. She raised her honest eyes to him.

"Pen, don't let me think this! Don't let me think that you might have been happier with me!"

Distressed, silent, she looked away, and the cool afternoon air flowed about them, and foghorns droned on the bay. Pen's thoughts moved upstairs to Kelly's studio; Isolde and Grandy would be running up and down, there would be the old laughter, inconsequential telephoning and marketing and talk of dinner. . . .

"Suppose I could take you down to Salvati's for minestrone and ravioli now, Pen, would you like it?"

"You're always so good to me!" she said in a whisper. And then, suddenly changing in tone and mood, "Ah, Kelly, it's no use now. And I'm late! Will you get my car out for me?"

"Can you imagine what it is, Pen, to love a woman—every inch of her, every tone of her voice—and know that you've lost her?"

Pen said nothing. And after a pause Kelly turned without a word to the line of parked automobiles. For endless minutes, it seemed to Pen, he backed and bumped the blue car gently to and fro; the dingy little green car in front of it moved a reluctant inch forward; Kelly got out and Pen jumped into the driver's seat.

"Thanks so much, Kelly."

"Will you think of me sometimes, dear, and remember that I'll never change? I'll never look at another woman."

She did not answer. She rubbed her bare thumb on the hand he had laid on the top of the door at her left, and their eyes met. "Good-bye!" she said. Then she was on her way.

A clock on Post Street said six-twelve. There was no possibility of making headway in the slow stream of home-going traffic. No help for it—she would simply have to be late. She had extracted from Isolde a promise to telephone the Flaggs that she would be late, but that wouldn't help much. Pen's mind was one confusion of troubles as she engineered her way down the hill and across Columbus Avenue, across Market Street, down Potrero, out into the highway rise toward the south. She was late; Jeff might have had a relapse; they would all be at the table wondering at her manners; Philip certainly saw in the Flagg connection fresh opportunities for sales, for borrowing, perhaps; she, Penelope, looked pale and draggled and would be breathless and unconvincing in explanations. Kelly. Kelly Quentin. He loved her, of course. She had underestimated the seriousness of that feeling, perhaps because it had awakened no responsive feeling in her own heart.

The miles were moving by with maddening slowness. The car's clock was certainly five minutes slow; all the other clocks along the way were later; six-thirty, nineteen minutes to seven, and not even to Millbrae yet!

"Fool, fool, fool that I am to let myself in for this sort of thing!" Penelope muttered. She was caught behind a lumbering van; no cutting out into the east lane here, with a traffic officer riding sedately at her side. Forty-five miles, not one fraction of a mile faster!

"It's nonsense!" she said suddenly, aloud. "Why should I be afraid of the Flaggs? What right have they to say that I shall be on time for meals?"

And then, as her thoughts took another turn: "The trouble is now that I don't belong either place. I couldn't go back home, and I don't fit in with them. Sooner or later I'll be one thing or the other . . ."

A sudden memory brought her up straight in the seat with the force of an electric jolt. Hannah had told her at noon today that the Flagg cousins from Milton were going through San Francisco on their way to some consular post in the Orient, and that understanding the circumstances of Jeff's accident they were merely coming down for a quiet family dinner, nothing formal or very social, just family—just as usual. They would be all gathered there when she, breathless and tired and draggled, went in.

"Well, what if they are!" Penelope said, speaking aloud again, turning the car up toward the gates at last. "Why should I be afraid of the Flaggs!"

The days went slowly for her. There was nothing that she could do for Jeff, except sit by him smilingly perhaps for a few minutes in the morning and evening, and let him hold her hand and ask the others proudly if he had not a beautiful wife. Penelope felt superfluous and awkward in the sickroom; Jeff's nurses took scrupulous care of him; his mother was a fine reader and loved to spend hours amusing him with detective fiction; Hannah and he had infinitely more to talk about than he and Pen had. She had times of feeling lonely and strange; times when she felt that her only dignified course, her only way to happiness, was to get out of all this at any cost. And at such times her old jealousy of the Flaggs rose hot within her; she didn't belong with them, she wanted never to hear of them again!

On the night after she had been late for dinner she came downstairs in good season, carefully dressed, to find some agitation in the group in the library. Most of the senior members of the family were there; Jeff's father was standing at the hearth with an opened newspaper in his hands. Aunt

'Lizabeth, as always close to Uncle Teege's wheel chair, looked up with a rueful smile at Pen as she came in somewhat shyly and sat down.

"See the evening newspaper?" Tom asked, looking up with his usual kindly smile.

"The newspaper?" Pen countered, at a loss.

"The whole story's in it!" Aunt Margaret said in her crisp voice. She was knitting rapidly. "Everything. There ought to be laws against that sort of outrage. It's a complete fabrication, of course, and yet it isn't worth exposing!"

"What is it?" Pen asked. Tom put a newspaper into her hands. She saw her own picture; a dreadful picture that had been taken because her mother had bought a one-dollar coupon from an agent, and had afterward insisted that someone pay the additional two dollars at the studio, and get six of the regular ten-dollars-a-dozen pictures at the bargain price.

Beside it was a picture of Jeff in polo attire, a photograph of the scene of the accident, a sketch of Flaggwood. The reading matter was sensational from first to last—a headline, "Life Crisis Wins Family Consent to Society Nuptials!" ran straight across the page.

The entire story of the midnight wedding that had followed the family's attempts to break up the engagement between Miss Penelope Fitzpercy and the scion of the Flaggs was laid bare. Jeff had been "desperate after Miss Fitzpercy's final decision to abide by the will of his family." Reckless with disappointment, he had had a serious accident. In his delirium only one cry had escaped him: "I want to leave my wife behind me, not my sweetheart!" The marriage had been performed in the sickroom by Judge George Flagg Farmer, great-uncle of the groom. The new Mrs Flagg was a beautiful ash blond, with a captivating smile and an air of great happiness.

"The audacity of them!" said Hannah. "Oh, it's sickening!" George's little wife said. Old Mrs Flagg shook her head.

"I don't like it," she said with distaste. "But I must say that we usually manage to avoid this sort of thing. It'll mean a flood of callers and telegrams—no help for it!"

"What I wonder is, where and how they *get* it?" Hannah said. "Once getting it, they can add that silly, sensational tone to it, no matter what it is. Jeff loathes this sort of thing, and of course it makes Gram——" She paused to smile across at Gram with the confidence of the most beloved granddaughter of all. "It makes Gram simply sick!" she said. "Doesn't it, darling?"

"Well, it's the sort of thing you avoid if you can," Gram said dryly.

"No reporter talked to you, Penelope?" her father-in-law asked sharply.

A sense of being alien from them, an ache of homesickness for her own people smote Penelope keenly, and she felt her throat dry and her eyes stinging. They never would speak the same language, she and these strangers.

"Penelope doesn't know anything about it," Tom said quickly.

"No, I haven't seen any reporter," Penelope said proudly and slowly. "But I presume of course it was my mother who gave them the story. They couldn't get the picture anywhere else, could they? She probably didn't see any particular reason for secrecy, and I confess I don't! After all, what the paper says is true. It seems too bad that everyone is so much—so much distressed about having the truth come out."

There was a full minute of frozen silence in the room. Penelope did not look at anyone; she knew how they would look. A fierce defiance possessed her. She wasn't going to excuse herself at her mother's expense, no, not for a thousand Flaggs! Her face still burned from the shame of the cheaply sensational article, but they shouldn't know it. She shrugged very slightly, looked at the fire, managed a faint ironical smile.

"Of course," old Mrs Flagg said presently, very softly, and with no particular intonation. Tom left his chair and came over to Pen.

"There's Jean announcing dinner," he said. "Suppose you and I lead the way?"

"If I hate them enough," Pen thought, rising, "if I hate them enough I won't cry!"

CHAPTER XIII

Chagrin kept her wakeful for the better part of the night. Penelope restlessly rehearsed in her troubled thoughts the scene in the library before dinner, when all of the senior Flaggs had been there, disgusted, annoyed, humiliated by the newspaper's gushing revelations concerning herself and Jeff.

They had known perfectly well, she told herself bitterly, or at least upon the slightest reflection they *should* have known, that it was her mother who had given the newspapers those details, that it was from her mother and no one else that at least one of those photographs had been secured. But they must pretend not to know, question each other and exclaim and lament so that Penelope, the alien in their midst, might thoroughly learn the lesson that the Flaggs did not like that sort of cheap publicity.

"Well, and do they think I do?" she asked herself feverishly, in the long watches of the night. "Do they think anyone likes that sort of stuff?"

And quick upon that thought came the realization that at least her own mother had not shown any particular aversion to it; evidently Mother had babbled along happily in her beloved poetic phrases about the soft lamplight that had shown upon the deathbed wedding, and the natural beauty and charm of the bride. Penelope, alone in the night, sighed heavily. There was no curing Mother; there was no common ground upon which she and the Flaggs could meet. Penelope's fierce instinctive Celtic loyalty might rush up to protect her, to defend her, but nothing she could do would ever explain the difference that lay between the two families.

After all, she was a Fitzpercy. Or was she? She had belonged only a few weeks ago to the cottage in Armitage Lane, to that easy lazy life that had included unwashed dishes and unpaid bills and unkept appointments. Now for a little while she had had a place in this other world of Flaggwood; an unimportant and even a somewhat unrecognized place, to be sure, but she was here, and she was "Mrs Flagg," and it was for her rather than for any of the others to decide whether she should remain here, or should slip back into the old life as if she had never left it.

There was nothing in it to tempt her to go back. After a few weeks of the different conditions, the different voices, the new standards and codes and ways of thinking, she realized that it would be very hard to go back. Her mother would oppose the nullification of her brilliant marriage; Persis and Phil and Isolde would think she was crazy. Coming back to nothing, empty-handed, when she had had it in her power to make terms with the mighty Flaggs!

"If I could slip away from them all, all of them!" Pen thought, tossing about, snapping up a light to look at the time, sighing as she snapped it off again. "If I could get a big movie contract—but no, that wouldn't make the slightest impression on the Flaggs. Well, then, if I could marry some immensely rich fine man, and have a place like this and all our family, and all some other family . . ."

And then back to first principles. "After all, I belong here. I'm one of the Mrs Thomas Jefferson Flaggs, if I want to be. Jeff loves me—he can't wait to be well enough to have his honeymoon and his home and his wife to himself.

"I probably love him as much as most girls love the men they marry. Everyone loves Jeff, when he's up and about. And if we loved each other, and had a little apartment in the city, while he finished with his law studies, and had his father and mother for dinner, and came down here week ends——

"But even then," her thoughts broke off despairingly, "that wouldn't mean that I knew by magic, overnight, how they like things done, and what they hate, and how words are pronounced in French, and how you speak to servants! They're no better than I am, but they're different.

"But after all," Pen reflected, fresh and breathless from a cold shower, when at last the morning came, brushing her thick soft pale gold hair, getting herself ready for a morning call on Jeff, "after all, I'm half Irish. We're adaptable, we Irish, if we're nothing else. My grandfather Fitzpercy used to say to Dad that an Irish third-rate scamp could pass as a gentleman anywhere in the world except in Ireland! There's no reason why I

shouldn't beat them at their own game sooner or later, be more of a
Flagg than Gram herself!"

This was the morning mood of courage, but the long day had a way of
wearing down her high spirits, filling her spirit with misgivings and dis-
couragements again. Pen didn't seem to belong anywhere in the scheme.
They were all nice enough to her, in varying degrees of civility or kindness,
but nobody needed her. Even Jeff did not need her; he needed his nurse
and he depended upon his mother for hours of spoiling, amusing quiet
family gossip, reading of books. For Pen he had only a sort of exaggerated
boyish jocosity. "There's my gorgeous wife! Isn't she beautiful this afternoon? You can only stay about five minutes, Pen, because Martha gets
mad if I don't get my sleep after lunch."

Pen's problem he sensed not at all. He was completely sure of her, and
that was enough. Once again Jeff was sure of himself as one of the in-
vincible Flaggs, and sure of Pen, and his mother, and his nurse; once
again the world was all right for him. "My harem," he called the devoted
women who lived now only for him. And of these perhaps he depended
most, at the moment, upon Martha Disco.

There was nothing of the siren about Martha. She was thirty-seven,
gawky, sallow-cheeked; she had long cool sanitary hands and prominent
dark eyes and a tremulous voice. She had nursed various Flaggs for fifteen
years; she knew them all, and liked to gossip with Jeff's mother or his aunt
Hannah about the family. The subject of herself was also of inexhaustible
interest to Martha. She related incidents of her childhood, her mother's
death, her adoption with eleven other flood orphans by "Mother Todd,"
her boisterous rejection of various offers of marriage. There had been two
other nurses: Miss Jensen, an exquisite blond Swedish doll, Miss Keith,
a smartly groomed and curled beginner, with an engaging lisp and dimple,
but these had vanished, and Martha was left alone in the field.

Jeff's affectionate overtures to his young wife, his wanting to hold her
hand and to ask everyone if she was not beautiful, embarrassed Penelope
when Martha and the others were witnesses. When she came in after
luncheon it was usually to find his mother there quietly reading, quite
content to have her boy restored to her; the past forgotten, the future all
serene, Jeff lying comfortably in his pillows, listening.

Later the other women of the family drifted in for short or longer
stays—Jeff's younger sisters, Peggy and Lucy, his cousins, Ann Merry and
Lucy Towne, Aunt 'Lizabeth, Aunt Hannah, Gram. Hannah was often
there; Amy came shyly in almost every day; George's superior little wife,
with her chatter of Washington and London and society, of this friend's
yacht and that friend's polo record, sometimes brought her fat baby
Lucy and the handsome Dutch nurse with the gold earrings for a call.

The male members of the group came in, too, and Martha was always
there in the intervals, very busy and adequate, and not entirely approving

of Jeff's having too much company, even that of his wife. Pen had a confused sense of never seeing Jeff alone at all.

On the afternoon after the newspaper episode his mother happened to go into town; Martha had gone out for her rigid daily constitutional; Pen found Jeff alone for the first time since their marriage. Hannah had been with him but had gone. Jeff was propped in pillows, playing patience with two small packs, his fine brown Flagg hands moving the cards about in little sheaves.

"Hello, darling," he said. "Are you beautiful? And did your mother step off the deep end with the press—oh boy, oh boy!"

"You heard about that?"

"And you sassing Gram."

"I didn't sass your grandmother," Pen said, feeling a sudden deep inclination to cry, and speaking coldly and stiffly to avoid tears.

"That's the way I heard it!" Jeff chuckled, removing a completed "spider," laying out another row.

"Would you like to play dominoes?"

"No, thanks, darling. Mother's coming in to read."

"Who told you about last night?"

"Oh, everyone. I gather," Jeff said, smiling absent-mindedly as he played, "that you are rather stirring up the clan!"

"It was all true."

"You mean you are?"

"Am what?"

"Stirring up the clan, bird-brain. Hit your telephone!"

"No. I mean that what the paper had all was true."

"Yes, I know." He said it in exactly the tone his grandmother had used when she had said "Of course!" so softly, so significantly last night. And he narrowed his dark eyes as she had, too, in an expression that said, "Penelope can't understand our point of view. No use getting impatient."

Anger surged in her. She wanted to hurt him, to triumph over him. But to start arguments, ask for freedom, go back to Armitage Lane? Ah, she must think about that.

"You'll get onto our ways," Jeff presently said, busy with another "spider."

"I'm not anxious to get onto your ways," Penelope thought. She was silent. "Your grandfather was over at the guest house this morning," she said. "They're getting your rooms—our rooms—ready."

"Swell, huh?" he said, with a keen upward glance and a smile. And she knew he was thinking of the hour when they would take possession of the new apartment as husband and wife. "Going to be crazy about me?" he asked. "It's going to be fun, moving in!"

"That depends." She was dull, unresponsive, heavyhearted. She could not help it. Whichever way she turned she saw only humiliations and doubts. She could not reach these Flaggs, make them feel her important, no matter what she did.

"Your fight with Gram got under your hide?" Jeff suggested amusedly.

"It wasn't a fight." Pen could have slapped him in her sudden hot anger.

"Telling her you didn't think it was important."

"Well, and I don't. You don't want me to lie to her, do you?"

"I love you when you get mad, Pen!"

He laughed, went on with his game. Pen sat still, trying to get control of her emotions. However serious her problems were, and at twenty-two they seemed to her insuperable, she perceived that for a while at least she would get no help from Jeff. Whatever energy he ever had possessed was in abeyance now. For ten days he had been lying completely idle, being waited upon, being spoiled by them all. He liked it. He would lie here in this airy comfortable room for at least another six weeks; he would be invalided for weeks, perhaps months, after that, keeping hospital hours of late rising and early going to bed. He liked that idea, too. His mind now ranged no further than the interest of the day's trays, the hours of listening to his mother or Martha as they read to him, the luxury of sinking back into sleep whenever he felt like sleep.

His mother came in with new books. Jeff was all impatience to have her go on with the story she had been reading to him yesterday. Pen, going away after a little while, asked herself impatiently why she had not suggested reading to him—not that she read very well.

She went down wide hall stairways and through airy passages out into the garden sweetness of late afternoon. Lawn sprinklers were wheeling in the long rays of descending sunlight, sending punctual sprays of diamonds through the still air. The sun was close to the rim of the western hills; just outside of the green shade of the great oaks columns of gnats were spinning up and down. Four or five children, little Merrys and Townes, and Jeff's fourteen-year-old sister Peggy, were lying like wet little seals along the rim of the pool, gossiping. At the edge of the lawn, in the group of basket chairs where Penelope had first seen them, some of the older members of the family were sitting together. Old Mrs Flagg, her brother Judge Farmer, Tom's invalid father and his gentle shadowy mother, handsome Aunt Hannah with her strong glasses and flying knitting needles. Penelope evaded them, turned off along a path blazing with flower borders, and wandered in the general direction of the farmyard and berry garden that led to the orchard.

It was all beautifully groomed and parked; there were white fences, fruit trees stockinged in white, white barns; the red chickens and red cattle looked picturesque in the formal setting. She came upon Jeff's grandfather, deep in consultation with his foreman; he reached a firm, strong old hand for Penelope's hand, held it while he finished with Roberts in a few brisk sentences, and turned with the girl to take the orchard path along the edge of the woods.

And quite suddenly she felt that out of all the world, husband, mother, sisters, brother, this was perhaps the only person in whom she could confide, this mild, kind, quiet old man was perhaps the only person in the world who could advise her.

They leaned on the orchard bars that led to the wood and talked together. It was not a long talk; what he said was characteristically simple, as was everything he said—completely unaffected, entirely quiet. He did not give her advice exactly; he said that he was not qualified to advise a—a young lady. He personally thought that Penelope was perfectly able to decide any question for herself; she might not have known it, but among her admirers was a certain old man. He had been watching her; he thought that she had a very hard road to follow; he would be glad to help her talk it over, if that would do any good.

Just this much helped, although her heart was too full and her spirit too troubled to let her say so. She had to talk guardedly, carefully, for fear that tears would interrupt her and break down all her defenses.

Leaning on the bars, looking down at the descent of the orchard and the roofs that showed between the plumes of the trees, she somehow managed to pour out the whole story, gaining steadiness and self-control as she went along. She had always liked Jeff, she said, in a casual sort of way, but she had told him she would not marry him without his family's full consent, had told him that only a few hours before his accident. Then had come the crisis of his illness, and her arrival here at Flaggwood, and their strange marriage.

Since then, Penelope rushed on impetuously, nothing had seemed right. She had not felt herself Jeff's wife; they were strangers; she was a stranger in this house. She wasn't needed; she wasn't liked. Oh, they were all kind enough to her, but it was obvious that her position here was a false one; it had been obvious from the beginning!

"Gram—Gram doesn't like me," Penelope pleaded. "I don't blame her! I'm not the sort of woman she wanted Jeff to marry. But we are married now, and that complicates it all. If our marriage is annulled, then that—that mark is on me forever, that I was married to some man whose family had the marriage annulled!"

"You and Jefferson want it annulled, eh?"

"No, we don't! Or at least I'm sure he doesn't, and I think I don't. That's just it. I don't really know what I ought to do, or what I want to do."

"What does your mother think?" he asked, after a silence.

"I can't ask Mother. She thinks it's all so romantic. She's so pleased about it. That's part of it, too," Penelope said, flushing a deep apricot pink under her ivory skin as she turned distressed eyes to her companion. "My family. They're—no help. They sort of—depend on me. They'll always come at the wrong times, and borrow money and—and all that. If I'm hurrying to get home they delay me. We don't do things as they're done here, and my own people don't understand."

Another pause, while the eyes of old Tom Flagg followed the course of a chipmunk into the underbrush.

"And you're homesick, eh?"

"No," Penelope answered after a second's reflection and speaking slowly as if she groped for words. "I'm not, really. When I go home, now, I'm homesick for Flaggwood, and for the way we—you do things here."

"Ah, well, that's better, then!" the old man said, brightening, and with an approving smile. "But the difficulty is," he went on, "that you're not sure it's Jeff that holds you?"

"Oh, exactly!" Pen said, in relief that he could understand so well.

"Give me a moment," Jeff's grandfather said then, looking away, frowning. For a while he did not speak, and the still beauty of the hour had its effect upon Pen's troubled spirit in spite of herself. "There's a sure way out of this, of course," old Thomas Flagg presently continued. "But you're how old—twenty-two? You're young to try it, my dear.

"But you're a Flagg now, after all, as my wife would remind you," he went on, with a hint of his mischievous smile breaking up the serene gravity of his face for a moment. "And the Flagg women have always been good fighters. Marriages are built, you know. They're built. There's no marriage that couldn't be a success, and no marriage that couldn't be a failure. It depends on the women who are in 'em!

"The thing for you to do now is the thing for us all to do, always. There's no other way to live and be at peace with ourselves. It's to take every hour as a separate job and be kind in it, and not to think of yourself at all. Just be kind, and don't let your pride be hurt, and don't be afraid. That's the whole secret."

A certain strange calm fell upon Pen with the words; she could not explain it then, or ever. Something stretched her soul; she felt the old boundaries break, and the strange light that never was on land or sea inundate her spirit. Just to be kind, every separate hour, and not let one's pride be hurt.

"But we have to come to decisions," she said, with the last flicker of her fear dying away even as she spoke. "One has to *do* things—one has to plan——"

"No, that's just what we don't have to do," the old man answered placidly. "The plans take care of themselves. We have to be as children. They never plan."

"No," she had conceded, struck, "children never plan."

And for a long while they two hung on the orchard bars, their back to the wood, their eyes on the rich rolling country below them, orchards, oaks, winding roads, the faraway village, and the nearer strips of emerald and pink that were the Flaggs' gardens and lawns.

"It won't change your destiny when your destiny moves," Jeff's grandfather said. "But it'll make you feel that you're equal to whatever comes. Time, my dear, time is the great solver and adjuster."

Thoughtfully, almost silent, she presently walked back with him toward the house. They stopped at a certain door among all the whitewashed sheds and fences, and Pen admired a beautiful, nervous red setter and a litter of squirming blind puppies. They stopped to speak to Mike about artichokes. They stopped when children circled out of the shrubberies with cookies in their hands, wild with excitement over some game. Pen's companion showed her pink and blue hydrangeas on the same bush, and oranges and orange blossoms hidden in the thick shiny leaves of the same tree. When Pen reached her room it was six o'clock; Hannah was idling there, waiting for her. The two talked together while Penelope dressed for dinner.

"You seem suddenly gay, Pen," Hannah said.

"I think I've got religion."

"I think I've got to tell you this about Emily—personally, I can't stand Emily," Hannah said. Pen listened smilingly to a spirited story.

"Does Tom like Emily, Hannah?"

"I don't think so. But she's his brother's wife, and of course he's always nice to her. Why'd you ask?"

"I don't know. Just thinking."

"Tom's coming down tonight," Hannah said in an odd tone. And quite suddenly Penelope knew what Hannah's tragedy was, and what Hannah's secret. She loved Tom, of course. With a sudden quickening of the pulse Pen wondered if Tom loved her. Cousins. The senior Flaggs wouldn't consent to anything like that!

For a moment she felt herself one of them, hearing the family gossip, studying the family histories. The sensation lasted only for a flash, but it was a good feeling, and it left its mark. She seemed to hear the old man's words again: "The Flagg women have always been good fighters." There would be a satisfaction in fighting, if one were sure of being right. Penelope felt sudden wings lifting her. She was one of the Flagg women now.

CHAPTER XIV

The next morning when she went down to breakfast at an almost prompt half past eight the chair at the head of the table was empty; the old head of the house had had his breakfast earlier, as he often did, and had gone his way to his all-absorbing barns and orchards. At the foot of the long table, in the chair nearest the swinging pantry door, Jeff's grandmother, sipping her coffee and reading her newspaper at the same time was flanked down the length of the board by the children, Frank and Bill Merry, Tom and Mary Towne; Lovey Merry, five years old, was raised on a leather cushion to table height; Farmer Towne, two years old, was royally noisy and happy in his high chair. Between the children's chairs were the various grown-ups: Lucy Towne; pretty Emily Flagg, George Flagg's young wife, sitting next to her brother-in-law Tom; Concy Forsythe, just back from New York and murmuring happily to her gentle Aunt 'Lizabeth about wedding plans; Jeff's sister Peggy and his brother Mark; Aunt Margaret, agitated and handsome, quoting political editorials; and Peter Flagg's nervous, beautiful young wife Amy with the redheaded, shy Sally, who was seven. Lastly, Hannah was there, of course, segregating the family mail, tossing letters to this one and that, bending her dark smooth head one way to hear little Bill's confidences, and the other way to catch the important whisperings of Mary.

Maids were going about with egg cups and plates of popovers and pitchers of chocolate, but the coffee was exclusively handled by Aunt Margaret, behind the urn, and Aunt 'Lizabeth operated a toaster that was always smoking. The children passed jam and cream and saucers of fresh red strawberries; at each end of the table were round platters heaped high with fruit—peaches, figs, apricots, cherries that looked artificial in their waxen perfection.

The setting for the scene was the long old-fashioned room that opened through three glass window doors upon a terrace glowing with red and yellow roses, shafts of blue delphinium ten feet high, and potted hydrangeas trembling in pale pink-and-blue beauty. There was a white-wood fireplace in the dining room, with a portrait above the mantel; there was a long sideboard set with old silver mugs and spoons; there was little else except the long table and the chairs. But Penelope sometimes thought it the pleasantest room in the house, and this breakfast hour the happiest she ever knew there. Sunshine was bright on the terrace on this warm summer morning, but it was shaded away from the room by cool striped awnings that somehow gave the hour a gala aspect; the day was fresh, the children's white shorts and short-sleeved shirts were fresh, their young faces shone with soap and water, and their dark hair was in damp order; everyone looked cool and rested and ready for the day.

Penelope found her place between Aunt Amy and Jeff's young sister Peggy; Tom, just across the board, caught her eye as she sat down and smiled at her. Beside her plate was a small silver bowl filled with great velvet-hearted pansies, purple-black, cream, palest lavender, gold.

"Oh—mine? Oh, who gave me these?"

"Grandfather!" Peggy said triumphantly, and Pen immediately became aware that almost everyone at the table was watching and listening. It was evident that the flowers were significant of something she did not understand. "D'you know what that means, Pen?" her little sister-in-law asked with a laugh of delight.

"I know they're beautiful. I'll thank him."

"No, but that means that you're Grandfather's guest! He never does that until he likes people—he's only done it twice before that I know of! You've made a hit with Grandfather."

"Congratulations, Penelope," Aunt 'Lizabeth, Tom's gentle mother, said smilingly from the other side of Peggy. "Father has made that a little custom. He had his breakfast this morning and went out. He was back in about ten minutes with those flowers; we were all teasing him, but he wouldn't be laughed out of it. He set them there himself."

"What is it?" asked the formidable grandmother, laying aside her glasses.

"Grandfather gave Pen flowers! Pen is Grandfather's guest!" a dozen voices said. Pen, seated now, raised the little silver bowl in both hands to display it.

"Ah, did he?" old Mrs Flagg said simply. She made no further comment; a grandchild had come about to her shoulder and was whispering to her. The other members of the group admired the flowers and smiled encouragingly at Pen, and she knew that she had received an accolade. She was one of them.

"How's Jeff?" the voices asked as usual.

"Fine. He had a good night. He's having his breakfast, and Martha says getting hungrier and hungrier."

Pen's smiling eyes turned toward Amy, sitting next to her. Amy was fair, if not as fair as Pen herself. Her hair was a golden brown, her eyes violet, her expression one of timid, woeful friendliness. Amy was Peter Flagg's wife, and Peter Flagg belonged of course to the older generation, brother to Uncle Mark and Aunt Hannah and "Teege." But she was twenty years younger than her husband, and so girlishly slight at thirty that she seemed much more akin to the group that included Hannah and Tom and Jeff. She did not catch Pen's glance; she was staring into space with the vaguely dissatisfied look that was characteristic of her. Aunt Amy was always kind and gentle, and sometimes quietly witty and amusing, but in any quiet moment she lapsed into this characteristic mood of dreaminess and abstraction, and always, when she saw her so, Pen thought that she was unhappy.

After breakfast she went upstairs to show Jeff her flowers and describe to him the pleasant little recognition of them at breakfast. Jeff, breakfasted and comfortable in pillows, reading his mail and his papers, waiting in that leisure that only the invalid knows for his bath and his mother's morning session of reading, was in a receptive mood. Windows were open; Martha had drawn a blanket up to his chin; she was flourishing about with fresh linen, pillow slips and towels and sheets. Penelope stayed only a little while and then went down to the little office that was a part of the old main house, to find Hannah. Hannah had said that she was going to rush into town this afternoon, and would take Pen, and drop her for a call on Isolde and the babies.

Usually Hannah was working in the office at ten o'clock; sometimes her grandfather, sometimes her grandmother was with her, or the house-keeper, Lindenborg. All the business of the household was transacted here; the household and farm and garden servants, the nurses and governesses were interviewed, engaged, discharged; Hannah wrote out typewritten menus every Monday; so many meals in the house, so many in the garden, a picnic supper packed for Friday night, carefully balanced trays for Mr Jefferson Flagg. If new croquet mallets or tennis balls were needed, if rugs had to be washed or new blankets marked, Hannah knew it, and memoranda in Hannah's dashing hand went in every direction.

This morning, strolling along the terrace toward the office door, Pen knew that she would not find Hannah within. Hannah was down on the drive, slim and dark and neat, talking to Tom. Tom had his light overcoat on, his hat in his hand; his attitude suggested, to Penelope at least, that he was upon the very point of leaving, continually arrested and held back by whatever Hannah was saying. He would nod, open the car door, glance at her again, and again nod. And always at this point she appeared to add the phrase that delayed him afresh. Finally he walked away along the drive with her, their heads close together, Hannah's dark beauty very vivid as she looked up at him.

The sight somehow stirred Penelope. Hannah had no brother, the Beville-Atwoods were without sons, and Hannah had once said to Pen that Tom was the ideal brother. But Pen knew it was not sisterly affection that was glowing in those dark eyes; it was not sisterly eagerness that was catching Tom back again and again when he would get away.

She kept carefully out of their sight, moving along the terrace in the shelter of the potted plants and the tall delphinium and hollyhocks that towered above the heavy massed border of stock and phlox and verbena, and entered the office with a last cautious glance toward them. No; they were still absorbed in talk; they had not seen her.

The office was empty; Pen took the revolving chair opposite Hannah's desk chair and reached for a newspaper that was folded on the flat top of the desk.

Moving the newspaper, she uncovered a heap of letters held down with a crystal paperweight. The top letter was in a familiar hand; the sight of it made Pen's heart beat fast with instinctive dread. It was her mother's handwriting. Without hesitation, indeed without consideration, she went about the desk and lifted the paperweight and read the letter. It was an appeal to old Mrs Flagg for a loan of "a few hundred." Clipped to it was a pink slip—a check for five hundred dollars.

"*You may imagine that it is frightfully—impossibly difficult for me to do this,*" Pen's mother had written, in her sprawling hand, on the blue paper with the dark blue bands. *"Only the most serious emergency could force me to consider it, and if you feel it necessary to refuse this request I shall of course understand. I cannot ask my darling girl to help me just at present, and so I turn to 'Gram,' of whom she so often speaks affectionately."*

There was more of it. A fulsome finish was signed *"with eternal gratitude, Ellabeth Fitzpercy."*

Sitting in the office, with the silence and sweetness of the summer morning like a sea of peace about her, Pen felt her throat thicken and the hot color come up into her face. Her heart beat fast with shame and anger and helplessness; her first impulse was to destroy letter and check and let Hannah infer what she would when she missed them.

She obeyed instead her second impulse, which was to leave the office as quickly and quietly as she could, conscious only of the need to escape to some place where she could think, could wait for a calmer mood in which to consider all the values of this new shock. She had had no right to read her mother's letter; if old Mrs Flagg had wanted her to know of it, Hannah would surely have mentioned it; the affair did not concern her except in that it hurt her and humiliated her almost beyond her powers of endurance.

Up in the green woods behind the house she found a fallen log and sat down upon it, her thoughts still in chaos, her face blazing, her breath coming quick and hard. Oh, Mother had had no right to do that! It was inexcusable, within a few weeks of that marriage that had been no marriage at all, to complicate Pen's already difficult problem with this thoughtless—this shameless appeal. What must they think of the Fitzpercys, these proud, fine, self-controlled Flaggs; what kind of a woman would they think Jeff's wife to be, when her people so promptly had shown them what their standards were?

"Oh, how could you, how could you, how *could* you!" Pen said aloud, to the whispering sweetness and stillness of the woods. Her mother's graceful easy phrases came back to her. " 'The Gram of whom Pen so often speaks affectionately,' " she said scornfully.

"The Gram who hates me, who couldn't stand the idea of a Flagg marrying me in the first place! I'll go see Mother this afternoon," she planned, her thoughts feverish in the race to find some way to undo what had been done. "I'll have her return the check, with a note—no, I'll have her telegraph to Mrs Flagg this afternoon saying that she no longer has need of the check—I'll be as gentle as I can! Just to be kind, every separate hour," she thought, sudden tears of pain and self-pity in her eyes, "that's what Grandfather said to do. Be kind, every separate hour, and not hurt anyone's feelings, and then the crises will take care of themselves! But not this crisis! Oh, dear, what shall I do, what shall I do!"

When she went back to the house it was almost lunchtime. Hannah looked rather pale, Penelope thought, and as if she had been crying. She was coming up the terrace steps at the same moment; Penelope joined her, forgetting for a moment her own distress.

"Hannah, nothing wrong?"

"Nothing wrong with Jeff, if you mean that," Hannah said smiling. "He was roaring to De Vecchio that he must sit up."

"But you look——"

"I'm all right," Hannah said, smiling, but averting her eyes suddenly, and with her lips trembling. "Just one of the days when my sawdust is all doll, as little Mary said," she added, laying a brown hand on Pen's wrist with a significant pressure.

"Hannah," Pen began on impulse, "I was in your office waiting for you this morning. When you were down with Tom on the terrace, I mean."

"Was it so obvious?" Hannah asked, still not looking at her.

Penelope was still, in sheer surprise.

"Tom's lucky, Tom's always a Flagg first, and everything else after that," Hannah went on bitterly, her fingers still on Pen's wrist, her eyes averted and lowered. "But sometimes I think I can't stand it. He's my first cousin; I'm three years older than he—very well! I admit it. I admit that he doesn't care the snap of his finger for me, really. You saw it, I suppose they all see it! I don't care."

Penelope had drawn her aside to the shelter of the flower-walled upper terrace. To have Hannah break—Hannah the marvelous, the perfect, the self-controlled—was to be thrilled and shocked and made oddly happy all at once.

"I didn't see anything, Hannah," she said. "You must pull yourself together; it's almost lunchtime. It was something else that worried me," Penelope went on, with a rueful and shaken laugh. "I was in your office this morning, Hannah. I saw my mother's letter."

Her face was scarlet again, but there was heart's ease in telling this other girl, this girl who was shamed and troubled, too, about it. Pen's eyes met Hannah's eyes honestly.

"Oh," Hannah said quickly, self-controlled again. "I'm sorry."

"I'm horribly sorry she wrote it. Mother's—a poetess," Pen explained lamely, with a little mirthless laugh, "and they—they see things differently."

"I'm sorry you saw it. Grandfather didn't want you to see it."

"She shouldn't have!" Penelope's smile was all forgiveness, indulgence for her mother—all apology for the mistake. "I think I'll tell her—ask her to wire your grandmother that she won't need that money."

Hannah, her composure now fully restored, looked earnestly at the other girl.

"I don't know that I would, Pen," she said slowly.

Comfort began to creep into Pen's sore heart.

"Hannah, I have to! If they'd do this before I'm a month married, they'd do it again. I can't—you've all been so generous to me with the

[157]

car and the allowance—Jeff's costing such a frightful lot—I can't let them——"

"They won't again."

"Oh, they will," Pen persisted gloomily. "You don't know my family. My brother will try to sell washing machines to Uncle Mark; my brother-in-law will send you tickets for piano concerts; my mother will write you letters like that letter!"

"Well, we'll take them as they come!" Hannah said cheerfully.

"Yes, minute by minute," Pen agreed seriously. "But that doesn't keep me from being ashamed," she said.

"Oh, I know how you feel," Hannah conceded, with a sympathetic look from her fine dark eyes. They went into the house together; coming through doors and in from porches and down the stairway, the family was gathering for luncheon.

"Penelope," said her mother-in-law, busily crossing the hall, eyeglassed and important, "did you say that you were going down to visit your mother this afternoon?"

"I thought I would. But if there's anything I can do for you, Aunt Margaret——?"

"There are two things you can do for me, my dear. You can take De Vecchio down to the Palo Alto hospital; he has to operate there at three; and you can stop at Roos Brothers and ask if Frank's belt has come back—they were to order one with his initials. His birthday is Tuesday."

"Gladly," Penelope said, grateful for distraction from her own thoughts.

"Father, you look very spruce this morning," Margaret Flagg said, presenting the old man with a cheek to kiss as he came out of the hot sunshine of the terraces into the wide, shadowy hallway. He was in cool pongee color; he had a spray of cherry leaves and thick enameled scarlet fruit in his hand.

"Pretty enough to go on any lady's bonnet," he said.

"You had an early breakfast," Jeff's mother said. "I was down by eight."

"I missed you, too," Pen said shyly. "But I loved my flowers. They told me about them—about your bringing them in, I mean. Thank you—Grandfather."

She had never called him that before. She saw that he noticed it. He made her a smiling little stately bow.

"You're going down to see your mother?" he asked. "I'll have one of the boys put some fruit into your car before they bring it around to you."

Old Mrs Flagg came in, flushed from the heat of her morning spent in the chairs on the lawn, breathing heavily, but gallant and energetic as ever in her plain white silk. Penelope went to her.

"Mrs Flagg, may I speak to you a moment?"

"Certainly." They were alone—the strong old woman with the white hair and browned skin, the slender tall girl with gray-blue eyes and flax-gold braids.

"I'm sorry—I'm terribly sorry my mother wrote you," said Pen. "I'm going to—I thought I'd ask her not to do that again."

Old Mrs Flagg halted on her stout cane. She did not move her head to look at Penelope, but rather continued to stare straight ahead of her, in the direction of the dining-room door.

"I wouldn't do that," she said, in a somewhat expressionless voice. "It's a hard thing to want money. Nobody likes to ask for it."

The answer was unexpected. It was neither the usual gracious evasion of thanks, nor was it criticism. Penelope was silent for a few embarrassed seconds, at a loss. Presently she said:

"Well, thank you. Thank you very much!"

"You're quite welcome!" the old woman said briefly, going on toward the dining room. Penelope stood still for a second and then followed her. How one could hate this old woman, but ah, how one could love her, too!

CHAPTER XV

It was about three o'clock when she reached her mother's cottage in Armitage Lane; the ugliest hour of the hot still afternoon. Broken toys lay about in the dry gardens, withered stems of tarweed and yarrow thrust themselves up between the shafts of the untended roses and bamboo. Mats of marigolds had passed their beauty; the blossoms were whitened yellow slivers against the pale green bushes. The very houses, cheap wooden houses that needed painting, looked dried and thin.

Nobody was in sight at the Fitzpercy house. Penelope, standing in the kitchen doorway, her face curved into a resolute smile of expectation, called the various names. Her eyes took in the details of the familiar disorder—grease on the blackened stove, grease and crumbs on the floor, dishes jumbled in the sink, odds and ends of food scattered on the plates on the table. The remains of an almost-drained bottle of milk were visibly soured; flies walked on the sugar bowl; eggshells and scraped crescents of watermelon rind overflowed the garbage tin.

She had been rehearsing stern reproaches to her mother as, talking pleasantly with handsome gallant old De Vecchio, she drove along. She had determined that all attempts to borrow from the Flaggs must stop. If her family couldn't respect her dignity enough to save her that sort of humiliation, then she would sever her connection with the Flaggs entirely. Her decision on this point was wavering, anyway; unless she could obtain her mother's—her brother's—solemn promise that this sort of thing would not go on, she would give up the fight. She would have her marriage annulled and go away—go away somewhere, anywhere, and carve out a destiny for herself. . . .

Thinking these thoughts, trying to steel herself to put them into execution, she heard a faint tremulous answer to her call. It seemed to come from upstairs. Pen walked into the kitchen and called again.

"Who is it?" somebody called back.

It was her mother's voice. Pen went into the hall and looked up the narrow stairway shaft.

"It's Pen, Mother!"

"Oh, come upstairs, Pen!"

Pen ran up, to find her mother half dressed, but prostrate upon her bed, looking pale, and with her fair gray-streaked hair in more than its usual disorder. Mrs Fitzpercy burst into tears as she kissed her daughter, but she smiled gallantly through them, and in a second was quite herself again and radiant with pleasure over the visit.

"My darling—and looking so beautiful—my queen rose in a rosebud garden of girls!" she said. "Don't mind my crying, darling; it's just that I was feeling blue, and it's so good to see you! I've been lying here making up my mind that I'd get up and straighten things out a little, and time has simply slipped by and I'm afraid you've found the house in a *mess!*"

"Headache, Mother?" Pen was sitting in a low chair drawn to the bedside now, holding her mother's hand. Ellabeth Fitzpercy's faded eyes watered again.

"I did have a slight headache, Pen. Better now. I took some aspirin. But tell me of yourself, darling, and poor dear Jeff. Is he better? What does the doctor say?"

Pen duly reported, more with a view to quieting her mother, who seemed inexplicably agitated, than because she felt the details were entertaining. Mrs Fitzpercy brightened at the description of the apartment that was being made ready for the Jefferson Flaggs; her eyes sparkled.

"Where's Persis?"

"She went in to stay with Isolde last Friday; she's still there. The twins have had bad sunburn. Isolde and Grandy took them out to the beach one of those terribly hot days."

"Oh, poor little mice!" There was a moment's silence.

"Pen, dear, I hated to do it, but I wrote Jeff's grandmother to borrow a few hundred dollars just for a few weeks," began her mother, somewhat timidly. "I was afraid you wouldn't like it, dear, but I didn't know what else to do."

Pen's heart ached fiercely with pity. She patted her mother's hand.

"That was all right."

"Indeed it wasn't all right, no matter how generous you are, darling. It was all wrong, and it never will happen again. But it was under such peculiar circumstances that I——" Mrs Fitzpercy stopped, hesitating; began again. "This is Wednesday," she said, recommencing. "You were here Monday, weren't you? It was Monday night that your father came home."

"My *father!*" Pen's voice was quiet, but her eyes came with the swiftness of arrows to her mother's face.

"I didn't let them tell you. It was just—well, it was just *too* much," Mrs Fitzpercy said.

"I thought—how many years is it? I thought he might be dead, Mother."

"We all did. I've not heard for almost six years. He was here, you remember? He was here seven years ago."

"Remember! I was fifteen."

"Well, of course you remember. He wasn't very well then; he was going down to the Texas oil fields, and he promised to let me know how he was, and how things were going with him. I had two letters, and then I had this old trunk of letters and clothes and things from Canada somewhere, and the letter from the man—you remember?—who said that Marvin had left all his things behind him and gone into the mountains months—oh, *months*, before, and that he couldn't have lived through the snows."

"But he did?" Pen hoped that the complete aridity of her soul had not reached her voice.

"He looks better than I've ever seen him; he's actually fat," Mrs Fitzpercy said, gaining cheerfulness and color as she discovered matters to be going well. "He had on a nice gray suit; he's quite *stout*, really, and he seemed so grateful to get home! Phil's taken him into town today to see Isolde and his grandsons—poor Marvin, he did look quite dashed when I informed him that one of his daughters was quite old enough to be a mother! But he hadn't one *penny*, his partner cheated him on a franchise for a mill or something; it's a long story, I didn't understand all of it; and I'm flat broke, it just happens, working on the new book, but of course no money until it's all ready. . . ."

Pen listened in a troubled dream, her face serene, her eyes even smiling, but her soul sick within her.

"So that if he can scrape together enough capital to get to Hollywood," the story ended, "and be sure of just a few weeks there, he'll probably get into something very much worth while. He was even talking of our moving down there if this thing develops, and I know it *will* develop, because men like Joe Case and Roger Thorpe don't put their good money into ridiculous schemes. No, this really seems an opportunity for your father at last, and my first thought when I knew he must have two or three hundred dollars was the Flaggs. If I can give them a sweet daughter, who saved their son's life, a few hundred will seem nothing to them! You didn't hear whether Mrs Flagg feels that she can send it to me or not?"

[161]

Penelope's eyes were thoughtful; she smiled at her mother, spoke gently:

"Yes, she did. I saw the check."

"Ah, that's good!" the older woman said, brightening. "I was going to have Phil go over to Martins' and telephone you tonight, and perhaps drive up with Daddy tomorrow and see you," she said.

"I'll telephone you in the morning, Mother, and we can arrange it. Have Phil call me up from the Martins' at ten."

"Goodness, I am so relieved about that money!" Mrs Fitzpercy said. "I knew she would, but it's a relief to be sure. Your father has talked of a thousand other openings, but this one seemed much the best—it's that camera patent someone is experimenting with. He'll leave in a day or two now for the south, and perhaps take Phil with him. He says there ought to be good opportunities for Phil down there, and while I'm not myself enthusiastic about the movie atmosphere—or what you hear of it, anyway—there are emergencies when any port seems good, and as your father says, we must be practical and do things with the future in view."

Again Pen listened, half smiling, but with somber eyes. Her father and mother would of course want to come and see her in her glory—the daughter who had married one of the rich Flaggs. And how could she bear it, and why *should* she bear it, this unwelcome appearance of the father who had visited his family only twice in her recollection, and then only to tell his hard luck stories and to raise funds for fresh absurd ventures? She imagined herself saying, "Hannah, my father. Aunt 'Lizabeth, may I present my father?" and her spirit shuddered away from the thought. Some ordeals were too hard; some efforts were impossible. Her own position in the Flagg family was peculiar; the introduction of her suave, talkative, obviously unsuccessful father would afford her only one more hour of discomfort.

Thinking these things, she lost the thread of her mother's talk, if indeed it could be said to have any thread. But that signified nothing; Ellabeth Fitzpercy was accustomed to rambling on unattended; she liked the sound of her own voice and could amplify the simplest statement with long poetical ramifications infinitely soothing to herself.

On this occasion she became so much comforted that she presently descended the stairs with Pen, and giving the kitchen up as a bad job, went out into the arbor, where mother and daughter sat for another hour of talk. Pen now produced the forgotten basket of fruit from the Flagg orchards; ah said her mother, on a great breath of pleasure, that was what she wanted. She had had no lunch, and only a cup of black coffee for breakfast, but the great black figs, the grapes and the mellow pears would be her meal.

Had Pen found her so, stripping the wet silky skins from the peaches, resting her faded pretty mouth against the tarnished muscat grapes as she sucked them one by one, she might perhaps have reproached her, might perhaps have begged her to reconsider her request for money. But the moment for that had passed. Mrs Fitzpercy was happy, her headache gone, the money promised, her adored Pen with her, and the little graceful compliment of the fruit assuring her that the Flaggs had not resented her appeal. The world was all serene again. Pen could not introduce any cloud.

Suddenly there were arrivals. Persis, looking draggled and weary, Philip in the old brown suit that needed pressing, and a stranger, a gray-headed, almost completely bald man with a walrus mustache. Penelope rose in confusion; she had meant to escape before this happened.

"Hello, darling, you look so lovely!" Persis said, kissing her, and looking, despite her smile, as if it would take very little to start her crying.

"Hello, Daddy," Pen said to the stranger, not evading his kiss.

"Well," the man said, sitting down, speaking with a great air of jovial heartiness. "It's our multimillionaire daughter, eh, eh, eh? Your Highness is well today, I hope? This is a condescension, Ella."

"How's Jeff, Pen?" Persis said, in quick distaste and embarrassment. Pen had not seen her father for seven years, but as she heard him and looked at him she felt as if it might have been only yesterday that he had been at home; smoking a great deal, sleeping late in the mornings and having his midmorning breakfast in the kitchen, in a dressing gown, with a handkerchief about his throat, and teasing her about fat Roy Paston, an odious high-school acquaintance whom she had always heartily despised. He was older—much, much older—and while he did not look dissipated, and in fact was not dissipated, as far as she knew, there was a certain bagginess and grayness about him that his jaunty manner did not hide. He did not look exactly shabby, but just as definitely as some men's appearance said success, so his said unsuccess. Older, grayer, still he was just the same. He had acquired a conversational habit of saying "Eh, eh, eh?" ruminating at the end of almost every phrase.

"I tell your mother it's not fair, eh, eh, eh?" he said. "Springing young ladies on me when I left her with only little girls, eh, eh, eh? Isolde with children—grandsons, eh, eh, eh? I tell your mother I didn't bargain on grandsons!"

"We didn't know how to reach you, Marvin," Mrs Fitzpercy said, with an amused air that did not conceal the fact that she was quivering with nervousness.

"No, listen, you quit your old trick of blaming yourself for everything, Ella!" the man said good-humoredly. "Same old sixpence, your mother is, eh, eh, eh?" he added, in his indulgent way. "Scared of her own voice! Whoo, Pen," he went on, rounding his faded blue eyes. "What an eyeful this lucky feller Flagg got when he got *you*! Family beauty, Mommy, eh, eh, eh? She's like your sister Dora, Ella. Exactly like Dora, only she's—by Jove, she is better looking!"

"You do look darling, Pen," Persis said in an undertone. "Let's get the conversation somewhere near honesty and simplicity," the younger sister's anxious uncomfortable voice seemed to imply. "This is insufferable; help me to bring it to normal. Don't be angry; that won't help!"

Whether Persis really felt all this or not, Pen didn't know, but her sister's quick apologetic asides and her uneasy smile reached her, and she said reassuringly:

"I've nothing to do these days except keep myself nice!"

"How about some beer, Phil?" They had brought some beer with them; now Phil went into the house to get glasses. Persis continued to nibble at grapes.

"Wonderful fruit, Pen. Where'd you get it?"

"Old Mr Flagg—Jeff's grandfather—had it put in the car. Most of it grows on the place; the grapes came from the ranch up in Sonoma County."

"The Hermione Mine, that's where the Flagg money originally came from," Marvin Fitzpercy said, taking a great draught of his beer, gasping and wiping his mouth. "They were New England folks, came out here without a cent and started farming in the Humboldt County. Napa County, I guess it was. They bought this mine over near Virginia City, and for a while they took a million a month out of it. A million a month! Tom Flagg—that's your husband's grandfather—who was a young man then, went on to Washington and had some sort of lawsuit—won it, of course. You can win any suit if you've got enough money, eh, eh, eh? Yes, sir, you certainly can."

"They must always have had money, Dad. They've portraits and rugs and china from Revolutionary days. Those things always have meant money."

"I've no doubt they've worked the government for something from the very beginning," Marvin Fitzpercy said. "Well, I'm glad my girl is getting the advantage of it, if we're fools enough to let the capitalistic system go on. Eh? I never had any privileges, never struck that sort of luck, or wanted to take money away from anyone else so I could have too much of it, but I don't grudge it to you." And he looked about the circle with his quick little complacent "Eh, eh, eh?" for a conclusion.

"I knew they had a place up in the Napa neighborhood," Penelope said. In one minute she would pretend to be amazed at the time and could go. But would he want to come and see her—would he want to come and see her?

"Teege, that's the one I knew; he's just a year or two older than I am," her father said. "Ever hear of him?"

"Oh yes, Uncle Teege they call him. That's Tom Flagg's father. The Tom Flagg who was here, remember, Mom? He's an invalid now, and has to sit in a chair. He's at home with the rest," Pen said.

"Well, I didn't exactly know him," Marvin Fitzpercy amended it. "You've got to go, eh, eh, eh? I knew a lot of the fellers he did. Oliver

Gough—Gough Street was named for his father—was one of them. Bill Hopkins, and Harris. All those fellers."

Persis got to her feet as Penelope did; her mother and father smiled good-byes. "I'll walk with you to the car, Pen," Persis said.

"I may have to go south," her father told her in parting. "I've a prospect down there. But your mother and I may run up and see you one of these days."

"Just let me know, so that I'll be there," she said, wincing deep inside, outwardly calm. Persis leaned on the door of the car for a moment's private talk.

"Pen, don't mind. I'll keep him from coming to see you if I have to drive a nail in one of the tires! Isn't he awful—isn't he awful?" Persis said quickly and urgently. "But he's going away! Why she ever let him *in*, when he showed up on Monday night! But he has to go south right away; he has some crazy scheme or other down there. Don't mind him, Pen; he'll go away again and be gone for years, the way he always has!"

Penelope looked down at her sister's tired, flushed young face, her heart aching so solidly that she could hardly speak.

"I mind for you, darling," she said. Angry, impatient tears came into Persis' eyes.

"Oh, I'll get through it," she said doggedly. "Only it makes me sick to have you dragged in, to have him talking as if he'd like to go up and be entertained at dinner by the Flaggs. And he would, too; that's the worst of it. He *would!* He's been trying to borrow money somewhere; I don't know whether he has or not. Gone for seven years, and then he comes back and wants to borrow money! But don't let it worry you, Pen," the younger sister again begged. "You're out of it, and you're all right, and that's all that matters! I just love—I just love to think that all this doesn't touch you," Persis said fiercely. "You're in a big house, with servants and gardens and a swimming pool, and gradually—gradually," she rushed on, her lip betraying her with a sudden trembling, "we'll get out of the way!"

"Persis, you're so sweet," Pen said, on a rush of love and pity. "I'm so sorry that it's all like this. Things don't seem to be arranged for us the way they are for other girls. Maybe we can gradually straighten them out; maybe we'll get the breaks someday——"

"Isolde, now," Persis said, as Pen hesitated, looking with troubled eyes at her sister, and rubbing Persis' hand with her own hand, "things are horrid there. Grandy goes on composing, but he doesn't get engagements to play, and if he does get a pupil the twins start crying or something; it's all such a mess! And I don't think Isolde manages very well; she doesn't seem to grasp things; they're too much for her."

"I feel so stupid about it all, Persis! I feel that none of us, none of us Fitzpercys really knows how to live. And there's no one to ask."

"I know that I wish I'd been born a Chinese rice picker or an Eskimo," Persis said darkly. Penelope, stooping forward for a good-bye kiss, touching the starter with her foot, laughed forlornly as she drove away.

CHAPTER XVI

Jeff was asleep when she peeped into his room an hour later. She went on to her own and began leisurely preparations for a bath and change. She was standing, her body curved, her head upside down so that the flying brush could penetrate the hanging curtain of her glorious golden hair when a quiet, discontented little voice near her said: "Sometimes I wish I hadn't cut mine!"

Pen flung the mane back, straightened up flushing and panting, and smiled into the serious eyes of Jeff's aunt Amy, the thirty-year-old blond wife of fifty-year-old Uncle Peter.

"Oh, hello, Amy!" she said, pleased. There was something very pleasant about the way the Flagg women went about among each other's rooms, calling. Nobody called Amy "Aunt," she was much too young. Even the children called her "Amy," and Pen with the rest.

"What are you and Jeff going to do about it?" Amy asked, with the idle, indifferent air that was characteristic of her. She sat down, lighting a cigarette.

Penelope was at her mirror, braiding the long strands in two plaits. She brought them into a coronet across the top of her head, pinning them snugly. They shone like polished gold.

"About what?" she said.

"Well, I mean," Amy said, with a little schoolgirlish laugh, "are you going on with it?"

"Jeff and I?" Penelope said thoughtfully.

"Yes. You know what I mean. It's some job," Amy added, significantly, "to be married to a Flagg. I didn't know whether you wanted to—take it on."

Penelope felt the blood creeping up into her face. She went on soberly with her hairdressing.

"They make an awful fuss about marriage," Amy went on. "They're not like other people. It's a life sentence, you know, if you do."

"If I go on, you mean?"

"Yes, if you go on." Penelope was silent, and Amy laughed her nervous little laugh again. "They don't expect you to," she said suddenly. "They think it's only Flaggs that carry things through. And I've been wondering. I can say this to you, Pen," she added rather timidly, "for I don't think you're any more in love with Jefferson Flagg than I am!"

"The circumstances of our marriage were so mixed," Pen began slowly, flushing and smiling.

"He would have bullied you into marrying him whether he'd been hurt or not," Amy said, with a touch of bitterness. "That's the Flagg way; they can have anything they want, because they're Flaggs!"

Penelope said nothing for a brief space. Presently she asked simply, "Were you bullied into marrying Uncle Peter, Amy?"

"Certainly I was!" Amy said passionately and promptly.

Penelope, surprised and distressed, had no comment ready.

"I was nineteen when Peter Flagg met M'ma, up in Reno," Amy said. "M'ma was there getting a divorce. The man she married, Lee Davies, was there with her; we were living at a sort of farmhouse outside the city; I was riding and having a beautiful time. Peter Flagg came up there on an inheritance suit and stayed at the same place. M'ma would have thrown Lee over like a shot to get him—everyone thought he liked her, when quite suddenly he told her it was me. That," Amy said, rubbing out her cigarette, dropping it into a tray, "finished *me*. I was married to Peter before I knew what it was all about—twelve years ago. And the old lady— Gram, I mean—didn't like it one bit better than she does your marrying Jeff! They hate that sort of thing, the Flaggs do. They hate girls they don't know. You'll see. Nobody'll make it easy for you. Hannah's always polite, and I love Hannah, and the old man gave you flowers. He never gave me any, but he likes you. But all that doesn't matter one bit! What matters is Gram, and she hates you, and maybe you'll go crazy, as I did, and run away from it."

Penelope, now in the processes of dressing, found all this of absorbing interest, found her courage challenged rather than lessened by it.

"How far did you run, Amy?" she asked, smiling.

"Oh, I went to Paris, with Emil le Touchard," Amy answered haughtily. "I thought you knew. I was there for four years."

Penelope, genuinely shocked and serious now, wheeled about on the dressing-table seat and stared at her.

"Sally was born in Paris," Amy said, with a sort of impatient superbness. "But after a while Emil went back to his family in Bordeaux. They do, you know. Frenchmen always go back to their wives and children. I didn't have any money; he didn't, either. I'll do him that much justice. He would have given it to me. The fourth day after he left, the old lawyer came and took back most of the jewelry. I didn't want it, but it made me feel queer. Sally was two, then, and for a year I did everything I could, shopped for friends of mine and wrote M'ma for twenty-five or fifty dollars at a time. And then Peter came over. There'd been no publicity, no scandal; he was one of the holier-than-thou Flaggs, the great American family that always does things right, and he asked me to come back, and bring the baby, and said that I never would be reproached, and that Sally would be one of the cousins among the rest!

"Come over here and I'll tie that for you," Amy said, interrupting herself, as Penelope merely considered her fixedly, without comment. "So he brought us home, and—because there's nothing else for me to do—I've been here five years," she went on. "Five years of it, birthdays and picnics, and Sally's music lessons—all the Le Touchards are musical—and having her teeth straightened, and going to Hawaii with Aunt Hannah, and knowing that it's always going to be like this! Give me another cigarette. Thanks. I hate the Flaggs," Amy said, trembling. "I despise them. So good, so perfect, so loyal. They're hypocrites, every last one of them, and Peter's the worst of the lot. He's never put his finger on me since he joined me in that Paris hotel. Horrible hotel, on the Rue St Honoré! Stairs and cats and smells. We were 'Mr and Mrs Peter Morris Flagg, infant and nurse,' on the boat coming home, but he never came into my room. I have birthday presents and furs and a checkbook, and they all hate me, and that's what I've done with my life!

"What you'll do," she added, as Penelope for sheer surprise was still silent, "what you'll do, if you're smart, is have your marriage annulled, and stick them for enough money to travel and live as you like for five years! You were talked into marrying Jeff; everyone thought he was dying; he's a completely spoiled kid, drinks and gambles, I don't know what he hasn't done to worry the wits out of them in the past two years. If you're smart you'll get out of it now, before you've got children to consider! I hadn't nerve enough; perhaps you have!"

Amy's breast was heaving now and her lip trembling.

"I don't know why I'm talking this way!" she faltered, suddenly bursting into tears. "I don't know where I'd be *without* the Flaggs! Women have had an awfully hard time trying to make a living in Paris these last years. I'm the one to blame; I can't settle down here and take them at their own pompous, self-satisfied values. They're too good, and it's all too smooth and friendly and happy, children and grandchildren and lunch on the lawn and charades after dinner! If nobody loves you," Amy stammered, busy with her handkerchief now, and speaking in a carefully controlled tone, "it's all such a *farce!* You do as you think best, Pen; perhaps you'll be the equal of the old lady. She said to Aunt 'Lizabeth today that she wouldn't give you six months with Jeff. 'There may be a woman somewhere who could manage him,' she said, 'but not that beautiful doll!' "

"Did she say that?" Pen asked quietly.

"Maybe I oughtn't to tell you."

"I'm glad to know what she thinks."

"Now," said Amy, "I'll go dress, and before dinner I'll sing three or four old Scotch songs for Grandfather, and then Sally'll come romping

[168]

in ready to kiss dear Mother good night. . . ." Her bitter ironic voice trailed away into disconsolate silence; she rose from her chair.

"You're the most beautiful person who ever came into this family, anyway," she said.

"I hear Gram alluded to me as 'that Irish girl.'"

"Did she? Who told you that?"

"Jeff. He thought it was funny."

"He *would* tell you. That's Flagg humor, pure and simple. They think that because one of them says it, no matter how rude it is, it's all right." Amy came close to Pen and spoke suddenly in the gentle friendly manner with which Pen had always associated her. "I don't know why I broke loose this way tonight," she said apologetically. "I'm horribly sorry already. I took my chance when I ran away with Emil, and I lost it, and that's all there is to it. Sally's lucky that she'll have money and a fine name to help her live it down. I've never done this before, Pen; I don't talk. I've never talked even to Hannah this way. I'm happy—honestly I am—most of the time. Only when I see them so smug over their samplers and warming pans I——" She stopped, her voice was rising again. "Well, I'm over it now, anyway," she finished mildly.

She raised her face, and Pen stooped and kissed her. A moment later Amy was gone, and Pen walked slowly across the big upper hall to Jeff's door. It was six o'clock; twilight was soft in the hall and in the great well of the stairway; lines of light showed under bedroom doors where various members of the family were beginning to think of dressing for dinner. A rabble of shouting children came upstairs, pulling themselves along by the railing, leaning over it at dangerous angles—brown, untidy, wearied.

Penelope went into Jeff's room and crossed to the bed and laid her hand on his.

"You look beautiful," he said restlessly, absently. And then, as she sat down in her usual low chair, "Pen, you're not going away, are you?"

"Going where?"

"Anywhere."

"Where would I go?"

"They let you into marrying me; that's what's eating them," Jeff said with inelegant urgency. "It's never happened to us before; they don't know what to do about it!"

"I don't know that it's their affair," Pen said mildly.

"Well, it isn't, it isn't!" he agreed eagerly. "But they're sort of trying to break it up because they don't think we can get away with it."

"They can't break it up unless we agree," Pen said, thinking.

"No, but maybe they think they could make terms to which you *would* agree, Pen. You see they know—shucks, everyone knows—that you're not as crazy about me as I am about you! And I'm sick now," Jeff said, breathless and perspiring with the effort to grasp her hands and to show

[169]

her by straightening up in his bed that his strength was returning. "I'm no good now, but give me a chance! I'll show them——"

"Jeff, lie down or I'll call Martha. You mustn't. De Vecchio said absolutely no effort—he didn't want you even to have a pillow——"

Pen, his hand still grasping hers, turned in alarm as he sank back with a wet face and closed sunken eyes. She had heard a step behind her; in a wave of relief she realized that someone was here to help her bring him back to consciousness.

It was his formidable grandmother who stood there leaning on her cane, her disapproving eyes on Pen.

"What's happened?"

"We were talking and he fainted. Oh, Martha!" Pen gasped, as the nurse came in. "Do something!"

"Talking too much, huh?" said Martha, her flail-like arms busy, her own upper lip perspiring as she changed his position. "This won't hurt him. That's right, Mr Jeff. You're all right."

"I thought he wasn't to be excited," his grandmother said. "I'll not wait now. I'll come back after dinner, Martha."

Without a word or a look for Pen she thumped away. The two younger women looked at each other, and Martha grinned.

"You'll never get the best of that old battle-ax!" she said affectionately. "You'd better get out; he's coming around. Well, what'd you want to jump around that way for," Pen heard her scolding. "Haven't you got any sense? Don't you know that you haven't any more vitality than a rat?"

A few minutes later she came out to where Pen was anxiously waiting in the hall.

"He's all right," she said. "I think his mother got him kind of worked up today telling him that it might be months before you and he could get started as real married folks. You've got your work cut out for you if you're going to stick it. You won't get much help from them or from him, either. They're the grandest people in the world once they like you, but it's like breaking into the movies for a while."

The upper hall was lighted now. Various doors were opening to show groups of pajama-clad, slippered children running about or jumping on beds; various members of the family were issuing forth to go down to dinner. Peter Flagg, square and gray and kindly looking, was just descending the stairway in the company of his old father and his wife. Amy was in pale blue; her smooth, delicate young shoulders were bare; under the soft hall lights her aureole of pale brown hair had turned to gold. Her violet eyes were deeply smiling at something the old man had said; Pen, joining them, saw that her little hand had dropped into Peter's hand as they went downstairs.

They went on to the music room, where a fire had been lighted against the gathering chill of a foggy summer night. Mark Flagg, sunk in a great chair, was reading the evening paper; his busy wife, needles and spectacles flashing, was knitting, a few feet away. On the broad davenport was George Flagg, with his arm about his young wife.

His grandfather took a chair always held sacred to his use; Peter stood at the fire, warming his hands at his back, his eyes contentedly studying the room. Amy drifted to the piano; her hands found chords, the lamplight fell graciously upon her blue flowing gown and her shining aureole of hair. She began to sing. She sang "Robin Adair," and "The Minstrel Boy," and "Norah Creina."

> "*Lesbia hath a robe of gold,*
>   *But all so tight the nymph hath laced it,*
> *Not a charm of beauty's mould*
>   *Presumes to stay where Nature placed it. . . ."*

Penelope took a deep low chair, leaned back and half closed her eyes. She was tired after the long day that had begun with the staggering discovery of her mother's appeal for money, had moved on through the revealing scene with Hannah, the drive with De Vecchio, the dreadful hot hour with her mother in the old cluttered atmosphere of home, her father's unwelcome arrival, the talk with Persis. Then had come later talks with Amy, and with Jeff and Martha, and with Martha alone, and now finally the day had ended with this peaceful hour of firelight and lamplight, the old man serene in his big chair, the young lovers murmuring and giggling on the davenport, the blue flowered figure on the piano bench.

"I may be licked," Pen thought dreamily, "but I don't know it yet!"

CHAPTER XVII

"I want to talk to you, Penelope," old Mrs Flagg said to her quietly a day or two later. Penelope realized suddenly that she was alone with Jeff's grandmother. They were down on the lawn; there had been quite a group there. Now the others had drifted away, perhaps at a nod from the old family despot. The girl raised her eyes for a steady look, looked away again at the green sweetness of the lawns and tree shadows.

"About Jeff, of course," the older woman said.

"About Jeff?" Penelope echoed.

"You and he have discussed plans?"

"Plans?" Penelope repeated again. "You'll get nothing out of *me*," she thought. Her heart was beating fast; she must feel her way through this talk with the utmost wariness.

[171]

"Your marriage," Mrs Flagg said. "I have been discussing it with his father, and with the boy. It was, of course, no marriage."

Penelope said nothing. Her eyes did not waver.

"It was not a marriage in the ordinary sense," the old woman elucidated it. "The boy was, as we thought, dying. De Vecchio and Cox both said so. Jeff tells me that you had repeatedly refused to marry him?"

She ended on an interrogative note. Penelope smiled.

"I didn't consider that Jeff had seriously asked me," she said, after a moment's pause. "I didn't suppose him to be in any position to ask me. I didn't take him seriously."

"Exactly. That's what he told me this morning. His illness," his grandmother said, speaking with something less than her usual assurance, speaking, Pen thought with a little thrill of scared triumph, as if she were even a little discomfited by the turn the conversation seemed inclined to take, "has made Jeff seem older than he is. It has changed him. But his mother and I both feel that that—that will not last. And we all feel—hem!—that *if* you and he are not to go on with this marriage, this is the time to end it. This—this annulment—could be explained. A later break would be—unfortunate."

"Isn't it, after all," Pen asked simply, "what Jeff and I feel?"

Old Mrs Flagg seemed taken aback for a second, but only for a second.

"Well, certainly," she said then decidedly. "You have a mother and sisters," she added, reverting, Pen knew, to some argument that had occurred to her before. "You might want to travel, follow some line of study."

"You mean money?" Pen asked flatly. There was a silence, and she saw the other woman flush. Then for the first time she saw a vulnerable, a human side to Jeff's grandmother. Old Mrs Flagg spoke hesitatingly, almost apologetically.

"If I do," she said, "I mean it only because you are—now, this moment, a Mrs Thomas Jefferson Flagg. You have your—your claim. You have done us a great service. This situation—this emergency—never has occurred with us before. We want to be fair. We want to be more than fair. You and Jeff are not man and wife in the ordinary sense. If you are never to be man and wife, that doesn't mean that you are not to—to at least —to gain—to have something——"

She stopped, confused, and Penelope realized that part of this woman's power at least came from her strange capability of seeing both sides of a question.

"I wish," she began again, as Penelope, looking at her thoughtfully, did not speak, "I wish you were in my—in our position. We don't know quite what to do. My brother, Judge Farmer, says that the marriage could quite simply be annulled. Jeff's mother, Margaret, would take him up to the Sonoma place for a long convalescence. He couldn't very well ask you to go there; it's a rough farmhouse up in the fruit country—it's **not**

[172]

comfortable. We both feel—we all feel, his grandfather and his mother and father and I—that an injustice was done you on that night when you came here. The doctors said that he was dying—you remember exactly what the circumstances were. Now we want to be fair to you, and of course to him. It may be months before he is anything but an invalid. He has not graduated from law school; he has not passed the bar. He has—he occasionally—in certain ways he still makes us very anxious. Unless you feel sure that you want to undertake it——"

She stopped again in some little confusion. Penelope had raised her head, her quiet look meeting the other woman's troubled eyes fairly. There was no insolence, no anger in the look. Penelope's clean-cut chin was held high; the magnificent plaits of her hair, still damp from a swim, and fastened coronet fashion across her head, shone gold in the afternoon light.

"You haven't discussed this with Jeff, Mrs Flagg?"

"Not at all. He hasn't been well enough. But now that Martha is going, we feel that we must settle it."

Penelope looked away through narrowed eyelids at the dazzle of the gardens, the mounting tiers of the terraces, the old-fashioned cream white house with green blots of tree shadows lying graciously upon it.

"I would like to think it over," she said.

"Surely, my dear!" The old woman's eyes were narrowed, too, and she was half smiling. "That 'my dear' means that she thinks she has me!" Pen thought.

She walked away slowly, across the green lawn, her head held high. Frank and Billy Merry, Tom and Mary Towne, absorbed in a desperate game of Cops and Robbers, came charging past her from some lair in the shrubberies. Mary, screaming like a maniac, caught at Pen for a shield, wheeled her about, dodging and panting, flung her aside and was gone again like an arrow, with the howling boys streaming after her.

"Aren't they savages?" Lucy said, descending the terrace's flowery levels with sturdy little Farmer's hands in hers. "I think I'll have to put that Mary of mine into boarding school in the fall! Come along, lover," she said to the baby. "There's Gram down there. We'll go down and see her."

Pen went into the cool airy hallway and ascended to her room. She closed the door behind her, crossed to one of the windows, and stood looking down at the gardens and stable yard and the oaks and pear trees that were sending long clean shadows across the lawn. It was Saturday afternoon; Tom and Ben Merry and young Mark and Concy's Gilbert were deep in a passionate game of croquet. Pen could tell who the partners were because Tom and Gilbert were continually moving off to confer secretly as to policy, and the other men kept together, too. At the side of the field Uncle Teege's wheeled chair was parked; he was watching interestedly, a group of young women sitting or lying on the grass near him.

Pen identified Hannah, Ann, the young Lucy who was Jeff's sister, Concy. Gentle Aunt 'Lizabeth was officiating at a tea table; the men came up and gulped ginger ale between shots.

Beyond the croquet lawn was a hedge, and beyond that berry bushes, the blackberries sending savage streamers into the air. Then came orchard, and a paddock where two or three riding horses and a pair of Shetlands were wandering loose. And then the high old-fashioned barns, and the sheds that were whitewashed as cleanly and trimly as a toy farm.

Her eyes fixed absently upon the beauty and peace of it, her senses unconsciously soothed by it, Pen fell into deep thought. She thought that these seniors of the clan had been pondering her affair, discussing it. She thought of Tom's advice, given her on the very day before Jeff's accident. They hadn't wanted her to marry Jeff, that was clear.

But now she had married Jeff; she had tasted this new sort of life; she had been, for a few strange weeks, with them but not of them. Some of them liked her, of course; Amy did, the children did, kindly, quiet Aunt 'Lizabeth did, and the old head of the house had put flowers at her place. But even these knew that she did not belong.

Yesterday her father and mother had come to Flaggwood for that casual call Penelope had been dreading, for that hour that had proved to be one of the most difficult of her life. Everything had been as unfortunate as unlucky chance could make it; the affectations of Ellabeth Fitzpercy had been increased and enhanced by the strain of the situation, and Pen's father, with his gallant assumption of magnificence, had put upon her the last bearable degree of shame. Perhaps feeling himself at a disadvantage, Marvin Fitzpercy had forced his cheerfulness, his familiarities, his miserably misplaced humor to a point which had embarrassed the Flaggs almost as much as it had Penelope; his dry little "eh, eh, eh?" had seemed to her never to stop. They had had cold drinks; they had been shown something of the place; they had gone. "You must dine with us some night soon," Pen's mother had said to Jeff's magnificent spectacled mother at parting. Aunt Margaret had made her lips smile graciously, had bent her stocky body in something like a bow. But Pen had known what she was thinking.

Standing in the window, she remembered all this. She remembered her own feeling of hurt and shame when at last the long call had ended—a wearied conviction that she did not belong to the new life and that she could never go back to the old. Where did she belong, then? Which road of the two hard roads was the way out?

She had said, only a few weeks ago, that she didn't love Jeff Flagg enough to marry him. But even while she had said it she had known that there were fear and pride in her answer to him. Fear that the dazzling prospect of entering the Flagg family as a member might be as suddenly, as capriciously, withdrawn as it had been extended; and pride that was ready to protect her in advance from that humiliation.

[174]

Well, all that was changed now. She was suddenly, bewilderingly, his wife. She had been a member of this household for six strange weeks; she had conferred with the other women of the family, Aunt Margaret, gentle Aunt 'Lizabeth, splendid, definite, dark-eyed Hannah. This world of fine voices, fine manners, of dancing, confident children in sandals and fresh sweet linen, of airy, orderly bedrooms where evening fires burned and fortunate little Flagg babies toasted their bare little toes, had been for a little while her world. Something deep within her hungered to be a part of it, to go on into the years sharing it, to give it to her children.

Jeff had seemed withdrawn from her since the night of their marriage. Nurses, doctors, an invalid's exacting routine had built a wall between them. Even now, with his last nurse dismissed and his full restoration to health only a matter of time, he needed Penelope less than he needed Mollie with the trays, Esther ready for his alcohol rub, his mother with the mystery stories.

But she could win him back. Penelope need only be tender with him, need only show him a readiness for companionship and affection to captivate him again. She had not shown him this because she had felt too insecure in her position, too uncertain of the next step.

But suppose she put hesitation and indecision behind her? Suppose, with Jeff's young love to help her, she accepted the conditions that made life difficult here? Suppose she attacked her task patiently, with grace and courage and, when she could manage it, laughter, disposing of each day's problems—the demands of her completely incalculable father, the watchful hostility of Jeff's formidable grandmother—as it came along?

A sudden light came into Pen's narrowed eyes; her heart rose on a wave of courage and determination. That was the way to go! The alternative, the annulment of her marriage, the smug acceptance of money in payment for the favor she had done the Flaggs, the wearisome proceeding of dispensing that money to pay Dad's bills, to pay Phil's bills, while the world said that Penelope Fitzpercy had been lucky, and could marry anyone she liked now, with all that Flagg money—no, it made her face flush with shame even to think of that road!

As for her feeling for Jeff, it was true, as she had told Persis, that nobody could dislike Jeff. Handsome, dark, sure of himself, full of laughter and nonsense, why shouldn't any woman love Jeff, as he grew older and steadier, took his place in the family firm or went on into diplomacy? If his wife's love were a matter of gradual developing, if their life and success and place in the family must be patiently built, slowly won, well, wasn't that the way the Flaggs did things, after all, steadily and with character and planning, not in emotional bursts, but building for tomorrow, and for the children of tomorrow, rather than for today?

Penelope could have laughed aloud in sudden ease of heart and mind. She had only to go straight forward now; life must be as she had decided it should be. It would conquer her no longer; she would master it instead and some day take her place as one of these cultured, these admirable Flagg women who were so pleasantly, so deeply secure in the dignified safety of wifehood, motherhood, womanhood.

"Well," she said aloud, "that's that!" And it seemed to her from that moment that it never could have been any other way.

After a while she raised her head, decision in her dark blue eyes. She went to her closet and took from it a certain gown; it had been Concy's; it was almost new. A full, delicate, gracious garment of creamy faint browns and golds, with an odd touch of burning turquoise here and there for relief. Penelope laid it carefully on the bed, went to the bathroom to run a bath, scattered crystals in the clear water that was green against the green tiles.

A little later she went into Jeff's room. She had asked him several times in the last twenty-four hours if he would like her to read to him, to work at a crossword puzzle, to play dominoes. He had always answered with a polite no. Martha Disco was gone; Jeff felt neglected and aggrieved.

Tonight she did not ask him. She brought the domino board and the tiles to his bedside and set them there, his eyes languidly following her. Before, without question, she began the game, she leaned over him, and her fragrance and sweetness, the touch of her firm young cheek, her lips in a kiss on his chin were his for a moment. She played better than he, but tonight she lost. Jeff was surprised when his dinner tray interrupted them at seven o'clock. Gosh, was it that late!

That night Penelope said she would teach him poker patience. He played very good poker, Tom said. She did not play poker, but she loved poker patience. Tom came in, and they played three handed; Jeff's mother mildly reproached them when she came up from a bridge game at ten o'clock to find them fighting hard. The sickroom was emptied then, but Penelope came back an hour later, perfumed and beautiful in her pajamas and robe, with her hair hanging in two splendid braids. She had a pillow and a comforter.

"Esther make you comfortable?" she asked. Esther was the brawny red-headed woman who for seven years had been Uncle Teege's nurse.

"What are you up to?"

"I'm going to sleep in here for a little while. I'll go back to my room if you get off nicely." Pen busied herself at the big couch. "Do you know that Cocky has slept at your door every one of these nights?" she asked. "Let's have him in just for a moment, tomorrow. Esther was telling me that he heard your voice tonight and nearly went out of his skin."

"Do you know that I've never seen you like this before?"

"Oh yes, you have! Remember the night I came down from the porch and we talked? But I'm glad if you've forgotten it. Now, remember you're to wake me, Jeff, if you feel in the least horrid, or can't get to sleep, or need anything."

She settled herself luxuriously in the pillows, drew the blanket neatly to her armpits, glanced over at him above her book.

"Want me to read?"

"Pen, why didn't you do this before?"

"Oh, the place was all cluttered up with nurses."

"Much more of this and I'll think you like me, Pen."

"You go to sleep, little boy. More poker patience tomorrow."

"And Cocky for a visit.

"This is kind of fun," he said sleepily. His sleeping pill was beginning to make him drowsy. "Don't go back in the night," he said. "I've gotten awfully babyish. I like someone to answer if I wake up all of a sudden and think that accursed car is sliding along that rock shoulder again."

Pen did not answer; she saw his eyelids lower. When 'Lizabeth Flagg slipped in, at six o'clock the next morning, she found them in the same positions; Jeff peacefully asleep, Pen curled deep in her comforter on the couch, with a gold braid hanging down almost to the floor.

CHAPTER XVIII

"Your Aunt Margaret tells me that you are taking care of the boy at night?" old Mrs Flagg said to her a day or two later, passing Pen in the upper hall. Jeff appeared to have a very special place in the hearts of the older women of the family, and his aunts 'Lizabeth and Hannah and his grandmother often spoke of him as "the boy," as if among the many boys he were unique.

"Well . . ." Pen said, temperately, warily. They looked at each other.

"Well!" the other woman echoed. She went her way and Pen went hers; the issue was fairly joined; the question Jeff's grandmother had not quite dared ask was answered. No turning back now.

Pen went downstairs to search for a certain magazine that contained a questionnaire that Jeff was anxious to try. In the library-window ingle were Hannah and Tom, talking. Tom was going into town; he and Hannah had not been discussing anything serious, at all events, Pen thought, for they separated easily enough, welcoming her.

"Hello, Pen. How's your sick man?"

"Uproarious. Throwing himself and everything else all over the place." Pen was looking over magazines at the long table.

"Tom, you'll be back tonight?" This was Hannah.

"Can't. Dinner for Petrie. Bore," Tom answered smilingly. "Good-bye, gals, be good! I'll telephone you as soon as I hear from Lucy, Hannah."

"I'll go out and see you off," Hannah said. Her dark face was alight; her dark eyes shone with mysterious inner radiance. Graceful and slender and light on her feet, her smooth black head inches below Tom's own dark head, she went away with him. Penelope went to the library window and stood looking out at them, on the terrace.

Rollin had brought Tom's roadster around to the drive. Tom and Hannah stood in the morning sunlight talking, smiling at each other. Penelope could see Hannah's uplifted face; Tom's face was partially hidden, for his back was turned, but from the outline of the hard brown jaw she knew when he was serious, and when that sudden smile of his illuminated his eyes and showed his white teeth.

"Wonderful to love any man as Hannah loves Tom!" Penelope thought. "Wouldn't it be wonderful to her to have him sick, and needing her, to be free to go up to his room and take care of him! If Tom were the one who had been hurt . . ."

The thought gave her strange pain; she did not know why. She thought it must be pity for Hannah, but the pity was strangely mixed with the memory of Tom's dark eyes crinkled into his kindly smile, of Tom's wide, firm Flagg mouth twitching with amusement. Frightening, to be in love with a man like Tom. Not like anything else in the world, the pain of caring for a man like that. . . .

"Penelope, I never was really in love with you before," Jeff said to her that evening.

"You thought you were."

"I know I did. But I didn't know anything about it. Having you come in here at night, and sleep on the couch there with your book—it's the darnedest thing that ever happened to me!" Jeff said. "I think about you all day."

It was ten o'clock. Jeff was settled off for the night; Pen had gone to her own room, had returned slippered and wrappered, and was now going about opening windows, extinguishing lights, arranging the invalid's bedside table. Presently she came back to her chair and to an idle last game of solitaire, and they talked alone together.

Jeff was in a state of great content, his Scotty was asleep on his feet, there had been an exciting prize fight on the air, and Tom and Mark and some of the others of Jeff's generation had come into Jeff's room and disposed themselves in a circle of chairs to listen to it. There had been betting. Jeff had laughed out with his old wild laugh, and Pen had seen again the quality in him that had been in eclipse during all these weeks since his accident—the quality that made them all love him and forgive him everything. He had been gay, witty, with odd flashes of power in his handsome dark eyes and new notes in his voice. Jeff was getting well.

When the others had gone, Pen sat at his bedside, working out her game of solitaire. Jeff, propped in pillows, was content idly to watch her moving fingers. "No, that goes on the stock pile," he would say; or, "You can play that ten-spot, Pen."

"Now the point is, Jeff," Pen said, still playing, "what are we to do?"

"What?" His eyes were instantly bewildered, troubled. "How d'you mean?" he asked.

"I mean that here we are, at the crossroads of our affair, and perhaps our lives," Pen said. She spoke quietly; Jeff hated things dramatized and made tense. "We either go on from here or we don't," she said. "We're married, and we're not married. How about it?"

"How about what?"

"Us. These last weeks," Pen said, "I've been asking myself, 'Do I love Jeff?' And the whole Flagg family," she added lightly, "has been asking itself, 'Does he love her?' Your grandmother, I think, would be glad to have us call it all off. You're only twenty-four, and you happen to be an especial favorite of hers."

"What are you talking about?" Jeff said gruffly. "Stop that damn game; let me hold your hand. What's all this?"

"Just that I think we ought to think it over, Jeff."

He was holding her hand now, smiling at her indulgently.

"Gosh, how women love to talk things over!"

"You see, it'll not be any too easy for me here, if we go on with it, Jeff."

"Go on with it! What else could we do? Listen, Pen, I love you. I told you so months ago; I love you more now than I did then. Listen. I've thought all day, these last days, of your coming in here at night. By gosh, that's why I'm getting well. It's because I'm happy. It's because you're here!"

"It was Martha last week," Pen said smiling. "It's anyone who takes care of you!"

"Oh, Martha! I'm crazy about Martha; she's a swell old war horse, and she used to rub my back, and throw me around like a sack! But you're my wife!"

He was eager, laughing, handsome in his blue-striped pajama jacket. Pen, looking at him, thought that it would be impossible for any woman to see Jeff quite unmoved.

"I'm beginning to like you so much, in spite of the fact that you're a spoiled baby!" she said.

"I'm not a spoiled baby. I'll do anything you want me to. But listen, Pen, why shouldn't we go on here, you and I, in the new apartment— I'm dying to see it! Then after Christmas I get back to work, graduate and take my bar exams a year from Christmas, or as soon as I can, take a holiday and go around the world or something and come home and settle down. Isn't that what they all *want* me to do?"

"I'm not so sure they want me in it. I think they don't feel very sure of me, and not at all sure of you! I think they feel that perhaps in a little while we'd throw the whole thing up, and have a Flagg scandal. Even your grandfather——

"I was talking to him this morning after breakfast, walking up and down on the terrace," Pen went on, as Jeff, still holding her hand, frowned at her and offered no interruption. "And even he seemed dubious. 'It all depends upon how much you love each other,' he said."

"They can all go to hell!" Jeff said simply.

"I think what I'm trying to say is this, Jeff: I hate divorce, but it's only fair to remind you that this wouldn't be a divorce, if you and I decided upon it. Our marriage could be easily annulled. Your grandmother'd like that, as much as any other solution. The whole thing has been too irregular for her. But that isn't the important thing. The important thing is, do we love each other enough to go on? To take that new apartment, and work hard, and go steadily ahead? It would mean your coaching from now on, working at least two hours a day. It would mean my biding my time, making friends with them all. There'd be terrible difficulties, you know. And my own family wouldn't help much! Isolde and the babies, poor little old Persis, Phil drinking and having accidents with the car, and now this delightful father I've told you about; they'd all be problems! And Mother, Mother most of all, because I never can hurt her, and she never will understand. All that—all that to handle somehow, and to make ourselves into fine people. Can we do it?"

He had been moving his lips and jerking his head impatiently when she started, as if he would interrupt her. But now he was looking at her very seriously, his brown thumb moving on her hand, his eyes thoughtful.

"I know I love you very much, Pen," he said simply; "if you go away from me it only means that I'll come after you. So that it's really up to you, dear. It's up to you to decide if you'll take the chance. I know you like me, don't you? Maybe you even love me. But you're not in love with me. Is that what scares you? I'm in love with you. Isn't that enough, to start on? I've been sick for seven weeks; I've not known what it was all about," Jeff went on, relapsing into the less elegant phrasing that was more characteristic of him. "But we start fresh from here. I've not had a drink for nearly two months; I'm going to stay on the wagon until I pass the bar, and then you and I'll go on a bender and tear up the carpets, huh?"

"Jeff, if we do it we mustn't fail in it! Sometimes it seems to me it's a good deal to undertake," Pen said. "There are a good many fine people in this family. There are six Thomas Jefferson Flaggs. They're all pitying us and discussing us and shaking their heads about us now. We're starting with a handicap. Can we do it? Do you want to think it over?"

"You fool!" the man said fondly. "You beautiful idiot! Of course we'll get away with it. We'll tell my dear old grandmother to take a long flying jump at herself. We'll tell the world tomorrow that we were married seven weeks ago, and move into our new house next week!"

"Jeff," she said, "it's a serious thing to do."

She had slipped to her knees beside the bed. Now he faced her with eyes as grave as her own, and laid his hand on her shoulder. Pen clasped her fingers about his free hand.

"You bet your life it's serious," he agreed.

"If we do it, we have to make a go of it, you know."

"I know what you mean," he said; "you mean that they all think we're going to fail."

"And she thinks so, especially. We can't let her be right, Jeff."

"We'll make a go of it, Pen. People do. I've been an awful rotter. Tom was quite right. I oughtn't to have married. But I've not had a drink now for seven weeks, and I feel like a fighting cock. As long as you love me, I'll not throw you down."

"I don't think you ever were so terrible a drinker, Jeff."

"Well, I used to boom a good deal."

"Your booming days are over," Pen said.

"You said it."

"Jeff," she said, still kneeling there, looking at him with thoughtful eyes, "do you believe in prayer?"

"You bet your life I do! I kind of do," Jeff said, the end of his sentence much less certain than the beginning. "Do you?"

"I think I do. We never went to any church, but Mother taught us our prayers. My grandparents, both sides, were church people. But I like to pray," Pen said. She looked at him with a sort of shamed courage. "Would you mind if I said a prayer now?" she asked.

"No, darling, and I'll say it with you," Jeff said, stirred.

"That we make a success of our marriage, and that we are always good."

"Right-o," he agreed. They said together the prayer beginning with "Our Father."

"Mrs Jeff."

"Mrs Lindenborg?"

Pen stopped, crossing the upper hallway, and arched interrogative eyebrows at the handsome old housekeeper.

"Would you mind steppin' into my room just a moment, please?"

"Surely not!" Pen went through a doorway she never had chanced to open before, and was in the back hallway with white arcades on all sides, and a glass door at the far end that gave upon an upper porch. Mrs Lindenborg escorted her to a square, pleasant corner room in which photographs of blond Swedish girls and babies and stalwart young men were everywhere.

"There was something I wanted to say to you." Mrs Lindenborg put forward a chair, and Pen sat down, and the housekeeper sat down, too. "You and Mr Jeff are moving into your own house on Thursday, aren't you?" the housekeeper asked. "I heard Miss Hannah telling the girls about making up the beds tomorrow and putting flowers about. I thought I'd like to tell you something. Has anyone ever told you of the sausage and apple pie party?"

"The sausage and apple pie——?"

"It's a great family for customs," the older woman said. "They like to do things the way they've always been done. And whenever anyone moves into a new house, they have the sausage and apple pie party."

"Oh, Lindy, I'm so glad you told me! I want," Penelope said, "always to do things like that. We move Thursday—when would we have it?"

"You'd have to have it Thursday night. That's it. I don't see that you could, not knowing the ropes, as it were, and with Mr Jeff so weak. But I thought it might be nice to ask them to have sausages and apple pie for the regular dinner in the house that night. I've forgotten," Mrs Lindenborg said, "just how it started, but it was 'way back in Puritan times. There was a young son married a girl, and the family I think was against it——"

"Ha!" Penelope interpolated, with a little rueful laugh.

"Anyway, the man's mother didn't think she was a good housekeeper. She might have had Indian blood, I'm not sure. So she told the mother-in-law that the day they moved into their cabin she'd have the whole family for dinner, and that was what she served them."

Pen was thinking, her brows knitted.

"Look here, Lindy, how many are we now? Fifteen?"

"I think there's nineteen when Mr Tom's down and the Merry children are here."

"Could we possibly have nineteen in that little place? What else would we have except the sausages and pie?"

"Nothing except bread and coffee."

"And could you get me the sausages?"

"Oh, they'd manage all that in the kitchen, Mrs Jeff, and we'd send the girls over with the silver and napkins and cups. But the thing is, would you want to try it, with Mr Jeff still weak, and so many to come over?"

"Lindy, I want to do it for a housewarming! And you must tell me exactly how it's always done. How do I ask them? And should Miss Hannah know about it, in case there's extra company?"

"Ah, but you see the whole point of it, Mrs Jeff, is that it must be a surprise."

Pen shook her head.

"How could we do that?"

"Well, that's where I was thinking you might really steal a march on them all. They wouldn't know you knew of it, much less that you were going to try it. Miss Ann, now, for instance," Lindenborg said, in her pleasant accents that from long years of association were almost as American as those of the Flaggs themselves, "when she and Mr Merry moved into their place here six years ago, they pretended to have forgotten all about it, they told Mrs Flagg that they were going to have an early dinner and go into town to dance. The table was set just as usual; they always do that downstairs, so that there won't be any hint. And then when the family gather for dinner Jean announces that dinner is being served in the Merry house, or at the Peter Flaggs', or wherever it happens to be, and they all go over there for their sausage and apple pie."

Pen's eyes were dancing.

"Lindy, you really think we might work it?"

"Well, I'm sure you could if you wanted to," the housekeeper said. "There'll be no hint of it; I doubt if even Mr Jeff'll think of it. I can have the girls smuggle the things over, and tell them in the kitchen that there isn't to be a word said. Indeed, I'll manage it all for you if you like. It was only that I didn't know how you felt about it."

"That's only day after tomorrow. You're sure you can?"

Mrs Lindenborg only laughed comfortably for reply. This was her business; she loved it. She was infinitely calmer than Pen was when the day of the Jefferson Flaggs' move came, and Pen and Teege's nurse carefully engineered the stretcher that two of the gardeners were carrying, carefully placed pillows and rugs, saw that Jeff was settled off for an afternoon rest after the excitements of the move.

"I've everything ready in the spare rooms downstairs," Mrs Lindenborg said, her faded Swedish blondness quite flushed with the conspirator's happy excitement. "Jean's settin' the table in the big house as usual, and there isn't one of them has any suspicion at all."

Pen was too restless to settle long to anything. She examined her new domain with infinite satisfaction. It was all perfect; her desk with its sheets of paper neatly engraved with the name "Flaggwood," the radio, the complete if tiny kitchen installed in a large closet, the great sleeping porch that looked into the woods. The aunts and cousins had made today an occasion for simple wedding presents to "Mrs Jeff." Pen saw her own monogram "P.F.F." on linen sheets and fat bath towels, would serve at least a few of her guests tonight with her own silver spoons. The tea and coffee service, on its heavy tray, came from Grandfather and Gram.

"They'll have their silver, I suppose?" the old woman had said grudgingly. "Of course they'll have it, Lucy!" the grandfather had answered. Pen had not heard the words, but she knew they had been said. Jeff's satisfaction in this particular present, and in all the presents, had helped to cure the hurt feeling that she was not entirely accepted by his people even now. The opening of every separate buff flannel bag had been delightful to him. There was a sort of exhibition in the afternoon, with the Merrys and Townes and Hannah, Aunt 'Lizabeth and Aunt Margaret and Aunt Hannah, Amy and Concy and various children coming over to look at Pen's presents.

When Jeff had had his six-o'clock supper Pen told him in cautious undertones of the great plan.

"Jeff, everyone's coming over here to supper tonight."

Jeff, his fork in a chocolate éclair, regarded his wife bewilderedly.

"What d'you mean?"

"Sausages and apple pie, dear!"

"Oh, for the Lord's sake!" Jeff ejaculated, after a stare. "I'd forgotten it!"

"Lindenborg told me."

"But you didn't—how the deuce——"

"It's all arranged downstairs here. Just as soon as I go to the house the maids will be over here. Everything's cooking at the big house; they'll just bring it over, and they've got napkins and plates and things all ready downstairs."

"Hannah fix it?"

"Hannah hasn't the slightest suspicion."

"Oh, look here!"

"I mean it. Nobody has! Lindenborg did it all. Jean's to make the announcement in the usual way, when he comes in to announce dinner. So be ready for the onslaught."

"You're taking this business of being a Flagg seriously, aren't you, Pen?" Jeff said presently, immensely pleased.

"Yes, I suppose I am. It seems to me a great adventure."

"Getting married to a handsome young man?"

"Well, that, too. But making something of—not of the family exactly; I don't mean that. But of being an American. Does it occur to you that your family is terribly American—what American families ought to be?"

"The old Hermione Mine is what set us up, Pen. My great-grandfather got hold of it in 1876. We never were rich before that."

"It isn't money only," Pen said, coming in and out of the sleeping porch as she went on with her dressing. "The Flaggs were always—*people*. In the Massachusetts days, when Hannah Carter made her sampler for General George Washington, and before that, when Dame Lucy Flagg opened a girls' school in Amherst—they were *people*. They worked hard and loved each other and believed in God. They made America. Someone —someone has to go on believing in America and thinking that the Constitution and the Declaration are great documents. It's—something to do."

Jeff was hardly listening. His thoughts had wandered.

"If you're right," he said, "and nobody suspects, it'll knock the old girl for a loop when Jean announces the sausage and apple pie dinner tonight!"

"Who else has done it, Jeff?"

"Oh, everyone! Ben and Ann and Uncle Peter and Amy, and Aunt Hannah after their new place was built."

"They wouldn't have told me," Pen said slowly, musing.

"Well, if they wouldn't, it's because they'd never dream that on the day they got me hauled over here on a stretcher, with nurses and hot-water bottles and everything else, you could entertain. How many will it be?"

"Nineteen, not counting you."

"Well, you see, they'd think it was out of the question!"

"Yes, I suppose they would," she said slowly. But a faint suspicion still lingered in her eyes.

When she was dressed she walked across the green lawn in early dusk to the house. It was September now, and lights were lighted in the hall. The flowers on the terraces were dim blots in the gloom; there was a wet chill already in the garden, and Pen found a wood fire blazing brightly in the library. A dozen of the older members of the family were gathered there; a chess game was in progress between Uncle Teege and his oldest son; Amy was at the piano; Gram, magnificent in flowing taffeta ruffles and lace tabs, the big emerald shining on her stout old hand, the Carter cameo at her throat, was in her usual chair. One by one the children began to straggle in, neat of head and respectfully lowered of voice, for Amy was singing "Adelaide," and old Thomas Jefferson Flagg was motionless, listening, his eyes watering.

Pen came in quietly and took a fireside chair, her white gown lost in its big embrace, her fine, long, nervous Fitzpercy hands clasped on the arms. Tom smiled at her over the chessboard, and when the music was stilled for a moment, asked her how her invalid had stood the strain of the day.

"Marvelously, Tom, thank you. He seems to feel wonderfully well."

"Gram was just reminding us of one more of the Flagg customs, Pen," gentle Aunt 'Lizabeth said in another interval.

"What one was that?"

"You'll think we've nothing but family customs."

"I love some of them," Pen said. She raised her gray-blue eyes to her husband's grandfather. "Flowers at breakfast," she said smilingly.

"Well, this one unfortunately we couldn't observe today, on account of Jeff's condition," Aunt Margaret, knitting busily, looking up with a flash of eyeglasses, explained for Aunt 'Lizabeth. "It's what we call the 'sausage and apple pie' dinner. It's always served on the night any family moves into a new house."

"Jeff and I should have had sausages and apple pie tonight, then?" Pen said mildly.

"Ah, my dear, we all know why you couldn't! The point is that it's served to the entire clan," Aunt Margaret said with relish.

Pen glanced about the library, caught Tom's eye again.

"A rather large order," she observed.

"Well, of course!"

"I remember the one at Aunt Ann's!" Mary Towne said animatedly. "'Member, Mother, when Tom put a sausage in with the goldfish?"

"The beginning of it," Aunt Margaret said, knitting, "was two hundred years ago when Amanda Flagg, the foster sister of the first Siamele, was moving into a new log cabin. Her mother-in-law didn't like her, she was a Poultney, and there'd been bad feeling, and she said that she didn't think Tom's house would be in order for a month, and she didn't expect to be asked to dine there for three.

"Somebody told Amanda—it was her daughter who married a Dutchman named Von Bagger, Tom, who was Amanda's grandfather," Aunt Margaret diverged to say, with a glance for Tom.

"I see," Tom said. Pen realized that Tom was supposedly to take Jeff's place as an admirer of the fascinating Amanda when she came to visit this autumn. She tried to read his face, but his expression betrayed nothing.

"Amanda," the narrator went on, "had two babies to raise, her sister's children. The sister had been killed in the raid where Siamele had saved the others. She had cotton and flax to weave and candles to make and fruit to put up and roots to get into her cellar. She wrote her grandmother in England a long letter about it—it's in our museum here. But she wasn't going to be downed by her husband's mother!"

In spite of herself Pen raised her eyes to meet those of Jeff's grandmother. Mrs Flagg was looking straight at her; Pen had known she would be. The look hung; the older eyes turned first.

"So, the night she moved in," Margaret Flagg was continuing, "Amanda sent a message to her mother-in-law, and to everyone else in the clan, that she would expect them to dinner. And she served sausages and apple pies to thirty-one of them, and she and her mother-in-law made up their differences that night, and became tremendous friends, and she wore the emerald for forty-one years!"

"At least that's the way we hope it ended, Aunt Mag," Tom said, sitting back after moving a chess piece. "This poor old man, enfeebled in wits as well as in body," he added, of his father, "apparently has walked open-eyed into my trap. He is suffering the torments of the damned!"

"Well, Tom, well, Tom," Uncle Teege said, scraping an aquiline chin with an invalid's thin clean hand, "I wouldn't say that, my boy. I wouldn't say that exactly . . ."

"Castle, Teege," the older Hannah said.

"Not out of check, if you *please*, Aunt Hannah," Tom protested.

"Oh, I didn't know!"

Pen looked at the board uncomprehendingly; she made up her mind that she would learn to play chess. Perhaps forty years from now, when she was Aunt Hannah's age, in this same library someone would be playing with her. She thought of her surprise, and her heart beat fast. This being a Flagg had its moments!

CHAPTER XIX

All nineteen of them were in the library half an hour later when Jean appeared at the door.

"Dinner will be served this evening in Mr Jefferson's house, madam," he said. Pen tried afterward to describe to Jeff the sensation that ensued. But the incredulous gasps, the laughter, the sudden outburst of clapping and exclamation, the enthusiasm with which the Flaggs set out across the lawn for the first hospitality of the new home were quite beyond her powers of reproducing. She remembered Hannah's amazed eyes, Tom's triumphant: "Ah, good for you, Pen!" and the old man's pride. "I knew she would if we gave her a chance!" he said.

"And what did Gram do?" Jeff demanded, eager for every detail.

"She just got to her feet—you know that sort of farmer's-wife squareness she has as she gets to her feet, as if she were going to put her arms akimbo and sell eggs or something—and said, 'Well! Will you give me your arm, Mark?' and she and Mark started off at the head of the procession. I was helping Tom with Uncle Teege's chair, so I didn't hear what she said, if she said anything."

"She doesn't like you, eh?" Jeff said thoughtfully.

"No, she doesn't like me."

"But why?"

"I can see why," Pen said, with a sigh. "But I'm not done with her yet!" she added, under her breath.

"What did you say?"

"Nothing."

It was after ten o'clock; the guests had streamed away in a laughing confusion of congratulations and thanks; an army of maids had removed the last traces of the plates and cups, the last bits of sausages and apple pie. The party had been a tremendous success, the completeness of the surprise starting it off in a burst of enthusiasm that had carried it well on its way.

In her sitting room Pen had had chairs for a dozen grown-ups ranged in a circle; three or four card tables had been scattered about; piles of forks, coffee cups and napkins were ready. It was a part of the tradition that the hostess should serve her guests herself; Pen had gone back and forth tirelessly in her plain white dress; Tom, acting host in Jeff's place, had been a tower of strength to her. And with their customary good breeding the Flaggs had played their parts wholeheartedly, Uncle Peter telling a story, Uncle Teege catching up the flung ball, Ben Merry and Jim Towne doing their share, the women praising everything, and Amy finally at the piano playing songs that everyone could sing for a last quarter-hour. And as a crowning event, Grandfather had solemnly read aloud "The Hanging of the Crane."

Now it was all over—another milestone in the Flagg history. Jeff, lying back in his pillows, and Pen, wandering to and fro at her undressing, discussing it happily. There was a low light at Jeff's bedside on the sleeping porch; the dressing room was lighted, and a little fire was burning there in the brick fireplace. Chill sweet air came in through the porch wire nettings; an autumn moon flooded the night with silver.

"It was all perfect, Pen."

"It was fun. I had nothing to do with it really, of course. If I'd had to make the sausages, as the original Amanda did, I couldn't possibly have done it. And yet I don't know . . ." Pen said musingly. "The things you actually have to do, chopping and sweeping and cooking, aren't half as hard as some of the other things. What are other Flagg customs, Jeff?"

"You'll have to ask Hannah. The ring, for one thing, if you call that a custom. The emerald Gram wears. It always goes to the next important."

"That'd be Uncle Teege's wife, then; that'd be Aunt 'Lizabeth? And then Tom's wife, if he marries?"

"Not necessarily. It's whoever Gram gives it to. She wasn't a Flagg, you know; her mother-in-law gave it to her. I suppose," Jeff added, "because she was the kind that runs things. Aunt 'Lizabeth ought to have it next, but she's so gentle and quiet she wouldn't wear it. Aunt Hannah's dying for it, but of course she isn't a Flagg now; she's a Beville-Atwood. Mother's the one that wants it. She was an Ogilvie, but her mother was a Farmer, and the Farmers all go back to the Flaggs. And what George's wife would like," Jeff ended, laughing, "is to have Aunt 'Lizabeth die and Tom not marry and the ring come to her. She's only twenty-two, Emily, but she's got her eye on it! It stands for something more than just a ring; it's a sort of sign. It's just one more of the Flagg superstitions," Jeff said. "You got away with the sausage and apple pie dinner one tonight with bells on, and I'll tell you all of 'em as I think of 'em, if you like 'em so much! Well, here we are in our own house, Pen; we've gotten that far! How do you like taking charge of your old crippled husband?"

She came, in her wrapper and braids, in her young beauty and sweetness, to sit on his bed and hold his hand. All the lights in the new house were out now except the reading light at Jeff's elbow.

"Jeff, do you speak French?"

"Oui, Madame."

"I mean, how does it happen you do?"

"They sent me over with Mark when I was fourteen. Aunt Hannah took us; she was just widowed then. Ann and Lucy were married and

Hannah was out in society and doing Junior League and things. We lived in St Cloud; we hated it, but we did get some French. I've forgotten a lot. The kids always go over. Didn't you hear them talking about taking Frank and Bill and Tom and Mary over?"

"Do you play chess, Jeff?"

"I know the moves. You've got to be born with a growth in the brain to play chess."

"Jeff, how much do you know about Shakespeare?"

"Say, what is this, a questionnaire?"

"No." Pen laughed, went away to bring his sleeping draught of milk made bitter with some sedative drug, came back to praise her little kitchen, went off once more, and came back again to say of it, as she had said of a hundred other details of the new house's furnishings that day: "It's so complete!"

But when he was drowsing off and she was reading a little later, the books she had carried to her bedside were a Spanish grammar and a fat red volume entitled *History and Civilization*.

In the days that followed, Jeff watched her moving about her little kingdom serenely and happily. He loved to see her brushing her glorious mane of pale gold hair; he loved to see her dressed in the new blue gown, the dull gold gown, fresh and perfumed and lovely, ready to go over to the big house for lunch or dinner. His people drifted through his sickroom; Hannah, fine, affectionate and amusing; Ann and Ben; George with his pretty, ambitious wife; strange Amy, fitfully gay, fitfully sad; Uncle Peter and the aunts, and his busily knitting mother. The grandmother came for a few minutes every day; the grandfather usually called immediately after breakfast when Jeff was having his own breakfast and his letters and his newspapers, and Pen was clearing things up, emptying cigarette trays into the fireplace, straightening chairs, sharpening Jeff's pencils for his crossword puzzles, or moving the card table nearer to the bed. It was cold autumn weather now, the days brilliantly clear and hot as soon as the inevitable morning fog had lifted; the nights sharp and cold, with fires blazing in the library and dining room and in the Jeffs' snug little apartment upstairs in the guest house.

Every hour Jeff loved his wife more. It became an idolatry, this feeling that the rapidly convalescing man knew for the tall, golden-crowned girl who came and went in his room all day long, and who knelt beside his bed every night and buried her head in her hands, and prayed that their marriage might be a success.

She came to love him, too, truly and deeply and satisfyingly to herself. It was not passion, but then a young wife could scarcely feel passion for the bridegroom who was so weak, who was still in the shadow of so serious an illness, who depended upon her like a child for his trays, for company and amusement, and to have his face sponged and his pajamas changed. Pen and Uncle Teege's nurse made up the bed freshly twice a day; when the day came that saw Jeff feebly walking to a blanketed and pillowed fireside chair, once more a living figure in the family group, he cried with weakness for very joy, and Pen felt her own eyelids prick, too.

Her mother and Persis came to see her, and he watched her handle that situation, too. Marvin Fitzpercy had gone to Hollywood now, taking Philip with him; Pen was happy to see her own people, was full of questions. They had taken a taxicab from the village, Mrs Fitzpercy and Persis; Penelope saw that they had the right things to eat and drink, showed them everything that she thought would interest them, including the family museum, and drove them home at five o'clock. It broke her heart to leave them at the cottage in Armitage Lane; everything there looked shabbier than ever, and more shrunken, and Persis seemed young and sweet to be condemned to that dry and ugly environment, but there was no help for it at the moment. Penelope drove back alone, planning. If she could have Persis for a visit—but no, that would not be possible. Persis would not be happy in the Flagg environment, and Penelope had her hands full without any further complications.

She went in to see Isolde, sharply resentful and unhappy over the prospect of another baby, and the sisters sat in the studio all through a rainy afternoon, watching the twins toddle and stumble about the drafty, splintery floor, and discussing the problems of women's lives. Kelly Quentin was living in the same building now; he presently came downstairs, and they had tea with canned milk in it, and bakery rolls, eaten from the end of the studio worktable, with its litter of papers and plaster and crayons and tubes. A collector called with a gas bill; three months—twenty-one dollars. Penelope paid it quickly, almost ashamedly. Isolde was still sweet, despite her ironies and bitterness of speech; but she was swamped, buried in duties and responsibilities that were far beyond her strength or capabilities. Pen thought she had been made a nervous and exhausted shadow of her old self.

"Grandy doesn't seem to think that this sort of thing is awfully hard on Isolde!" Pen said to Kelly, when he walked down with her to her car.

"Why, they seem to me terribly happy!" Kelly said, elevating his eyebrows.

"It isn't that. They're devoted enough, and I think in her heart she'd rather have Grandy get an engagement to play at a funeral than have—well, any amount of money," Pen began. Kelly interrupted her, as she glanced at him for approval. His expression was rather one of surprise.

"Why, you know darned well she would!" he exclaimed.

"I suppose so," Penelope agreed, letting the subject drop, and with a sense of dissatisfaction suddenly pervading her being. Life had gone flat. If to be rich like the Flaggs was still to have problems and difficulties, to be struggling in San Francisco's Bohemia with twin babies and an impecunious genius of a husband was a little too much the other way. Never a dull moment for Isolde!

"You seem very happy, Pen," Kelly said, in a tone of casual politeness.

"I *am* very happy. Jeff's almost well, you know."

"Shall you go on living with the other family?"

"I don't think so. I believe," Penelope said, at the wheel of her car now, "I believe that Jeff and I are to have a holiday in Hawaii, and then come back, just before Christmas, so that we can get a good start at law school in the new term. We'll have a little place in town here."

"Honolulu, hey? Things have changed, haven't they?"

"Things have changed." She raised her dark eyelashes, and he saw the quiet smile in her eyes. He wondered if she was acting.

"Has he—your husband, much law work to make up?"

"About three quarters, I think it is. He could take his bar examinations next year, if he's well enough to work."

"And meanwhile you go to Honolulu?"

Her eyes shone as she nodded. There was a pause, then Kelly said: "He's lucky."

"I'm lucky, too," Penelope said. And quite suddenly she felt that it was true; she *was* lucky to be able to escape from the old uncertain world of debts and doubts and unpaid bills into the Flagg world of order and plenty, steamer reservations, new luggage smartly banded with the Flaggs' unvarying green and white.

"If it hadn't been for that accident to Jefferson Flagg, Pen, you might have taken your chance with me," Kelly said, in a low, shamed tone. "You remember that Sunday night when we talked, and you said that at least you didn't like anyone else better?"

"Ah, but that was before—that was a long time ago!"

"Ever think of it?" he persisted unhappily.

"Well, not now!" she said, with an uncomfortable little laugh. This mood in Kelly distressed her. For years Kelly had drifted through the home scene, a lounging slender figure in painty old cords and a thin shirt; she had taken him and his adoration for granted. She didn't like to be reminded of the ease with which she had brushed it aside; she didn't like to think that Kelly had a right to resentment. There was even a faint resentment on her own part in the feeling this reproach from him caused her, and she told herself—and almost for the first time—that it was Jeff that she loved, of the two. If occasionally, in considering her marriage to Jeff, she knew moments of vague doubt, they were nothing to what she would have experienced had she renounced Jeff, and had there been no accident to precipitate matters, and had she married Kelly!

"You're happy, aren't you?" he said jealously, watching the expressions that crossed her face.

"I am happy," Pen answered gently. He had had no business to ask it, of course, but she was sorry for him, and answered as kindly as a mother might. There was a moment's pause, then the man said suddenly, abandoning the conversation almost roughly,

"Well, good-bye then!"

"Good-bye, Kelly!" Pen said. Immediately she was driving away, emitting an audible "whew-w!" of relief as she went. It was good to have that conversation over. It was good to feel that the few minutes' talk with Kelly had cleared the air for her, had dispersed the various little uncertainties that had fretted her when she thought about him. She didn't love Kelly; she never could have loved him, really. And discovering that would make it all the easier to love Jeff wholeheartedly. She felt loyal to Jeff; she liked the feeling of being loyal to her husband. Kelly's manner had invited complaint; she had made no complaint. She loved Jeff—yes, even seeing his faults and knowing his weaknesses, it was impossible not to love handsome, assured, masterful Jeff. It was good to be going home to him, to regale him with the home news, to make the Fitzpercys' makeshifts and compromises amusing.

"When you are glad to go home to a person," Penelope said half aloud, driving along, "that's proof that you love that person. Or like him, anyway," she presently added, in her thoughts. "I wonder if marriage could be a success," she mused, "if the husband adored the wife, and she only liked him tremendously."

Presently she was thinking of her own family. Her visit to them had left the usual sting; contacts with her own people, with her old life, were invariably hurtful. She could do so little for her mother, for Isolde and Persis, and they did so little for themselves! They drifted along, never quite finished with the housework, never putting into execution the plans that they made so readily, never quite fully dressed, never wholly out of debt. A great impatience toward them all possessed her, yet under it she felt the pain of love and loyalty stronger than ever.

She had a brown dress with a checked brown-and-cream silk blouse, and a loose brown coat to go over all, and a brown hat. She had three evening dresses, and some white silks for the beach. There were tickets; there were things to be sent to Stateroom B 32. Jeff was well again, and he and she were going on their honeymoon. Jeff had a letter to a Honolulu bank; they were to be gone thirty-seven marvelous days, rich and young and just married, free to buy what they liked and do what they pleased as they traveled away into the sunshine of the blue seas.

"Mom, if you could go!" Penelope said. "Or Persis."

"Oh, shut up!" Persis countered. "This is your trip. I'll have mine!"

To Penelope it all began to seem somewhat dreamy and confused. Things, she mused, were not what they seemed in this life. To go off to Honolulu for a month's holiday would have sounded like the maddest of dreams a year ago. Now here she was actually sailing, with the letters of her name marked smartly on her luggage, and flowers in her stateroom, and friends on the pier laughing and flinging streamers of paper ribbon into the air. And yet something was aching inside; in her soul she was longing to share this with Mother and Persis and patient Isolde; longing to take the two baby boys along and give their small pale faces the benefit of beaches and sea air; in her soul she was perhaps a little unsure of this buoyant new husband, who was already greeting old friends and making new ones on board, who already seemed to have escaped from her care, and to have returned to the mood of that Jeff Flagg whose wild moods had so worried his mother and father a few months earlier.

When the city, spread upon her hills, was left behind them, and they had passed through the Gate into the western sunset, she and Jeff examined every inch of their gay pink chintz cabin, negotiated with the stewardess for vases, read letters and telegrams, unpacked their belongings. On a shelf above Pen's bed, she ranged her books; her brushes, her jars of creams and powders found their allotted places. All this was incredibly gay and thrilling, and now that she was committed to the trip, and by no miracle could Persis or her mother share it, she abandoned herself to the joy of it with a free heart. Everything enchanted her, and Jeff, who had made ocean voyages before, was enchanted with her delight.

In that milky dusk that spreads over the ocean at the close of day they walked about the almost deserted decks. The ocean looked cold and wintry; the line of coast off toward the east was to be placed only by the occasional wink of a lighthouse. A few uncomfortable travelers, well rolled in rugs, and preferring the fast gathering cold and night to the odors of cabins and dining rooms, were in their chairs.

Pen and Jeff leaned on the rail and stared at the water that was rushing so swiftly away into the dark. A gong sounded behind them, dressing call. Jeff, his arm tight about her, gave a shudder of sheer excitement and happiness and said: "Do you realize that we're alone at last, and married, and off on our honeymoon, and that this is our wedding night?"

"I think I've been realizing it all day," Pen said, turning toward him, for a moment in the gloom, the shine of her dark eyes; turning away again.

"I'll tell you something else," he said. "We're going to celebrate with a quart of wine at supper."

"Oh, Jeff, no!" She was back in her old mood for a moment. "De Vecchio said no wine, you know!"

"De Vecchio is enjoying his own dinner and some Tipo Chianti at this very second," Jeff said with a laugh. "Forget De Vecchio, darling! I'm going to have wine with my dinner. If he has Imperial Crown '21, then I'm going to have Imperial Crown '21."

"Now, Jeff, that would be crazy. He said so. And you promised me that you'd surely be on the wagon until you passed your finals in law school."

"Oh, come, but not on my honeymoon! Listen, don't go righteous on me, Pen, and begin to watch me, and worry about what I do! Be a sport.

We've got to drink our own health tonight, and Mom and Dad, and your people. I'm well, now!"

"Jeff, no wine. Positively."

"Well, we'll see. Come on, we have to dress for dinner," he said. And Pen knew from his tone that he was really annoyed.

"Married to one of the Flaggs," she said to herself, as she dressed. "Married to one of the Flaggs and off to Honolulu for a honeymoon. Mrs Thomas Jefferson Flagg."

She looked at Jeff, still a little sulky as he got himself into his dinner clothes; and she looked at the dark sea rushing past the ports, and heard the dinner gong in the passage. And it was all so strange that she felt as if she never had seen this man before, as if she were not Penelope Fitzpercy at all.

CHAPTER XX

"Oh, Jeff, what a lot!" Penelope ejaculated, when, upon their return from Honolulu, she and he settled down for their first discussion of ways and means. The allowance that Uncle Mark was making his son seemed to her enormous.

"It would be if we had it," Jeff admitted, in a moment of deep sudden gloom.

"How d'you mean 'if we had it'?"

"Well, gosh, we owe so much money, Pen!"

"Owe money? How? Jeff, we can't!" Pen was aghast.

"That feller has my note, you know," Jeff said. "The poker game."

"That man on the boat?"

"Sure. And then—oh, well, I like buying you things," Jeff said. "Don't worry, Pen," he went on with a laugh, as she looked anxious. "It'll all work out. I'll pay it off. We'll get a lot of checks for Christmas."

She thought of the things he had bought her on their Honolulu trip— a delicious lacy white stole, some pink-white corals, a great tapa cloth worked in angles of brown and paler brown. He had been overdrawing, of course.

They mustn't begin this way. Pen looked very serious.

"Dad would clear it all up, now that we're really getting started," Jeff said. "But I hate to touch the old boy again."

"*We'll* clear it up," Pen said determinedly. "I'll do my own work, we'll not buy a thing. With five hundred a month, Jeff, we ought to be simply rolling in money!"

And even as she spoke she remembered that her mother had quietly "borrowed" twenty dollars from her a day or two earlier, and had told Penelope quite frankly that Persis, who had a job in a Palo Alto bookstore now, was buying a two-hundred-dollar fur coat on the installment plan.

"I thought maybe big sister would like to pay the balance and give her a happy surprise," Mrs Fitzpercy had suggested. Penelope had only smiled in rather sickly fashion, in reply. Rent was ninety dollars, any sort of maid would expect nearly that, and Jeff was reckless in such matters as telephone calls, sending his suits to the cleaner, jumping into taxis, bringing home flowers to his wife. Problems again, life seemed to be nothing but problems!

They had found a small apartment on Washington Street in San Francisco, with a bay view. Its four rooms were squarely and unimaginatively set—bedroom, living room, dining room, kitchen; there was nothing particularly attractive about it. But it was clean and bright and not too oppressively furnished, and as Penelope was to do most of her own work and Jeff would be working hard, it seemed entirely adequate. They moved into it in late October, and on the first of November Jeff reported to his law classes and settled down to hard work.

Jeff's father and mother, the stout dictatorial "Aunt Margaret" and quiet "Uncle Mark" of the group, came up to have dinner with their son and his wife, and all the other members of the family called in due time, even the grandmother stopping in on an afternoon to exchange a few remarks with Jeff and to listen to what Pen said with her usual air of wariness, before declining tea, declining anything else to eat or drink, and going upon her way.

Tom came in often; only for a few minutes, perhaps, but always with his air of quiet and affectionate interest. Hannah came twice a week, at odd hours. Sometimes she found Penelope busy in her little kitchen at ten in the morning; sometimes she found Persis there, for Persis loved to come in and lunch with Jeff and Pen. Once for two days Penelope had the Tasker babies to care for; Hannah with characteristic kindness talked of a change of diet for them. "You ought to be as fat as butter balls, boys," she told them seriously.

Jeff came home for lunch, and liked it to be hearty; Penelope had no trouble here, for fine shops were close by, and everything connected with housekeeping was made easy for her. Lima beans and peas came shelled in neat white cartons; applesauce and fig puddings and corned beef hash were available at any moment in cans, and Jeff's favorite soups merely had to be heated. She could have an ice whenever she liked by merely mixing it and putting it into her refrigerator; and she had the services of a well-trained young colored maid in the afternoons.

Luncheon was easy, but clearing up after luncheon in the quiet of early afternoon took perhaps an hour. Dishwashing, brushing away of crumbs, putting away of plates and napkins and china, darkening of the kitchen and final adjustment of odds and ends in the refrigerator—these things were all trifles in themselves, but they had a way of mounting up into real work, and Penelope would be flushed and tumbled and spotted and breathless by the time she had finished them.

Then what? A bath and a walk, perhaps a movie alone, or a call on Isolde. Or perhaps they could get Isolde's Mrs Machini to keep an eye on the boys, and Isolde would go to the movie, too. Movies always were longer than the sisters expected them to be. Somehow one always thought of a movie program as taking two hours. But if there were a vaudeville show, or if the feature picture were important, it was always after five o'clock when they emerged, weary and dreamy and drugged with entertainment, into the street.

Then the procedure was hard. Penelope had to think. What was it that she had written down on that careful list at breakfast as necessary for dinner, and where was the nearest place to find it? The trouble with lists was that almost invariably she forgot to put them into her purse.

She was a bad manager and made unnecessary work for herself. She would stand in the street in the windy coolness of the late afternoon, trying to decide.

"I told her I'd bring home artichokes," she might tell Isolde. The reference was to the colored woman who came in at five to cook dinner every night.

"But it's nearly six, Pen," Isolde might protest. "They take almost an hour."

"Yes, and Jeff likes them cold, too. I ought to have all these things in the house; sometimes I do. But today Mother came in and wanted me to go shopping with her, and we lunched downtown. . . . I don't know what we'll have."

But Isolde was never anxious. She had no such strain to encounter; Grandy did not care what time dinner was served, and rather liked to help prepare it. He could always waste a completely happy half-hour at the piano, or he would sit spooning cereal into the little boys with perfect patience. Sometimes the Taskers did not dine until nine o'clock, and then it was a comfortable meal, dragging itself on into the night indefinitely.

It was different with Pen. Jeff came home hungry and jaded and had nothing of which to think except his food. "When do we eat?" he would ask, even while Pen and Carolyn were hastily and guiltily washing the new potatoes, or tying a string about the bundle of raw asparagus. With the superabundant meals of Flaggwood for his standard, it was quite natural that he should like certain things served in certain ways; he was quite unconscious of being in the least critical or exacting, and Penelope acquitted him of either feeling. But his quiet assumption that crab legs always came in a bed of ice with quartered lemons about them, that a green salad must have a hint of garlic and a sprinkling of chives, and that grapefruit were naturally halved and seeded and delicately loosened from shell and fiber, made difficulties for Penelope. Breakfast and luncheon she could manage, but the dinner struggle broke her spirit and tired her thoroughly.

Carolyn did not come on Thursday nights. Pen was stunned by the rapidity of their recurrence. On Thursday nights, when the smoke from broiling chops had faded from the kitchen, and the potato salad from the delicatessen shop and the cheese cake from the bakery had provided a satisfying meal, there was the monotonous problem of clearing up to face. If she piled things in the sink, then they would all be there, down to the last spoon, the last bit of greasy paper, the last cigarette ash and burned match, for consideration in the bright fresh morning. The toast would taste of mutton, and the congealed grease in the broiling oven melt and smell; the coffee percolator must be cleaned. It was not pleasant to sit down to breakfast in a litter of dishes and crumbs.

Perhaps she had managed to slip into the bedroom just before serving dinner, and freshen herself, brush her hair smoothly, get into a lacy housecoat. Now she must change again; one couldn't wash dishes with orchid and turquoise ribbons dangling into the dishpan.

"I simply marvel," she said, "that millions of women do this every day. If you could only do it for eight hours on a stretch, and then be done for three days! But it's like a chain pulling you back all the time."

"We always did it at home," Isolde offered.

"Ah, yes; but that was different! Everybody came drifting into the kitchen at all hours and fried an egg or cut up a tomato. If there wasn't any bread we took crackers or made waffles. I remember Mother and I living on French toast last winter, because it was easy and Kelly's uncle had sent him that big can of syrup. It's quite different when you have to think of soup and meat and vegetables and salads and desserts and coffee, and keep them all moving."

"Maybe you feed him too well, Pen."

"I don't think so. I certainly don't begin to give him as much as the menu in the paper says every morning. We only have two, or at least three, courses. But twice a day seems to leave no time in between at all. Or at least it wouldn't, if I did everything I ought to do. I'm always forgetting to put milk bottles out, and letting things sour, and running out of vinegar or sugar or something five minutes before dinner!"

"Ah, well, you've not got twins to manage, too," Isolde commented. Pen looked at her with speculative eyes.

"I don't see how you *do* it!"

"You do it because you *have* to do it!" Isolde said darkly.

CHAPTER XXI

She and Jeff began to form a habit of dining at Carlotta's on Thursday nights. To reach Carlotta's they left the apartment house's big brick doorway in the early evening breeze, walked three steep blocks downhill, crossed an arterial avenue of movies and Italian and Chinese shops, and entered a small alley. They must be there at six o'clock sharp or at seven o'clock sharp; Carlotta served meals only at the two hours, and admitted no stragglers. The *antipasti* were slammed down in a thick white platter; the *minestrone* came smoking and plentiful and delicious in a great bowl. The bread was sour and fresh; there was no butter, but there was good hot meat or fish, and a salad glittering with pure olive oil, and there were always weazened but eatable apples or oranges or pears for a finish, with soft creamy cheese and sweet strong coffee. And the charge was fifty cents.

The Flaggs always paid more for their dinner, however, because Jeff liked a bottle of red wine with the meal, and a cocktail to start it. To see him drinking made Pen uneasy, but it didn't seem to harm him, and he was in much better spirits the moment the heating alcohol rested and invigorated him. Both tired, they would grow sleepy over their meal and sit idly talking long after it was finished. Jeff always had law studying to do at home, but often they did not start for home until nine, and nine o'clock was exactly the hour when the second show began at the movies.

"Let's see if it will be on tomorrow night, Jeff, and then we can have a light early supper and you can get two good hours of work in before nine o'clock."

"Or let's slip in now and just see it, Pen, and then tomorrow we won't come out at all."

They loved each other; they were very happy in their little home. Jeff was perhaps most the lover, and Pen's attitude toward him still partook somewhat of the nurse and mother, but they were much too content to analyze their separate reactions too closely, and when Jeff asked, as he continually did: "Do you love me, darling?" Pen would stretch her cheek up toward his kiss affectionately, and answer quite honestly: "You know I do!"

Arranging their books and silver, they laughed a great deal; he caught at her hand and kissed it as she passed him; she stooped, going behind his chair, and rested her cheek against his dark head. They were always going to do great things; get up early on Sunday mornings and take long walks, paint the back porch, get next term's law course and study it in advance, and so be ready for it when the new term began.

But just living and loving occupied them fully. Whenever there was a holiday they slept late, dawdling over their breakfast and their newspapers at ten o'clock; perhaps then they would walk over to Isolde's, waste another hour or two in idle talk and laughter, discover with consternation that it was three o'clock, and depart hastily so that Pen could do her breakfast dishes and Jeff put in a really serious hour of work before it was time to go down to Gram's. They dined at Flaggwood every alternate Sunday night; sometimes there were only a dozen at the table, sometimes thirty. Jeff's father would perhaps ask him a question or two about his law work, but otherwise they felt themselves free from all observation or restraint; nobody asked them how they spent their allowance, or how Jeff was progressing. Whether he would coach in midsummer, or whether they would take all those long months for a holiday, was a question to be settled only by themselves.

Other Sundays they might drive down to the cottage in Armitage Lane, or Philip would drive his mother and sister in to dine with them, or there might be a salad and canned corned beef at Isolde's, with Kelly added to the group. Jeff liked the freedom of the studio and the cold beer; he and Pen were always late in getting home on these occasions, and Monday usually started with long heart-rending yawns, groans, and a general sense of dragging and weariness.

Now and then as the brief Western winter melted into spring, and the hot Easter holidays were upon the city, he took too much to drink, and became garrulous and truculent; once at Carlotta's table, and once at Isolde's, and at another time, but on this occasion not so noticeably, when some old friends came in to call before dinner, and there was a dice game on the dining-room table. Penelope's fine jaw began to tighten a little grimly at the new problem; she was not going to be a moralist or a "dry" or anything like that, but she did not propose to go through with Jeff what a woman had to bear when her husband drank! She hated Jeff in that condition. Not that he was ever disagreeable to her, but he was silly and unmanageable, and his serious heavy asseverations and protests were only a little less annoying than his sleepy, laughing apologies the next morning. It wasn't anything terrible, but it was so idiotic!

They had not been married long before old friends of Jeff found them; certain young couples like themselves, whose families were financing them through the first hard years of bond or insurance selling, certain detached young men who formed a habit of dropping in at the Flaggs' late in the afternoon for what Penelope continued to call "tea." She called it tea even though tea was never served. Cocktails and little crackers with cheese browned upon them and potato chips were popular; and after the roulette game was introduced, the men drank highballs abstractedly, their eyes on the green cloth.

It was Ned Truax who brought the roulette game; one of the factors that blinded Penelope in the beginning to its insidious danger was the chance that Tom was there that afternoon, and Tom seemed to understand everything about roulette, and insisted that if they play at all they play with a revolving bank, and for an almost inconsiderable stake. Five-cent bets, Tom decreed, and everyone cheerfully bought twenty chips, and started off with great laughter and casualness. Ned, small and redheaded and lisping, was in law school with Jeff; everyone felt that Ned was clever, but he was of the engaging, incurable, attractive-scamp type, and Penelope never felt quite sure of him or comfortable about his influence on Jeff.

Ned said that a friend of his had had the roulette wheel, and did not use it any more because it had broken him, and so had said that Ned could borrow it.

"Can't buy 'em in the shops!" Ned told Pen.

"Some you can," Tom said abstractedly, busily counting chips into stacks.

"Illegal, though."

"Sure, it's illegal."

"Oh, Tom, why?" Penelope asked.

"Well, when they kicked out the tables in France," Tom said, "they said that on the races a man lost his own money, and that on the roulette wheel he lost the company's money."

"But not this kind of a silly game at home," Pen said.

"Oh no; and we're changing the bank around, so that everyone gets a chance!"

That was in February. Within a few weeks' time it had become the custom to have a roulette game every afternoon. Half a dozen, ten players would come in; often the men would bring a bottle of gin or whisky, so that the young hospitality of the Flaggs would not be too seriously strained. Six o'clock, seven o'clock, eight o'clock often struck before the eager, intent group broke and the players began to scatter.

Penelope had never seen a roulette wheel in her life before. She knew nothing of it except that it was the game that made Monte Carlo so famous, and that men had won and lost fortunes at the wheel. But from the beginning she did not like it; it made her uneasy. Gambling of any sort was bad; the men laughed as they complained of losses of ninety cents or a dollar and a quarter, but she noticed that they became as excited over these ventures as they could possibly have been over real stakes.

She never played herself. Once she spoke to Hannah about it. Hannah laughed.

"What do they buy, the original stake, I mean?"

"Twenty chips for a dollar. Usually they start with a dollar. Or maybe a man will play with silver dimes."

"Do you play, Pen?"

"Oh, never. And I wish Jeff wouldn't! But the thing is, Hannah, if he doesn't play here, maybe one of the others will start it up, and that means he won't be home."

"Isn't Jeff working pretty hard?"

"Yes, he is, really. He studies hard in the evenings, unless he gets sleepy. And Thursday evenings we usually go to a movie. This is just for an hour or so before dinner."

"Well," Hannah said after thought, "it probably won't last. It may be like miniature golf or one of those things people play like mad for a while. I wouldn't worry."

"Well, I'll be glad when it's over!" Penelope said, somewhat reassured. "I loathe it!"

Yet the days upon which, for one reason or another, there was no game, seemed oddly to lack spice, and when Penelope cleaned the dining room after luncheon she always set the green cloth and the wheel with its ivory ball in readiness for the afternoon. When Jeff came in he might have Ned with him; others would presently come up the stairs. Talk of yesterday's luck, of the number that repeated three times, of the number that hadn't come up during a whole afternoon's play, was absorbing to them all.

"I think we ought to play the zero—or the double zero, anyway. You can't in a home game. I don't think we ought to take chits; chits are the things that ruin you. The columns are all right unless you're simply out of luck, as Marge was the other night. You can't beat that kind of luck. The first time she stayed off the middle column two came up, and when she was out in the kitchen with Pen, if two didn't come up again, and she'd been on two for three nights running to my personal knowledge! Can Marge afford to lose fourteen and eleven and nineteen dollars every week that way, Jeff? Red Miller hasn't stopped, don't you fool yourself! What he did last night was go downtown and get into a real game."

The zinging clatter of the ball, the rattle of chips, the men laughing ruefully as they took new fives and tens from their wallets, all became routine. Yet Pen never felt easy about it. In her sleep she saw the sharp ridges and the numbers: red, black, red, and the sticky glasses and the hard young hands.

"It's—whoopee, it's red!" cried the croupier. "Take your hand away, Jeff, and let's see it! There she blows—my little baby! Gol dern it," some man would mutter under his breath, "she refused me. Hung right over it and went on. Count me out ten bucks more, will you, Pen?"

The men all liked Pen, and the women adored her. She was simple, friendly, sympathetic. But she soon discovered that where gambling—even this modest informal sort of gambling—reigned, every other human emotion was subject to it. An accidental addition to the group, an unexpected caller, might look on amusedly for a spin or two. But eventually the fever caught them all one by one, and the money was forthcoming, and with a little laugh of excitement the new victim had pushed his way into the tense circle and was watching red and black, odd and even, with the rest.

Pen and Jeff had their first quarrel over the roulette game. It came late one night when the crowd had stayed to play until almost eight, when Pen and Jeff had gone out to too heavy a dinner, with too much wine, and when after a poor movie they returned to the flat at midnight to find the undisturbed ashes and poker chips, torn chits, tumbled chairs, dirty dishes and empty glasses. White and tired, Pen merely glanced at the disorder with a face of distaste, trailing through it to the bedroom. Jeff looked at the green cloth.

"You little spiteful pellet!" he said addressing the ivory ball. "You played me for a sucker, didn't you?"

"How much did you lose, Jeff?"

"Oh, I don't know. The third column didn't come for sixteen spins. Can you tie that? I kept doubling on the other two. After the fifth time the third column didn't show, I thought it was a cinch. Lord, I don't understand how a contraption like that can be so contrary."

"But weren't you ahead once?"

"Sure I was—couple of hundred."

"Well, it seems to me," Pen said wearily, sitting down to remove a shoe with a dropped hand, "it seems to me senseless to risk so *much* money when you're winning. If you're losing you'll play quarters; that's all right. But I never can get this theory that when you're winning you ought to stack on chips the way you do. It made me sick to see Red raking it off!"

"He's got a chit of mine for something, too. Forty-two, I think it is."

"Well, you're spoiling the game, gambling so high!" Pen said in sudden bitterness. "We can't afford it. And we're in so deep now that we have to go on to get it back! We can't let Rose and Ned stop now; Ned says he's a thousand ahead."

"Ned's crazy!"

"You're crazy," Penelope said, still bitter at the memory of those red and blue chips piled so high, before the very last spin, and destined to be swept away like the leaves of autumn. "You're crazy not to salt a little down, every time you win! Last night you had one nickel left and you put it on eleven, and eleven came. If it had been a five, look what you'd have won!"

"Well, don't blame me when she runs that way!"

"Well, I certainly didn't start this roulette thing!"

"Yes, but you're glad enough to have the money when we win!"

"I am not! I'm nervous all the time and excited all the time, and it's your fault! If you were like most men, and took your responsibilities *seriously*—instead of drinking too much and gambling all the time . . ."

They were off. It was completely terrifying to Pen; she never had quarreled this way with him or anyone else before. She was presently crying violently; she flung herself into bed and buried her face in the pillow, sobbing. It seemed to her that she had nothing worth while for which to go on living, and the thought of Red triumphing over his winnings stung her like a nettle.

There was a long silence. Jeff, who had not started to undress, went into the bathroom. Later she heard him in the other rooms jerking chairs, snapping off lights. Pen dried her eyes and, still breathing hard, opened her book and made herself read.

"Want a drink of water?" Jeff called.

"No, thanks!" Her heart began to beat normally again. He wasn't angry.

Presently Jeff, undressed and buttoning the frogs of his pajamas, came about the bed and knelt down beside her and put an arm about her. Pen, reading on her pillows, her hair loosened into a gold coil on her shoulder, her discarded clothes in a ring on the floor, raised her eyes from the page, and they smiled shamefacedly at each other.

"Don't be mad at me, Pen."

"I'm not mad at you, Jeff!" Her arm was about his neck and her cheek against his. "I'm a fool," she said penitently.

"There's one thing about roulette, Pen. If you lose it one day you get it back the next."

"I don't know . . ." she said doubtfully. But as it chanced, Jeff was lucky the next afternoon, and won everything in sight, and Pen, still not comfortable, still convinced that all this was unwise, was nevertheless restored to spirits again.

Their utter freedom, hers and Jeff's, amazed her. They could take a day off when they felt like it, and drift about the bay on Red Miller's little boat, eating sandwiches, drinking long cold drinks, and listening to the radio. They could sleep all day Sunday if they were tired, stay up all night, decide against dinner in favor of a movie and late supper, invite the roulette group to stay on for scrambled eggs and coffee.

"Do what you want to, have a good time!" was Jeff's easy creed.

"But, Jeff, oughtn't we be working and worrying about something?"

"Ah, that's your New England, my dear, battling with your Irish! If you were all Irish you'd know that all you have to do is what you like to do. And if you were New England you wouldn't want to do anything but work and pray and run the flag up on the Fourth of July. As it is, when you're good you think it's dull and you're wasting your time, and when you're bad you worry!"

"I presume the way we are going on *is* completely immoral," Pen said dubiously.

"Well, Ben Merry, with his nose stuck into his father's lumber business, might think so, and George might think so, because George hasn't ever stepped off the beaten track in his life! But you wouldn't want to marry Ben or George."

"Tom, now. Would Tom think we were crazy?" Tom had been in the East for two months; Pen had often wondered what he would think of the roulette developments.

"Oh, well, no. Tom's a good sport! Tom'd think it was all right," Jeff said. He laughed, and after a moment repeated, "Tom's a good sport," in a tone that said plainly that only a good sport could possibly think so.

"I wish I knew where we are going," Pen said. "We appear to be on our way."

"I wish they'd send us abroad this summer," Jeff said. Instantly her face lighted.

"Jeff, is there the slightest chance of it?"

"I don't think so."

"But suppose you graduate from law college with honors?"

"Ha!" Jeff said. "I may not graduate at all. I may have to coach all summer and take the bar exams sometime next spring!"

Pen experienced a moment of chill.

"Oh. But wouldn't that disappoint them terribly?"

"It's much wiser," Jeff said, scraping a freshly shaven cheek with his big hand. "It's much wiser to skip a term, and take 'em when you know you're ready, than flunk."

"Oh." A silence of enlightenment on her part. "Ned Truax, will he flunk?" Pen asked then.

"Ned wasn't laid up the way I was for three months."

"I wish they were over, and you in the firm!" Pen sighed.

"I wish they'd send us to Rio," Jeff said. It was still another exciting thing to hope. Pen's gray-blue eyes glowed again.

"Is somebody going?"

"If we get the light-and-power case, and if Carter comes home."

"Jeff, wouldn't that be glorious!"

"Darn it, I have to get through first!"

They were on their way to spend a week end at Flaggwood. Tom had been in town the night before for a dinner; he would call for them and take them down. Jeff kept him waiting while he hunted vainly for a law book. "I ought to do some reading tonight," Jeff said. Pen somewhat timidly asked Tom, as they drove down through the country that was now in the full flood of early summer glory, if the bar exams were very hard.

"Pretty stiff," he answered with his pleasant brief smile for her.

"Did you have a terrible time with them, Tom?"

"Well, no; not as bad as I thought. I'd been dreading them, as I daresay Jeff is. But we Flaggs more or less *have* to pass the bar," Tom said. "Afterward we do other things, politics and diplomacy and business. But we're all lawyers first."

"Do you *like* the law, Tom?"

"Love it!"

"I don't think Jeff does."

"Ah, well," Tom said, "he's been cramming now, that's always bad. But just as soon as he's passed he'll feel like a new man."

Penelope was silent, painfully aware that Jeff had not done any cramming at all, that he had forgotten his books for days at a time, that he had done no work at all at night. But then Jeff was bold and he was lucky; perhaps he did not have to study the way the other men did. Jeff was lucky!

When they reached Flaggwood it reminded her of her first sight of it, now nearly a year ago. It had seemed another world to her then, an unattainable world in which super beings flitted about in white frocks on green grass; mellow shadows made a setting for brown children at a pool; maids came and went with trays of cold chicken and bowls of salad.

Now she belonged there. Now someone was ready to carry her bag and Jeff's to "Mrs Jefferson's rooms," now the various exalted members of the once impressive group welcomed her: "Ah, hello, dear. Hello, Jeff. You're just in time to swim if you want to swim; the children have gone to get into their suits. Mother, here are Jeff and Penelope. Change into something cool, Pen, and come down on the lawn; it's much cooler. Uncle Teege and Uncle Mark are finishing their chess tournament there, and it's quite thrilling."

This last was Hannah; she paused for a moment, dark eyes on Tom's face.

"Hello, Tom. It seems too good to have you back in the picture again!"

"Two months away were plenty," said Tom. He and Hannah walked toward the big house together, and Pen heard the notes in Hannah's voice, saw the look in her brown face. The tides of the big family's life began to wash about her again; here was her brisk mother-in-law in charge of a small grandnephew, the two-year-old Farmer Towne; here was Uncle Teege, waving a hand that held a captured pawn; here was her brother-in-law Mark, introducing a pretty girl named "Jimmy."

"Law finals next week, poor Jeff!" old Judge Farmer said.

"Is he worrying horribly, Pen?"

"You know Jeff. He never worries about anything."

"But he gets through," said his little sister Peggy jealously.

Pen went on to her cool airy rooms, where there were spikes of blue delphinium and pink roses in bowls, to match the blue and pink of the wallpapers. There were guests in the downstairs rooms for this week end; she could hear a man's laugh and smell a cigar. The smell, or the hot trip, or the shade after the blazing sun, made her feel suddenly ill and she lay down for a moment, closing her eyes, resting.

Amy came in to see her—a strangely excited and restless Amy, who could seem to settle down to nothing, answered Pen's questions absently, studied herself in the mirror almost uninterruptedly. Later Pen thought that the presence of a handsome British captain, Desmond Dunne, who was one of the guests, had something to do with it. Amy, perhaps, was embarked upon another affair. Whatever the cause, she was certainly rejuvenated, and Penelope began to perceive that she really was beautiful in her discontented, delicate way.

After dinner they went to the gallery and had charades. There was a low platform at one end of the gallery, and a curtain, and footlights; back of these were two or three rooms used for dressing. Penelope was in a charade with Tom and young Lucy and the Merry children. The word was "pioneer." Pen, in improvised hoop skirts and a scoop bonnet, guiding little Frank and Bill across open praries, talking of Indians and water holes and covered wagons, was so lovely that there was complete stillness during the final performance, and Ben Merry even forgot to draw the curtain.

"Gram was delighted with 'pioneer.' She said you were a born actress, Pen," Hannah said, afterward.

"Did she say that?"

"Indeed she did."

Pen would perhaps have said that she despised her husband's grandmother, but she was oddly touched and pleased with the praise, and a little later when she found herself near the old woman, as the audience settled itself for a last charade, she ventured, quite unexpectedly to herself, upon a timid smile in her direction.

"That was a fine charade, my dear," old Mrs Flagg said instantly. "You and the little boys looking toward the West."

"I was thinking how wonderful those women were," Pen said simply.

"Wonderful!" There were actual tears in the old woman's eyes. "I could have watched you a long time," she said. "I like to think of their courage. No other nation produces women like that!"

Pen, to her amazement, as the lights went down, found herself settled on a pillow almost at Mrs Flagg's knee. And somehow she liked sitting there.

The last charade, performed to a chorus of hysterical squeaks by Mary and Thomas Towne, aged eight and ten, and the two Merry boys, was "resolute." Whether it really was funny or not Pen could not tell, for the children's acting was so bad and their own mirth so contagious that she and the entire audience laughed until they cried. The first syllable was illustrated by Mary as a colored Mammy urging her white charges to res' themselves; the second was Franklin in a poor imitation of Ed Wynn's "So-o-o——"; the last was celestial in character, with redeemed souls playing lutes as they wandered about in long togas made of sheets. The acting of the entire word the audience found beyond all bearing: four giggling, stumbling, ridiculously clad children representing themselves as travelers to Vesuvius, vigorously clad in large flowered hats, eyeglasses, dusters, an evening hat, galoshes, expressed themselves as resolved not to see the volcano. Mark Flagg, impersonating the volcano under a pyramid of chair legs and rugs, obligingly flung handfuls of cornstarch into the air at appropriate intervals.

CHAPTER XXII

The little apartment in Washington Street, with one big fly buzzing over unwashed dishes in the sink, and the roulette disorder occupying the darkened dining room, seemed very far away to Pen, and once again she wondered if she and Jeff were abusing their new freedom, wondered if they were wasting hours, days, weeks whose opportunities might not come back again. Somehow one felt differently about these things at Flaggwood.

Persis and Phil came to luncheon on the lawn the next day; Persis' beauty was open sesame everywhere, and Pen thought she had never seen her brother so quiet, so nice, so generally satisfactory. There was only one bad moment between the sisters, and that was when Penelope, ashamed that she had not seen Isolde for several days, asked Persis what the plans for the summer were.

"I don't think Isolde'll come down," Persis said.

"She's not going to stay in town!"

"Well, there's the new baby coming in late August, Pen. She can't count on getting in to her hospital and doctor on time. The car's usually out of order. She's made arrangements at St Luke's; I think it's only ten a week. But there'll be someone else in the room with her."

"Perhaps we ought to manage to get the boys away from her for a while, and give her a good rest."

"I would, but Mother simply can't. She's having these headaches, and she's nervous; she's not heard from Dad for weeks, and she's always afraid he'll come in."

"I'll try to get over to Isolde's oftener," Pen said soberly. She had not been very faithful, now that there were so many hot days, and so many nights when she was too much excited and tired to sleep. She had not felt particularly energetic, and the punctual demands of breakfast dishes, luncheon flurry, marketing, brushing crumbs and making beds, attacking luncheon dishes again, had been burdensome of late.

"I'll see Isolde tomorrow," she said, more in promise to herself than to Persis.

"Shall you and Jeff be here all summer, Pen?"

"I imagine so. He's dying to travel somewhere, but I think we'll be here."

"Travel!" Persis echoed. "Where could you possibly travel that would be as wonderful as this! The pool and the garden and fruit and cream and fresh eggs and the library and the woods!"

"I know; it is lovely," Pen said, ashamed again.

When the Clines had taken them home after supper that night, Pen said to Jeff: "Would anything be gained by our stopping the roulette short, and your digging like mad for the rest of the term?"

"Who's been talking?" Jeff asked.

"Nobody. That is, nobody about you. But everyone talks of the finals as if they were pretty stiff. And the bar exams after that!"

"The beauty of them is," Jeff said, with a rending yawn, "that you take 'em in March, and you don't know until September if you've passed 'em or not!"

"Oh, Jeff, how horrible!"

"Isn't it? Dad," Jeff continued, snapping the top from a bottle of beer, and pouring it foaming into a tall glass, "says I ought to go into the office this vacation, and work around and get the feel of it."

"In town here?"

"Yip."

"Oh." It was not a thrilling prospect. "Just for practice? Then that means we stay here."

"Go down to Flaggwood week ends."

"Jeff."

"Huh?" he said. He had been walking away with his beer. He turned and looked at her. Penelope was sitting at the kitchen table; she had taken off her white hat, and her hair was crushed. The kitchen was in complete disorder from a hurried luncheon the day before; Penelope looked about at it and sighed, brought her tired eyes again to Jeff's face.

"I think I'm elected," she said simply.

"Huh?" Jeff said again. He stared at her aghast. "You don't!" he whispered.

Penelope said nothing. Tears came into her eyes. There was a silence.

"I feel rotten all the time," she confessed presently.

"Oh, gosh," Jeff murmured, sitting down. He looked awed. "What makes you think so?"

"Amy thinks so."

"What'd she say?"

"Oh, she was talking to me last night when we were dressing for dinner. You were playing croquet, remember? She said it was hellish," Pen said with a rueful laugh. "It wasn't definite. She just hoped it—it wasn't."

"Ha! She would. D'you mind so much, Pen?"

"Well, just now—before you've passed your bar, and while things are so unsettled. It means expense, and my being laid up. . . .

"I hadn't thought about it; I guess that's what scares me," Pen added, as Jeff fell suddenly thoughtful and stared into space with a knitted brow.

"As far as the expense goes, the old man'll take care of that," Jeff said absently, after a moment.

"He may not like it."

"Oh, he'll be tickled to death. First grandchild. Uncle Teege has two grandchildren, and Aunt Hannah's got a pack; he'll like it as far as that goes! But it's a complication," Jeff said.

"It may not be so," Penelope observed. "It is, though," she added with conviction.

Her increasing discomfort and languor confirmed the suspicion hourly; she managed an early luncheon a day or two later and went to see Isolde. The day was hot and still; Penelope felt her forehead wet as she climbed Isolde's stairs. Her sister was lying down; she looked weary and ill. The little boys were inexhaustibly active, bumping their heads, entering upon violent baby quarrels, cramming their small hands into the unwiped little mouths where teeth were pressing through the hot gums.

"Come on, Sis, let's take them out to the Park!"

"I couldn't, Pen. I feel too utterly rotten. If I could just get about an hour's sleep—without *hearing* them, and *worrying* about them——" Isolde said.

"Where's Grandy?"

"He has to give his lessons in Breuner's studio—too much noise here. Take that away from him, Pen."

"I *think*——" Pen said half aloud. The rest of the phrase was not expressed. She wiped her nephews' faces with a wet towel, put on their rumpled jackets. She drew down the shades of the studio and put a light rug over Isolde's feet. "Come on, boys," she said, "we'll go bye-bye."

The double perambulator was downstairs, chained to a ring in the wall under the area stairs. Penelope, panting now with the exertion of managing two babies and her handbag, wheeled them out into the street, found a shady bit of sidewalk and meditated. Now what?

Her own apartment was not very far away, but the streets went steeply up and down between it and Isolde's house, and even when she reached it there would be nothing to do with the babies there. So she went to the Park instead and managed to fill two endless hours, jogging the carriage as the other women did when the babies fretted, moving on to another neighborhood and another bench when they roared, and thankful beyond all expressing when they finally fell asleep.

"I ought to do this every day or two," she mused. "Poor Isolde! Twenty-six years old, and all she wants is just to sleep and rest!"

When Jeff came home at five that afternoon he found Penelope sound asleep in the bedroom, and several of the roulette group being elaborately quiet in the dining room as they stacked chips and whispered about "hunches." Pen aroused herself smiling and bewildered, her hair in a tangle, her neck and forehead sticky.

"Was it terrible?" she asked, of the law-school finals.

"Not so bad." He was lucky that afternoon, and wanted to take her to the "Palace" for dinner. But Pen was too tired to go; she lay on her bed sipping hot milk and presently sent him out to dinner. She heard him telephoning a friend; he did not return until after three o'clock in the morning. Through the hot hours she lay wakeful and nervous, wondering where Jeff was and what he was doing. When he finally came in, trying to be quiet, stepping about with elaborate caution in dim light, she was lying on her side with shut eyes, apparently asleep. Penelope did not speak to him then; it would have been useless. He would retain no memory of it in the morning even if words meant anything to him now.

The main difficulty in this particular crisis, and it was not the first of its kind, was that Jeff really had two natures. When he was not drinking, when he was shaved and fresh and studying hard and enthusiastic about his meals, he was one man. At his worst, he was quite another. It seemed to him, and even at times it seemed to Penelope, unfair to blame the fine, sober, self-respecting better partner for what the other man did.

"I know, I know, gosh, don't rub it in!" Jeff would say, stricken and bewildered, when she reproached him. "Why don't you stop me when I start in?"

"Because you don't *hear* me then, Jeff!"

"I know. I'm rotten. But I'm on the wagon now, until after the exams, and then we'll go down to Flaggwood for two weeks' vacation anyway, and they'll keep an eye on me there."

So for a few nights there was no roulette; Jeff dined simply at home and afterward got at his law books. On that Sunday he went to the library, coming home jaded and hungry for a late dinner.

"Is it going all right, Jeff?" Pen had spent the day amusing the Tasker babies, spoiling Isolde; she was as tired as he.

"Not a prayer!" he said.

"You mean you may not pass?" Penelope demanded in consternation.

"Not a prayer!" he said again.

Five days later they went down to Flaggwood. The big family group welcomed them as usual. Splashing and laughter sounded from the pool; tennis balls were snapping on the court; Tom and three other men were deep in a furious game of croquet. The day was the perfection of summer glory; flowers were blazing everywhere, and lawn sprinklers flinging their punctual jets of diamonds over the green lawns.

"Gosh, it's good to be here!" Jeff said. He glanced at Penelope, who was slowly going about unpacking. "Don't be mad at me, Pen," he said. "I'll get hell the minute my mother sees this eye. Stand by me!"

"What are you going to tell her?" Pen said coldly and wearily. "We might as well get together."

"I'm going to say that you and I were dining at an Italian restaurant and a fellow got lippy and I socked him."

"Be sure to bring me in."

"You can't make me feel any worse than I do."

"I was at Isolde's," Pen said stonily, "keeping salad cool for you, waiting and waiting. You came in with a rag on your forehead and a policeman! I don't know what to do, Jeff! It's awful. Nobody could stand it."

"You were awfully kind to me. I'll never forget it."

"I despise myself for being kind to you. But what else can I do? I can't make a scene before Grandison and Kelly. I can't come out into the street yelling like the Italian grocery woman. I certainly," Pen said, trembling, "I certainly wouldn't be nice to you if I knew anything else to do! And this morning," she went on, summarizing her wrongs in a low, steady voice, "this morning you tell me that you never took your finals at all."

"Well, listen, Pen," Jeff said, dogged yet ashamed, "it's no excuse, but the reason I got pie-eyed is because I slipped up the exams. And the reason I fell off the wagon was to forget the whole damn thing! D'you think I wanted to go tell the old man that I'd flunked, and that that was on my record? I've got a pretty hot record as it is, what with flunking last year, and being laid up for three months! I talked it over with Rogers, and he said he thought I'd be much smarter not to take 'em."

"You mean it's all to do over again, next fall?"

"Well, it ought to be a pipe next fall if I coach this summer."

"Jeff, your father will feel terrible! But where were you, then, all Tuesday and Tuesday night? You said you were going to somebody's house to study. You didn't come home to dinner; you were late at Isolde's yesterday——"

"I know."

"But where *were* you?"

"Oh, booming, I guess."

"Ah, Jeff," she said slowly, softly, looking away. Tears came to his eyes.

"I got into a game with some fellers. I had no business to play; I couldn't read the dice."

"Lose?"

He nodded, and Penelope's heart turned to ice.

"Much?"

"Yip."

His manner was more and more terrifying to her. This was bad, or he would not have broken it to her in this way.

"How much, for instance?"

"Oh, a lot. About seventeen hundred, I guess."

"Seventeen hundred!" She sat stunned. "But we *have* it, Jeff?" she asked anxiously.

"Have it? How d'you mean?"

"Well, we have—I mean our allowance, and Aunt Hannah's birthday check, and Uncle George's check?"

Sitting handsome and haggard on the edge of a chair with his white trousers on and his white shirt unbuttoned, Jeff made an eloquent gesture with spread hands.

"Gone!" Pen whispered, aghast.

"*Aw* gone!" Jeff announced with little Tom Cline's air of baby triumph. But he did not smile.

"Jeff, it couldn't be!"

"It is. Why, what d'you think we've been doing it all on, the cocktail parties and all the rest of it? Some afternoons those fellers got away with two bottles of gin! And there were always flowers and taxis, and our rent's a hundred."

"You mean—but then—but then you'll have to ask your father to pay your gambling debts?"

It seemed like an echo from some story she had read; not like herself speaking. Married to a rich young man whose father had to pay his debts.

"Looks so," Jeff said briefly.

"My clothes, I suppose, and having the maid," Penelope presently said slowly, thinking.

"Everything counts up."

"We haven't done what they hoped we'd do, Jeff."

"Here's the thing," he said; "if you'd let me tell Dad about the baby everything'd be swell."

"How do you mean?" A flush had come into her face. "I thought we wouldn't tell anyone for a while," she said.

"His first grandchild. He'd be tickled pink, and Mother too. They'll let us off everything."

"I hate to do that. I'm hardly sure myself."

"I'd tell 'em you oughtn't to be agitated and excited, see? How about it?"

She still hesitated. "I hate to do that."

"Well, we'll have to do something, or we'll be out of luck."

"I blame myself, letting things get into this jam," Penelope said, thinking.

"You're not to blame! I'm the one that's to blame."

"Stupid, stupid, stupid of me!" she murmured, not speaking to him. And in the weary heat of the afternoon and the physical discomfort that was her first signal of approaching motherhood, she realized vaguely, yet with strengthening conviction, that she would always have one supreme responsibility, one oldest child, and that the responsibility and the child were Jeff.

She looked at him seriously, thoughtfully. He was talking, telling her about last night's events.

"It started in with quarters, Pen; I give you my word. This man Ross, whoever he is, took the bones out of his pocket and just said casually, 'If we're not going to Brewer's let's roll dice for fifteen minutes.' He said he had to get home by six, and it was after five then."

"And when did he get home?"

"Well, about the time I came to Isolde's the next day. He telephoned his wife; she was all right about it; and I went to sleep, and I thought I'd feel fresh when I waked up, and go home too. But then when I waked up I said I'd stay for three rolls, and it was all coming my way, and I got the dice. And I give you my word, Pen, I couldn't lose 'em until— well, I was pretty deep in when it broke again. Then I won some back. I wouldn't quit forty-five hundred loser."

"Jeff, don't you realize what that *means!* Don't you realize that there are people in the world to whom that would be a *fortune?*"

"I could have made it as well as lost it, Pen."

"But do you mean now that your father or someone will have to pay all that good money over to a man you just happened to meet and roll dice with?"

"Oh, we'll fix it up someway," Jeff said. "It's getting you mad that worries me. Don't be mad at me, darling. I love you so much, honest I do."

He was kneeling beside her, his arms about her. Pen laid a hand on his shoulder and drooped her face so that it touched his.

"I know you do, dear," she said gently.

"Jeff!" Tom's voice shouted outside. "Croquet!"

"Oh, coming!" he shouted back. And in another moment he was gone. Penelope slowly dressed, her face very grave, and followed him out to the lawn.

CHAPTER XXIII

The holiday life of the clan was moving in full swing. Small babies staggered and stumbled on the shadowy stretch of the lawn; four youngsters in their early teens were on the tennis court. At the side of the croquet field an audience was grouped, old Mrs Flagg dominant in it, other younger women in white and light colors watching the game, commenting upon it as the players came up to rest between bouts.

Concy Forsythe and the man she was to marry in a few days' time came across the grass; they had been to a wedding together; Concy looked flushed and lovely. Mary Cline, Tom's younger sister, had a magazine questionnaire and a pencil; she was filling in all gaps with questions. "Amy, George, Jud, of what national language are the following words?"

Uncle Teege was working out a chess problem, staring thoughtfully at a board upon which a few pieces had been set. Jeff's mother was knitting; once she called a small child who was skulking past under cover of bushes and tree trunks. "Sally, come here and let me measure this!"

"I'll be capshered, Aunt Mar'gret," Amy's redhead said pathetically.

"No, you won't be captured! I want to see how this is across the shoulders."

Penelope, joining the circle, smiled rather uncertainly at one after another, answering greetings only in monosyllables. She sank into a chair, and when Mary's enchanting Tom, aged two, came to her knee, she drew him up and began once again to tell him the story of the naughty bowwow who barked at the pussy and tried to eat up the cream.

Tom and Frank Merry, Bruce Bannister and Judson Forsythe Flagg were playing croquet. Jeff was nowhere in sight. Pen awaited a moment until Tom, panting and deeply concerned over the game, was near enough to have her speak to him without being overheard.

"Tom, where's Jeff?"

Tom gave her a serious glance. He was a little out of breath; his white shirt was open at the throat; his brown, hard legs emerged from white shorts.

"Want to see Mother's prize-winning phlox?" he asked.

Pen immediately rose, and they walked toward the stretch of border flowers near by.

"The ones I entered in the show were larger than any of those, Pen," Tom's gentle mother called after her.

They looked at the phlox.

"Jeff's in awful shape," Tom said then. "I sent him back to bed to make up some sleep. I don't know whether we can do anything for that eye or not. I asked Esther to take something up to put on it. He went off the reservation, eh?"

Pen nodded; tears came into her eyes.

"Walk on with me here; be looking at the delphinium. There, those low things—what are those? I never remember flowers."

"Stock and wallflowers," she said steadily. "Those cr-cr-creamy ones are st-st-stock."

"Don't cry, Pen. We've got to go back; it's my shot. Pull yourself together. It was the finals, I suppose? He had to celebrate?"

She could only look at him; she dared not trust her voice.

"I'll come up to your place just before dinner," Tom said quickly. "Take that chair next to Mother and talk flowers. She'll talk about flowers all night."

"Jackson," Aunt 'Lizabeth said without preamble, as Pen sank into a chair beside her, "Jackson should have all the credit. He's really a remarkable gardener. He has been splendid." She lowered her tone. "May I ask you something, Pen?" she asked, with a cautious glance about.

Pen's heart sank. Her wet eyelashes had betrayed her, or perhaps something in her color or expression told this older mother that there was to be a baby. But no . . .

"I don't want him to hear me—I don't want him to see my lips move," Mrs Flagg was saying. "But tell me, do you think your Uncle Teege is looking ill?"

"Uncle Teege?" Pen echoed in surprise. She had been too deeply absorbed in her own problem even to see Uncle Teege; he was there in his wheeled chair, working at his chessboard, but she had not looked directly at him. Now she did so, and instantly and involuntarily turned startled eyes toward Aunt 'Lizabeth. "He does look rather pale," she said. "Has he had a cold?"

"The doctor said that he was in absolutely perfect health except for his —lameness," his wife said quickly, anxiously. "Lameness," Pen thought, was hardly the word. Uncle Teege had been completely crippled in one arm and one leg for twenty-one years. He could not stand. "You think he's pale? But then the others are so burned!" Elizabeth said.

"You had the doctor, Aunt 'Lizabeth?"

"Well, he happened to be here. Emily's baby swallowed something. Your Uncle Teege talked to him. I didn't know it at the time."

"You mean he wanted to see him?"

"But that doesn't mean anything, Pen," Elizabeth Flagg said quickly. "Do you think it does?" she asked.

Pen knew that she lived only for her husband; that none of the others, not her own family, not her children, meant anything to Aunt 'Lizabeth. Her whole life circled about his wheeled chair.

Aunt Hannah was talking, evidently on an old grievance.

"I was born a Flagg," she said, "I marry a Beville-Atwood, but even when I am widowed, I lose my own name! I'm no longer a Flagg. I consider it entirely unfair for the woman to be robbed of her name. It's the women who keep the traditions, who preserve the family relics. Look at the museum. Where would it be except for Mother? It's Mother who has preserved everything, gathered everything together——"

"And my mother-in-law before me," old Mrs Flagg put into the pause.

"Well, exactly—the women! I was married thirty-eight years ago," said Aunt Hannah. "I've not had the right to call myself a Flagg since I was nineteen years old. And yet I was born a Flagg, and I love the name!"

"Maybe Mary'll marry a Flagg," her daughter Lucy suggested. Mary, aged eight, took up the subject animatedly. "Who will I marry, Mother? What will I do, Mother?"

"I should think that for a hundred persons three hundred sandwiches would be ample," Hannah said abstractedly, working on a penciled list.

"The children will eat ten apiece," Lucy Towne said.

"How many are coming to the wedding, Hannah?" This was Pen. For a moment she had forgotten her own uneasiness.

"Only family. We never have anyone but family. About a hundred," Hannah answered. "The Robert Flaggs get here tomorrow from Portland. The Forsythes arrive Thursday; we'll have every bed full. The men will build a sort of platform against the hydrangeas there, and we'll decorate it on Monday."

"Two more Jensen bowls," Concy said. Her mother laughed adoringly. "Darling, you can set a beautiful table!" she exulted.

"Married in white, Concy?"

"Oh yes; we're always married in white," Concy said. Young and lovely and protected and confident, she was about Pen's age. Pen thought of her jealously. Gilbert de Puy was an irreproachable young Frenchman; Concy would be the nineteenth vicomtesse. Concy would have no sordid worries about her own family—an idle, borrowing father, a brother who was a constant care, a little sister cheated out of all the beauty and fun of youth, an older sister burdened and disillusioned and worried about rent. Concy's husband would not gamble, would not have to appeal to the grownups for money. Pen came back to the reality of her own position with a sigh and found herself walking toward her own house with Tom and Hannah.

"Will you come in, Hannah?"

"No, I'm going on. Tom says he wants to talk to Jeff. See you later!" Slender and straight in her blue dress, with her black hair as always flawlessly smooth, and her shoes smart, and her dark eyes pleasant, Hannah went on her way, and Pen took Tom up the little side steps that rose among the vines and shrubs of the garden, and to the wide bridge that went from the bank to the apartment above the guest rooms. Jeff was just waking up.

It was not real awakening. He was heavy and stupid. Pen felt sorry for him when she saw how clearly Tom read the situation, and how futile were Jeff's efforts to pass it off as quite natural and agreeable.

"Hello, Tom, old boy! How'd the croquet go?"

"Fine. They got us, but it was on one rotten shot of mine. Four rover game. Well, Jeff," Tom said, sitting down, "you've kind of gotten yourself bunged up, haven't you? What happened?"

"Oh, I don't know," Jeff said, suddenly and wearily abandoning pretense. "I cut my finals, you know, and made a general fool of myself."

"Cut the finals?" Tom looked serious.

"Rogers advised it."

"Did, eh?" said Tom. "Told Uncle Mark?"

"No; I was going to tell him tonight."

"Listen," Tom said. "You've got to quit this sort of thing. You can't keep it up, Jeff. It isn't fair to Pen."

"I know that," Jeff said, somberly.

"Worries your mother horribly, too."

"That's not all of it, either, Tom. I lost some money."

Tom looked up from his linked hands, looked down at them again. Pen anxiously studied his face.

"Roulette? Where'd you go? Pebble Beach?"

"No; just a crap game—big chump that I was!" Jeff said.

"You ought to pull yourself up, Jeff, and let that sort of thing alone," Tom said mildly, after a silence in which Jeff looked away through narrowed lids. Tom continued to study his locked fingers, and Pen watched him. "They've gotten you out of it a dozen times; they will again. But there's no percentage in keeping this sort of thing going. You've got a lovely wife now—you ought to think of her."

And Tom raised his eyes with his friendly smile to Penelope. The smile seemed to go through her entire being like the cut of a tangible knife, and she felt herself tremble, and the palms of her hands grow wet. For a second their gaze held, then Tom turned to Jeff again.

"Anyway," he said, "you can't come to dinner looking like that. Tie something on it tonight and you'll be all right in the morning, but you'd have 'em all guessing if you showed up this way. Have a cup of soup or something——"

"Gosh, I couldn't touch anything," Jeff interrupted. "My head's splitting. I've taken ten grains of aspirin."

"Well, then you're sure to sleep," Pen said. She presently went into the other room with Tom. Jeff had fallen off into a heavy doze; they could talk without disturbing him.

"You're not to worry about this, Pen," Tom said then. "It's not your fault. Poor fellow, he—— Poor fellow."

"I feel as if it were my fault in some way. I ought to have run the money end. I blame myself for that now. I left it all to him. And roulette, Tom— remember that you were there the night they brought the wheel? We've been playing every night."

"Lost money?"

"No. But I think it kept him in the gambling mood and interfered with his work. Now he has to tell Uncle Mark about it, and he's sick with nerves."

"How'd he get the shiner?" Tom asked abruptly. Pen laughed forlornly at the unfamiliar word.

"I don't know. He met some men; I suppose they were drinking. I sat up waiting for him all night, wondering——"

"H'm!" Tom muttered, looking away. "Well, he'll get out of it," he said briefly.

"It'll be the last time, Tom. He swears that. He says that if they'll just help him this once he'll never fail them again."

"He's lucky," Tom said, still not looking at her. "He's always been lucky."

"Jeff lucky?" Her tone was surprised. In what possible way could Jeff be considered luckier than Tom?

If her words were a question rather than an ejaculation, Tom did not answer them. He looked at her and smiled, and with a final "See you later!" was gone. Penelope went back to the sleeping porch; Jeff was unconscious, snoring heavily. Quietly, not to disturb him, she set about dressing for dinner.

Rather nervously, half an hour later, she presented his apologies. He had a blinding headache and was not coming to dinner. Aunt Margaret accepted the explanation sympathetically enough and passed it on to her mother-in-law. But Jeff's father greeted the message with a displeased "Hum!" and Pen, stealthily watching the grandmother, saw her brow darken. She felt ashamed and anxious. Jeff had been behaving badly before their marriage, but perhaps they had all hoped that she would have a steadying influence upon him.

"Finals," said Uncle Peter. "He's been cramming. I hated 'em!"

"Oh, dear," Pen thought, one of the big group in the library waiting for the dinner summons, "if only he were like the rest! If only he'd graduated from law school and we were proud of him! This puts it off until late fall at least; it means he has to coach this summer."

CHAPTER XXIV

Like every other dreaded hour, however, the bad hour passed, and she and Jeff found themselves an accepted part of the household for the summer, the matter settled and dismissed without recriminations, or any reproaches except the first. Pen felt humiliated and ashamed for a while, but Jeff settled down to coaching in real earnest, and Amy told Pen, by way of consolation, that Jeff's Uncle Peter had twice failed in the attempt to pass the bar examinations. About the gambling debt the family in general did not know. Pen understood that Uncle Mark had been very severe with his son on the subject, and that Jeff had been required to give his note against some inheritance known as the "Carter patent money," which would be his when he was twenty-five.

There was nothing about which to feel satisfied or proud, but the episode passed as all others did, and the various events that would be landmarks in this summer quickly swept it from first place in the family minds. Constance was married in a flurry of white ruffles and lilies of the valley; Tom Cline, aged two, burned his microscopic thumb badly on fireworks smuggled in by Tommy Towne. Bruce Bannister took young Lucy dancing in the city, and they had a blowout on the way home and did not get in until three.

"I've never let her do it before, and I certainly never will let her do it again!" Aunt Margaret said afterward.

"I never let Concy do it—not once," Aunt Constance Forsythe said complacently, and Pen saw the glance the two women exchanged.

The children went off to the beach cabin for a week's change, Hannah and Pen as escort. Pen loved this. She loved the rambling shingled brown cottage where they all somehow stowed themselves away; she loved the freedom of their meals, for no servant went along, and above all she loved the shore; soul and body seemed to be rested and refreshed by the nearness of the rolling green ocean, the sweetness of the soft salt airs.

The Merrys, the Townes and the Clines, with the bride and groom, Lucy, Peggy and Mark Flagg, Frank and Billy Merry and Tom and Mary Towne went off on a packing trip into the High Sierras in August; the big house seemed deserted with only a dozen persons drifting about and the long table shortened to a more reasonable size. Pen was somewhat thrown into the company of her mother-in-law and came to know all the older members of the group better. Persis, asked to spend a month with friends in Santa Barbara, could not have gone if Pen had not managed a check for clothes and fare; it was one of the happy moments in Pen's summer when she went down to help the excited and expectant Persis pack her bags for the trip.

So Pen's heart, always full of them, always fretted because she could do so little for her own, was at rest where Persis was concerned, and as her mother was almost constantly with Isolde she could feel content about the older sister, too, to a certain extent. Now and then she drove in to see them, making a cheerful report on Jeff, wishing always that they might have the comfort, the spacious sleeping porches, the quiet service, the restfulness of Flaggwood.

The summer days drowsed by. Tom came down for week ends, and he and Jeff and George played croquet. Nurses went about with the toddling babies who had been left behind by the camping party: Lovey Merry, Farmer Towne, Mary's Tom. Little redheaded Sally Flagg moved like a sprite among them all; she was a reserved child, not unfriendly, but needing no company but her own and that of the mother who darkly, unhappily adored her. Pen knew now that Peter Flagg had not spoken to his wife, except when the presence of others would have made the silence noticeable, for five years. He had brought her and her child home from Paris in that same silence which enveloped him now. He had not forgiven nor forgotten, but Amy was a Flagg, and the child was a Flagg, and as long as they needed and would accept his protection he would extend it.

She learned that Jeff's mother and Hannah's mother, Aunt Margaret and Aunt Hannah, were deeply jealous of each other, both watching on

Gram's fat, strong, fine old hand the emerald that meant leadership, each suspicious of the other's moves. She liked Tom's mother, Aunt 'Lizabeth, best. Aunt 'Lizabeth took her about the flower gardens and conservatories and talked to her about Uncle Teege. He was not so well, or he was a little better. How did Pen think he looked?

Uncle Teege was dying. They all knew it except Aunt 'Lizabeth, and, they told themselves, himself. But Pen, looking into the wise, humorous eyes, thought that Uncle Teege perfectly appreciated that his days were drawing to an end, and that all their goodness and carefulness could not cheat this particular Thomas Jefferson Flagg of a dignified death.

"He doesn't come to the table any more," his wife said. "But that really means nothing. The first summer after he was ill he never even used his wheeled chair. We couldn't make him. We all thought then that Thomas couldn't live. We really did. Don't remind me of that time. I can't bear to think of it. Mary was only three months old, Tom and George little fellows. We were in the East, you know; Thomas was in a war camp. They brought him home—I was with my own people in Englewood, New Jersey. They brought Thomas home. I won't talk of it; I still dream of it nights! He'd been so big, so fine in his olive drab! I was so proud of him. But we won't think of that time," gentle Aunt 'Lizabeth would conclude nervously, "for he's all right now; he's wonderfully well and he enjoys life more than many a man who can go about, play golf and do everything!"

And over and over again she said: "I'm not in the least nervous, and it's a good thing, for he'd see it, and there's nothing in the world the matter with him!"

"What'll she do when he dies?" Pen asked Hannah.

"Oh, don't!" Hannah said. "She'll die, too."

"Well, I really believe she will."

"She's had something."

"Something?"

"I mean she's not been cheated out of it all," Hannah said. "She married the man she loved—she was Gram's secretary, you know. Didn't you know that? She was Betty Pierce. Gram had known the Pierces, and she was doing a lot of charity work or something, and she needed a secretary, so she asked Betty to try it. So you can imagine what a fairy story it all seemed to her!"

"She says they've never had a quarrel."

"I think that's true. It's hard to imagine quarreling with her, or with him, for that matter. He's one of the calm Flaggs, like Tom," Hannah said, guiding the conversation as usual to Tom. "George and Mary are the peppery sort."

"Who was Richard Flagg? Someone spoke of Richard Flagg."

Hannah hesitated, her face growing grave.

"He was another uncle," she said presently, looking up from her knitting. She and Pen were alone on the lawn, both in basket chairs, both knitting. "He came between Mother and Uncle Mark," she said. "He was a fascinating sort of person. He died ten—oh, eleven years ago."

"Not married?"

"No." There was another pause; then Hannah said again: "Wild."

"That's why somebody said Jeff was like him," Pen said, with a rueful laugh. Hannah answered simply.

"Jeff is like him in certain mannerisms and looks. But that doesn't mean that Jeff's nature is like his. Uncle Dick was very lovable," Hannah added; "we children all liked him when we were little. But he was quite unmanageable, a constant anxiety," she finished. "And then, you know, in the end we think he killed himself."

"Killed himself!" Pen echoed startled.

"Oh yes. And it almost killed *them*," Hannah said. "It was never made public, of course. Grandfather still thinks it was an accident. But he drank a whole bottle of sleeping stuff."

"Was he in pain? Was he sick?"

"Well, he had been. And he'd done something either awfully stupid or actually crooked— Oo, la, la," said Hannah, "we must talk of something else. Here comes Emily."

Emily Flagg had been Emily Jennings of Washington. She was Penelope's age almost to a day. She was extremely pretty, in a Dresden shepherdess sort of way, with brown eyes, light brown hair, a cream-and-rose skin. She was the wife of Tom's younger brother George, and had a baby daughter, Lucy Farmer Flagg.

"Hannah," Emily said radiantly, sitting down, "I've been trying to find someone to tell the news! My uncle, the old duck, that's Senator Jennings, of course, thinks that he can manage it!"

"The diplomatic berth, Emily?" Hannah said pleasantly; but Pen knew that Hannah liked Emily no better than she did.

"Wouldn't he be the old darling!"

"But wouldn't George have to take his bar first?"

"Not necessarily, he says. It would mean—what fun!—our going to Washington for a few months. But after all," Emily said, very busy and important, and speaking in a gay rush, "all my friends are there, of course, for I was married there only two years ago. It would be the greatest lark, getting home! And then if George should be sent to Spain or France, my French and Spanish, you know—George's French is all right, but it makes him so mad when I talk Spanish and he doesn't understand a word. He'd pick it up in no time, though. I wouldn't move Lucy," Emily said, considering, "until October, at least. I wouldn't take her into that heat. But Mother's got a lovely nursery waiting for the first grandchild. 'Don't be disappointed not having a boy,' she wrote me. I told you that, Hannah. 'All the Jenningses start with girls,' she said."

"We'd miss the baby," Hannah observed.

"The baby," Emily said, "must get used to moving about. Diplomatic babies have to be good travelers! We might even fly East with her. We'll certainly fly from Paris to London if it's London, for I hate that Channel trip."

There was a great deal more of it. Pen listened in silence. She was no match for Emily.

"You'll have to get married, Hannah," Emily rattled on, "and come and visit us in Europe! It's such fun in the diplomatic circle. You meet everyone!"

"Who's to get married?" Tom asked, joining them and taking a chair.

"Hannah!" Emily said, with her little high laugh.

"Hannah? Oh, we can't spare her," Tom said, glancing up at her with a smile.

"If I were a man I'd be in love with you, Hannah," Penelope said, involuntarily, and with a smile. Hannah smiled back at her, and from that moment, although she did not know it for long years, Penelope in Hannah had a firm champion in all the family councils.

"He doesn't hear that sort of thing," Hannah said, walking beside Penelope toward the house.

"Tom?"

"No. I don't exist, to him. I'm his sister—his schoolteacher—part of the wallpaper. I'm anything and anybody he doesn't see!"

Hannah spoke in a hard, half-laughing tone, as if she were amused at her own hurt.

"How long has it been like this, Hannah?"

"How d'you mean 'like this'?"

"I mean your—liking Tom?" Penelope spoke a little timidly, yet knowing that Hannah spoke to no one else on this matter, and that she liked Penelope to probe into it.

"It began——" Hannah said, and paused for a moment's thought. "Oh, I used to adore him at baby parties, when he was eight and I was twelve," she said. "I never can remember the time when I wouldn't have died for Tom. But the awful part began one Christmas holiday. It was just after my father died. I'd been abroad a year and come home, and Tom was coming. We were all in the library, and it was bitterly cold and there was a big fire going. Tom came in with Mark and Uncle Mark; they were all cold and rosy and laughing, of course, and unbelting their coats and being kissed. I don't know whether it sounds like anything, but I always remember it as it was that afternoon. Cold and getting black dark outside, but with the house all lighted up and wreaths around, and the smell of pine wreaths, and Tom—smiling and talking to everyone, and then coming over to me. I burst out crying, of course—I'd adored my father, and I wasn't here when he died, and I tried to get away, but Tom held me with his arm tight about my shoulders, and he wouldn't let me go. He just talked on until I was quiet again. And that—that began it. And that was—well, more than five years ago. He was about twenty-three or four. But he was a man even then."

She left Pen at the corner where the drive turned about the zinnias, and Pen went on up the path toward the woods, and mounted the stone steps where the hollyhocks and dahlias were drooping after the hot day. She went upstairs to her shaded, orderly sleeping porch. One of the dreary hours of life had suddenly seized upon her; she felt sick and discouraged. Other persons' lives seemed to have been so successfully managed, or at worst their problems were problems of dignity and honor. She could not seem to grasp the right thread to begin to untangle her own.

Emily, for example. What had Emily done that she should be the one adored daughter of the rich Jenningses; her distinguished father, her uncles, her mother, her brother all forming a society whose only reason for being was to spoil and worship her? Emily would go back to Washington and wear broad white hats and Paris frocks designed especially for her own small person; she would dine at the White House, chattering Spanish prettily with the Ambassador; she and George would presently sail, with little Lucy and Lucy's uniformed nurse, for great adventures in strange lands. Well, that was Emily's luck. One mustn't be fool enough to be jealous. But why couldn't it have been Persis?

Penelope thought of the campers in the High Sierras. She had but a vague idea of what they were doing, but she knew that there were horses in it and campfires and swims in cold mountain lakes. All so happy and secure, these Flaggs, proud young parents with their brown children riding along beside them, happy young lovers, contented old folk.

But in the end her thoughts came to Tom—Tom arriving home cold and eager for Christmas holidays, when the house was lighted and trimmed with scented fir, and the fires were blazing, and as she mused, a softened expression came into her eyes, and she was presently deep asleep, with a half-smile on her face.

CHAPTER XXV

"Gram wants to know if you will be her hostess on Friday," Hannah said to her one morning.

"Did she say so?"

"Suggested it to me. It was her idea. She'll speak to you about it tonight before dinner."

"She didn't ask you to sound me about it?"

"Oh no, no! You're to be surprised. She has some very special company coming on Friday, and Mother and I'll be at Tahoe. There'll be you and Uncle Teege and Aunt 'Lizabeth, and Uncle Peter and Amy and maybe Sally and Lovey."

"Why not Amy?"

"Amy's no good as hostess; too fluttery. Aunt Margaret's going to a club dinner somewhere. Aunt 'Lizabeth never comes over until the very last minute with Uncle Teege. Tom'll be down; he'll help. Emily and George will be here, but she asked for you. That means something, Pen!"

"Well, if she asks me," Pen said.

She was elated when she told Jeff, but she managed to mask her feeling and to answer with nothing more than quiet politeness when her husband's formidable grandmother approached the subject just before dinner that evening.

"Penelope, would you mind being a little early on Friday night, and taking charge of some guests of your grandfather and myself, Major and Mrs Gerald Chandler and their daughter, Dolly Rudd? Tom's bringing them down, and neither Maggie nor Hannah will be here."

"I'd love to," Pen said composedly. "They're staying?"

"Unfortunately they can't. They're sailing the next morning for China; he's on a special mission there. We'll send them back to town that night."

"But they'd like a room to rest and freshen up, if they're just off the Overland Friday morning," Penelope suggested, urged on by a touch from Hannah's foot. For the first time she won from the old woman a quick surprised glance of approval.

"Well, maybe they would. You and Hannah arrange that. She goes off to Tahoe tomorrow."

"That last remark," Hannah said to Penelope later, "is a distinct sign of favor. She knows," Hannah said affectionately, "what I know, that you're the smartest of the lot, that that Irish spirit and—well, whatever it is of yours—makes you worth Ann and Lucy and Emily and Mary all boiled down together! Tom sees it, too. You're getting Gram so that she'll eat out of your hand."

"Bite it, more likely," Pen said with a laugh. But her heart was lighter than it had been in many days. Jeff was working hard and steadily, going in to town to pore over law books and attend lectures, playing croquet and tennis, sleeping long, drinking little, when he was free. That fear was laid for a while.

Physically she began to feel better, too. Often in the mornings she was weak and miserable, hungry without being able to bear the smell of food, weary without having made the slightest effort. But now that her hope of motherhood was known to the older women of the family, she found herself being a little spoiled. Her morning tray, holding just enough iced fruit, smoking hot coffee, dry thin toast to make any normally hungry person long for more, came over punctually at eight o'clock, and after that she often fell into another deep, delicious sleep and awakened somewhat ready for the drag of dressing at ten or eleven. Jeff's mother had been crisply satisfied with the news; she had expected, of course, that the new Mrs Thomas Jefferson Flagg would have children. But his father had been deeply touched; had tried to show his affectionate pleasure and concern to Penelope in a hundred somewhat awkward ways which had touched her in turn.

He had never shown her any friendliness before, Mark Flagg. She knew he had felt no happiness in his oldest son's sudden marriage and the events that had led to it. But the prospect of holding a grandchild in his arms had reached this rather silent, most businesslike of the Flaggs. He told his wife that he often thought how pleasant it would be to have another little baby about. "Of course some of the others have small ones," he said, "but this one will be ours."

When Margaret Flagg told her son this, Jeff told Penelope, and Penelope was deeply pleased with her latest conquest and felt that things were somehow straightening themselves out. Matters between herself and Jeff were adjusting themselves, too; when he worked so hard and behaved so well, and showed in so many ways his passionate devotion to her and his dependence upon her, and when the circumstances of their lives were outwardly so felicitous—music and laughter and gardens, meals beautifully served in the old dining room or out on the lawn, everyone kindly and life always distracting and amusing—she must have been hard to please not to return to him some of the love he lavished on her, and to feel quite sure that he and Isolde had been right, that she was one of the women to whom true wifely devotion only comes slowly and after marriage.

Before Hannah and her mother departed for ten days at the Lake, Hannah gave Penelope careful parting instructions.

"Come over to the house about five and wait on the terrace. They get here around five, and Gram won't show up until half past six."

"And show them round a little?"

"Yes; just the gardens and pool, but not the theater, because there's to be a picture in the theater that night. It seems the Chandlers have never seen the picture that was taken on that trip four years ago, and Lindy's getting a man from town to run it. You don't have to bother about that; she'll set the chairs and everything. It's just to see that someone meets them and takes charge of them, and that they're shown to a room."

"I'll be over by quarter to five. I'll wear my blue."

"Oh yes, wear the blue, and be ready at five. And then, about quarter past six, be sort of hanging round downstairs to take them to the library."

There was apparently a little formality to this business of being Gram's hostess, Pen reflected, rousing herself from an hour of idle reading on her bed on Friday afternoon. It was three o'clock, much too early to get started. But the sense of importance, the excitement persisted, and she looked approvingly at the blue gown, blowing gently to and fro on a hanger, pressed and ready for the night's festivities.

Once she had the Londoners safe inside the library door at half past six, she need feel no further concern. Gram and Aunt 'Lizabeth, Uncle Teege and Uncle Mark, Tom and Peter and Amy would all take charge of them then; there would be music and talk and glasses of sherry. Up to that point she was responsible.

She would wait for the car on the terrace. The September afternoons were infinitely soft and gracious, with steady sweet light upon the gardens and the odor of brush fires delicious in the thinning air. She would go forward smiling at the newcomers and at Tom.

"Mrs Chandler? How do you do, Major . . ."

And then, when Jean had sent the bags upstairs:

"You sent the bags up to Mr Jefferson's old room, Jean? That's right. Would you let me show you just a little of Flaggwood, Mrs Chandler, since this is your first visit here?"

Rehearsing it, she got up and freshened her face with cold water and began to brush her soft thick gold hair. Looking at herself in the dressing-table mirror, she reflected that her beauty had its good times and its poor times, and that this was one of the good times. Tom and Jeff and all of them wouldn't be ashamed of her tonight——

Her telephone rang, and she reached for it. She knew the voice instantly, and knew that Jeff had been drinking. Her heart plunged downward, downward.

"Yes, Jeff? This is Pen."

"Pen, I'm in trouble. . . . No, not bad trouble, but I'm in kind of a mess. Are you dressed?"

"All but my dress."

"What are you doing?"

"Getting ready for the Chandlers. They get here in about an hour."

"Who said they would? They won't be there a minute before six. Isn't Tom bringing them down?"

"Yes, but Hannah said about five."

"They won't be there at any five. Hannah's cuckoo."

"What about it, anyway? Where are you?"

"I'm at Rosner's. Know Rosner's? 'The First Empire'? Three miles in toward the Skyline, up past the dog hospital on the highway?"

"This side of San Bruno?"

"Yep. I'm there. Pen, I want you to come get me, now, right away, without telling anyone, see? Listen, if you tell anyone you get me in Dutch with the old man, see? Now listen, Pen, I had two cocktails, but I've not been drinking. But if he has to send for me he'll raise hell. You come get me."

"Jeff, I couldn't. Where's the car?"

"It's there at home. George brought me in this morning. Remember I thought you might want to go see your mother this afternoon?"

"But how'd you get to this place?"

"Oh, a fellow brought me down. Friday night, see? And we were both sort of glad that Monday's a holiday—Labor Day. So he asked me if I knew this place. I've not been here for years; it used to be run by a colored man, but it's changed hands or something. It's a nice place; it's not rough or anything, but now this fellow's gone, and I can't walk two miles to the bus, and then maybe wait an hour, and maybe be late. It won't take you fifteen minutes to get here."

"It would take me half an hour at least, and it's five minutes to four now. Jeff, I can't. Isn't there someone else here—one of the men——"

"He'd have to ask Gram or the old man. They're awfully strict about anyone else giving orders. Come on, Pen; we'll be back in thirty minutes, I swear we will!"

"Jeff, you know I'm Gram's hostess this evening. She made a point of it. Hannah's not here, and Gram didn't want Amy or Emily. It'd be crazy——"

"Listen, Pen. You know what it'll mean to have the old man mad at me again. I'm stuck here. I give you my word you can do it in fifteen minutes. Look, it takes you ten to get to Belmont. Jump into the car and come along —we'll be back in loads of time, and it isn't a matter of life and death, anyway. Lindy'll show them their rooms, and you'll be there by the time they've washed their faces."

"Jeff, telephone for a taxi—there must be some place near. They must have had to call dozens. You'll have to do that. I honestly don't want to risk it."

"Here's the thing, Pen: I've got to have five dollars to get out of here. My check's no good. Prent and I had a bottle of wine, and I must have left my wallet somewhere. I haven't got a cent. I've got about thirty cents to pay for this call. I feel like a fool, Pen, but honestly I'm not drunk, and I don't want to get in wrong with Dad. He'd think it was all off again. If you'll slip down here and pick me up we'll be back in loads of time, even if Tom gets there anywhere near five, which he won't. He was to pick them up at the Hotel Fairmont in the city at four; he'll get into a lot of traffic; he'll probably whirl 'em around and show 'em the Cliff House and the Golden Gate; you know Tom. All this time we're talking you could be here! I've thought and thought, Pen, and this is the only way we can get out of it without everyone knowing——"

"I'll be there!" she said abruptly. She pulled a silk dress over her head, caught up her loose soft coat. Her purse, and a glance into it to see that there was money there, and she was flying down the drive in the blue car; she was out of the gates and on the highway.

Now, if everything would only go well. If everything would only go well. The car moved smoothly and lightly; the gauge showed plenty of gas; the miles began to go by. Penelope's heart beat fast, and her thoughts flew as fast as the flying wheels.

Rosner's at four twenty-five, one minute to pick up Jeff, off again. Back to the highway at half past four. Belmont, San Carlos—they could easily be home again by quarter to five. Two breathless minutes to tear off her dress and slip into the blue, and then a run to the house across the twilight grass, and a breathless query to Lindy: "Company come yet?"

"Not yet, Mrs Jeff."

And then everything would be all right, and she could settle down and breathe deep again.

She took the turning; there was no mistaking it. A small sign with a pointing hand said "Rosner's. French Dinner. Dancing. Three m."

"Having written all the rest," Pen said aloud, "you'd think they could spell out the 'miles.' Three miles—three miles—I'm going an even fifty— that means about four minutes. And it's only four twenty-four—that clock's right. . . .

" 'I'm sorry, Gram. I had to go get Jeff. Why didn't he come as he had arranged with Tom? Well, a friend offered to bring him early, and his car broke down. Near Belmont, wasn't it, Jeff? However, I hear Lindy took care of you, Mrs Chandler, so it was all right. Only I was sorry not to be here.'

"Why should Gram know at all? As a matter of fact she needn't. Who will tell her? I certainly won't. Rosner's, one half mile. Up the dirt road? Up the dirt road we go . . . that must be it. Jeff ought to be out on the steps. Park here. Park here. Slam the door. Leave the key; we won't be here a moment; nobody'll steal it. Café and Cocktail Room. That would be it. But where's Jeff?"

Running up a flight of steps, crossing a porch, she looked into the big room that was evidently used as a barroom and restaurant and dance hall. At the tables scattered about it a few persons were sitting: a French family, the little girls wearing manes of straight black hair, were enjoying an early dinner. Two policemen were talking quietly to a man who appeared to be the proprietor or head waiter; their eyes, and the eyes of others, were upon a man who lay with his gray head on the cloth.

Pen gave them but a swift glance. Where was Jeff? A wheezy clock struck half past four. She went to the head waiter.

"Just one, madame?" he asked automatically, his interest only partially withdrawn from the disgraceful old reveler at the table.

"No, I'm not dining. I wanted to ask you—was a gentleman here a few minutes ago who had lost his purse? There was some wine to pay for, I think. A dark man in a light suit?"

The waiter was experienced and wary.

"I do not remember, madame."

"I mean a man—two men, and one went away, and they owed for some wine?" She opened her purse. "I'm only about thirteen miles away from Flaggwood," she thought; "that's nothing, if Jeff only was here."

"I think they both went, lady," the waiter said. He was paying her but partial attention. His real interest was centered in the gray-headed old man who was sound asleep with his head on the table. "I don't want you to run him in, but he says he hasn't any money, and I won't have him here overnight," he said to the policeman.

"How much does he owe you, Gene?" one of the policemen said.

"That isn't the point," the restaurateur answered. "The point is I don't want him round."

"I wish you could tell me if two men——" Penelope was beginning, when the old derelict raised his head, and she saw that it was her father. Their eyes met. Marvin Fitzpercy stirred himself, smiled. There was a silence.

"Well, Penelope, my dear child," her father said amiably, ending it, "what are you doing in this place at this hour?"

Penelope turned sharply to the police. Her face had whitened, and she felt her spine cold.

"What has he done?" she asked.

"He hasn't done nothing," one of the officers hastened to explain. "Me and Joe were on our way home, and we stopped in here for a beer, that's all. And Gene happened to say he didn't know where the old gentleman belonged."

"He owes you something?" Pen asked the waiter briefly.

"It is not zat," Gene assured her politely. "He comes here at two o'clock," he said. "It is now five. He seem to wish to z-leep."

"He'll go with me." She paid his seventy-cent bill, did not forget the tip. "Come on," she said, touching her father's shoulder. He had lapsed into drowsiness again; he roused himself.

"Yes, surely, my dear. Certainly! I was about to go anyway."

He stumbled slightly as he walked, and she steadied him. They went out to the porch, Marvin Fitzpercy holding tightly to the railing of the steps as they descended. Penelope guided him to her car, opened the front door, shoved him upward, lifting his right leg in after him, closing the door. Then she went around to the driver's seat, slammed the other door, bent forward to the board lights to find her key. A moment later the car's lights picked up the bushes and the gravel in the early dusk; they were gliding down the narrow dirt road. It was not quite dark.

Penelope drove along slowly, thinking. What to do with him? She wasted no time upon questions or reproaches. He was here, and he was completely unfit to take care of himself. It was distinctly her problem now, whatever it might eventually be.

A hotel? No; that was out of the question. He would give his name there, and be identified, and she would be identified too. The obvious solution would be to take him down and leave him with her mother, but

Pen's heart shrank from that. It didn't seem fair to introduce this trouble into that little household that was so burdened already.

Of old Mrs Flagg and the dinner party she thought only dreamily, as of something far away which concerned her not at all. Of course she should have been there at five o'clock, of course she should not have been racketing over the lonely country roads in the late cold afternoon, but such considerations seemed to have no weight.

"This is the third or fourth time I've thrown her down," Penelope thought. "I was late once before, I forgot the telephone message, my mother borrowed money and talked to reporters, my brother tried to sell her a cooler or heater or whatever it was—I don't care!"

The shock of finding her father, the keen anxiety and responsibility that had accompanied the shock, had banished all lesser considerations. Two policemen watching him when she had chanced to go in; two officers not quite sure whether or not they should "run the old man in"!

"I hate him," Penelope thought. "No; of course I don't hate him; he's my father. He brought Persis and me little blue and pink silk parasols once. He used to sing 'Bedelia' to Persis when Persis was a baby. He can't help it. He's weak. And I'm weak; or I never would put up with Jeff. I'm weak, or I never would have come out at all tonight. Then my father probably would have landed in jail, and probably not the first time, either! 'Father of Mrs Jefferson Flagg Pleads Unemployment.' He would have dragged me into it. They all drag me into everything and leave me there! If there were somebody—*somebody* I could meet now who would help me out. There's nobody. I can't think of a single soul in this world who realizes that I've had a rotten break, and that someone ought to stand by me. Jeff, my father, Phil—they all throw me down."

Her passenger was very quiet beside her. Perhaps the cool evening air was sobering him, or perhaps he had fallen into a doze again; Penelope could not tell. Now and then he slightly lurched against her, immediately straightening himself again.

"Are you taking me to your own house, my dear?" he said presently, with his finest manner. "I don't feel myself exactly dressed for any contact with strangers."

"I'm taking you home to Mother, Dad. Unless there's some place you'd rather go?" Penelope spoke quietly, without expression.

"No, I don't think of any place. I would have been glad to treat you to a little supper . . ." His voice trailed off drowsily. Penelope drove on in silence. Her dial clock said ten minutes to six when they reached the cottage in Armitage Lane.

There were lights in the kitchen; Persis and her mother were there, sharing a can of pea soup, the toasted end of a loaf, and a dark fruited slab of bakery cake with icing on it. Their delight at seeing her was one more pang to Penelope.

"Oh, Pen, you darling; you've come to supper!" Persis exclaimed. "Listen, we've plenty of eggs; I'll fix you cocoa, or tea, or something."

Pen kissed her mother, pressed her firm cold cheek against the softly withered cheek.

"Hello, Persis; hello, Mummy. I'm so sorry. I've got Dad here."

"Your father! He said he wouldn't be home tonight."

"Oh, then he's been home again?"

"Since—when was it, Persis? Since Tuesday."

Pen experienced a certain revulsion of feeling. He had been home this morning, and he probably would somehow have engineered himself home tonight. She might have left him at Rosner's, paid his bill and given him a few dollars. She would not have found Jeff, of course, but she might have gotten home in time to save something of the situation that was now hopelessly lost. Too late to think of that now.

"Phil's got an awful cold," said Persis. "He's been in bed two days."

"Phil has?"

"Yes. Go in and see him, Pen. I asked him if he wanted milk toast at five, but he seemed sleepy."

"I've just thought of something," Mrs Fitzpercy said. "Why can't Pen take me to a train? Isolde wants me to come in, and I was wondering how I'd get to a train," she said.

Marvin Fitzpercy, tousled and red-faced and sleepy, stood in the kitchen door.

"Well," he said amiably, "I'm a lucky fellow to have a pretty daughter pick me up and get me out of a jam. How's the boy?"

"Better, I think. We didn't count on you for dinner, Marvin. Where's the car?"

"The car will be delivered tomorrow morning completely repaired."

"Repaired!" Persis echoed.

"Nothing at all, nothing at all," her father said reassuringly. "I had a little trouble, fender bumped and one light broken. It was entirely the other man's fault. Now don't anyone worry about dinner for me. Anything will do. I'm quite accustomed to looking out for myself."

"Pen, if I change, will you get me to the train? I'm worried about Isolde. We had a postcard from Grandy this morning saying that she was not so well. And any time now——"

"Just hurry, will you, Mother? For I have to be home for dinner."

"Home for dinner?" Persis echoed. "Why, what hour on earth do they have it?"

"Seven thirty-eight. There's special company tonight. The London representative of the firm and his wife and daughter." Penelope felt no special concern as she said it. Things had gone beyond that point now. She went into the dark bedroom and lighted a lamp. Philip, lying on his back, regarded her steadily.

There was about him the neglected, unnatural look, the pathos of a person who is ill. His bed was rumpled, he had not shaved, the air in the dark little bedroom, against whose two windows garden shrubs pressed, was close.

"Phil, you feel rotten!"

"Not so good," he said in a hoarse whisper, not smiling. "Where'd you come from?"

She sat beside him, aching to do something for him, trying to amuse him with bits of gossip and family news.

"Isolde's laid up, too, Mother said."

"That's not serious now, Phil. She just gets tired easily. Jeff and I are moving back into town next week, and then I'll see her often, and perhaps be able to take charge of the boys when the new one comes."

When she went back to the kitchen her father was asleep again in the position in which she had first seen him tonight at Rosner's, his arms on the table, his face hidden. Persis, in strong and obvious distaste, said that she would see that he went to bed immediately. Penelope and her mother went out to the car.

"Oh, Persis, Persis, darling!" Ellabeth Fitzpercy called a moment later. Persis came running out into the dark, apprehensive that something had gone wrong.

"Tell her, sweet," the mother said. Penelope, already at the wheel, said with an embarrassed laugh that she had just told her mother a bit of news.

"My dear, if anything in the world could make me happier!" Ellabeth said, emotionally.

Penelope, trying to be patient, echoed in her soul what Persis, with a little rueful laugh that robbed it of its sting, said dryly:

"*You* can say that, Mother, of all people?"

"Ah, you only say that to be modern, darling!" her mother countered reproachfully. "But it's a very good world to live in, after all!"

"Get into the car, Mother. I'm going to telephone and send old Mrs Flagg a message that I'm late."

CHAPTER XXVI

Just an hour later, at a quarter to eight, young Mrs Jefferson Flagg came into the library of the old house, dressed for dinner. She looked her loveliest in her blue gown, with faint shadows about her blue-gray, black-lashed Irish eyes, her flawless skin colorless, her lips a pale scarlet, and her glorious coronet of gold freshly brushed and braided. Her only apology was to her husband's grandmother, and that was delivered simply, without elaboration:

"I'm very sorry to be late."

Old Mrs Flagg, magnificent in violet brocade and lace, looked at her thoughtfully.

"You had my telephone message that I couldn't be here?" Pen said.

"Oh yes, about an hour ago," Jeff's grandmother said, faint significance in the words. Jeff himself, impeccably dressed for the evening, had come up to put his arm about Pen; in a sort of stupefaction she turned and saw him. Her tired beautiful eyes widened.

"It was partly my fault," said Jeff. "She went out to pick me up, my car broke down. But then what happened to you, Pen? That was two hours ago."

"I met my father, quite by chance," Pen said, in further explanation to the older woman. "He was ill."

"Ah, I'm sorry," old Mrs Flagg said politely.

The conversation hung. There seemed to be nothing else to say. Pen and Jeff went over to the London visitors; she held her head high; two scarlet spots stained her cheeks.

"Gosh, you are a sport, Pen!" Jeff said. "The feller I was with had only gone to get his car, but I was kind of woozy and I thought he'd run out on me. He came back just after I telephoned you, and paid the bill and brought me home. I thought those asses there would tell you! He said— Prent said that we'd be sure to meet you on the road, but we missed you. I telephoned Rosner's, but you'd gone."

"It's all right," she said patiently.

She sat at dinner between George and Tom. Penelope was inclined to like George the least of the Flagg men, perhaps because she fancied him affected by his diplomatically ambitious, complacent little wife. George was always polite to her, but he never had very much to say. Tonight he and Bruce Bannister, who was on Emily's other side, were deep in aviation talk. Bruce had his own plane.

Emily always sat next to George. They had been married two years. Emily's attitude was that of the politically minded wife who shares with her husband not only his heart, but his interests, his leisure, his plans, his life; she made it a point to sit beside him at meals, to listen to him, and now and then to quote her father, the Judge, or her uncles, the Congressman and the Senator.

Presently Tom turned from young Mrs Rudd, the Chandlers' daughter, to say to Penelope, without preamble:

"What went wrong?"

"Nothing very serious," she answered lightly.

"Uncle Mark was all ready to get worked up because he thought it was Jeff," Tom said, handsome and serious and sympathetic. "But evidently not? For Jeff came in fifteen minutes before you did."

"Didn't he give any explanation?"

"Just said that you were dressing, and would be along."

Pen mused upon this as she ate her fish. Jeff had somehow gotten home, straightened himself out with bromo and cold shower, managed to reach the library at almost the right time, casually alluding to her—to Penelope, who was scouring the dark countryside for him, for all he knew—as being a few minutes late, but shortly to put in an appearance.

And the maddening part of it was that she *had* put in an appearance; no one had been alarmed or concerned. She had forgotten her engagement with Gram's guests, that was all. Pen was always late and careless. Her family was like that, poor girl!

"Something did go wrong," Tom said, watching her. She smiled again.

"It's all right now, anyway."

"Jeff late?"

"It was my father," Pen said presently, after reflection.

"Oh, I'm sorry. Not sick?"

"No, not sick. But I had to pick him up—somewhere, and bring him home."

"And Jeff wasn't back with the car yet?"

"No, Jeff wasn't back, but the car was here. And then I was delayed."

"Too bad, this special night!"

"I suppose your grandmother was displeased."

Tom was infinitely tactful. There was no shade of hesitation in his manner.

"I don't think so. At all events everything is all right now. Things come up; accidents happen. If you had to go out and Jeff wasn't here, she'll understand. Just as long as it wasn't Jeff's doing! Pen——" he added impulsively, and stopped. She raised her somber eyes to his.

"Tom?"

"I was going to ask you if you'd let me tell Uncle Mark that. That Jeff wasn't the reason you were so late."

Her eyes were fixed on old Mrs Flagg, magnificent in violet brocade at the top of the table. To protect Jeff—never to let them know he was in it at all. To play their own game with the Flaggs . . .

"Why?" she asked simply.

"Because he's apt to be so critical of Jeff in spite of the fact that the old boy has been making a tremendous effort lately. Uncle Mark came into my room at about five-thirty and asked if Jeff had come down with me. Then he walked over to your house. Nobody there. And then he began to fuss. It's Friday night, you see, and Monday a holiday—just the time Jeff would take for a break. Now if I could assure him, or you would speak to Gram——?"

Tom stopped, on a questioning note.

"I don't want to. I'm afraid of them. Jeff's father doesn't like me," Pen said slowly.

"He isn't demonstrative with anyone. But you mustn't think he doesn't like you. Ever since he heard of the baby coming he's been trying to be kind to you," Tom assured her, in his brotherly, concerned way. "But he's always been hard on Jeff. He feels Aunt Margaret has spoiled him, and I suppose she has, in a way. He worries more about Jeff than anything else in the world, and God knows he's got enough business worries, these days."

"Jeff really is trying to get started. But his father can't expect him to be an angel all at once."

"You got a telephone message and went to bring your father home after he'd had a smash—well, a sort of a smash. That's true, isn't it?"

"That's absolutely true."

"Well, that'll be a great relief to his mind. And if Jeff goes on as he is now, he's going to make himself very solid with his father."

"I sometimes wonder——" Pen began, and stopped.

Tom's eyes met hers; he bent toward her.

"Wonder what?"

"Wonder what they think of me, the grown-ups," Pen said, wishing, even as she heard her own words, that she were not quite such a fool as to open this subject. "Whatever happens, whatever I do, I'm in wrong with them. They know—you all know—how I happened to marry Jeff! I've not done anything since to make them dislike me. But I simply don't—*click*. What do they really think? Do they think I'm after alimony? Do they think I planned Jeff's accident——"

"Now go easy, go easy," Tom said warningly, as her voice thickened.

Pen subsided. She sighed, faintly shrugged her bare shoulders, sat back.

"I'm in disgrace tonight," she said. "I couldn't help doing what I did. There are times—— But what does it all matter?" she ended, wearily. "It's all at cross purposes anyway. And I needn't bother *you* with it."

"You're not bothering me," Tom said. "And I think you'd be surprised, Pen," he added suddenly, in a low quick voice, "to know just exactly what some of us do think of you—what one of us does, at least. To me you're the finest person I ever knew, the sweetest and the most—the most wonderful. I see you with Hannah, and with my mother, and with the children, and I think that you're—you're contributing something to the Flaggs that they've never had before, and that they've needed very much!"

"I don't mean to make you say things like that, Tom," Penelope said in a low tone, not looking up.

"That isn't just a pretty speech." She did look up now and saw the dark flush on his face. "And at that," Tom said, with an uncomfortable shred of laughter, "I didn't mean to say it."

"But I hope it is true," she said, very low. "If you believed in me, Tom, I believe I could go on; I believe I could be wonderful, someday!"

"Believe in you!" he said on an abrupt laugh. "Whatever you want to think of my opinion of you, Pen, you'll not realize—you can't . . ."

He had not meant to say so much, indeed to say anything of this at all. She hardly knew what she was hearing. They looked at each other bewilderedly for a moment or two, then Pen turned to speak to George, to make him talk to her, and after a moment heard Tom talking with little Mrs Rudd.

It was Mrs Rudd who told her mother later that young Mrs Flagg must have been terribly tired before dinner, for as soon as she had a little food she regained her color and sparkle, and was altogether the most beautiful woman Dolly Rudd ever had seen.

CHAPTER XXVII

"Do you realize that I've been studying, gosh darn it, for about twenty years?" Jeff demanded. Penelope, looking up over her sewing, laughed unsympathetically.

"Put that way, it sounds awful."

"It is awful. I'll be twenty-six in March, and I started to school when I was five."

"Yes; but you didn't do much studying."

"I did, too! Twenty years ago, and gol dern it, here I still am with books and seminars and lectures, and finals in two weeks!"

"I don't remember ever studying anything very hard," Pen said thoughtfully.

"You finished high school."

"Oh yes; I got through. But examinations never were very dreadful to me. It's the spasmodic way you go at them, Jeff, which makes them so hard for you. All through the Christmas holidays you didn't open a book."

"Is that so-o-o-o? I read a lot, down at the house."

"Well, you did read a little. But considering how important next month is——" Penelope stopped, driven suddenly into her own thoughts. Next month would be February; her child would be due then. And Jeff, if he could, would pass his bar examinations. It was a milestone in their lives, this coming month. She found herself wishing that both ordeals were over.

She and Jeff had come back to the city apartment, Jeff determined to set a new record for himself, Penelope making no audible promises, and yet so changed within her own soul that sometimes she hardly remembered the old Penelope. It was hard now to go back even a year or two and try to remember what emotions, what impulses had actuated her. As for the real past, the lazy girlhood days of dreaming and idling under the little grape arbor in the shade of the Parsonses' windmill, they were all another life. The ignorance of them, the strange inefficiency of them, the lack of any driving principle or formed ambition amazed her in retrospect. Unmade beds, unwashed dishes, unexecuted plans, unnoted hours and hours had drifted by, her nineteenth, twentieth, twenty-first years had passed and left no mark.

If upon a certain day her mother had not decided that the silly old sampler ought to come out of its frame, she might be back there still, in Armitage Lane, with agreeable episodes with Kelly Quentin to afford an occasional welcome break, and disagreeable crises with Phil to provide shadows. Just on a chance she had come in the burning heat to Flaggwood, to see if the Flaggs wanted the sampler, and all the rest had followed.

When her musings reached Tom's visit of warning, Jeff's accident, the strange days of vigil at Flaggwood, and the sudden marriage in the sick-room, the analysis of her old feeling became harder than ever. What had she thought she was doing, marrying this dying man? What did any girl think she was doing when she married? What did any two persons know of each other, before they had experienced the months of close companion-ship, the sharing of meals and rooms and name and joys and sorrows, the awakening that was marriage?

Had she ever loved Jeff? She did not know. She knew that they were man and wife now, snugly warm in their little Washington Street apart-ment on this wet January night; the man sleepily digging into law books, the woman embroidering tiny pink roses on little cotton nightgowns. She knew that Jeff could be amusing and adorable when he wanted to be, and that then she was happy and ready to enjoy anything that life offered. And she knew that he could be otherwise, professing deep passionate love for her even while not altering by one iota his plans to play poker or to go on stag parties, irritable and sensitive under any reproaches afterward. And she knew that for the most part he was in neither one mood nor the other; usually he was just a human being, hungry for breakfast, interested in the sporting news, getting a late start for his lecture room, coming home grimed and tired and hungry at night. He was wearily appreciative of a good dinner and wearily critical of a poor one. And after dinner the scene, twenty-five nights a month, was what it was tonight: colored Lily doing the dishes, Penelope sewing, Jeff absorbed restlessly in law books.

Sometimes at ten o'clock they went to a late movie, but this was too tiring to be a regular custom; Penelope tired easily and liked to get to bed early. Sometimes, on week ends, they went down to Flaggwood. The gar-dens were bare now in the cold winter airs, and some of the trees leafless; there could be no more sleeping on the sleeping porch; such visitors as the old people had occupied the guest rooms in the big house, where radiators clicked all day long and big fires blazed. There were waffles and sausages for breakfast, and brisk walks in sweaters and heavy-soled shoes; if the sun were shining, the women, playing bridge or backgammon in the warm library, would hear the croquet balls clicking on the lawn. George and Emily had gone away; Uncle Teege was soon going on a longer journey than any of theirs. Aunt Hannah and Aunt Constance were on a trip around the world; they would see Concy and her French husband in Paris; George and Emily might have been sent to Paris by that time, too. The clan was scattered.

But Hannah was there, always sweet and companionable, and there were plenty of others to fill the long table with the dark-eyed olive-skinned Flagg faces and keep the conversation moving. Lucy, in her sophomore year in Stanford; Peggy in her last year in a smart finishing school; Lucy and Ann and their children; Uncle Mark sighing over business conditions; Aunt Margaret, animated, spirited, protestant and knitting; Amy, drooping and gentle and sad.

Hannah and Penelope formed themselves into a sort of guard for Aunt 'Lizabeth. Uncle Teege was failing fast, but his wife would not see it, or would not admit that she saw it. But she never left his side unless the girls coaxed her into taking a short walk, or coming down to see the begonias in the hothouse, or the new arrangement in the museum.

Jeff's old grandfather and grandmother still reigned, or rather the old woman did, for the senior Thomas Flagg lived very quietly in his eighty-second year, walking through the stable yards and gardens, inspecting new calves, new puppies, new foals, spending contented hours by the fire with his books and newspapers or his solitaire. It was his stalwart old partner who still occasionally went into town for a day's shopping, penetrated into her own kitchens to see what was going on, wrote endless letters, on a sloping little rosewood and purple felt desk set on her knee, and had a hand and a voice in everything that occurred.

Penelope saw her family often, never having good news from them. She wished sometimes, a little wearily, that just once they would send her home heartened and optimistic about their affairs, but they never did. There was never any money in the cottage; there was always poignant need of it. Customarily she emptied her purse while she was there. "Here, darling, I'll pay the rest on the hat. Give me that bill, Mother. I can let you have five, Phil."

She had no reward, for they thought her much richer than she was; thought her resources were practically inexhaustible. Sometimes when she had strained her credit to the utmost to help them, Persis would say innocently: "We're not like you, Pen, who just have to ask for it!" or her mother would murmur complacently: "I wouldn't take this, dear, if I didn't know that neither you nor the Flaggs will ever miss it!"

As a matter of fact the Jefferson Flaggs would only have been able to make ends meet by constant watching and good management, and as Pen knew little of good management, and Jeff refused to follow any system at all, they were always in money difficulties. This distressed Pen for more reasons than one. It hurt her pride to have Jeff appeal to his family, as she knew he often did, and it hurt her affections to see her own people in need of necessities while so much money was being wasted.

But there was no use fretting about what she could not change. Pen had learned to keep her mouth shut about what was incurable. She reasoned with Jeff; she was as gentle, as tactfully persuasive as she could manage to be. But when she failed, she accepted failure philosophically; perhaps order and reason would emerge from all this confusion someday. For the present she could only act for each minute as if that minute were the only one, and be patient, and hope.

Twice Jeff had failed her in the six months before her child was born. Once, in November, he had not come home on a Saturday night, and it was only on Sunday afternoon, and after she had suffered a real agony of nervous apprehension, that he had come unsteadily into the room where she and Tom had been trying to play cards. Tom had been helpful; there had been few words, and afterward Tom had gone away without comment. Jeff had been sorry, of course, and had started upon the straight and narrow path of good behavior all over again.

The second time had been in early January, when he had lost a Christmas check at roulette; five hundred wonderful dollars that would have meant so much, Pen had thought, to her own people. She had been angry then, bursting out in nervous exasperation, saying bitter things she had not meant, reminding him that her marriage to him had taken place only because of the innocent misrepresentations made by the doctors after his accident.

Jeff had been so crushed that he had actually frightened her. He had turned white; he had been afraid to speak. Afterward, when she was silent and shaking and sick with revulsion from her own fury, he had knelt at her chair, and locked his arms about her, and pressed his wet face into her knees.

"You've got to forgive me, Pen, because I love you. I can't live without you! I know what a scut I am, but I swear it was for you, Pen, that I wanted to double the money. I wanted to give you a check for three thousand for the baby, Pen, so we could move into a bigger place, and have a little nursery for him, and everything! I went into Art Lewis's place, and they had a wheel there, and we played nickels, and I was so damn lucky, Ned said we ought to go get into a game somewhere. I didn't know where there was one, I'll swear that, Pen. I hadn't the faintest idea where there was a wheel in San Francisco. I hadn't played three times before I was up to seventeen hundred—fool that I was not to quit! But I'd just gotten there, and I had a stack left from the original stake, and I said I'd play that. And she came up zero seven times in thirty rolls."

For a day or two she had maintained silence; she had been completely aloof from him. But this never worked with Jeff; he knew too well how to dramatize it. He was meek, hard working, gentle. He brought home a tiny pair of moccasins for the expected baby. He abased himself; he could not call himself sufficiently severe names. And in the end she forgave him, and they went down to Flaggwood in a softened mood to each other; Jeff's perhaps not very deep, Pen's perhaps not very confident, but the forgiving, the penitence, the forgetting infinitely refreshing to their souls.

On a certain February night when Jeff had finished his work and was yawningly watching Penelope play her last game of solitaire, Ned Truax came in. He was a small man, sandy-complexioned and redheaded and amusing; Penelope did not like him. But Jeff was so bored with his work and so sleepy that even Ned was welcome to her tonight; he would afford Jeff a break, and they could talk their unending boxing and tennis and golf championship gossip together.

They said they were hungry, and, as Lily had gone home, Pen went into the kitchen and scrambled them some eggs, bringing in the golden heaps and a pot of hot coffee just as the clock was striking eleven. Penelope watched them start into the supper, and then excused herself; she was sleepy and was going to bed.

"Don't you keep Jeff up too late, Ned."

"Five minutes," Ned said with his mouth full.

Penelope went to bed, creaming her face, stretching her stiff young body that was so twisted and dragged out of shape, brushing her thick long hair. She took up her book, read for a few minutes. But the presence of the two men in the adjoining room fretted her; she could not read herself sleepy. Why didn't Ned go home and let Jeff come to bed?

She was out of bed and at the door; she would put her head out and say merely, "Midnight, gentlemen!" They couldn't object to that; she didn't care if they did. Anything was better than this lying awake, cold and restless, waiting for Jeff.

But when she opened the door a crack to peer into the living room she saw that it was empty. They had not finished their eggs and toast; they had not put out the lights; they had simply and quietly departed.

Penelope was angry; she hardly knew why. Jeff and Ned had a right to go out for a turn about the block if they wanted to. Perhaps Jeff was only walking with him to the street car. But she was angry, shaking with chill, sleepy, tired just the same. She wished Ned Truax wouldn't come in and see Jeff; she thought that Jeff might have had the common decency to tell her they were going out.

Perhaps they thought she was asleep. But all Jeff had to do was to push open the bedroom door to see that she was reading. There was never any good in it when he went out with Ned Truax. Oh, why shouldn't they? They were grown men; they had a right to do as they liked. Why should a man consider his wife's comfort when she had lost her beauty and was tired and irritable all the time?

Pen sat on the edge of a chair in the dining room and hugged her chilled body in her arms; she was in her thin silk nightgown, she had not reached for a robe, and now she needed it and would not move to get it.

[240]

She yawned wearily, and hooped herself so that the curve of her back rested against the chair.

Lights were burning brightly; the half-eaten supper, cold eggs and bitten toast, the curdled cups of creamed coffee and the cigarette ends were unlovely in the bright glare.

"Cold," Penelope said, on a yawn. "It's frightfully cold."

Her mind began the clearing up, piled dishes in the sink, set a kettle to boil for her hot-water bottle, extinguished lights. But she did not stir.

"They've probably gone somewhere where there's gambling. Well, if he's that way he's that way. If his father and mother and grandparents and wife and the prospect of a child won't steady him . . ."

Moments ticked up. She seemed held like a person in a dream. In her heart was a deep resentment of Jeff, yet every fiber of her longed to have him return, to hear his stealthy key in the lock and the beginning of his apologies.

Oh, if you could only do something with life, instead of having it eternally do things to you! It would be so wonderful to be molding it, making it fit to some plan . . .

"I can't sit here, I'll get pneumonia. Hot water for my bottle, that's the first thing."

Her fingers gripping the table edge to give her a lever against the ungainliness of her figure, she rose. And instantly pain rose too, a breathtaking, shocking wave of it, and Penelope, frightened, feeling the blood stop in her heart and wet drops spring to her forehead, sat down again, panting.

It had come, had it? She had known it would come. But now it was here, which was somehow a completely terrifying and unexpected thing. The pain went away blissfully, ebbing and dying like a scream, and there was peace, and electrified into activity now she availed herself of it.

"What to do now? I have to do something; what to do? The doctor—no, the hospital first. Telephone the hospital—but if that pain comes again when I'm at the telephone," she said clearly and aloud. "It doesn't matter; I'll have to do something. Mother—she has no telephone. Isolde—it wouldn't do any good. The Flaggs—Tom—Tom's in town; he'll find Jeff for me anyway. . . ."

She telephoned the hospital; they were all ready for Mrs Flagg. She talked to the elevator boy downstairs in the apartment house; he would get her a taxi, yes, ma'am. Then she called Tom's club. Mr Thomas Flagg, please, and say it is very important; it is Mrs Flagg calling.

Two minutes of shaking cold and suspense; then blessedly, like a warm flood of light upon her chill and nervousness, Tom's voice.

"Hello, this is Tom. Mother? Is it Dad?"

"No, it's Pen, Tom. Penelope. Jeff's out; he went out about an hour ago with Ned Truax. And I—I don't feel well."

"You don't feel well!" Here was one person at least to whom her welfare was important. His words were like pistol shots.

"I'm going to the hospital, Tom. I've telephoned there; that part of it's all right. But I didn't know how to manage the rest."

"I'll come for you at once, of course. I'll be dressed in five minutes—I'll be there in ten minutes!"

"No; I've a taxi here; I've packed a bag. I'm all right; it won't take me five minutes to get there, and they expect me. But it's getting hold of Jeff——"

"You mean you're all alone?"

"Yes. Lily goes home nights, you know, and Jeff went out."

"Ha!" What Tom thought of it all was evident in his tone, but he made no further comment except to say: "If you can get to the hospital perhaps you'd better not waste any time. I'll see what I can do about Jeff."

Pen packed a bag with trembling cold fingers, dressed herself, got into a big warm coat. She scribbled a note to Jeff, went down to the street. The taxi was waiting under the cold night lights, but as she crossed the sidewalk another car drew up behind it and Tom leaped out. He caught her bag from the elevator boy.

"Pen, I was in time! Here, I'll take that. Wait a minute."

He went to dismiss the taxi, came back, and settled her with her bag in his car. When she was on the front seat he leaned over the door.

"All right?"

"F-fine," she said with chattering teeth.

"You're cold!"

"No." She laughed uncertainly. "Just—nervous, I guess. I'm all right."

"We won't be a minute." He went about to the driver's seat; the door slammed; they were on their way. Pen huddled in her big coat in silence; she did not speak during the short trip.

Bewildered, she was absorbed into the smooth hospital routine. The big halls were clean and bright; everyone was quick and efficient; the tones of her doctor and her nurse were matter-of-course and reassuring. She was going to be a marvelous patient, Miss Partridge said. Miss Partridge made no fuss and asked no questions; she put two comforting hot-water bags into the high flat bed, and brought Pen a cup of thin delicious chicken soup.

Pen was presently warm, relaxed, idle; lying in the dimly lighted empty room that smelled of carbolic and ether, watching the nurse folding things, opening cardboard boxes, coming and going noiselessly, in her pipe-clayed white shoes and stiff uniform. Miss Partridge was pretty, with a strawberry mark on one cheekbone.

Queer hours were recorded on the face of the little clock that Miss Partridge, at some half-forgotten long ago time, had wound and set with quick movements of her capable little hands. Three o'clock was not afternoon; quarter to seven was morning, with the hospital waking, and the lights out. Pen was nervous and tired now; she talked and moved restlessly. She felt frightened and desolate, and yet kept hoping that Tom wouldn't come back, that the family wouldn't begin to come in, that Jeff wouldn't be found. Much better to be alone in all this.

After a while there was a message from Tom. Everything was all right, and he and Mr Flagg would be at the hospital soon. So he had found Jeff? But Jeff had been gone for days. No; it was only yesterday—it was only last night that Jeff had been sleepily watching her play her last game of solitaire beside their fire, and Ned had come in.

She forgot them all. She was fighting hard; sometimes droning meaningless words, half under the blessed drugs; sometimes acutely awake, her wet face working, her hair—heavy and soft and gold—pushed off her forehead and pinned under a white towel.

"We will have to do something about this," the doctor said sympathetically, and the nurse murmured admiringly: "She's being so brave," and she knew that neither meant it; that there was a great deal more of this ahead and that they were trying to cheer her without meaning for one moment to help.

Fortunately, she thought breathlessly in a moment of respite, fortunately one became too much absorbed in the business, too sleepy and weary and angry, to care what they said or what they did.

"Your sister, Mrs Tasker, is here," the nurse presently told her. In a lull, Isolde came in, white and pitiful and affectionate; she held Pen's hands, and gritted her own teeth, and said through them: "It won't last, darling," when Pen was seized upon by a fresh wave of agony. "Keep your eye on the clock—it won't be forever!" said Isolde.

The city whistles shrilled and droned for noon; but Pen did not hear them. It was almost one o'clock when she opened her eyes to a strange sweet world that was without pain. She was afraid to move for fear the agony would come back; she was warm and safe in blankets, no sheets, no pillow; she was drenched with sweat. But it didn't matter; the pain was over.

Somebody told her that she had a little daughter; the fact seemed to belong to events that had taken place long years in the past. She remembered dimly that there was to be a boy or a girl; it seemed odd to have it settled. A girl. "That's a very cute little daughter of yours. The nurses were all laughing at her, she put up such a fight."

Pen was conscious only of wanting to be left alone, to drowse, and get rid of the sticky sweet taste and smell that drenched mouth and nostrils, and rest. If she moved she might hurt somewhere; she would not move. Perhaps she was dreaming all this; perhaps she was lying on the sitting-room couch at home in that odd state between waking and sleeping that had so long made her days unreal, and dreaming that the baby had come. No; she wouldn't dream so definitely of a daughter.

Isolde came back; she had gone home to see to her own babies; she looked tired and pale.

"Tom Flagg is downstairs," she told Pen. "He sent you his love, and said that Jeff will be in at about five. Where's Jeff been all this time?"

"Out of town," Pen said simply.

"It was Tom Flagg who telephoned me at about eight."

"It's over," Pen stated, speaking to herself.

"It's just beginning—you wait!" Isolde said, with a little laugh. "But then you've only got the one, and a good maid," she added.

Miss Partridge came in with flowers; boxes and boxes of them. There were messages with them from all the Flaggs, Ann Merry, Lucy Towne, Mary Cline, Aunt Hannah, Aunt 'Lizabeth, Amy and Hannah. There were baby roses from the Merry children, and a little china lamb filled with daisies from tiny Tom Cline. There were pink roses, two dozen of them, with a card on which the names of Mr and Mrs Thomas Jefferson Flagg had been scratched, and a firmly penciled "Gram and Grandfather" had been written. "God bless the dear little girl and her mother," Gram had written underneath.

Pen, after sleep, and more soup, and ice cream, was in such spirits late in the afternoon that when Mr Thomas Flagg was announced she asked to see him. They were alone for the two minutes Miss Partridge granted.

"How are you?"

"Marvelous!"

"It was awful, wasn't it?"

"Partly because I was such a fool I didn't know what I was in for."

"I wanted to tell you," Tom said, "that Jeff's all right. He's asleep now, and he's going to be here about six. He's all right. I didn't tell them anything—I mean Aunt Margaret and Uncle Mark—about his having been away last night."

"You saw them?"

"Oh, they've been here and had a peek at the baby! First grandchild, you know. I saw her, too. They hold 'em up at the door of the room, and you look through the glass."

Pen smiled languidly.

"Is she cute?" she asked indifferently.

"She's one of the Flaggs, all right. Black hair. She was waving her arms and legs, sort of slumped into a blanket. You can't see much, but I thought you might like the report of an eyewitness."

"Thank you. Tom, was Jeff drunk last night?"

"Yep."

Pen sighed, looking away.

"Why do we all protect him?" she asked.

"I suppose to protect *them*," Tom answered, after a moment's frowning thought.

"And life has always protected them," Pen said dryly. "That's reason enough, I suppose."

"Well, doesn't it make it smoother for everyone?" the man asked in a troubled voice.

"It certainly makes it smoother for Jeff," she said bitterly. Miss Partridge, unobtrusively stepping around the screen, ended the conversation.

"I think, Mr Flagg, that I'll have to——"

"Yes, yes, yes," Tom said hastily, getting up. "Jeff'll be in a little later," he said in farewell to Pen.

"All right. And thanks so much for everything, Tom. That's my husband's cousin," Pen said, in explanation to the nurse, when Tom had gone. "He was the only one I could get hold of last night. We didn't expect the baby for another ten days, and Mr Flagg was away."

"I think that's one of the handsomest men I've ever seen," Miss Partridge said dreamily. "I love that dark ugly type—I don't mean ugly— but with the jaw stuck out that way, and big teeth. I'll bet he's nice."

Later she asked Pen if she would like to see the baby, and Pen leaned over a little to look down on a dark, pulpy, angry little face, with heavy closed eyelids.

"Frog," she murmured.

"She's a wonderful baby," said the nurse. "Vigorous. She's the liveliest thing I ever got hold of."

But Pen was tired now, and felt suddenly depressed and sick; she ached when she moved, and her head hurt. She tried to go to sleep again, failed, twisted about, complained to the doctor, and felt the nurse rubbing her arm with cotton as a preliminary to a hypodermic. When Jeff came they would not let him disturb her; she slept until midnight, was hungry, laughed for the first time, slept again.

CHAPTER XXVIII

The baby was named Elizabeth for Penelope's mother, and Pen liked to think that it was for Tom's gentle mother, too; it was one of the Flagg names. She was christened in the little wintry church that was nearest Flaggwood, Tom and Persis accepting the responsibility of godparents. She wore the famous Flagg christening robe of delicate yellowed handkerchief linen heavily embroidered and set with panels of fine lace. Penelope was amazed at the smoothness with which one more baby was fitted into the life of the clan. Every woman in the family took an affectionate interest in the little Elizabeth, and when Pen went down in March for a visit and a rest, one of the younger maids was delegated to help her with the baby. Jeff's mother was especially devoted; Pen saw a new side to the brisk, dominating character of her mother-in-law. Margaret Flagg came to Pen's apartment twice a day; immediately after breakfast when the pulpy, well-behaved Elizabeth was having orange juice, was being bathed and dressed and bottled before her long midday sleep, and again at six, when much the same routine was preceding her extinction for the night. She loved to handle the baby, to lay the soft little fragrant face against her own dark cheek; she would hold Elizabeth while Pen and Marie busied themselves with the elaborate paraphernalia of the modern nursery.

Elizabeth was a modern baby. She knew nothing of colic, croup or rashes; she rarely cried, and then only in an argumentative, drowsy fashion, when placed on her face for sleep. She developed fast, her dark eyes following her mother about the room, her button of a mouth struggling to form sounds before she was four months old. The Flagg men photographed her on Sundays, the tiny expressionless face close up against Pen's beautiful one.

Penelope loved her with a passion that possessed her completely. She feared, she hoped, she planned incessantly for Buff. Lily, the colored maid who took care of her kitchen in the city apartment, had named the baby by beginning with a careful "Ellabuff." After a while it was Buff to everyone; Pen fancied that it fitted the dark, small, energetic girl, with her silky black mop.

She hung over her child asleep; she caught Buff up against her face and kissed the little temples, kissed the soft sweet back of her neck, kissed the small square feet when it was bath hour. Buff's goodness, her smallness, her helplessness wound chains about Penelope's heart; the world was her baby. She looked at the young Flagg mothers—Amy, Mary, Lucy, Ann— with new understanding. No wonder they looked complacent when the children were tearing about over the lawns and through the shrubberies; no wonder they said so often to the nurses: "I believe I'll take him up and put him to bed tonight!" The possession of compact, complete, soft little Elizabeth, her velvet weight, the snuffling little sounds she made close to her mother's ear, her turtle-raised dark head in the crib when she was awakening, were all so many miracles of delight to her young mother, as was every other minute of her day. She contrasted Elizabeth's royal beginnings with the troubled start of the three small nephews in Isolde's cluttered studio, and her heart ached for them. Presently she sent Isolde the birthday check that dying, magnificent old Uncle Teege had given her. But Isolde and Grandy, while affectionately appreciative, did not spend the check for a nurse's wages, as Pen had suggested; they rented a houseboat in Belvedere for two months, and spent the summer fishing little boys out of the bay.

Through the first weeks of Elizabeth's life, Pen did not speak to Jeff except when it was unavoidable. She would not discuss his conduct on the night of the baby's birth; she did not complain; she told no one what had occurred. Wearily, politely, coldly, she ignored her husband as much as was possible. In the city apartment she changed his sleeping quarters to the little extra room that had been described by the agent as a "den," and that some of the tenants used as a servant's room. When he hinted that he would like to go downtown to see "a feller for a minute" she bowed her head; when a few minutes later he decided not to go, but to stay at home and study, she did not give him the word or glance of praise for which he was hinting.

Buff was too small to make much personal appeal to her father, but Jeff, wanting to placate his wife, would praise her and tease her somewhat self-consciously when he came in late in the afternoons. Sometimes Pen permitted this, herself looking boredly into space while it went on; sometimes she said, "Don't distract her now, please, Jeff. She's just being settled off." On Sundays she often left the house in midmorning, taking the baby with her to Isolde's. She would spend the entire day there, not happy, but absorbed in the care of the four children, and in talk of them, and in family gossip. And late in the afternoon she would return, showing no sign of interest if Jeff, working hard, were pathetically glad to have her return, and no sign of resentment when he returned if he had gone downtown to dinner.

"You hate me, don't you?" he asked her once.

"Not at all."

"You don't love me, then."

To this Pen made no answer.

"Is it because I threw you down the night Buff was born? But, good Lord, Pen, I didn't know. It's rotten to rub it into me for something I never meant to do. I know it was a rotten thing to do——"

"It's not that I'm rubbing it in," she said once, when there had been a great deal of this. "It's simply that I don't see the use of letting myself worry about you any more. You're going on saying that you're going to pull up, and not doing it, and promising me things, and not meaning it, and I simply get tired of it, that's all."

And she rose, with the baby in her arms, and went into her own room with no further comment.

When they went down to Flaggwood in June, Jeff's mother asked her, in one of their nursery hours one day, if he had taken his bar examinations.

"Oh yes!" Pen said confidently, although she really did not know.

"Have you any idea how he got along with them?"

"I haven't, really, Aunt Margaret."

Margaret Flagg sighed.

"Funny if Mark passes the bar examinations before Jeff does. Jeff's twenty-six now, and Mark only twenty-four. But I believe Mark's going to distinguish himself. My father was Judge Ogilvie; Mark's very like him. Are you worried about Jeff's work, Penelope?"

"Not a bit," Penelope said serenely. Her mother-in-law looked relieved.

"Then you think he will pass?"

"I don't know."

That was all of that. But it was not long after this that Penelope's recently acquired self-control was put to a sharp test, and incidentally she discovered that Jeff had once more avoided the risk of flunking by not attempting the final law-school examinations at all.

She said to him one day quietly:

"Jeff, Hannah happened to say something today about my 'allowance.' I didn't say anything, but I didn't understand. Is your grandfather making me an allowance? Hannah spoke as if he made it to all the girls."

"You knew that," Jeff said, over his shoulder. He was at his bureau, looking at ties.

"Since when?"

"Oh, a few months. Since Buff came. The idea being a nurse's salary, I believe."

"Yes; but they pay Marie."

"Because she's here anyway."

A silence. Penelope looked at her husband's back, and warned herself in her heart: "Don't go to pieces. Don't go to pieces. You'll only frighten Buff."

"How much is it, Jeff?"

"You know how much it is, because I told you, and you knew I was paying off some bills and put it in the bank!"

Steady now, steady.

"When did you tell me?"

"When they sent it, the first month. Sometime, anyway. In the hospital maybe. I don't know!" he said impatiently.

"You never said one word of it, Jeff."

A pause. Then he said smoothly:

"Oh yes, I did, and you've forgotten it. What's the kick, anyway? We said we'd always pool our money, didn't we? I've never held out on you. I want to get out of debt, and I want to get a job, and I thought you'd just as soon help me out."

Remembering all that the Flagg money had done for her, and that her very wardrobe as a bride had come from them, she was silent.

"You say you want to get a job? Aren't you taking your bar exams next fall?" she presently asked.

"Not next fall!" he said airily and began to whistle. Penelope sat looking at him thoughtfully; she did not speak.

But silence became too difficult to maintain, especially when they were established for the summer at Flaggwood and the family chatter was all about them. It began to seem senseless and priggish to Penelope to hold this aloof and moral attitude toward Jeff when they were alone, and to be graciously conversational when the others were within hearing. He was boyishly proud of himself as being "on the wagon" now; she knew that the effort at self-control made him feel nervous and upset. Suddenly, one day when he was watching her finish Buff's bath, she went to him and laid the freshly dressed, fragrant baby in his arms, and as she did so stooped and brushed a kiss against his dark forehead. Instantly he sprang up, mother and child in his embrace, and little Buff was almost smothered between her father's shaken tears and her mother's shaken laughter.

Just what mental and spiritual processes had brought her to this moment of forgiveness, Penelope did not know. It was an impulse she had had to follow at the moment; afterward she was glad, for Jeff was gay and happy again, and the atmosphere between them was pleasanter than it ever had been. Her disapproval never seemed to have much effect upon his actions, but his mood suffered under it very much, and he was so touchingly grateful to her for her forgiveness that Pen's own heart was soothed and satisfied, and the bitterness temporarily washed away.

They talked over their problems that day, and Jeff promised to tell Tom the whole story and to abide by Tom's advice. Should he face the music, give up the law, try to find an opening in some business? Or should he tell his father that once more his summer must be spent in coaching, that he owed gambling debts again, that he must start all over again?

Jeff was so lovable, in this penitent, honest mood, so eager to be forgiven, so lavish with promises, that Penelope somehow felt very near to him, even while her mind told her that his reformation was no more likely to last than it had been before, even while she despised her own weakness in believing in him.

One day, clad in the heavy brocade pajamas that the Flagg women almost always wore in the mornings, she was crossing a dewy lawn in mid-morning toward the big house when Tom called her from the croquet field.

"Pen, what you doing?"

"Going to find Hannah. She ought to be in the office."

"She's not. She's gone to market. Come over here and play croquet."

"Oh, I'm awful, Tom," Penelope said, pausing near him and smiling up at him. With him were Jim Towne and Uncle Peter.

"You're no worse than Uncle Pete. Come on. I'll take you, and Jim can take Uncle Pete. We'll pack you round!"

"What are you doing at home at half past ten in the morning, Tom?"

"I have to be in court in Redwood City at two; it wasn't worth while going in. Take a mallet, Pen."

"Well, I'll play," Pen agreed, "but I'm awful."

"Pete's awful," Amy said, from the side lines. She smiled shyly at her husband. Peter did not seem to hear her.

"Take the black and start, Pen."

"We're off," Jim said.

The game took a long hour and a half; the June day was warm. Pen's forehead was wet; her gold hair plastered itself against it in spirals. She played with desperate concentration, gasping with excitement when a shot went right, wailing apologies to Tom when she missed.

"Oh, Tom, I'm so dumb! I'm making it so hard for you."

"I'll save you," Tom said. Their eyes met, and they laughed at each other. Pen could only marvel at the way he did save her; his long shots spun straight across the big field and went home with unerring force; he played the balls as he liked, placing them in the different strategic positions long before he needed them, following up through wicket after wicket to play them trimly in turn. He was a rover; he was back at Pen's wicket to help her. She began to feel less fear and more excitement.

"And Uncle Peter's dead on him, Tom? And he has to sock? Well, then, why shouldn't I come to you?"

An audience had gathered now; Uncle Teege had been wheeled down to a post in the shade, Aunt 'Lizabeth beside him. Lucy, Jim's wife, with little Farmer, who had been ill, was there; Hannah, back from the village; Aunt Constance; Jeff's little sister Lucy, her new beau Lieutenant Draper; Ann Merry, expecting a fourth baby. Lastly, Gram and Grandfather came down in time for the thrilling last plays, they were there when Penelope made the one remarkable shot of her game. She made it blindly, in complete discouragement, for she was far from Tom, through a stupid misplay, and the red and blue balls were together.

Her shot curved up the field magnificently; her ball struck the red ball, fell close to her wicket.

"Pen," Tom said, in the hushed ecstasy only the croquet player knows, "are you alive on it?"

"Absolutely. Dead on the other two. Shall I make my wicket?"

"Make——?" Tom was dazed with the magnitude of the triumph. "Of course that's your wicket," he said. "Of course you'll make it. All *that* shot was, was the game! Go through. Hit it again. You're marvelous. Give it to me and play blue."

Ten minutes later the game ended in triumph, and Tom walked over to the chairs beside Pen.

"Champion timber here, Grandfather."

"It looked like it, Tom. That was a magnificent shot!"

"That was an accident," said Pen, flushed and happy.

"Yep, but the tyros don't have those accidents," Tom reminded her. And again they looked at each other, and a slow wave of deep joy arose in Pen's being and seemed to float her off her feet into some place of aerial delight.

Tom threw himself down at his mother's feet; the long lean body stretched out in its white flannels, the dark head darker against Aunt 'Lizabeth's white dress. Pen sat down, trembling with a feeling that was like nothing she had ever felt in her life before. Tom. Tom. Tom. All this beauty of summer lawns and gardens, and deep green shade under the trees, and whir of water sprinklers and flash of birds was made miraculous because Tom was there.

That evening, when she and Jeff went into the library, Tom was already present, sitting on a sort of hassock at his grandmother's knee, talking to her. Pen saw the firelight and the lamplight shining on his brown, serious face; she saw the face change into a smile as he got to his feet to include Jeff and herself in the circle.

"Sit here, Pen," he said. Pen, with an answering smile, took the big chair he indicated; she was silent tonight, sometimes glancing about the big old-fashioned room that was filled with drifting figures, sometimes staring dreamily at the fire. A feeling of complete content possessed her. She could have sat on here forever in the olive-green velvet gown, with the logs blazing in the fireplace, and the lamps softly shining, and the various Flaggs talking and laughing in their subdued before-dinner voices. Nothing mattered now; nothing else but that Tom was in the world and would now and then speak to her or look at her.

The enchantment went on and on; it irradiated her days with light, and the problems with which her own family was eternally confronting her and the nearer problem of Jeff receded into the background, were forgotten. For a while Pen did not know what the new magic was; then she did know, and could not change it, could not stop it. She made no attempt to do so. To feel as she felt now was to have all life singing and shining and thrilling; her entire being was possessed with it; she could have checked her heartbeats as soon as drag herself back to the old troubled drabness of living and leave this enchantment behind.

There was no outward sign between them as the summer days went on in flower scents and tree shadows, splashing of pool waters and click of tennis balls. No sign, at least, of which they were conscious. But Tom had a fashion now of being near her in the group; perhaps not to talk to her especially, or even address her directly at all, but there. Her eyes met his across the long dinner table; he had only to say her name to set her senses adrift. Her own voice saying his had cadences that had never been there before.

Tom was one of the handsomest of the dark Flaggs; tall, lean, his gray-black eyes keen under the heavy Flagg brows, his skin burned an Indian tan. He was, with his Uncle Mark, at the head of the family affairs in the San Francisco office, and managed the estate of his invalided father and mother as well. It was a large estate, Pen learned, for Aunt 'Lizabeth, once Gram's demure little secretary, had presently become, through an uncle's death, an heiress. Tom, at thirty, carried these responsibilities gallantly; nothing ever worried him, as he sent cables here and there, made air trips to Seattle or Los Angeles; he was always free for croquet with the other men or chess with his father. They all respected Tom's opinion, and

Pen gathered a general impression from the conversation of the uncles and cousins that Tom was considered the most brilliant member of the clan.

"Tom ought to run for Congress," Hannah said. Pen, when she first had heard this, had thought how Hannah would like to have accompanied him to the capital as his wife, and what a distinguished couple they would be. But now that Uncle Teege was growing feebler and feebler every day there was no talk of anything that would take Tom away from home.

The Carter Flaggs were coming up from Rio this summer; they came every second or third year; everyone was very careful to avoid any suggestion that this visit was because of Uncle Teege's failing health. Carter Flagg was Uncle Teege's son by a long-ago early marriage; his mother had died thirty-seven years ago, when the baby was born, and it was several years afterward that Uncle Teege had met Aunt 'Lizabeth and had been comforted. Carter was therefore Tom's and George's and Mary Cline's half-brother. Pen was interested to see one more Flagg and his wife and their two little girls and their boy baby. Carter had been married twice, too; his first wife had been a distant cousin, Mary Carter Farmer, so dear to Gram that while she lived there had been no question as to who next should wear the emerald ring. But lovely Mary had died when her second daughter was born, and the boy baby was the child of a new wife—Tedda.

They five were coming up from Rio; they would arrive in San Francisco in the cool fogs of a July morning; somebody had to meet them.

It was arranged that Tom would drive his car in as usual at eight; Pen would put Buff through her usual little program and follow with Hannah and her car at ten; they would meet at the boat at noon and divide the Carter Flaggs in any pleasant way; little girls with Hannah and Pen, father and mother and nurse and baby in Tom's car with him and Jeff; or Jeff driving Pen's car—or no, Hannah with Tedda—or no . . .

They discussed it, as they often did, at the long breakfast table, the children taking keen, excited interest in the arrival of almost-forgotten cousins; Lucy Towne pleading her sick little Farmer as her excuse for not meeting them, Ann pleading her impending new baby.

Pen, with an unexpected wrench at her heart, left her own baby for the first time. But immediately she forgot Buff in the novelty of driving up to town in the fresh sweet morning, and finding her way down to the big dock. She drove carefully between the crates and bales, the trucks and drays of the wharf; strange, thrilling odors were drifting into the cool, foggy, midsummer sunshine, odors of roasting coffee and tar and sea water washing on the barnacled piles. The *President Jackson* was not in, but there was plenty of shipping about, tooting of whistles, shouting of men, screaming of cranes and ropes.

Tom came over to the car through the checkered shade and sunshine of the pier.

"Where's Hannah?"

"At the last minute she couldn't come. Jean Porter's mother died last night, and Jean telephoned for her."

"Mrs Porter died? Gosh, that was sudden."

"Awful. An embolism, they said, if that means anything to you."

"We're being deserted. Jeff went home on the eleven-o'clock train."

"Jeff did?"

"He was miserable with rose cold or hay fever, or asthma, or whatever that is he gets, poor fellow. He said he was all right, but he didn't want to sneeze all over the Carters."

"Well, he'll take that stuff and sleep and be all right," Pen said cheerfully. "And it's good to have somebody down there with Marie and Buff. When will we see the *President Jackson*, Tom?"

"I was just asking. She's late. Maybe you and I ought to go uptown and have some lunch."

Pen got out of her car, and they walked together on the oil-soaked, spongy floor of the long roofed dock. They looked at the ships and the cargoes that were being so busily packed and unpacked. Pen never had made a long sea journey; her honeymoon trip to Honolulu had been her only experience of the sea. Tom said he liked the Panama trip almost the best of any he ever had taken; he showed Pen a Norwegian boat, and they agreed that with congenial companionship and a few good books that long slow trip would be a great experience.

"Do you suppose the food would be all cheese and salt fish, Tom?"

"Oh, Lord, no! They say it's perfectly delicious."

They found a taxi cruising along the Embarcadero and went uptown to the Fairmont Hotel, whose dining-room windows commanded a view of the giddiest, the most sparkling of all cities. Flags hung limp about Chinatown's turrets and pagodas; boats crossed the bay with long lines of foam; gulls wheeled and swooped and piped in the cool foggy winds.

"We can see the *Jackson* coming in from here, and we can be down there long before she's alongside," Tom said.

He had stopped in the hotel lobby to buy her gardenias; their heady, heavy sweetness was in her nostrils. There were scented flowers on all the tables, and on a round table near by, set for ten, there was a great pyramid of fruits: black plums and figs, golden pears and flushed peaches, orange-tinted apricots and sprawling purple and red grapes.

Penelope put her beige bag and her beige gloves beside her plate; she knew a tip of the creamy straw hat and the blouse she wore with her brown suit were becoming; she would have known it even without the testimony of Tom's eyes. Music, a violin, a 'cello, piano, began to play softly; her heart swelled with sheer unbearable felicity. Life was suddenly too sweet.

Tom ordered the luncheon with no reference to her; she liked that, too. He talked, as they lunched, of the Rio de Janeiro Flaggs, and of the case that had preceded his case in court that morning—a custody case.

"Poor little kid, he was only five, and he didn't know what it was all about," he said.

"But, Tom, if they both want him, the aunt and the mother, it must mean that they love him!"

"I don't know. There's a big estate involved. I don't know which had the harder face."

"It's a tragedy," Pen said, looking away, thinking of Buff and of Isolde's boys, and of the Flagg babies safe and sheltered in their sunny winter nurseries and on their shady summer lawns. "A sad childhood is a terrible tragedy, isn't it, Tom?"

"The worst of all."

"Is the father of this child dead?"

"Killed himself. The mother left him and took the baby with her, and he killed himself."

"And which are you representing, Tom?"

"Oh, neither! I was early in court and listened to some of it. It's a dirty business altogether. My case was an insurance question," Tom said. "We weren't in court fifteen minutes about that."

The enchanted moments went by. The players closed the piano and put their instruments into their cases and went away. Tom went away to telephone the steamship company; the *President Jackson* might be in any moment now. They went back to the dock and were presently immersed in the confusion of landing. Penelope knew Carter Flagg when she saw him because he was so like Tom. The half-brothers, both lean and brown of skin and black of hair, met grinning. Tedda Flagg was pretty in a Latin way; she was Brazilian born, with smooth, small, plump, brown-pink hands and a child's full soft figure. She was all concern for the children; "Jen, Maria, Tomé," she kept saying distractedly, occasionally bursting into very gushes of Portuguese with her Portuguese nurse. She smiled in wide-eyed admiration of Pen's blondness and tallness, discovered at once that this was the mother of the newest Flagg baby, and elected to drive down with Pen and the children. By the time they reached Flaggwood they were fast friends, but it was not this little adventure that lent the light to Pen's eyes and the singing notes to her voice that night, but rather the one that had preceded it. The thought of that luncheon hour with Tom stayed with her; it ran like a dreamy undercurrent of ecstasy beneath all the other hours of the day, and when she was alone with her child in the twilight, and Buff, drowsily pulling, half-asleep, was finishing her six-o'clock bottle, Pen deliberately brought it to her mind and relived it, detail by detail, word after word.

There were two facts in the world now: the first, composed of all the other realities lumped into one; the other the amazing, the transfiguring truth that Tom Flagg cared for her. Pen gave even her child but an absent-minded attention; she deeply, dearly loved this soft little lump of well-behaved babyhood, but as she kissed Buff's pulpy small cheek she

[254]

thought of Tom. Would he come up in the morning for a peep at the baby; would she meet him when she crossed the lawn for luncheon?

They did not meet daily, for Tom stayed in town most of the week, but he came home much more often than he had last summer, ostensibly because of his father's rapidly failing health, and whenever he was at home he and Penelope managed to talk, perhaps only for a few minutes, perhaps on entirely indifferent subjects, together.

At noon they always joined the swimmers by the pool; Tom straight and brown and unsmiling as an Indian in his black swimming trunks; Pen a girl of gold in a yellow suit with a yellow cap. They would lie on the grass of the "Lido" with the others before and after the swim, murmuring, silent, conscious of each other's presence and of that of no one else. Pen loved this hour, with the hot sun beating down, the birds silent, the flowers scentless in noon heat. Maids would be moving over the grass, setting bowls of salad and plates of cold chicken on the long table; every member of the big family, babies, children, youngsters, young mothers, and the older folk, would be scattered about; the pleasant Flagg voices were calling and laughing and murmuring everywhere.

One night there was dancing at a party for the Rio Flaggs. Pen danced with Tom for the first time; afterward they went out to the terrace and took basket chairs under a hot moon and looked up at the stars.

Jeff had gone early to bed tonight. He was reporting every day to the family law office in the city now and evidently being kept hard at work. He came home tired and often turned in immediately after dinner. He had elected to do this tonight, excusing himself as soon as the meal was over. Pen had stayed on, to dance with Johnny Cline and Jim Towne and Ben Merry and Mark, to dance with Tom's half-brother Carter, and finally to be asked by Tom to dance.

He had not asked her earlier in the evening. He had been engaged in a long conversation with his mother and Amy after dinner. Pen and Hannah had had their hands full, starting the younger crowd into dancing and talking together. Even with the Flaggs alone the group would have numbered forty; as it was, a score of young neighbors had been asked to come in; the big room was comfortably filled with the circling figures.

These were early parties. This one had been moving toward a triumphant ending at midnight and Tom had come over to where Pen was sitting and had signaled to her without words an invitation to dance. She had surrendered herself to his arms in equal silence, and for a few dizzy moments had felt them about her, had given herself to the joy of the movement and the music in his strong, big hold. Then he had brought her out to the terrace.

At the far end of it there was a little space screened off like a balcony with potted hydrangeas. They sat there in the tempered gloom, the moonshine washing and whitening the gardens which fell away on either side of the terrace steps below them.

"God, what a moon tonight!"

"I'm not so fond of moonlight. I like starlight."

"You look like something made of starlight tonight," Tom said, with a glance that immediately turned away again. "What is it? New?"

"Old. It was old when Concy gave it to me. But it's French," Pen said, with a fond glance downward at the glimmer of frail ruffles.

"Concy's, eh?" he said, lighting his cigarette.

"When she was married she gave away dozens of gorgeous gowns. She and Aunt Con went to Paris every year and went crazy buying new dresses."

"Does she care more for that sort of thing than most girls?"

"Oh, I don't think so. Well, perhaps a little more. Or they have more money."

"They haven't much money. They probably," Tom said dryly, "haven't as much as De Puy thinks they have."

"Oh, Tom, I thought he was rich! I thought he had a place near Paris."

"He has a place near Paris," Tom conceded briefly, after thought. "Hannah," he added, "is Hannah crazy about clothes?"

"Not the way Concy and Emily are. But Hannah always looks smart; she never wears anything cheap."

"But you," he said, "the most beautiful of them all, wear Concy's old dresses."

"Well," she countered, above the sudden uprush and flutter of her heart, "isn't that part of being one of us?"

"Pen," he said suddenly, not hearing her, "if Jeff had died that night after he was hurt?"

She was silent a moment, trembling at his tone rather than at anything he said.

"Then I never would have seen any of you again," she presently said lightly.

"If I had known—that day I went down to talk to you about Jeff!"

There was a long silence. Then Pen, resolutely taking the conversation to safe ground, said nervously and awkwardly:

"Hannah always spends a lot of money on what she does buy, but she doesn't buy as much as some of the others."

"She always looks lovely," Tom said, in a flat voice.

"Were you ever in love with her, Tom?"

They had said the word between them; it trembled in the air.

"With—with Hannah?" he stammered then, not knowing what he said.

"When you were kids?"

"Oh yes. Well, I think so. But we weren't such kids. That is, it was only about five or six years ago—one Christmas holiday. I was still in Harvard law school, but I came home, and Hannah and I—I remember theatricals and trips to town and buying her violets."

"Hannah doesn't forget," Pen said, the syllables falling slowly, with infinite pity.

"Maybe she says she doesn't," Tom said restlessly. "Don't girls like to think they go on caring?"

"Ah, but if you once care, you do," Pen said. She was speaking of herself now, and her voice betrayed it. There was a silence.

"Strange, isn't it?" Tom said briefly, almost reluctantly.

"Yes," she said in a whisper, "it's very strange."

The night of velvet and silver throbbed on; the stars wheeled; the lowered glimmering scarf of the Milky Way was just over the lawn. From the house came the sound of music; they were playing a waltz. A breeze sighed over the garden, and the scent of sleeping flowers, drenched with dew, moved in the warm air. Pen, silent in her deep basket chair, her gown spreading in a dim blot of color in the milky moonshine and inky shadows, felt herself trembling in every fiber of her being. Tom leaned back in his chair, flinging away his cigarette, locking his arms behind his head. She saw the little arc of fire circle in the night's blackness, disappear. Moments went by; time went on; neither spoke. Penelope felt that this hour had had no beginning and would have no ending. She and Tom—she and Tom —shut alone into a globe of night and stars and sweetness.

After a while he moved suddenly, was on his feet.

"Come on, dear. We'll go back to the others."

She started up, her fingers in his hard, big hand.

"Tom, I think I'll go home. It's late."

"I'll walk across with you to your house, then."

They went down the terrace steps together, Pen's ruffles trailing. She thought that he might kiss her at her own door; she wondered if he was thinking that, too. When they got there the cottage looked theatrically beautiful in the last of the moonlight, with vines draped on the white-washed wood, and one dim lamp burning upstairs.

They stood there, their hands still linked, and Penelope looked up at him and smiled and saw the glint of his dark eyes near her own. She felt the quick wrenching of his fingers on hers; then without a word he went away, walking quickly down the stone steps toward the path, his figure now clear in light, now lost in shadow, presently gone.

Penelope went upstairs. It was the dressing-room light that had been shining through the drapery of the vines; everything else was in darkness. Marie was sound asleep on the cot beside Buff's crib; Jeff sprawled heavily on his own bed on the sleeping porch, his face darkly flushed and his breath coming stertorously.

Undressed and in her light housecoat and slippers, with her hair in braids, Penelope went about the rooms quietly, hanging up Jeff's discarded clothing, putting away her own gala gown. Her senses were still surging, her face hot, her hands shaking and cold. Jeff and his animal-like sleep did not disturb her. She straightened his big figure in the bed, took away a pillow, lessened his covers. He half awakened and grunted a recognition.

"Thanks, Pen. I've got a lousy headache. Will you give me an aspirin? Oh, Lord, I wish I were dead!"

"Jeff, don't say that."

He did not answer. He had not meant what he said, or even thought what he was saying. Sleepily he took the medicine from her hands, gulped water, plunged back into bed, digging his black head against the pillow, jerking the covers over his shoulder. Penelope got into bed and turned up her reading lamp. But she could not read tonight.

CHAPTER XXIX

After that she and Tom walked in a world of enchantment which was encompassed by that other familiar world of rooms and lawns and gardens, voices and figures moving in summer sweetness, and yet that was far apart from it. They never spoke of love to each other; they could see each other unrebuked; they could add what cadences they liked to Tom's cousinly "dear," or to Pen's mere pronunciation of his name, and for the time that was enough.

At breakfast she often poured him his coffee when she poured Jeff's, walking out afterward to the sunshine of the terrace to see them both off for town. In the late afternoon he frequently came to her house, sometimes with Hannah or one of the others, to take a look at Buff. Buff would be lying in her pen on her back, waving her arms, gurgling, trying to roll over; or perhaps Penelope might be in the dreamy quiet mood that accompanied the six-o'clock bottle and would look up to smile at Tom with eyes heavy with happiness.

A few minutes later she would walk with him to the Teeges' house, to see the invalid, to spend a few minutes with Aunt 'Lizabeth, poor, pitiful Aunt 'Lizabeth, who was always so sure that he was better.

On those rare days when they did not meet earlier, Pen always found Tom dressed and waiting in the library for the hour before dinner; they could talk to each other then, perhaps not overheard, perhaps a part of the group; it didn't matter. The thing that was said between them in every instant when they were together needed no words.

It was mid-August when Hannah said to her one day, with that slightly self-conscious manner in which she always managed to introduce the subject of Tom:

"Tom may go to Rio, you know."

Penelope, lifting Buff from the bathtub, enveloping the child in a soft big towel, could let a full minute elapse before she asked, with careful lightness:

"Tom may? I hadn't heard that."

"Which makes it all the more maddening that I'm not his sister," Hannah said. "If I were his sister I could go along and nobody care!"

"Would he—will he go with Carter when Carter goes back?"

"No; sooner. Right away. As soon as Uncle Teege——" Hannah stopped short, interrupted by a sharp sigh. They all loved Uncle Teege.

"For how long?" Penelope asked.

"Oh, a long time. He was saying that maybe Aunt 'Lizabeth would go, too, but of course he can't say that to her. She won't believe even now that Uncle Teege is so ill. But now that George and Emily are in Washington, and Mary's married, there isn't so much to keep Aunt 'Lizabeth here."

"Tom?" Penelope said, her heart dying within her. "Who decided that he ought to go?"

"He decided it himself; he was talking to them about it yesterday, I think it was. You see, we've the law business of two or three big coffee firms down there, and someone always has to be there to run that end of things. There's always been a Flagg in Rio; Uncle Peter was there for a while, and before him Gram's nephew, Cousin Peter Farmer. Now it's to be Tom."

"You mean to live there?"

"Well, for a while. Years anyway."

"That would be too bad," Pen said slowly. Buff was in a microscopic shirt and a pinned undergarment now, content, enjoying her ten-o'clock bottle, swooning off into light sleeping, awakening to begin a furious attack on the receding slope of the milk again.

Hannah had walked to the railing of the sleeping porch and was looking off through the netting at the opening to the forest. Sunlight filtered down into it only in rifts and blots through the heavy-layered leaves of the redwoods; gnats spun and buzzed in the shafts of light.

"It just seems to take the sun out of the sky."

"It wouldn't matter if we were of different nations," Hannah said restlessly; "he's not in love with me. But he isn't in love with anyone else, either," she presently added, still looking away through the wire screens into the hot sweet silences of the summer-morning woods. "I know that. And just of late, Pen, he seems so happy, and so gentle. I see the greatest difference in Tom; he's waking up; he's different. And all that might mean . . ."

Pen was hardly hearing. The world had gone blank. Tom going away —Tom going away! There would be nothing left.

That night she brought the subject up when she and Tom were supposedly playing backgammon in a sheltered corner of the library.

"I heard something today." She inverted the leather cup, lifted it and

[259]

looked at the dice. "Six one, my bar point," she said levelly, moving two men.

"What'd you hear?"

"That you might go to Rio."

He raised his look deliberately; their eyes hung together.

"Yes," he said, "that's true."

"When was that decided, Tom? Your play," Pen said.

"It isn't decided. But Carter and Tedda would like to stay here; her mother's come up for some treatments in San Francisco. She has cataracts, I believe, and it's going to be a long, slow job. Tedda wants to be near her, and Carter'd just as soon stay. He's been away eleven years. Somebody has to be down there."

She spoke slowly, not looking at him, looking instead at the fine nervous Fitzpercy hand that was moving the white ivory disks.

"But not you."

"It might be wise," he answered, in the light detached tone she had used.

"Tom, not you." She did not know what she was saying; she would not, in her senses, have said this. But her senses were all in confusion now. Penelope had been carried away from all her moorings. "No," she said trembling, her hand, with the leather box in it, resting on the edge of the board, her eyes far away. "I can't go on—I can't go on, if it's you. I'm so horribly lonely, Tom," Pen, speaking in a low voice, rushed on blindly. "No one helps me, no one stands by me, except you. My mother— my father, he's at home again, and in trouble again; my sisters—Isolde, always needing money—they all do, and everything else with it, jobs and advice and clothes, everything! Jeff—Jeff's no help. I'm never sure of him. I'm always worried about him. You know how it is. I need you! I don't want anything except to have you for my friend—just my friend! Don't go away. Please, Tom."

Tom inverted his cup precisely on the red and yellow points. He made his play.

"If it could stop there," he said evenly.

Pen tried to meet his eyes; he was not looking at her.

"But of course it will stop there!" she said in a quick, hushed voice.

"Will it indeed?" Tom said civilly, lightly. There was a long silence. Pen sat motionless, chained to her seat. The room went round in slow circles. Raising her eyes to Tom's with an effort, she saw his dark look full upon her; he had leaned back in his seat, and there were beads on his forehead under the dark rich line of his hair. For a long minute they looked at each other. "I am miserable, Pen," he said then simply. "Miserable."

She played blindly, moved the disks.

"We can't be," she said in a low tone. "We mustn't be." But even as she said it, in fear and amazement, a wave of pure joy went over her that it was with Tom that she must meet this new problem. It was theirs—theirs together. He had not disclaimed it. He was miserable.

"I was never going to say it, Pen. I can hardly believe I have said it now. There's nothing to do. Of course there's nothing to do. And so I'm going away."

"Play, Tom; I think they're watching us. You're going away to forget me?" The simple, simple words. She had read them in hundreds of books, heard them in hundreds of movies. They never had had meaning before.

She saw a smile on the dark face.

"Not that," he said. "I wish it might be that. Men aren't going to forget you, Pen, once they have found you. But I'm going away."

"Who's ahead?" Hannah said, strolling up to watch them.

"We both are," Penelope said confusedly, blood hot in her face. Had Hannah heard anything, perhaps suspected something? Would she notice the oddity of their manners, here in this rather dim corner of the library?

Dinner was announced; they all went out. The meal was presently interrupted. Pen and Tom had something else to think about. Every one of the older persons left the table, and the others made but a poor pretense at eating. Tom went away swiftly, first of all, with his mother. Uncle Teege was dying.

That night and during the next strange day, when a heavy mist lay over Flaggwood like the visible presence of the change that was coming, Pen and Tom were often together and spoke together constantly with the intimacy of a sister and brother. Of their new-found love they never spoke. To Pen's infinite satisfaction Aunt 'Lizabeth seemed to like to have her near in these hours which were filled with insufferable agony. Pen waited on her like a daughter, and when there was nothing to be done found a seat in the shadows near her and awaited her opportunity to be of use again.

Uncle Teege's house was filled with quiet family groups that formed and melted and formed again. There were big fires in the fireplaces as the cold summer night wore on, and now and then maids with serious, sympathetic faces came through with trays of coffee and plates of toast. Hannah did everything, was everywhere. Her mother, Aunt Hannah, was strong in comfort for Teege's old mother, and for his stricken son. But Aunt 'Lizabeth seemed mercifully unaware of what was going on. She looked very white and old and clung to Tom with pathetic need, but she answered questions gently, as always, and if she could be in the invalid's room, went in quickly and quietly, with perfect self-control, to sit at his pillow and hold his hand. George and his wife were in Washington; Mary and her husband were away with friends on a mountain trip; Tom was the only child available, except Teege's older son, Carter. Both men were on duty all night long, going about the changed house, murmuring, sitting, smoking by the fire.

Penelope went home at about one o'clock and had some hours of sleep before Buff awakened at six. After breakfast she went back to Uncle Teege's house. Aunt 'Lizabeth was lying down; De Vecchio had given her something to make her sleep. Gram was there, enthroned in the spare room next to Uncle Teege's sickroom. There must always be someone with her, and part of the time it was Pen.

"Gram, you had some breakfast?"

"Yes, my dear, I think so. Something. Someone brought me over a cup of something. It's your grandfather I'm thinking about. He was restless last night, and was sleeping so sound when I got up this morning that I wouldn't waken him."

"He was having breakfast with Ben and Uncle Peter when I had mine. He's coming over soon."

"Ah, that's all right, then." Fog pressed at the windows. They had left a lamp lighted in the dim room. Old Mrs Flagg was in a wide comfortable chair. She looked very badly, Pen thought, leaning back against the chintz, her eyes closed.

Peter and Jeff and both the Marks, and young Peggy and Amy came and went. The women moved noiselessly, whispered the question that was in all their hearts. Tom came in, looking tired and white, and smiled at Pen.

"Do you and Gram mind if we leave you alone awhile? Hannah and I are going to have some breakfast."

They went away. Pen sat on in a dreamy silence, her elbow on the arm of her chair, her cheek resting on her hand. Presently the old woman spoke.

"Teege—we called him that because there were so many Thomases—is my oldest son, you know. Johnny Flagg—you've not met him, they live in London—was four years old when I married Tom Flagg. Teege was born fourteen months later. We wanted a girl because we had the boy— John was a beautiful boy, and I'd known and loved his mother. But the minute I saw my own boy I knew I'd wanted him.

"That's sixty-one years ago. We lived in Connecticut then; it was the bitterest cold winter I ever saw. The snow was up to the dining-room window sills in my mother's house from Thanksgiving almost to Easter. We kept the baby down in blankets; my mother used to call him her little cocoon."

Penelope had raised her head; she was listening respectfully. But she knew that Jeff's grandmother was not talking to her. She was only thinking, remembering, aloud; she was trying to forget today's pain in the thought of other days.

"Little boys wore dresses in those days," she said, "scalloped Holland aprons. I remember the feel of them when they'd come upstairs hot from the irons on Tuesday nights. And he wore his hair in a big silky curl over his forehead; I used to make it on my finger and thumb. We were with my mother that winter because my father had died and she needed us; Tom was like another son to her. We were so happy, my sister Hannah and I, with our husbands and our babies. The war was over, and the world was all to start fresh. It was sad enough for my mother, but I was young and giddy, and I remember Hannah and I had plaid silks that winter, and we thought we were about the best! I had a fur cap and a tippet, and we used to skate, and have molasses stews. Ah, dear, it was a long time ago!

"My mother had played the piano, but she never touched it again after the news came from Andersonville Prison. But we girls used to play and sing 'Juanita' and 'Bright Things Can Never Die,' and 'Champagne Charlie.' I had three sisters, and we all married soldiers and lived close together."

"All dead now, Gram?"

"No; my sister Bessy lives in Baltimore. She was here two years ago. Hannah died when she was only thirty-one, and Mary of flu, after the war. And now, my dear, my dear, my dear," the old woman said, in an undertone, "it's my big boy going. My first boy. Always such a good son to me!"

"My heart aches for Aunt 'Lizabeth," Pen said, to distract her. Her eyes brimmed tears; she shook them away.

"Ah, yes. She's been a wonderful wife to him. Teege was married to a third cousin first, you know. Mary Farmer, my uncle's son's daughter. That was Carter's mother. But she died, and afterward he married Mary Pierce's little girl—we were so surprised—she seemed such a child—she was my secretary. . . ."

The old voice droned away into silence. Pen glanced at her companion cautiously; had she perhaps fallen into a doze? But no. Mrs Flagg was sitting erect, her old hands meeting on her cane, her bright dark eyes fixed on the fire.

Teege died at five o'clock in the afternoon without a word or a sigh, his head drooping against his wife's shoulder. At seven, going into her darkened bedroom to talk to his mother, Tom, seating himself beside the bed, laid a hand on another pulse that had stopped moving too. Pen was in the hallway with Hannah when he came out. They went together to tell the old people, and Pen never forgot the groan that was torn from Jeff's grandmother as she realized that the loved daughter-in-law had gone away with the husband she loved.

Pen had seen the family in gala mood; now she saw its soberer side. Everything seemed changed, with the dignified figure of the invalid gone, and Aunt 'Lizabeth's gentle shadow never crossing the lawn any more, her soft voice no longer taking its share of their councils. Serene as their influence had been, somehow they were more missed than some of the noisier members of the group would have been. Tom was grave now over new business worries and responsibilities, quiet in his double sorrow, and Pen knew how sadly he came home at night to the household which no longer held his father and his mother.

CHAPTER XXX

In mid-September the Jefferson Flaggs moved back to their town apartment. Penelope assumed full responsibility for Buff, and Lily, the colored maid, came back as cook. Jeff had definitely abandoned the law and had taken a position in a real-estate office. He seemed immensely relieved to be done with studying, and his personality and gaiety and charm seemed likely to make an immediate impression upon his clients and ensure him a success. For five or six weeks he worked with great enthusiasm.

Then the cold weather shut down and prospective buyers of property grew fewer. November was rainy. Jeff formed a habit of leaving the office at about four to go to his club, where he played cards and drank highballs until six o'clock or later.

His new employers were lenient with this program because young Mr Flagg unquestionably was at home in the finest social circles and might be supposed to find patrons there, and because he was on a very small salary, with a commission, and so was not a great loss to the force. So Jeff was free to spend his late afternoons as he liked, and perhaps twice a week was persuaded by one club friend or another to telephone home to his wife that business was delaying him, and to play another rubber and another after that.

Tom went out to see Penelope every day. When she had first moved, his visits had been less frequent, and for each of them he had some sort of reason to present. Hannah had sent the baby something; there was family news to report; Gram wanted to know at what time the Jeffs were coming down on Saturday.

But after a week or two these excuses had dropped away, and Tom came every day without offering any explanation at all. He would find Pen tucking Buff off for the night; as the child grew older, and into exquisite beauty and responsiveness, Penelope sometimes delayed the hour of bedtime, and Buff, eight months old, nine months old, beginning to radiate all the enchantments of healthy babyhood, would lie luxuriously in her mother's arms in the firelight and doze off to the sound of familiar voices: Mother's voice, Uncle Tom's voice.

When seven o'clock came, without bringing Jeff, Pen would rise with the baby in her arms.

"I'm just having soup and a salad, Tom. Will you stay?"

"Jeff not here?"

"He telephoned, but Lily took it, and she never is quite sure. But I don't think he's coming."

"I couldn't take you downtown for supper?"

"Not tonight."

Jeff, coming in at ten o'clock, might find them still talking over the fire; Penelope beautiful in the old blue velvet, Tom dark and quiet and serious.

"Hello, Tom. I'm sorry to be late, Pen. But I got into a game at the club with a man who wants to find an apartment house; I haven't landed anything for him yet, but I don't want to let him go."

He would have been drinking; he had always been drinking, and sometimes was hardly able to articulate. But he would take his own chair and ask about the baby, and perhaps reiterate painfully and frequently his elaborate explanations of his absence. Tom listened; Pen listened. Afterward Pen might ask quietly if he would like some black coffee.

No; he was going to turn in. Would Tom like a drink? Tom never would drink with him.

Pen and Jeff did not always go down to Flaggwood on Sundays, as they had done a year earlier. They had no car now and must depend upon Tom to make the trip coming and going. Pen had no nurse, and must pack and unpack Buff's manifold necessities herself; the basket and blankets, the bottles and garments.

More than that, Jeff preferred to stay in town. He could sleep on Sunday morning, a luxury his grandparents' rule never permitted; he could drift down to the club in the early afternoon, always to find some sort of game in progress: poker, bridge, dice. He told Pen that he made more money at the club than he did at his business.

She was kind to him in these days—indifferent and kind. She was too ecstatically happy, too deeply absorbed in her own affair, to care very much what he did, one way or another. He left her free to follow her own path, and she paid him a similar compliment in return. Sometimes his apologies for having drunk too much, or for having been reckless and unfortunate at cards, left her politely bored. What Jeff did or thought or felt was no longer important.

Her family saw little of her. Love monopolized all her time; there was nothing in her life but Tom. Jeff's father and mother came often, but only for brief visits. If her mother came to see her and the baby, if Persis used her apartment to rest and change between afternoon and night engagements, if Phil came in to borrow money, Pen was kind. Now and then, if Lily were working in the kitchen, and it was safe to leave the baby, she walked over the hill to see Isolde. But to Isolde's plea that they have long days together in the old way, she returned evasive answers. Buff was so small, and so much trouble to move.

Isolde's life had fallen into difficult ways. She was a poor manager. Even her utmost efforts and Grandison's good-natured help could not keep the slipshod household, the drafty floors and cramped studio kitchen, the long hard flights of stairs, a comfortable home for three delicate boy babies. The Taskers' studio was not popular with the other tenants of the big ramshackle building; there was always crying, slamming, screaming going on there. Isolde never knew a moment's real rest or peace. Once Pen found her father there; he had evidently been hungry when he arrived. He was finishing a great plate of bread and butter, a can of corned beef, a pot of coffee when Pen came in. She gave him ten dollars. "I wish I had it to get a big laundry done and get started fresh!" Isolde said to Pen, when he was gone.

Pen obligingly opened her purse again. From the beginning they had thought her much richer, her resources much larger than they were. It did not matter. Tom would be at home when she got there; they would stand talking a minute by the fire. Then she would go to take off her street clothes, and make herself lovely, and carry Buff out for a fireside half-hour with Uncle Tom.

If Jeff came in before dinner, Pen usually fell silent; not that she ever talked very much. But with the two men there, it was better to let the conversation go on without her. Jeff never would join in a three-sided talk.

When they were alone she and Tom talked of everything and of nothing. At first they had talked much of his parents. Gradually other topics crept in. He brought her books, and they discussed them; he sent her flowers; sent her the new blankets for Buff's crib, a new percolator, a new lamp. No day went by without its gift: playing cards, a handkerchief, a magazine, a special sort of cheese, an exquisitely balanced basket of winter fruits or a gay tin of Nuremberg cookies.

When on a December afternoon at last they brought the thrilling, trembling thing that was their love for one another out into the open, it was done quietly, without an embrace, without joy. It was done gravely, almost with reverence. Pen was in her chair; Lily had carried the baby away; it was almost six o'clock. Tom was standing at the fireplace, one arm laid along the mantel, his face only half turned to Pen, his eyes on the fire. One lamp was lighted; but most of the room was in soft umber shadow.

"We have to talk about something, Pen."

"I know."

"Are we going to do anything about it?"

A silence.

"We can't—do anything about it," she said then, faintly. And after a while, "What would it mean, Tom?"

"I've been thinking. Reno for six weeks, Pen. You'd simply have to face it. You'd take Buff and a nurse; it wouldn't seem long."

"I've thought of it, too. He'd never consent."

"Jeff wouldn't consent?"

"Never. Not to giving up Buff."

"I never think of him as especially fond of her," Tom said dryly.

"No. But it's his hold on me. And he's proud, Tom, terribly proud. And in his way he loves me. He wouldn't want the family——"

She paused, narrowing her eyes, looking into the fire, a faint frown wrinkling her forehead.

"Have you thought of the family, Tom? What it would mean to them?"

"Does it matter?"

Pen laughed forlornly.

"Can it be a Flagg speaking?" she said. "I don't know, Tom. I know that I can't—I can't let you go away in January. That's next month! I can't stay here without you."

"The family will care, terribly," Tom said. "It isn't the sort of thing we do. But you and I and the baby will be in Rio. And years from now, when we come home, everything will be different. Gram and Grandfather gone, Aunt Margaret running things——"

"Aunt Margaret is Jeff's mother," Pen said, and laughed briefly again.

"Against all that, Pen, is the reality of our caring for each other. There's nothing else. It's with me every hour of my life, burning me, eating me up. The thought of you, and your hair and your hands, and the way you lift your eyebrows when you smile, is never out of my mind. Well," Tom said, interrupting himself impatiently, "there's no use saying that. You know that. The question is, what are we going to do?"

"It comes down to Buff, Tom. I couldn't share her. It isn't fair to any baby to share her," Pen began, speaking slowly, finding words. "Jeff never will let me go while he can hold me with Buff. Otherwise it wouldn't matter. He'd be just as happy here in a bachelor apartment as he is with me; he'd be free then to dine at the club as often as he liked. He could go down to his mother and father week ends if he wanted to. They'd not miss me; they've never really loved me as your father and Aunt 'Lizabeth did. Gram doesn't count, either. She's seventy-eight. She's bound to feel the conventional thing about it all, that it's a scandal for the Flaggs—that to divorce one cousin and marry another and to take one of the grandchildren completely out of the group is a terrible thing. I don't know that it matters! But it's Jeff. The minute he suspects that we have our plans he'll be twice as stubborn as ever. He'll never give in."

She had gotten to her feet and was standing at the mantel facing him.

"Your marriage to Jeff wasn't the normal sort of marriage," Tom reminded her. "He's never taken his responsibilities seriously; he's never thought for you, or saved you. He got drunk the night Buff was born; he's never had a check yet, nor any money yet, that he hasn't gambled away. You owe him nothing, Pen. You're an angel of sweetness and generosity to him; he doesn't appreciate it.

"Suppose he does fight?" he said, as Penelope was silent. "We can fight back. He'll not make any public scandal; he's too proud. You won't have to claim intemperance and gambling and nonsupport. You'll only have to say mental cruelty, or incompatibility; one of those things. It'll all be handled for you quietly; I know a man in Reno who will do it. You've given him his chance to make you love him, Pen. You've given him a thousand chances! There's another thing, dear," Tom said, his arm about her now, and her eyes close to his, "once you are my wife and before we leave San Francisco, we'll straighten out poor little Isolde's affairs and we'll fix up your mother and Persis. That worry'll be over forever. When you sail you'll have Buff and her nurse, and you'll know that your own people are secure. Won't that mean something? A good nurse for Isolde and the boys, and a better outfit altogether, perhaps in town here, for Persis and your mother?"

Her magnificent gray-blue eyes rested on his thoughtfully. She was in his embrace, her head turned to look up at him.

"Tom, darling, everything. For I'd be gone, you know, and they'd miss me."

"Then do you think you can make up your mind to face the music?"

"I think I can. If we can make him give me Buff."

"The court will give you Buff. The minor child always goes with the mother. It will be horrid for a few weeks. And then it'll be all straight sailing, and I promise you, Pen, you'll never be sorry. This first marriage of yours will come to seem like only a bad dream."

And tipping her head back, and drinking deep of her young beauty and sweetness as if at a river bank, Tom kissed her. Her hand crept to his shoulder, was tight about his neck; their beings seemed to fuse in the first mad ecstasy of the first kiss that was a lover's kiss. He had kissed her hand, he had brushed his cheek against the crown of her hair. He had never kissed her lips before.

Afterward Pen gave herself to his arms; rested her head against his shoulder, spent and dizzy. And for a while neither spoke.

CHAPTER XXXI

It was only a day or two later that she and Jeff found themselves talking about it. By what steps the conversation immediately had grown violent, Pen could not remember; she had certainly spoken quietly enough. They were at breakfast; it was morning; Lily had not yet arrived; Buff was asleep in the bright December sunshine of the nursery.

Whatever Pen had said was completely swept away in the sudden rage with which Jeff received it. A hint sufficed him; the whole situation was plain to him at once; his wild fire of words dazed and shocked her beyond any power of retaliation.

"Jeff!" she whispered, staring at him, her fingers at her cheek, "Jeff, *don't!*"

"You're to get a divorce and the baby," he shouted. "You're going to call me a drunk and a gambler! All *right!* But what am I doing all the time? Sitting back and taking it on the chin, huh? Don't you *fool* yourself," Jeff said, his tone suddenly lowering to one of menace and triumph, "there are such things as countercharges, you know. I'm not going to be held up for everyone to grin at——"

"Don't talk that way! There never was any idea of——"

"I don't care what there was any idea of! D'you think I'm a fool? D'you think I'm not onto what's going on between you and Tom? D'you think I don't know that he's here every day, that you're wearing the earrings he gave you, that you're planning to marry him the minute you're rid of me? But it's not quite so simple," Jeff said, speaking in the quiet of white heat. "It's not so damn simple. You can't go one step without my consent, and I'll never give it. My grandmother—my father and mother —they'll all stand back of me——"

"This isn't a matter for them to decide," Pen said hotly, as he paused for breath. "Our marriage was a mistake; I've always felt it so. You're not the sort of man who ought to be married to anyone! You're never home. You have no sense of responsibility. You've left everything to me——"

"All right. But when it comes to Buff, she's mine. She's as much mine as yours. You'll see; they'll all stand by me. The baby's a Flagg, after all, and the Flaggs don't get divorces to marry each other . . ."

"You can't talk to me like that, Jeff," Pen said, after long minutes of it. She was very pale. "You've not been a good husband to me. You know it. I don't care how much your family stand by you, I'm finished. If you want to drag your own daughter's name through the papers into a scandal case, I'll fight. It isn't only the drinking and the gambling and cruelty—mental cruelty—and neglect. It's Marie too. You thought I didn't know about Marie. But she told me when she left."

"Marie! Maybe I kissed her once or twice——"

"You admit you made love to the baby's nurse!"

"And what about you and Tom? Is anyone going to suppose that you could go as far as making arrangements to get married, before you'd ever spoken of a divorce to me, without going a lot further? That Muriel who was here when Lily was sick told me a long story about a week ago."

"Muriel! The word of a servant!"

"You telephoning Tom in the mornings, and Tom bringing out oysters for lunch, and your sitting talking for four hours, and his going away before I got here; you didn't know that I knew all about that?"

"Once," Pen whispered, her face ashen. "That happened *once*. I don't

[269]

deny that Tom and I have come to care for each other. I don't deny that we plan—perhaps—someday——" She stopped.

"But that has nothing to do with my wanting to be free now," she ended briefly. She was shaking with fright now. That he would retaliate had never occurred to her.

"Oh no; not at all!" Jeff said. "Nothing to do with taking my baby to Rio, either. You wait until you put it up to the family."

"I see no reason for putting it up to the family."

"Well, Tom will! It's the family that will send him to Rio, if he goes. It's the family that will settle everything. If Tom goes against Gram and all of them, he cuts himself off from the whole clan. He won't do it. None of us would!"

"And you are going to represent to the family that you've been a good husband, that I have nothing to complain of?"

Jeff fell sulky, his dark Flagg skin flushing.

"No, I'm not going to do anything of the kind," he said resentfully. "I don't care how much of a rotter I am. I don't care how much you've had to put up with. That doesn't mean that I want to give up Buff. She knows me now; she likes me. I—I had a terrible accident two years ago, and I think they shoved me back to work too soon," Jeff complained, putting his elbows on the breakfast table and his forehead in his palms. "If they'd sent me to the Sonoma place and let me loaf around for a while none of this would have happened!"

"The Sonoma place wouldn't have given you any character," Pen said sternly. But her heart was oddly shaken at the sight of the black head in the brown hands, and the sound of the grumbling, little-boy voice. "An old fruit ranch ninety miles from nowhere," she went on, "with nobody there but a caretaker, as far as I can find out——"

"It's a swell place," Jeff said. "If we had gone there, if that damn roulette business hadn't started up . . ."

There was a silence. Pen, trembling, poured herself a second cup of coffee. In her mind she was already putting this to Tom, wrinkling troubled brows at Tom, gripping fast to Tom's comforting hand.

"But listen," Jeff suddenly added, getting to his feet, shoving his chair back to the table, and hanging his head doggedly as he looked at her lowered eyelashes and gravely abstracted face. "Don't fool yourself that you'll ever get the kid away from me. If you go to Rio with Tom Flagg, not one member of the family'll ever speak to you again, nor to him, either! And I'll have Buff. That Muriel Palisades or Pumpernickel or whatever her name is will go as far as I like about you and Tom. You can't deny he's been making love to you, my wife and my own cousin, and that you plan to get married. It'll be a big scandal that won't do you or Buff any good, but I'll go through with it before I'll let Tom Flagg put anything over on me!"

Pen sat as if turned to stone.

"Tom Flagg is one of the best friends you ever had," she said; "he's gotten you out of trouble a thousand times."

"Yes, he sounds like my best friend, in a pig's eye!" Jeff said. "You start something and you'll find it isn't so easy to finish!"

The door opened, closed; Pen heard the outer door slam. He was gone.

She sat on, dazed and bewildered. She had never thought of Jeff as fighting back or as having any ammunition with which to retaliate. His accusations left her feeling a little sick. He could not possibly make such charges against her, and yet, if he did, there would be plenty of reason for a scandal-loving world to believe them. Tom *had* been at her house every day for months; Tom *had* made her handsome presents; Tom *had* planned with her a future in which her husband played no part!

She went to the telephone.

"Tom, something rather—bothersome has happened. Could you come out a little early tonight so that we can talk about it before—I mean while we're alone?"

"Are you alone now?"

"Yes. Jeff's gone. I'm just going to get the baby's morning routine started."

"I'll be there in five minutes."

"Oh, Tom, *can* you?" The blood had come back to her heart; her senses were swimming in the high blue seas of rapture again. Now that Tom was coming, everything would be all right.

Penelope put on a fresh dress: plain blue dots, plain broad organdy collar. The blue made her eyes bluer; her cloud of flax-gold hair was as soft as that of a baby. When he came in, her hands caught at Tom and held his own hands tight.

He listened to the story with a face whose seriousness somewhat aroused her fears.

"He won't do it," he said at last. "Jeff's decent, underneath. He was just trying to bully you. He can't pretend that yours was the usual sort of marriage. He won't dare to claim that he's been a good husband."

"Yes, but, Tom—if he does?"

"He won't."

"Yes, but suppose his father and mother—Aunt Margaret and Uncle Mark—stand by him, and Mary and Lucy and Peggy, and Aunt Hannah and Uncle Peter?"

"Oh, they'll *stand* by him fast enough," Tom said absently, thinking.

"You think they will?" she asked, her heart sinking. "Why shouldn't they stand by you? You're worth ten of Jeff!"

"You know the Flaggs, Pen. Buff's a Flagg; Jeff's a Flagg. You can't imagine my grandmother saying anything else than that it's out of the question, that this sort of thing simply isn't done, that any wife who allows another man to make love to her is as guilty as the husband——"

Blood burned in her cheeks. He had had his arm about her; now she drew away and looked at him with darkened eyes.

"But, Tom, you know it wasn't anything like that!"

"I know it wasn't, darling." Tom laughed. "Don't be cross at me; I'm talking for my grandmother!" he said. "I'm talking for the whole crowd of them, my sister—Hannah—Amy."

"And do they matter?" she asked proudly.

"Not at all. You and I are rich, Pen; we can do as we like. If I go to Rio it'll be ten years before we see any of them again, and by that time they'll have forgiven us. The only thing we have to worry about," Tom went on, "is getting Jeff to agree. And I really think Aunt Margaret will talk him into that, rather than face a scandal. The catch is that Buff is the only grandchild, and she and Uncle Mark don't think or talk of anything but Buff. How often does she come to see Buff?"

"Oh, three times a week—oftener, maybe. Sometimes when I leave Lily here, I come in and find that Aunt Margaret has arrived and let Lily go, and has the baby herself. And you know yourself that Uncle Mark stops in on his way home almost every night before you get here. He goes home at about four. If we're at Flaggwood they're in and out all the time—oh yes," Pen conceded in dissatisfaction, "they're crazy enough about Buff. But then why haven't they raised Jeff with some character and some sense!" she finished.

"Jeff was delicate as a kid. And Uncle Mark's never been very close to him. Pen," Tom said, "I want to talk this over with them."

"With them?"

"With Aunt Margaret and Gram. Just those two, and perhaps Uncle Mark, and of course Grandfather. But he won't say anything."

"Tom, why?"

"Because I think they may talk him into it."

"Wouldn't they be the very ones that would talk him out of it?"

"I don't know. They ought to hear your side, anyway. Grandfather's awfully wise. There's just a chance he might say to Jeff, 'Give her rope. You'll get more of the child by keeping the peace with Penelope than by antagonizing her.' Gram will do anything to avoid notoriety. She hates divorce, but if we have to have one in the family, she'll want it quiet, with no discussion. Let me put it to them, Pen. Let me remind them what a rotten row you've had to hoe, gambling debts, flunking law school, drinking. They know I've stood by Jeff, that I'm not knocking him for the pure pleasure of knocking. You're coming down to Flaggwood Saturday, aren't you? We'll settle it all on Sunday morning."

Pen was unpacking Buff's paraphernalia in the spare room a few days later when Hannah came in. It was a Saturday afternoon in December, balmy and sunny. There were cosmos and chrysanthemums still blooming in the garden borders, and on Pen's dressing table a glass bowl of delicious double white violets. Outwardly Flaggwood was what it had always been on a fine, soft winter day. The children were chattering of Christmas; the scent of baking mince pies floated from the direction of the kitchen. But inwardly Pen was quaking, and nothing seemed as it had ever been.

"Hello, Pen!" Hannah said, with a kiss. "Hello, beautiful, beautiful Buff! Who brought you down, Pen?"

"Tom."

"Anything up?"

"N-n-not that I know of."

"Jeff came down last night," Hannah said, arranging flowers, taking off Buff's wraps.

"I know he did."

"There's a feel of something in the air. Old people getting behind doors and buzzing," Hannah said. But as Pen showed no inclination to confide, she went on quite cheerfully to family topics. Pen changed her dress; Kate, the nurse, came in to take charge of Buff; the two young women went downstairs together. Croquet was going on; Tedda Flagg had two small nephews from São Paulo with her and was explaining the game to them. Neither Tom nor Jeff was playing. Pen did not see either. Children were everywhere; kindly aunts and uncles opened doors and came up and down stairs; maids announced things; fires blazed. In the big bedrooms mothers were putting babies to sleep; elderly women moving about; voices sounding. Teege and Aunt 'Lizabeth were gone; George and Emily and Aunt Conny, little Constance and her new husband were not there. But they would sit down thirty-one to dinner just the same. Life went on simply because it did not stop. But to Pen it was terrifying now. Her heart would not come down into its rightful place. Every time anyone spoke to her it jumped and fluttered with fear.

"They can't take Buff away from me; I'm free, white and twenty-one; Tom wouldn't let them," her thoughts said over and over again in a jumble.

It was after dinner that Tom came for her; she jumped up from her place in a fireside group with her face whitening.

"Aunt Margaret and Uncle Mark want to see you," Tom told her, in the hall. "Why, Pen, don't be so frightened!" he said, smiling. "It's all going to be all right. They can't eat us!"

"What do they say?"

"I don't know, my dear. I know Jeff talked to them practically all afternoon. It really doesn't matter what they say, Pen, except that they may influence him to refuse a divorce. But even if they do we'll not give in, and after a while they'll see."

"I hate this," Pen said in a whisper, as he put his hand on the knob of the upstairs sitting-room door.

It was a small room. Jeff's grandmother spent much of her time in it, writing letters, resting, having special conferences with this member of the family or that beside the fire. She was there now, in her great winged chair, an imposing figure in the black-and-silver brocade with the lace lappets; her stern eyes went for a moment to Pen and Tom as they came in, returned to the flaming logs. The Flagg emerald glinted on her soft, fat old hand.

Opposite her, in the companion chair, was Jeff's silver-headed grandfather. He did not look up; to Pen he seemed aged since last she had seen him; he looked broken.

Jeff's father was standing at the hearth, a puzzled, angry expression on his face; Aunt Margaret, sitting next to old Mrs Flagg, eyeglassed and knitting fast, had evidently been crying. Her eyes were ringed with red; her mouth was trembling; her lashes wet. The only other person in the room was Jeff, who stood at a window, looking down at the winter night, his back to the room.

"Come in, Tom; come in, Penelope," old Mrs Flagg said. She indicated seats in the circle, and Pen slipped into one, Tom standing behind her with one arm across the high back of her chair. "Jeff told us what your plans are last night," his grandmother went on. "It's been a great sorrow and a great shock to us." She stopped short.

Nobody spoke for a moment. Then Pen said falteringly:

"I've been very unhappy, too."

"Yes, I know you have been!" Aunt Margaret said sharply, nervously, as one who will be just at any cost, and there was another pause.

"I had no idea that the boy was—was worrying you again," his father said, impatiently. "I've seen you often, been up there to see the baby four or five times a week. You never spoke of it."

"There didn't seem to be any use in speaking of it," Penelope said simply, fighting a maddening inclination to cry. Tom's hand came down and touched her shoulder, and she felt her courage come back. "I'm not blaming Jeff," she went on appealingly. "I don't think he can help it. We were married—you all remember how we were married! Perhaps we didn't love each other enough; I don't know. But we're—we're not happy!"

She began to cry on the last words, and took out her handkerchief and blew her nose and wiped her eyes, not looking at anyone.

"But surely," Mark Flagg said, "after so short a trial—you've been married only two years—surely time might make a difference? Young people make up their quarrels; that's part of marriage."

"We don't quarrel," Penelope said. "It's not that."

"Penelope," Jeff's mother said, in a broken voice, "if you can't forgive Jeff—and he has tried you terribly, we all know that—for Buff's sake, for all our sakes, won't you give him another trial? This is—this would be such a cruel blow to us all! To have the baby taken out of our lives—your uncle Mark and I are so fond of her——"

She stopped short, her throat thickening, and knitted furiously, her eyes on her needles.

[274]

"You forget, Aunt Margaret," Tom said, from behind Penelope's chair, "that I'm in this."

His grandfather looked up, benign, silver-headed, quiet.

"No, no, no, Tom," he said in an undertone, looking down again, "no happiness there, my boy. No woman could ever give her marriage a fair trial while she was thinking of another man."

Penelope looked from face to face; her gaze stopped on that of Jeff's grandmother.

"What would you have me do?" she demanded. "What do you think a woman can do, when she has had nothing but neglect from one man, nothing but kindness from the other? I've tried with Jeff—you know I've tried! I've made mistakes, but I didn't mean to. We have a baby. Do you suppose I wouldn't do anything in the world to save Buff what she'll have to know someday? I didn't want to come to care for Tom, but he was like a big brother to me, always helping me—always helping us both. How could I help caring for him? Now—now am I supposed to say, 'I'm sorry, Tom. We love each other. But because the family hates divorce, and because you happen to be Jeff's cousin, and because your people love Buff, you're to go away to Rio without me, and I'm to stay on here worrying?' *Worrying!*" Pen broke off to ejaculate bitterly. "About money, and gambling, and where Jeff is at night, and cards, and whether Jeff's driving the car when he's been drinking! I love this family," she finished, crying now, but keeping her chin up, and speaking in angry bursts through her tears, "but I can't sacrifice everything that makes life worth living because this family thinks I ought to!"

Jeff had come over from the window. He sat haggard and weary on a hassock at his mother's knee; she held his hand as she said tremblingly:

"Pen, Jeff and I have been talking all morning. This would be different, dear. This would be different! We'd all help. We'd all be with you in trying to make it a success. Don't let an angry mood now undo everything Mark and I have tried to do for him. I blame myself, Pen! I am bitterly to blame. But he tells me, and I believe him——"

"Don't, Mother," Jeff said gruffly, looking away. Margaret Flagg was silent, her face wet with tears. Mark Flagg began to speak, stopped abruptly.

"I don't know," old Thomas Jefferson Flagg said mildly, looking from one to the other, "I don't know why this couldn't be adjusted. Jeff's in earnest now; Pen isn't going to be hard on him."

"And what about me, Grandfather?" Tom said.

"I don't think you're in this, Tom," the old man said. "I don't think you're in this, my boy."

"I think you're all wrong," Jeff's grandmother said quietly. There was a moment of electric silence. They all looked at her.

"I say that I think you're all wrong," she reiterated. "Penelope here has had all the difficulties to bear, and no one to help her. We've all helped

[275]

a little with money; it isn't enough. She has a right to her own life and her own way. She's a woman who could marry almost any man she chose, I should think; we have no right to hold her. What she decides to do is her own affair. I should be sorry," said Lucy Farmer Flagg steadily, "to see Tom and Pen marry; there's never been anything like that with us, cousins marrying cousins, and the complications, especially where Buff is concerned, would be hard on us all. But that's their affair; they'll settle that without any reference to us.

"I've watched her struggling with the problems of her life; she's done her best with them. Her father and mother, her sisters, her husband, haven't been much help. There ought to be better times coming to you, Pen, and I hope they'll come, my dear. If you and Tom really love each other we'll all do what we can to make the situation come out right. The only thing I would ask you is that you wait a little while. He needn't go to Rio for another year; meanwhile let us keep the thing as quiet as we can."

"Ah, Gram!" Tom said, going to her chair, kneeling down to take her hand and put it to his lips. Pen was crying quietly. Margaret Flagg spoke through a sudden flood of tears:

"You're right, Gram. You always are. But we—Mark and I—can't bear to let our baby go!"

"You'll have other grandchildren," old Mrs Flagg said sternly, unsmilingly. "Mark and Lucy and Peggy'll marry. This boy may marry again, when he knows better how to appreciate a wife and a child. But her child is hers. If ever she wants to bring Buff here for a visit, she knows how welcome she'll be. But no one else has any claim on her. You see that, Mark? You see that, Jeff? You've lost the right, my dear, to make conditions any harder for her than they are. No woman is happy doing this; it's not easy! We all want to love the father of our children."

She stood up, reaching for her cane.

"I've made this a matter of prayer," she said. "You'll all say it doesn't sound like my way of settling things. You're right. It isn't my way. But I suppose my way could be old-fashioned and wrong, and the new way right. A woman had to stay with her man no matter what he did, once. Perhaps she was happier; women *are* happy in self-sacrifice sometimes. But we've all taken Pen for granted; we've not been fair. In any case I'm only saying what I think. You can all help her decide. But if she goes away from us she'll only be doing what I think I'd do in her case!"

Pen sat back in her chair, spent and silent. Her face was shining with tears. She looked at the magnificent old figure that was beginning to stump toward the door, and into her heart for the first time came the knowledge of what made this woman's greatness: not the Flagg millions, not the prestige of great names, not her natural genius for command. It was some deeper quality; it was something that was honest and brave, generous in victory and unconquered in defeat.

[276]

She turned from Jeff's grandmother to Jeff; he was standing; he looked tired and pale, but there was an expression in his face that Pen never had seen there before. He came to her and knelt down, and she put her hand on his shoulder.

"No use, Pen?" he said huskily. She looked at him long and thoughtfully, and the other figures in the room stopped moving, and there was a silence. Pen pressed a hand over her eyes.

"Wait a minute," she said presently, in a faint tone. "Give me a moment, Jeff."

CHAPTER XXXII

It was extraordinary that life could go on after that. It was unbelievable to Pen that she could sleep that night as she eventually did in the room adjoining the porch where Jeff slept, and that a Sunday morning exactly like all the winter mornings that had ever dawned there could break over Flaggwood. She was early awake and at the window.

The spare room was luxuriously warm, although the garden was frosted, and old Martin, the head gardener, walking along the terrace with the dogs, was beating himself with his leather-coated arms and smoking at the mouth as he went. Pen took Buff with whispered thanks from little Farmer Towne's nurse at the door at seven o'clock and performed her ablutions and dressed herself in the baby's company. Jeff was still asleep, rolled into a cocoon on the sleeping porch. He and Pen had not talked much upon coming upstairs after the family conference. She had felt jaded and discouraged and blank. She felt jaded and discouraged and blank even after her night's rest. There was so much talk, there was so much talk, and she was so tired of it! Everything was all wrong: herself, Jeff, Tom, the critical, anxious family, everyone! There was no way out.

She had been fool enough to think that she and Tom could ignore the family. Nobody could ignore a family like this. To cut herself and Buff and Tom away from it, to close the doors of Flaggwood to themselves and their children was too comprehensive a program. She did not have the courage to do it; she was not sufficiently sure of herself to attempt it. One could do anything, if the road were clear. But to defy them all, to say to Tom: "I'll make up for everything you lose," to say to Buff: "I'll be father and mother and grandparents; I'll put something into your life finer than Flaggwood and the cousins and the theatricals, the pool and the gardens!" was different again. She could not promise that. She could not promise anything in this mood of confusion and despair and shame and doubt. Even Tom could not help her now.

Listening to old Mrs Flagg's completely unexpected defense of her, hearing the decision that was like Solomon's decision of old: that this young wife of Jeff's *had* been unfairly treated, that she *was* entitled to her liberty, and that her child must be hers alone, Pen had heard something else, too. Something that went deeper, that was not to be said in words. She had heard the voice of courageous womanhood speaking, womanhood that studied its problems from some higher standpoint than that of mere happiness, that was honest and brave and simple. And that challenge had stirred her to the deeps of her being.

Impulsively, not thinking, she had interrupted the decision. She had put one hand over her eyes, pressing it there, and had stretched the other blindly toward Jeff, toward that repentant, voluble, loving Jeff whose brief conversions, whose brief reformations she knew so well.

"Wait a minute," she had said huskily. "Give me a moment, Jeff."

A moment for what? She had not quite known then; she did not know now in the crisp early winter morning. Nothing between Jeff and herself had changed; she had known that if she tried him again, if she gave him another chance, it would be without any hope of his altering. But she had known, too, that the smug, neat arrangement she and Tom had planned, the quick divorce, the triumphant departure as Tom's wife for Rio, with Jeff's baby, leaving father and grandparents, cousins and great-grandparents behind, would never come to pass. Shame that she had dreamed it had burned her face, had made her feel almost one with Jeff in failure. And she had known, to her further confusion and humiliation, that Tom had been ashamed, too. Bared before these watching eyes the affair had seemed to be almost equally discreditable to them all; the faulty husband, the intolerant wife, the attentive cousin. It was a sordid enough version of the old triangle.

Whatever she had thought of it, whatever had been sheer excitement and happiness musing alone in the little San Francisco apartment, waiting for the little double ring which meant Tom, she could not think here. Here, with Jeff's father and mother so concernedly listening, so anxiously watching, with the luxury and beauty of Flaggwood for a setting, and the things Flaggwood represented behind that beauty and luxury, she had seemed less and less the outraged wife, and more and more the undisciplined girl who must plead her "happiness" for her excuse. Generations of hard-working, hard-thinking men and women had built this clan; the four-poster beds and portraits, the silver and the samplers were but the guinea's stamp, after all. Whatever Jeff was, whatever the trials of her marriage, with Flaggwood for a background life should go on with an unruffled exterior; that was the Flagg way. A wife stood by her husband; a child possessed his father; grandparents rejoiced to the third and fourth generation; children grew into their heritage of beauty and companionship and joy in the big family circle.

They could not ever adjust themselves to the divorce and the remarriage that only a day or two earlier, to Tom, she had so breathlessly declared was the only way out. To the Flaggs, that had seemed no way out at all; they would not consider it. Take Mark and Margaret's grandchild away; drop all responsibility for Jeff; marry the cousin who had been like a big brother to him all his life; kill one branch of the family completely, as far as the root was concerned—that would be no solution! That would be only to complicate the situation afresh, to cause infinite heartache to them all.

But it was not that consideration only that had moved Pen to reconsider, to stretch out that forgiving hand, to burst into despairing tears, with her wet face still held away from Jeff's eager embrace, and her voice thick with resentment. There had been a deeper reason; there had been the Irish Fitzpercy pride, burning hot within her. They had been successful wives, these other Flagg women; they had weathered whatever difficulties life had brought them. They thought her different; if she did this thing they would always feel that what had not been too hard for them had been too hard for her; Jeff's wife had been beautiful and young and undeveloped, poor dear child, and she had broken under the strain.

As for Tom's share, well, they would minimize that; they would make that chivalry; they would call that Tom's generosity. Of course he liked and admired Jeff's wife; of course he was sorry that Jeff had behaved so badly; they all were. But as to considering the claim that Pen's divorce and her marriage to Tom would clear anything up, that was preposterous!

Thinking this, in that strained, dreadful hour of conference, and later, in the still watches of the long winter night, Pen had come in natural sequence to the decision of Jeff's grandmother, to that totally astonishing verdict, seriously delivered, that took her child away from one of the Thomas Jefferson Flaggs.

"Mark and Margaret will have other grandchildren . . . her child is hers . . . there ought to be better times coming to you, Penelope . . ."

Leaving Buff in the nursery pen with little Tom Cline and Farmer Towne, Penelope went slowly down to breakfast. She did not want to face them all at breakfast. There was nothing else to do. She felt a weary boredom in body and soul. There would be more talk this morning, more promises from Jeff. She would see Tom . . .

But even from the thought of Tom the life seemed somehow to have vanished. Tom. Tom Flagg. The two syllables of his name had thrilled her once; now the stolen sweetness of those talks by the fire in the city apartment, those luncheon meetings between Buff's ten-o'clock bottle and her two-o'clock awakening, was all gone. Only a troubled impatience remained, a sense of utter boredom, an angry inclination to say: "Oh, why

[279]

need they *talk* so much! Whose business is it except mine and Tom's!"

The dining room was flooded with sunshine that streamed in through the old-fashioned crossed swiss of the curtains, and danced on silver and glass, on the children who were twisting and sliding in their seats, seizing their silver mugs in both hands, building cream and cereal islands in their silver bowls. Amy was there, murmuring discontentedly to Peter, her lip trembling with some inner anger at his good-natured replies.

"You'd let *anyone* walk on you!" Pen heard her mutter.

Mary Cline, Tom's sister, was there, with little Tom in a high chair beside her. She was spooning the porridge from his joyously sputtering little mouth, replacing it firmly between his pearly new teeth. Jud Flagg and the Merrys, with two of their children, Aunt Margaret and Uncle Mark, Aunt Hannah, little Mary Towne, old Judge Farmer, Jeff's brother Mark and his sister Lucy were all in their places; there were plenty of vacancies left. At the head of the table facing her old husband far down its length at the foot, was old Mrs Flagg. She looked up sharply when Pen came in; she did not speak. Pen slipped into a chair; she was not hungry, but her hot thin tea was welcome.

Presently every fiber of her being stirred. Tom, looking tired, had come in and had taken the seat next to her. He nodded and smiled about the table, said only her name, as he shook out his napkin: "Pen."

After a while, under cover of general conversation, she could look at him, speak to him:

"Tom, you look terribly tired. Didn't you sleep?"

"No, I was walking. Yes, I guess I got some sleep. It was after five, though. It was almost dawn."

And then, after an interval when he talked to Lucy on his other side, he said:

"We can't let any of them decide this for us, Pen. That's what I've been thinking. You see that?"

"Oh, I see that," she agreed faintly, looking away.

"It's too serious, Pen. It's going to affect our lives too much. What Aunt Margaret and Uncle Mark think doesn't matter any more."

"Your grandmother," Pen breathed.

"Gram's with us."

"She's fair," Pen said, as if to herself.

"You heard her. She knows you've had a rotten deal. Could we go out and walk somewhere and talk, Pen?"

"What, right from the table?" Pen shrank back a little.

"After they all begin to go." In a few moments quite simply they left the dining room together. In the hall Tom gave her a leather coat, a soft old felt hat of Hannah's that happened to be in the downstairs closet. His quiet, authoritative manner fluttered Pen's resolution afresh; she laid a quick hand on his sleeve.

"We can walk up and down the side terrace here, Tom. There's almost

[280]

nothing to say. My job's with Jeff. That's all there is to it; this is the end. Jeff and I talked together when we went upstairs. We're going up to the Sonoma place, for a while, anyway. You and I love each other—but that doesn't matter!"

They had come to an angle of the terrace that was comparatively sheltered. Tom took her by the shoulders, squared her about.

"Pen, are you thinking of us, you and me, or of the others?"

"I don't know. I only know that I can't go through with it, I can't face it."

"But Gram said——"

"I know what she said. I know what she meant. She'll make it easy for me to get rid of Jeff; I'll have my child. But my share of it would be to let you alone. Didn't you understand that? I'm the sort of woman all men fall in love with; I could be a success on the stage; I'm not a Flagg! That was what she meant. That's understood. Not said, just understood. I've failed Jeff and Jeff's failed me, but I'm not a Flagg, so I'm to get the best of the bargain. Only—hands off the other Flaggs! I can't do it, Tom. You see, if I were free I *would* marry you, no matter how hard we tried to stay apart, and they'd shut us out forever, like the Livingston Farmers and Uncle Carter. I won't do it to you, or to Buff. That's all."

Pen ended breathlessly, turned toward the house as if she would leave him.

"I love you," Tom said simply. "I've never loved any other woman. Couldn't you and I carry this through?"

"I don't know, I don't know," she said, breaking. "I only know what I have to do now, that this is the way I have to do it! Tom, it's only this," Pen stumbled on, tears running down her cheeks now, her cold fingers held in his big warm hands. "It's only that I don't want you to think it's easy—that I don't care! I want you to tell me that this is the right way!"

"I can't tell you that," he said. "I can't let you go. You're the only thing I have in the world. What else matters than that?"

"Everything!" she said feverishly. "Ties—things—reasons—go deeper than that. We have to live for ten years from now, and twenty years from now, and for the years when we'll be old, like Gram and Grandfather. It's all right now, for a little while. But Buff will grow up, and we'll grow old, and it'll always be there—that we fell in love with each other while I was Jeff's wife . . ."

She was standing at his shoulder, pleading. Tom had half turned away from her; his arms were folded on his chest; he was looking into space.

"It can't be that this is right," he said in a hoarse undertone, as if he spoke to himself.

Penelope spoke slowly, deliberately.

"It means putting every bit of happiness out of my life," she said. "It means just darkness—where I can't breathe. But it may—it may come out differently, after a while, Tom. It's only now—just today and tomorrow —that I see how it has to be. We—mustn't see each other again. You'll go to Rio, and Jeff and Buff and I will go somewhere—to the place in Sonoma, maybe. So this is good-bye, Tom."

The last phrase was almost inaudible; Penelope looked at him timidly after she had said it, but he did not turn. The tall figure in the worn leather coat, with the folded arms and dropped dark head, made no move. After a moment she went away from him, walking quickly, lightly across the terrace where fallen leaves were scattered, and where a fine pearling of frost still lay on the old red bricks.

She passed somebody—more than one person—as she went into the house, but she saw nothing, felt nothing, heard nothing, until she was busy with Buff's bath, until the familiar ritual of the nursery was moving about her, and in the silence of the winter morning she could hear the village church bells ringing for ten-o'clock services a mile away.

When the baby, well rolled, had been deposited on the porch hammock for her midday sleep, Pen came back into the bedroom to find Jeff's grandmother sitting quietly in the winged chair by the fireplace. The old Colonial carved woodwork of the mantel, the old Pembroke candlesticks, the Dresden jar of violets and pale pink winter roses, the portrait of some long-ago Flagg above the fireplace, the old Hessian fire dogs in their red coats suddenly made Pen feel as if she and this splendid straight old lady might have been transported to some other Flagg household of a hundred, of two hundred, years ago. Just so had other mothers, grandmothers, daughters, women of the family consulted together in quiet Sunday houses where babies were sleeping, children setting out railway tracks and splashing in paintboxes, girls gossiping of their wedding plans and their winter frocks, older women quietly coming and going in the big peaceful place, maids carrying away the breakfast plates, and the good odors of cooking permeating through the pantries and into the lower halls.

"Have you and Jeff made up your minds what you are going to do?" asked old Mrs Flagg, pleasantly enough.

"I wonder," Pen said, sitting down pale and determined opposite her, "I wonder if you meant what you said last night about my leaving Jeff and taking Buff away?"

The other woman countered with another question.

"It wouldn't mean that Margaret and Mark would never see the child, I suppose? Have her for visits?"

"If Tom and I were married it might mean that."

"If you and Tom were married, yes," Gram said, a little dashed, but steadily enough. "But I think you would not do anything that would cut him away entirely from his own people," she said. "We all love him, and he loves us."

"He loves me," said Penelope simply.

"He does now. And he would always love you, perhaps," his grand-

[282]

mother said. "He's like his father; Teege was like that. But there comes a time when you want the other things, too. You would want to come home here for visits, bring your children here."

The vision of herself and Tom together, with children, was too much for Pen. She leaned back in her chair, spoke in a whisper:

"I think perhaps you think it is easier than it is."

"I don't think it's easy," said Lucy Flagg.

"You think it would be a terrible thing for us to marry each other, that it would haunt us, that we would never be happy?"

"I think the time would come when you would see it so. You're very fine, Pen, and Tom is fine. The time would come when you'd look back upon all this as a fever, as something that carried you out of yourselves. A woman needs her self-respect, she needs faith, she needs prayer after a while—after a few years."

"I've never had any faith; I've never been taught any religion," Pen answered, almost sullenly. "And I'm half Irish. We don't take changes so seriously. We're not Flaggs! The Flaggs are American—American—American—through and through! That means they're rigid, they're Puritans; they judge everyone by their own little narrow standard. I'm different."

"The Flaggs are American," old Mrs Flagg conceded, "but it's because they're everything else, too. That's what American means. It doesn't mean only the groups of English who settled New England, Jamestown and Baltimore. I've real American blood in my veins," Lucy Flagg said, "from the first Siamele; she was an Indian. Hannah's a quarter Italian, and John Cline's father was one of the finest Jewish lawyers we ever had here in the West."

"Hannah Italian!"

"Hannah's your aunt Hannah's niece. Her father's name was Di Varsi; her mother was Hannah's sister Mary. Both her father and mother died when she was a baby."

"Then Hannah's not Tom's cousin!"

"Only his cousin's cousin."

"And half Italian!"

"American," the old woman corrected it. "As much as any other. Amanda," she went on, "who's probably going to marry Jud, is Dutch only one generation back, and Con's husband is a French vicomte. As for Scotch and German, they're everywhere! All the bloods are ours, Pen, and the Irish as fine as the rest. Your father realizes that," Mrs Flagg said with a reluctant half-smile, "for when I spoke to him one day of the Daughters of the American Revolution he said, 'I doubt if there's a revolution anywhere that Pen couldn't get in on! Trust the Wild Geese for that!'"

Pen laughed; found her eyes wet again.

"I don't know what I want to do," she said forlornly.

"You can't forgive Jeff?"

"Oh, forgive Jeff!" Pen muttered resentfully. "As if that mattered!"

There was a silence; then Pen got up and began to move about the room, straightening it, putting away the litter of blankets and tumbled clothes that always accompanied Buff's morning toilet. After a while Gram, who had been sitting quite peacefully staring into the fire, said calmly: "I'll send you in someone and have this built up, my dear. Even with the furnace these rooms get cold in the afternoons," and without further remark went away. Pen stood for a long time in the center of the floor when she was gone, staring aimlessly ahead of her. It was all so regal. "I'll send you in someone," and "Hannah, we need more blankets, Lindenborg says," and "Lucy, why don't you and Jim take Farmer and take that trip through the canal?"

"But you'd let me get out of it, would you?" Pen murmured aloud. "I'm not a Flagg; I don't have to play the game, eh? Well, maybe there are things in life that count more than being happy."

Late that afternoon, when everyone was in the library before dinner, Tom came in, in his overcoat, and with his gloves and hat in his hand. He and Ann's husband, Ben Merry, were going in to the airport to leave for Salt Lake City. He said good-bye to the others; he and Pen were ignored; he could draw her aside for just one look, for one touch of his strong big hand. Then he and Ben were gone, and the interrupted conversations, Uncle Peter's chess game with his father, the backgammon game in which Hannah and Uncle Mark were absorbed, the parchesi contest on the hearthrug, could go on.

Pen sat quite still; there seemed to be a dreadful stillness over the room, and over the winter night, cold and black on the terraces and gardens outside, and over the world. Tom's voice and the touch of Tom's hand were with her still; she must preserve them now; they would not come again.

"I didn't hear you," she said faintly to Gram.

"Baby go off nicely tonight?"

"She was angelic."

Wheeling of worlds in flashes of black stars; Tom going away, and away and away . . .

"I didn't hear you, Gram, I'm sorry."

"I asked why Jeff was late."

"He and—he and Tom were walking all afternoon, and he came in at five and went to sleep."

"Pen," said her mother-in-law in an undertone, from the low rocker beside her chair, "you have made Jeff's father and me very happy."

"I'm glad," Pen said briefly. She felt a prickle behind her eyes. She had been crying all day; everyone knew it, although everyone did not know why. Now she was going to cry again! Very well; it didn't matter; if everything worth living for was drained out of one's life, one cared little.

Jeff came down, groomed and quiet and pale; he would not have any sherry. His mother on his other side, he took a low hassock at Pen's knee, possessed himself of one of Pen's hands. A strange quietude suddenly enveloped her. Her heart was broken; she had been dragged through the lowest dregs of shame and humiliation and discouragement and pain; she was broken now. Jeff must be happy; his mother must be happy; Penelope Flagg's happiness mattered not at all. In the deeps of her spirit there was a strange sense of being crushed, destroyed, driven out of her own entity, a feeling that might almost have been peace.

She saw Tom only once again. It was in the foggy early morning of the next day; Penelope was going down to breakfast when Tom came rapidly up the big main stairway. He had his overcoat on, his gloves and cap in his hand; he was going away. They stopped short on the landing and looked at each other.

The morning was so dark with heavy ocean mist that soft lights were lighted in the big warm Flagg house. Babies were stirring behind the bedroom doors of the upper hall; below the dining room's wide doors were open, and a glow of firelight and lamplight came out from the bright confusion of silver and glass and flowers within. Penelope was conscious of the house like a wrap, like a presence, about her. Her face had paled when she had first seen Tom; she stood on the step above him, their hands linked, her breath coming quick and shallow.

"I thought you had gone, Tom."

"Going now," he said in a whisper.

"To the city?"

"No, I'm taking the nine-o'clock plane to Los Angeles. I'll be there a few days and then probably—go on."

"To South America?"

"Probably."

They said the words and the words seemed to mean nothing.

"I'm going up to see Gram now. Will you go in and see her sometime this morning, Pen? She feels badly."

"Yes. Yes, I will." Oh, she loved him so, the brown face and the white teeth when he smiled, the smooth black hair and the broad shoulders, the thin, fine brown hand! Pen felt sickness, weakness, overwhelm her. His voice went through her like the cutting of knives. She held tightly to his hands.

"Good-bye, my dear," he said.

"Good-bye," she whispered.

There was nothing more to say. They looked at each other as if they could never look enough. Then Tom abruptly dropped her hands and went on upstairs, and Pen went down. She was crying bitterly.

She could not go into the dining room; she went blindly on through the lower hall, around a corner where there was a table with a great jar of chrysanthemums on it, and to the closed front door. It was not much used, in winter; everyone came and went by the side door on the terrace;

this hallway was not lighted this morning; there was dim twilight there, like the light under water.

Pen stood at the door, looking out through its frame of glass panels at the dim greens of the garden and the looming, soft undulations of the fog. She was conscious not so much of pain as of confusion and shock. A great blankness seemed to envelop her; she felt bruised and weary in spirit, as she might, after an accident or a long illness, have felt in body. She did not know how to go on from here, how to begin to live again.

Presently someone was standing beside her; an arm was about her. Hannah had perhaps come out from the dining room and had seen her; anyway, Hannah was here, strong and bracing and silent. Penelope began to sob.

"Pen, I only knew this morning," Hannah presently said. "I knew from something Aunt Margaret said. Pen——"

Penelope was making an heroic effort to control herself. Her head ached, her ears ached, her throat ached with the strain she put upon them. She did not turn; she could not speak. But one hand, with her wet handkerchief in it, groped for Hannah's hand, and they stood there for a full long moment without speaking.

"He loves you," Hannah said, after a while, in a whisper. "I never guessed it!"

Penelope's hard-won quiet was shattered again. Her lip trembled, and her eyes flooded. She still kept her back turned to the other woman.

"Ah, Penelope," Hannah said, "you have everything! And that, too. Tom, too."

"I have nothing," Penelope said thickly, in the silence.

"Oh, my God!" Hannah said. "Then what have I?"

Pen turned her head now and gave the other woman a somber glance, conscious perhaps for the first time that Hannah was suffering, too. Immediately she averted her eyes again and spoke falteringly and hardly audibly:

"I need him so!"

"I know," Hannah said. And for a long time neither spoke. In the silence they could hear, far behind them, the chatter and rattle of breakfast still going on in the firelight and lamplight of the dining room. Outside, fog moved stealthily over the garden, like a pall.

After a while Penelope resolutely dried her eyes and blew her nose and turned to put her arms about Hannah and kiss her.

"You're awfully kind to me, Hannah," she said, brokenly.

"Want me to bring you some breakfast upstairs?"

"No. You've not got any powder? Is there powder in the little dressing room here? Come in with me, and then we'll go and have breakfast together."

"Tom's gone," said Hannah.

[286]

"Yes, I know. I saw him come down and get into his car with Uncle Mark. Tom's gone," Penelope said.

CHAPTER XXXIII

In the early sweetness of autumn morning, the air sparkled like crystal. Moisture lay heavy on the fields that had been burned and drenched since the first hot days of June. It had been a dry summer, but the nights had been fresh and chill, and each sunset had seen heavy dews soaking the orchards and the grain fields, lying like a crust on the deep gold dust of the country roads, jeweling the heavy apples and the purple prunes and the young squash vines with opals.

The ranch house stood stark and bare in the midst of the ripening, mellowing loveliness of the year. There were great maples and poplars in the yard; there were barns silvered into age; fences, haycocks, a windmill picturesque in the setting of great trees, the sloping rises and dips of the hills. There was a stream that rose in the canyon a mile back of the farmstead and came churning out of the woods to spread into sunshiny shallows in the open and slip away again into the tangle of oaks and madrones, wild lilac and hazelnut and huckleberry bushes below the house. All the world was beautiful in autumn, even more beautiful in spring. Penelope found strange beauties even in its emptiness and coldness, its stripped poverty in winter. But the ranch house itself never was anything but a blot on the landscape, and in the burning summer months she hated its four square shabby big rooms, its dry odors of food and wood and grease and ashes, its stiff inadaptability.

But summer was over now; September's last days were going by in a final back-fling of hot middays. Today, Penelope reflected, when she came down to the kitchen at seven o'clock, would be warm. But by five o'clock this afternoon there would probably be a general demand for sweaters, and there would be a fire in the sitting room stove after dinner.

Ola, the Mexican woman who helped with all the household work, whose days were one long contented drudgery for the Flaggs, was already in the kitchen. A good fire was burning in the big stove, and butter and milk and a basket of great peaches were already on the kitchen table. Ola was beating up something in a bowl; there would be brown biscuits or popovers for breakfast. In a few weeks there would be country sausage and waffles and hot cakes in the icy, hungry mornings, but the memory of the burning summer was still too fresh to permit of any such thoughts now.

The room was plain and grimy, stained and nicked and spotted and worn from fifty years of hard use. But it was at its pleasantest now, with the screened open western windows in shadow, sunshine striking joyously in through a pantry window against which red roses pressed their velvet faces, and the stir of breakfast preparations giving every old chair and pan and towel a reason for being. Penelope began her share of the work with the ease of old practice. Milk was poured, eggs broken, napkins and silver mugs put on the checked red cloth of the kitchen's center table. She and Ola worked comfortably together, without many words.

There was much to do. Meals at a farmhouse, Penelope had discovered, were achieved at the cost of constant labor. Things did not come canned and prepared to the ranch; eggs must be gathered, milk strained and skimmed, potatoes dug from the ground and fruit plucked from the trees. A pot roast must cook for a whole day; the shelling of peas was a long job. Penelope was busy all day and usually so tired that she was glad to go to bed at nine o'clock for ten hours' delicious sleep.

What the women on the other ranches did, how they managed, she could not think. She had Ola; she could send all her wash away to the village every Monday, a very mountain of it, and expect it back again fresh and white on Friday morning. Just to put it away, just to carry towels and sheets to their places in the old-fashioned awkward shallow closets was a long half-morning's work. Penelope's neighbors—the nearest lived more than two miles away—considered her a fortunate woman, far from overworked even in fruit-picking season, even though Penelope herself never felt wholly rested for more than an hour or two, never felt her work completely done. But that was the price one paid for living in the country, for having children, and she liked living in the country, and loved having the youngsters, her own and those of other women, about.

They began to appear: Isolde's Don and Davy, a sturdy six years old apiece now, serious, dark little boys whose small square shoes were always stubbed gray at the toes, and whose faded blue slacks and shirts had seen many a washing, were the first. They came down into the kitchen carefully; they must never run the risk of awakening Uncle Jeff, if he chanced to be sleeping late. Buff followed them, an exquisite dark child with the brown skin of an Indian, blazing soft black eyes ringed and lashed in black, a gypsy tangle of black silk curls. She was dressed as the boys were in faded blue, with worn sandals on her fine little feet.

With her came a redheaded child of eleven or twelve who looked eagerly at Pen as she came into the kitchen. "Aunt Pen, mayn't I get Teege?"

"But I think he's asleep, Sally." Pen's eyes went to one of the kitchen doors, and Sally approached it cautiously and opened it and peeped into the room beyond. A second later she had darted in in a very shower of affectionate ejaculations, to emerge presently with a bundle of blankets held in her thin little arms, and squirming and thrashing among them a blond boy of perhaps twenty months, who gave a shout of excitement as he saw the other children.

Pen established him in a high chair, after having indulged in a little ritual of kissing and straightening, and he had a brown crust to chew while the business of filling bowls and pouring milk went on. The kitchen was astir with life and movement now; Pen hauled small forms up to raised seats at the table, tied bibs, wiped little mouths as fresh and sweet as the scarlet strawberries that were in the creamy bowl. Peaches, strawberries, melons, figs and apricots, purple loganberries and purple prunes, the ranch ran over with fruit all through the summer months. There was an immense new refrigerator out in the big laundry now; it looked oddly out of place among all the other old-fashioned features of the place, but Penelope loved it, she told Jeff, like a living creature. "It ought to have birthday and Christmas presents!" she said of it gratefully.

This morning she inspected its contents carefully; bowls of gravy and odds and ends of meat and vegetables came out and were scraped into the soup pot; there was pie crust; there a third of the famous black chicken aspic that she made only on great occasions.

She had brushed her fair thick hair off her forehead, wound its heavy plaits high on her head; hair was only an annoyance on a hot morning. Her shoes were white and low and comfortable, her cotton dress, faded to the same mild blue as the children's garments, was fresh and crisp. A tall, sweet, busy woman, coming and going between refrigerator and pantry and stove and sink, she presently looked up with a smile as Jeff came in.

"Jeff, I thought you might be asleep!"

"No, I was down looking at the ram." The ram, a mysterious banging in a buried tank on the creek, was one of the absorptions of Jeff's life, and one of the fetishes of the children. Pen was sure that the boys imagined it to be a real live ram bucking and kicking down there, and Buff would never go near it alone.

"You look picturesque in that outfit, Jeff."

"I'm beautiful and I'm good. I was up at five, by gum."

"Teege wake you?"

"Didn't hear him at all. How late did he sleep?"

"Well, he was fussing at about five, and I gave him a drink. He went off like a lamb, and I did, too. But I always wake about seven."

Jeff sat down next to Teege's high chair and grasped his son's fat brown foot with a thin hand.

"Hello, feller," he said.

"Yo," said Teege, with a solemn look that was somewhat marred by the oatmeal on his brown round little face.

"We're feeding ourself this morning," Pen said.

[289]

"Here, let me put this in for you." Jeff began to feed the child. Buff came jealously about to bump herself and her silver bowl against his knee.

"Feed me, Dad!"

"Get up on your chair, then. I've got to be up in the woods with Joe most of today, Pen. There's a lot of wood up there, and we're going to get it ready to drag down next week."

"Far?"

"No, the piece beyond the old vineyard."

"Where the dead sycamore is?" Pen put a cup of smoking coffee down beside him, looking at him thoughtfully. He looked young and hard and handsome this morning, despite the band of pure silver that marked his black hair. "Eat your eggs, Jeff," Pen said. "You fool with those children and let your breakfast get cold! You'll be back for lunch?"

"I was thinking that maybe I'd take a sandwich along and not try to get back for lunch."

"Or better yet, we'll come up and picnic with you. I've a lot of chicken for sandwiches, and there's spice cake. Get started as soon as you can, and we'll be along with the provisions as soon as we're through here."

Pen had been on her feet for two hours now; there had been no break. The moment had come when she could conscientiously sit down, her own cup of golden brown coffee smoking beside her, the popovers, the sweet butter, the sugared strawberries waiting. The children had been satisfied and had straggled out of the room; Ola was attacking the first relay of dishes; the soup for tonight's dinner smacked and bubbled on the stove.

"Not so hot today, Jeff."

"No, thank the Lord we'll have cooler weather now!"

"That great big hard tooth of Teege's is almost through."

"Poor kid!"

"He'll be all right now that it's cooler. I love autumn!" Pen said. "Let's cut a lot of brush this autumn."

"You've gone crazy on brush-cutting!"

"With my little curved saw, and the children along, I love it!" Pen admitted with a laugh.

"You're a wonder!" Jeff said simply. He looked about the unlovely ranch-house kitchen, the discolored walls, the open pantry door through which the shelves could be seen, with their bowls of spice tins and ranged high lines of jams and jellies. "I love this place," he said under his breath. "I've been so many other places where I didn't belong. I belong here."

"That's a wonderful thing to have you say."

"Some people are geared up for different things, Pen. I'm always in low gear. I like helping with the dishes and puttering around the place and hearing what's been going on in the orchards or with the stock. That's my level. I like it."

"I like being so busy," Pen said. "I couldn't stand Lucy's—Concy's sort of life, with committees and bridge lunches. I don't entirely blame Amy for running away."

"D'you suppose Uncle Peter'll take her back this time?"

"He did before, and Sally, too. Yes, I suppose she'll come back sooner or later."

"Does Sally believe she's in a hospital?"

"Absolutely."

"But didn't she get a postcard from Tahiti, or wherever Amy and this attractive Danish gentleman were?"

"She asked me if the hospital was in Tahiti, and I said yes."

"Ha!" Jeff mused.

"You don't mind having her here, Jeff? It seemed so much safer to get her away from servants' talk and telephones and all that. And Aunt Margaret simply jumped at the idea."

"I love having her here! I wish we had ten kids here. When's Mother coming up again? Did she say when she telephoned?"

"No, she just wanted me to send her glasses down."

"And kind of hint that she didn't want us to be farmers forever, was that it, too?"

Pen raised grave eyes.

"On the contrary, Jeff, I believe they're reconciled to our being here now, being agricultural Flaggs again, as we all were in the beginning, in the American beginning, you know! Two or three times she said, 'You all seem to be so happy, Pen!' as if she were glad of it."

Jeff looked at his wife thoughtfully; Pen poured herself a second cup. After a while he said, out of musing:

"'Member how blue we were when we first came up here?"

"Oh, don't I!" Pen laughed.

"Smells and dirt and kerosene lamps. Well," Jeff mused, "it's come out all right. It's worked."

She considered this temperately.

"It's worked all right," she said simply, after a pause. "That's the main thing."

"For me it has," the man said. "You've had a pretty rotten deal for a woman who was talked into marrying me in the first place."

Penelope looked at him over the rim of her cup.

"Delicious," she said, setting it down. "There's nothing like coffee in the morning. Why are you bringing this up now, Jeff?"

"I don't know," he said.

"I like my life," Penelope said.

"Yes, but that's because you're like that. You'd like some other sort of life better. You'd like to be Emily, giving big diplomatic parties in Paris, or Hannah, traveling with Peggy, or Lucy, having a swell time with the navy set in Hawaii."

"Sometimes I would," Pen agreed thoughtfully, looking at her hands.

Dishwater, dust, mud, chicken feed, brooms were not good for the hands.

"But what made you think of all this now?" she added.

"I don't know," he said again. "Seeing you get everything started, I guess. Thinking that we've had four years of this."

"We've accomplished something," Pen mused.

"Not much. *You* have," Jeff said. "I haven't."

"We've had a pretty good time," Pen said.

"Peeling potatoes and washing didies," the man contributed dryly. His tone was lighter than his words, but the mood was unusual and made Pen uneasy.

"Something wrong this morning, Jeff?"

"Nope. Just thinking. Realize that you're twenty-eight tomorrow, old girl?"

"My birthday! So it is. I remembered it last week and then forgot it again. Twenty-eight. It sounds old. No, but Jeff," Pen said, returning animatedly to the first topic, "even if we don't seem to have done much, living on an old ranch and raising children, we have done *one* thing that I'm proud of."

"Buff and Teege?"

"No, not Buff and Teege. I'm proud enough of them, but then all the girls have children, so that's nothing new for the Flaggs. No, it's this. They thought we couldn't get away with it, Jeff. The family, I mean. They thought that with my background, and you throwing them down every ten minutes, on the minute, we'd not make a go of it. They've been waiting four years for the crash. We've gone on; we've not complained or reported or asked for their opinion; we've paddled our own canoe. I'm proud of that!"

"Oh, you, you," he said, getting up and putting the pipe in the pocket of his old leather coat, "you've got a lot to be proud of!"

He went out of the kitchen door and was greeted with a cackle of children from the yard. Pen called after him.

"We'll be up with lunch at about noon!"

"Is it a picnic?" Buff asked rapturously, her small form silhouetted against the brilliant light of the doorway.

"If you're all very good and help me!"

CHAPTER XXXIV

She had finished her breakfast. It was usually the one quiet moment between the children's early awakening and the noon siesta. Now she gathered plates together with an expert hand, disappeared into the downstairs bedroom for a few moments to return with a great basket of crumpled baby linen, brushed the stove with a turkey wing and pulled forward the heavy soup pot. The grocer was at the door. While she gave him her order she was swiftly washing dishes, carrying them to the pantry. Ola swept the linoleum carefully. It was only three years old; to Ola it still shone with the pristine beauty of its youth. Penelope brought big loaves to the table, sliced the rich firm chicken of the aspic into sandwich form, spread jam. By half past nine o'clock the kitchen was darkened and in order, except for the small radius of dropped toys and crumbs about Teege's chair. He was a majestic and dignified baby; sometimes he reminded her of his great-grandfather, that oldest Thomas Jefferson Flagg, who was still moving contentedly about among the gardens and kennels and stables at Flaggwood. Little Teege would always wait in silence while matters concerning him were afoot in the kitchen; he knew that the comforts of bath and mid-morning collation were ahead. Pen carried him into the bathroom dangling on her hip; her hands were filled with his fresh clothing, his microscopic scuffed buckskin sandals, his own special soap and towel.

She left him sitting in the tub, came back to look at the soup; presently Teege was luxuriously asleep in the middle of her bed, and she could lie down beside him for a stolen moment. Ola, hanging out wash, was meanwhile under promise not to let the twins or Buff out of her sight, but the children were harmoniously playing milkman this morning and showed no inclination to scatter.

Pen relaxed her body warily on the wide bed; to stretch herself into a position of comfort might be to awaken Teege, and an awakened baby was often a desolately bewildered and crying baby. She managed to draw a pillow under her head; she stared at the discolored old ceiling dreamily, indulging in a long yawn. She would not go to sleep, but it was luxurious to snatch even ten minutes of rest.

"The tomatoes," she thought, "they ought to be picked over. We could have scalloped tomatoes tonight; they all love them. His sun suit—we left it hanging on the windmill. Sally'd get it for me. It's eleven; I needn't move for ten more minutes, as long as they're all good.

"I wonder what got into Jeff this morning?" Pen mused on. "He hasn't talked like that for years. My birthday, probably. . . ."

Twenty-eight. She and Persis would have thought that old, once. It didn't feel old. Twenty-eight, and buried for four years on an old ranch up in the Napa Valley. Only it had not been buried, really. There had never been a time when she and Jeff had felt that it was a permanent solution for all the stinging and confusing problems which had driven them into exile. It was only going to be a stopgap, a makeshift.

Jeff had been shamed and broken; Pen had been bitterly ashamed, too. The easy escape of which she and Tom had been mad enough to dream changed its appearance; it had come to seem to her what it had been, a cheap exchange of one husband for another, a cheap plea for her happiness, a defense of her pride, an utter weariness of the struggle with Jeff, her love for Tom.

All this, looking back, seemed incredibly weak to her now. What had she thought would happen—that all the Flaggs would blandly accept the arrangement, that her own people, Phil and Persis, Isolde and the babies, her mother and father, would let her step gracefully out of their lives, carrying with her Jeff Flagg's baby, the Mark Flaggs' idolized grandchild? Life wasn't like that. One raged, one wept, one burst into furious onslaughts of protest, and then in the quiet foggy morning one dried one's eyes, and took an aspirin tablet for headache, and worked the thing out on much less romantic grounds. Marriage, after all, was a definite thing, like breaking your leg or being born with brown eyes; it was a long and delicate business to get out of it.

Had Jeff's grandmother known, when she had made that incredible defense of Jeff's wife, that Penelope wouldn't accept the offer of escape? Penelope sometimes thought that the old family dictator had been quite smart enough to achieve her ends in this indirect way. Whether she had or not, her opinion had had an immediate effect upon Penelope. Penelope could not afterward remember exactly what her own mental and emotional processes had been, but she had seemed to see the family as a whole; for one illuminating moment she had seen all America's families as one, working toward stability and unity, holding to the code, however vaguely appreciated that code might be, growing into a group that was not merely American, but that *was* America.

She had seen herself, young, strange, placed by a series of chances in this group, heavily handicapped from the very beginning by the fact that she did not belong, winning her way slowly in spite of everything, in spite of the dragging claims of her own people, coming to be beloved by the big group that was scattered about in the cottages of Flaggwood, that belonged to the old four-posters and silver spoons, the highboys and Spode, the Copley and the Stuart portraits as much as all these things belonged to them.

The tradition of fine manners and fine voices, the family rejoicings at weddings, the family excitement over the arrival of babies, the splendid crowd of little brown cousins laughing and racing and plunging into the clear pool water, and murmuring like bees in the upstairs nurseries at night, these were all part of it, and while she clung to it she was part of it, too, and her child would grow into her birthright. No impulsive departure from it could end in anything but chaos; Jeff's child in Tom's house, Jeff's wife become Tom's wife!—ah, that wasn't the way the Flaggs did things, and she had become a Flagg now.

So quietly, and with a white face and tear-darkened eyes, she had come to the family council on that important Sunday morning four years ago and had announced that she and Jeff wanted to start again. They would

[294]

like to go up to the Sonoma place for a few months, vegetate and rest, and think things out. If Jeff's people thought that a good idea.

"Why not Honolulu, why not a long trip?" the eager, grateful voices of Jeff's parents had suggested. Penelope had declined these offers. She and Jeff had decided what they would like to do, for a while anyway.

She remembered the soft smothering fog in which she and Tom had walked on the terrace for an hour; that had been the end. Penelope had not seen him alone again. She and Jeff, on Monday afternoon, in the very week before Christmas week and all it meant at Flaggwood, had climbed into their car, Buff in Penelope's lap, and had driven away to their hazard of new fortunes without explanation or argument.

"For a while anyway," Pen had said, thinking in her heart that that would mean until Tom was gone, until she had had time to cool her shamed cheeks, think out her thoughts to their definite ends. Until the people at Flaggwood had something else about which to talk.

But after that the weeks had whipped into months and the months into years without ever releasing her from the tie she had knotted herself. Her father, elegant, penniless, hungry, had come to stay with her. Puttering contentedly about the ranch, he and Jeff had become good friends, working together at the thousand and one fascinations of farming in the wintry days; painting, splicing ropes, mending machinery, tending the stock, riding up to the ridge to round up the calves. And at night there had been the good farmhouse dinner, and a sleepy game or two of dominoes by the fire before bedtime.

From the beginning Jeff had been happy. With his old boots, his old gun, his soft old felt hat awry, his dogs trailing at his heels, he had fitted into the life of all lives that was right for him without a sigh for anything left behind. Penelope had had the one business talk of her life with her father-in-law, before this. She must handle their income now; she would not have that uncertainty added to the endless difficulties of the new life. Jeff must concede her that; if he had no money he would be the less likely to gamble money away.

Rather silently, rather grimly, they had entered upon the arrangement. Pen had forgotten any feeling she had or had not for Jeff for a while; she had been an automatic woman, spurred into action by the thought that these other women, these older Flagg women, had felt that she must fail, determined not to fail, if human courage and ingenuity and patience could avert it. She had remembered the advice of her husband's grandfather, given her when she had first been married, six years earlier: "Marriages are built, you know. They're built. There's no marriage that couldn't be a success, and no marriage that couldn't be a failure. Just be kind. Don't be afraid and don't let your pride be hurt. That's all there is to it."

Before she had fully grasped the tangle that was life in the farmhouse there had been other crises to weather.

In the lush sweet rush of the western February spring, Isolde had come to her, sick, with three baby boys, and presently it had been decided that when Isolde went back she would leave Don and Davy, "just for a while." They had been Aunt Pen's boys for more than three years now; the Taskers had gone East; Penelope heard only occasionally from Isolde. But she and Jeff loved having Don and Davy, and Buff adored her cousins. The little boys had grown strong and square and brown; at six they were delighting Pen by the need of ten-year-old clothing; she thought with a wrench of fear at her heart that someday Isolde might want them back again.

The enlarged family had presently stretched itself afresh to take in for a few June weeks Pen's happily excited mother, a soberer Phil, and a happy Persis. Persis had been married to her elderly sweetheart in Pen's house. Grayson Polhemus' years were fifty-five to Persis' twenty, but he was stalwart and kind and generous, and Persis had immediately proved to be the sort of little-girl wife who likes her role. Her husband was manager of a steamship line; Persis had a beautiful home in Piedmont waiting for her, two stepsons who adored her, and prerogatives that took even Penelope's breath away. Persis and Gray had gone to Honolulu and Japan and Manila on their honeymoon, taking the two boys who were like the little bride's gawky young brothers, and now, at this very moment when Penelope lay on her bed in the warm midmorning, with one hand flung out to protect little Teege, her mother and father were enjoying a trip around the world as the guests of their new son-in-law.

"It doesn't cost me a cent," Grayson had assured her. But Penelope knew better and was inclined to think very favorably of Persis' husband.

Lying on the bed, she thought of all these developments; she had not been twenty miles away from the ranch for almost two years, but that was partly because of the sleeping baby lying beside her. Teege had chosen to arrive at Christmastime, ending all plans for a Christmas at Flaggwood; then there had been measles in the Merry and Towne nurseries; one thing had conspired with another to keep the Jeff Flaggs in their isolation.

"It won't go on forever," Pen thought, wondering a little at the same time if she would mind years of it, mind very much growing middle-aged on this same spot. "After all," she followed it up, "what more can any woman have but her children, and to be needed, and to be always busy? I wonder if I'd be any happier in—well, say in Rio, with a nurse for the children, and parties all the time."

And she tried to banish the reality of the stark old wooden house with high-walled, shabby rooms, dooryard of packed smooth earth under willows and poplars, barns stretching up toward the woods, and orchards clothing the slopes of the hills below, and to see instead the walled streets and big dim houses of a Brazilian city where women practiced scales all day long, brilliant tropical flowers crowding against iron gates, wide aprons of negresses flashing white in hot noonday sun. Tom was down there in all that. His grandmother sometimes sent Pen his letters, and she read every word of them, and tried to read between the lines. "*My love to Pen and Jeff when you see them,*" Tom always said. Often he added this message in ink to a typewritten letter. Pen would pore over it, wondering if the three letters of her name meant to him as he wrote them what the name "Tom" always meant to her.

An uproar in the kitchen brought her off the bed with a jump; Teege awakened with a frightened cry; everything was in confusion for a while. Then, with the children's faces wiped clean, and after drinks of water all round, the cavalcade set forth for the creek and the dead sycamore. The spot where they were to meet Jeff was only half a mile away, but Pen knew that it would take them the better part of an hour to get there.

They moved without haste; there would have been nothing accomplished by any display of haste except perhaps a complete defeat of the entire expedition. Teege was in the light barrow cart—a box sunk between high rubber-tired wheels; the luncheon packages were disposed about him. Sometimes Buff climbed in with him to ride a few feet until her natural restless energy caused her to climb out again.

The little boys and Sally rushed to and fro, covering the course several times like foraging puppies. They stopped at every butterfly, every ant-hill and lidded spider hole. They gathered branches and dropped them again. When they came to the creek there was a long delay in the sweet September shadows under the redwoods, across which shafts of shy light filtered down.

By this time Pen's forehead was wet. She produced the little collapsible cups for drinks from the clear dancing water. Pebbles on the bottom flashed through the ruffled currents; schools of minnows jerked to and fro. The sound of the men's voices came to them now, the barking of the dogs and the snapping of branches.

"Here we are!" Pen called, coming into view. Portuguese Joe came down to help her push the cart over the last ridges on the forest floor. The children were as instantly absorbed as chickens in a fresh grain field; their little forms went tirelessly back and forth, hanging over the water, peering into miniature jungles, conferring over microscopic discoveries on the logs. Jeff sat down and wiped his forehead. Pen was content to sit for a while with her back braced against a great fallen tree and her hands idle, resting.

After a while she opened the lunch boxes, distributed the sandwiches, boiled a coffeepot on a gypsy fire. The hours dreamed themselves away. It was two o'clock, three o'clock; Teege slept perspiringly in her arms. Jeff and Joe and the children went after logs, dragged them through the crushed underbrush, piled them for the wagon. Sally stopped to kiss her, fell over her, awakened the baby.

"She's my mother and I can kiss her, too," said Buff.

"Ha, she's my yant!" Sally countered in scornful amusement.

"We'll get started back, Daddy. It takes us longer than it does you and Joe, and there's dinner to think of."

"We're going now. Wait a sec, Pen. This is all we can do now, anyway!" Jeff helped her stow away the remains of the meal, the children's superfluous sweaters, in the barrow cart; he lifted Teege to his shoulder; they all went down the hill together. But before they got to the barnyard Teege was finishing the day's journey as he had begun it, sitting in regal state in the barrow cart.

"Gosh, that feller weighs something!" Jeff said.

"We are sights!" Pen said, her hair disordered and stuck with leaves, her face and hands dirty from soot and dust. The boys were grimed as only small boys can become grimed. Sally had torn her brief cotton dress; it hung in a loop toward her heels; her red hair straggled free; she had lost her ribbon. Davy had managed a nosebleed when he fell in the creek; his small upturned Fitzpercy nose was plastered with red; the rest of his dirty little face was an unearthly white by contrast.

"But what a grand picnic!" Pen said.

"You'd picnic at the North Pole, Pen."

"Why, but that'd be the very place for a picnic! If ever you wanted hot food it'd be there. Come on with us to the house, Jeff; Joe'll milk. If we aren't the filthiest lot of gypsies that ever— Oh, dear," Pen said, in the kitchen doorway, "where's Ola? Flies over everything and the door left open and something burning in the oven."

Pandemonium set in. The children were tired and hot; there were bee bites, scratches, sunburn suddenly to remember. Teege was bumped in getting into his high chair and wept bitterly; the twins brought the sick puppy lovingly into the very center of the scene. And in the midst of it all arrived the last horror and dread of Pen's life. Company!

CHAPTER XXXV

She saw the flash of a shining automobile in the yard; she heard voices. Seated on a kitchen chair, stripping off Buff's creek- and mud-soaked garment, a garment abbreviated at best, and now reduced to a grimy string, Pen looked up to see her husband's grandmother in the kitchen doorway. Old Mrs Thomas Jefferson Flagg, aged eighty-two; Frank Merry, a great-grandson, aged eighteen; Jeff's pretty sister Peggy, aged twenty.

In a bad dream Pen saw them standing in the streaming afternoon light that was the ugliest time of all on the ranch. Every dust hole, fluffed by the Plymouth Rocks under the shabby willows, every chipped board and stained dish towel in the kitchen, every freckle and mosquito bite, every streak of grime and smudge of dust on the children's faces stood out as under a microscope. Their rough heads, their stubby little blackened fingernails, their faded and spotted clothing were all in bold relief against the cool perfection of the visitors' appearance. Peggy and her grandmother were in spotless white. They had been driving for three or four hours; it made no difference. Frank—he had been one of the brown-legged shrieking little boys who had been splashing in the pool at Flaggwood when Pen had first called there more than six years ago—was also in white.

"We came up to the Peasley wedding in San Rafael," said Gram, "and we had to come the rest of the way and say hello."

She sat down, an imposing and even beautiful old figure on a kitchen chair. Peggy attempted friendly advances toward Teege, who burst into fresh terrified roars. Buff announced another nosebleed on the part of Davy. Flies circled and settled, remains of food in the picnic basket sent forth a dry odor. Jeff had stopped at the barns to milk; there was no one to help Pen.

"Usually Ola is here, and this place in order," Pen said. Despair and anger were in her heart. If the old dictator of the family had had to surprise her, why couldn't it have been in one of their happier moments, when the children were all having breakfast in the fresh early morning, for example, or on one of those evenings when they moved the supper table out under the oak, and watched the big disk of the moon come up over the haycocks. Why couldn't they have come an hour or two earlier and joined the picnic party, to find everyone scattered about in the picturesque noon beauty of the woods; the children making continual pictures of themselves in the mellow sweet gloom, the baby delicious in sleep; the campfire burned low, Jeff happy with his pipe. This was one of their disgraceful hours!

She did her best. But it was not to be a fortunate occasion, and nothing she could do would straighten it out. She brought a dripping ice-cold glass of water; the children must all have sips after Gram had gratefully drunk half of it.

She caught at dirty little garments, stuffed them out of sight anywhere, wiped Teege's sticky little face and carefully unraveled a burr from the gypsy mop of Buff's black hair. She tried to send Don and Davy on errands; they returned instantly, always with disheartening news. They "cudden fine" Uncle Jeff and the other people; they cudden fine any eggs; they obviously wanted to be in the kitchen, where the excitement was going on.

Peggy and Frank had gone off to find Jeff; Ola was nowhere. Penelope felt savagely in her heart that she would like to fire Ola. It was ridiculous to come home tired and hot and mussy and find the place all flies, doors wide open, and the crusts that were to be crumbs for the scalloped to-matoes a smoking mass in the oven.

"Was it a pretty wedding?—Not now, dear. After supper. No candy be-fore supper! Did you say 'thank you' to Gram?"

"I haven't seen this young man since he was eleven months old, last Christmas."

"I didn't hear you, Gram—Turn that water off, Don, and get down. You'll be all sloppy again. Give that to Teege, Buff, and let him chew on it.—He's cutting those great big hard side teeth," Pen said to the other mother, "and he's had a hard time. Last week was terribly hot.—Davy, don't pull the tablecloth, because that pulls the egg bowl, dear.—I don't think you ought to put the tracks down, Don. It's going to be suppertime soon. Why not go out into the yard, all of you? Don't you think that would be nice? I can't read 'Little Black Sambo' to you now, Buff. . . . Well, because Gram is here, darling, and she's come a long way, and we want to talk.—Tell me some news, Gram. We've not seen anyone for weeks. Uncle Mark and Aunt Margaret didn't come up last week because of Ann's chil-dren's measles. It wouldn't do to take them from one family to another. Oh, children, children, what are we going to do about these dreadful flies! Sally, will you look for the swatter? Not very nice entertainment for Gram, but better than flies. As a rule," Pen said to the other woman, with a nervous little laugh, "we never have a fly in here! But Ola has apparently gone off suddenly, and she left the door open. We'll be in order—— Not that, Buff; how did she get that down, Sally? That's your party dress; you can't wear that now.—Tell me," Pen added, again addressing the visitor, "what's the news of Hannah, and is she happy in her Settlement House?"

While she nervously talked, leaping from one subject to another, and constantly interrupted by the children, her hands had been busy. At the sink, at the stove, at the small buttons of the children's garments, any-where, everywhere, with no sequences and no plan, she had straightened, changed, darkened, brushed, ordered. Permission to turn on the yard faucet for exactly two minutes had taken the smaller children streaming out under the trees; little Sally lingered. She remembered Gram; she hov-ered about Gram's chair.

"Gram, has my mother come back from the hospital?"

Gram's eyeglassed look was serious upon her. Old Mrs Flagg never took a conversation with children lightly.

"Yes, dear, she's home. She has that same room next to mine."

"Where the goldfish were in the hall between?"

"Yes, that room. And I think," said Gram, "she might like her little girl back, one of these days."

Sally's small triangle of a face was flushed with pleasure, but she went to stand by Pen's chair and lay her cheek against Pen's shoulder.

"You'll have to speak louder, Sally; Gram couldn't hear," Pen had pres-ently to encourage her. The curly red hair went down.

"Couldn't Mother come up here?" Sally whispered.

Mrs Flagg looked at her speculatively; when she spoke again it was to Pen:

"How goes the French?"

"Pretty good."

"I wonder if you'd understand this phrase; *'Je voudrais vous parler seule.'*"

"Sally, go find Uncle Jeff, will you, dear, and tell him I need figs for supper, and to get them into the refrigerator as soon as he can!—What is it, Don? . . . Does it hurt? . . . No, it's not bleeding at all; it's just a little red scratch. . . . Well, she didn't mean it. I don't think she meant it. Buff, tell Don you didn't mean to be so rough. Now all go out again, all go out again, you too, Buff, you too, Davy—go on, all of you, for I'm giving Teege his supper and you only distract him, and Gram is tired. . . . Because she went to a wedding. . . . No, they're not all tiresome. . . . No, not for the people who get married—go on, now, go out, all of you! They never," Pen thought, "they never have been so tiresome! They're as bad as the flies—oh, my God, what is it, what is it, what is it!"

The last was a scream. She slid Teege unceremoniously into his chair, caught frantically at Ola. The Mexican woman was pallid under her leather skin; her black straight hair was wild; she had been crying and began to cry again as she spoke:

"Carmela—havva feet—Carolina she crazy—Carmela——"

"Oh no!" Pen whispered. Without a backward glance she ran, ran out of the kitchen, down the steps, across the yard, the bulkier Ola following. The children remained, bewildered, staring at their father's grandmother. Old Mrs Flagg picked up the silver spoon that had "T.J.F." engraved on it and began mechanically to spoon string beans and baked cereal into Teege. She presently told Jeff that she hadn't done this for a long time, but that one didn't forget how to scrape prune off their little faces.

When Pen came back the air was cooler, the lances of sunset had begun to fall graciously through the thinner light of the back yard. Jeff and Peggy had somehow managed to serve the children's supper; they were animatedly eating; old Mrs Flagg was in the rocker, her great-grandson in her lap, Teege's fat brown legs rolling upon a wedding gown that had lost its pristine freshness.

"Child all right?" the old woman asked.

Pen saw herself reflected in the new dishpan.

"I look like the witch of Endor," she thought. "Oh yes," she said aloud. "But Carolina's baby has had two fits before this, and we can't lose any time when they start. She had one an hour ago, a light one, and then this second one that almost scared poor Ola to death. She's all right now. It seems that the uncle, Tío Pablo, gave her a package of popcorn, and she ate the tin horse that was the premium."

"Ate a tin horse," Gram said, in the mother's tone of quiet resignation.

"It was very tiny. About the size of——" Pen picked an illustration from Don's plate. "A lima bean," she said.

"A big one like that, or a little one like this?" Don asked.

"Mother, did she eat a lima bean?" Buff demanded excitedly, crowding into Pen's lap.

"I don't think we ought to stay for dinner. I think it's an imposition," Peggy Flagg said. "Look, Pen!"

"Oh, that's the engagement ring, is it? It's a beauty; I've not met the young man, you know."

"Oh, he's dar'r'rling," said Peggy.

"You've not been down to Flaggwood for how long, Pen?" This was Gram.

"We've tried to, Gram. But if it isn't one thing it's another. Teege two years ago—whooping cough that summer! It was last Christmas, and then only for two days."

Things were blessedly quieting now. Jeff had carried Teege off to bed. The other children could hardly wait to have their napkins untied before the candy was carefully counted into their hands and they could escape into the yard for that twilight riot that is the cream of the country child's day. The scalloped tomatoes bubbled in the oven; Ola, horrified at the idea that the visitors had found them with a meatless dinner, had instantly sacrificed tomorrow's lunch to the occasion, and was doing something knowing with kidneys, ravioli, cheese. Jeff and Frank carried plates out to the table that had been set out in the yard; several chickens, usually in bed at this time, noted the unusual preparations and lingered. "And I know what they'll do to her white shoes!" thought Penelope.

But everything was going much better, and her disturbed spirit grew calm. She went in to kiss Teege in his bed, and slipped on a fresh gown. She had been saving it for the club opening tomorrow—no matter.

"I want to talk to Penelope alone for five minutes," Gram said flatly, when the meal was over. Jeff and his sister obediently went indoors with the children; young Frank joined Joe Riveras, who was setting gopher traps. There was dusk in the yard now; the air was cool and sweet and dewy after the long day. Penelope had put on an old sweater; she sat at the head of the table, with the older woman at her right. Their arms rested on the checked cloth; their eyes met as they talked in the deepening dusk under the oaks.

"Tell me how you feel about Sally," the older woman began without preamble. "Amy's home again; Peter went to get her two weeks ago."

"Amy's home again! She didn't write Sally."

"No, she seemed to feel badly, almost ill. She's better now."

Pen spoke after a long significant glance. One did not discuss Amy's affairs with that mother-in-law who was almost half a century older than she. But Pen and her companion understood one another.

"Does she want Sally?"

"She will soon, I think. That's one of the things I wanted to speak about. Is she much trouble here?"

"She's no trouble at all. She's a help," Pen said. "I love having her."

"You've your sister's boys, too."

"I've had them since Isolde moved to Baltimore. She has the younger one. She couldn't manage all three."

"And your father, is he still here?"

"I've a new brother-in-law now," Pen reminded the other woman smilingly. "He's vice-president of the Pan-Orient Line. My father and mother are on their way to China now; he arranged it."

"No trips for you, Pen," the old woman said thoughtfully. Pen felt an odd plunge at her heart. The tone was a mother's tone, regretful, loving. Her eyes came up thoughtfully, smilingly.

"Not while the children are so small."

"D'you get lonesome?"

"Lonesome!" There was no plea for sympathy in Pen's laugh. "I'm *flying*, from morning until night," she said.

"We'd like to see more of you at Flaggwood."

"Ah, and you will. We'll be much freer now that Teege has got a good start."

"Nice to have that name back among us again."

"Uncle Teege wouldn't mind his having it, I'm sure. He's a prize baby."

"When do you plan to come down to us for a long visit?"

Pen considered it. Dusk was soft and dim in the yard now; a tunnel of light poured across it from the kitchen window.

"Jeff is happier here," she said finally. "Perhaps—by Christmastime . . ."

Her thoughts went to Flaggwood as it would be at Christmastime. The big, comfortable rooms; the firelight and lamplight that would shine on the library books and the old portraits; the quiet coming and going of maids; her children joyous and expectant with the others, awaiting the revelations of the Christmas tree; above all, the luxury of company, of talks with the other women, of conferences and laughter over breakfast cups or during winter walks, again. In those first troubled months of her marriage, she had glimpsed, had sensed what oneness with the family might mean; she had won her place there now.

"Whenever you want us, but not for too long," she added. "Jeff is happier here. This is his kind of life. We know when we're well off."

"Jeff is a man," his grandmother observed, out of thought. "You've made a man of him!"

"Jeff begins to be quite an authority here," his wife said. "I wish you could hear him at the town meetings! He'll be mayor someday."

"Margaret's beginning to be very proud of him," the old woman said. "She loves to have you come down."

"Yes, I know. And that's a consideration, of course. We will surely be down for Christmas," Pen decided. "And then we'll see."

"You've just this one Mexican woman helping you?"

"Ola, yes. She's fine, too. We all like her."

"But doesn't that mean a good deal of work for you?"

"I like it." Pen would not be pitied. "I grudge every bottle anyone else gives Teege," she said, "and every bath anyone else gives Buff. They're growing up much too fast as it is."

"I remember feeling that way. As if I couldn't have enough of them while they were small." Old Mrs Flagg was silent for a minute. Presently she returned to her point.

"But, Penelope, surely you can be more comfortable here! A good cook, a woman to look after the children, someone to get your garden into shape —another bathroom, perhaps——"

Penelope laughed.

"Oh, yes. Jeff and I talk of tearing this place down and building a real Spanish farmhouse here someday!" she said; "low roofs and whitewashed adobe walls, and this old pepper right in the patio. But servants and money-spending weren't what he needed when we came here," she added, with a touch of significance in her voice; "they aren't what he wants, now. That way—that way's too easy, too cheap. He wanted to do it himself, chop wood and drive nails and rake. It was that that saved Jeff—saved us both. There's never been a time—he doesn't know this, or if he does he doesn't think about it—when I couldn't have put servants in here, changed everything. Uncle Mark has been only too generous to us. But there's been no money side to it at all. We don't talk of money here. We have our linoleum and our refrigerator and our window screens—you have no idea how the other women in the valley envy me my window screens! We're rich."

"So rich that you could manage the Millers, too?" Gram commented dryly, after a moment. Pen laughed in embarrassment, feeling the blood in her face.

"Who told you about them?"

"The woman wrote me—or rather I got your letter by mistake. I sent it back to her. But I'd read it. Is she better?"

"They're both better, she and the child who was ill. And he has work. So everything's going very well with them."

"How long has it been?"

"That we've been here? More than four years."

"They've not been all unhappy?"

"They've not been unhappy at all. Women," Pen said unemotionally, "women love pioneering. I've been pioneering. I've had my children. I've not minded any of it. And now, to have had Persis married here, and to have Isolde's boys with me, all that makes it seem like home. Really home.

And that reminds me, I'll have to bring Don and Davy with me at Christmas."

"Well, certainly," the other woman said, in quick protest that was almost impatient. "They're family," she added simply. "Penelope," she went on, rather more hurriedly, and with a change of tone, "there's one thing more. I did you a great injustice on that Sunday morning—do you remember it, four years ago? When it was decided that Tom should go off to Rio, and you and Jeff try this experiment for a few months."

"I remember that morning. Foggy."

"Foggy, yes, in more ways than one!" Gram said with a grim laugh. "There was a great deal that you had to forgive Jeff then," she resumed. "Did you know that I thought—that I believed until a few days ago—that there was something he had to forgive you?"

Pen's eyes came to hers; in the gloom just beyond the light from the kitchen window they shone like stars.

"I think I knew you thought that," she said slowly.

"You didn't tell me it wasn't true."

"No."

"Why not?"

"I'm not quite sure," Pen said, hesitatingly. "Because it *was* true, in one way," she presently offered. "I mean, I did love Tom; I felt myself as much his as if we had been married for years. My mind—my thoughts—everything had gone away from Jeff and were with him. Isn't that much the same thing?"

"Well, no, not to my generation," Jeff's grandmother said, after a moment's thought. "It may be to yours. It may be that to want to give yourself to a man is much the same thing as actually doing it. But in my day we made more of the fact. Less of the spirit, perhaps, more of the letter."

"I had failed Jeff in every other way than the actual one," Pen explained. "I wasn't going to take any credit to myself for having stopped short of the mere physical infidelity."

"But then why," asked the older woman, with a keen look through the soft early dark, "why should you have done it? All this, I mean. Coming up here to an old ranch house, washing dishes, working day and night, bearing Jeff another child. Why?"

"I don't know," Pen said again. "Or if I do, it's hard to explain it. It was—it was loving Tom as I did," she said in a lower tone. "And feeling that he came of a line of women who *didn't* give up, who stuck to things, and put them through, that they'd earned it—earned their places in the story. Oh, I know," she interrupted herself, with a thick little laugh, tears suddenly in her eyes, "I know what this must seem to you, this visit. Flies and freckles and heat and bumps and nosebleeds, my sister's children landed on me, my father and mother just what they always were, shiftless and—and irresponsible, my brother working in a gas station, Ola's daughter's baby having fits—it doesn't sound like much, does it?

"But to me," she went on, dashing the tears from her eyes, and smiling uncertainly and defiantly, "it does mean something. It means that I've worked out my problem; among all the Mrs Thomas Jefferson Flaggs who ever were, I've pulled my weight! No one can ever say that our marriage was a failure; Jeff loves me now as he never did when we were first married, and I love him. We need each other. We've children, we've a home, we've kept up some of the customs, if we haven't kept up them all, and because we have, Buff and Teege and Don and Davy will all have different lives!"

Mrs Flagg made no comment. She sat immovable; there was a silence.

"D'you know what opened my eyes as to what you had done, Penelope?" she asked, after a time.

"You mean Tom and me? Isn't it rather," Penelope offered, "what we *hadn't* done? We loved each other," she went on simply, "and I think we hoped, for a little while . . .

"But that wasn't the way," she presently began again, as the other woman fell silent. "That wasn't the way."

"I never told you that Tom wrote me—oh, a year after he went away," his grandmother said suddenly, with apparent irrelevance.

"Didn't he always write you?"

"I meant a special letter. About you."

"About me?" Penelope said, flushing.

"Yes. He said in it that he was unhappy. He said, 'Never to have had anything but those few hours. Never to have kissed her but once!' That," said old Mrs Flagg, "was what I hadn't understood."

"We weren't happy about it—we couldn't be!" Pen said slowly, her back half turned to her companion now, the words coming hesitatingly, over her shoulder. "After all, there was Jeff."

There was a short silence before the older woman spoke again. When she did so it was simply, as one speaks of a thing in the long past. It was almost dark now under the trees.

"I didn't know. I'm sorry."

"I think that no matter how reckless I might have been willing to be," Pen said, "Tom—Tom wouldn't have let me."

"I think you both behaved well," old Mrs Flagg said. She was silent for a moment. Penelope continued to sit twisted in her chair with her back half turned, looking away. "There's one other thing," said the older woman.

"I think I know what it is," Pen said, in a pleasant, normal voice, and with a sudden change of manner, as she turned her chair and fixed her smiling eyes upon Jeff's grandmother. "You mean Tom and Hannah?"

Old Mrs Flagg was watching her narrowly, almost apprehensively.

"He wrote you?"

"No, she did. I had a letter only a few days ago. Nothing definite in it, only she said that she was happier than she ever had been in her life before, and the moon was shining on Gloria Hill," Penelope said, with a smile almost maternal in her blue eyes, "and she and Peggy loved Rio more than Tahiti or Rome or anything else. That made me think that something was going on!"

"Well, I imagine you are right," said Lucy Farmer Flagg. "Your aunt Hannah had a letter, too. Hannah wrote her mother that she was almost thirty-eight and felt sixteen, and that Tom was the most wonderful guide two travelers ever had. We think that when she and Peggy come home for Christmas he may come, too."

"For a wedding," Pen said.

"We think so. Your grandfather," Mrs Flagg said, "was anxious—about you. About how you would feel."

"About me?" Pen was touched. She remembered her old friend of the breakfast pansies; she remembered being "Grandpa's guest." "Tell him that nothing would make me happier than to have Tom happy," she said. "And that there's no woman in the world I love as I do Hannah. This is the right thing, and it'll turn out to be the happy thing." Her eyes shone with a quiet content. "Tom and Hannah," she said. "She's waited a long time—she's never loved anyone else."

"But he, Penelope. What of Tom? Mightn't your seeing him—mightn't it be wiser to have the wedding—if they actually do plan to be married—down there in Rio?"

"Oh no, Gram! Think of Christmas at Flaggwood, with my Teege beginning to walk, and Tom and Hannah and Peggy all arriving in their big coats, with the green and white stripes on the trunks, and the tree, and all the children, and Buff flirting with Grandpa again. Don't cheat Tom and Hannah out of all that! The big fires," Pen said, "and the turkey dinner, and Lindy going about asking if we had enough blankets in the night—why, I've dreamed of every minute of it! And Tom and Hannah will only make it a little more perfect. Let's all have Christmas and the wedding at Flaggwood."

The old woman's eyes were fixed upon her. She seemed to come out of a moment of trance. She cleared her throat as she spoke:

"It means all that to you, does it?"

"Flaggwood!" Pen exclaimed, surprised that she could ask. "Doesn't it to us all?"

"I hope so—to some of them, at least, to some of them I've been a good many years hoping that it might."

"It's a wonderful thing to think that we've—we've earned holidays like these Christmas holidays," Pen said. "Arriving, with the children all bundled up in the car, and seeing everyone—and Amy, too? You say she's back."

"Peter went to get her; she'd come back as far as New Orleans. She was very ill."

"What's the answer there, Gram?"

"Simply that they love each other, I suppose. In some strange way that isn't like other husbands' and wives'. She loves him; she needs him even when she's completely carried away by these—these affairs of hers, and he forgives her because he needs her, too." Old Mrs Flagg gripped the chair arms with her blunt, brown old fingers, got to her feet. "You forgive me for thinking what I did of you, Pen? I forgave you—I understood. But I thought that much was true."

"Don't talk of forgiving!" Pen said, a little huskily, tears in her smiling eyes. "The fact doesn't make such a great difference, does it? It's the feeling that matters."

"Perhaps so. Well," said Lucy Farmer Flagg, "we must go in. I have to get started. We've a long way to go tonight."

"You're not going all the way back tonight?"

"All the way to my own bed, my dear. At my age, and if I live until November I'll be eighty-three, you like to wake up in your own bed, with the sunrise coming in the right window, and your Bible where you can put your hand on it. Yes, we'll drive back tonight. Peggy and the boy will sit and laugh and whisper in front; they've got a radio; we'll have jazz bands from Hollywood all the way. I've pillows, I'll doze on the back seat, and we'll be home by midnight."

"You're a wonder!" Pen said, with an affectionate laugh. The other woman put a firm, warm old hand on her arm, and they went into the house together.

The dishes were done now, and the kitchen in order, but both it and the living room were so hot that for the few more minutes of the visit it was decided that they would all sit on the porch steps. But first Sally had to escort Gram into the little downstairs room that opened from the sitting room.

"Look, Gram, this is Aunt Pen's museum. Look, that's the painting the man did of Buff and Teege."

"He was a wandering Belgian," Pen explained, standing with an embarrassed smile in the center of the poor little collection. "He was working here with Jeff for a while, a year ago, and when the crop was in he painted the children. It's like them, but I don't know how good it is."

"And looka this, Gram," Jeff said. "This is an egg ring. Ever see an egg ring?"

Old Mrs Flagg was serious and respectful.

"No, I never did, Jeff, what is it?"

Pen took it into her fine, nervous fingers, displayed it.

"It's a little bog-oak ring that my great-grandmother Fitzpercy used to take to market, in Cork. My father had it in an old box. If an egg went through the ring she wouldn't have it."

"It's extraordinary." There was a table in the little room, upon which the ring had lain. The older Mrs Flagg picked from it a red glass decanter with a heavy ball stopper.

"Just one of the old American glass bottles," Pen said. "It was knocking about our house for years, and when Mother moved into the city apartment she gave it to me. The quilt Mother herself knotted, when she was a little girl. And this—this is Dad's patent life preserver. The model of it. It never was put on the market. It has a food container and a water flask, and three rockets. But it never was made. And that's about all we have in our museum so far, isn't it, Sally?"

" 'Cept the ball of hair out of the cow's stomach," Sally supplied promptly.

"Oh yes, poor Whitey's ball of hair!" Pen said.

"I see," Gram said gravely. They all went out to the cooler air and darkness of the porch. The moon was rising, a pale, great globe that floated up above the oak. Soft, diffused light streamed in mealy shafts through the foliage of the trees.

"A lovely night for your drive," Pen said.

"And when do I see you again, children?"

"We'll be down for Christmas," Jeff said.

"Or if you would drive up for Thanksgiving dinner, we'll kill three great big turkeys," Pen suggested.

"Oh, Aunt Pen, not Dorothy!" Donny gasped.

"No, not Dorothy, of course. She's too good a layer. Three of the young ones that we don't love yet," Pen promised.

"I don't think your grandfather could," Gram said, stooping to kiss Sally. "But we'll see. Good-bye, Jeffy. Your mother and father will be up sometime this week. Good-bye, Penelope, give me a kiss, my dear. Get started, Frank; we've a long way to go."

"Good-bye!" the Flaggs called from the steps. The motor lights picked up tree boles and fence rails sharply, wheeled, were steady on the curve of the drive. The noise of the engine died away into velvet silence, and the little sounds of the night began to creep back; peepers chirped from the spillway at the trough, sleepy birds murmured in the side garden, boughs creaked and were still, and now and then the windmill's flanges moved far up in the dark with a rusty squeak and a splash of water.

"Some old girl, Gram," Jeff said with a laugh. Pen had gone as far as the stairs with the little boys and Sally; they had trailed up to bed; she had come back, and she and Jeff were alone.

"Imagine her, at eighty-two, going to that wedding, and then coming on here!"

"They must have left home at seven."

"About eight, she said. She's been twelve hours on the go, and just as fresh as a daisy."

"It's that she's so interested in everything," Pen said. "I know why she came up here today," she added, after a moment. She felt Jeff's sudden tension without seeing any evidence of it.

"What d'you mean?"

"To tell me—tell us—about Tom and Hannah," Pen added.

[309]

"Hah!" Jeff said, somewhat at a loss. "How d'you feel about it?" he went on cautiously.

"Glad," Pen said. "She's loved him all her life. They're wonderful people. They'll have one little girl named Hannah, and honestly think she's smarter and prettier than our six put together!"

"Are you bluffing, Pen?" Jeff asked, in the most serious voice she ever had heard him use.

" 'Bluffing,' you idiot!" she said amusedly.

"My God, I wish I could think you weren't!" he said.

"Well, you'll see," Penelope answered. "You'll see how glad I am to see them, and to show off Buff and Teege. You'll see how much the Jefferson Flaggs are a part of the picture this Christmas!"

"It seems to me kind of fine of the old girl to come up and tell you herself," Jeff said. Penelope laughed ruefully.

"I hope she likes what she saw!" she said. "I've never seen the place in such a state! I've never seen the children such *sights!* I was a *fright.* And the kitchen in such a mess, and the boys asking to get out their railroad tracks, of all times in the world to get out railroad tracks, and poor old Teege one mass of mosquito bites and hunger and mad and sunburn, yelling so that we couldn't hear ourselves speak! And the sink was covered with ant powder, and dead flowers all over the living room!"

"She likes all that," Jeff said, on a contented laugh.

"Then—to make it complete, I must needs rush off with Ola; I couldn't stop to explain."

"She was feeding Teege when I came in. Don was finishing off his nosebleed on her skirt, and Buff had just gotten a splinter in her knee."

"Trust Buff," Pen said fondly. "Oh, well," she added, "if she'd let us know she was coming it'd have been different!"

"It was all right," Jeff assured her, in a contented voice. "And the grandest thing is to have them gone again," he went on, "and everything quiet. I feel so—so damn peaceful all the time here, Pen," Jeff told her, speaking a little awkwardly, and with a little laugh. "My wife, my kids, my trees and horses and dairy, and every day just one day more of it, and nothing to worry about! I never was geared for the city and the law. And I know who gives it to me, Pen," he said, on a lower note. "I don't kid myself. You've given me all the happiness I've ever had in my life, I know it. I had no right to take it, but I did take it. And it breaks me all up when I think you're happy, too, that you're getting some of it back."

"Well, make me cry, why don't you?"

Her tone was laughing, but in the moonlight he could see the sudden shine of tears on her cheeks.

"We got away with it," he said. "What a funny feeling it gives you, to work it all out and to—to get away with it!"

"A good feeling," Pen decided.

"You bet your life it's a good feeling!" His hand moved on the worn step, and their fingers locked.

"We'll go down for Christmas, Jeff; we'll be the Jefferson Flaggs; we'll see everyone and get steeped in the home gossip, and then we'll roll Buff up in the bearskin, and put Teege into his squirrel zipper, and get into the car with all the presents, and the fruit cake, and come home to the kitchen, and big fires, and supper, and our ranch again! And it'll all smell of wood smoke and wet leaves, Jeff, and we'll hear the rain on the roof, and the wind high up in the trees."

She was speaking dreamily; as her voice died away a hint of the winter she was anticipating suddenly brought a cool breeze down from the vast darkness above them. Jeff got to his feet, extended a hand. There was an interruption.

It was Sally, who had padded out in slippers and pajamas to stand before them like a little ghost.

"Aunt Pen——" she began.

"Baby awake?"

"Oh no. But he has his thumb in his mouth again."

"Boys want me?"

"No, it was Gram," said Sally.

"Gram?"

"She gave me something for you. She said that when I was undressed I was to bring it to you. She says you're to keep it always."

"Something for me?"

They had been crossing the porch; they were in the kitchen doorway now. Pen looked down at the object, small and firm, that the child put into her hand. The kitchen lights fell upon it; the great emerald sparkled up at Pen as a wrinkled old face might smile.

The Kelly Kid

"Glory be to the everlasting glory of God, but some harm will come to that child if they don't lock him up safe in jail!" said the Widow Cahill, with bitter feeling.

"They'll get 'um yet!" added the Widow Murphy, darkly.

Ellen Murphy laughed her fresh, delicious laugh. She found her mother, and her mother's gang, as she called it, extremely amusing. Ellen had come in, on this balmy June afternoon of lingering warmth and lingering summery odors, to make the usual daily report upon herself, and her sister Lizzie-Kate, and Lizzie-Kate's young family, all of whom lived some three blocks away from the maternal household. Also, she wanted to find somewhere the last summer's hat that might be cleaned and dyed, and she had seized the opportunity to wash and iron the real Irish collar and cuffs that made her thin dark silk office dress look so smart.

"You're a grand lot of glooms!" she told the elderly women, as she pressed the hot iron carefully upon the steaming lace. "I wonder you wouldn't sit in the hot kitchen, a day like this!"

"These are bad days out-o'-dures, wid all the flu that's in it," said the little cracked voice of the Widow Cahill, over the large, plain white china cup from which she was drinking strong tea. Mrs. Cahill's bereavement had occurred some eleven years before, but never had an actress entered upon a congenial part more whole-heartedly than had the relict of Jarge Cahill assumed her weeds. He had been a bad husband living, but he was magnificent as dead, and Mrs. Cahill still wore fountains of crape, shiny black kid gloves that kept even when empty the imprint of her lean little work-worn hands, and a heavy face veil that fell all over her shoulders in shrouding folds.

Still, cackling little Mrs. Cahill was an optimist in the rather indirect

Copyright, 1923, by Kathleen Norris.
Taken from THE CALLAHANS AND THE MURPHYS.

Irish way, and Mrs. Murphy, her hostess this afternoon, was a pessimist, pure and simple. Both these wrinkled, bereaved, stupid old souls looked to Ma Callahan, the third and last of the group to-day, for inspiration and guidance.

"I don't know is he bad, or is he just wild and free with the bold spirits that's in him," Mrs. Callahan offered, now, of the Kelly boy, whose neighborhood escapades were under discussion. "I seen him yesterday," she resumed, after one of those mild pauses that marked all the conversations between these women, no matter how vital, "and I tuk it upon myself to stop him, and give 'um a word. 'Robert,' I says to 'um, 'yure good mother that's dead would turn in her grave if she could see the way you'll be carrying-on,' I says. He give me a bold, ugly look out of his bold face——" she finished, her voice drifting into silence regretfully.

"Oh, he's a bad one!" Mrs. Murphy contributed with feeling. "But this new cop on the beat, Hamilton, will get 'um!" she added, with vindictive enjoyment. "Ould Falley would never touch wan of thim boys, and they streelin' all over the place like Ayrabs! But this feller's a mean sort of weasel, and he'll get 'um. He got Jawnny Fay last week, and Big Jawnny give 'um such a lickin', when he heard that he'd been took to the Juvenile, that Rosy Fay come runnin' in here, the way she wouldn't hear the child holler!"

"Yes, and I think it was a dirty shame to arrest young Johnny," Ellen Murphy said, with warmth, as she pressed her iron gently along a scalloped edge. "It's the Kelly boy that's the ringleader, and he always goes scot-free. When Falley was on the beat, of course the whole pack of them knew they were safe," added Ellen, now holding the snowy fresh frill to the light, and scrutinizing it with keen blue eyes. "But this Hamilton is another pair of shoes——"

"I don't know where ever a cop would get a name like Hamilton," Mrs. Cahill mused, dreamily.

"He's none of our sort," Mrs. Callahan remarked. "He's a hard, mean kind of man, and God help Robbie Kelly the day he lays hands on 'um. Well, Robbie has a very ugly stepmother—she's a noisy, wild sort, Daze," she finished.

"He had a good mother," Mrs. Murphy said, dolorously, "and she had him in Sunday School, and she dressed him very nice, until the very Sunday she was tuk, God rest her. And Mack Kelly wouldn't have been a bad father to 'um if he'd lived. But Daze has got that young boy of her own that's never been right since he had scarlet fever, and him teethin', and she's hard on Robbie. Sister Felix says that the child has a good heart in him, but he's wild. And he'll end in jail, and I'd never raise hand nor fut to keep him out of it!"

"Mama's never forgiven him about the baby goat," Ellen said, laughing. "Mama's old Kitty had a kid here one spring, and all the Eyetalians are crazy about young goats in the spring, and Robbie Kelly drove the baby goat over to the Baldocchis', and told Gemma Baldocchi that Mrs. Murphy sent it with her compliments. Mama went down there—and the yelling!—and the screeching!—it was Duke's mixture, all right!" finished Ellen, enjoyable reminiscence in her eye.

Ellen's beauty and brightness had suffered a brief eclipse in the spring from the humiliating treatment of Mr. John Beatty. But she was quite her radiant self now, and life once more was a brimming cup of sweets and excitements. She had rallied the more rapidly, from the smart and the shame, because his eyes had been so often upon her, and because it had been possible by presenting an invariably poised and indifferent front to humiliate him a little in turn.

He would ask her to a swell country club just to play a part, would he? Ellen's thought had hummed as her flying fingers danced on the typewriter. He'd try to make a cat's-paw of Ellen Murphy! She rejoiced in open warfare as she had never rejoiced in unacknowledged love. She pushed her persecution of him to the limits of common charity, and beyond. Impassive, she stood beside him pointing out his errors, questioning his contradictory statements. His embarrassed laughter, his fumbling explanations, evoked no answering friendliness from her. Ellen, triumphing in her merciless young soul, told herself that she'd learn him to get fresh with her!

She was exhilarated with her rôle, and the united families of Murphy, Flint, and Kane admitted dispassionately that Ellen "had a healthy look on her, these days," or even that Ellen "tuk after the Florences in her looks, and they were a well-favoured lot."

Ellen's old grandfather, however, who was sitting in the elm-shaded bare backyard this afternoon, with two of the Callahan grandchildren, often told her outright that she was beautiful, and Mr. Clement Aloysius Riordan, whose company and adoration Ellen capriciously turned off or on like a hot-water faucet, was temporarily in favour at this time, and spared neither adjectives, panting breaths, deep, agonized flushes, nor brief, abashed laughs in attempting to assure her of her preëminent charm.

So Ellen was happy and indulgent this afternoon to "Mama's gang of perfect forty-fours"; her radiant youth had little concern with their dismal and funereal reminiscences, but she liked occasionally to spend an hour or two in their company, if only to make Dan, her brother, "die laughing" at her report upon them afterward.

"I'll tell you what," she said now, still in reference to the Kelly boy, "I don't know that it would hurt that kid to be sent up for awhile. He might learn some common sense. He's got no parents, his step-mother is going to marry again, and he says he won't live with his Aunt Lily in Troy. He'll go on this way until he kills someone, and then it'll be jail!"

"You'd wonder he wouldn't live with his Aunt Lily; she's a fine woman," said Mrs. Cahill, her veil thrown back, her lean little liver-spotted face flushed with tea and sociability. "She has a good job in the liberry, and he could set there evenings, reading a story out of a book, until she'd be going home. She'd give him a good home, and she'd like to have him for company. Lily is a fine ger'rl," added Mrs Cahill, thoughtfully; "the Sisters had her for the Blessed Virgin wanst in their tabloos; she looked very elegant."

"Well, wouldn't you wonder at him?" agreed Mrs. Murphy. "I'll go to the Judge myself, one of these days," she said, impressively, "and tell him that if ever there was a lad that a few years on the Island would do a world's world of good, me young gallant Robbie Kelly is the lad. I will so! I'll tell 'um that the boy could have a good home, with a fine ger'rl that's his own mother's sister, Lily Boone, but that he's so wild he wants to run the streets, stealin' goats off of decent, respectable people that has need, God knows, of every penny——"

The conversation rambled up and down comfortably. Soft, warm early summer lingered kindly over the unlovely neighborhood, and the light, streaming through young leaves, pleasantly entered the shabby, dark, smoke-stained kitchen. The tin spoons and colanders that Mrs. Murphy began in a desultory manner to employ in the first dinner preparations were black and shapeless with wear; some of them she had used for ten years, some twenty; she never thought of replacing them. A wire strainer with no handle had burned her fingers regularly three times a week, since Ellen was a baby; Dan had made round wooden knobs, clumsily botched together with wire, for her sauce-pan lids ten years before. Ellen and Jule and Lizzie-Kate had grown to womanhood, taking for granted the struggle with casseroles that leaked through cracks, coffee-pot tops that wedged in too tight, or else blew off entirely in a puff of brown foam; a chopping-bowl that had to be tipped up beyond the split that ran down one side or was useless, and an egg-beater that hitched and stuck once in every fifth revolution. Their mother always used a favorite little vegetable knife that had only the denuded spear of rusty steel left where once the wooden handle had been.

Mrs. Callahan had the rocker so placed that by a long arm she could reach the teapot; Mrs. Cahill sat at the end of the table; she occasionally cut a wedge of fresh bread from the loaf that was not yet quite free of the thin wrapping paper and the tangle of pink bakery string. Granulated sugar was in an open yellow-glass bowl covered with large, opaque glass warts; the sugar spoon was crusted with dried brown crystals from which the loose white sugar sifted. Mrs. Murphy prized the sugar-bowl, which she had selected from a Wheel of Fortune at a Fair.

"I ought to be going, Mrs. Murphy dear, to get the young children home," said Mrs. Callahan, without stirring. "Poor Annie's going to take Martin up to visit Josie in Albany awhile, that he shouldn't be too well-informed as to what's goin' on——"

She gave a mild, significant glance toward Ellen, before whom Annie's unborn child might not with propriety be mentioned. The other elderly women nodded, and sighed, and there was a silence. Annie Callahan Curley had been widowed six months before, and the arrival of her fifth child was thus more than ordinarily a solemn event.

"Martin, mind you, is an angel of God," Mrs. Callahan hastened to say of her foster-son, "but the child's eleven, and 'tis just as well he should be out of the way for awhile. Annie may go off to-night; she'll have a good visit with Josie and John, and when she comes back may the Lord send her a little comforter!"

There was no distinct "amen!" to this. But the others broke into an audible sighing and murmuring, with some shaking of heads, and much tut-tutting of lips. Mrs. Callahan wiped her eyes. Mrs. Cahill said, "Whatever!" on a long, dolorous breath, and Mrs. Murphy: "Betune us and all har'rm, the help of God help the poor ger'rl!" And there was a sorrowful and sympathetic pause in the conversation.

It was broken by a stir in the yard, the approach of disturbance and danger sensed rather than actually seen. The women exchanged apprehensive glances; Ellen made an indeterminate move toward the door.

Voices in the yard; then hammering steps upon the porch. Then the door was torn open, and upon a sobbing shout of defiance, fury, terror, and tears, a thin, dirty, torn, and tousled boy of perhaps twelve or fourteen rushed in. He was stammering and crying like a frantic little hunted animal; he saw neither the kitchen nor its occupants, but he saw the drophead sewing machine by the window and got behind it, and braced it between him and the door he had just entered.

"You dirty big liar!" he sobbed, his face streaming with tears and blood and dirt, his thin little chicken-breast rising and falling as if it would burst with the storm. "I never done it—you dirty liar! You can kill me—you can kill me—but you won't send me to jail! I'll get a pistol, and I'll blow your brains out—and I don't care if I do go to the chair—I don't care if I do go to the chair—you dirty big dirty liar——!"

His back was toward the stupefied occupants of the kitchen. But every one of them knew him, of course: the Kelly boy.

Mrs. Murphy automatically soused the end of a mud-colored towel under the cold-water faucet, and as she addressed her unexpected guest she was wiping his forlorn, still-sputtering face. She had not lived in this neighborhood forty years for nothing, nor was this her first experience of this sort.

"Here, what's all this to-do?" she demanded, equably. "This is a fine way to bur'rst in upon a Christian woman! What have you been up to now, Robbie Kelly? I shouldn't wonder if the police are after you again!"

The cold water had somewhat sobered the child, but he was still panting as he clawed her hands with his own lean little hard ones, and gasped:

"Oh, Mis' Murphy, don't let him get me! Hamilton's after me—the cop's after me and Lenny Spillane! Oh, Mis' Murphy, honest to God, I never done nothin'. It was them big fellers that was foolin' with the switch, and Len and me was just lookin' at what they done——"

"My God! There's been a train wreck!" shouted Mrs. Cahill.

"No, there wasn't no wreck!" the child said, quickly, his face white when the dirt and blood had been washed away. "But the cop says there might have been, and he says he's going to have me up before Judge Casey—and Casey told me last time, he'd send me up to Randall's Island! But I'll kill him first," gritted little Robbie Kelly, his teeth set, his tears breaking forth afresh as he turned his desperate eyes once more toward the door.

"It's a pity you wouldn't think of that, Robbie, before now," Mrs. Callahan said, mildly. "There's some that loved your good mother that thinks maybe you'd be better off for a few years, until you'd be eighteen or so, shut up where you couldn't do anny harm. Manny's the time I've disputed you about it, that you should go to your good aunt, and be a comfort to her, and sell a few *Posts* like Martin does, and grow up a decent man. But no, you'd be stravagin' the neighborhood, like a wild Turk that has no God itself, and now look what's in it!"

"I'll go to Aunt Lily—say, if you'll lend me the money for my ticket I'll go, if you'll just get me off this once!" Robbie promised, breathlessly. "Honest I will—I know the way! If you'll get me off with the cop——"

"So that you can run off wid me goats again!" Mrs. Murphy interpolated, drily, in the troubled pause.

"Mrs. Callahan, won't you *please*—won't you please, for the love of God and the Blessed Virgin——!" the Kelly boy begged her, beside himself with terror and urgency. "I'll go to my aunt, and I'll help her—I'll split wood for her and run her errands—you'll not be sorry—honest—*honest*—I promise you if I never promised anything in my life——!"

"For Heaven's sake, Robbie Kelly," Ellen said, impatient and distressed, "why on earth didn't you think of all this before? You could have gone to your aunt when your mother died, and entered school there, and tried to make something of yourself. And now you come in with your promises and everything, when the cop's after you, and he's a new cop—nobody likes him, and his hand is against everybody! You got the Fay boy into trouble, and that was the very first time, and you've been up twice before Judge Casey, and you know how mad anything with the railroad makes him, because they're all down on him, anyway——"

She put her ironing-board away with a bump, and there was a long silence in the kitchen. The Kelly boy still panted; his eyes roved despairingly from one face to another. Mrs. Murphy had pursed her lips, taken a chair, pressed a weazened little hand over her shut eyes, and was swaying from side to side with a rotary sort of movement indicative of utter helplessness. Mrs. Cahill cleaned her teeth with whistling sounds of her lips; her sharp, faded, scrutinizing gaze resting impassively upon the agitated face and the shabby, dirty, tumbled young figure. Ellen rested her shoul-

[318]

der against the bedroom door, her arms folded, her face exasperated and yet sympathetic, and Mrs. Callahan, in the low rocker, had a big hand planted upon each knee, her magnificent leonine head dropped a little forward, her handsome black eyes thoughtful and troubled.

"I could go with ye to the Judge, Robbie," she suggested, after awhile. "But I think he'll send ye up—the third time. I declare if your good mother wouldn't rather see you in your grave——"

Robbie's face wrinkled, all the fire and fight died out of him, and standing shamed and forlorn before them he began to cry great tears that ran down his freckled face and crept saltily into his trembling mouth. He was little, guilty, helpless, and inevitable punishment faced him.

"I tell you I never done it!" he said, stubbornly.

"You've done enough, God knows," Mrs. Cahill reminded him, inexorably, but without rancor.

"But I never done that!" sobbed Robbie, "and if he takes me and sends me to jail, I'll *tell* him I never done it! He can send me to the chair—because he's a big liar, but I'll tell the Judge that if my mother had lived I'd tell her the same thing—and if I was dying I'd tell it——"

The frantic, incoherent threats died stilly into the air. Robbie gulped, sniffled wetly, and gratefully grasped the handkerchief that Ellen supplied. Young, thin, shabby, and friendless, with the great machinery of the law set in motion to catch him, he wept into Ellen's little blue lawn handkerchief with the orange butterfly.

"Whisht!" breathed Mrs. Cahill, electrically. "There's the cop in the yard!"

An instant change took place among all present. Stepping with the silent agility of a deer, Mrs. Cahill opened the door into the bedroom, three feet from the yard door. The Kelly boy's tears dried, his eyes flashed courage and defiance again as Ellen laid her hand upon his shabby shoulder, and he and she vanished through the bedroom door like smoke.

Mrs. Callahan was comfortably enjoying a cup of tea, and Mrs. Cahill pulling on her dismal black gloves, her veil down as preparatory to departure, when Mrs. Murphy stepped innocently to answer an authoritative rap upon the porch door.

She blinked at the visitor, a tall, stalwart, freshly uniformed young man with a truculent red face.

"Well, God bless us, it's Officer Hamilton, will ye step in?" she said, with an air of pleased surprise.

Officer Hamilton sent a lightning glance about the kitchen, smiled with no warmth, and stepped in. He sat down in a low chair, and dandled his cap upon his knee.

"Mrs. Callahan you know, and me friend Mrs. Cahill. I misdoubt ye don't know the whole pack of us hereabouts," Mrs. Murphy said, socially. "You wouldn't have a cup of tea while you'd be talkin'? And now what is it—it isn't the Fourth of July barbecue yet awhile?"

Officer Hamilton looked from one to the other with a dreadful and unhurried smile. The smile said that they knew why he was there, and they knew that he knew they knew, and that business as important as his, authority as unquestioned, might suffer an occasional pause, but could never evade satisfaction.

"Come now—come now——" he said, with an indulgent smile. The three women exchanged glances almost too exquisitely bewildered.

"Well—whatever is it—all this is very strange——" said these innocent glances.

"Did ye see me ould father out in the yard that we had anointed awhile back?" Mrs. Murphy questioned him conversationally.

"Yes, I seen Mr. Florence, and lookin' extremely well and hearty, too," said the officer, leisurely indulgent, inexorable. "I'm after the Kelly kid. Where is he?"

"After——? Is it young Robbie Kelly?" Mrs. Callahan asked.

"Him and young Spillane," announced Mr. Hamilton, with a brief nod, as one who appreciates that he imparts—as indeed he was imparting, well-known facts. "It's the first time Spillane has been caught, and I left him off again. But me young friend Robbie," he resumed, grimly, "goes up to the Judge on Monday, and I don't doubt they'll learn him to evade the law before they're done with him!"

"I wonther that you could be doin' all that, and you widout a warrant or annything whativer," Mrs. Cahill said, the soft accents of the Tralee mountains wrapping each word as in cotton wool.

"He's here all right, I seen him bolt into the yard. Where is he?" the man persisted, brushing aside these mild diversions.

"I don't know why you would chase the poor child, annyway," Mrs. Murphy said, with some decision, from the sink, "but whativer you do, it's neither sign nor sound of 'um you'll find in my kitchen. He'd be conthrivin' to pass out of the neighborhood entirely, I should presume, and not loither about the way you'd put hands on 'um. He's a very spry young lad, if I have 'um rightly——"

"Come, now—come, now!" Officer Hamilton interrupted her in a slow drawl, with significantly smiling eyes. "You give me your word he's not here," he added, with a first touch of asperity, "you give me your word he's not here, and I'll believe you!"

"Where would he be?" Mrs. Murphy asked, in elaborate innocence. "Look in me little butthry—you couldn't be hiding a young cat and his kittens in there!"

She flung open the door of a large closet, where indeed nothing more concealing than an open flour barrel met the officer's quick and dissatisfied glances.

"Mama——" began Ellen, from the bedroom doorway. "Oh, how do you do, Mr. Hamilton?" she interrupted herself, with a smile that made her dazzling young beauty even more radiant. "Mrs. Cahill, would you

step in here and say good-bye to Aunt Susie, and you, too, Mrs. Callahan?" she asked, with a glance straight into each woman's eyes in turn.
"Did Mama tell you me aunt is in there quite laid up with the arthritis?"
Ellen continued prettily, as the two guests lumbered obediently into the
bedroom. "You'll want to look in there," she added, to the officer. "These
boys in the neighborhood, they're an awful care to you, I daresay," Ellen
continued, obliterating from the impressionable heart of Thomas Hamilton with a suddenness that made his senses reel, an imprint lately left
there by Miss Rita O'Connor of Centre Moriches. "I'll take you in there!"
she promised.

"I'll be stepping on along home, Mrs. Murphy," Mrs. Callahan said,
comfortably, from the bedroom doorway, "for it's small use a house has
for company, with the police in it! Your aunt looks better, and I don't
doubt she'll be up amongst us, and herself again, in a day or two, and
God grant it!"

"And I'll go along wid Mrs. Callahan," Mrs. Cahill said, following.
"Faith—I left me bag on the bed!"

She dove back into the bedroom, and immediately afterward the two
widows departed, murmuring together, and stopping to speak to old man
Florence in the yard, where Mrs. Callahan gathered up her two staggering
grandchildren.

"Stop in whin you're passin'!" Mrs. Murphy shouted after them hospitably. "Now, sir," she said somewhat truculently to the officer, "you've
looked into me butthry, and you've druv me friends off of me house, and
what else can I do for ye?"

Officer Hamilton was watching Ellen Murphy with shrewdly smiling
eyes.

"Did you know that I delayed on my way here to ask Officer Burns to
just keep an eye on your windows, Miss Murphy?" he asked.

The girl flushed honestly and indignantly.

"Well, I don't know why you'd do that, Mr. Hamilton," she said, coldly.

"So that nobody could help anybody else out of one of them, for instance," he told her, with a sort of quiet triumph.

"There's nobody in that room there but my Aunt Susan, sick in bed,"
Ellen asserted, stoutly, with a shrug. "I don't know what you're driving
at!"

"And if you arrest that child—and you with neither warrant nor writ—
a child that's got no mother, and whatever has he done but just a few
thricks that would make a decent man laugh at 'um, let alone arrest
'um—!" Mrs. Murphy began shrilly.

"It's my business to see that the law is respected," Hamilton said, inflexibly. "If he's not here, I'm sure I'm sorry that I broke up your tea-
party. And if you'll let me give one look at—that—sick—aunt—of yours,"
he added, addressing Mrs. Murphy, but with his eyes fixed on Ellen, and

his drawling tone full of meaning for her, "then I'll thank you, and take my leave!"

"Saving your presence, my aunt's not young, and she's sick in bed," Ellen offered, with a reluctance so betraying and so undisguised that Officer Hamilton suspected that a distressed and hopeless shaking of the head would begin, on the mother's part, and smiled again when he detected it.

"It's no use, Ellen," said Mrs. Murphy's frightened lips, making no sound. Ellen gripped her mother's arm with firm fingers, and the officer of the law with only a premonitory rap opened the bedroom door.

"Run, Robbie—run for your life!" the older woman shouted. Afterward she denied having said this, and added that if the child had been there, which she well knew he wasn't, she thought he might as well make a run for it.

Thomas Hamilton opened the bedroom door, and stood there, with one watchful eye never leaving the kitchen. He saw a shabby, plain room, with no place in it that would hide even the aforementioned young cat "and his kittens," with a narrow iron bed protruding into the center of the floor, and in the bed an indubitable old woman.

There was no mistaking her wrinkled old face, her thinning grizzled hair, her claw-like old hands. No Robbie Kelly—were he the child Coquelin—could assume that mask, that cracked old voice. The invalid wore a sodden but brilliantly flowered kimono; there was no suspicious hump of fugitive childhood at her feet, the floor under the bed was empty except for a collapsed hat-box, a heap of Sunday newspapers, a brick, two pairs of crushed and shapeless shoes, a string of empty cereal boxes long used by some child as a cart, and several curls of dust that lay shamelessly upon the unpainted rough boards.

Hanging on the wall opposite the door was a forlorn row of garments, but from under them no Kelly boots protruded. And through the small panes of the one window Officer Hamilton could see the back of Officer Burns, elaborately casual—and loitering up and down the block.

That was all. There was no wardrobe, no closet, no other door. Officer Hamilton flushed, and scratched his head, and glanced dubiously into the kitchen again. There was a third room, but the window from this gave upon the back porch, as the kitchen door did, and the doorway into it had been quite frankly open all the time. It contained a dark jumble of comforters and boots and odd meaningless garments, and was known as "Grandpa's room."

Officer Hamilton, without moving, glanced toward the street, and blew his whistle, and Officer Burns immediately straightened alertly and came into the shanty.

"The boy's here somewhere, Burns," said the harassed Hamilton, "and we've got to find him!"

"If you weren't the best dancer ever, Frank," said Ellen Murphy to

Officer Burns, with a killing glance, "I'd have you both arrested for breaking into Mama's house, and scaring the wits out of us all."

"Here's the thing, Miss Ellen," returned Frank Burns, kindly regretful. "The boy's been making trouble for everybody. It'll be for his own good that he's shut up awhile; it'll teach him a lesson!"

"Teach him all the lessons you want to, Frank, although I'll bet you weren't any Child Ignatius yourself, if I remember rightly, when you were his age!" Miss Murphy began, smoothly. "But don't waste time running around annoying people worse than a hundred Kelly kids could annoy them——"

"And him a posthumious child that never seen hide nor hair of his own father, that died on him before he was born——!" her mother added, in a high wail.

"Do you know what he did?" Frank Burns demanded, fiercely, as his colleague trampled sternly through old man Florence's lair. "Him and young Spillane was monkeying with the railway switch. Now—if you have an accident there, Miss Ellen," he pleaded, with a sudden change of tone, his handsome, clean-shaven, kind young face gravely concerned, "it's manslaughter. You don't want anything like that breaking loose in our neighborhood. Now, do you?"

Ellen was visibly moved. She looked down.

"But don't you have to have warrants, and search-warrants, and all that sort of thing, to do this, Frank?" she asked, with a sudden upward and most disquieting glance.

"Isn't it better to have him in a corrective institution for a few years, instead of in jail for life?" Frank countered, grasping at phrases that edified and surprised himself as well as everyone else.

"Ah, but there's no harm in a child like that!" Ellen pleaded in turn.

"Cellar?" said Thomas Hamilton to Mrs. Murphy, indicating a trapdoor in the floor with his big, shining boot.

"There is not," returned the mistress of the house, "and lucky thim that needs thim in these days!" she added, darkly.

Hamilton, incredulously, opened the flap, discovered a neatly embedded bathtub, in which some onions and turnips and a can of kerosene were odorously stored, and looked apologetic and somewhat foolish.

"Well, now, where is he?" he asked, looking about with a slight amelioration of his harsh attitude. "He run in here—we both seen that. You can't hide him forever; it can't be done. I'll nab him the minute I lay eyes on him, and it'll only go the worse for him if I have to tell the Court that he run off on me. Resisting the law——"

"A kid runnin' away from a cop isn't resistin' the law," Ellen interpolated, smartly. "I'll bet you used to run from them yourself, and think nothing at all about it! The child didn't do anything; he said himself that he and the Spillane boy——"

"Aha!" cried Officer Hamilton, triumphantly, "he *was* in here then?"

The girl flushed, bit her lip, looked up, looked down.

"Well, what if he was?" she demanded. "He run off again. He just run by, through the yard, and through the back gate out onto the hill."

"There's a pat' goes down past Harrison's place, that you'd be takin' and you steppin' to the market," Mrs. Murphy supplied circumstantially.

"He did not," Officer Burns said, good-naturedly and flatly. "I never took my eyes off the house."

"Well, wouldn't you think we was all the one for lies and inthrigues," Mrs. Murphy commented, in almost admiring wonder. "That's the police for it," she added, "they'll find you a murther as aisy as you'd pick up a button you'd dhropped on the flure. 'Clap him into jail,' says they, 'and we'll find means and ways to keep 'um there!' There was a feller back in the ould country, and him a dacint, God-fearin' lad that had a cousin at Maynooth itself, and the good mother he had on him——"

"Come on, where is he, Miss Ellen?" Frank Burns said, coaxingly, uninterested in this moving recital.

"Do you think, if I knew where he was, which I don't," Ellen said, briskly, "that I'd let you haul out that poor little fellow, and keep him in the Juvenile Detention two days—among thieves and God knows what, and then have him up before old Casey, to ruin his life on him? Shame on you! You and Mr. Hamilton are in a fine business chasing a child around the block, with the speeders right here on South Street killing nuns and Eyetalian babies and dear knows what all——"

"God help your husband, Ellen, when you get going!" said Mr. Burns, admiringly.

"Well, I hope He will!" the girl responded, warmly. "I'll go out and bring Grandpa in, Mama," she added, turning her back upon the forces of the law. "If you've both looked your fill of my aunt's room," she said, witheringly to the men, as she left the kitchen, "I hope you'll excuse my shutting the door, she's trying to get some sleep!"

"This'll all be told to the Judge——" Mr. Hamilton warned her, baffled and bewildered, but still determined, and somewhat red in the face.

"You'll tell him more than your prayers, I don't doubt that," Mrs. Murphy muttered, bitterly, again busy at her sink.

"Say, Dan, you help us out here," Frank Burns said, good-naturedly, as Daniel Murphy, thirty-five, weazened, looking alertly from one to the other, came home after his hard day.

Daniel kissed his mother.

"How's Aunt Susan?" he asked, sitting down at the table.

"Better. She's had aspirin, and she's drowsy," Ellen, now tenderly engineering her old grandfather in his armchair, answered briskly, as her mother looked a little vague.

"Here's the way of it, Dan. Hamilton and I don't like to butt in here," Officer Burns said, uncomfortably. "But you know that kid in the neighborhood that they call the Kelly kid?"

"Sure. Knew his mother," Dan responded, his weasel-bright eyes still travelling from one face to the other as he rapidly and lightly chewed gum with his front teeth.

"Well, he and that Spillane boy were monkeying with a railroad switch to-day——" Officer Burns pleaded, almost pathetically.

"Holy Nelly!" Dan said, gratifyingly impressed. He stopped chewing.

"States Prison offence!" Officer Hamilton supplied, with a grim nod.

"I'll tell the world!" Dan affirmed, beginning to chew again.

"Now, he's got to answer for that," the other officer said, logically. "I want to run him in. You've got to break up that gang of his, you know. Isn't it better that one kid should be punished, and scare the daylights out of the rest of them?"

"Sure," Dan conceded, nodding noncommittally as he chewed.

"Well, he run in here, into this house," pursued Burns. "We both seen that. Hamilton whistled for me, and I come in the other end of the block; he didn't pass me. And he never walked out the path at the back of the house, either, I seen that as I come along. We've got him, Dan, wherever the ladies has hid him. There hasn't been a soul come in or go out——"

"Come through, Mama, where is he?" Dan said, grinning. "They won't do him no hurt, Ellen. Cough him up. Maybe the Judge will let him off, anyway."

"He haven't set fut here or hereabouts," Dan's mother asserted in her high, shrill, plaintive wail of a voice. "I never seen nor heard the like of the questions these two officers has been askin'! They've waked yure aunt out of a sleep that might be life or death to her——"

"What's under them rugs?" demanded Officer Hamilton suddenly, his eyes fixed upon a nondescript mass of bedding, floor-covering, old carpets, and variegated garments that formed a sort of mountain against one wall.

Instantly Ellen was standing before it, her eyes flashing.

"It's just nothing but rubbish!" she said, with an excited laugh. "It's —it's—Dan—Mama——"

"It's been there this fortnight, until I could sort it all out for the Sisters' Rummidge Sale they're going to have," Mrs. Murphy said, bewilderedly. "Sure you couldn't hide a Galway pig there——"

"Just kindly take my word for it——" Ellen said, fiercely, to Frank Burns, as he looked at her inquiringly.

"I'm sorry I can't!" Hamilton had seized a broom, the heap was rifled in a few seconds.

It revealed old coats thick with age and hard wear, old derby hats pathetically dented and browned, old collars tied together with a boot lace, a jumble of paper patterns, faded cottons, disreputable boots, and one or two worn, small crêpe nightgowns in which yellowed ribbons still were knotted.

Ellen's face blazed as to a murmured accompaniment of embarrassed apologies she restored some sort of outward order to the unsavory heap.

"We've had enough of this nonsense!" she said, sharply. "Probably the Kelly kid has made Brooklyn by this time; I hope he has! He's got cousins there, and there's plenty of people he knows there! If you'll be so kind as to vacate the premises, I'll get my grandfather's milk toast ready for him——"

"That was a queer turn, Frank," said Officer Hamilton, as the two walked slowly down the block. "She's double-crossing me somewhere, that girl. The kid ran in there, and I didn't turn my back two minutes, I'll swear that. I looked over your way, and I run about twenty feet with my back to the house——"

"Well, I guess that was the time," Frank Burns said, yawning, and deciding to buy a dollar ticket for St. Rose's Ball and Raffle a week from to-night, and see for himself who was running with Ellen Murphy just now. "She's a beauty, isn't she?" he said.

"Yes," the other man conceded, still abstracted and still smarting. "I'm going to watch that house, Frank," he threatened. "And I'm going to tell Moore to. That's all I can do. And soon or later I'll get that kid."

"I'll bet on Ellen Murphy," young Burns said. "You'll see that nothing'll happen there to-night."

The prophecy was fulfilled. Unless, mused Officer Hamilton, walking up and down under the summer stars, and the street lights, and the softly moving new foliage of the elms, unless the arrival of old Mrs. Callahan and her adopted son was an event. Hamilton knew little Martin Callahan, who was as good a boy as the Kelly kid was bad, using his spare energies normally in ball-games and tramps and the building of tepees and forts.

"Hello, Martin," he said, as they passed him, "I thought you was going up to your aunt's in Albany to-night?"

"I may go to-morrow," Martin said, shifting the bundle he carried.

"My daughter got off to-night, but he may foller her and he may not," Mrs. Callahan contributed, politely, as they went on their way. Hamilton watched them suspiciously; had there been laughter under those demure voices? Laughter at what?

Had he followed them into the Murphy kitchen his vaguely uneasy question would have been fully answered. For there was laughter there.

Dan Murphy laughed in little violent squirts that convulsed his shrewd little lean face and wrinkled his apple cheeks. Mrs. Callahan laughed with a great shaking, as of an earthquake, and anon wiped her eyes, and anon burst out into crying laughter and choked and sobbed with the sheer felicity of it all over again. Ellen laughed until she had to lay her bright, bobbed mahogany head down on the table. Young Martin laughed sympathetically, looking from one to the other a little curiously with his nice boy's eyes, and even Mrs. Murphy laughed sourly and reluctantly, her mouth bursting into wrinkles, and her frowning forehead relaxing.

The old man was long in bed and asleep, but there was a sixth person in the kitchen, and she laughed, too. Old Mrs. Cahill, again veiled and shawled after her brief incarceration in Dan's bed, sobbed, sputtered, whimpered, and gasped with the rest.

"He—he looked——" Mrs. Callahan's handsome, good face, with its motherly, sweet-tempered lines, broke suddenly into crinkles. "Oh, the dear Lord preserve us!" she whispered, under her breath, ashamed of her uncontrollable mirth, and assuming a dignified expression that made the others laugh again. "Whin Hamilton give me a good clear look, as we wint out," she said, rapidly, and with shaking accents, "me heart died on me! And whin Robbie Kelly walked with me into me kitchen, dressed for all the world like a widow that's lost her husband—well, I thought Annie Curley would drop dead where she stud!"

"Did he get off with Annie?" Mrs. Murphy asked, for the mere pleasure of hearing it all repeated.

"As easy as kiss your hand," the other woman assured her. "He had Mart's old overcoat onto him, and they walked out of the house as quiet as birds. And they got the six o'clock from town; he'll stay at Josie's to-night, and go to his aunt to-morrow, and nobody the wiser. The poor child! He kissed me good-bye as solemn as a priest. I wouldn't wonder would he be a Bishop yet!"

"When Hamilton asked what was under the carpets——!" Ellen sobbed joyfully.

"My God, the dirty look you give him, Ellen!" her brother said, admiringly, "when you let out that you'd seen the kid!"

"Oh, but the best of all, Dan," his sister said, exulting, "was when you walked in and asked how was Aunt Susan! I thought I'd faint away——"

"Hadn't I just met Mrs. Callahan, and had it all out of her, and she running down the street to get the child a cap?" Dan demanded, in high feather. "'Go home, Dan,' she says, 'and see what-all's in it, with the Kelly kid and your mother and Ellen and all!'"

"So I did," Mrs. Callahan said, solemnly. "Those were me words!"

"I stipt back into your room, Dan," Mrs. Cahill boasted, "and I joomped out of me old dress and t'rew the veil over his head. 'Beat it,' I says. Wid that, Mrs. Callahan begun to talk to 'um. 'Mrs. Cahill,' she says, 'will you l'ave me have a tasteen of your buttermilk the night?' she says. Oh, dear Lord, preserve and defind us by the glory and goodness of God!" exclaimed the widow, "out they walked, wit'in t'ree inches of Hamilton's nose itself——!"

"We'll miss the child," Mrs. Murphy said, solemnly, in a long pause.

"We will that," Mrs. Callahan agreed, sighing. "Never will I forget the night him and the Spillane boy tuk two old carriage lamps, and wint out onto the highway," she mused. "And whin a car was comin' along in the dark, wouldn't they move up to it as if they was another autymobile until they was within fifteen feet, and thin the two of them split, and one go each side of the poor feller that was tryin' to drive——"

"The day he took Annie's baby and put Katie Oliver's kid in the coach," Ellen added.

"Oh, the Lord be good to us, that was a day!" said Annie's mother.

Mrs. Murphy, having swabbed up every possible dark, damp, and dingy corner of the sink and table with a muddy rag, and having carefully spread the rag, greasy, odorous, and warm, across the bottom of the inverted dishpan, now showed signs of tears. She seated herself on the foot of the old red box-lounge, where Dan was spread luxuriously, and he drew up his feet for better accommodation. His mother would sleep here, later, but now the piece of furniture was merely a lounge.

"Bad luck to the police that'd run him out of the neighborhood!" she said, resentfully.

"I was thinkin' I might have him down for Christmas wid Rose's children," Mrs. Cahill said.

"He could run around with Martin," suggested Mrs. Callahan. "There's no harm to the child."

"I'll send Lily Boone a fiver, next Christmas, and ask him down," Dan contributed.

"We'll get Josie and John to keep an eye on him, and see he has a good time," Ellen added.

A long silence fell. Dan smoked, and Ellen manicured her pretty hands. She and Mrs. Cahill and Mrs. Callahan were simultaneously entertaining vague ideas of departure; young Martin was exultant at finding himself out of bed at half-past nine; Mrs. Murphy, whose nose was always moist, sniffled, rocked to and fro, sighed, and clicked her false teeth.

"Oh, well, they're always persecutin' somebody," she conceded to the cruel world, suddenly. "Look at the way they treated the Lord!"

Keeping Ellen Out of It

"There's times that Ellen will talk very wild and bold, but she has a very good, lovely mind on her!" her mother observed.

For so long a time after this remark there was absolute silence in the Murphy kitchen, that an unseeing listener might have supposed the old woman to be alone, and soliloquizing.

But presently the bundle of neutral-colored garments in the rocker that encased the form of the Widow Cahill stirred slightly, and with a sniff the widow responded, in a tone of somewhat grim satisfaction.

"It's well some has, with the way the ger'rls is nowadays!"

Mrs. Cahill had been making a somewhat protracted call, and the welcome time for tea had arrived. At almost any moment now Mrs. Murphy would shove her kettle forward upon the rusty old dilapidated stove, and shake the green tin caddy as if to ascertain the amount of its contents. This last gesture was pure atavism, an instinctive, inherited fear from the women of the old country, who had had to husband the precious leaves. For Mrs. Murphy "cud have had a pound a week off the grocer, and it done up in gilt and pitchers of Japs," as she often observed with gratitude and pride.

Having done these things, she would set forth upon the bare old scarred wood of the table the mismatched china cups: the big one with roses that had been a prize for tea-coupons, the hand-painted blue one with the apple-blossoms on it—this had lost its own, and stood upon a scalloped pink saucer—and the two thick white ones. And she would take from a clean tea-cloth the delicious crusty loaf of bread.

Mrs. Cahill would then rise to go.

"Set down, set down," the hostess would say, "we'll have a little taste of tea."

"I don't want ye should be put to the bother," Mrs. Cahill invariably answered, as automatically as she said Amen after the last prayers at Mass.

"Oh, I'm goan to, annyway," the other always responded. "Papa likes his tea—it's all he takes, barrin' a taste of mush in the mornings, and maybe a bowl of bread-and-milk that you'd give a young child at noon! I can't get anny meat into him; it don't lay good on him. You're goan to have your tea, Papa!" she added, to-day, loudly, to the subject of these remarks, old Tom Florence, who in his eighty-seventh year was afflicted with a slight deafness.

The ancient, sitting dreaming, on this blustering, bitter November day, in the ingle by the stove, lifted blue old smiling eyes, and nodded. Old Tom did not speak much, but it was not because he lacked either the energy or intelligence. Perhaps it was rather that he had discovered the utter superfluousness of words: so many said—so little accomplished by them! Lovers needed them not, nor young mothers brooding over their babies, and Tom had joined these in a happy zone of peaceful thought and prayer, and only fixed his keen old blue gaze upon the babbling women now and then with deep and infantile amusement.

He had an old red comforter wrapped about his legs, and on the arm of his chair was his Bible, with the big spectacles resting upon it. And presently he would have one of the big white cups filled to the brim with strong, fragrant, smoking-hot tea, and cream and sugar, and his daughter, slopping a fifth of it into the saucer from which he would presently loudly drink it, would have no idea that he either heard or understood the conversation that was going on about him.

"Ellen," she presently added, returning to the subject placidly, as if there had been no hospitably filled interval, "is as innocent as the babe itself!"

This proverbially pure and unborn child was well-known to her hearer, and Mrs. Cahill nodded approval.

"And a good thing, too!" she said.

"She wouldn't know what you were talkin' about," continued her mother, "no more than if it was French!"

"She'll make the better wife for it!" returned Mrs. Cahill, in the tone of one making familiar responses. "There was a ger'rl back home," she added, after a peaceful time of tea-drinking, "Lizzie Cuddahy. She was a pretty ger'rl, with no kith nor kin, as was well-known, and she had a wild, innocent sort of look—she wasn't bright at all. Well, what did one of me bould young lads do at a Fair but lay hands on her, and try cud he kiss her a good, bould kiss on her mouth! And mind you—all of us was streelin' about and we seen the whole thing!" the widow interrupted herself to say shrilly, in a triumphant tone. "Lizzie—and well do I remember the little red shawl she had on!" resumed Mrs. Cahill—"let a yell out of her, and she give him a little clip—you might say—on the side of his face, and she pucked me brother Jawn, that was passin', by the ar'rm——"

"I'll bet Jawn Reilly kilt the poor feller!" Mrs. Murphy said in a tone of high relish, as the other paused, lost in pleasant reminiscence.

"Kilt, is it?" said the narrator. "He knocked him down and jumped on him, and kilt him—and when me gallant lad got up—saving your presence!—he had a nosebleed on him would amaze you! 'You take a ger'rl that has a father and brothers, and you with your kisses and hugs!' Jawn bawled at him, and all the young lads that stood by cried out the same. And I give you me solemn word on the stren'th of me oath," finished Mrs. Cahill, impressively, "that that was the last Lizzie Cuddahy ever seen of him, from that day to this—and she dead two years later with the tubercular consumption," she added, thoughtfully.

"I'd like to see the one that'd get fresh with Ellen," Mrs. Murphy contributed, after awhile. "Do you want some tea, or don't you?" she added, apparently to space.

This question was followed by a brief silence, which was broken presently by a most terrible and desolating moan. There was the blue twilight of a snowy November afternoon in the kitchen now, and the women's tea-table was lighted only by the cold, opaque oblong of the undraped window.

But across the room, upon the stamped velours of the lounge that was sometimes, in an emergency, or when Ellen was home, a bed by night, in a welter of newspapers, garments, an old comforter, a shabby old buggy-robe, a sewing basket brimming with socks, an empty market-basket, and various other ill-assorted objects, there might still be discerned, in the gloom, the prostrate figure of a girl.

It was from the girl that the bitter cry had proceeded, and that the two old women, mothers and grandmothers both, could remain totally unmoved by it, was a strange thing to see. But they went on with their tea-drinking without so much as a glance in the direction of the lounge.

Mrs. Murphy's next remark, however, was undoubtedly inspired by it.

"Yes, and she'll do more cryin' and wailin' before she is done, that one!" said she, darkly.

At this loud sobs and choking sounds came from the lounge, and the girl who was weeping there sat up, and brought her feet to the floor.

She was young, she was just seventeen, and she was so small that, as she sat there with her black curly mop tumbled and falling about her tear-stained little white face, and her swollen red lips trembling, and her thin, childish shoulders bowed, she might have been a little girl of twelve or fourteen, caught cheating in Arithmetic and up before the maternal court for a possible whipping. Her dress was a plaid skirt and a green sweater, and there was a string of yellow glass beads about her babyish, soft little throat.

That Mother Nature, with a world to choose from, should have needed such a poor little instrument for her great designs, and that the cruel springs of her trap should have clamped themselves upon the half developed body of little, orphaned, ignorant Kitty Spillane, was one of the simple truths that makes life so hard to understand. All about Kitty magnificent women in the twenties, in the thirties, baby-loving, intelligent, physically perfect women were moving upon their defrauded and sterile way. And Kitty lay upon the Murphy bed-lounge, without a dollar, a friend, a husband, or a coherent thought to help her—and hers!—to face the bleak and enormous world.

With her black eyes almost lost in the pasty great shadows that encircled them, and her throat dry, and her red lips sore from being bitten in her agony, and her cheeks washed with tears, Kitty thickly implored a hearing.

"Mis' Murphy—will you leave me speak to you!"

"I will not," responded Mrs. Murphy, promptly and dispassionately. "You'd like to, I'll be bound! And you'd say more than your prayers, too! But the time for you to speak, Kitty," she added, neatly, "was months back! A great, big ger'rl like you, and bringin' shame and disgrace on all that knew your good mother," she went on, in a low, cutting tone. "My free and fair advice to you is that you'll do no talkin' whatever for awhile —there'll be talk enough, without you doin' it! You can say your prayers, over at the Reformatory, and take it to heart that no decent man will ever look at you—you with a young child taggin' you that has no father to him at all!"

At this frightful summary of her miseries, present and to come, poor Kitty's courage failed her again, and in a fresh storm of sobs and crying she flung herself face down on the malodorous contents of the lounge again and abandoned herself to shame and grief.

Nothing further was said until the knob of the porch door was quietly turned from the outside, and wind-blown and rosy, Mrs. Callahan came in. It was not unusual to have her appear at this hour for her own share of gossip and tea.

But her manner and expression to-day were unusual. She looked grave and concerned, and when her quick glance had swept the tea-table, and passed old Tom, who was dozing, and reached Kitty, her look came back to Mrs. Murphy again, and her lips shut tightly, and she nodded. She sat down at the table, and loosened the strings of the shabby, drooping widow's bonnet she wore, and automatically stirred her tea. Her eyes and those of the other older woman met, passed each other, and met again. Nothing was said.

When she had had her first scalding draught, however, Mrs. Callahan set down her cup, sighed, and shook her head. The other women perfectly understood, of course, long before this, that the news of Kitty Spillane, entrusted to nobody, confided to nobody, betrayed to them by Kitty herself, only a few hours before, had filtered, in mysterious fashion, to Mrs. Callahan's kitchen. And here was Mrs. Callahan to sit in judgment.

"Well," said the visitor, finally, in a mild voice, and with a long sigh, "you'd wonder at Gertie Spillane's ger'rl!"

There was no verbal response to this. But bitter sobbing recommenced on the lounge.

"Papa and Mama brung up Richard Foy's father, from the day he was a young infant eleven days old!" Mrs. Murphy said, with a sidewise nod toward her old father. "Didn't they bring Bernard Foy to America, and rais'm?" she demanded, mournfully.

"I know full well they did!" Mrs. Callahan affirmed. Mrs. Cahill clicked her tongue, shut her eyes tightly, and shook her head from side to side. "It's well Gertie didn't live to see this day!" Mrs. Callahan added, bitterly.

Poor Kitty could bear no more.

"Mrs. Callahan——" she stammered, her face running with salt tears. "Here's the way of it! Here's the way of it! I—I says—I says we was goin' to get married—and I—I—says——"

"Never mind what you says!" Mrs. Callahan interposed, gravely, as Kitty's narrative degenerated frankly into crying, hiccoughs, and choking. "It's always the same story!"

"No—but—but he says he loved—he *did* say he loved me!" Kitty sobbed, coming, young and awkward, to stand before them. "He—he says he had an aunt—that—that lived in New Jersey!" Kitty struggled on, fighting her heaving breath and trying to control her trembling mouth. "And he says we would—we—we would talk about the weddin'!" she stammered, "and he ast would I go—go over—go over and have Sunday dinner with her! And I ast Mrs. Reynolds—the lady I work for!—and she—she says yes, I could go. And I and May Baker and Oliver Wolf was goin'! And then May—May says she wasn't goin' any further—and I—I says——"

"Where was this, Kitty?" Mrs. Callahan asked, sternly.

"This was Trenton. And May says it was two o'clock, and she wanted to get back—and I never knew why she wanted to go!" Kitty resumed, crying freely. "And he kept sayin' his aunt would be mad if I didn't come—and I do love him, and I'd be doin' my work thinkin' how much I loved him, and that we was goin' to be married!" broke off the little creature, sobbing bitterly again as the full measure of her wrongs and her disillusionment rushed over her.

"And when was this?"

"This was in August!"

"And this mornin'——?"

"This mornin' Mrs. Reynolds seen me hangin' up the children's rompers on the line, and she—she told me I could get out!"

"And Richard Foy?"

"He's enlisted. And next week he's goan to Ar'zona!" ended Kitty. And for a few minutes there was absolute silence in the kitchen.

"Drink your tea," said Mrs. Callahan then briefly. And Kitty, trembling and gulping, and with downdropped eyes, sat timidly down on the end of a little bench, and obeyed.

Perhaps the hot fluid revived her, for presently she raised her tear-bitten eyes to the older woman, and begged falteringly, and with a sort of frightened earnestness:

"Mrs. Callahan—don't leave them send me to the Reformatory! I loved him so—I never had a bad thought about him! Leave me work somewhere —I'll work for nothin', and I've learned lots—and leave me act like I was married, and had a right—had a right to be the way I am! Please, won't you—that knew Mama—and how proud she was of me! It ain't fair that he should go off to Ar'zona—and me stay here and have them say that Gertie Spillane's girl was in the Reformatory!"

"I don't know whatever else we can do, Kitty," Mrs. Callahan answered, mildly and sadly, after awhile. "You've lost your job; and the way you are you can't take another. 'Twould be very mortifying entirely to the other young ger'rls, that wouldn't look at a king, and he making eyes at them, that you should be living round among them—like one of them! Sure, it's very hard, but it's always been like that. I wouldn't want my Mary, or Mrs. Murphy's Ellen, to know annything about this—it isn't for young ger'rls to know. And how could we keep it from them, with you right here? There was a time you sh'ud of thought of that, you poor girl you!"

Kitty, passionate, panting, and eager, when the kind, wise voice began, had chilled and shrivelled visibly as it proceeded. Now she shrank down quietly in her seat, her young childish elbows on the table, her dark rich curls spilling over the white hands that gripped her forehead.

"Yes, I see," she said now, lifelessly. And presently, as no one spoke in comfort or defence, she went desolately across the kitchen, and sat down on the couch again.

"She'll stay here for a night or two, until we see. Ellen won't be over in all this snow, and Daniel was very fond of her poor father, God rest'm," Mrs. Murphy told the others, rather than Kitty herself.

"I told her, seven months ago, when her poor mother died," Mrs. Callahan began in a low tone. " 'Kitty!' I said, 'I wonder you wouldn't stay with the Sisters awhile, for the sixteen months until you're of age,' I told her. She seemed very cast down entirely, and she says she wanted to earn a little money, the way she would have it to spend! And now look what's in it!"

Kitty Spillane, as the older women began to stir toward departure, shrank from the glare of the kitchen light like a little sick animal. Old Tom shut his eyes. But another young woman, not much older than Kitty, stepped into it without hesitation or fear.

This was Ellen Murphy, come over from her sister Lizzie-Kate Kane's house, with the ninety cents for the three tickets Mama had sold them a week before. It was dark outside now, and had begun to snow again, but Ellen had had as escort and guide to the very door the eager and trembling Clem Riordan, and Clem had piloted her safely enough, although, to be sure, they had wasted the best part of half an hour on the four blocks that lay between the two houses.

Ellen had on her round fur hat and the long dark coat with the dark fur collar; her cheeks blazed, her mahogany hair curled up in tendrils against her hat brim, and her blue Irish eyes had a frosty bright sparkle, as if they were giving off light themselves.

Snowflakes lay on her shoulders, and she was out of breath, and laughing. Ellen always radiated life and youth and beauty; even in the wilting days of August she was softly cool and blooming, but in winter, with her blood thinned and dancing, and her cheeks bitten into blazing color by icy, still air, she had all the glow and velvety brilliance of a child.

"Hello, Mama, hello, Mrs. Callahan, how-do, Mrs. Cahill!" Ellen said, gaily. "Do you love Ellen, darlin'?" she tenderly inquired of her grandfather, kissing the thin silver parting on his old head.

"Walk out of here—travel——" said her mother, with simple directness. "Go on with Mrs. Callahan—she's just going. Go on. I'll talk to Lizzie-Kate later, but I've me own good reasons that you shouldn't stay here now!"

"Mama, for Heaven's sake!" Ellen said, astounded, looking from one to another. Her eyes reached the couch, and Kitty sat up, and they stared at each other. "Hello, Kitty," Ellen went on, then, in a different tone. And a different sort of color crept up from her fur collar, and spread to the roots of her hair. "Hello, Kitty, I didn't see you!" Ellen said, again, slowly.

"Now, will you move along please, and mind your own affairs," her mother said, nervously. "Go on, Ellen, Kitty doesn't feel very well, and we're talking about matters that don't concern you——"

"You come with me, Ellen," suggested Mrs. Callahan, kindly. "I pass right by Lizzie-Kate's door. Good-night, Mrs. Murphy. Mr. Florence, be sure you don't lay awake, frettin' and dreamin' again. Good-night, Kitty. I'll be over to-morrow."

"But what's the matter, Mrs. Callahan?" Ellen demanded, pathetically, as they went through the dim, snowy yard.

"Kitty's had a little trouble with her employer, that's all!" said Mrs. Callahan, comfortably. And for the remainder of the short walk through the lazily falling and pausing snow she talked cheerfully of other matters.

They parted at the Kanes' side-gate, and Ellen went into her sister's kitchen. Lizzie-Kate was upstairs, it appeared, settling little Joe for the night, but Flurry, the boisterous four-year-old, was staggering about the floor, waiting for his father to come home, and Ellen found her older brother, Dan, smoking his pipe, his prematurely weazened little shrewd face somewhat serious and his beady blue eyes fixed on the oven door.

She flung her outer wraps into the hall closet, and returned to kiss her brother, and take the rocker near him.

"I've just come from Mama's. It's snowing out," said Ellen. And in an odd tone she added, "Dan, Kitty's there."

"Kitty Spillane?" he asked, with a quick glance, as he readjusted his pipe. "So someone was tellin' me."

"Mama bounced me," complained Ellen. "Mama'll find out that I know about Santa Claus some day," she added, resentfully, "and she'll drop dead!"

"Well, that's all right," Dan approved calmly, but with a quick, suspicious look. "You can't do nothin' about it. It's too bad. But it's none of your pie."

"Oh, Lord!" Ellen sniffed. "Flurry, don't blow that awful whistle!" she adjured her nephew, crossly. "The girls have been talking about Richard Foy going with Kitty for I don't know how long!" she added, scornfully.

"Well, it's nothing for any one to talk about, and it's none of your business, and it's none of mine," Dan said, finally. "I'm sorry for Kitty, if she liked him," he added, watching Ellen keenly over his pipe. "But it's none of your affair. You keep your hands off, Ellen. I wouldn't touch it with a ten-foot pole! Now you mind what I say!"

Dan rarely used this tone. But when he did Ellen was suddenly reminded that he was the head of the family, after all; she was bound to be "said" by Dan. And she realized now that, as far as she was concerned, Kitty Spillane was merely a lovelorn lass pining for her soldier lover.

"Well, you know she's only seventeen, Dan," she persisted, more quietly, "and Richard did say that they were going to be married—they were engaged, you know!" Ellen finished, rather scared, as Dan shot her a warning glance.

"Well, you keep out of it!" Dan said again.

"If there's anything to be done," Lizzie-Kate said, gravely, once more in her kitchen, and busy about supper-getting, "Mama and Mrs. Callahan will see to it!"

"Miss Crowley at the liberry couldn't do anything could she, Lizzie-Kate?" Ellen presently asked. "I mean, she knows so much about the laws, and she knows those Juvenile Court people!" she added, as Lizzie-Kate looked surprised and showed distaste.

"I don't know what she'd have to do with Kitty losing her job, and falling in love with Richard Foy!" Lizzie-Kate said, unencouragingly.

"Well, I don't think much of your precious old Captain Doyle," Ellen said to her brother, after a discontented interval of silence. "You're always boasting how smart he was, and how decent with the men."

"What's Pat Doyle got to do with it?" Daniel asked. He had once been a sergeant in the National Guard Company in which Pat Doyle had served as lieutenant before entering the regular service.

"Well, nothing much. But he's the captain of the company Richard

Foy's been put in—don't you remember someone said so, and you said you were going down to Governor's Island to see him? If I was you, you bet I'd go and see him, and I'd tell him about Foy and have him lay him out. It makes me so sick—everybody sitting around and saying there's nothing to do!"

Dan looked at his sister queerly.

"You girls talk very reckless nowadays, Ellen. What has Foy got to do with it?" he said.

"Well—well——" She had to take to cover. "Kitty was in love with him," she hesitated.

"Yes. And what of it?" Dan asked, coldly.

"There isn't anything to do, Ellen," Lizzie-Kate said, in calm disapproval of the entire topic. "You can't understand it, and it wouldn't be right you should, and that's all there is about it!"

"Yes—but suppose it was me——" Ellen began, eagerly. Her sister fixed her with a cold, unyielding eye.

"Suppose it was you—what?"

"Well, that—well, that——" Ellen floundered.

"Well that *what?*"

"Well, if I fell in love with a fellow that enlisted, and lost my job——" Ellen amended it lamely.

"You'd come to some older woman, like Mama, and ask her to advise you, and that's what Kitty has done," Lizzie-Kate summarized, sternly.

"Yes, and if it was me, you'd be streaking over to Miss Crowley, and up to old lady O'Brien——" Ellen mumbled, unimpressed.

"Perhaps," said Lizzie-Kate, mildly turning her face away from the pouring steam of the saucepan, as she drained the potatoes, "perhaps you'll tell me what old lady O'Brien has to do with it?"

"Well, weren't you and Kate Oliver talking about how you'd like to get a nice girl to stay with her, and just keep her company, and that her son would pay three dollars a week——"

"Yes, but you'd have——" Lizzie-Kate recollected herself. "Are you going to stay and have supper with us, Dan?" she asked her brother, elaborately dropping the distasteful topic.

But Dan had fallen thoughtful, and made no response.

"We'll have to have our talk before Ellen gets in," said Mrs. Callahan, the next day. "Does she know anything about it, Lizzie-Kate?" she asked.

"I don't think so," murmured Lizzie-Kate, giving Flurry a little spank of pure love on the back of the clean romper into which she had just inserted him. "She thinks Kitty was in love with Richard Foy, do you see? And that she feels bad on that account."

The meeting was in Lizzie-Kate's house, that Kitty might not overhear what was said. The women all looked very serious; Mrs. Cahill had cupped her spotted, lean old chin in her spotted, lean old hand. Mrs. Callahan sat idle, big hands on her big knees, a troubled expression upon her handsome face.

"I'll not have Ellen come home again until Kitty is off and away with herself!" said old Mrs. Murphy, firmly.

"What Kitty Spillane needs, you'd think, is a good spanking," Mrs. Callahan said. "You look at the child, and she doesn't seem much older than Kate Oliver's Bernadette, with the simple look she does be having! And now—the poor thing, she's let herself in for it, and there's nothing we can do for her at all!"

"Nothin'!" said the Widow Cahill, dismally.

"I went over to see Miss Crowley, at the liberry, this morning," Lizzie-Kate said. "I named no names, of course. And she said she could speak to some friend of hers that's in the Juvenile Court Social Work. But I don't know will she do much good!"

"I thought maybe I'd go see old lady O'Brien," Mrs. Murphy added, in her sad and lingering whine. "Lizzie-Kate was sayin' that Ellen suggested—the poor innocent child!—that Kitty might work there."

"Richard Foy has got such a hard, mean mother on him," Mrs. Callahan, whose thoughts had been following another line, said suddenly. "She's buried seven before Richard, and she's——"

"She's embithered, that one!" Mrs. Cahill supplied, simply, as Mrs. Callahan paused.

"Oh, she's very soured and solitary," Mrs. Callahan resumed. "She lives all alone in that big house with that fortune-tellin' servant she's got, Rosy O'Farrell—and what she does with herself at all you'll have to tell me first if you want me to tell you! She'll step out to Mass, and so back with her again, and never a 'good-morning' out of her! Her and Rosy talks of nothing but signs and superstitions! Why them two women don't blue-mould, moonin' round them empty rooms all day and all night, has me beat!" Mrs. Callahan finished, musing.

"It's the pride she has," said Mrs. Cahill. "Richard was a great trile to her, wild as he was, and not livin' at home much, and whin I heard he'd enlisted himself into the army, to be a soldier, I thought it'd be a grand thing for her, to know where he was nights! But whin she hears of all this to-do, she'll be as wild as a wild hawk!"

"I wouldn't wonder did she know it, and she and Rosy put him up to enlistin', that he'd be out of the way for awhile," Lizzie-Kate suggested, with a significant nod.

"Well, I wouldn't wonder meself!" Mrs. Murphy said, in a silence, struck. "He's all she has," she added, thoughtfully, "and to have him mixed up in annything would break her heart. Sure, doesn't she keep all their rooms, just like they always was, and his with them?—Rosy O'Farrell's cousin was tellin' me so not a mont' ago," continued the widow. "She has Richard's room always waiting, and what does she have but Bernard's room, and the children's room, with their dolls and toys, and poor old Mr. Foy's room, and his pipe and the green satin sash he used to wear in the pe-rades, and Aggie's First Communion veil draped over her pitcher in the parlor, and she won't leave anny one move them!"

"She was always a very superstitious one," Mrs. Callahan contributed. "She'd not walk through a funeral, or pass a pin, and it layin' in the street. And she never got over it that little Aggie cut her finger, on the day of her First Communion, and got blood on her white dress, and that poor Bernard, the day before he was kilt, picked up a peacock feather in the street, and come runnin' in with it. 'Oh, Mama,' he says, 'look what Burnie found!' She says the heart turned to curds inside her. It's well known she's very superstitious," the speaker rambled on. "Ellen was tellin' me the other day that she'd tell the children years ago never to walk under a ladder, or look at the new moon face forward!"

"Rosy O'Farrell told me that a black cat come into the house the day of old man Foy's bein' tuck sick," Mrs. Murphy pursued, in the same half-mournful, half-dreamy tone, "and the instant her eyes fell on it she give a screech—and she fell back into a chair, Rosy said, as white as a bowl of lard and she says, 'Go for the priest, Rosy, he's dying!' And him with no more than a cold, mind you. And that day hour didn't he lie dead!"

All this was an old story, but the women tut-tutted dutifully, and relapsed into gloomy silence.

"There's nothin' to be done with *her*," said Mrs. Callahan, finally; "I doubt is she very strong entirely in her mind. You say a word against Richard, and she'd show you the door! Sh-sh!" she added, warningly, "here's Ellen!"

Here was Ellen indeed radiant with the prospect of the free Saturday afternoon, with a free Sunday to follow, and with the knowledge that Clem Riordan was waiting at the gate, in the sunshine and snow, to suggest delightful amusements and distractions for both.

"Hello, Mama!" said Ellen. "How's the Perfect Forty-Four Club? I've just come in to change my hat, and then you can go back to the discussion of Sister Ignatius' Golden Jubilee! Say, Mama, can I go in— back home—for five minutes to speak to Grandpa?"

"I don't know why you couldn't," Mrs. Murphy said, her little owl-like face screwed up and her old eyes blinking rapidly. "Kitty's gone up to Mrs. Reynolds', to get her clothes!" she said inconsequently.

"I didn't want to see Kitty," Ellen answered, innocently. "But I just wanted to speak to Grandpa. Does Kitty feel happier?" she asked, artlessly.

"Kitty'll be all right," said Mrs. Callahan, gravely.

"You know I think she was in love with Richard Foy!" Ellen added, brilliantly enlightening.

"That would account for her feelin' so bad, thin," the Widow Cahill commented, mildly.

"Mama, don't you think maybe his mother would do something for them?" Ellen pursued. "She has plenty of money!"

"We were just sayin' that she would have nothin' to do with annything of the kind," Mrs. Murphy said, repressively. "She's a very cold, hard woman, and Richard's her only child. I wouldn't tackle her, I know, and there isn't anny one I know that would thank you for the job! Now, go along, Ellen dear, do, for Heaven's sakes, and don't bother!"

"Mrs. Callahan, dear, would you speak to me out here a minute?" Ellen asked politely, a few minutes later, when the hat had been changed and she was taking her departure. Obligingly Mrs. Callahan stepped into a small square passage known to Mrs. Murphy as "the butthry," where empty tubs smelled strangely of stale suds, and old brooms congregated with a salt-rimed ice-cream freezer.

"You know, about Kitty——" Ellen began, eagerly, when they were there alone. The older woman's face darkened. "Why wouldn't you go and see Judge Casey about it?" Ellen pleaded. "You nursed his little girl through the diphtheria, and you laid out his wife, and you tell him that Kitty is a good little girl——"

"Why, Ellen, you talk very wild!" said Mrs. Callahan, disapprovingly. "What would a Judge have to do with it?"

Ellen flushed; she saw she had overstepped the limits of her supposed knowledge, and she looked down in some confusion.

"Go on," said Mrs. Callahan, inflexibly. "Why should Kitty's losing her job, and falling in love with the Foy boy, have anything to do with Judge Casey?"

"I don't know," Ellen said, abashed.

"Well, I should think you didn't!" Mrs. Callahan said, in admonitory triumph. "You be a little more careful how you talk, Ellen!"

"Yes'm," Ellen answered, dutiful and impressed. The older woman returned to the kitchen well-satisfied. But she presently sank into a brown study, and surprised Lizzie-Kate by emerging from it suddenly to ask if the court-house was open on Saturday afternoons. Lizzie-Kate said yes, it was, why? Mrs. Callahan made no response, but ten minutes later she picked up her shawl and pulled forward three inches the dragging weight of her crape-draped hat, and took her departure, still thoughtful.

Ellen, escorted by Clem, spent only the sanctioned five minutes with her grandfather, and was gone again long before the heart-broken Kitty, dragging her old yellow "leather-type" suitcase, returned to the Murphy home.

Grandpa had been dozing, but Ellen relentlessly had aroused him, and a whispered conference ensued.

"You knew his father, and his grandmother, too!" Ellen had presently been saying eagerly. "If I brought you an envelope, couldn't you write Richard Foy?"

"His grandmother was me own cousin, Bessy Willitts, and didn't your grandmother and I bring his father up like one of our own?" the old man had wheezed, his blue eyes bright from sleep. "But I can't do nothin' now, Ellen. Poor little Kitty——! She's *pretty*, Ellen—she's very *pretty!* Yes, sir, we tuk Bessy Willitts'—me own cousin's—baby, and didn't we bring the poor child to America with us, and it eleven days old! And that was Richard Foy's papa. Well, well, sick and cast-down, and widout a friend in the world to stand friend to her, you can't help pityin' the poor child!"

This had not been satisfactory, and Ellen had abandoned all hope where Grandpa was concerned.

But after she had gone, and before her mother had come back, old Tom suddenly had roused himself, and sat thinking. And presently he had hoisted himself stiffly from his chair, and went into the dark tumbled lair that was his bedroom, and fished from under his bed his treasured strong box.

A key dangling on an oily scapular cord, about his neck, opened this, and the old man had sat fingering the contents for a long time.

There were some securities in the box, destined to amaze his heirs, for he had never mentioned them. There were also worthless and almost worthless papers in envelopes. There was the deed to the shanty. There was an insurance policy.

And there were real treasures besides. A thin old blue-and-white check kitchen apron, which he lifted to his old face and pressed there for awhile. A prayer book bursting its yellowed ivory covers. A book of souvenir photographs from the Chicago Fair, in 1893. A letter signed "Ellen" in staggering letters—this only some fifteen years old—and another letter signed "Nelly," forty years older.

But he had put all these aside. And presently he had in his shell-like, gnarled, clean old hand a pencilled note written on ruled, coarse paper, undated, and signed "Bessy." Old Tom had put away the box again, had locked it and hid it, and had come back to the kitchen, and put on his glasses.

For some time he had sat dreaming, the paper in his fingers, his eyes far away. Then finally he had cleared his throat, and had pushed his glasses once more into place, and, holding the paper at varying distances, until it had been rightly gauged, he had read it, half-aloud.

"Bernard dear," it said, "this is Bessy writing you, and the baby's here, and he's very pretty, and so little your heart would go out to him. And may God bless you wherever you are for coming back to give him your name, dear. Nelly and Tom is here, and they're going to take the little child to you, in America, because of my feeling so weak and queer. And it may be I'll follow you both, if I get strong again.

"BESSY."

Old Tom had read it twice, had wiped his eyes, and folded it, to see the pencilled superscription on the back: "Bernard Foy." It was with this message that little dying Bessy, fifty years before, and so many thousand miles away, had sent to the new world Bernard Foy, junior, the eleven-day-old scrap of humanity that was to be young Richard Foy's father one day.

"I wonder what Bernard Foy's cold, black-faced widow would say to that?" old Tom had mused. And then suddenly, and more kindly, "I wonder what the lad himself would say? There's no real harm in Bernard's boy!"

Ellen had meanwhile given her grandfather up as a bad job, and returned to Clem, on the sidewalk, again. Nor did her concern and discouragement where Kitty was concerned keep her from a full enjoyment of two separate movies, two chocolate sundaes, a hearty dinner with Lizzie-Kate and Lizzie-Kate's husband, the patient and silent Joe Kane, and an evening of innocent dancing and flirting at the Friendly Sons' Annual Ball. She returned home, exhausted with felicity, at a quarter to five in the morning, staggered out to "seven" more dead than alive, and spent the quiet, snowy Sunday morning browsing over the papers, and reading the Katzenjammers to Flurry, seated fat and exacting, in her lap.

But in the afternoon she paid a call.

She sat frightened, yet determined, in the terrible parlors of the Foy house, when the crisping footsteps of Rosy O'Farrell had died away into a sepulchral silence, and told her fast-beating heart that anyway, Mrs. Foy couldn't kill her. She looked at Aggie's picture and Bernard's, on easels, and the fearful crayon enlargement of the late Bernard, senior, over the black marble mantel. The furniture was walnut and horsehair covered with white lace tidies. The bay-window was draped in hideous fringed green rep. The shades were drawn. A clean white scarf lay across the heavy white marble top of the center table. There was a green book of religious poetry, and on top of it a presentation copy of "May Brooke."

After awhile Ellen heard a dull booming far away, like the sound of voices through barriers of cold earth and gravestones, she thought, and then silence fell again, a silence punctuated and underlined by the solemn plock, plock, plock of a big clock, and by the whine of surface cars in the cheerful streets so far away, where men and women and girls and boys, and small babies in Sunday coats, were walking.

Her heart leaped; a black-clad, white-faced woman, with black eyebrows, had come silently in, and was standing close behind her.

"Ellen Murphy?" said Mrs. Foy, in a dead voice.

Ellen had meant to begin with a few pleasant words of introduction, about old school-days with Bernard and Agnes, but this recognition discomposed her, and she stammered and laughed somewhat awkwardly as they both sat down on the slippery edges of chairs.

The conversation that followed was supremely unsatisfying to Ellen. Richard's mother seemed to suspect something amiss from the first, and anticipated any possible hint from Ellen upon the subject by volunteering the remark that Richard was a fine son, although people seemed to be amusing themselves of late with lies that nobody could prove and any weak, bad girl could say of any decent man!

But when Ellen, rather low in spirits, and hot of face, had departed, Mrs. Foy remained standing motionless, for a long time. Then she went out to Rosy O'Farrell, in the bleak, orderly, airless, and foodless kitchen.

"This Murphy girl says she had a dream of me, Rosy—that's a funny thing!" Richard Foy's mother said, presently, after some half-hearted irrelevancies. "I don't know why she should come here to tell me about it! I wish she'd stayed at home with her queer talk!"

"Betune us an' all har'rm!" said Rosy, expectantly.

"She says she came because this dream frightened her," said the other woman slowly. "I don't know what it could mean. There's many a one would tell you there's precious little sense in dreams! It isn't like what you'd be seeing or picking up!" she added, uneasily.

"Oh, moy!" Rosy differed, shaking her cold, oily, neatly braided gray head, "there's a lot in thim! Wasn't me cousin's young lad—three days old, cot up on her——"

She cited instance after instance, but she and Mrs. Foy had been over this ground many times before, and the other woman did not listen. She sat staring into space, with a sober face.

"She says—this Murphy girl says——" Mrs. Foy began again, painfully, when at last there was a pause, "that she was walking on the sand——"

"The sand is the future!" Rosy promptly interpreted.

"And I was there," said the other, wetting her lips and swallowing with a dry throat. "And there was a—there was a white snake had holt of me!"

"My God!" said Rosy, turning pallid. "White—that's a woman you're jealous of!"

"And she dreamed," resumed Mrs. Foy, "that there was a sort of a voice, crying out and bewailing!" She stopped.

"May God have mercy on us all through the everlasting mercy of God!" Rosy ejaculated, blessing herself.

"And she thought it cried out——" Mrs. Foy said, and stopped again, panting. The dark hairs that formed almost a moustache on her upper lip were wet.

"_What!_" Rosy asked, in a piercing and terrified whisper.

"She thought it cried out," the other woman said, swallowing: " 'The bitter curse you put on your son's nameless son will foller him and his to the last hours of their life!' " Mrs. Foy, also whispering, her eyes wide-open and fixed upon Rosy's, said slowly.

"On your son's son!" Rosy echoed, bewildered. "But for God's sake who could that be?"

"If this Spillane girl isn't lyin'!" Mrs. Foy said, significantly, and trembling. Rosy looked struck. "If you could have heard the Murphy girl—the way she said it!" continued Mrs. Foy. "And mind you—she's as innocent as buttermilk! Didn't she ask me a few minutes before how was Richard, and she says, 'We all thought he liked Kitty Spillane,' she says, 'that's so pretty and good,' she says, 'but I guess Kitty's too young to think seriously about anybody!' she says."

"My God!" said Rosy. "The snake had ye, did he?"

"By the leg," the other supplied, fearfully. "God help me!"

"That's bad," Rosy admitted, simply. "Was there a storm in it?"

"She said the wind was howling."

"Then there's death in it!" Rosy prophesied. Mrs. Foy's teeth chattered, and she could not speak. "There's death in it," repeated Rosy. "God be good to us all! 'Nameless'—that's what it is. And you jealous of her!"

"Oh, I never was jealous of—never—I never had a jealous thought of her!" Mrs. Foy cried, on a great windy wail. "Why would I be jealous of the poor weak wicked thing! All I done—all I done——"

"You'd twist like a heretic, whin he was off on Sunday, to see her," Rosy reminded her mistress. "And you'd say to me: 'Rosy, is she so pretty?' And what did you tell him—and he weak and wild enough annyway, God knows!—what did you tell him but that if he tuk up wid trash like George Spillane's ger'rl you'd cut him out of his father's money!" Rosy reminded her, sternly. "And what were you doin' here three weeks back, when he come in an' tould you the fix he was in, and he reconnoitherin' the street the whole time, that the ger'rl shouldn't foller him here. It was you put him up to enlistin'—and runnin' away on her! Jealous! You'd 'a' cut her heart out of her aloive!" Rosy muttered, in conclusion.

Mrs. Foy, during this mumbled tirade, had looked stricken. Now she rose weakly, forlornly, to her feet.

"Well, I done it to save the only son that's left me old age!" she said, trembling. "God knows I'd go on me knees to the girl, that there'd be no curse on him!" She left the kitchen with no further remark. But the subject broke out again at supper, and again in the early evening, and when Rosy passed her mistress's door, at eleven o'clock, she heard the unaccustomed scraping of a pen upon little-used writing paper.

Ellen, to the satisfaction of her family and group, had apparently entirely washed her hands of the troublesome subject of Kitty. She went upon her accustomed way rejoicing, and although Lizzie-Kate was one evening indiscreet enough to mention at the supper-table that Mrs. Callahan had been talking to Judge Casey, Ellen seemed not to notice the slip, nor did she ask embarrassing questions when her mother inadvertently betrayed that Mrs. Cahill had been investigating a possible position for Kitty with old lady O'Brien.

Lizzie-Kate had her own secret: Miss Crowley's friend, at the Juvenile Court work, had been unexpectedly firm and resourceful.

If the girl was under age, and really had a letter beginning "My darling little wife-to-be——" and if—and if——

Dreadful terms peppered the conversation, and Lizzie-Kate, timidly and anxiously repeating them to Mrs. Callahan, learned that Judge Casey had not been sparing of frightful and enlightening phrases, either. Weak, alone, young, Kitty Spillane might be, and only the shadowy little thought of a human being might be the child who was to follow her, but still, it appeared, these had their rights; in the great thundering machinery of the commonwealth there was a tiny cog here and there that had to do with Kitty and her baby.

The women looked at each other seriously, debating these things. But they kept them from Ellen, and when presently Dan went down to Fort Jay at Governor's Island, where the barracks were, to have a chat with his old friend and captain, Charles Montgomery Doyle. Ellen was not informed of the step.

And the afternoon gathering of women congratulated themselves that the affair, whatever its outcome, had been abandoned by her. On the day that Mrs. Callahan was to see the Judge for the second time, and Mrs. Murphy was going with Mrs. Cahill to see old lady O'Brien, and Lizzie-Kate had determined to wheel the baby over to "the Juvenile," and see if anything had come up, didn't Ellen most providentially get a half day off from the office, and take not only herself, but Grandpa away, on a visit to Lucy Fallon at White Plains?

Grandpa had not had so ambitious an outing for months. But Ellen was strong as an ox, her mother said, and 'twas only one change of cars, at the Grand Central. She had said that she would have him back in his chair, with his milk-toast, at five o'clock, and she did, exchanging, as her mother noted, not so much as a glance with the subdued and silent Kitty, who was obscurely sewing in the kitchen when they returned. Mrs. Murphy's own heart was so bursting with an elaborate plan, and a dazing secret, that she paid small attention to either, but Grandpa seemed well, and full of chuckles and content, and Ellen fairly glittered. To be sure, the old man more than once spoke of White Plains as "Governor's Island," but then he often wandered a little in his speech.

On the following Sunday afternoon, after a fresh fall of snow, Ellen Murphy invited Clement Riordan to accompany her on a walk. She so visibly brimmed with mystery and amusement and mischief as she did so, that Clem's suspicions were aroused, and as she took familiar turnings, he regarded her with kindly superiority and contempt. But she passed the favorite candy shop, and the favorite "movie" theater, and Clem began to wonder where she was going.

To his amazement she climbed finally up the steps of the church and took up a position where she could see without being seen: screened by the wide columns that flanked the entrance. Then her glance bade him wait.

Presently toward the open doorway a group of women, shabbily clad, but brisk and cheerful, made their way. Clem recognized them all: Mrs. Murphy, Mrs. Cahill, Mrs. Callahan, Annie Curley with her new baby, and Lizzie-Kate Kane. With them, silent and somewhat pale, was an extremely pretty girl of perhaps seventeen, with Ellen's old mushroom hat hiding her eyes. "Kitty?" Clem said to Ellen. Ellen nodded.

They all went into the church, and in a few minutes two more women came along, one wearing heavy mourning, and with a mouth emphasized by a faint moustache. And with them was a youth in olive drab, with the heavy service overcoat: a rather weak-faced boy, but handsome, and today with an expression unmistakably determined. And these went into St. Rose's, too.

Ellen then began to behave strangely. She turned about in an agony of nervousness, she laughed, she buried her face in her gloved hands. Then she would suddenly catch Clem by the shoulders, and perform a sort of dance before him. Finally she fell to sending anxious looks alternately toward the church door and her wrist watch, and all this time she said nothing, and did not seem to hear Clem's natural questions.

After perhaps fifteen minutes of this Clem, who was getting chilly, proposed that they either go into the church or walk on, but Ellen only said: "Oh, wait—wait!" and laughed mysteriously again. And presently the party, all together now, came out of the church.

Clem and Ellen were near enough to see the faces; the women looked shaken yet happy. Parting, in the bleak afternoon wind, the sound of their voices came broken with quiet laughter.

The soldier shook hands all around; and the dark-faced woman kissed him, and stooped perhaps a little awkwardly to the little girl in the mushroom hat standing beside him, and kissed her, too. She did not smile as she did this, nor as she said, so clearly that Clem and Ellen could hear:

"Will I see you again, Richard?"

Richard Foy was pale, excited, happy, more important, in his new uniform, and with his new wife, than he had ever been in his life before. He did not hear his mother.

But the girl in the mushroom hat did, and she timidly pulled at the sleeve of his olive-drab coat.

"Richard. Your mother spoke to you."

"Sure, Mike!" said Richard, cheerfully, then. "My leave is till Toosdy. We'll see you Toosdy. Say, thanks, Mom," he added in a lower tone, touching his pocket. "You were awful generous to think of the cush!" He kissed his mother again, but his eyes were on Kitty. "You'll—you'll take care of her, won't you, when I'm at camp?" he faltered, suddenly, with watering eyes.

And with wet lashes he laughed at himself, waved at the other women, who were now filtering away, smiled at his mother and Rosy, and put his big arm about his wife. Kitty shrank up against him, and put her little new glove in his; there was peace in her eyes, and a wonderful flush of peach-color had come into her face. "Come on, dear!" Richard said, and they went down the cold, dark street together, and turned at the corner without a backward glance, and were gone.

The dingy widows' veils of the wedding party blew in a restless wind, and Ellen heard her mother say: "Won't Ellen be fit to be tied—wit' us not tellin' her a word till it's all over and done wit'!"

Then the street was empty, and Ellen looked up at Clem, with her adorable sapphire eyes a little dimmed, and her husky sweet young voice a little thick, and she laid her warm hand on his arm, and said to him— she, the proud, the unapproachable, the cold!—the words that he would never pass St. Rose's portico without remembering.

"Kiss me, Clem!"

Prisoner's Base

Ford looked so savage as he came in that Dina did not dare say anything to him, much less mention what was really on her mind. Instead she put dinner on the table—the one o'clock dinner of sausage cakes and hot biscuits, sweet potatoes and stewed tomatoes, apple jelly and fig pudding. Ford liked hearty, hot, greasy food on these chilly spring noons; sometimes he would eat three or four doughnuts while he was waiting, and fall upon his meal with his appetite apparently unaffected.

Today he did not have to wait; Dina was ready for him. She sat down opposite him, eating little herself but watching keenly to see that he had plenty of butter and that the cream and sugar were handily placed for him.

"You cook these?" he presently asked, with his mouth full.

She nodded yes, anxiously adding a question: weren't they all right?

"Sure they're all right," Ford said. "Cash don't do any cooking, does she?" he added suspiciously.

"I don't believe she knows how to cook."

"That's not what I asked you."

"No," Dina answered quickly, apologetically. "Poor old Cash, she just clears up."

"I don't want any murderer seasoning my food!" Ford said.

"I don't know that they proved anything on her, Ford. She denies she was there at all that night. She says she wasn't allowed to put her witness on the stand."

"They all say that." Ford's first wild savagery of appetite was a little appeased now, and he attacked his second helpings more slowly. "Can't trust any of 'em!" he said, picking his teeth with a rotary movement of lips and tongue.

"I suppose you can't." Ford Huddleston was warden of the prison whose shadow lay across Dina's dining table, and her kitchen and her bedroom. Its great brick walls rose above their lives like barriers between them and all the rest of the world. At their meals they talked about little else than the prison, and at other times they talked hardly at all. "How's that Mexican girl?" Dina asked.

"Got her in a jacket."

"Ah, poor thing. More coffee, Ford?"

"I don't know why you always ask me that. I always take it, don't I?"

Dina said nothing as she poured the smoking amber fluid into his big cup. She had talked only to half-crazed Lily Cash, her convict washwoman, that morning; she would have been glad of some little interest or distraction in a fresh conversation. But Ida Snow, the wife of Ford's assistant, had gone to visit her folks in Cleveland, and there were no other women near. Larkin Flat, the town, was two miles away.

"Oh, I had a letter from California," Dina presently said. She said it deliberately, bravely, but with a fast-beating heart.

"How d'you mean, you had a letter from California? That don't make sense."

"Well, I meant from—from Lin's folks. I knew you didn't like me to talk about 'em much."

"I suppose you got to tell me Chester is O.K.," the man sneered, wiping a walrus mustache after a long draught of coffee. "Head of his class in kindergarten and getting on fine. All right, I know it."

"Lin's brother Thomas is coming East as far as Chicago," the woman said. "He and Het are driving. He said he'd bring Chester and leave him here for a month, if you're willing."

"What's the big idea taking him out of school?"

"Oh, this wouldn't be until vacation, Ford!" Dina was so eager that her color fluctuated painfully, and the thin hand on the table trembled. "This wouldn't be for 'most two months!" she said.

"Well, no use getting excited about it until the time comes."

"I don't know, Ford. It's April now, and those California schools close in June."

Ford Huddleston scowled, staring away into space. He finished picking his teeth and took out his pipe. Dina rose and got him matches and an old leather bag of tobacco. She sat down again, anxious and eager, her eyes glued to his face.

"No," he said suddenly. "I don't want him here!"

"Oh, Ford, don't say that, if it was just for a month! He'd have such a good time here."

"I'm not thinking of him. I'm thinking of you. I don't propose to have my wife forgetting everything else but a kid of five. When you had him you hadn't any use for me."

"That's not true, Ford," she pleaded mildly. "But he was only a baby then, he wasn't four. And the understanding—the understanding was,"

Dina stammered, made bold by desperation, "that he was to be with us."

"You mean before we were married?"

"Don't you remember, at Cousin Julia's? 'Member saying that he'd be just like your own boy?"

"Yep . . . Well, fellers say funny things when they're after a woman."

"But he's been in California seven months now, Ford, and that's an awful long time in a little boy's life."

"They're good to him, ain't they?"

"Well, I guess they are. But I never knew Lin's folks. I guess his brother Tom's kind enough. He's a doctor, and he don't live at the ranch with the old lady. But since he and his wife are willing to bring Chester along with their children he must be kinder goodhearted." Dina stopped; her voice sank to a note of wheedling. "He won't be any bother to you now, Ford," she said. "He's getting to be a big feller. If I had him here for a month seems 's if I could go on. He——"

"Seems 's if you could go on?" the man echoed. "What you talking about? What are you going to do if you *don't* go on? You women can talk more like fools than anything I ever saw! What more do you want than you got? Your husband run off and left you, didn't he?"

"He might of come back, Ford. He was killed in a log jam. That wasn't his fault."

"He wouldn't er come back! His kind don't. He was through, all right. He'd had enough of his own kid whining and crying around, I don't know why I should put up with it! His folks said they'd take the baby——"

"Because you wrote 'em, Ford! You wrote 'em a year ago. I never would of! I never had had him away from me even for one night till you and I were married. I never thought I'd have to give him up. When you and I first began going together——"

Dina stopped and assumed a good-humored smile. When she spoke again it was lightly.

"Anyway, if I could have him for July this year," she said, "I'd send him back to Lin's folks in August without saying a word."

The man—he was a large, gross man whose two-days growth of heavy black beard, added to the effect of the straggling mustache and thin disordered hair, made him look unkempt—was watching her thoughtfully as he chewed on his empty pipe. He was in his shirt sleeves and vest; his big figure bulged shapelessly at the belt. His small eyes were narrowed into a suspicious smile.

"Better leave him where he is," he said comfortably.

"Oh, Ford, but it's such a chance to see him and feel like he's mine again!"

"Yes, well, that's just what 'll upset you and get you half crazy again, the way you were last fall. No, you leave him be, where he's lucky. He don't miss you by this time, and he don't need you. I know more 'n you do about things like this."

"But don't you remember, Ford," Dina said patiently, in desperate courage, as he fell into self-satisfied musing, "the Sunday we fixed it all up that we were going to get married, that you and I walked past that corner house, back in Somersville, and you says, 'Wouldn't you and your kid like a home like that? Won't you do it for Chester's sake?' Don't you remember that, Ford, when I was sick and couldn't go on teaching?"

His small eyes moved over her ruminatively. Again he worked his tongue to clean his teeth.

"Nope," he said flatly. "All I know is, we gave the kid a fair chance. It didn't work. When his grandma wrote from California I happened to open the letter, and I wrote her. She said she'd gladly take him. I don't know what more you want."

"Yes, but I don't even know if he's well or not, Ford! This letter this morning is only the second I've had."

"Listen," the man said. "One man walked out on you because you were always sniveling and whining. You look out you don't find yourself looking for a job again!"

He got up and walked into the adjoining bedroom. Dina could hear the bed creak as he flung himself down upon it. In another few seconds his heavy deep snoring sounded throughout the cheaply built house.

It was a one-story house, one of a row of five. Two of them were empty; a third was the Snows', temporarily deserted now; a fourth occupied by bachelor assistant wardens; and the fifth, the largest and the corner building, was the Huddlestons'. To all five the prison walls supplied a back fence, and from all five the great rise of the northwest wall shut away the late afternoon sun.

Two miles from the prison the little prairie town of Larkin Flat lay open and level, crossed by railroad lines, boasting only a few two-story buildings, only a few trees. In the summer it sent a dazzle of alkaline dusty heat to the white sky; in the winter it was bare, brown, beaten down by rain and broken up into mudholes that reflected the homely little frame houses and the bare whips of the cottonwoods. Here and there, in a cottage yard, some homesick woman had planted geraniums and marguerites, but water was scarce at Larkin Flat, and gardens did not flourish there.

The town, forlorn as it was, however, was a haven of coziness and comfort compared to the prison that was reached by a bare stark ribbon of highway across the prairie. There was no green at all here; there was nothing here but the harsh squareness of unrelenting cement and brick, of barred windows, of clanking doorways within doorways, of cold sanitary smells of carbolic and antiseptics and hideous warm smells of cheap food, bodies, defective plumbing. There was a sack factory, a storehouse, a flagged gray yard for exercise and for the desolate activities known as "sports," and there was the row of five gray-painted cottages—that was all.

One of the big buildings housed the electric chair and the row of cells for the condemned.

Dina was not an imaginative woman. Her years were but twenty-nine to her husband's forty-eight; her type had been, and in many ways still was, girlish, simple, confiding, uncritical. She was a little woman with pale gold hair and a transparent skin; tears, wakeful nights and hours of hard work and harder worry had shadowed her blue eyes and robbed them of color, and constant thought of her child had given them an eternally anxious, asking look, but she was still, in some odd unchangeable way, a comfortable, an essentially wifely little creature, and she managed to make homelike even the dreary environment in which she found herself.

But she wondered sometimes how it all had happened. How had she happened to marry Ford? Even sick, penniless and with little Chester to care for, it must have been a strangely blind hour that saw her promising herself to the big, blustering, conceited man. She had known Ford Huddleston to be one of the idlers, one of the bullies of Somersville— green, tree-shaded Somersville, with the big elms arching over it, and the good Sunday dinner cooking so decorously in Cousin Julia's house; Somersville with green trees and gardens, with women sauntering home from club afternoons and baking smells floating from kitchen doorways.

Nothing good had ever come of the Huddleston blood. And yet Ford had seemed to be making an effort to be worthy of a wife; he had stopped drinking, he had been wonderful to little Chess. . . .

Then the prison appointment had come. Why? What had Ford ever done in his forty-five years except hang about drinking places, gamble, brag of his political influence? Why, quite suddenly, had this last boast been made good and he been appointed warden at Larkin Flat Prison? Ford, with powers of everything short of life and death in his hands! Dina and he had been married on the strength of the new job and had come together to this hideous place more than two years ago.

One hundred and fourteen men in his power now, and the possibilities of graft and abuse and favoritism and bribery infinite! He could drink all he liked now, and still he would be obeyed. Nobody could talk back to Ford in these days.

Dina roused herself from musing, began the usual clearing away; she stacked the dishes neatly in the sink, darkened the dining room just as Cousin Julia always darkened hers after a meal; set about dishwashing and dinner preparations methodically. Corned beef and cabbage for dinner, reheated biscuits and blackberry roll. The meat had been simmering all morning, filling the house with its gluey, unsalted smell. Dina took down from a shelf a jar of blackberries of her own preserving, poured the black liquid contents into a bowl.

It was just then that the telephone rang sharply, and at the same moment the voice of the prison siren rose in a great shriek and swept above the house like a shrill howling wind, bringing Dina's heart into her mouth with terror, and bringing Ford forth from the bedroom still half asleep, his face florid where it had touched the pillow, his fingers fumbling with vest buttons. He snatched the telephone.

"Who is it?" he shouted more than once. "How long ago? What the hell have you fellers been about that you leave it wide open?

"It's Pool!" Ford said to his wife, hastily concluding only the essential part of his redressing. "Five fellers' time was up this morning, and we let 'em go. Luke says they think he slid out when they did."

"He's got a good chance then," Dina contributed, half to herself. She couldn't help it; when they escaped she always hoped they'd get away. "Murderer, Ford?"

"Killed a feller that got fresh with his sister. I don't know what it was——" Ford rushed away, and Dina followed him to the door and stood there, staring out at a world so bare and level that even a cottontail could hardly expect to escape across it in any direction, especially with the siren sweeping it with a wild alarm of warning, and the townsfolk running to their doorways two miles away to share the excitement of a getaway.

"I wonder where he is; they'll kill him if he's a lifer," Dina thought, her heart hammering. "Oh, poor fellow, poor fellow, what could he possibly do? Where can he go? They'll get him, and Ford 'll talk to him that awful, awful way he does. . . ."

She went back to her kitchen; knelt down. She was a praying woman, though there was small encouragement for trust in God here. Now she very simply asked her Father not to let Ford talk to the man the way he always did; not to say, "Well, by the time we get through with you you won't feel like running so fast! Tie him up, Luke, and let's have a little party to celebrate his getting away!"

Standing up, opening her eyes, a little dizzy, she saw a mud-spattered, dirty man in stripes standing in the kitchen door.

Dina was not frightened for herself; men in stripes were a commonplace with her. But a swift protective pity for him tore at her heart.

"For God's sake go give yourself up while there's time," she said in a sharp, furious whisper.

The man was staring at her.

"Say . . ." he stammered. "What do you know! *Say!*"

She looked at him now, and her knees grew weak, and her mouth filled with salt water. Dina sank slowly into a chair, never moving her eyes from his.

"Oh, my God in heaven!" she whispered.

He had a cup of water at her lips; she swallowed some with an effort that brought tears to her eyes. Her look did not leave him.

"Say, what a break *this* is!" he said. "Dina!"

"Lin," her lips said without sound. She sat staring at him weakly, broken.

"What are you doin' here?"

"I'm—I'm Huddleston's wife."

"Oh, my Godfrey!" Lin said. She remembered the old oath. "I bin here two months," he added. "Funny I never saw you."

"I don't go over much. I'm in the women's end a good deal, but Ford don't like me to see too much of the men."

"You ain't married to *Huddleston*, Dina?"

"For 'most three years now."

"You haven't had much of a break with your husbands, I'll say that," the man said after a pause. The siren was still now; the world very still. A chicken looked in the kitchen door, clucked reproachfully, went away. Dina panted; she was very pale. "You got a divorce?" the man said.

"There isn't any divorce if you're a Catholic," she reminded him, speaking vaguely, almost apathetically. "We thought you were killed, Lin, when the jam broke. The boys came back and said you and old Cap Cutter and three of the Portygees were washed right down the river. They found the bodies and there was a funeral. Then I took Chester and went to Cousin Julia's for a spell."

"I didn't go back," he said. "I wanted to get out. I was sick and Chester was sick all the time. I've paid for it, Dina. I've never had a happy moment since. I've wanted to go back and tell you I knew how mean I'd been. I always thought I'd make good and then come get you."

"How'd you come to murder anyone, Lin? Ford says it was someone insulted your sister. And when 'd you take the name Pool?"

"Curt Pool," he said. "I never done it, Dina."

"They all say that."

"But this was a frame-up. Dina, where's the kid?"

"Out in California with your mother."

"No?" the man said. And into his sallow, haggard young face a strange light suddenly came. "Is that right? Did you take him there? She's got a nice little prune ranch up in the Santa Cruz range; it's just about a living for her. Is he there?"

"Ford sent him. He can't stand Chester. When we were married he said he'd always give him a home——

"Lin," Dina said, interrupting herself in sudden agitation as the siren began to whine again high up in the sun-washed air of the chill spring afternoon, "you've got to get out of this and I don't know how I can help you! They'll shoot you down like a dog if you put up any fight, and there isn't a place between here and Larkin Flat that 'd hide a cat. What 'd you do it for? You can't get away with it!"

"I gotter have clothes," the man said.

"There isn't a thing—he'd kill me if I helped you, because there was three escapes and that Baretti thing last month, and he's scared to death of his job!" the woman said. "He isn't going to let anyone else get away. Oh, why did you do it?"

"Lissen, Dina. If I can get to Larkin Flat for the five train—it's after three now—I'm all right. I'll get West to Ma, and she'll hide me away until things blow over. Huddleston ain't anxious for any more breaks to be reported from Larkin Flat. Get me an overcoat anyway, can't you?" He came nearer, and she remembered the look in his eyes and the tones of his voice. "Look," he said. "Whether they get me or not, here's something I want to know. Will you forgive me, Dina? If I get away I'm going to do different now. Honest I am. I'm going out to Ma's and run her place for her, and try to give the kid a break. Will you just say that you aren't mad at me?"

She looked at him, trembling. June color flooded up under her fine skin and a young light softened her tired eyes.

"I've always loved you, Lin," she said thickly, very low. "You weren't ever unkind to me. You were sick, and Chester was sick—— Oh, my God, that's Ford!"

She broke off in a terrified whisper and went quickly to the dining room, closing the kitchen door behind her. Ford had thundered up the front steps to the barren little porch; three or four guards were with him.

"See anything of him?" he shouted.

"Run this way?" Dina called back.

"Sure he did. The boys seen him. He was hiding in the storehouse; he'd tunneled into it somehow. They knew he was in there for an hour; they didn't think he'd dare make a break for it. But he run out, half an hour back, when the siren began! Circle the house, boys, and look through the Snow place," Ford directed in an excited shout.

"He may be in one of them empty houses!" one of the men called.

"Oh, where is he? Where could he get to?" Dina's frantic thoughts ran. "The flour barrel—under those quilts in the closet—up attic—there's not room to stand up there, but he might have swung himself up through the trapdoor and be lying flat. He's fighting for his life now, sure enough! I guess you're wishing you'd let well enough alone now, Lin."

"Didn't see nobody?" her husband demanded, following her into the kitchen now as the men forged to and fro like hounds on a scent, their voices echoing up and down Warden's Row. The siren was silent again, and all other noises sounded loud.

"I was out in the kitchen, Ford. You know how awful that siren makes me feel!"

"He's a tough bozo, all right!" Ford was searching the closets, the laundry; he leaped down the cellar stairs. "He dropped his gun as he ran," he said. "So we're not going to have any trouble with that baby!"

Dina stood still on the kitchen doorstep, with the great walls of the prison rising to shut off her vision a hundred feet away. The zoom of the mail plane sounded far overhead; that meant three o'clock. It would come to earth in twenty minutes at Ridley, nine miles away. The free, graceful thing flashed white against a whiter sky; twinkled in the cold spring light. Dina's eyes followed it westward until the harsh roof line of the prison shut it from sight. Oh, to be in it, to be up in the clean cold air, to be anywhere but here!

At any second they might find Lin now; at some one of these ghastly seconds they would find him. They would drag him in, helpless and whining. "Aw, have a heart, Warden, you'd have done the same thing!" Lin would perhaps be muttering as he was hustled over to the jail again, to such limited mercies as Luke and Ford chose to extend. They had hosed Baretti until he was half conscious and then flung him into "solitary" until he raved and frothed and died—but no, there was no use being sorry for the men in the prison, there was nothing to be done about it, it was just that way!

The hunt went on. Men ran across the little back yards of the Row, jumped fences, looked down from upstairs windows, called back and forth. Ford ran to the prison, came hurrying home again. Dina thought that she never had seen him in a worse state of excitement and anger.

"If he don't show up pretty soon I'll get the dogs from Plaquette!" he said, jerking the telephone dial about with his fat forefinger.

"How'd he make the break, Ford?" Dina was sure, by this time, that Lin had somehow gotten himself into the attic. Impossible to think how he had managed it in the few minutes between her seeing Ford and his violent entry into the kitchen, for a dozen men were scouring the place now, and every garage and chicken house and porch corner had been turned out; but somehow he had managed to hide himself. She attempted to engage Ford in conversation as often as she could; wherever he was, time was an important consideration to Lin.

"He must have got into the storehouse when the men went out this morning. We let five fellers go today; they made the noon train from Larkin Flat, and he probably fooled himself he could get away with 'em. But nix. Luke checked 'em—they don't put anything over on him! This feller Pool—he's a lifer—got himself into the storehouse through a window in the back that's been blocked up for years," Ford went on, his eyes searching the open space before the Row as he and Dina stood on the front porch, his voice absent minded and lowered to little more than a growl. "He shoved the boxes around and squeezed in. Maybe he thought he could live in there for a while," he said. "Luke didn't miss him until the boys come back from lunch and then he asked Harry, and they scouted around a little—I was over here—and they seen his legs through the front window of the storehouse. But he run through and jumped out the back window—they didn't know it was there—and by the time they got Red and Tex he was running this way. He got behind this row of houses all right, and Tex come for me—I was just back in my office—and I says, 'No rush, boys, a flea couldn't get away 'cross these flats, and we'll do this thing right,' so we went down and checked 'em all over and locked 'em up. I don't want no more trouble here," the man ended. "That business last month didn't do me any good. When we get hold of Mr Curt Pool he'll wish he hadn't been quite so tricky."

Dina saw the three o'clock train pull itself like a shining little snake free of the village. Two miles away, every inch of the road open to the merciless prisoner inspection, and Conway, the stationmaster, vigilantly on the lookout. No, no hope there! She had talked to Lin ten minutes ago; no man could make two miles in that time—no man in prison stripes, with his sinister history written in his haggard face and terrified eyes.

"I should think he'd kill himself," Dina said, wondering if he had, in one of the empty rooms of the two untenanted houses. Was that going to be the end of Lin Forrest, the lean, good-natured boy who had bought her a Florodora sundae at Witting's so many years ago, and had walked home with her, and told her that she was the cutest-looking girl he had ever seen? Poor Lin, who was just getting a start in the lumber mill when Chester had arrived, and times had gone hard, and Lin's health had given way. He hadn't been able to eat or to sleep; he had grown depressed and cross; "getting you and the kid into a mess like this!" And then had come the terrible wet day of his leaving her, and a week later the log jam and the sullen rush of the swollen river, and six men—and Lin among them, swept away in a jumble of raging, coffee-colored water and churning logs—logs leaping into the air, logs standing on end, logs hammered together as they had gone roaring down toward the rapids.

Weeks afterward, with their clothing torn and washed away and their faces obliterated, some of the men's bodies had been found. There had been a funeral, with Mrs Lin Forrest as one of four widows. To no one, least of all to terrified little penniless Dina, had it occurred to doubt the finality of that hour.

"But I surely liked that lumber town," Dina thought, staring at the bare prairie and the twinkling distant roofs of Larkin Flat. "The big trees, when they were wet, and the way the smoke smelled, and taking our lunch up to the falls in the summer."

"Got him!" Luke, the guard Dina especially disliked, shouted at this moment. He charged past the Huddlestons, husband and wife, thundered across the porch to the kitchen. Dina and Ford followed him. "He's up here in your attic, Mis' Huddleston!" Luke shouted.

"He can't be," Dina said. "I was right here in my kitchen all the time the siren was blowing!"

"He's here, all right!" the man repeated. "Looka the—looka that trap door!"

"Ford!" Dina caught at her husband's arm. "Don't let the boys shoot at him! You've got him—he can't get away. If you kill him there'll be an investigation, and after all that trouble last month that won't do you any good. Robertson wrote you he wasn't any too well pleased——"

"Get out of my way!" Ford shouted, jumping up on the gas stove, extending big arms toward the trap door. But he had heard her. "Don't shoot, boys," he said as the other guards gathered in an excited group in the kitchen. "He ain't got a gun. If he gets funny with his fists knock him out, but we don't want the governor over here again. You picked up his gun, didn't you, Tex?"

"Red did," Tex answered in a soft thin wheeze oddly at variance with his gorillalike person. "He din' have nothin' in his hands when he run."

Ford mounted the ladder someone had brought and placed beneath the trap-door opening. With that strange unimaginative courage that had before this surprised Dina in him he thrust his head up into the dusty darkness above.

"We got you, Pool!" he called. "Come on down here. You can't get away with it!"

"Maybe you have and maybe you haven't, Huddleston!" Lin's voice sounded from somewhere under the low raw pine shingles. There was a crash of glass. "You ain't any more anxious to have more trouble here than I am!" Lin added. Ford withdrew a dusty head, yelled incoherently to his men. "He's out on the roof—he's got away. Get out there, some of you—get a move on—hold onto this ladder, Tex——"

They all rushed out to the front of the house again, Dina following. She ran down past the forlorn straggle of the garden, looked up at the roof. The guards were swarming along the Row from porch to porch now, yelling at the man's figure that was running fleetly from roof to roof above their heads. The five cottages stood close together. The man ran up the slope of one roof as if it were a little hill, ran down the corresponding slope and lightly jumped the five-foot space between the gutters to repeat the performance on the next roof. He was swifter than the clumsy tumble and scramble of the guards below; he reached the empty end house, sprang from its roof to that of the garage, bounded to the earth and was clearly to be seen running like a deer across the slight rise of the bare field beyond.

Lost, of course, but how he ran! Lin had been a famous runner years ago, and he had a hundred-yard start on his pursuers now. Dina thought of the plane that had moved so steadily westward half an hour earlier. Ah, if it had been against the cold white afternoon sky now, and had swooped down toward that straining figure, what an escape there might have been!

But there was no plane. There was only the open stubbled prairie bleak before the first breath of spring, and filled with mudholes where the men had dug rocks or played their cheerless ball games. Twice she saw Lin fall; both times he was up and away again like a hare, but both times the panting, shouting, cursing following of the guards was closer.

"Don't shoot!" Ford had bellowed after them. She went back into the kitchen and knelt down and covered her face with her hands. No hope, no chance for him. No God to pray to! Lin to be soused with icy water, punched and beaten, flung into the bitter exile of "solitary," and her little Chess, who so loyally loved his mother, who couldn't believe that "Mom" was sending him away even for a visit—little Chess seventeen hundred miles away! And herself presently to listen to Ford gloating upon the capture of his prey, and to serve corned beef and cabbage for supper.

"You couldn't do anything about this, God, and I'm not going to bother asking You," Dina said. The hunt was over now; they were bringing Lin back. She could hear their voices; she looked from her kitchen window and saw them crossing the field, the muddy figure walking uprightly enough, but tightly gripped by the big hands of Charlie and Red. "No, Lin, you couldn't make it; you never had a chance," she said.

She stuck a fork into the corned beef that was gently turning pink and gray, in the frothy, slowly boiling water. Dina was a good cook; that was all Ford wanted, and a woman. His meals had to be hot and prompt and hearty, and his wife hard working, silent, capable, and at night affectionate —there was Ford's whole idea of a mate.

The siren again; three short blasts. Silence, and then three more. That meant that the fugitive was captured. That screamed to all the farms and villages within reach of its hideous voice that there was no more danger from the runaway; wives could turn their children loose in dooryards again, and small boys go off to pastures to bring in cows. He was caught. Warden Huddleston was a darned fine warden in spite of that cruelty story last month. A lifer got loose today at noon and they landed him before four o'clock. . . .

Blackberry roll for dinner. Dina stooped toward her flour barrel, scooped up a sifter. Blackberry roll. "Oh, God, I hope they aren't going after him with the hose. God, help him! I went over to Mrs Goldberg's when Chester was born, and Lin came creeping in—he was crying. There never was a mean bone in his body. . . .

"Don't I remember how funny his face looked with tears all over it, and I wiping them off with my hand! Didn't it feel good lying there, and hearing Chess fussing! And the smell of tea when Linda Goldberg brought me in a cup. That was a long day. Four o'clock in the morning when Lin and I walked over to Goldbergs' and got Joe Goldberg out of his good warm bed. . . .

"Ford's certainly having a good time with Lin now. Well, if they kill him, like they did Baretti, there 'll be an investigation this time, sure enough! You'll not feel so good, Mr Ford Huddleston, if the governor comes over. . . .

"I wonder what Ford 'd do to you, Lin, if he knew what I'm thinking? If he knew I was remembering that day I wore my cross-barred organdy and my white hat, and we walked from the church down toward Mill Lane, and you took the key of our cottage out of your pocket? You said, 'Now don't you get scared, Mrs Forrest, I'm just the same Lin's been keeping company with you for three years. I haven't waited for you this long to scare you now. You and I'll get dinner together like we have at Julia's dozens of times. . . .'

"Seven years ago. My Lord, that seems more than seven years ago!"

Five o'clock, and Ford due home for dinner any minute. Lin was lucky if he had been flung, cold and muddy and supperless and aching from blows, upon the black verminous floor of the solitary cell. But it took the boys a lot of time to wreak their vengeance upon anyone who broke jail; they liked excitement, they adored a hunt, but none of them enjoyed the necessity of sounding the siren that notified all the surrounding country that another man had evaded their vigilance and was making a desperate rush for freedom. The "caught" siren was always sounded with especial fervor and repeated with what, to Dina at least, was nauseating gusto.

The telephone rang. The sheriff and the station agent and the authorities generally wanted to know if Pool had been captured. Yes, they got him, Dina answered patiently. They had him fifteen minutes ago— half an hour ago. Mr Huddleston was still over at the prison but they probably weren't answering that telephone now; it was after five, and there wouldn't be anyone in the office. She began to wish feverishly that Ford would come home, ending the episode, ending the horrible suspense of not knowing what was happening to Lin.

"I guess I'll stop praying," Dina thought.

A sudden new doubt assailed her. With Lin living—living beaten and soaked with cold water and flung into solitary confinement, it was true, and subsisting on water and dry bread, yet still alive—what was her status in Ford Huddleston's house? What could Ford do to her if he ever discovered that she was deceiving him, that she had not been genuinely a widow at the time she and Ford had married?

"He couldn't put me into jail, I should think. It wasn't my fault. The priest married Lin and me and read prayers over Lin's body with the rest of the boys that were drowned when the jam broke. Maybe I ought to get away. I've got 'most two hundred dollars saved. I always thought I'd use it for Chester's education, but it 'd get me someplace Ford couldn't find me. But if he found out he'd be meaner 'n ever to Lin. . . ."

It was almost six o'clock; the table was set and the supper ready when Ford's heavy foot sounded on the porch. The spring night had closed down dark and chilly, and Dina had lighted a fire in the black iron "airtight stove." Her kitchen was brightly lighted and warm, but the passage was dark, and at first she could only see that a man was with Ford; he was bringing someone home for supper.

The man followed him to the kitchen door; a lean man, with a rather white face and gentle sad blue eyes, and long clever hands. A man whose brown hair was wetly brushed, and who was clothed in worn garments obviously never selected to fit his thin breadth and his inches. Lin.

Lin. Dina stood staring, the color ebbing from her face. She was too

[361]

completely stupefied to disguise her amazement, but fortunately Ford, who was in a boisterous, jovial mood, saw nothing.

"Got enough dinner for two hungry fellers?" he asked.

"I got plenty, I guess," Dina said in a third attempt to speak.

"This is Tom Mack, the feller we were chasing today."

"I thought it was Pool you were chasing."

"Well, we did too!" Ford said with a forced, hearty laugh. "Come in, Mack," he said. "Set down. Yes," Ford expanded it with relish as his shapeless, gross body itself expanded comfortably in a big chair, "we certainly got things balled up today. Mack's time was up this morning, and he left the pen with the others."

"Oh, 'sat so?" Dina said politely, setting another place. Her face was pale and her hands were shaking, but she did not look at Lin, and Ford never really looked at anyone. "Where's—where's Pool?" she asked.

"Well," Ford said, taking his knife from his pocket and paring his nails, "he's got away. He must be hiding out round here someplace, in some barn or silo, and I ain't going to make any fuss about him. We'll get him. The sheriff 'll have to know. I'll stop in and talk it over with him tonight, but I don't want the boys to blow the siren again. It does nothing but frighten the women. We'll get him, all right."

"Mrs Huddleston looks like she'd like to know how I got back into rocks, after I was let out," the visitor now said. It was Lin's remembered voice, and now that he had abandoned the hideous filthy striped prison apparel the men called "rocks" he was indeed Lin again, only older and thinner; he was the man she had loved so eagerly years ago, after her lonesome and bewildered girlhood—indeed, the man she loved still.

"Pool stole his clothes while he was washing up down at the canal," Ford explained. "Get a move on, Dina," he remonstrated. "Can't we eat? I've got to get Mack, here, to the seven-ten."

"I was discharged with four other fellers this morning," Lin explained, falling upon the corned beef with vigor. "Warden, here, drove 'em over to the noon train, but I walked. I been shut up for a year, and it felt good to me to walk where I liked again."

Dina moved her trusting, weary eyes to his face questioningly.

"I got a year for being mixed in with a gambling racket," he said.

"You weren't a lifer, then?" the woman asked mildly.

"No, but Pool was. And Pool worked a break while we was busy getting the boys discharged this morning," Ford said. "He must have hid in them cotton woods where the maller bushes are, down at the canal back of the grain elevator, and when Mack, here, stopped to wash himself and clean up he stole Mack's clothes. Mack had to get back into the rocks or go naked, and he come back here to explain to me and borrow some clothes." Ford gulped down masses of hot meat smeared with mustard, forkloads of steaming cabbage, wiped his dripping mustache. "Then what 'd you do, that you got caught in the storehouse, Mack?" he asked.

"Well, I followed Red in there when he went in for some beans. I wanted to talk to him," Lin explained. "But the minute he saw the rocks he went out again, and the door slammed and shut me in. Red and Tex and some of those others stood guard, and they sent for you, Mr Huddleston. I was afraid they'd shoot, and I wasn't sure they'd seen me, so I lay low. Well, after a while I saw the back window, and I thought I could sneak round here and explain, but the boys seen me and it was all up. Maybe," Lin added, with an apologetic smile for the warden, "maybe I shouldn't of been so scared. But I ran without thinking what I was do-ing——"

"You should of yelled that you wasn't Pool," Ford said genially. "But you boys get so you can't look no one in the face!"

"I know. But when you've been in the pen awhile you sorta lose your guts," Lin apologized simply. And as Ford's bullhead was lowered over a second mammoth helping of food he winked at Dina.

"Where you goin' now, Mack?"

"I'm going West. I've got a wife and kid—well, my wife ain't there just now," Lin said. "But I'm expectin' her to join me," he added.

" 'Sat right? Know you was sent up?"

"Does she know I was in the pen? Yep, she does," Lin answered after a moment. He split open a fifth biscuit. "Home cooking surely does taste good, Mrs Huddleston," he said.

"I guess it doesn't make any difference to her," Dina said. "If she thought you were dead she might of married someone else, but as long as you were living she'd know she was your wife."

"In that case—if she thought a man was dead, and married again—a woman would just have to leave a letter for the second man, explaining that she was no bigamist," Lin said. "And get out. He wouldn't have no claim on her."

Ford was not listening.

"Ain't there something else?" he demanded.

"There's a blackberry roll. Wait a minute." Dina carried plates into the kitchen, came back with the smoking pudding and the graniteware coffee-pot. The men finished their dessert hastily; it was quarter to seven now, and the dirt road to town was filled with mudholes. Ford went around the corner to get the car; Lin and Dina had a moment together on the porch.

"How'd you get him to bring you to supper?" the woman asked in a quick, furtive undertone.

"Oh, the boys had turned the hose on me and they were getting pretty rough. I guess he felt a little ashamed, and nervous maybe, on account of Baretti passing out on him last month. He don't want any more trouble."

"Why'd you do it, Lin? You're smarter than he is. You didn't have to hide in the storehouse and make that getaway. All you had to do was walk into the office and say, 'I'm Mack.' "

Ford had driven the muddy car to the floor of the garden twenty paces away; Lin was leaving.

"All right!" Ford yelled.

"Say this over to yourself until you understand it, Dee," Lin said hastily, shaking hands in farewell. She remembered the little name of their early days together, and the little shack at the lumber camp, and the smell of wood smoke and wet redwoods, and her heart began to dance in a way it had long forgotten. "Say this over till you get it," said Lin. "Pool is a friend of mine and a good feller; I've known him seven years. He done what he did—well, never mind that, but there was reason! He killed a skunk, and his wife's dying of tuberculosis, and there's children. He's got a hide-out up in the Canadian woods where they'll never find him. He's got a name fixed and a place and everything. And his brother-in-law is the mail pilot—get that? The mail pilot that went down at Ridley at three-twenty, see? I had to keep things going until three-twenty. After that I knew he'd be all right. He had four hours to walk nine miles. We swapped clothes at the canal, and I spattered my face with mud. I took care they wouldn't recognize me——"

"Come on!" shouted Ford. Lin ran lightly down the steps, waved a hand from the car.

"See you again someday, Mrs Huddleston!"

"See you again!" Dina echoed. She leaned against the doorpost and looked up at the wheeling stars in the dark blue sky of spring; there was a new moon and she thought it seemed friendly, as if it was smiling down at the tired little woman in the shabby kitchen apron in the shadow of the big prison. When she brought her eyes to earth again she felt as if she had been praying—really praying, not just making herself say the words of prayers.

The lights of the town twinkled on the prairie, two miles away. Dina could see the train pull in, a caterpillar of little lights, could see it draw away again, toward the Far West.

Lin was on his way West now, on his way to the mountains and the redwoods, and the frosty mornings green and shadowy, and the long summer days scented with tarweed and prunes. Chester was out there, little slender, anxious, affectionate Chester in his belted sweater and stubby little shoes, waiting for "Mom."

"Gee, it is certainly one sweet night tonight. I guess we are going to have spring early after all!" Dina said aloud. "I guess it does you good to pray even when you've kinder stopped for a while," she said.

[364]

The Heart of a Mouse

The old Peacock place, the housewives of Friends' Landing would have told you, was a disgrace to the village. Fortunately, from their point of view, it was not, strictly speaking, in the village; it stood in a scattering of shabby houses down toward the shore, beyond the sandbanks, only really visible when one looked for it or caught sight of its untidy environs from the waters of the river. It was a wooden house, two-storied, with a wide porch going all around the lower story. It had a crazy windmill which tipsily supervised a tangle of unpainted barns, chicken houses, woodsheds, dovecotes, tool houses and rabbit boxes, and a very maze of rusty and rebellious wire fencing, sagging gates and tottering railings. This region sloped gradually to the sandy shore and the lisping waters of the busy river, where there were further embellishments in the way of a float, a crooked and rotting pier, two small sunburned bathhouses leaning against each other for support, and such barrels, logs, ropes, anchors and crates as the kindly river had brought to the small greedy hands of Tony and Minny Peacock, and Bud and Hume McKay.

In the yard were further treasures. There were more ropes, all sorts of ropes; more planks and barrels and boxes; there were bicycles in every stage of dissection and rust, wheelbarrows and coasters, old skates and coils of wire, hammers and nails and staples. There were the remains of more than one old wagon, old milk cans, farm machinery long past usefulness, chains and odd wheels. Against one side of the woodshed there was a neat arrangement of paintpots; half-a-dozen variegated swings dangled from the lower branches of the great maples and elms. Everywhere that children's hands could be busy children's hands had been busy, setting up a little enterprise in horse chestnuts with the old fringed buggy top for a stall, constructing harnesses or carving boats, painting, digging, climbing, tying ropes. The earth in the yard had a bare, packed look; whatever green or blossoming thing the children had not trampled and scraped and denuded had fallen to the rabbits, chickens, dogs or cats. Up the trees were platforms, and down in the soil were caves, for such times as Minny, Tony, Hume and Bud elected to be Bandar-log or prehistoric savages.

The Peacock children's mother, the widow of the older Anthony, six years dead, was a lean, vigorous, black-eyed woman, large of bone and deep voiced, perhaps in her middle thirties, though the children thought her extremely old. She was a hot-tempered, despotic, energetic, impulsive person, given far more to deeds than words, and always briskly busy. No one ever loitered, delayed or philandered in the neighborhood of Mollie Peacock; tradespeople gave her their messages in nervous haste, village women stammered stupidly in their anxiety not to anger her. They said that she would almost as soon spank a small child as speak to it, her hands rather led than obeyed her tongue, and there was short shrift for some youngster every time the lamps were not filled, or the woodbox empty, or the porch unswept. Minny and Tony and their cousins leaped through their daily tasks with passionate zeal, and eyed their mother nervously whenever she unexpectedly bore down upon them. Sometimes, said the women of the village, she whipped them terribly.

The women of the village were almost as one in their disapproval of whipping, although they varied a trifle in their ground upon the question. Mrs Hallowell said that her children were too logical to make it necessary, and Mrs Treanor that Pippsy Treanor was always guided quickest by love, but Mrs Leroy went further and stated, even occasionally from platforms, that corporeal punishment caused a malignant reaction in a child's moral tissues and disturbed his norm until Fear had been vanquished by perfect Love again. They talked of these things at the club frequently, but Mrs Peacock did not come to the club and so did not hear them.

She pleaded that she had not time for the club. Beside her children she had Crazy Lucy and Grammar Peacock to care for. The latter was her husband's tremulous, clean, feeble old mother, who sat in the sunshine all day long throughout nine months of the year, and beside the kitchen stove when the weather was chilly, and knitted and darned and peeled apples and shelled peas in a contented dream that enwrapped seventy years of helpful and sad and happy memories. Crazy Lucy was the cook, a pale, silent woman whose husband had deserted her; unrivaled in the making of gingerbread and rice pudding and graham rolls and all the other inexpensive edibles that the Peacocks consumed by the square yard. Once Mrs Hallowell had mildly expostulated with Mrs Peacock on the subject of Lucy.

"Does thee really think it safe to leave thy dear children with that queer girl?" she had asked.

"The children won't hurt her!" Mrs Peacock had hardily returned. Mrs Hallowell had looked a trifle nonplused and had said no more.

One day some sprightly program chairwoman had suggested, as a means of attracting young Mrs Peacock to the Village Improvement Club, that gentle old Quaker Mrs Peacock be asked to read a paper of reminiscences before the members. Grammar Peacock had known Friends' Landing long before the railroad came, when Indian camps were lingering in the western hills, when the mail came through once a week on horseback, and when some of the bearskins that now graced the floors of handsome brown bungalows had been wandering the woods on the backs of their original owners.

So Grammar came to the club and tremblingly launched into her memories, and for half an hour—even for an hour—feminine Friends' Landing listened with bright respectful interest, with laughter and applause. But when the clock struck five young wives began to slip away, and the maid who was to serve tea at five began to rattle cups in the reception hall, and still Grammar talked pleasantly on and on and on. At half-past five a flushed and harassed hostess of the day asked young Mrs Peacock if she couldn't just, perhaps, give her mother-in-law just a— well, just a gentle hint, but young Mrs Peacock pleaded vivaciously, and in a whisper, that Grammar was having "the time of her life." So Grammar talked on, past six o'clock, and until half-past six, and until ten minutes of seven, and then finished waveringly with a halfhearted fear that perhaps she had tired "the ladies." The diminished audience was by now too much exhausted to rise to a polite lie, but the gallant daughter-in-law said heartily, "Not a second too long!" and led the proud and weary old woman tenderly away, to an evening of praise and hot tea and more reminiscences, in which the subject of time was never even mentioned.

She was always kind enough to the old lady, it was conceded, in her flighty and despotic way. But oh, said the mothers of Friends' Landing, and especially said the women who were not mothers, how frightfully she talked to those children! How she grabbed them and hustled them and jumped them into the shabby car and out of the shabby car, what warnings she hurled at them, and what punishments she threatened! It was dreadful, in this day of analyzed and interpreted childhood, to realize that a well-to-do woman, and an intelligent woman, could possibly be so far behind the times. In their shabby garments the young Peacocks and their cousins brought wood and milked cows and tramped into town for the mail much as did the Italians and Poles of the lower river settlement; they rode on watering carts and hay wagons, did hair-raising things in their catboat, and apparently were free to start a fire and cook a meal wherever the fancy took them. They did not go to village parties or the dancing school, or even to the Louvre when there was a carefully supervised children's matinee, with a fairy tale and educational films. Altogether they were a neglected lot, and if it had not been for their mother's genuine goodness to their old grandmother, Friends' Landing would have said her to be a decidedly heartless woman.

There was, however, one other person who had never had anything but tenderness and gentleness from Mollie Peacock, and this person, although he was aged only eight and had known her but ten intoxicating days, was deeply convinced that she was the most remarkable woman in the world and had the most endearing manner. Yet little Paul Craig had known a great many women and a great many changes in his hundred months of living, and was perhaps as shrewd a judge of human nature as might be found in all Friends' Landing. In actual years he came between seven-year-old Minny and eight-year-old Hume and considered Anthony and Bud, who were nine and ten, dizzy heights above him, but in experience he was as old as all four of the harum-scarum youngsters put together.

He had been standing listlessly in a corner of the playground one morning, ten days ago, when he first saw her. She had come out across the bare clean porch of the Children's Home Shelter and down the bare, clean steps and into the sharp clean May sunshine, with Mrs Younger, who was the matron. Mrs Younger had been carrying a bowl very steadily—it was filled with Irish Moss custard, which the matron had been sending to old Mrs Peacock.

There had been other children in the yard—clean, quietly playing children, in blue checked blouses and pinafores—but they had retreated from Mrs Younger. Not that the matron was cross, exactly, but she was Authority, and, unlike other children, these little mavericks in the Children's Home Shelter had no refuge from Authority, no spoiling indulgent arms, no sheltering lap, no competent grownup to stand between their tender, lazy little bodies and the inexorable routine of disciplined work and play, washing and eating, sleeping and waking.

Paul had not retreated from Mrs Younger. He had come only two months before from a place that made the Shelter seem safe and happy and secure. They had said, the decent people who had investigated and exposed that other place, that he was fortunately too little to remember much of it. But he remembered it all and would carry the dim memory into manhood and fatherhood, and would think, when he was dying, of the dark room where two infuriated grownups had faced down a helpless little boy who knew his mother was dead and could not hear him, and that these big people were going to hurt him. He had never talked about it, he was afraid to talk about it, but he had been thinking about it as he stood idling in the healing sunshine and had watched Mrs Peacock and the matron come toward him, and, incidentally, toward the gate.

"Here's a nice child, with such a serious little face!" Mollie Peacock had said. "I'll bet you this is a boy that never cries!"

And as she had stooped toward him he had not noticed that her black hair had been slipping untidily under her dowdy hat, nor her brown lean face freckled, nor her hands muddy from driving. He had only seen something that had melted his frozen little heart almost painfully and had made him touch her hand with his stubby, cold little red hand and smile timidly at her.

"Do you, now, Mouse?" she had said cheerfully. Paul had answered her honestly, if shyly:

"I haven't anybody to cry *to!*"

Mrs Younger had not heard him; he had thought perhaps the other lady had not heard him either, for she had not looked at him. But after a moment the visitor had said suddenly:

"Mrs Younger, will you be a darling and lend me this boy? He'll hold that wonderful custard steady in the car," she had added quickly, "and he can play about with my Siwashes, and I'll bring him back tonight or in the morning. Would you like that, Mouse?"

Authority had hesitated. They didn't like to have the children away at night. Perhaps some other day . . .

Paul's emotions had almost nauseated him. He was cold, he was feverish, he prayed.

And so it really had come to pass. He had got into the front seat of the muddy little car, and taken the bowl between his shaking little red hands, and nearly strangled himself because his breath came so spasmodically and so shallow. The women had chatted, perhaps for three minutes, but for Paul it had meant three eternities in which any second might end the dream, might find the matron suddenly unpropitious.

It had been a golden morning, getting warmer toward noon, with shadows of flickering young green across the road, with breezes kissing Paul's face, with perfume pouring into his little lungs. Mollie Peacock had been silent as they drove along, but when they came to the village she told him what she had to buy at the grocery and asked him if he liked chocolate. Paul had told her that he had had chocolate with silver paper around it once, and he had put the silver paper in his mother's prayer book because it was so pretty. He had been deeply interested when the grocer's boy put butter and potatoes into the car, and when they drove on he had said smilingly, out of deep thought, to Mollie:

"He thinks I'm your boy!"

Then they had come to the old Peacock place and had got out, and Minny and Hume had taken charge of him, and they all had played "milkman," a delightful game in which everyone dragged cans about on the cart and slopped water in and out of all kinds of containers. Bud had given him an old strap, and Tony five heavy bolts of differing sizes, and Minny had helped him button his shoes after they had all been wading. And, best of all, Hume had told him that they would be "podners on everything," and have secrets from the big boys.

At lunch his little heart had sunk a degree—just that much of his wonderful day had gone! Lunch had been at a long table at one side of the kitchen; the old lady had moved only a foot or two from her rocker to reach her place; Lucy had commented and advised while she served the hot, delicious food; Mollie Peacock had not removed her hat, had eaten casually while she telephoned to some insistent woman that she could not take part in a rummage sale. The sunshine had streamed in on the blue bowls and the big loaf, the stove had sent forth an appetizing odor of smoking griddle and browned pudding; the children had seized cookies to bear into the yard, to devour there while waiting to be summoned in for dishwiping.

They had been so good to him! He might feed the rabbits, and he might put his eager little hand into hollows in the hay where there were surely eggs. And he needn't wipe dishes, nor sweep the back porch, nor rake the road; indeed, they would not let him do anything, though he really longed to help. And they had clustered about their mother to beg for a gypsy supper on the riverbank, "because Paul is here!"

How fast the radiant afternoon fled! To Paul it had been dreadful to see it go. It had been drawing toward sunset when suddenly the miracle had occurred. Minny, who had been cross before lunch and drowsy after lunch, had been pronounced by Lucy and Grammar to be "sickening for something." When the doctor and Minny's mother had been called in consultation they said, "Possibly mumps."

These magic words had brightened the children's faces as steadily as they had clouded the grown-up sky. From "no more going for mail" and "no school" the older boys' litany of thanks had risen in joyous crescendo to "Paul can't go back!"

Paul, Mrs Peacock had decided, with one hand on the shoulder of his heaving little checked shirt, certainly couldn't go back. No, even if it wasn't mumps, the doctor had said—and it proved indeed not to be— better not let the child go back into the institution for a week or ten days.

That was ten miraculous days ago now. Ten days of joy were a long time to Paul, even though these days flew in a perfectly new and amazing manner, from the hour when he wakened in the alcove of Anthony's room, to the long warm spring twilight when, dusty and muscle-tired and ecstatically happy, he stumbled to bed again. They all knew that he was happy, but how heavenly happy they could not dream. It was all a matter of course to the Peacock children, dearly as they loved it. But to Paul the kitchen, fragrant with breakfast, his own chair between Grammar and Hume, the laughter that accompanied the emptying of blue bowls, the soft haze of an early summer morning over the river, the muffled sound of whistles from the factories a mile away, the splash of some invisible fisherman's oars, the pink rose that Aunt Mollie stuck into the strap of his new blue overalls, were alike touched with an exquisite enchantment that would never fade from his heart.

He would wander out with the boys into the yard, almost always silent, except when the rich, surprised little chuckle they all loved escaped him, but eagerly and breathlessly helpful with all their daily duties. He ran for a hammer or a broom as if his life depended upon it, he raised logs that were fully half his own weight, and raked rubbish or picked up chips with a passionate ardor that brought unaccustomed red into his pale little cheeks. When Grammar's knitting ball rolled away, or Lucy wanted a needle to sew up the stuffed chickens, it was Paul who leaped down from his Lotto card or his Parchesi board, only anxious to serve. Grammar in return let him help her cut out cookies, a rapturous and breath-taking responsibility, and Lucy showed him how to weave worsted chains through a spool. The two women, in the endless hours they spent together in the kitchen, or on the back porch that grapevines were beginning once more to screen, agreed that he was a dear little fellow.

"The way them little legs of his 'll run, the minute you call him," Lucy might muse, slopping comfortably over the dented dishpan and the cooling suds. "Run to see what you're after, I mean, not make for the shed or the fence like them other Ayrabs!"

"A body could do sompin' with that young one," Grammar, holding her needle and thread between her squinted eyes and the light, would agree comfortably. "He'll talk to ye like he was eighty. And he'll run to do ye a good turn when Tony and Bud 'll set like graven immidges! 'You fellers 'll blue-mould in your tracks,' I says to 'em yesterday. 'You remind me of a feller your grandpa used to tell about. . . .'"

And so on and on into the sweet fragrant morning, while the bread baked, and the cherries simmered, and the lilacs about the door rustled in their clean green foliage. The warm, shining dishes would be stacked away, and the children murmur and scold over their planks and ropes and wheels, and Grammar, still talking, would move her rocker out of the path of Lucy's mop and pail. It was a homely little community, isolated and primitive, yet it knew utter peace and content, and the presence of the wistful little alien somehow was making these days oddly happier for them all. Paul's deep eyes, glowing with joy, and Paul's wide mouth, that somehow could not so quickly lose its betraying lines of unchildlike solemnity, were the salt that seasoned the carefree days that had always been so gaily taken for granted.

As for Mollie Peacock, whose busy comings and goings were apparently so briskly practical, she was experiencing curious and poignant emotions because of the stray little boy that chance had brought into her own group. When he laughed his rare little reluctant laugh, she oddly wanted to cry, she felt her lashes sting with the tears that had come so rarely and so painfully since Anthony, the tender, big, splendid husband who had been so patient with her untrained and impatient beginnings, had died. Anthony had died despite the desperate prayers she had poured out, her black head bowed against his knees, and five days later, the ashen-faced and stony-eyed Mollie had seen her first-born son go into the darkness, too, the Tommy that had brought father and motherhood to Tony and herself in a golden springtime eight years before, the Tommy for whom they had bought, before he was born, the little moose-skin moccasins from the old Indian woman and the silly alphabet plate at the Hollybridge Fair.

After that there was a dazed time, when Grammar was very good, and little Minny always cried when her mother cried, and traced the tears with a fat forefinger down Mollie's thin cheek. And then a busy, brown-skinned, capable widow had taken the place of the laughing, radiant wife, and they had come to this old house of Grammar's by the river, "for a while anyway." When Aunt Sally died Bud and Hume had come too; when Lucy's husband deserted her Lucy had come.

So six years had gone by, and to Mollie, as is the way of widows, it still seemed only half a life. Her soul seemed still straining on toward that fuller life of daily talk, daily laughter, daily confidences that is happy marriage. She still felt that the cloud might somehow break, that Anthony might slip a big hand under her elbow in the old way, carry her off for some happy city visit filled with strange impressions of restaurants and theaters. He was somewhere, and his "girl"—he had always called her that —was blindly and stupidly seeking him. Why, before she knew Grammar, before Minny and Tony were dreamed of, there had been Anthony, there had been fat, bad baby Tom throwing napkin rings and spoons to the floor of the little Wakely cottage down by the bridge. Grammar and Tony and Minny had never seen that cottage; it had burned down one night, and today the old roses and hollyhocks of Mollie's bridal days were smothered in mallow and willows and rank grass. Sometimes she walked by it and wrung her heart with the bitterness that no one could know or share.

She had shut it all into her heart, and there it had been locked, cold and dark and heavy, beyond bearing, for a long, long time. Mollie had treated her grief as she treated Tommy's little old shoes and Anthony's few letters. She took it into her hands sometimes, but she dared not look at it: she could only shut her eyes and bow her face against it in agony of spirit. No, she was not living now, she was stunned and defrauded, she was like some pathetic little sea creature left high on a rock, waiting, shriveling, suffering for the blessed return of the tide.

And now this solemn little orphan from the shelter, this "mouse," with his stubby, willing red hands and his eager dark eyes, was somehow making her want to cry again, and, incidentally, to laugh again, and to do other normal, simple things that are as wholesome for the soul as fresh air and sunshine for the body. Through Paul's eyes she saw for the first time that the kitchen was a pleasant place to be, that the yard was a children's paradise, and that the routine of porridge and pudding, of overalls and swimming suits and small shabby pajamas had a soul of its own.

For the first time it began to dawn upon her, in an undefined yet infinitely healing way, that out of the wreckage of the old perfect life had grown another life, as complete in its way, and, if less radiant, perhaps more useful. She was not all the lone, lorn woman of her wakeful nights and solitary musings; she was, after all, the center of four children's universe, and the means of making a weary old woman and an ill-treated young wife contented, at least. That this was supremely worth while Paul showed her. Paul was healthy, he was decently clothed, his adenoids had been duly removed, and his Catechism pumped in. But no institution could give Paul or any other little boy a back yard, and chips to bring in, cookie cutting and trotting for the mail, a Grammar and an Aunt Mollie. Tony and Minny and Hume and Bud had always had these things.

"Dear Lord, the poor babies that haven't!" thought Mollie on a shuddering breath, when she came to this point in her reflections. And that night—it was Paul's seventh night under her roof—for the first time in six years, she prayed that God would spare her for Grammar and the children, and keep them all safe in their paths of pleasantness and peace.

"Perhaps I am reaching out for something that I never will have again," mused Mollie. "Perhaps Anthony was just himself, and no other—no other husband could ever mean so much!"

And she thought of Lawrence Rossiter. She had been obliged to think about him a great deal of late. He had told her once that he was one of the men who will not take no for an answer, and he had not taken it. Mollie found it difficult to regard Lawrence and his suit seriously; she felt in the matter unexpected impulses toward girlish flippancy and girlish airs. She did not quite like herself when the dashing, handsome, persistent man was beside her. What did he want her for? she would ask in half-petulant surprise. What would her life be, in a strange city, as the wife of an almost strange man? Certainly her modest three hundred a month—for when the young McKays' board was subtracted it was only that—was not a tempting bait for so successful a man? But, Mollie wondered honestly, could a brown-skinned woman of thirty-eight be the real attraction?

She did not love him of course. He did not expect her to feel for him what she could never feel for anyone but Anthony. But she would be a married woman again, there would be companionship, there would be the blessed plural again in life. She had been so lonely, and the years had been so long.

Grammar was the problem. For Lucy, after all, was not Mollie's responsibility, and the three boys were old enough for boarding school. Minny, of course, would stay with her mother. . . .

"But it's too silly, my planning this way!" Mollie would interrupt herself with a smile. "I'm a fool, and he's no more in love with me than—well, than I am with him! He—he hasn't got in his whole body as much love and tenderness—and gentleness—and goodness—as Anthony had in his dear old clever right hand!"

And perhaps she would surprise herself by bursting into tears.

After all, she reasoned half impatiently, what was to be gained by any change? She had a full life and a most interesting one, here. To become a good man's wife might indeed be a promotion for some lonely girl, but she, Mollie, was a woman—why, just to belong to her and to share her children's privileges had seemed heaven itself to the little Mouse.

"Lucy 'n me's been tellin' you all this for two years," Grammar said placidly, when Mollie, in a confidential mood most unusual with her, tried to express herself to the old woman. "There ain't a woman breathin' any luckier than you—be shoo she may. You got Anthony's memory——"

"I know I have!" Mollie said quickly.

"And you got Anthony's children! You got plenty and runnin' over to live on, even payin' ten cents for a cauliflower and raisin' no more than half your greens——"

"I know it, Grammar!" Mollie's face burned. "But—but it is certainly odd, and it makes one feel—feel young again," she stammered, "to have a man—and he is a prosperous man, too—to have him . . . And it isn't as if I was a rich woman. . . ."

"Maybe there's oil in them lands of yours, upriver, as there was in the Widder Wilson's," Grammar suggested at random.

"Oh well, if you're going to be ridiculous!" And Mollie left the kitchen haughtily. But the disquieting doubt persisted—was strengthened, indeed, despite her air of injured assurance.

On the eighth day of his visit Paul, climbing cautiously into a pantry window under Tony's whispered directions from the geranium bed, stepped firmly if gently into a pan of setting milk. The splash that followed the little boy's agitated jump to the floor affected a sheet of hot gingerbread and seven clean dish towels, and a pyramid of tins clattered after him.

The uproar brought everybody on the place to the scene, Mollie leading. They found a Paul with terrified eyes, as white as the plaster wall against which he was backing blindly. Seeing Mollie, he burst into frightened tears. She gave Lucy and Grammar and the gathering children a look full of compunction and knelt down beside Paul.

"Why, Mouse—Mouse—Mouse," she said tenderly, in a voice that the others had never heard before. "You mustn't be so silly! I'm not angry at you, darling. I'm not going to punish you—it was an accident, that was all!"

Paul dug his wet face into her crisp gingham. He was shaking with sobs, choking with fear. For a long time it was impossible to quiet him. Mollie carried him to the shady side porch and sat down with him in her lap. She banished the audience with a glance, and for a while of silence kept her arms about the dusty little body, and felt the heavy droop of the little rough head against her shoulder.

"Listen, Mouse," she said when the heaving heart so close to her own was quiet, and the tear-stained little face had been wiped dry, "you mustn't be afraid of me. You've had too much scolding and punishing in your life, you poor little scrap. I'll *never* punish you, Paul, when you come to visit us. My darling, do you think I could be angry at a poor little scrap of a child that hasn't got any mother, nor any home of his own? You've seen me punish Tony, and I sent all three boys to bed without their supper last night, but that doesn't mean *you*. Don't ever, ever, ever let me see you so frightened again!"

She had told him that she wanted Mrs Younger to let him come to them soon again, for another visit, and Paul had nodded, even though he had feared in his secret heart that this dream of bliss might not be. The matron had telephoned every day to know when the child was coming back to the Shelter, and Paul knew what the phrases "discipline of the institution" and "upsetting the child's mind" meant to her.

Now Mollie, sitting in the peace and silence of the porch, with the morning sunshine flickering through the leaves and falling gently on the worn old sunken flooring and the big pan of greenings and the benches where the children had most of their summer meals, began to think of something new. She pondered and reasoned it in her quick mind for only a few moments before she said:

"Your mother is dead, Paul?"

"An' my daddy too," Paul said, by heart, contentedly, from his refuge.

"Then somebody *could* adopt you, Mouse?"

"If they wanted to," Paul agreed.

"Mouse," said Mollie, "don't set your little heart on it, but I am going to ask them—mind, they may not, now!—I am going to ask them if you may not come here to me, to be one of my boys."

Paul got down from her lap, and Mollie's heart contracted with pain at the sight of the anxious, incredulous little face that questioned her own. For a full half minute they looked silently at each other. Then the child said, trembling with eagerness:

"I would try to be very good, for you! And I would bring in wood and sweep the yard for the kids—every day I would! And I'd do anything you *ever* ast me to—even if it was sumpthin' nobody else would do!"

Mollie laughed rather shakily as she kissed him.

"But you won't set your heart on it, Mouse? There are rules and regulations about these things."

Bud called him, and, full of his great news, he fled. Mollie, looking after him, felt a sudden qualm of doubt. What about Lawrence? Wasn't it enough that he was undaunted by the prospect of two children, without her risking the introduction of a third? Well, perhaps what Lawrence thought was of no consequence. Yet sometimes she felt as if a current as firm and resistless as that of the near-by river was bearing her toward this man and all that his coming into her life implied.

[375]

Paul prayed that night that he would never risk Aunt Mollie's anger again. But it was only the next day that another unpleasant episode occurred. He could not feel that he was exactly naughty in this connection, but he knew Aunt Mollie was displeased with him, and his heart sank correspondingly.

They were all in the front garden, making one of their spasmodic efforts to beautify it, raking, burning, digging and sweeping busily. It was the first day of June, balmy and green, cool in the shade, but so hot in the sun that the children panted and glowed with the heat and cast shabby sweaters and hats behind them as they worked. Grammar's chair had been brought out beside the lilacs, and Lucy, who was picking chickens, occupied the lowest porch step.

Presently Lawrence Rossiter stopped his phaeton at the gate, and Mollie, unpinning her turned-up skirt, leaned her rake against the fence and went out to talk with him. She invited him to join their labors, since he apparently had nothing else to do, but Lawrence smilingly declined and asked her instead to come and drive with him; he was looking up some securities, and she was only wasting her time with these children.

However, Mollie could not go, and she had come back into the garden, wondering a little just what his business was anyway, and what "looking up securities" meant, when Paul was found to be white and trembling and close to tears. The stern need of discovering who had been "mean" to the Mouse immediately engrossed her.

Paul, recovering his equilibrium rapidly, explained that he thought maybe Mr Rossiter had come to take him "back there."

Mollie sat down on an upturned hydrangea tub and questioned him in surprise.

"Back *where*?"

"To—to Mrs Smith's," said Paul in a whisper.

"You mean that villainous place where you were before you came to the Shelter?" Mollie questioned. "The place the police closed in Manville? But what—what has this gentleman, Mr Lawrence, to do with that?"

"He was one of the d'rectors," Paul said readily.

Mollie eyed him a moment in silence. He knew, in his sick little heart, that somehow he had displeased his goddess.

"*Who* was?"

"Mr Rossiter was."

"Oh, was he?" Mollie questioned. The Smith scandal had been duly aired in a virtuous press. But she did not remember his name in it, perhaps because she had not known it then. Of course a man might be a director and still not know that they had chanced to place an unscrupulous and half-crazy woman in charge of an orphanage. . . .

Still, the directors should know. Who else could stand between the children and abuse? Of course Lawrence was a bachelor, had perhaps been drawn casually into the directorship. For that particular institution

[376]

had had several of the prominent people of the neighboring town of Manville upon its directorate, and a man who, like Lawrence, was both socially and politically ambitious, might be glad to be included among them.

Still, the directors should know. Mollie looked beyond Grammar, knitting peacefully under the lilacs, and into the hideous memory of those newspaper revelations. Babyhood crying with fear; little stammered explanations met with a whip; little bodies wet and neglected; little appetites gnawing and fainting and gnawing again in locked rooms. Of course he hadn't known that. . . .

Still, he *should* have known. Mollie turned troubled eyes to the disgraceful yet happy garden, and she shuddered as if the warm sunshine shook her after the passing of a heavy cloud.

"You are sure this was the same man, Mouse?" she asked. Paul was very sure.

"Because Joe Sullivan talked to him," he said.

"And who is Joe Sullivan, dear?"

"He was a big boy that used to go with Mr Rossiter to hold his horse," Paul explained, "when Mr Rossiter was driving up the river. And Joe told him about it—that they were mean to us kids—and asked him if he would tell his aunt. Because Joe couldn't write to his aunt—they wouldn't let him."

"And what was he doin' up the river?" Grammar asked suddenly.

"He was buying a lady's farm, but after, Joe said, they made him give it back to her, because her husband was dead, and she didn't know about oil wells," Paul said in his innocent voice as he leaned against her chair.

"H'm!" Mollie said, facing Grammar bravely, as was her wont, but with reddened cheeks. "And did he come to see you after Joe Sullivan talked to him?" she asked.

"No," said Paul simply.

"Not when Joe told him you were all unhappy?"

"I don't think he said we all were," Paul said scrupulously. "But he told about Rosy Mason and the Butterick baby."

"The Mason Girl!" "The Butterick Infant!" Mollie knew their names by heart. She had seen them many a time, in glaring print. And already she vaguely realized that a shadow had indeed passed over the garden and out of her life forever.

It made her feel oddly shocked and shaken, even a little ill. She put Paul gently aside and went slowly into the house, and all the rest of that day, and for the few moments that they saw her on the next, she was strangely silent; "mad," Paul decided uncomfortably. She went away from the house very early in the car and came home very late, and she spoke to nobody except Grammar.

But on the following morning she called Paul to her and said:

"This is the day you were to go back, Mouse. I'm going over to Manville now to see a lawyer, and this afternoon I shall be at the Shelter, to wait until the directors' meeting is over, and when I come home I shall know—about you. But you mustn't hope too much, dear!"

"No," said little Eight sturdily, looking straight into her eyes. "I'm not!"

"Well, I am," she said with a shaken laugh, "and if they disappoint us this time we will try again, won't we?"

"Yes, please," said Paul. But she knew he did not believe it. "You'll be back around—around four, I should think!" he hazarded.

"Not so early, for I have to go see a very, very sick lady after the meeting," Molly said, wondering what there was about this child that gave everything he said so oddly sweet a flavor. And as she drove away in her mud-splashed car she reflected wonderingly upon a civilization that found scores, and hundreds, of other objects worthier of time and money than the preservation of a Paul.

For a while after she left he was very silent. His little fortunes hung in the balance, and although the warm, silent spring day might proceed placidly in spite of them he could not quite keep pace with it. He sat on the step for a full half-hour, dreaming and hoping, in his little-boy way, and when Lucy came out with a basket and told him that the children were down on the old pier, fishing, he merely followed her silently down to the three twisted cherry trees and helped her gather the first cherries. He helped her set the table, too, and when luncheon was over he swept the porch and filled the salt and pepper shakers.

Two o'clock. Paul looked at the clock; he thought it had stopped. He asked Lucy if she thought Aunt Mollie would like to have the inkwell cleaned. Grammar immediately put her hand on his forehead and said she thought the boy had a walking fever. She settled him beside her on the shady porch with a box of fascinating double photographs and a stereoscope, and the crackle of her starched and lacy afternoon apron and the sleepy sputtering of hens fluffing in the cool dust of the yard were forever mingled in his memory with the colored views of Yokohama and Benares.

But after a while Minny came in crying, with a nosebleed. The boys had refused to play with her unless she would let them pull her loose tooth, and had pushed her down. She and Paul were immediately given two saucer pies and were amicably looking at pictures when the repentant boys came after them both. They had rigged a square platform to the high branches of the maples, a platform that moved just above the ground, on four long ropes, with a thrilling and rotary motion.

For an hour, or until one of the ropes broke, catapulting Bud violently against the side of the barn, the children enjoyed the swing. During the few moments when they feared that Bud was dead their shrieking and laughing was silenced, but immediately afterward they recovered their gaiety of spirit and made a fire in the mud oven and baked apples and potatoes.

Large quantities of these, half cooked, and eaten with almost equal amounts of salt and cinders, made them all feel ill, and Lucy at four o'clock reported to Grammar that they were all lying on the riverbank, telling stories. Lucy went into the village with the grocer, to be sure of getting her spices for the cherries next week, and Grammar fell peacefully asleep in her chair.

It was some minutes after old man Fleming had made his kindly gift that the children dragged themselves lazily up from the riverside to look at the half barrel of tar.

"What do you s'pose he gave us this for?" Anthony asked suspiciously, looking down into the turbid depths of the heavy mixture.

"His daughter is going to get married, and maybe he doesn't need it any more," Hume offered lucidly, and after a grave exchange of glances the children accepted this as the simplest solution. Minny advanced an exploring finger to the black surface and drew it slowly up with a fascinating little tent of tar drawing after it. The boys began to jump about, dropping lumps of the soft black substance from hand to hand.

"Golly, she sticks!" Anthony laughed excitedly.

"Jiminy, you bet your life she sticks!" Hume shouted.

"Gosh, she certainly is sticky, all right!" Paul echoed, almost fearful of the adhesive black that caught and caught at his stubby little fingers. And for some five minutes the quintette repeated these words delightedly, with infinite variations, as they danced about with the tar.

When Minny first dropped her sagging lump on the weather-whitened boards of old man Fleming's pier there was immediate consternation, and the place was not only scraped with a board, but stamped and rubbed with ten sturdy boots. But later the children became less scrupulous, and a passing hen was deliberately decorated with a saddle of tar, to her own scandalized excitement, and Lucy found tar that night on the back "stoop," and indeed for several days was continually making unwelcome discoveries of the same nature.

The original inspiration, to tar the side path from the gate to the porch, was abandoned almost immediately. The tar might indeed be spooned onto the gravel, but smoothing it, even with the kitchen broom, was out of the question, and the children even thought it wise to remove themselves and their tar barrel far from the scene of the experiment and to appear to have no interest in, nor connection with, the unseemly blotch upon the path.

They went out near the hay barn and sat down in a rough circle and eyed their treasure thoughtfully.

"It's darn lucky," said Bud McKay seriously, "that there isn't anybody in this village who's been stealing something, or murdering somebody, or something!"

"Why, Bud?" piped Minny, who did not have sufficient self-control to pretend, as the boys instantly did, that this sentence was comprehensible.

"Why?" echoed Bud, with a truculent look about, and in a manly tone, "because they'd find themselves in trouble, that's why!"

"If they stole this *tar*, they would," Anthony, who was six months younger than Bud, hazarded warningly, with an uncertain look at his senior.

"If they stole *anything*," Bud affirmed, enjoying his cryptic utterances to the full. Minny eyed him curiously, like a robin, with her little bobbed head cocked inquisitively, but was only vaguely aware that she was missing the point. The boys exchanged furtive glances for a full minute before Bud said, "They'd get tarred and feathered, that's what *they'd* get!"

This tremendous thought pleased everyone, and the children nodded significantly at one another. Tarring and feathering . . . !

"What would they feather with, Bud?" Anthony asked with a glance at a passing white minorca. The minorca, suspecting the worst, skittered out of sight, and Anthony, picking up a dropped white feather, touched his finger to the tar and stuck the feather thereon, eying it meanwhile in a thoughtful and abstracted manner.

"Feathers!" Bud said. "Like what's in those old pillers up attic," he added thoughtfully.

Then there was a moment of ruminative silence. Paul, who had picked up another feather, stuck and freed it on every finger of his left hand in turn. His small body, gaining in rotundity daily, leaned comfortably against an empty and upturned trough. Minny, her legs dangling, sat on the trough, Hume beside her. The older boys sat on the chopping block, their knees almost as high as their shoulders, the tar barrel between them. A perfect spring afternoon was descending graciously upon the old Peacock place, shadows were lengthening upon the hammered earth, and great shafts of sunlight piercing the thick new green of the maples and willows. Grammar, pausing at the window of her warm bedroom over the kitchen, looked out and thought the children singularly well behaved. Lucy, hustling into supper preparations, with the grocery boy's pleasantries echoing in her ears, also glanced at them and saw nothing irregular in progress. Presently she heard Anthony going up the attic stairs and asked what they were playing.

"Bud says we can play hoss thieves," said Anthony after a pause. Lucy said nothing more, and the conversation closed.

It was a gracious and gentle Mrs Hallowell who picked Mollie up, when the second tire burst, and offered to take her home. Mollie was most appreciative. Six o'clock, and she had been gone all day from Grammar and the children; she had been at the Shelter, and she had seen old Mrs Ebright. . . .

She was chattering cheerfully, if wearily, when the shining Hallowell car turned into her yard, and it was in her hostess's face, to which her own was turned, that she first read the warning of something amiss. She turned, with a familiar sinking of the heart, to identify—who was it? Pitch, had they gotten? Lumps of it in—which child's hair? And their faces! Good heavens, and the porch . . . and the dogs . . . !

"Thee has never heard in thy life such a dressing down as she gave those dear unfortunate children!" said Rachael Hallowell to her husband that night.

Indeed, Mollie completely forgot her and forgot everything else in the world except the five wrongdoers before her.

"Bud McKay! And Anthony Peacock—you great big strapping boys, that certainly ought to know better!" Mollie began with deadly aim, as she slapped and shook and scraped and wiped angrily. "The very idea . . . when your mother is away. Don't touch me with those hands, Hume. You naughty, *naughty* disgraceful children—all over Lucy's porch! Now stop whining, Minny, you're quite old enough. Throw that away, Hume—every bit of it—and, Tony, you go get that pail of kerosene out of the barn. You stay where you are, Bud! Do as I *tell* you, Tony! Give me those hands, Paul. I don't know *what* I'm going to do, Anthony, but you may be very sure that you won't hear the end of *this* business for many and many a day. Now put your dress on, Minny, you naughty girl, and Paul—you're done!—you pick up your shoes, and you two streak it right *straight* upstairs and get right *straight* into bed. . . . Put your foot into this bucket, Hume! Of all the disgusting—— Go along, Paul and Minny, and don't let me hear another word out of you!"

"Thee would have wanted to cry—to see them creep off like little mutes," said Rachael Hallowell, finishing her description. "They were frightened to death, poor children, and no wonder!"

Yet Rachael Hallowell had not seen the radiant face that one of the children wore as he went upstairs, nor the ecstasy that shone in his eyes and swelled in his heart. Her sixty years were not as shrewd as his eight, and she could not know that in the familiar motherly scolding he read aright the news of his acceptance; that, supperless and smelling of kerosene, and in disgrace, Paul Peacock could have sung for very joy as he climbed untimely into bed and lay awaiting the penitential bread and water that marked him no longer a child apart, but one of the dear unfortunate children in the old Peacock house.

The Mother of Angela Hogan

When Angela Hogan left the Hamilton Home School for Girls, on her eighteenth birthday, Miss Schofield and Mrs Allenby told each other that in one case, at least, their careful training had borne good fruit. To Angela, at eighteen, after thirteen years of their supervision, they felt they could point with pride. Angela had gentle manners, she played the piano, she wrote a clean legible hand, she had had domestic science and stenography courses, and she had a nice little nest egg in the bank to tide her over the time of looking for employment. Altogether Angela was far better equipped than were most of the Hamilton girls for the struggle of life.

And yet their mutual reassurances as to the launching of Angela somehow lacked a genuine ring, even as their quavering good-bys to her lacked spontaneity. Angela, considering what a timid, silent little creature she usually was, had made them uneasy at the very last moment with a very fusillade of interrogation. She had delivered her questions alternately to Mrs Allenby and Miss Schofield; but they could not answer her of course; she had seen that. She had become silent as abruptly as she had turned vocal, her burning thin little face suddenly white again, her manner once more the timid, quiet manner they knew.

This little final scene, however, did not really flaw the fineness of Angela's record at the Hamilton, nor the confidence of her protectors in her future. She was one more girl saved from the unfortunate circumstances of her birth; she would always be a credit to them and to herself.

Angela, a little dazed with freedom and with the strangeness of being alone in the streets just at the hour when the girls were getting ready to file in for lunch, walked along in autumn heat for some time without any consciousness except a feeling of profound relief. Ah, it was good, if a little terrifying, to get out of the Hamilton once and for all, after a long thirteen years! Thirteen winters, summers, autumns, springs in that one atmosphere of polished halls and mutton stew and chowder; those dormitory cubicles scented with girls' rubbers and serge skirts, those lavatories smelling of carbolic acid!

Angela breathed deep of the sweetness of liberty. Hansen had taken her bag to Mrs White's; she was unburdened. The girls were eating beans and stewed dried apricots now; this was Thursday. She was done with beans and stewed dried apricots forever! She went into a Childs restaurant and sat timidly silent for a long time at a long marble-topped slab. After a while she ordered fried soft-shell crabs, hot butter cakes, coffee, ice cream. It was all delicious; nothing tasted in the least as all meals tasted at the Hamilton.

Courage and confidence returned with the food, and Angela planned as she ate. She was not going to live at Mrs White's, she knew that. Girls from the Hamilton always went to Mrs White's; there would be girls she knew there; girls who knew that Angela had been a Hamilton girl. She must get her bag away from Mrs White's at once, without arousing suspicion. Afterward she could find a safe place to live; one could always go to the Sisters and ask their advice. But not Mrs White's, with everyone saying that she had been an orphan, a girl whose "home influences had been unfortunate"; no, she couldn't stand that! Much better to make a fresh start somewhere else, where nobody knew anything.

Not that the girls knew anything specific of Angela's long-dead mother and father; for that matter, Angela knew almost nothing herself. But the girls who were placed by generous patronesses in the Hamilton Home usually had one history. Without the generous patronesses they would have been city foundlings. Owing to the wonderful founder and supporters of the Hamilton, they were given a better chance than that; they were educated in manners and voices as well as in book lessons, they were nicely dressed, they went up to the Hannah Hamilton Camp in the Adirondacks every summer. And at eighteen each girl was given one hundred dollars, found a good position and placed with Mrs White.

It was a wonderful charity, and Angela hoped that she was duly grateful for it. But burning in her heart were resentment and shame; she had been resentful and ashamed for many years now, ever since she had been old enough to know just the type of work the Hamilton did. She could not shake that shame and that resentment fast enough from her skirts. She must cut away the past. And perhaps after years she might forget it, might come to believe that her mother had been only one more good woman in a world of good women, an honored wife, a happy mother.

"Who was my mother? What do you know about her? Why did I come here?" she had passionately demanded of Mrs Allenby and Miss Schofield. They had tried to pacify her, to put her off. They had said, after swift oblique glances at each other, that they did not know. They did not know anything about any of the girls. They never did. No, there were no letters, no documents of any kind, except of course—except of course, in Angela's case, that nice bank account that meant that she could buy herself a lovely home someday.

Angela's face had flushed darkly at the mention of the bank account. Ten thousand dollars! Her mother had never saved that sum, that was clear. Angela was a white-faced, silent little creature, but she was not dull. Even to her unsophistication the neat finish of the amount said something significant; it had been paid by someone to someone. It had originally been written in one check. She hated the thought of it; she never would touch it!

Strolling along after her luncheon, she bought herself a wet pink rose in a spray of asparagus fern, a bag of chocolate caramels and a movie magazine. She sat in the shade in the park and read her magazine and watched the children and the nurses. At four she went in a taxi to Mrs. White's.

She stopped the taxi three doors away and looked at the White house. It impressed her unfavorably. Brownstone and shabby and one of a long row, it might have been a child of the Hamilton itself. Angela asked the taxi man to go and ask for Miss Hogan's bag and say that she was not coming tonight but they could telephone Mrs Allenby about it. Eventually she could, of course, escape from Mrs White, but it would be better to escape now, in the very beginning.

The man came back in two minutes with the familiar bulging bag. Angela could hardly believe her eyes. It was as simple as that, once one was eighteen! Mrs White was out, it seemed; she had probably gone up to the Hamilton to see why Angela was delayed. A colored man had delivered up the bag without question or comment.

Angela stopped at a drugstore to telephone; then she got back into the taxi and gave a Bronx address.

She was tired and nervous and whiter than ever when she reached Mrs Loughborough's kitchen. The heat of the day, the excitement of her adventures—lunch in a restaurant, a ride in a taxi, the capture of the bag—had exhausted her spirit. Angela, coming unannounced into the dim, hot, smelly, cluttered place, was conscious of a great need to cry.

But they soon cured that. Mrs Loughborough opened her great arms to the wanderer; Torey, ironing a white linen dress in the center of the kitchen, was instantly friendly, not to say sisterly.

"Look, Ma," said Torey. "Tom's not home. Hook me out a couple of sheets from the wash there and I'll iron the hems and we'll fix up his bed for Angela. Look, Angela, I've got a date for tonight and Saturday and Sunday, see? But I can break 'em off or else ask Jerry to get hold of another fellow. . . ."

Angela sank into this atmosphere with those ecstatic shudders that beset the freezing who are suddenly restored to warmth and shelter. She could not savor it enough; the loving big capable mother, the beautiful clever daughter who had a fine job, the mismatched plates and shabby chairs, so different from the furnishings of the Hamilton!

Torey had a box of collected savings stamps; she and Kane O'Malley were going out to the office to select a premium. Angela went with them. They saw a movie on the way home and bought a watermelon and ate it in the kitchen. Ma had been to church; sure Angela could go wit' her to siven in the mornin' if she'd get up whin the alar'rm wint off, she assured the guest cordially. It was all intoxicatingly free, it was deliriously exciting, the way the Loughboroughs lived, the things they could do, the things they didn't have to do! Angela, a fish that had at last fought its way to a great stream, swam in it ecstatically.

There was one bad minute. It came when Angela, wiping dishes, had to explain to her hostess for the third time how she happened to come to her.

"I remembered Mamma saying that if ever I needed a friend I was to remember you. But that was when I was only a little girl; Mamma died when I was six. I was at the Hamilton then. Mrs Allenby told me Mamma had died, and let me sit in her room all day and look at her travel books. So today I was afraid that you had moved, but I telephoned old Sister Ligouri, that came to see me twice, and she said to look for Thomas Loughborough in the telephone book, and that was how I knew." Angela went this far and then, trembling a little and lowering her voice, asked quickly: "You knew my mother, didn't you, Mrs Loughborough?"

"Oh, Blissed Mother, tell me what to say to the child!" Ellen Loughborough prayed. Aloud she said: "I did that. But not so well. Because she lived down on Eighth—or was it Christopher Street—an' then they wint to Erie to live, an' my children were little. . . ."

Angela was looking at her keenly. How much does she know? each woman was asking herself.

"Did you know my father, Timothy Hogan?"

"No, that I didn't, dear'r. He died—God rist him—befoor I knew yure mamma." Mrs Loughborough rubbed the bone of her nose. "I knew some of the other Hogans, Joe and Robert," she said. "But that was later."

"Later than what?" Angela demanded.

"After yure mamma died, dear'r." Mrs Loughborough was floundering in deep water, but her quietly reminiscent tone gave no hint of it. "What you've told me today about the place they put ye," she went on, "makes me think I cud well have gone up to see ye once or twice! But the truth is ye wint out of me mind entirely. I knew poor Kitty Hogan was dead, an' I hear'rd they got ye into a very grand place, an' that was the whole of it! Didn't nobody iver go to see ye, or take ye a dolly or whativer?"

"Never!" Angela answered. But the tears that suddenly splashed on the dish she was drying were not self-pitying tears. They were tears of despair. Once again she had crept up to this subject of her mother; once again she had been evaded, put off. "Why did you call her 'poor Kitty'?" she wanted to ask. She did not dare.

For a long time she made no mention of her mother again. She fitted into the Loughborough clan quietly, as a drop sinks into a stream, and within a few weeks they were taking Angela as much for granted as they did themselves; Torey, Tom, Ellen and Paul and their children, Will and Ag and theirs, George and Eileen and their little boy.

To the Loughboroughs, at first, she was merely a homeless little mouse who paid Ma five dollars a week, worked in the Y.L.I. and couldn't get enough of churchgoing. "One of these days she'll joomp off an' be a nun on ye!" Katty Fealey, noisily drinking tea on a Thursday afternoon, predicted, and Mrs Loughborough agreed to that solution readily enough. No girl could do better than that, if only the creatures had the sense to see it.

But certain odd developments not exactly encouraging to this theory presently took place in the case of Angela Hogan. For one thing, when she got a little weight and color, she quite suddenly turned out to be a beauty, in a quiet way. Her eyes were deep Irish blue, her mouth had an irregular and indeed an irresistible charm, and the rich mahogany of her hair curled against temples that were as white as Carrara marble, and threaded with the same blue veins. There was a faint hoarseness to her voice that was infinitely engaging, and she had a confiding little trick of touching for a second with her own small hand the hand of anyone with whom she was talking that appeared to be entirely free of coquetry and that yet was devastating to the male heart. Before anyone fully appreciated what was going on Con O'Shea was the avowed slave of little Angela Hogan, who lived at Loughboroughs'.

She did not entirely live there now, for Tom had come back to his room, and Angela was lodging two flights upstairs, with Mrs Con Loughborough, Torey and Tom's Aunt Lizzy. But Aunt Lizzy had her meals in the big twin building next door with her married children, so Angela had her breakfast and dinner with the Loughboroughs and went to church in the evenings with Ma. She never wanted to be out of Ma's sight at any second when it was possible to be near her; her starved little heart clung to Ma; the others in the group were only shadows.

Even to Con O'Shea she paid but casual attention. The richest, the most eligible man known to the Loughboroughs, or to anyone else in the neighborhood, Con was handsome too. He was the only son of rich Mrs Connors O'Shea; he had once been a little wild. But it was funny to see him come back into line and get up for early Mass and attend Benediction when he had a chance of seeing Angela. As for escorting her, that was out of the question; she never went anywhere with any man. The mere thought struck her new roses from her ivory-smooth cheeks.

"I don't know what you'd want better than Con," Tom Loughborough told her.

"Oh, don't say his name to me!" Angela begged, the tips of her ears coloring scarlet as she bent over the dishpan.

"Why shouldn't I say his name to you?"

"Oh, because I don't ever want to have anything to do with him!"

"What's the matter with Con O'Shea?"

"Nothing, nothing, nothing! Only, if I ever was to fall in love, but I never will—but if I ever *was* to . . ."

A long pause. Tom dragged comfortably on his pipe; Mrs Loughborough put away hot plates.

"Don't tease her, Tom," his mother said.

"I'm not teasin' her. I was just wonderin' what was the matter with Con O'Shea. And what was the rest of that, Angela? If you ever was to fall in love—what, eh?"

"Nothing! I've forgotten what I was going to say," Angela said hastily.

"Why, you know that's a lie," Tom said in his pleasant brotherly way. "You know that's one big lie. And you in a state of grace—I'm surprised at you!"

"Well, if it was a lie I'm sorry for it, but I'm not going to tell you what I was going to say!" Angela, backed up against the sink, red-cheeked, but game, like a cornered child, said unashamedly.

"She's goin' to be a little nun, this one is," Mrs Loughborough said affectionately.

It worried her somewhat to discover, as the weeks went by, that Angela had no intention of becoming a nun. Virginal and shy and holy she might be, but on the only occasion when Mrs Loughborough dared question her about it she was quite definite.

"You that don't like the men at all and 'll niver raise yure eyes to thim, is it wit' the Sisthers ye'll be goin'?" Ellen ventured one night when she and Angela were walking home from Benediction. "Sure, ye're niver happy but ye're in chur'rch, or doin' somethin' for someone——"

"Oh no, I'd never do that!" Angela's soft, hoarse little voice said quickly in the dark street.

"Ye might have a vocation?"

"I haven't. I know it full well. I'd no sooner take my vows than I'd be thinking of men," Angela answered astonishingly. "I'd be longing that somebody'd kiss me or that I'd have the feel of a child in my arms. It'd come over me like a tiger tearing at me," the girl went on simply. "And I'd go the way my mother went!"

Sheer amazement robbed Mrs Loughborough of the power of speech for a full minute. Presently she asked:

"How d'ye mane, the way yure mother wint? D'ye mane ye'd come out of the convent? Yure mother niver was a nun, Angela."

They were going in the house door now; they were climbing the stairs. Angela made no answer.

But when they were in the kitchen, and Mrs Loughborough was sitting panting in a chair at the table, and Angela had given her a cup of water, the girl pursued the subject.

"I'm like that," she said.

"Like what?" the other woman asked uneasily.

"I act the way I do with men because I'm afraid," Angela persisted. "I'm afraid. I'm afraid of myself."

"A good little angel of a ger'rl like you has no call to be that," Mrs Loughborough muttered, distressed.

"So that's why I'll never marry anyone," Angela said.

"Con O'Shea is turnin' into a fine feller," the older woman offered hesitatingly.

"Oh, him!" Angela said scornfully. "There's others I'd have before ever I'd look at him. But I'll never marry a one of them!"

"You were tellin' me you'd like to have a child in yure ar'rms."

Sudden tears were in Angela's eyes.

"Not for me," she said in a whisper. And, turning toward the sink, she had for a moment her back to the room. Suddenly she wheeled and faced her companion.

"D'you know what's almost the last thing I remember of my mother?" she demanded. "It was Easter, and she was working in the candy factory all night on big rush orders, and she came for me to the Hamilton early in the morning and took me to church. And on the way home she said, 'We'll stop and say "Happy Easter" to your father's mother; she doesn't like me, but she'll want to see my little girl in her white dress and her pink hat.' So we went to some place out toward the Concourse, and up in an elevator, and into a room. There were two women there; one was my grandmother—she's dead now, and the Lord has dealt with her—and the other was an aunt or cousin of mine, I think.

"Well, I forget how it started," Angela said, pale and tragic as she recalled it, "but in a minute Mamma was answering back, and the other woman, the younger one, was shoving her toward the door. And Mamma called out something about my father, that he had left his mother and that he hated her. It was then——"

The girl was no longer thinking of her listener. Her voice had sunk to a whisper, her eyes were gazing into space.

"It was then she called Mamma—terrible names," she said. "My grandmother did. She said that my mother was—bad. She said things—about me. She sat in her chair, hammering on the floor with her crutch and shouting, and the other woman went on shoving Mamma out and locked the door.

"We went downstairs, and Mamma showed me Easter eggs in windows, but I was crying, and she was shaking all over. She took me to a movie, and afterward we had ice cream, and then she took me back to the Hamilton. We never talked about it. I never saw her again.

"But I've remembered that. And it makes me feel that I'll never be like the other girls—like Torey and Ag and Eileen. It's inside me, like a curse!"

Her tone rose wildly. She stopped, and was silent. Mrs Loughborough cleared her throat before she said mildly:

"Yure grandmother Hogan was a very violent woman, God rist her. It's thrue that she drove Tim Hogan forth from the house an' there was bad blood betune thim. But what a child rimimbers, Angela, wudden't mane annythin' at all had yure mother but lived to laugh at it wit' ye. If ye brood over it, sure we're doin' the very thing yure mamma wud want ye to stop. There's none of us dares look back at the past an' do that. All we can do is shut the dure on it, an' go on, askin' the Blissed Mother that she'd kape us from makin' the same mistakes over again. Now you say yure prayers," Mrs Loughborough concluded, encouraged to see that her words were having some effect, "an', if ye don't want Con, ask St Joseph to send ye some other good man, an' go yure way like the rist of us, doin' yure bist, an' raisin' the childern. . . ."

Angela's mood seemed softened. She came over to Mrs Loughborough and got into her lap as a child might have done, and cried a little on her shoulder.

But after that the days went on and were weeks, and Christmas came, and there was no change in her. She still trembled away from anything like serious attention from any man; she still liked best to go to church in the evenings or to disappear early with a book. Con O'Shea took his dismissal hard; after all, girls did not refuse men as rich as Con O'Shea lightly, but Angela never weakened. There were other nibbles, one or two from highly eligible young men; none seemed to make the slightest impression.

Angela moved about the Loughborough kitchen like a transforming genie. The sink boards shone white; the dish towels twisted in ivory purity on the pulley line outside the window. Tom formed a habit of smoking his evening pipe there instead of going around the corner to Pete's, and he and Angela had long talks.

"I've known girls like you before, afraid to get married," Tom told her. "They think it'll scare them to have a man always about. But take a chance—take a *chance!* Marry the next guy that asks you, and you'll be so busy keeping his shirts clean and rinsing bottles that you'll forget it."

"Maybe someday I'll try it," Angela said lightly, but trembling, as she filled the salt shaker from the red box.

"No, but what are you afraid of? Don't you want him to kiss you? Don't you want your husband to love you? You're a queer one!"

"I'm happy as I am," Angela said.

"Yes, you are! No girl's happy without a man running her!"

"That's not true."

"You'll never have that nice family of little boys and girls the way you're goin' on," Tom said. "Oh, you make me tired!" he added under his breath as Angela walked into the bedroom without replying. When she came out she had on her small brown hat and the big brown coat with the fur collar. "What is it tonight?" he asked half impatiently.

"Vespers. Advent," his mother, following Angela, answered briefly.

"Oh, for the Lord's sake!"

"Exactly. For nothing else," Torey said neatly. Torey had been getting dressed to go to a movie with Lew McGill. She now telephoned the long-suffering Jerry Whalen that she wouldn't go out with him tonight after all, as she had forgotten a most important engagement that she couldn't possibly get out of.

"How about you and me goin' to the movies with Lew and Torey?" Tom said unwillingly, and almost ungraciously, to Angela.

"Oh, I'm going to church with Ma, Tom."

"I know you are, I know you are!" he said gruffly. "But I said, how about goin' to the movies?"

"Instead, you mean?"

"Well, what d'you think? You can't take the movies to church."

Angela, looking somewhat frightened at his tone, slipped out of the kitchen with no answer. Torey narrowed her mischievous blue eyes at her brother's gloomy and preoccupied face, and laughed.

Two weeks later, when the New Year was proceeding upon its icebound, gray-shadowed way, Mrs Loughborough discussed the matter of Angela with Mrs Whalen over a cup of tea. The day was overcast and bitter cold; occasional flakes of snow fluttered down the gloom of the airshaft outside the bedrooms; through the kitchen windows the backs of tenements could be seen lightly powdered with it. The lights of the theater were lighted early; for eight hours the great signs would fluctuate punctually up and down, up and down, against the dreary shadows of the night.

"I wint to see thim at the Hamilton," Mrs Loughborough confessed suddenly. Mrs Whalen's little monkey face wrinkled into dubiousness.

"About Angela," she stated simply.

"I can't make her out," the other woman said in affirmation. "I thought likely they'd give me a tip."

She filled her guest's cup; her own cup. Their worn hands reached automatically for the cream, the sugar. Mrs Loughborough held the blue bowl comfortably in the palm of her left hand while she spooned forth the white sweetness. Mrs Whalen dipped her teaspoon into the cream and tasted it critically. Cream had a way of souring in these hot kitchens.

All up and down the big tenement, and in the twin house next door, and in all the houses round about for blocks and blocks, kitchens were warm and hospitable in the late afternoon. Even the children, coming in with wet, frozen, red hands and apple-red cheeks, had their heartening mugs of milk and sugar and weak tea. Lights shone out on clotheslines and fire escapes and vegetable boxes powdered with snow; the outer world was at its coldest and most forbidding season. But in the kitchens there was warmth and noise and the odors of tea and bread and butter.

"What 'd they tell ye about her?" Mrs Whalen presently asked.

"Oh, they talked a lot," the other woman said with a sigh.

"They wud."

"They had char'rts an' lists on her in a box."

"They'd not get far wit'out their catalogues, whativer *thim* are," opined Mrs Whalen.

"I tolt thim she'd been here six mont's—but sure they knew that annyways; she'd wrote thim that. An' I tolt thim that she was a fine ger'rl wit' a good hear'rt on her, an' that she was grand wit' the childern. But I ast thim did they know why she'd be so agin the boys that she'd niver look at a good lad like Con O'Shea, that cud dress her in silk the longest day she'd live!"

"The dear'r knows!" Mrs Whalen muttered, shaking her head.

"An' I wanted to know did she know about her own mother," Mrs Loughborough added with a cautious look about the kitchen. The other woman also lowered her tone.

"Kitty," she said simply.

"Kitty. I didn't know did she know about her or didn't she."

"Did they tell ye?"

"They tolt me nothin'. They tolt me no more than that they cudden't tell me annythin'. 'Tis a rule of the home. They know nothin' of anny of the ger'rls, they've no records; they'll give ye no satisfaction. ' 'Tis a protection for thim,' she told me. 'Does the ger'rl know what her mamma done?' I ast her. 'I cudden't tell ye annythin', I don't know meself,' this Mrs Allenby said. She's a big fleshy woman wit' eyeglasses that hooks up against her on a spring. 'I cudden't tell ye meself,' she says. 'I don't know.' 'Does the ger'rl know?' I ast her again. 'Well, that I cudden't tell ye,' she says. 'But I'll show ye the new liberry wing we've built on,' she says. 'I've come to see no liberries,' I says. Wit' that she tolt me that she thought the ger'rl was conditioned."

Mrs Whalen's eyes came up with a startled look.

"Angela!" she exclaimed. "Ye'd wondher," she added after a moment's stupefaction, and in rising indignation, "that they'd say that sort of thing agin a decent ger'rl that never done a thing wrong, but runs off to church the minute she gets the dishes done!"

"They don't mane that," Mrs Loughborough said, not very sure herself what they did mean.

"What else wud it be?"

"They said it meant that the child had been—well, ye cud call it scared-like, whin she was yoong," Mrs Loughborough explained.

"Ye don't scare thim into that condition," Mrs Whalen objected firmly. "An', if they'd ask me, it's a mane thing to say of anny ger'rl, much less this wan!"

"All they mane is that she don't like men because whin she was a baby someone said somethin' or done somethin' that put her off thim," Mrs Loughborough persisted.

"Is that all it is?" Mrs Whalen's little walnut of a face wrinkled in concentrated thought. "Well, that's nothin'," she said dubiously.

"They tuk it very serious. 'Angela,' she says to me, 'may have her'rd somethin' whin she was on'y a baby. But it's there in her hear'rt, an' it 'll niver come out,' she says."

"Thin you mark my wor'rds, woman dear'r, she knows about Kitty," Mrs Whalen said with a nod of conviction.

Mrs Loughborough's great bosom moved on a deep sigh.

"It's that," she said; "but who'd tell her, Jule?"

"She'd guess it."

"She cudden't guess all Kitty done. There was no one knew it but you an' me an' a few that's dead. Poor Kitty!

"L'avin' Tim for a merrid man, runnin' out in the night, an' after he threw her off goin' into consumption," Mrs Loughborough mused, scarcely above a murmur. "D'ye mind how sad she looked wit' her hair in braids on the piller whin me an' you wint down to see her in Bellevue? There was always good in Kitty; she had a kind little hear'rt on her. Poor ger'rl!"

"It was bad look for her that the divil she run off wit' had money," Mrs Whalen said thoughtfully. "If he'd been a poor man there 'd have been no bank account for the child, an' she'd have gone to the Sisthers, where they wudden't have talked about 'conditions' for a fine clean ger'rl who niver looks twice at anny boy, be he rich or poor!"

"It's that tin thousand in the bank worries her," Mrs Loughborough said. "She don't know where it come from, an' it frets her. An' then there was her father's mother, old Mrs Hogan, that was very cross-grained an' crabbed. Angela don't talk to me or to annyone," she went on. "But this she did say whin we were talkin' the other day. 'Ma,' she says, 'me father's mother cur'rst me mother an' me an' drove us out of the house, an',' she says, 'I'll niver take that cur'rse on to anny child of mine!'"

"The dear'r Lor'rd bliss us!" Mrs Whalen said on a tut-tutting whisper. "An' Tom wants her too. Well, she'd bring ye some more fine grandchildren, Ellen. She's a good ger'rl."

"Tom!" Mrs Loughborough said from the stove in the tone of one awakening. She stood still, feeling the sword in her heart. Tom!

After a while Mrs Whalen bundled herself into an old coat trimmed with mangy bands of black fur, settled her widow's bonnet, pulled on cotton gloves neatly darned at the finger tips, and went her way. She left

Mrs Loughborough apparently quite the same as usual, beginning preparations for the children's dinner.

But Mrs Loughborough moved as one in a haze. The solid earth was rocking under her feet. It was all clear to her now. Tom, her magnificent, tumble-headed, steady, wonderful boy was in love with Angela Hogan.

He had liked girls before; he had been dashing and confident and teasing and witty and dominant with girls before. But this time it was all different. Fool, fool that she had been not to see it! Tom. Tom in love, and perhaps going to be married, and give that great heart of his to another woman. It made his mother feel strange and chilled and old; she was trembling a little when Tom came in and touched her warm soft cheek with his hard cold one and went on into the bedroom to wash his hands and comb his hair.

She studied him furtively when he came back. Tom had only been cleaning up in this scrupulous way for a few weeks. He had never done that sort of thing before; that was a sign of course. His hair wet and brushed, his big hands scrubbed; he even went so far as to clean his nails. Very handsome he looked when he came out and sat down with the evening paper to wait for the girls and for his supper. Her heart yearned over him; she wanted him to be small, mischievous Tom in the ragged cords and the red sweater again, begging to go down into the dangerous street for play in the late afternoon.

"Aw, lemme go down, Ma, will you, Ma, will you? Go on, Ma. Lemme go down with Ray and Johnny, will you, Ma?"

"What are you thinkin' about, Ma? You look queer," Tom said. She came back to the kitchen with a start, back to realities. He was a man now; he was twenty-four years old. And he was in love.

Torey came in, jaded and pale; Torey dropped into the nearest chair, piled overshoes, coat, gloves, hat, bag together on the floor under the kitchen table, rested her elbows on the cloth and covered her face with her hands.

"I'm dead!" she said briefly as she did nearly every night.

"Go to bed right after supper," her mother said, also for the thousandth time.

"I've got a date," Torey, completing the usual exchange, answered wearily. She seized a part of the paper; the meal was all ready to be served fifteen minutes later, when Angela came in.

Ellen Loughborough watched Angela, watched Tom. The girl was her usual eager, cheerful little self; mildly amused at the events of the office day, quick to spring to the stove or the sink in service, lovely in her quiet content at being here with these friends she so loved.

But the man was changed. He was clumsy, he was silly in sudden spurts of words, he was almost savage in silences. He annoyed her with contemptuous teasing and was violent with Torey when she joined in on it. Finally, crossly and indifferently, he asked Angela if she would like to go to a movie, and upon her accepting, for there was no church service that evening, he became his sunniest, his dearest self, affectionate and amusing and natural again. In short Tom acted like a man in love, and his mother could only marvel that she had not seen long before this what was the matter with him.

"Tom likes Angela, I wudden't wondther," she observed tentatively to Torey when they were alone.

"You're a born detective, Ma, with a nose for news!" Torey jeered good-naturedly. It was as obvious as all that then.

"I doubt does she like him."

"She's crazy about him," said Torey. "But she'll never marry him. Tom's going away—he can't stand it."

Mrs Loughborough, dazed that matters had progressed thus far under her very nose, stood at the sink regarding her daughter bewilderedly.

"Tom's goin' away?" she breathed.

"Well, can't you see that she's driving him crazy, Ma?"

"Tom," his mother murmured, thinking.

"She's got him jumping sideways," Torey observed simply.

"There's no ger'rl alive 'd say no to Tom."

"Mamma, wake up. She's told him so."

"She hasn't!"

"Don't you fool yourself. Tom's been crazy about her since the moment she set foot in this house. But Angela's afraid," Torey explained.

"Afraid?"

"Yip. She's afraid her mother—marked her," Torey said mysteriously.

"Mar'rked her!"

"Yip."

"What way wud she mar'rk her?"

"Well, some of those girls from the Hamilton Home come from queer families, you know. And then there's that ten grand she has in the bank. She went up to the bank and tried to find out who put it in there for her. Of course they said they didn't know."

"She wint to the bank? Angela did?"

"Indeed she did."

"An' she tolt you all this?"

"No, she never told me a word of it. But she happened to say she'd been up in the neighborhood of the bank, and I guessed the rest. And of course that's why she won't marry Tom."

"She likes him?"

"Oh, Ma, she's crazy about him! Now, not the petting kind of crazy, but just a deep-down kind of—well, *fire*, burning inside her," Torey said. "It's as if she was his mother and his sister and his grandmother and all his aunts rolled into one. Can't you see how uncomfortable she is when he acts like a fool, the way he did at dinner? Can't you see the way she always asks for what *he* wants when you're talking about dinner? It's just that she's afraid to let herself go—she's afraid of married love——"

"We'll go no further than that, if you please, Torey."

"I know. But that's the situation, Ma. Lissen, Ma, did you know her mother? She was all right, wasn't she?"

"Kitty Hogan—she was Kitty McQuaide—merrid Tim Hogan whin she give up her job in the box fact'ry," Mrs Loughborough, busy with the dishpan, answered readily. "Tim was a fine boy; he'd a job up in Erie, an' I niver seen much of thim afther they was merrid. They'd only the one child, an' afther Tim died Kitty come back here an' wor'rked in a candy factory. I'd ought to of looked her up, but me childern was small an' I'd me hands full. The next was that Kitty was dead, an' the child put in this place—God hilp the poor little thing!"

"Then where 'd the money come from, Ma?"

"Well, I don't know why Kitty wouldn't have a friend—some kind old woman who'd pay the thousand to get the child into the home an' give her a nest egg aftherward! There's people doin' that all the time, an' no scandal attached to it. The wor'rld is too aisy to take the bad of it," Mrs Loughborough said.

"It isn't the world now, Ma, it's Angela. If you get talking to her someday you tell her you knew her mother and that she was all right," Torey said. "She and Tom love each other—at least I imagine that Angela calls it love, and Tom's got it all right. But she'll go away and give us all up before she marries anyone, the way she feels now. She thinks that with her blood she might go crazy after she was married."

"With her blood!" Mrs Loughborough echoed scornfully.

"Well, you talk to her, Ma."

"I will," the older woman said decidedly. But she took her time about it, meanwhile watching Tom with a heavy heart. He was so desperately, so pathetically in love. He was so wretched. He was vouchsafed by Angela so few crumbs with which to comfort his misery of hunger.

Angela was his whole world; of the mother who had borne him, who would have had her hand cut off, and gladly, to give him his heart's desire, he was only vaguely aware.

"Thanks, Ma; gee, you're kind, Ma," he said to her sometimes in a quick, dry voice, like a person talking in a fever. It was a fever, his feeling for this deep-eyed, low-voiced girl. Tom had to be near her, had to hear her voice, had to watch her moving about his mother's kitchen, or hold her cool little unresponsive hand while they sat through hours of movies; but being near her was torture only a trifle less acute than the torture of being away. Angela's mood was his barometer; if she was at all kind to him he went into a sort of drunken ecstasy of happiness; if she were anxious and burdened and cold he snarled and jerked himself about like a wounded animal.

One night his mother heard him crying and came padding out to the kitchen in her bare feet to find him at the table, his head dropped on his outflung arms. She touched his shoulder and he raised his face unashamedly, and she saw the tears wet on his face and on his black eyelashes, and heard the break in his gruff whispered voice.

"I've got to get out, Ma," he said.

She sat down, whispering back:

"Why d'ye say that?"

"Becuz she won't look at me," Tom said briefly. "No, nor at any man," he presently added darkly, as his mother made no answer but stretched out her hard scarred hand and laid it on his. "She, that's dyin' to be in my arms, where she belongs, that's dyin' to have a child of her own, while she's kissin' Ag's children, an' Ellie's children!"

"Why won't she, thin, Tom?"

"Oh, becuz of some nonsense!" he said impatiently. "Becuz her mother was this or that! What do I care what her mother was? It's Angela I'm after, not her mother, nor her grandmother either! I've got so I can't work, Ma," Tom went on, looking down at his big knotted hands, a shadow in his eyes. "She comes between me an' everything I try to do. I keep seein' her hands, the way she cuts bread for you, and her quick look up when anyone speaks to her."

"Where 'd ye go, Tom?"

"Pittsburgh, maybe. Vic Connors is there. He'd get me in."

"I cudden't have ye l'ave me, Tom."

"I'd come back to you someday, Ma," he muttered, his eyes evasive.

"I cud tell ye the whole story of her mother, Tom. She was a good sweet ger'rl, to begin wit'. But afther Tim Hogan died on her——"

"I don't want to hear it," he interrupted grimly. "It hasn't anything to do with me and Angela. If I could once get her into my arms I'd make her forget that a lot of old biddies gossiped about her mother. Suppose her mother *was* a fool? That used to count in the old days. But now—why, Ma, half the girls——"

"Don't tell me about it, Tom!"

"I know what kind of a girl *she* is," the man went on moodily. "She's the kind that if once she let herself go—my God, Ma, the man she married would be in heaven! Ah, but it's no use," Tom interrupted himself impatiently. "She's afraid. 'I'd be too happy with my man and my children and my little home,' she told me yesterday. She didn't want to go see Gemma Walsh on Sunday. 'No,' she says, 'they're just married, an' she has everything the way I'd like to have it, little dotted curtains in her kitchen, an' a baby comin', an' all!' An' she begun to cry, the poor little thing!"

His tone was one of infinite pity; tears stood in his own eyes.

"Tom . . ." his mother began and fell silent. He looked at her expectantly, tumbling his rich hair with his hands.

"I wondther," she began again, after thought, "I wondther cud I talk to her? I wondther if I tolt her that her mother was fine and good wud it change her?"

"She wouldn't believe you."

"I'd make her believe me. There was nothin' vicious in Kitty," Mrs Loughborough went on musingly, "there was nothin' tough about her. All was, she—but I belave I'll not tell ye annythin', Tom, an' thin ye niver can throw it up at her. Whativer it was, it's long ago, an' all that knows it now is me an' Jule Whalen, an' she's got the charity of God in her, that one. She'd niver bethray ye."

"Ma," he said, hope lighting his honest blue Irish eyes, "could you do that?"

"I cud, an' not lie neither," Mrs Loughborough said thoughtfully.

"Lie if you have to," said Tom.

"I'll not. I'd not do that for annyone. But I'll talk to her." There was determination in Mrs Loughborough's tone. She sent Tom off to bed immediately, new confidence in his heart, and presently went to scramble down in her own untidy lair of blankets and coverlets. But until she heard his strong familiar snore she did not sleep.

Three days later her chance with Angela came. It was evening. Tom was working late at the foundry; Torey had gone out with a beau. Angela, very tired after the dinner dishes were done, was at the kitchen table, undecided as to whether she would go around the corner with Mrs Loughborough to Confession for First Friday the next day or go upstairs to bed.

"I always hate to miss a visit to church," she said, trying to keep her eyes open.

"Ye niver got that off the neighbors," Mrs Loughborough, putting broken bread to soak in milk for hot cakes the next morning, answered casually. "Your dear mother was one you'd always find in chur'rch."

"Mother," Angela said softly, half aloud.

"She was very good, Kitty was," the older woman added. "Whin I go on I hope she'll be the one to meet me in heaven an' get me in."

"I guess you don't have to worry, Ma. I wish," Angela said in a little courageous rush, "you'd tell me about her. If she was good, what did she do that made my grandmother hate her?"

"Yure grandmother Hogan was a reckless one wit' her tongue, Angela. There was manny she hated besides yure poor mother."

Angela was silent a few minutes, looking into space. Presently she said: "Leave that and I'll wash it."

"It's done. It was just a rinse."

"Did my mother ever do anything wrong, Ma?" The girl's voice was sick with fear and pain, but the words came steady and clear.

"Niver, in the course of her whole life!"

"Ah, but you mightn't have known!"

"I knew that. Her hear'rt," Mrs Loughborough said, "was as pure as

that of anny saint you'd be readin' about in a book. I niver knew annythin'
but good of her. There's manny thinks of her and says prayers to her to
this day."

Angela's usually pale cheeks blazed scarlet. Her stupefied eyes were
upon the older woman's face.

"My mother!" she gasped in a whisper.

"Yure dear mother. Where you iver got the notion that it wasn't that
way, Angela, I'll niver know. Good she was, protectin' you . . . guidin'
you . . ."

"Oh, I knew she loved me!" Angela said breathlessly. "But I thought
. . . I used to worry . . . nobody told me . . .

"And then, being at the Hamilton, where so many of the girls had
funny histories," she went on, speaking in an almost apologetic tone now,
"and they never told us anything—they always said they didn't know anything of our people——"

She stopped short, spreading her hands in a gesture of appeal.

"They'd do that to protect the poor ger'rls that had nothin' but bad
news to lear'rn, Angela."

"Well, they might." The exquisite colors of April were in Angela's face;
her eyes were shining through wet lashes. "But you never told me that
Mother—that Mother—was so good," she stammered.

"Ye niver ast me, dear'r!"

"Oh, but you knew—you knew how it was worrying me to think that she
—that perhaps I might someday go that way—that it was in my blood
too!" Angela said confusedly.

"How wud I know that?"

"But my being in the Hamilton—someone paid for that."

"Yure mother had manny friends you niver knew nothin' about, Angela.
She's done favors for tins and dozens of thim that I know of. There's
manny a kindness she's done me. There niver was a betther human woman
that iver lived than she, no, nor more beloved either!"

"But if—if they loved her so, then why wouldn't they come see me in
the Hamilton? I grew up feeling shut out—different from girls who had
homes and friends, out in the world——" Angela stopped again.

"Well, Angela, it's har'rd to say," Mrs Loughborough said after a moment. "But people's as quick to forget favors as to ask thim, we all know
that. Here's me, that owed yure dear mother so much, an' I niver tuk
the throuble to look ye up. The wor'rld is like that, dear'r. Look, somewan
put all that money into the bank for ye; that looks like ye had a friend."

"You don't know who that was?"

"I'd lost sight of her for years, d'ye see, while ye lived up in Erie. I don't
know what friends she had or whativer it all was. But this I know, that it
was yure good mother guidin' ye from heaven that brought ye here to me
an' found ye friends an' a home—yes, an' a good man to love ye, too, an'
you puttin' up yure hands to hide yure red face while I say it! If yure as

good as yure mother, ye'll be one of the bist of God's creatures, an' me oath on that."

"You mean it!" Angela whispered, her eyes stars.

"I mane ivery wor'rd of it."

"Oh, but why didn't someone say all this to me before! You mean she was—she was like other women—like Ag and Eileen and Ellie—she was like you——"

"She was betther than I iver was," Mrs Loughborough said humbly. "Whin ye think of her, Angela, think of someone who knew bitther sorrow an' bore it well, an' loved her child, an' tasted the full grief of parting."

Angela had crossed the kitchen now; she had her arms about the older woman; her wet face was against Mrs Loughborough's face.

"Oh, my God, I'm so grateful you told me this!" she said, laughing and crying. "Oh, God forgive me that I ever thought any different of her! It was living in that place where they were all so cold and hard, and thought the worst of everyone—that all girls were naturally crooked, and all women doing wrong! I'll never think of her again except to bless her and ask her to protect me. And there's nothing in my heart to be afraid of except to be good!"

"That's all, Angela. An' what 'll ye do wit' all yure money? Buy yuresilf a little home someday that you'd own?"

"I was never going to touch it! But now," Angela said radiantly, "d'you know what I'm going to do? I'm going to give it to Lizzie and Jerry Moore. He's crippled, you know, and he can only do odd jobs, and they're buying that double house in Long Island City. That 'll mean they have a home, and some rent coming in, and she'll not worry any more! That's what I'll do, and good riddance to it, and all my worries beside! Oh, Ma, I feel so light I could dance—I could go right straight up into the air——"

It was upon this last phrase that Tom came in, tired and grimy. His eyes brightened as he saw Angela's transformed face; his whole aspect brightened when he returned from ablutions in the bedroom to find Angela alone, setting his dinner upon the table in good wifely fashion, brewing him tea, sitting down opposite him to smile at him while he ate.

"Not goin' to church with Ma, hey?" Tom asked.

"Not tonight, no. I thought maybe you and I could go to a movie later, Tom," Angela said simply.

Meanwhile Mrs Loughborough had gone around the corner and up the snowy steps into the great warm edifice that was dimly lighted, that was stirring with well-bundled forms. Children were half walking, half running in the aisles, whispering, genuflecting ostentatiously.

When she got there, there were a good many people in the church. But she stayed on her knees a long time, and the big place was almost deserted when she went up the left-hand aisle to the altar and knelt before the statue of the gracious young woman in the blue robe, with a white veil falling lightly over her braided hair, and her arms outstretched to all the suffering, the sorrowful, the lonely and unfortunate women of all the world.

Before her the tiny lights of a hundred red candles wavered in the soft, incense-scented air. Mrs Loughborough knelt down and looked up at her.

"Mary, help an' save us all," she said in a whisper; "those wasn't lies I tolt her, dear'r. Ain't ye her mother as much as iver poor Kitty was? Haven't ye been guidin' her an' watchin' her for all of her life? That's all I tolt her. I said ye was good an' had done manny an' manny a favor for me an' for others; that's thrue, isn't it? Sure, where wud we all be if ye wasn't Mother to us, lovin' an' helpin' all along the roads we go? D'ye mind that I mixed ye up wit' another mother that's maybe long ago forgiven an' safe wit' ye for all time to come?"

The radiant vision made no audible answer. But in the dim candlelight there might have been upon her face a smile of infinite tenderness and understanding as she looked down on a homely old woman in a shabby winter coat, kneeling below among the troubled shadows of the world.

The Longest Way Round

"She said if she married him she'd likely have to spind most of her life in the kitchen," Mrs. Considine said, setting down her teacup, sucking her dental plates into firmer position, and sighing.

"Where would she want to spind it, thin?" Mrs. Moore asked, with mild surprise and contempt in her soft County Clare voice.

"Well, you'd wonder." Mrs. Crowley, the third woman at the kitchen table, was somewhat younger than the other two, and young for her own fifty years. There was no thread of gray in the slick black hair that was swept firmly off her fresh, open face and twisted into a tight knot on her neck. Her cheeks were rosy and full, her small black eyes deep-set and bright, her mouth heavy and prominent and filled with large, crowded white teeth. Sarah—she pronounced it Sayrah—Crowley's skin was still of the firm whiteness known only to the petals of white roses and the skin of Irishwomen.

She might well express surprise at any woman's objection to life in a kitchen, for most of her half century of living had been spent in one kitchen or another. She knew the low-ceiled, smoky, peat-scented kitchens of the old country, with rain trickling on the thatch and with the sharp smell of pigs drifting in sometimes from the sty and mingling with the good odor of strong tea and baking potato cakes.

The rocking steerage in which, at twenty, she had crossed the ocean had held no kitchen that she ever saw, or cared indeed to see, but her cousin Marg'rit, amazingly established in the New World, had dazzled the weary little emigrant with her first sight of a gas stove, glass-enclosed cupboards, milk sealed in bottles, rice and beans in "nate little boxes." And then had come the Warrington kitchen with Sarah an underling of the underlings therein amid the breath-taking whiteness of tiles and ice-boxes, glass-topped tables, enamel and stainless steel.

"Sure, you'd think it was a surgery you was cookin' in!" Sarah used to say of it later, in amused indulgence.

Her stay in this magnificence had not been long. It had lasted little more than a year, during which time she had never penetrated even as far as the dining room to which the triumphs of Mrs. Doolan, the cook, had mounted. She never knew who crashed indifferent forks into the crab aspic or the raspberry mousse, nor saw the young ladies' bedrooms with their frilled beds and long-legged dolls. John Crowley, who drove the big car for the Warringtons, had lost no time in wooing the pretty, shy kitchen maid, and in establishing her on a Long Island farm.

And here, upon four shabby acres, in a weather-peeled, flimsy, ten-room rattletrap of a house entirely innocent of plumbing, with two apple trees, seven chickens, a goat, and a young maple tree, Sarah Crowley had come into her kingdom, with her kitchen for its apartment of state. A succession of heavy-headed, black-haired little boys and vivacious, gray-eyed girls with dark curls had promptly joined her there; "the creatures," as she called them, had apparently had no doubts as to the choice of a mother.

The oldest of them, the incomparable Julia, was now older than her mother had been when she arrived, and twenty-eight years of wifehood and widowhood had passed over Sarah's black head. But in all of them she had never gotten far from her kitchen. John and she had discussed in this kitchen the wisdom of his resigning as Mr. Warrington's chauffeur to accept a position in the grocery seven blocks away. Here babies had lain, nursing comfortably in their mother's arms; older children had whooped with whooping cough in this kitchen; bitter cold and anxiety had reigned here for brief moments, laughter and tears, fighting and loving, scolding and praising had seasoned the stained old walls and the worn linoleum of the floor. The room was saturated with years of homely living, homely meals shared; twenty thousand times or more had Sarah Crowley put the sugar bowl and the cut bread and the oatmeal upon the table; one hundred thousand cups of social tea—perhaps that many more—had been poured by her steady, work-worn hand into the waiting cups.

The women were drinking tea now. Not straight cups of it, but a half cup, and a quarter cup added to it, and a bit more top milk and a taste more of the tay and a bitteen of sugar whilst yure hand is on the spoon, Aggie. Every afternoon of their lives they had something vital to discuss, and this afternoon it was an orphaned young protégée of Mrs. Crowley's—Lizzie Garvey's Betty, who had recently come to live at the Crowleys'.

They had approached the matter delicately; it was a delicate matter. Birth and death they could discuss freely and calmly; ger'rls, once safe in wedlock, had babies whether they wanted them or not. Old folk died whether or not they longed to live. Families were evicted when they

couldn't pay the rint; children broke windows, arms and legs, were ex-
pelled from school, acquired meningitis or infantile. Big boys did terrible
things, things involving loud crying and prayers on the part of the women,
and perhaps visits from cops. Or even dreadful, shameful, tongue-tied
visits to courtrooms and jails.

About these things they could talk. But today's subject matter was different. Mrs. Considine had opened it with a natural, casual query: "Yure
Betty, thin. Is the child ateing her males?"

"She is not," Mrs. Crowley had returned briefly.

"It wouldn't be yure Tom that she's quarrelin' with?" Mrs. Moore had
asked as a matter of routine. She knew the answer, but the question had
to be gotten out of the way.

"She hasn't give a look to Tom these three weeks," Mrs. Crowley had
answered automatically. Whatever it was, they all knew it wasn't any trouble with Tom, who was only too obviously infatuated with little Betty.

Then there had ensued a silence in which all three women, refreshed
by a newly made pot of tea, had sighed in turn.

And it was then that Mrs. Considine had observed that the unapprecia-
tive Betty had been heard flippantly to observe to "our Ellen" that if she
married Tom she'd likely have to spend most of her life in the kitchen.

"Does Julia know annything about it?" Mrs. Moore presently asked.
"They workin' in the same office, and Julia bein' like a big sisther to her,
it's likely she wud."

"Betty'll not talk to annyone," Mrs. Crowley said. "She was cryin',
upstairs in her room, last night, and our Ellen wint up to her. But she
couldn't make sinse of anny of it!"

"If there was more of thim like Julia!" Mrs. Moore put in, shaking a
grizzled little head in a draggled widow's bonnet and veil. The late
Clement Moore had been anything but a comfortable housemate; his wife
and children had regarded his arrival home on Saturday nights with un-
mitigated fear and dread. But for sixteen years Aggie Moore had dutifully worn for him the badge of mourning.

It was always good to get back to Julia, the oldest of the Crowley
brood. Julia was strong and sweet and good, lovely to look upon, and presumably suitably and sensibly engaged to Martin Mhoon. For nine years
Julia had been a breadwinner, and most of her steadily increasing wages
had gone to satisfy the family's demands. Mrs. Crowley was a widow
too; there were six other boys and girls beside Julia, and the profits from
a boardinghouse whose management was at best unbusinesslike would
never have kept them all housed and fed without help from the oldest
son and daughter. Mrs. Crowley in her heart sometimes wondered what
on earth she had ever done to deserve these paragons of children.

But it would never do to admit that. So when Mrs. Moore sighed, "If
there was only more of thim like Julia!" and Mrs. Considine, her smiling
eyes filling with tears, added, "The darlin'!" Mrs. Crowley merely said:

"She's stylish-lookin', Julia is; she's a good child. But sure, I wish they'd all stop puttin' that red on their nails," she complained. "It's like young tigers they look, reachin' for the bread acrost the table!"

"There's some puts it on their fate," Mrs. Moore remarked after the tut-tutting noise that introduced most of her remarks.

"And who'd see their fate?" demanded Mrs. Considine. "These ger'rls that ain't even married yet! And sure, even whin I was married to Frank Considine, and me a big ger'rl of twinta-two," she went on musingly, "wud I let him see the bare fate of me? I wud not! I'd joomp into me bed and pull the covers over me! I niver tolt him yoong Frank was comin' until iv'ryone else in the neighborhood was onto me hopes and fears, as they say——"

"That's the secret that don't ever kape anny too good," Mrs. Crowley observed with an indulgent smile as the speaker, beguiled by these long-ago memories, let her voice die away into silence. "But the way they talk now, you'd think the ger'rls was the old women and the old women was the ger'rls. 'I don't know that you'd like the pitcher, Ma,' Genevieve or Stella'll say to me whin they come home from the movies, 'It's kind of rough for you,' they'll say. Well, it was my good mother, God rest her, that kept the devil away from me, not me from her. But these days——"

"Hello, girls." It was Julia in the doorway, back from work. Mrs. Moore and Mrs. Considine smiled at her; her mother, her heart bursting with love and pride, merely said patiently: "Whativer have you done to yure hair now?"

"Nothing at all, Mom, except that it needs a shampoo."

Julia came in and sat down at the table, a fine, beautifully made creature whose plain clothes could not disguise the splendor of her long slender limbs, the thin wrists and finely turned ankles. Julia had wide-open gray Irish eyes and a creamy, colorless Irish skin; her lips were strawberry-red; the rich curves and waves of her tawny, thick hair had reddish lights in them. Competence, humor, self-possession spoke in every line of Julia's person, in every tone of her voice. One generation removed from the cabins of rural Ireland, there was no door in the world that might not someday open to Julia, and no position she might not grace.

"Tay, darlin'?" asked her mother.

"Thanks, no. D'you mean to say," asked Julia, standing at the sink and helping herself to a glassful of cold water, "that you tea guzzlers will go home now and put a good hearty dinner on top of all these buns and jam?"

The three women laughed guiltily.

"All I do at night," Mrs. Moore explained, "is stand up by the stove whilst the boys is gettin' their dinners, and maybe take a taste of this and that."

"We don't ate now until close upon nine o'clock," Mrs. Considine said. "Pether have the late shift these nights. And the ger'rls will always be waitin' for him. They thinks the wor'rld and all of him."

"As for Mom," Julia said, coming over to sit with them at the table, "she never eats any dinner. She'll serve us all, and put two pieces of asparagus on her plate, and look at them all through dinner."

"If I have me bread an' tay," her mother offered in her soft, amused voice, "there's little else I'd want beside. Sure at home in the old days we'd not thank you for anny supper unless maybe it was a piece of bread an' drippin' late at night. It was tay, an' potato cakes——"

"Mom," said Julia, "if you tell me once more how the sweet Irish butter dripped out of those potato cakes——"

The women all laughed. The visitors were now getting ready to go. Julia sat on at the table, dreaming, until she and her mother were alone.

"Martin telephone, Mom?" she asked then.

"He said he'd be in afther sivin, and yu're not to ate yure supper, becuz of his takin' you and Kate and a lot of thim to Clancy's."

"A-ha." Julia accepted the plan absently. "I think I'll take a bath," she mused.

"Hard day, deary?" Her mother was at the sink, busy with the teacups.

"It's this sudden change into spring weather. It was hot in the office today. Mr. Monroe brought in a lot of lilacs from Locust Valley. Where's everyone?"

"Well, I think the spring's got the whole lot of thim, too," Mrs. Crowley said. "Ag come over wit' the baby, but she had to go back to start Harry's dinner. Ellen's upstairs, layin' down, and Willy's over to the candy store seein' if he can't get a job there. Brother Anselmo thinks he's goin' to flunk out of school. Joe's playin' wit' the boys over on the hill, and where the ger'rls are I don't know unless they'd be stravagin' the streets seein' cud they pick up a coupla sailors——"

Julia interrupted the trailing monologue with a laugh.

"They're too young for that! But where's Betty?"

"I don't know. Didn't she l'ave the office whin you did?"

"She stopped at about four o'clock and said her head ached. She didn't come home?"

"I didn't see her come in. Maybe she stipped over to the liberry," Mrs. Crowley murmured, absorbed in draining the water from soaking peeled potatoes. "What ails her annyway, Julia?" she asked.

"Ails Betty?"

"There's somethin' gone wrong wit' her."

Julia looked out of the kitchen window, pursing her lips thoughtfully. She did not answer.

The scene outside no longer showed the plain, shabby slopes, winding mud roads, straggling fences that had once surrounded the Crowleys' four-acre farm. Civilization had crept from the big city over new bridges; first in the form of lines and lines of stained and dripping garbage trucks.

Sarah Crowley had looked out upon dumps through all the years when the children were little. Cans and rusty bedsprings and the eternal ashes of which everything had tasted and with which everything had been powdered had been her environment for ten years.

But the dumps and the ashes were all gone now, and ranks and ranks of red brick tenements had taken their places. As far as the eye could reach stretched the battlements of three- and four-room flats. At the street levels were shops: markets and beauty parlors and theaters and dairy restaurants; tile and marble and glass and cellophane had replaced the old grocery which had once worn the name "Crowley and Connors—Staples." Poor Jawn had felt sad to see his business go, swallowed up by one of the smart new chain stores—stores run by bright young men whose orders were never to cash anyone's check or let even the smallest, shabbiest child plead for a few days' credit on the bill. Jawn had given credit to half the families of the neighborhood—of course he had; any grocer with a heart in his body would! He had entered the half pound of lard and the two loaves of bread in little brown books that dangled on strings behind the desk.

So the trade for the first three weeks of the month had gone to the cheaper "chains," and when money ran short, in the last week, Jawn's customers had come pleading back to him again. "Mama says will you charge it?" had said the little voices he could not refuse.

He had lost his store, lost his place in the world; he had sat brooding in Sarah's kitchen for a few months, and then, because of thin old shoes and weary job hunting and bitter winter weather, he had been able to make no struggle against the swift-striking onslaught of pneumonia that had put so many of the families all about into black.

But Jawn's children had prospered with the prospering neighborhood. Julia had been working since her seventeenth year; Tom, two years younger, had never lacked employment. Barstein's Manor Flats had brought with them the need of hundreds of workers; they young Crowleys had profited by that need. Everything had favored them: the big new schools and playgrounds, the improved streets, the rise in real estate prices. All but half an acre of the farm had long been sold; Sarah Crowley had burned the mortgage papers in her own kitchen stove. She set the potatoes to boil upon this stove now.

"I thought maybe, wit' Betty workin' in the same office wit' you . . . ?" she presently ventured, with one of many anxious glances at her daughter's face.

"Betty acts," Julia pronounced presently, speaking in a puzzled, deliberate manner, "as if she was in love."

"Well, that's it of coorse!" her mother agreed promptly.

"You think so?" the girl asked with a surprised look.

"What else? It's so thin she is, an' as cross as a bear whin poor Tom spoke to her last night, an' not atin' more than a taste of this an' that at her males."

"Think it's Tom?" Julia offered with a slight frown.

"Tom! She cud have Tom tomorra if she'd look at him!" the older woman said scornfully.

"And would that make you mad, Mom?"

"I don't know," Mrs. Crowley said in an oratorial drone, "why I'd be mad that a poor child that lost her mother whin she was three and her poor father, God rest him, but six months ago——"

"And after all, Aunt Julia was going to marry her father, only he was killed, Mom. That sort of makes her Aunt Julia's stepdaughter."

"Well, then that makes it she wudden't be within the forbidden degrees of kindred that she'd marry Tom!" Mrs. Crowley said triumphantly.

"Mom, you make me laugh," observed Julia. "But if it isn't Tom that Betty's crying and carrying on about," she mused, "who would it be? Not Martin, I suppose?"

This last was said in joke. The complete devotion of Martin Mhoon to Julia Crowley had begun with her high school days, had continued, only deepening and strengthening, with the years, and was presently to lead to an autumn wedding.

"I think you'd know well," her mother answered dryly.

"I?" Julia's thick dark eyebrows went up in puzzlement. "What are you getting at, darling?" she asked.

"You being right in the office with her," the older woman repeated with patient insistence.

"You mean it's someone in the office?" Julia asked bewilderedly.

"It's Kenneth Monroe. That's what's ateing her hear'rt out," Mrs. Crowley stated firmly.

Julia looked staggered.

"Ken Monroe!" she exclaimed, annoyance, incredulity, amusement all battling in her tone. "Mom, he's forty-four! He has a wife and two boys. Surely that little *idiot . . . !*"

She fell silent, staring at her mother with awakening eyes.

"That might be it!" she admitted in an electrified whisper.

"She sees him every day, don't she?"

"Well—no, not every day," Julia said, lost in speculation. "Well, yes, I suppose she does. But Betty—why, all she does is file letters and sort mail—the poor little simp—the poor little *half*-wit! I don't suppose he speaks to her once a week."

"Less than that'd do!" Mrs. Crowley said simply.

"But how'd you happen to think of it, Mom? She didn't say it was Mr. Monroe?"

"She? She doesn't say nothin'! But you'll notice, Julia, that, whativer way the talk goes at dinner, he comes into it. It's Mr. Monroe has a new boat, and if the boys say annythin' it's 'Oh, Mr. Monroe said this or that to Mr. Jim Monroe the other day!' Or she'll say 'The Monroes always goes up to Maine for the summers,' or—well, now, what was it she said to our Ellen night before last? 'Mr. Monroe writes his name the way you'd think it was copper plate,' she says."

Julia delicately nipped at a polished fingernail with her teeth without removing her eyes from her mother.

"If she has any ideas about Kenneth Monroe," she presently said, "she's just a little crazier—she's just a little *younger*—than I think she is! But I don't believe it!"

"Well, God hilp her annyways!" Mrs. Crowley said piously. "I wish I knew where she's got to now!"

"Oh, she'll turn up!" Julia drifted upstairs, past the bare, orderly rooms with their variegated beds and ill-assorted chairs and tables. Everything was clean and spacious and shabby; the floors were painted a dark, brownish red and had strips of carpets and odd rugs strewn about for their only covering.

Ellen Crowley, nineteen and gentle and invalided, was lying on one of the two single beds in the big front room she shared with Julia. Both girls had always felt that their home was the most comfortable in the world, and themselves lucky beyond the lot of all other humans. They loved their airy room, and if it was innocent of the touch of professional decorators, Chinese wallpapers, chromium chairs, period desks, it was still the prettiest apartment in the house. The dotted swiss at the windows was fresh and stiff, and on the beds were peach and powder-blue taffeta comforters.

Ellen had drawn her comforter up over her thin little pipestem legs and feet; she smiled at Julia as the older girl came in, and watched her lazily as Julia threw off her office attire and got ready for her bath.

"I don't know whether there's hot water. Miss Mag took a bath about four."

"There's plenty. Mom said Ag was in with the baby."

"And is she getting cute!" Ellen's voice, as frail and sweet as herself, trailed the last word into two syllables. Now she waved her arm, and Julia saw the unexpected gesture in the mirror and turned to face her sister with puzzled eyes. Ellen was signaling significantly toward the adjoining hall bedroom, pointing that way with a digging little emaciated finger. Betty's room.

Julia's eyebrows went up and asked a question, and a quick motion of Ellen's fingers and Ellen's handkerchief said, "She's crying!"

"Oh-h-h?" Julia commented voicelessly. Aloud she said, loud enough to be heard, "Where's Betty? Why doesn't she come in here and talk to us?"

As she spoke she opened the connecting door and looked into Betty's little cubicle, and immediately she stepped through it and closed it behind her. Betty was lying flat on her bed, finishing a very thorough job of sobbing her heart out. Julia went over to her and sat on the edge of the bed and patted Betty's shoulder. Betty jerked away.

"Ah, don't," said Julia good-naturedly, in the voice of wisdom, experience, big-sisterhood.

"Get out, please get out!" said Betty thickly, her face still buried.

"Don't cry, honey," said Julia. "No man is worth it!"

Betty, with flushed and swollen face, reddened wet eyes, blubbering young wet mouth, straightened suddenly. Her hair, hanging in lovelocks around her head, was in tangled disorder.

"It isn't a ma-*han!*" mumbled Betty, gulping.

"Of course it's a man," Julia said composedly. "And you're nineteen, and you're going to do a lot of crying over men before you're twenty-six, I can tell you that!"

"You're engaged to Mart, and Mart's making sixty a week," Betty said resentfully, swallowing, sniffling, blowing her nose and doing what she could for her hair. "You should worry! You've never cried over any man! They're all ker-*razy* about you from the minute they lay eyes on you! Mart's been in love with you since you were sixteen. He said so!"

"They all say that," Julia observed dispassionately. "They all think they knew all about it from the beginning. But they don't. Four or five years ago, when I was about twenty-two and Mart was twenty-nine, I used nearly to go crazy because he was in love with Uncle Flurry's Ellen, she that married Wolfe O'Connor and had the little boy that died. Remember Mom was streaking up that way last Christmas? Well, whatever Mart Mhoon says now, he was crazy about Uncle Flurry's Ellen, and if he says he wasn't—come on into my room and do that at the mirror, Betty, you can't see what you're doing here—if he says he wasn't, he lies."

Betty laughed shakily, her swollen face contorting for a second.

"Mart would punch your face in if he heard you say that!" she said thickly.

"Wouldn't he though?" Julia said complacently. "I expect to be dragged all over the floor by that lad about once a week! But, Betty," she went on seriously, "you mustn't get silly ideas about love. It's the most natural thing in the world to fall for someone—someone you perhaps see every day and don't know anything about——"

She watched Betty keenly as she spoke. Betty flushed hotly.

"Oh, I know I'm a fool!" she muttered, looking away.

"Is this the first time?" the older girl asked keenly.

"Oh, God, yes!" gasped Betty, tears starting afresh.

"Don't you let Mom catch you saying that. She's death on the third Commandment."

"Well, don't think I haven't per-*rayed* about it. I was praying then," Betty said with a touch of sullenness. Julia regarded her thoughtfully.

"Is it someone you see every day, Betty?"

A flash of resentment from the reddened eyes.

"I can't tell you, Julia. There's things—things——"

"He's older?"

"I don't know how old he is! Who—who told you anyway?"

"Nobody told me. But I suppose you know that he's married and has two kids?"

The blue, blue eyes under Betty's black thatch widened. She was obviously shocked. But she rallied to answer calmly:

"It doesn't make any difference if he's married ten times!"

"Look here, Betty," Julia said persuasively, "you're just making it hard for yourself, thinking about a man that you'll probably never really know, much less have a chance to marry! So you do your hair and come along into the bathroom with me and wash your face and cheer up. You'll get over it, honestly and truly you will!"

"I wish people would shut up and mind their own business!" Betty said in a low voice, staring at herself dully in the mirror.

"I know how you feel," Julia said mildly from the doorway, departing.

There was company for supper, no unusual thing in the Crowley house; the visitor was a cousin of Mrs. Crowley whom everyone liked and whom they rarely saw, and there was a great welcome for Cousin Batty Mc-Govern.

They sat down thirteen. Mrs. Crowley was at the head of the table; Tom at the foot. On one side were three boarders, the Misses Keohane, Annie and Mag, who worked in the post office, and Mr. O'Meara, who was invalided and quiet and had just come in as a boarder. Also on that side were two sons of the house, Willy, fifteen, and Joey, ten. On the other side were Betty, next to Tom, whose eyes she would not meet, and Ellen, seated on a brown pillow from the parlor couch; also Genevieve and Stella, daughters of fourteen and twelve, eternally whispering and giggling together and utterly oblivious to the world about them. Julia and the guest carried the line back to Mrs. Crowley.

The talk for a while was all family talk, but eventually, as all the younger members of the family knew she would, Cousin Batty got on the subject of the Louis Carteret McMichaelses, and then everyone had questions to ask, for the incredibly rich and prominent and aristocratic Mc-Michaelses had, quite unconsciously, been court jesters to the Crowleys for all the twenty-seven years that Cousin Batty had been their house-keeper.

She had gone to them first when "Mr. Gerald" and "Mr. Lou, Jr.," and "Miss Eleanor" were young children, and after the older couple's first divorce had stayed with the wife. Later she had followed "Miss Eleanor's" imposing fortunes and taken on the management of her Virginia farm, her Park Avenue apartment, her Adirondacks camp. Batty was a family institution with all the McMichaelses; what they never dreamed was that they were a family institution with all the Crowleys.

The Crowleys knew them all by name and nature, and reveled in a sort of joyous pity of the limitations, stupidities, and discomforts in which the other half lived.

"Fred Fredricks said in his column that Eleanor's getting a divorce now from King," Tom said. Tom was a big, rough-looking, gentle fellow with a head of crisp waves of coal-black hair, and coal-black hair sprouting from ears and nostrils and showing dark blue on his heavy-shaven jowls.

"That makes four to the three of them," Annie said interestedly, cleaning her teeth busily with her tongue.

"Yes, that makes four to three," Cousin Batty admitted. "An' if Mattress—that's Mr. Lou, Jr.'s, wife's Frinch maid—is tellin' the truth, he's goin' to be divorced again too."

"Well, they don't get much happiness for all their money," Mrs. Crowley said on a long sigh. She gathered what remained of a platter of young spring chicken smothered in creamy gravy, half a sweet potato, three tiny braised carrots, and held the spoonful toward Tom. "Come on, Tom, finish it for me!" she said.

"Oh, God, Ma," protested Tom simply.

"Don't use the name of the Lord in vain," his mother reproved him. But because it was Tom, and because of the way she felt about him, she added, "darlin'!"

"Gerald McMichaels married that rich Philadelphia ger'rl, din't he, Batty?" Mag Keohane reviewed it. "And they had a boy?"

"They had two of the finest boys you ever see," Batty supplied. "Gerry and David. I don't know what they're like now, for they've been batthered about from one school to camp and camp to school until all they'd ever see of their mother is whin she'd take thim into Abercrombie and Fitch's to get thim their outfits off a list printed in one of thim little books! 'Twas afther Mr. Gerald and her got their divorce—becuz of him runnin' after a ger'rl in his office——"

Julia's magnificent gray eyes moved slowly to meet her mother's eyes. It was no accident that brought Cousin Batty and her gossip to the Crowley board tonight then? She looked on to Betty's young, still tear-stained face. Betty was hanging on Cousin Batty's words; she had no eye for Julia. Mrs. Crowley, with a great air of innocence, was still pressing the last remains of the dinner upon one and all.

"Finish up this tasteen for me, Mag. Willy, you'll have it? There's nothin' to it."

"Now I tell you," Cousin Batty was saying impressively, "Mr. Gerald sewed the wind and he ripped the whirlwind, as they say. And him with children! Their boy, little David, had just had his ninth bir'rthday par'rty whin she noticed—the wife noticed—that he'd changed. He was runnin' afther this pretty ger'rl in the office; Norma Patterson, that was her name. His wife put deteckatiffs onto him; I don't know what she paid thim— they said it was twenty-five dollars a day!"

"It would be," said Tom, relishing at once the story and the contents of the big spoon.

"It was all Norma," the storyteller went on. "Oh, he was in love at last—din't I hear him tellin' his brother, Mr. Lou, Jr., that?—and sure it wud be a pity that all three of thim should be unhappy and what a mother Norma'd make the boys! Well, that was the end of father and mother, too, for the boys. He married his Norma and she never let him so much as see thim again, an' din't the first wife marry a man fifteen years younger than she was, twinta-one, he was, an' her own boy only five years younger?"

"I thought one of thim boys died in school?" Mrs. Crowley mused, shaking her head.

"That was Miss Eleanor's boy—Tim Russell. Afther she got her divorce she wint to Europe an' left the children wit' the grandmother and me. Well, old Mrs. McMichaels was livin' wit' her thir'd an' she wanted to go to Reno and get another divorce, so she give it out she was openin' the place in Honolulu and was goin' there. She was a little ashamed of that divorce," Batty explained, "for the marriage hadn't lasted but four months. Her maid told me that the night they were wed he tolt her it wud cost her a million to get rid of him, and I think that's what it did. So she sint me ahead wit' the little ger'rl an' she kep' the boy. And 'twasn't a month before I had the cable sayin' that little Tim had died—cryin' for his mother, they said. He wasn't but six, God help the poor little feller. Iv'ry night he'd ast me, 'Batty, is Mummy comin' back? Batty, why did my daddy go away?' Well, Miss El'ner had her count—she's the countess, if that's what she wanted."

"Yes, but Harry Russell, the man she married, started the whole thing, didn't he?" Annie Keohane prompted.

"He did," said Cousin Batty. "Like all the rest of thim, he met the beautiful, lovely, virtuous ger'rl that was goin' to give him the fir'rst love an' happiness of his life, an' he broke up his home an' give up his children to get a divorce and marry her. And two years later he threw the whole thing up at her. . . . He said she was the one who made him do it, an' wrecked his life, an' separated him from his mother—for old Mrs. Salisbury Russell niver wud speak to her or him ayether—and her an' her little boy was suin' the other day through the lawyers that he'd niver paid up the alimony—what it was I don't know, but it never taught him nothin'. I seen in the *News* that Harry Russell was goin' to marry that Doris Carey Lilienthal Barker an' if he does he'll be payin' three alimonies come this time five years, now you mark my word!"

"But—but——" It was Betty, scarlet-faced, stammering, seeming terrified already at the sound of her own voice. "But maybe people do really—sometimes—love each other," she murmured, abashed, her head drooping.

"What'd you say, Betty?" Tom was attentive; he bent his dark head toward his little neighbor.

"I was saying that people—maybe people love each other!" Betty burst out, choking on tears. And sobbing loudly, with her face bent down on her covering hands, she rushed from the room.

Tom whistled softly, shrugged his big shoulders.

"And I hope you think you were smart, Mrs. Crowley," Julia said to her mother later.

"God help the child, I didn't know she would take it so har'rd!" Mrs. Crowley said. "'Twon't hur'rt her," she added, unabashed.

"If there was any good old skeleton in the Social Register that Cousin Batty didn't dig up tonight . . ." Julia said musingly. She sighed a little wearily. She and Mart had been dancing and had won the place in the semifinals of the big tournament; that was expected. But competition had been spirited and the spring evening was warm. "It seems to me you kind of rubbed it into the poor kid," she said sympathetically.

Her mother was moving about, making more than spotless a spotless kitchen. Sarah Crowley had been trained in the stern school that wasted no drop of buttermilk, no smudge of flour. Now she had set the breakfast cereal to soak, had placed sparkling milk bottles outside the door, had "wrenched" her dish towels and wrung and jerked them half dry, and pinned them on the kitchen line. Everyone else in the house was asleep; it was midnight.

"Julia," she said seriously, "there's true love betwixt a man and woman, as well you know. What you and Mart have felt for each other these three years is what I mane. Whin I married yure father—God grant him eternal rest!—the love talk waited until afther the priest had had his say. What we talked about was whether we cud afford to get married an' wud the blessin' of God rest on us an' our children! Well, times is changed, but hear'rts hasn't, an' whativer stuff this feller is pourin' into poor little Betty's ears isn't love. It's poison, that's what it is!"

"Mom," Julia said patiently, "how do you know he's ever said anything to Betty? Why, the poor little cluck didn't even know he was married until I told her tonight. That's what she was crying about, not Cousin Batty's yarns about what Eleanor Russell said to Harry the very day week Timmy come down wit' the maizles."

"Look out you don't mock no one," Mrs. Crowley put in mildly.

"I thought you were so proud of your brogue," Julia said with her lazy laugh.

"I'd be ashamed of manny another thing befoor I'd be ashamed of me good brogue," her mother answered simply. "Do you kape at her, Julia," she urged, returning to the problem of Betty. "Yu're the head of the office; you do what you can for her!"

"If I hear much more nonsense like that," Julia said disgustedly, "I'll fire her from the office."

"You'd not fire Lizzie Garvey's Betty becase a man made love to her?"

"I'd fire her for getting such crazy ideas in her head!" Julia said warmly.

"Why, she hardly ever sees him! I don't know when he'd ever have a chance to annoy her!"

"Tom tolt me," Mrs. Crowley, her thoughts off on another tack, said mysteriously, "that Billy Dugan, who works on the *Star*, tolt him tonight that tomorra there was goin' to be a big scandal bur'rst—the papers are goin' to have it. That Lily de France is divorcin' the Mexican bullfighter she married last year."

"Honest?" Julia asked, diverted and interested. The movie star's trilogy of marriages had been so many front-page sensations. "I thought that was the great love affair of the world," she mused, shaking her head and staring into space.

"It was, last year," her mother answered briefly. "Now she wants to get back her two little ger'rls by the first marriage, and the stepfather—the second man she married—says she gave thim to him, and their real father wants to get thim, too, becuz he's divorced again. An' I'll read it all to Betty at breakfast, ivery wor'rd of it, and ivery mor'rnin' I'll give it to her. How they had the whole wor'rld thinkin' they couldn't live without each other—and him givin' her a new pear'rl for her necklace ivery Thur'rsda', becase it was on Thur'rsda' that they met——"

"Mom, when a girl like Betty falls in love it's a real thing; you can't just dismiss it as a piece of foolishness," Julia took advantage of a pause in the triumphant recital to submit mildly. "*Sometimes* men and women stay loving each other!"

"Not whin it star'rts wit' a forty-five-year-old man makin' love to a little ger'rl in his office, Jule. Oh, they can buy emeralds," said Mrs. Crowley, "an' they can tell ye that it's bethter for one woman to be unhappy than to have all three of their lives rooned. But that don't last six mont's. It's then that they begin to think of the children, an' how comfortable it was at home, without all this bustin' up of where they'll be, an' who'll have the baby, an' who'll pay alimony and support. There's no passion—an' that's all it is—can stand much of that. You tell her all that, Jule, an' I'll be readin' her this an' that from the papers, and betune the two of us——"

"But I think it's all *imagination!*" Julia persisted impatiently as they darkened the kitchen and made their way toward the stairs. Betty, she told herself, was just the sort of little simpleton who would build up a story like this from nothing, and work herself into hysterics over it. She determined to keep a sharp eye on Betty; it would be a great satisfaction to prove to Betty herself that it was all nonsense, and to see that Betty was moved to some other office.

Betty and Julia worked in the big Chase insurance office, Betty as a humble beginner, Julia as the most trusted of the clerks, and virtually the manager of the dozen young men and girls. What Miss Crowley said was law.

So when she turned back, a few days later, at noon, when everyone else had streamed out to lunch, and found Betty still loitering at her desk, it was in the order of a command that she said sharply, "Come on, Betty. I'm going to the cafeteria. You come along with me."

Betty did not move. Her cheeks reddened. She looked defiant.

"I was waiting. I wanted to see someone," she said, breathing hard. Julia sat down opposite her, spoke in the gentle tone of a mistress of novices.

"Don't you see how silly this is, Betty? Don't you realize that you're making the whole thing up from nothing? What on earth are you breaking your heart for, over a man who hardly knows you're alive?"

"I'm not in love with him any more, if that's what you mean, Julia," Betty said breathlessly. "I—I hate him! Aunt Sarah's been telling me—all these days she's just been rubbing it *into* me—that a married man is just—just pul-*laying* with a girl when he talks so sweet to her—and kisses her—and never tells her he's married——"

"Kisses her!" Julia echoed, her face paling. "He didn't!"

"But he did, Julia. Right here in this office! The day we were late, looking for those policies."

"Kenneth Monroe kissed you?" Julia asked slowly.

"Mr. Monroe!" Betty repeated, scandalized.

"You just said so," Julia whispered.

"No, I didn't! I said Mr. Heffernan——"

Julia gripped the younger girl's wrist, brought her face close.

"Are you by any chance talking about Aloysius Heffernan?"

"Wishy Heffernan—yes," Betty stammered, bewildered. "I always liked him, and he liked me too. Ma knew he did!"

"Ma knew he did?" Julia asked slowly.

"Yes. But he was sort of going with Aggie Quale," Betty said, "and then when you said he was married——"

"I never said Wishy was married," Julia said absently as Betty paused.

"But you *did*, Ju, and that he had two children!"

"No. I was thinking of someone else. So it's Wishy, is it?" Julia mused. "No, he's not married. I can get hold of him—I'll have him at the house Sunday. Tom may not like it, but I'll fix Tom."

"Why wouldn't Tom like it?" Betty asked innocently.

"Because—well, Tom likes you," Julia answered simply.

"Tom does!" Betty was suddenly scarlet.

"Don't you know it?"

"But, Julia—Julia—but Tom's——" Betty stopped, breathless. "Everyone's crazy about Tom," she said. "All the girls are."

"And Tom likes you," Julia repeated it.

"But I never—Tom," said Betty. The last word was added on a dazed whisper, after a pause. Julia laughed.

"Wishy's better-looking than Tom," she said.

"He is not!" Betty said warmly.

"Well, you can look at the two of them Sunday," Julia promiscd her.

"Well, but no—looky, Julia," Betty began in some confusion, "here's the thing. Don't ask Wishy for a while—I mean, maybe a week from Sunday, see? I mean——"

"O.K.," Julia agreed amiably. She laughed again, and suddenly kissed Betty. Betty's face was radiant. "Mind now," she said, "if Tom takes you out sometime, you don't act silly and high-school-girly with him."

"Oh, Julia!" Betty breathed ecstatically, and Julia was answered. "But, Julia," Betty went on after a moment, "if Wishy Heffernan isn't married, why did Ma have Cousin Batty to dinner, and all that talk about the Mc-Michaelses, and how these divorced people were always so unhappy, and their children died, and they married the wrong people?"

"You say Mom knew you were carrying a torch for Wishy?"

"Well, yes, because I told her. It sort of slipped out, when I was feeling bad one day."

"And you were onto it, were you," Julia said reflectively, "that she put Aunt Batty up to all that talk Sunday night?"

"Well, yes, becuz Aunt Batty kept looking at me."

"Ha," Julia commented noncommittally. "She's deep, that old saint is."

"Aunt Batty is?"

"No, I was thinking of Mom. Well, you trot out to lunch, Betty, I've got some letters to finish. Do you pray about this?" Julia asked.

"Oh, I do, Julia."

"All right then. And pray for me, too, will you?"

"*You*, Julia! Why, but you and Mart——" Betty stopped short, surprised and puzzled.

"Yes, I know. But you pray for me, will you? Don't forget now." Julia kissed the younger girl again, and Betty, comforted and excited and hopeful, went on her way. "You go ahead," she said, "and I'll follow."

But she did not follow. Instead she remained at the desk where she had happened to seat herself, staring into space with pursed lips and narrowed eyes. Once or twice she sighed.

When the girls came back Miss Crowley was hard at work, seeming quite her usual self. The busy office hours followed their usual course. It was late afternoon and everyone had gone when Julia Crowley threaded a space of desks and railings and quietly opened an office door marked "Kenneth Monroe, Jr. Private."

In the beautifully carpeted and curtained sanctum a man sat at a wide flat-topped desk, telephoning. Julia sat down in a great swivel chair facing him.

"Hello," he said, smiling, glancing up. "One second." He hung up the receiver, came swiftly about the desk, dragging his chair with him, sat down and took both her hands. "Now this," he said in a manner almost reverent, "is an event. D'you realize that this is the first time you've done this? You had my letter?"

"A week ago." Julia had a momentary struggle to find her voice.

"And did it surprise you, dear?"

"It—stunned me," said Julia.

"It's all come so suddenly," he began, his tone reassuringly quiet. "First our liking each other, after so many years when we didn't seem conscious of each other's existence. Then—only a few weeks ago!—my happening to catch you when you were going out late to dinner, and that talk in the restaurant until—when was it? Midnight? And then ever since the feeling, growing stronger and stronger, that it might be—it might be—that some-day you'd make me the happiest man in the world. I've been so lonely, Julia. Oh, I know. I know about Phyllis and the boys! But in just these last few weeks I've found out what happiness is, what life could be, and don't think for one instant that I'm ever going to let it go!"

Her gaze broke over him with a sort of puzzlement.

"You mean—your letter said—that you'd really go to Reno, get a divorce, Ken?"

"What else could I offer you—offer your mother's daughter?" he asked quickly. "I'm being moved to the coast office. Phyllis won't go; that's flat. I get things started in San Francisco, slip up to Nevada—it's all so simple!"

"No," she said soberly, "it's not so simple. As far as Mom's concerned, the divorce and the talk and the scandal would break her heart anyway. But it isn't that. It's that I just—can't do it. I've always thought I could do anything—get away with anything. But this is different. That's—that's my answer to your letter."

"Then that miracle the other day—that didn't mean as much to you as it did to me?" Kenneth Monroe sat back in his chair, folded his arms, looked at her through narrowed eyes. "Our finding each other?"

"You'll never know what it meant," Julia said soberly. "You'll never know the way my heart—my heart seemed to be swimming all the time," she went on hesitatingly, feeling for words. "The way the waves kept going over my head."

"Ah, then, darling——" he began eagerly. But she interrupted him with an appealing glance.

"It isn't even that I'm afraid I couldn't hold you, Ken," she said. "I think perhaps I could. No, it's all the other things. Your mother—it'd take me years to win her, and then what'd I have? Just that an old lady who didn't like me for a while had begun to like me. I'd work hard," Julia went on thoughtfully, "for anything I wanted in this world. But why start handicapped and have to win back every person who ever loved you? Meeting the family's friends in California, having them say, 'She's nice, even if she did get Ken away from Phyllis.' Seeing it in their eyes. 'She was in his office, and I suppose she saw herself with furs and a big establish-ment——'"

[419]

"Oh, shut up!" he said gruffly, with a laugh. But he was not pleased.

"Your sister Jane," Julia went on. "She likes Phyllis; they were in school together; they were each other's bridesmaids. She'd ask us to dinner, but she'd never like me. And perhaps it's the boys most of all. You'd want them with us; I would too. But after what their mother and grandmother and aunts had told them about me, how far would we get with them? A few movies and the circus, and both of them watching us the way little boys watch grownups——

"And then there's my family, Ken. Ag's husband works in the shipyard. My brother Willy's always in trouble; Mom takes in boarders. You don't know them yet. I want—I want anyone I marry to be crazy about them. I don't want to feel anxious when my husband and I go to have dinner at home. Even if Mom would ever want us to dinner, you being divorced!"

She shut her eyes and two tears slipped down, even though she tried to laugh.

"No, I can't do all that," she said. "Having a charge account at Tiffany's wouldn't make up for it, no, nor the opera box nor your uncle Laurence's yacht. I like you—I like you better than any man I've ever known, Ken," Julia said, freeing her hands and, as she and the man stood up, laying them lightly on his shoulders. "You've spoiled me for any other man, God help me, and I lost Mart Mhoon when I told him so. But there's lots of other happiness beside honeymoon happiness, and I've put them both into the scales, and I know which side comes down.

"And so it's good-by, Ken, and all luck to you! I'll not see you again— no, don't come with me. This is good-by."

"Good-by, Julia," he said quietly. He walked to the window and looked out at the deepening dusk. Julia went through the chain of offices and downstairs in the elevator, and somehow she got home.

Somehow she got home, and found her mother just dishing dinner and as usual entertaining company. Tonight it was big, rangy, sandy-haired Myra Keenan, nurse to the Percy Schuylinghauser babies. Myra was already at the table, talking to the Keohane sisters and Betty.

"Tell that again to Julia, Myra," Mrs. Crowley said, coming in with a great smoking platter. "It's about Louise Schuylinghauser wint off wit' the doctor, Julia," she said, "and how the boy that was in prep school tried to kill himself for shame that his mother was livin' up in some place on Par'rk Avenue——"

Julia greeted the guest, kissed her mother.

"It's a poor general that wastes his ammunition after the battle's won, Mom," she said wearily. "I'm not having any dinner; my head aches."

She went upstairs. The big dim shabby room was empty when she entered it, but after a while Ellen came limping in and looked about in the dusk and slowly approached the bed.

She knelt down beside it and groped for one of Julia's hands, and put it, strong and young and warm, and wet with tears, against her face. "Ah, don't Ju! You're so wonderful, Ju," she said.

The Hand of God

"Every night when I go to bed I ask myself why I don't kill Genevieve,"
Tom Crowley said thoughtfully.

"Somebody ought to," Julia agreed.

"Now that'll be about enough of that," their mother put in severely.
"It's a very thryin' age she's at."

"Trying what?" Tom countered.

"Trying to pretend she's grown up," Julia supplied. "Fourteen, and
buying a new lipstick with every dime she can get! Talking about boys
with Maudie Kelly while they're supposed to be doing their homework.
Frizzing that hair of hers until she looks like a Zulu with a ring in its nose."

"It's that superior laugh of theirs that gets me," Tom said. "I can
stand anything but that! I was over in Corona the other afternoon ordering some lead pipe and if I didn't see Gen and Maudie wandering along
the street, piping everything——"

"In Corona!" Mrs. Crowley's big hands stopped their activities for a
moment, and she looked patiently at her son.

"Sure," Tom said. "A couple of sailors were right in front of them,
and whether they were trying to pick them up I don't know, but anyway,
when I saw Maudie and Gen here that night I thought I'd give them a
tip. I said that it wasn't any of my business what they did, but there
was no percentage for them in that kind of thing. Gosh, you should have
heard them laugh! They whinnied with their heads up like a couple of
horses, and Maudie says, 'Now don't get upset, darling. He says himself it's
none of his business!' 'Well,' Gen says, sighing, 'I wish sometimes my
family had something else to do except spy on me!'"

"Oh, they drive you mad!" said Julia.

"You wasn't anny St. Agnes yourself whin you was four'rteen, Jule,"
her mother said mildly.

"I know I wasn't, Mom. But I'll be darned if I was like Gen. Eating until she's forty pounds overweight, giggling over everything, never taking a bath but putting on a lot of perfume——"

"Look at Stella," Tom said as his sister paused. "She's only two years younger than Gen, but she's so pretty and gentle and dainty. The boys are already crazy about Stell."

"To hear Genevieve and Maudie talk, every man they see is crazy about *them*," Julia added. "They talk nothing but boys, and the movie stars they're crazy about."

"Well, I like Gary Cooper meself," Mrs. Crowley said stoutly. "He has a face as kind as a priest!"

"That's all very well, Mom, but you don't write him letters."

"Well, they don't either."

"But that's exactly what they *do*. Or if it isn't to him it's to some other Hollywood star. At least from the way they talk, I'm sure they do. And I know Maudie's told her mother that Tom's crazy about her."

"Our Tom?" Mrs. Crowley asked, startled out of her pose of calm and giving the big boy a glance.

"I've got plenty of company," Tom grinned. "Maudie was telling me the other day that Hogan, the soda jerker at Shapiro's, was making her life a burden with his attentions——"

"Tom, she didn't have the nerve to say that!" Julia interpolated.

"She did. And she has some aviator down in Florida who writes to her every day. And didn't she tell Gen some long rigmarole about Val Casey's uncle from Buffalo?"

"Mom, that's dangerous," Julia said virtuously, looking expectantly at her mother. "Maudie's only fifteen, and with her head filled with that sort of rubbish! Writes to her every day! I know who she means—she means Joe Duffy. Writes to her every day! I don't suppose he even ever sent her a postcard of an airport!"

"Oh well—ger'rls," Mrs. Crowley said patiently. But she was not happy.

"I'll tell you the only thing I mind," Julia began again with sudden spirit. "They can use as much make-up as they like and walk around telling each other about their love affairs, but it's the *lying* I hate. Genevieve simply doesn't know the truth when she sees it any more. She pours out all sorts of silly gush without ever stopping to think if there's one shred of truth in it. Remember last year when she had the Kellys thinking she was an adopted child and that you had some baby clothes with beautiful French embroidery on them—clothes she had on when you found her? And remember when she told you that Mr. Chalmers was really an English duke but he was hiding here in America because he thought he had wronged the cousin who would inherit his estate?"

"Gosh, I never heard that. Where'd she get that?" Tom asked with an appreciative grin.

"Oh, that's nothing!" Julia assured him, warming. "I think now that

[422]

that story of how she and Maudie heard some woman moaning and cry-ing upstairs over the bakery was all lies, Mom. And I *know* it wasn't true that before Sister Sebastian was moved to the Albany house there was a handsome man hanging around the convent."

"She'd ought to l'ave the Sisthers be," Mrs. Crowley said uneasily.

"Sister Anastasia says that Genevieve isn't going to graduate; she told Gen that today. And Maudie Kelly, too," Stella Crowley said over a piece of bread and applesauce. She had come in from the hall, having gone upstairs to change her school dress to a play dress, and had entered the kitchen almost unnoticed. Now she joined the group and the conversation, taking a seat at the table.

Stella was approaching her thirteenth birthday. Always a pretty and dainty child, with her socks firmly held to her round little legs and her small wrists set off with spotless trim cuffs, she was advancing almost im-perceptibly now into exquisite young girlhood. Her silky black hair was taking on an added luster; her cheeks wore an apricot glow; where her sturdy little form had been flat and compact it was blossoming into soft curves, budding and blooming into the miracle of womanhood. Stella would be lovely someday; not as tall, not as beautiful as Julia, but with something of Julia's assured manner, something of Julia's innate wisdom, much of Julia's beauty.

"Sister said that Genevieve's and Maudie's conduct was far from edi-fying," Stella reported without any special feeling, "and that a Produstant gentleman told Good Mother that he was surprised that Catholic girls would set such an example."

"That Protestant gentleman!" Julia said impatiently. This mythical character, with his moral commentaries, had been a familiar figure in her schooldays too. "He's always there and he's always being disedified! No, but seriously," she went on, as Tom gave a great laugh, "I think you ought to talk to Gen, Mom. Now one day this week, maybe it was Mon-day," Julia added in sudden recollection, "where was Gen after school? Maudie had a cold, and she wasn't at school and she telephoned twice. Gen got in to dinner, and someone asked her where she had been——"

"And she said 'taking my feet for a walk,'" Stella supplied, deeply interested, but more concerned in the opinions of her elders than in her own.

"Gee, she certainly has a good supply of those wisecracks!" Tom ob-served. "'Down on the tracks trying to put a train on my skirt,' and 'I'm as old as my tongue and months older than my teeth!' and 'If I don't graduate I'll quituate.'"

"Hello," said Genevieve from the doorway. "Who's quituating?"

"You, probably, if you don't get next to yourself," Tom answered.

"Don't tell me that this gathering of my very reverend and assured good masters is all about me!" Genevieve said airily.

"Tom's wor'rkin' tonight and Jule's home ear'rly," her mother explained.

Genevieve, overweight, with a bad skin, thick, dry, curled hair and too much make-up completing the rather flashy effect of sweater, scarf, striped short skirt, and tricolored latticed shoes, went to the pantry to help herself to some of the bread and applesauce. But she did not bring it back neatly on a plate as Stella had, and instead of using the two-days'-old brown wheaten loaf that waited on a trencher, she slashed two hot, palpitating crusts from the afternoon's fresh baking, and returned with melted butter and applesauce dripping upon her fingers and her sweater.

"It's a divine day," she said with her mouth full.

Mrs. Crowley used that adjective for one class of thoughts only; she winced when it was belittled for lesser use. But she could not further discredit Genevieve in the eyes of her sisters and brother now.

"You'll wor'rk har'rd," she predicted, "an' gradj'ate wit' the rest of thim."

"Who said I wouldn't?" Genevieve demanded amiably. "My Godfrey, look at my sweater!" she added disgustedly. "I had an engagement for to-morrow night, too. I'll wear Ellen's."

"What's your engagement?" Julia asked with a keen look.

"Would you not like to know, sweet sister?"

"Don't say 'my Godfrey'; I've told you that before," said her mother. "It's like somethin' else it does be soundin'."

"Yes, S'ter," Genevieve said as if absent-mindedly. Reproof must never seem to reach the inner fastnesses of her superiority.

"You're not talking to the Sisters," Julia reminded her, annoyed by the casual form of the reply. "You're talking to Mom."

"Thanking you for the information, I'm sure," Genevieve returned courteously.

"I'll not have you goin' out wit' boys, Saturda' night or no Saturda' night," her mother told her when Julia had gone upstairs, Tom had departed for the ironworks, and Stella was busy with homework in the adjoining room.

"Mama, will you *kinely* tell me why you objec'?" Genevieve demanded in a patient voice.

"Because yu're only a little ger'rl. Yu're not fifteen itself yet."

"Your own mother was married at fifteen," Genevieve argued.

"Thim was different times an' different people. We'll have no talk at all of that, if you please." Mrs. Crowley scattered handfuls of flour on a white scraped board, lifted to it from a white bowl the shining wet mass that was biscuit dough, patted its pebbled surface with a knowing hand. "Where do you go these days, afther school?" she asked. "I know you was doin' nothin' bad, but there's manny a fix a ger'rl can get herself into, an' her not knowin' the danger there'd be in it."

"I don't do anything," Genevieve said after a moment.

"But where do you go, lovey?"

"Oh—walking."

"Maudie wasn't wit' you, for Maudie was at home sick."

"No," Genevieve conceded. She looked dreamily into space, laughed lightly. "I should say Maudie *wasn't*," she said. And she added in an undertone, "Poor Maudie!"

"Where'd you walk?"

"I *ought* to walk," Genevieve began on a sudden virtuous note. "I ought to walk off ten pounds, if I'm to be St. Cecilia in the Christmas cantata. I walk round the cemetery out to the air base. That's more than a mile!"

"Did Sisther say she'd let you be St. Cecilia?"

"She promised me. The girls," Genevieve went on without undue haste, "don't know yet. I don't know when she'll tell them. It's on account of Superior not liking me."

"Why wouldn't Mother Superior like you, dear'r? She's very fond of Julia an' Stell an' all of us."

"Oh, it's on account of that Constantinople business, I guess," Genevieve said carelessly.

"Constantinople?" Mrs. Crowley connected this word with nothing but a foolish bit of gibberish heard now and then in the course of a long life and ending with "a nople and a pople and a Constantinople."

"Mother Superior," Genevieve began, spacing her words firmly, as one who adds simple fact to fact, "was in the Constantinople convent for years. *And*—when she first came here she called me out of class one morning—*and* she asked me if I had relatives in Constantinople. *And*—I said not that I knew of."

"Not that you knew of!" Mrs. Crowley said, stupefied, and pausing with her biscuit cutter in air. "What possest her! They'd be blacks, I wudden't wondher!"

"She said never to mention it to you or anyone else," Genevieve, her eyes darkling and glowing in a very spate of thoughts, said smoothly, "and so I never did. That was all there was to it anyway. She put her hand on my shoulder and sort of whispered to herself 'How like, how very like!' and then she told me to go back to class and forget all about it. But since that time she's been especially kind to me in a hundred little——"

"I thought you said she didn't like you?" the thoroughly bewildered older woman put in at this point.

"She doesn't," Genevieve conceded promptly, "but when a nun doesn't like you she makes a special effort to be nice to you. All the girls notice it."

"Then she'll probably let you be St. Cecilia, you think?"

"Let me be? Oh yes, *that*," Genevieve said, recalled.

"If yu're really tryin' to take off fat, ye musn't eat hot bread," Mrs. Crowley said mildly. "It'll do ye no good to walk to the flyin' field an' back if you fill up the minute you get home."

"Darling, I love you!" Genevieve smiled as at the vagaries of a child, gathered her hat and purse, pounded her way upstairs. "You're delicious!"

she called back. She swept into the room where Ellen was lying on her couch, a newspaper folded at a crossword puzzle in her lax hand, her eyes filled with dreams. "Where's Julia?" the younger sister asked.

"Taking a bath. She's going out with Mart."

Genevieve dropped her coat and books, twirled about in the center of the floor, her hands locked above her head, and indulged in a gay mysterious laugh. Suddenly she sank with one extravagantly graceful motion at the side of the couch and caught Ellen's hands to her cheek.

"Oh, Ellen, Ellen, Ellen, what do you do when men are fools enough to fall in love with you?" she demanded.

Ellen looked at her gravely. She was the only member of the family who conscientiously tried never to laugh at Genevieve, scold her or criticize her, and she felt in the maintenance of that attitude a real responsibility. But sometimes it was heavy going.

"Don't tell me anyone has fallen in love with *that?*" she said half humorously, lifting to view the black fingernails of one of Genevieve's stout young hands.

"Oh, that!" Genevieve shrugged, dismissing it scornfully. "Ellen," she gushed, "I'm having such thrills!"

"Tell me," Ellen invited her, bored in advance.

"He's an aviator."

"Not the one whose picture you cut out of the rotogravure a while back?"

"That's the one." Genevieve's giggle was filled with triumph.

"But how'd you ever meet him?"

"I walk up that way now and then. And day before yesterday——"

"But you were with Maudie that afternoon, weren't you?"

"I said I was." The second word was slightly stressed. There was no perceptible pause between question and answer. "But I was at the field with Ed," Genevieve said.

"It isn't 'Ed' already, I hope? He looks—how old is he? He looks thirty-five."

"Thirty-four," Genevieve said after a second. "And oh, is he darling! Ellen, do you think fifteen's too young to marry? Mom's mother was only fifteen. I'll be fifteen in August."

"Much too young," Ellen answered seriously, "and you're very silly to even think about it. He's not in earnest. He thinks of you as a little girl."

The exultant, affected laugh again. Ellen felt her teeth on edge.

"That's all you know!" her younger sister declared. "But, believe you me, we're both in earnest now. I wish you could see the letters he writes me! I showed Maudie one yesterday. Wait!"

She reached for her bag, extracted the newspaper picture of the aviator, showed with it a much-folded typewritten letter on unmistakable stationery. The little winged ship was engraved at the top with the imposing caption of the aviation company in brilliant red and blue.

"'Darling, can't make it today; making up reports,'" Ellen read. "'Wish your beautiful eyes and the soft mouth I love to kiss weren't always in my mind. See you Thursday at our own meeting place.'"

It was signed with two initials: E.B. They matched those of the name beneath the picture—Edward Burns.

Ellen looked keenly at her sister, looked back at the letter and then at Genevieve again. Was there any truth in this? If there was not, then Genevieve had deliberately—anyone could secure a piece of flying-field stationery, of course—but would Gen deliberately . . .

"You've got to stop this," she said. "Mom would be perfectly wild if she thought you were carrying on with an aviator more than twice your age. You pay more attention to your schoolwork——"

"Oh, schoolwork!" Genevieve moaned. She pushed the stiff brush of her overcurled hair this way and that, hiding her face. "Ellen, I can never go back to school," she said. "I wish I could. I wish to heaven I could! But don't you understand—*won't* you understand—that I'm not a child any more! I'm a woman, and paying the price for being a woman." She pressed her hot face, still entangled in the black curls, against Ellen's neck. "The moment he touched me, the moment his arm was about me," she whispered, "I seemed to go weak all over! I tried——"

"What on earth is going on?" It was Julia's clear, amazed voice that cut across the confession; Julia, her beautiful body wrapped in an old cotton kimono, her beautiful tawny hair loosened, her beautiful eyes shining with laughter and scorn like two star sapphires, was in the doorway. She toweled her hair vigorously, shook it back to stare again at her sisters.

Genevieve, discomfited, sat back on her knees, reaching for the love letter and the portrait.

"Nothing," she said sullenly. "Nothing you wouldn't laugh at. Because naturally," Genevieve continued, gaining a certain oratorical force and ease as she went on, "naturally everyone would be in love with Miss Mary Julia Agnes Crowley if she was in the picture at all! So don't let anything that could happen to poor me disturb you!"

She swept from the room with the last words, banging the door of the adjoining apartment after her. Julia raised her eyebrows at Ellen, shrugged.

"Nice age," she commented dryly.

"You don't suppose there'd be any harm in her picking up an aviator out at the airport?" Ellen asked uneasily.

"Does she say she did?" Julia was busily arranging her hair at the dressing table.

"She met one of them, and—and sort of—liked him, I think, and he wrote her a letter," Ellen said hesitatingly.

"See the letter?"

[427]

"Yes, she showed it to me. She seems to be gaga about him," the younger sister added simply.

"She would be; that uniform would be enough. But I don't believe any one of them would look at her," Julia said thoughtfully. "Too many other girls around."

"But if she sort of—goes after it," Ellen submitted timidly.

Julia frowned, her hair perfection now, her face delicately touched with powder, her lips delicately crimsoned.

"That's the sort that don't get it," she said. She stepped into a pleated black frock, drew it up about her slim hips, and buttoned its many small gold buttons scrupulously. A scalloped white collar was turned down at her throat; more tiny gold buttons held white cuffs in place. Julia looked at herself critically in the glass, tipped a small ribboned hat to an irresistible angle.

"Is it Mart again tonight?" asked Ellen.

"Mart," said Julia with a sigh.

"You—you don't feel any happier about that, Ju?"

"Nope," said Julia briefly. In a moment she said, "Good-by, darling," and left the room. Ellen lay thinking for a long five minutes, then she pulled herself up with a little wincing and struggling, straightened her own hair, and descended for the family dinner.

But the family dinner was being postponed, and an instantly perceptible tension held the lower floor. The boarders, three in number, and little Joe and Stella and the married daughter of the family, Ag, and Ag's husband, Harry Kane, and Tom, were all milling about restlessly between kitchen and dining room; Julia and Mart were loitering in the lower hall, and loud hysterical voices were coming from the closed door of the parlor. Ellen stopped in consternation.

"What's up, Ju?"

"Heaven knows!" Julia said. "But Mom's in there, and Genevieve, and that precious Maudie Kelly and Mr. Kelly and some man! I wish someone in the family had the wits to notice what's going on right under their eyes."

"Well, all I saw," said Stella with a virtuous stressing of the pronoun, "was that Maudie was yelling and crying in the kitchen, and Genevieve came in and said, 'You big tattletale!' to Maudie, and then Mr. Kelly and some man came to the door and Mom said for everyone to come into the parlor and she'd see if she could make head or tail of it, and then Genevieve said, 'You keep out of this, Stella Crowley!' and slammed the door in my face."

"Maybe Gen's killed someone like Willy did!" little Joe said with relish.

"Willy never killed anyone, Joe, and that's the last dime you get from me for the movies the longest day you live if ever I hear you saying that again," Julie said, drawing her small brother to her with a firm grip of strong young fingers and speaking in a low voice.

"Who's the man?" Tom asked. He had returned with an unexpected evening of leisure, after finishing a job that had taken but a few minutes, and was enjoyably contemplating the prospect of taking his girl to a movie.

"Nobody knows," Julia said. "He looks like a wife beater, I'll say that for him."

"Tom," said Mrs. Crowley in a tired voice from the parlor door. Tom sprang to obey, went into the parlor. The door was closed again. Ellen, sniffing, went to the oven and rescued the biscuits in a state bordering closely upon burning; Stella, with one eye to the parlor door, began to set the table. Little Joe, struck with a sudden inspiration, went cannily out the side entrance, noiselessly mounted the front porch steps, and stationed himself outside the parlor window.

They could all hear Maudie's high-pitched voice and Genevieve's deeper, sullen tones. Now and then Mrs. Crowley spoke questioningly, the man talked, and once laughed most disagreeably, and presently Tom was talking, firmly and quickly—violently even.

Then the door into the hall was abruptly opened; a male form was rapidly propelled to the street door by Tom's big hand. There was the skittering sound of a body descending steps by bumps and wild handgrips, execrations were poured out by a figure staggering to the street, and in the parlor a brief résumé and finale to the episode preceded the departure of Maudie and her father.

The family had only to wait now, and not stop the inevitable flood of information by any discreet questioning. Julia and Mart remained only long enough to hear Tom's first angry summary.

"Fools! Gen and Maudie put a matrimonial ad in the paper, and all that loafer had to do was to hang around the post office until someone came and asked for the mail! Fourteen years old, and they haven't the sense of Ag's baby! He walked in on old Kelly tonight and tried to blackmail him, and precious little Maudie has to streak over here and drag Genevieve into it! She's the one that thought it up!"

"But it was half my money that paid for the ad!" Genevieve said honestly, hotly. "It was all a joke. We didn't know——"

"You don't know anything," Julia said coldly, departing. "I never heard of anything so silly! Can't you wait to get a husband until you have a little sense?"

"I know this! I'll never speak to Maudie Kelly again!" Genevieve said passionately, seeking sympathy.

None was accorded her.

"Perhaps the less we say about the whole thing the betther," Mrs. Crowley said wearily, absorbed in belated dinner preparations and moving about her kitchen without meeting anyone's eye.

The boarders tactfully withdrew to the parlor, to busy themselves with the radio and await summons to the meal, but in the kitchen the purgatory she knew she could not escape engulfed the unfortunate Genevieve.

"What'd you think you were doing?" Tom, at ease with the evening paper at the kitchen table, asked amusedly.

"We thought it would be fun to read the answers," Genevieve answered, choking. "We didn't think anyone could find out who we were."

"Peel thim for me," her mother said, putting a pot of smoking sweet potatoes down beside her. The girl seized the knife gratefully, dropping the hot silky skins on the floor and on her pleated plaid skirt, grateful only to be employed.

"Gen, do you *want* to get married?" little Joe demanded.

"No, of course not!" she answered angrily. "It was just for fun. It was just to see what they'd say!"

"So you call yourselves 'Blondes, eighteen, recently in model and chorus work; steady income from government bonds'?" Tom reminded her.

"I hate you," Genevieve said thickly.

"That's enough teasin', now, Tom," his mother said briskly. "They done a fool thing an' wasted their good money, but he hadn't no business to bother them, an' I'm glad you threw him out."

"Mom, he couldn't have made Gen marry him, could he?" Stella asked, angelic sisterly anxiety in her uplifted eyes.

"Oh, shut up," Genevieve muttered from a cloud of steam.

"Well, of course he cudden't. But at the same time it's cour'rtin' danger to have anny association whatsoiver wit' the like of him," Mrs. Crowley answered. "Evil communications corrupt good manners, as they say. Go tell thim everything's ready, lover. Put a lump of butther in that, Stell, an' don't bur'rn yure hand. Clear out of me way, Joe avick!"

There was a brief lull for Genevieve, for dinner was late and everyone was hungry, but she knew it was not for long. Tom presently burst out with a muttered "Gosh, it makes you feel dirty even to touch a fellow like that! 'Maybe the little ladies would like to pay a little something to keep this out of my lawyer's hands?' His lawyer's hands, pah! He's the kind that takes damn good care to keep away from lawyers!" growled Tom.

"There isn't a month that the detective magazines wouldn't have some story of a poor girl being led astray and murdered by one of them in cold blood," Mag Keohane, who had worked in the post office seventeen years and had boarded at Mrs. Crowley's exactly that long, observed thoughtfully.

"As if there wasn't trouble enough in the world," twelve-year-old Stella said in an audible aside to her mother. "He might have told them to meet him somewhere, mightn't he, Mom? Mightn't he, Mom?"

"I'll bet that boy knows how to fire a pistol, oh boy, oh boy, oh boy," Joe soliloquized.

"'Meet him somewhere,'" Genevieve repeated in trembling scorn. "What do you think I and Maudie are?"

"Well, really it's hard to know what you and Maudie are sometimes," Tom said, shaking his head. Genevieve was wondering if she could refrain from tears long enough to say proudly, "I hate you all!" when Ellen came to the rescue. Ellen was as shocked as everyone else at her younger sister's latest escapade, but she was always for the underdog, and she knew the misery of shame and helplessness that was overwhelming Genevieve. So she said kindly:

"You know, I've often wondered, Mom, what sort of men answered those matrimonial ads. I don't blame Gen for taking a chance, just for the fun of the thing. Of course she and Maudie couldn't know that this sort of a man would follow them home. D'you suppose those marriages ever turn out successful?"

"Well, not with that one it couldn't!" Mrs. Crowley was an experienced peacemaker, too, and she had begun to feel uncomfortable over the laughter and teasing to which Genevieve was being subjected. "It was a silly way to waste money," she added mildly, "but if none of ye ever does wor'rse, I'll thank God on me knees."

The tide had turned, and Tom good-naturedly contributed his share to the change of tone.

"Lord, you can get matrimonial bureau booklets full of pictures of girls and men," he said. "You'd die, reading 'em. They're all home-loving and lonely and needing sympathetic companion with money to invest——"

There was a laugh that seemed to clear the air, and Genevieve was sufficiently recovered to say sulkily but apologetically, with stinging eyes:

"If he'd followed *me* instead of Maudie, you bet I'd never have dragged Maudie into it the way she did me!"

"Poor kid, she was probably scared out of her seven senses," Tom said leniently. Genevieve's eyes brimmed; she could sustain their contempt only by a conscious effort of pride and will; their kindness was too much for her.

"It was a fool thing to do," she conceded thickly.

"But do you want so much to get married, Genevieve?" Stella demanded innocently. "You're only fourteen. I wouldn't want to be married until I was at least twenty-five."

"I thought you were going to be a nun, Stell?" Tom, perfectly sensing the effect upon Genevieve of Stella's question, asked surprisedly. This was carrying the war to new ground. Stella's clear little lovely face flushed.

"I used to think I would," she answered briefly.

"Well, wouldn't it sort of haunt you all your life if you didn't?" Tom queried solicitously. "Wouldn't you always remember—I mean, saying that you got a job and had beaus and got married—wouldn't you always feel that you'd refused a vocation?"

"No, I wouldn't!" Stella asserted, red-cheeked. "Would I, Mom?"

"You was only a child when you used to say you'd dedicated yourself to Blessed Marg'ret Mary," her mother began pacifically, wondering what had gotten into all the children tonight, anyway.

"I was only ten!" Stella put in, ready for tears.

Genevieve rose unsolicited and began to clear away plates for the pudding. She felt blind adoration in her heart for Tom and stopped behind his chair to kiss the waves of his thick, curly black hair. But this caused a trickle of gravy from a tipped plate to spill upon his shoulder, and Tom was annoyed and followed his sister into the kitchen, where with hot water and a clean towel they spent some minutes repairing the damage.

"Gosh, if you'd look where you're going once in ten years!" Tom grumbled. Genevieve was speechless. There was no use trying to extricate herself from the accidents and embarrassments of life; they had lain in wait for her ever since she could remember anything at all; they would always lie in wait for her. Everything she said made matters worse, and in attempting to mend them she only involved herself the further. Any impulsive emotional gesture she made was likely to turn out horribly, with ink being spilled or glass broken or a lamp falling on someone's head. Or else she herself fell full length over a rug or a schoolroom form. If people gave her letters to mail she always forgot to mail them and was always discovered, and if she wrote a sentimental note to Maudie, Sister Domitilla inevitably found it and read it to Genevieve in her sweet passionless voice, and recommended that schoolgirls refrain from extravagant expressions of affection among themselves.

However, tonight's searing experience was ending in the blessed routine of dishwashing and evening gossip; Annie and Mag Keohane came into the kitchen to talk to Mrs. Crowley about the mission while she set oatmeal to soak and put together the dry ingredients of breakfast's corn bread; Joe yawned over his homework; Stella settled down with schoolbooks in the dining room; Ellen limped upstairs and Tom went out. Genevieve presently disappeared int the welcome obscurity of her own room and devoted herself to algebra, Bible history, peanut brittle, and a radio turned down almost to inaudibility.

And the next day all was forgotten. It was a singing day of high clouds and cold sunshine; Genevieve felt invigorated and excited by it. She found on her desk at noon a twelve-page letter from Maudie; but she did not glance toward Maudie as she put it into her pocket, and when school was over she did not wait for Maudie, who had been kept in to explain why she had been late that morning.

No, Genevieve went home, where she read the letter with thrilled delight. Maudie explaining and apologizing and anxious to be friends again! Well, that was certainly a change. Genevieve plastered seven soda crackers with butter and strawberry jam, and sallied forth into the afternoon streets at peace with the world.

Julia was coming in the gate as she went out, and of course had to ask her where she was going.

"To the Homeway for Mom," Genevieve answered smoothly, "and then for a walk!"

"You'd better look out where you walk; it gets dark early now," Julia warned her. Genevieve walked away without acknowledging this sisterly solicitude.

"Poo-ey on you-ey!" she said aloud with great satisfaction to the unanswering streets. For a few minutes she loitered; she was known in this neighborhood. Then she walked briskly, entered a crowded bus, and for some fifteen minutes sat staring out of the window, in a dream of conquering Hollywood.

But she was not too lost to the present to descend at the right place, turn corners, cross streets, and presently ring the bell marked "Day," that flanked a big columned institution doorway. Inside was a dark, unfurnished, spotless hall and a small parlor containing only six rigid chairs and two framed colored religious pictures. Here Genevieve was joined by two women in voluminous black, who sat one on either side of her, talking earnestly. Genevieve's share of the conversation was for a while confined to a respectful "No, S'ter" and "Yes, S'ter" but she presently had her opportunity to speak.

"You say you know Mrs. Harney well, Genevieve?"

"Yes, S'ter. I met her last month when she was at the little girl's grave in the cemetery. I was walking through."

"Someone you love is buried there?"

"No, S'ter. I was just walking. And she was crying, and I talked to her and made her go home. I mean I took her home, and sort of stayed round helping with the dishes and all that. Until her husband came back."

"Sister Paul and I stopped there yesterday," one of the nuns said quietly. Genevieve's eyes widened with fear.

"You told her!"

"No," said the nun with the faint hint of a smile touching her grave wise mouth. "No, we are not sure but what your plan of keeping all this a secret is the best. She did not even suspect what order we come from. We said that we were tired, which was true, and a long way from home, which was true. And she offered us tea. We thought it a very pleasant home, and she is a good woman. And the husband," the Sister Ligouri added after a second's pause, "is a good man. It was sad to hear them talk of the child."

"They were married ten years before they had Rose," Genevieve offered, her eyes anxious. "He—Mr. Harney—wanted to adopt a baby a year ago, when Rose died. But she—she says she wants to wait for the hand of God."

Her voice faltered into silence. The nuns looked at each other.

"I've been there—oh, often," Genevieve pursued. "I talk to her, and sometimes we go round the corner to Benediction. But she—she almost lost her mind," she finished simply.

"I imagine you have been a good friend to her," Sister Ligouri observed mildly, after a pause. "She told us of you, without our having mentioned you. Sister and I thought we had better not say anything of knowing you. She said you had come to them in their darkest hour and that she felt she could not have gotten through the last months without you."

Had Julia or Tom seen Genevieve's face now, in the dim filtered light of the sparsely furnished, clean little parlor, they might not have recognized their sister. Her eyes were shining, there was life in the dull heavy features, there was power in the poise of the curled head.

"Thank you, S'ter," the girl said thickly. And then bravely: "But you think you'd—you'd rather not give her a baby?"

"No," said the nun, "we think perhaps we will let you try it. We can go in now and then, as if accidentally, as we did yesterday, to see that the little boy is flourishing. Mrs. Harney told us yesterday that the priest and the neighborhood nuns often come in to see her. We believe it will be a safe home for him."

She turned to the other religious and they exchanged murmurs.

"It is little Peter, Sister?"

"Peter. Yes. Sister Infirmarian said that she would have him ready."

Genevieve did not speak. She was in tears. But she was smiling, her cheeks still wet, when she descended the flight of stone steps to the street, a blanketed bundle in her arms.

There was another bus ride in a new direction, the girl sitting stiffly, pleased that the casual glances of fellow travelers so simply took her for a proud young mother. Presently she descended in a humble neighborhood and walked slowly along, thinking out the next steps of her undertaking.

Her heart was beating hard as she made her way through deepening dusk toward a row of plain cottages, each with its rose tree and geraniums in a patch of garden, its curtained bay windows dark, its kitchen region showing angles of light.

Into a certain gate Genevieve slipped; she came out again a moment later, breathing like a runner, but with empty arms. A stout little acid wail followed her as she fled through the early dark.

She turned a corner, walked a block or two slowly, her senses swimming, entered a bright market where late shoppers were hurriedly selecting sausages and Saratoga chips for supper. Genevieve took her time, put butter and soda and soap flakes into the wheeled cart she pushed ahead of her. After a leisurely fifteen minutes she went to the telephone.

"Mrs. Harney?" she asked when she had dialed her number. "I'm at the Homeway on my way to the house, and I've forgotten whether we need anything except soda—— What?"

She had been interrupted by a stream of half-coherent, tearful, and laughing words from the other end of the wire. Genevieve listened with an odd expression on her face, but her words were properly incredulous and amazed.

"When? Just now? . . . But who? . . . I don't believe it! Is Mr. Harney home? . . . But wasn't anyone with him—but I'm coming as fast as I can!"

Carrying a bag of groceries, she retraced her steps along the street, went in at the gate she had entered before, raced about to the kitchen yard, and opened the door.

In the light and warmth within a woman of perhaps thirty-eight or forty was sitting with an infant in the curve of her arm. Her face was thin, her eyes marked with old sorrow, but there was a radiance of joy about her.

"Look, Genevieve!" she whispered. "Look at him! I heard him crying, out on the porch, ten minutes ago, and I—I couldn't believe it! He's only six weeks old, the letter says, and his name's Peter. His father and mother are dead, and she—'A friend of Peter'—that's what she signs the letter— she says she wants me to take him. Oh, Genevieve, didn't I tell you and Robert that God would give me back a child! Ah, my little boy . . ."

She had a milk mixture in a cup; she was tenderly feeding him driblets of it from a spoon. The baby, who was small but sturdy, with a shock of silky black hair, ate greedily.

"I haven't a didy," Mary Harney said, her wet eyes shining, "but the crib's in the garage and I've the sheets and blankets—left, from the one that—didn't come! That's it, Peter—that's right, my little boy——"

A man, a plain, hard-worked, weary little clerk, opened the outer door and stood staring at the group. His face was tired and sad too, but it brightened suddenly as he saw his wife.

"What have you there, Mary?" he asked.

"God sent him to us, dear," the woman said. And then, as he knelt down and put his arms about wife and child, she faltered on: "I had to wait for God's hand, Rob. I'd never have done it on my own. But he has no one—he's ours, and feel the grip of his fingers already! That's Daddy, Peter, who's going to take you fishing someday!"

"Well, Mary, prayers are heard," the little man said when both had laughed thickly and both had wiped away tears.

"Oh, God is good," Mary Harney said. "Lend me your handkerchief that I don't drop tears on him, now he's just come! I've written you a list here for the drugstore, Rob, and you'll have to get the crib out. There's cotton and oil and a rubber sheet we'll need, and three bottles and a strainer—I wouldn't use any of the kitchen ones on him, and see if Robinson's is open for safety pins and didies——"

"I'll get them for you, son," the little man said. "It's a long time we've been waiting for you to come home."

Genevieve silently closed the kitchen door, closed herself out into the chilly dark. She was late for dinner now, and the bus was crowded and slow. Well, no help for it!

But by some luck, when, coatless and hatless, she glided into the kitchen and breathlessly and inconspicuously began to lend such aid as she could to dinner preparations, it was to find that everyone else was late, too, and that her absence had hardly been noted. It appeared that her married sister, Agnes, proud wife of Harry Kane, had added a second daughter to her family only an hour or two earlier, and Mrs. Crowley, who had at once gone over to Ag's to take charge, was not to return for dinner at all. The new baby absorbed the conversation; admiration and congratulations for Ag were mixed with pity.

"I'll bet Harry was ready to give the baby to the orphanage," Tom chuckled. "He has seven sisters and no brother!"

"I don't know why a person is always pitied if she has only girls," Julia said sharply. "If I had forty I'd want them all girls."

"Oh, the Lord help Mart!" Tom said. Julia gave him a steely look. The younger girls chuckled, and Genevieve caught her breath and composed herself and began to think with great satisfaction of the events of the afternoon.

"Genevieve," Ellen took occasion under cover of a loud general conversation to say reproachfully, "how could you tell me that yarn about Mr. Burns?"

"Mr. Burns?" Genevieve echoed, puzzled.

"Ed Burns, the aviator. Julia happened to say today that she saw him when she and Mart were dancing somewhere last week, and that he reminded her that his wife used to go to school with her, and that they have two babies."

"Oh?" Genevieve said, temporarily dashed. "Oh well, I was just fooling," she added airily.

"Well, I want to say that that's dangerous fooling," Ellen said severely.

"Gen, next time you go out don't soak yourself with my three-dollar toilet water," Julia said at this point.

"And don't dog-ear library books," Mag Keohane, one of the boarders, added. "Nelly O'Dea spoke to me about it yesterday."

"You took my skates and left me yours with the broken strap and if you don't put mine back I'm going to tell Mom," Stella contributed.

"Well, I'm popular!" Genevieve said, rising with a handful of piled plates. "Put your bouquets on the mantel, folks. Foo-ey on you-ey!"

"Nothing you say reaches her these days," Ellen confided to Julia in discouragement a few days later. "Now last night, when she slept in your bed because you were over at Cousin Batty's, if she wasn't beginning one of her yarns, after we had the light out. How she met some woman in a graveyard——"

"She's cracked on graveyards!" Julia put in appreciatively.

"And she got this woman home——"

"A corpse, did she mean?"

"Oh no, some woman crying over a dead child. Gen, it seems, got her home and jollied her up and talked to her and her husband, and comforted them. She's been over there practically every day, and they think she's a sort of angel. She tried to talk them into adopting a child, but the woman said she just wouldn't have the courage to take the step. But Genevieve told them they'd be glad, once they did."

"I suppose," Julia said in mild impatience and amusement, "that's the kind of thing she'd *like* to have happening to her!"

"Well, that's it, poor kid. The angel in the house."

"So then what happened?"

"Well," confessed Ellen with a little shamed laugh, "I lost the rest of it. I was dying for sleep, and I said, 'Oh, shut up, Gen, I'm dying!' and we both went to sleep."

"She's hopeless!" Julia said with a sigh. "Look, Ellen, don't you think this fingernail stuff is too dark?"

Peter Stops Walking

Vonnie Considine was a good woman. Even her pessimistic, wizened little mother-in-law could not find any fault when her son fell in love with the superior Miss Veronica Teresa Agnes Cullen. It was a surprisingly good match for simple, hard-working Peter to make. Old Mrs. Considine was secretly a little afraid of Vonnie, but she could look forth from the swathing folds of her dingy widow's veil with great satisfaction upon Vonnie's housekeeping and baby raising.

Vonnie and Peter had two children—daughters. Marie Dolores Veronica was ten; Geraldine Anne Virginia, eight. Geraldine had been dutifully named for Peter's father, Francis Gerald Considine, but she was usually called Jerry and he had always been known as Frank. Vonnie did not like either the name Frank or the name Peter; she said to her best friend, old Miss Donovan of the Girls' High, that she was glad her children were girls, and that if she had had twenty children she would not want any of them named either Peter or Frank.

She was unlikely to have twenty children. She had two, and there she stopped. The neighboring women, struggling along with broods of eight and ten, watched her with a slightly resentful admiration. Their kitchens were never in complete order; their nights were never unbroken; they had neither time nor money for beauty parlors. But not so Vonnie.

"It's very fortunate the way my children are spaced," she said sometimes in quiet satisfaction.

"Spaced!" said Mrs. Clem Moore in the sanctuary of the Crowley kitchen. "Wherever did she get a word like that one?"

"Ye don't space children," Mrs. Crowley commented thoughtfully, "ye *have* thim."

"She said she wanted a girl first to name for her mother," Julia Crowley contributed from her place at the kitchen table. Julia was doing things to her nails with clippers and paints, and enjoying the older women's desultory talk. "Then," Julia resumed, "she wanted another girl to be a companion to her, she said. And she said that was *enough*."

"Did she say what hour in the morning she wanted thim?" demanded Mrs. Crowley in high dudgeon.

This sally was received with much chuckling among the tea drinkers. Julia grinned.

"There isn't any question," she said reflectively, "that Vonnie has got everything worked out——"

"That'll be enough," her mother cut in sharply. The girl subsided, smiling over her manicuring. Unmarried women, even when they were twenty-six years old and experienced office managers like Julia Crowley, did not discuss family limitation in this atmosphere.

"As far as namin' the child Marie for Pether's mother," Mrs. Moore reopened the conversation, "Mamie Cullen was known as Mame for the whole of her life excipt that the Sisthers called her Mary!"

"Ye'd think Mary'd be good enough for thim," Mrs. Crowley offered, after thought. "It was good enough for the Lord. But no, they must make it May and Marie and—what's this Lizzie Dolan calls her child?—Maysie. Maysie! And as for Vonnie Considine——"

But the topic had to be abruptly dropped, for old Mrs. Considine came in at this moment. She reported that she had been at Vonnie's and seen the children, just in from school. But she sighed as she said it; things were not going any too well at the Considine house. Peter was a steady fellow; he didn't drink; he gave his wife everything the heart of woman could desire in the way of household equipment and personal possessions. Vonnie had a brand-new stove and a new radio, new bedcovers and new parlor curtains; Marie had music lessons, and the family enjoyed the use of a small but efficient car. But for all that . . .

"Maybe a ger'rl like Vonnie can be *too* good a housekaper an' *too* smart a manager," old Mrs. Considine said with another sigh. "Whin ye've taught domestic science in high school like Vonnie has, sure there's nothin' ye don't know. There's talk about budgets an' food values, but Pete looks very tired an' cast down entirely. Vonnie wud niver be tired tellin' ye of domestic science, but there's little talk goes on betwixt the two of thim these days. Ye'd think allergies an' antipathies—whativer they may be, God between us an' har'rm—was mush an' milk! She had me dishtracted the way she wudden't let the children have limonade at the circus—what else cud they do, the creatures, an' maybe be sick at home later, an' what har'rm to thim?"

"What indeed?" said Julia Crowley gravely. Later she said to Ellen that Von Considine's house gave her the creeps.

"It's perfect," said Julia, "but it's dead. 'Member the lampshade she was so crazy about that Peter gave her for Christmas? Well, it's always *here,* and the desk *here,* with a feather pen sticking in a little vase full of bullets, and one of those rockaby blotters just *so.* They've a furnace, of course, but Von's got a gas log with gray fringe hanging on it in the parlor, just for looks. Curtains crossed of course, like unmentionables, and a fern with green crinkled paper around it."

"I s'pose they never use the parlor?" Ellen asked, laughing.

"Indeed they do. Von won't let them sit in the dinette, evenings. She says the parlor is to sit in. So they go into the parlor, and the kids do their homework, and Peter reads the paper, and Von sews. And the next day she dusts everything and fixes it all perfect again——"

"Those vile ash trays in the morning!" Ellen put in, shaking her head.

"Ash trays nothing! Peter can't smoke in there. Peter can sit," Julia said with an unfeeling laugh, "and look at the six books on the table with the elephant book ends against them and the painted leather bookmark hanging out, and at the taboret that used to be in the Cullen house years ago, and the round Chinese mat under the lamp, and the Chinese glass bracelets to pull down the window shades, and the chocolate set."

"Just like Mom's parlor!" Ellen commented in high irony.

"Especially whin the ger'rls have had a candy pull an' are coolin' off in there," Mrs. Crowley contributed.

"Or Tom brings Hugh Harrison home to sleep on the couch."

"Or Tigey has kittens behind the piano."

"Or a rainy Sunday with Ag and Harry and the baby here, and the funnies all over the place!"

"Von's mother lives with them too," Julia presently said.

"And she's awful, isn't she?"

"Paralyzed. She used to get about a little, but now she can't even talk so you can understand her. She doesn't know anyone."

"Well, order or no order, and budget or no budget, I don't think I'd like to live with Vonnie," Ellen said. "I should think it would all but give Peter a nervous breakdown."

"It may not be a nervous breakdown," Julia answered soberly, "but it's something. Something's wrong over there. And Pete's a nice little fellow and I'm sorry about it."

"Not divorce?" Ellen asked, her eyes clouding.

"Oh, not from Vonnie! She'd never face anything like that. She's the sort that never will admit anything's wrong—with her, anyway. It'd always be Pete's fault!"

"Well, I wudden't think it'd be Vonnie's fault," Mrs. Crowley said in a troubled voice. "Her president of the Children of Mary an' all that. Maybe they're wor'kin' Pether a little too hard at the wor'rks."

"They *are* working Peter too hard. He's been moved into the office now and he gets sort of bothered and confused with the bookkeeping," Ellen said unexpectedly. Julia looked thoughtfully at her little invalided sister. Peter had come to see Ellen once or twice of late, sitting beside the couch on the porch where she spent most of the autumn afternoons—not talking much, as far as Julia could discern, but apparently deriving some comfort just from Ellen's presence.

"Peter liked the foundry best, though he got less money," Ellen said. "He worries now. His boss is Andy Buckley, and Andy's awfully mean."

"You apparently have the whole story," Julia commented.

"Well, I know Peter walks the floor nights sometimes," Ellen admitted, "and that it makes Vonnie mad."

"I should think it might, with all that furniture in the room, to say nothing of Von's mother and the children." Julia mused a moment. "But I don't know what else Vonnie could do," she said thoughtfully.

"Probably Vonnie thinks everything is lovely," Ellen said with a rare note of impatience in her voice. Julia laughed and left it at that. There was no use trying to change Vonnie Considine!

Vonnie Considine herself might have agreed with this verdict if she had ever seriously thought of changing herself at all. Like all women who are lavish in suggestions of change for anything and everything else, Vonnie rarely extended her critical observation to herself. She had been buoyed up by a consciousness of rectitude, capability, and reason from the day when her mother first presented her, as a tidy, watchful little girl of six, at the gate of the Notre Dame Convent, to begin her education. From that moment she had been admired, a leader, going on quietly, composedly, from triumph to triumph, finally to become the most valued young teacher in the Girls' High, inevitably slated for principalship.

Marriage had prevented this promotion, though it had not stopped—it had merely deflected—the course of Vonnie's progress. She had proved more than equal to the new demand. Vonnie had not only done everything that could possibly be expected of a housekeeper and a mother, but she had felt herself qualified to advise countless other women as to their duties and responsibilities.

Until very lately, that is. Now something was wrong, and Vonnie's most conscientious examination of her own discharge of her duties, of her table, budget, house, of Marie's and Jerry's actions, had failed to reveal to her any slightest thing awry.

So it must be Peter. And it became her duty, gently, kindly, firmly to guide Peter back to his old happiness and serenity.

For he was an inexacting little man. Vonnie was some inches the taller of the two; it gave her a sense of command. He had not needed much commanding. He had admired religiously everything she did for the twelve years of their marriage. The various flats she had selected and furnished had inevitably represented unbelievable luxury and beauty to him. His mother's home had been shabby and crowded; Vonnie's apartment never was that. His mother had had nothing in her five poor rooms that was not used and abused to an almost unrecognizable point; china, blankets, rugs, curtains all reduced to one state of common grayness; saucepans blackened, china chipped and mismatched, meals eaten at any and all hours from the end of the kitchen table.

So that Vonnie's orderly kitchen, her nicely stocked linen closet, her ways with dishtowels and mixing bowls and toothbrushes, her tidy arrangements of six roses in a green glass vase, had all seemed miracles to Peter. And his clean good babies had seemed the supreme miracle of all.

They were now in the nicest flat they ever had had: a flat with two bedrooms, a bathroom, a parlor, kitchen, and dinette. The dinette was a square space marked off from the kitchen by a low-standing wall that had china shelves on the kitchen side and bookshelves on the dinette side. It was filled by a narrow table and two carved and cushioned benches. It saved Vonnie innumerable steps and much effort to be able to pass things over the low wall or place them on it.

Otherwise it was not quite as useful as a regular dining room because it opened into the kitchen, and Vonnie had a theory that school children should not breathe the air of kitchen and dining room after meals. So Marie and Jerry did their homework in the parlor. Also in the parlor there sat, day out and in, the stony, silent figure of Vonnie's mother. Peter helped Vonnie drag and lift and push the figure into the front bedroom at ten o'clock every night.

The front bedroom had once been his room—their room. But now Vonnie and her mother had shared the double bed for six years, and Marie had a cot in the corner. Peter and his younger daughter had the other room. That was the best way to work it, and that was the way Vonnie worked it.

And when her friends and neighbors noticed that Peter was getting cross and glum and silent, and was very unlike his old self, Vonnie saw it, too, and she did something about it. She scolded Peter lightly, kindly, and when that elicited only most unwonted rudeness, Vonnie, lapsing into sullen silence in return, took other steps. She wrote to Dorothy Davenport. Her husband upset the nerves of the whole family by walking the floor at night. What would Miss Davenport suggest?

Miss Davenport's picture, about as large as that of Washington on a stamp, adorned a column in the newspaper every morning with her solutions of domestic problems. Peter never read this part of the paper, so Vonnie felt quite safe. Using a fictitious name, she sent a letter to Miss Davenport, and a week later she had a printed reply. Vonnie's eyes brightened at the thought of so simple a solution.

That night was cold with the first touch of winter. Radiators in the Considine apartment house smelled and clanked, and when Peter got home it was dark. He had been delayed over some question of a balance in the office; Vonnie considered this none of her business and was in the process of serving a good dinner.

Up to this time Peter had not noticed any change. But when they all went into the parlor, and Vonnie began her usual encouraging and advising of the children with their exercises, he looked around in weary surprise. The table was in the center of the room instead of against the wall; the old lady's chair stood right in the only free space that was left; the couch was pulled out at an angle.

When he restlessly rose, from sheer habit, and took a few paces he was blocked and sat down again. Vonnie kept her eyes religiously upon her mending, but her mouth twitched. Peter got up again and said he thought he would go to bed.

So it did work, to a certain point. But not wholly, for he remained as remote, as silent and unresponsive as ever, and on the third night he suddenly shoved all the furniture back into its old places and began his pacing again. Vonnie said nothing, but she was not beaten.

This time she wrote to Lisa Lotta Leonard, who managed a radio program called "Is Yours a Failure?" Various husbands and wives were interrogated on this program; each told his grievance and some lucky man or woman suggested the cure and received a big ten-dollar bill for the answer, amid shouts of laughter from the audience.

Vonnie wrote in her question in a carefully disguised hand; she awaited the next Thursday afternoon with a fast-beating heart—the Thursday after that. On the third Thursday night here it was! Lisa Lotta was actually reading her letter aloud, and the laughing noisy crowd was eager to suggest answers. Let her move the furniture about, let her have friends in every night, let her tell him he had to stop or sit in the kitchen, said various voices. Last of them all came the ten-dollar winner, who had, it appeared, cured a badly addicted husband of that very trick. Vonnie listened, the light of determination in her eyes.

The next night, a bitterly cold night of early winter, found the Considines grouped in the parlor as usual, with old Mrs. Cullen silent in her chair. Peter looked tired tonight; Vonnie hoped that he would not slip off to bed at eight o'clock as he sometimes had done of late, because that would put off the cure until the following night.

"I wish now I'd had this rug cleaned before summer," she said to him, to break a silence. "But we were having Marie's tonsils out, and I wanted to pay up the hospital on the minute."

Peter said nothing. He had dropped to his knee the hand that held his paper; his eyes were on space.

"Mrs. Moore at the grocery was saying that the President has put himself into a very undesirable position," Vonnie began again. And again Peter was silent. "Gracious, what makes them so cranky!" his wife thought. Aloud she said: "That mosquito bite still shows on Marie's cheek; did you notice?"

Marie's beauty was an important thing to her father. Now he called her to him, caught her fair little face in his big hands, and scowlingly studied the scar.

"You hoyt!" Marie protested, squirming free.

"I'm sure now that it was a ringworm," Vonnie observed.

"Ringworm!" he said in bitter scorn. Marie was whispering to her mother, giggling, and looking toward him.

"Wait and see," Vonnie told the child smilingly.

Peter turned his brooding eyes toward the gas log; it was unlighted, but it stood in the mock fireplace and it seemed natural to have his chair face it. He looked about the room, with its fringes and dark materials, its stuffed dark chairs and orderly shelves. Gift books and photographs of the children in their First Communion clothes and vases and the standing lamp: everything in place. He got suddenly to his feet and began to walk to and fro with his hands clasped at his back.

This was the moment for which everyone evidently had been waiting. Vonnie got to her feet, Marie and Jerry, with bursts of half-smothered mirth, jumped to theirs, and all three, hands clasped behind them, paced after him. Through the chairs and past the table they paraded, their heads bent as his was, their steps exactly following his except when they had to make shorter turns to keep out of his way.

It took Peter a turn or two to perceive what was going on. Then he made a brief growling noise in his throat and went out of the room. He slammed the door behind him, and a moment later they heard the bed-room door slam.

There was a moment of complete silence in the parlor. The children looked expectantly at their mother.

"Shall we do it again tomorrow night?" Geraldine asked, a little uncertain.

Vonnie swallowed visibly, but she spoke quietly.

"Yes, we'll do it again tomorrow night, and every night that Papa walks the floor. Now you both settle right down to your compositions, and I'll try to find out what Grandma wants."

She thought: "Well, it made him good and mad but I don't care! It makes me good and mad to have him carrying on like a caged tiger that way."

"Maybe he wanted to lissen to the baseball game," Marie ventured. "Don't you 'member he said one time he wisht all the programs he liked didn't come just when we were doing our homework?"

"You go on with your homework now," Vonnie said briefly in answer. Her interior arguments went on. "All right, the house is small for five people and there isn't any place Peter can be by himself. But what of it? Have I got any place to be by myself? All right, he works hard in the office and Andy Buckley is as mean as a snake. I *know* it. Is that *my* fault? 'We're running over expenses a little.' So what? Peter spends money just as much as I do. I'm wearing a coat that my aunt Maggie wore for three years. There isn't a woman alive could have gone on cooking on that stove, I don't care what anybody says! A dollar a week! I've been married twelve years and I'll be forty my next birthday, and I can't buy a new stove at a dollar a week without driving him crazy!"

Presently she looked into Peter's room. It was time to get old Mrs. Cullen to bed. The children were working quietly, if with many yawns and many intervals when their small heads rested wearily on the table. Peter's abandoned newspaper seemed somehow to reproach Vonnie, but she could not quite think why. Peter had been the one in the wrong. Certainly if a man is so little in control of himself as to walk the floor in a room sixteen by fourteen feet square, his wife is not to blame if she attempts to turn this bad habit into a jest?

Peter was not in his room. Vonnie felt a second's panic. But almost immediately he came in—evidently from the street, for there was light snow on his old coat—and helped her quietly with the inevitable evening task of settling off the old woman. He was always gentle with Vonnie's mother; he was gentle tonight. But he did not speak to Vonnie or look at her, and she began uneasily to wonder if the advice of the articulate Lisa Lotta was infallible.

A day or two later she came to the frightened conclusion that it was not. Peter walked the floor no longer, but his grim silence in the house, and his disappearance after dinner every evening, were warning to Vonnie that she had gone too far. She felt bitterly aggrieved. She was not young now; her trimly braided hair had gray streaks in it; her colorless face was innocent of make-up; her eyes were always concealed by glasses. Vonnie was a plump woman who liked and who set an excellent table, but Peter seemed to have small appetite now. She began to wonder what was going to happen. He wouldn't leave her: he wouldn't shame her, and break the children's hearts?

"Peter's worried," she would say now and then anxiously to friends. But nobody cared what his worry or hers was about. Those who had worries of their own—and that meant almost everybody—immediately and eagerly enlarged upon them. Those who hadn't had forgotten that there was any such thing.

So a few more wretched weeks dragged along—Peter silent and brooding in that dark anger that is Irish resentment, Vonnie silently martyred in that mood of selfrighteousness that is Irish pride. They addressed to each other only occasional lifeless monosyllables; the children lived in that infantile purgatory that is the house of quarrel.

And then the unthinkable happened. Vonnie lay awake all night beside her crippled mother, trembling, weeping, hearing the drunken breathing, smelling the dreadful breath of the hulk of a man slumbering so heartily in the next room. Peter drinking! That was it. He was on the downgrade now, and her life was to be one of ruin, debt, shame, want, like the lives of other women she had known! She had pitied them, perhaps a little despised them. Why did they put up with the brutes? And here she was, faced with the terrible choice that had been theirs: to abandon a worthless husband in spite of vows and duty, or to let him wreck her life and her children's lives!

Early in the morning, feeling as weak in soul as in body, she crept through rainy streets to the earliest Mass. There was always healing here in the dim, shabby old church that smelled of a sweetish disinfectant and of dust and decaying wood and wet garments. Umbrellas dribbled pools into the pews; there were very few persons at "six" on this unfriendly morning, but of course Mrs. Crowley was there in the third pew on the Gospel side.

Vonnie, intermittently crying and staring vaguely and wearily ahead of her at the single candle on the altar, was not conscious of deriving any comfort anywhere. But she did study Mrs. Crowley's familiar dark red felt hat with the bronze feather around it, and Mrs. Crowley's broad black-clad shoulders spattered with rain. She knew the hat, for it had entered that pew more than a thousand times; she knew the shoulders, too, and that they were strong enough to carry other troubles than those of their owner. And she knew that that very day she would take the horror and shame of her problem to Mrs. Crowley. Just deciding upon it made her feel somewhat lighter of heart, and she spattered home in the rain with a softened expression in the eyes behind the scholarly glasses.

Peter was dressing; he made no apologies when he came into the dinette at half past seven; she exacted none. They did not, indeed, speak to each other at all. The children came out, thoughtfully bringing raincoats and rubbers; Peter declined an offer of eggs with a faint shudder, and Marie commented interestedly that Daddy looked awful pale.

Then he was gone, and the children were gone, and Vonnie was moving through the familiar domestic routine just as if this morning were like any other dark wet winter morning, just as if the solid earth had not cracked beneath her feet. Once or twice she stopped in her steady going to and fro and pressed her hand on her heart; once or twice she said aloud, "Oh, God, help me!" Otherwise everything was as usual and the house in perfect order on the stroke of ten. The ordering, the preparing of vegetables and the dessert must, however, wait today; Vonnie had an important errand.

She found Mrs. Crowley's house also in order; at least the kitchen was unwontedly neat, and its mistress apparently in a mood as near that of leisure as she ever knew. Ellen had not come down yet; the others were all away at school or work; Mrs. Crowley was stringing beans into long slivers on a board, using a small knife that had been sharpened into a thin scimitar of steel.

"Well, Vonnie, God bless you," she said cordially in welcome. "L'ave yure umbrella drip in the enthry, there, an' come in. I was askin' Pether's mother about you this few days agone. Tom was tellin' me that he don't think Pete looks so good."

This was Vonnie's cue to seat herself at the kitchen table, rest her elbows upon it, and burst into tears. They were the more terrible to her because Vonnie seldom cried and had supposed herself, after the agonized hours of the night, to be cried out. But Mrs. Crowley did not stop her busy slicing, and the glance she gave her guest's bowed head was more compassionate than surprised.

"What's Pether been doin', thin?" she presently asked.

Vonnie looked up, red-eyed, blotched of face, gulping, trying to laugh. "How'd you know it—it wasn't one of the children?" she stammered.

"Nobody doesn't ever cry that way over the children," the older woman pronounced confidently.

"Peter's drinking," Vonnie said in a burst, and was still, her eyes upon her hostess.

"Pether Considine!" Mrs Crowley exclaimed.

Vonnie nodded wretchedly. She began to recount the whole story.

"He was head of Goodman and Meyer's old foundry, you know, and doing so well and liked by everyone—you know how quiet Peter is, but everyone likes him—and then last August they promoted him—put him in the office on the routing—seeing what was the easiest way to get goods to Albuquerque or Toronto or wherever it was—and he had a five-a-week raise——"

"And that made it what?" Mrs. Crowley asked interestedly in the pause.

Vonnie's plaintive voice took up the story.

"That made it fifty-five a week," she said. The other woman nodded seriously.

"You could do good on that."

"Oh, we were. We were getting along so well! And now this."

"He's been comin' home drunk to you?" Mrs. Crowley made a tutting deprecatory sound between tongue and teeth.

"Oh no!" protested Vonnie in horror. "It was only once—last night. That's—that's what made it so *terrible!*"

"Well, maybe the boys was celebratin'," the older woman submitted mildly.

"Oh, celebrating!" Vonnie echoed impatiently. "No, he was mad. You see, he's been walking the floor lately—he's gotten into the bad habit of walking the floor. He comes home at night perfectly glum; he won't even speak to the children. He eats his dinner like a petrified mummy and then suddenly jumps up when they're trying to do their homework and begins to march around like a crazy man. It's gotten me so worked up," continued Vonnie, getting further from tears with every word, and closer to anger, "that I've just made up my mind that he's got to stop it. So I wrote to Dorothy Davenport. I didn't sign my name of course."

"Her that writes the colyum," Mrs. Crowley commented thoughtfully.

"Yes. And she put an answer in. She's only a young girl, they say, and I think it's remarkable how she solves things for people! And she said to move the furniture all around differently, so that it would seem unfamiliar to him."

"Well, it *is* remarkable how she solves things," the older woman observed dryly. "An' her a young ger'rl, too! An' did ye thry it?"

"I did," Vonnie answered, encouraged, seeing nothing amiss. "I mixed up everything. But Peter just pushed them back in their old places and it only made him mad."

Mrs. Crowley made no other comment than a deprecatory sympathetic tut-tut.

"So then," Vonnie pursued, "I thought I'd try Lisa Lotta."

"On the radio? But Pether might have hear'rd ye."

"Oh no, I didn't give my real name! I just wrote in, as lots of them do, and told her I listened in on her 'Is Yours a Failure?' every Thursday, and that my husband had changed and got gloomy and quiet," Vonnie explained, "and I asked if any other woman had had to solve the problem of a man's walking the floor in the evenings."

"Oh," said Mrs. Crowley, interested, "an' what did she tell ye?"

"She brought the question up last Thursday night, and I was so scared," Vonnie, who was beginning to enjoy these confidences now, said eagerly, "I was so scared that she'd use my name that I almost went through the floor! She had four women answer it and the last one got the ten dollars for the way she'd cured her husband of doing it."

"An' what way was that?"

"To get up and follow him around," Vonnie said, "and have the children do it too. I jumped up the moment he began, and Marie and Jerry came marching after and we played follow-the-leader just as hard and fast as we could! I don't know what the Brophys, downstairs, thought we were doing."

"An' that wor'rked?"

"That," said Vonnie, suddenly tragic again, "was what made him *furious*. He went out and slammed the door, and for weeks he didn't come home until the last minute and then he'd go right out again, and now this!"

"An' this mornin' he cudden't get up?"

"Oh yes, he got up and went off to work. But he looked like a wreck."

"Well, thin, he was not drunk," Mrs. Crowley pronounced firmly, "even if he had drink taken. He'll not do it again on ye."

"He'll not do it again, believe me!" Vonnie said, with her nostrils dilating. "Now I'm going to a psychiatrist!"

Mrs. Crowley's eyes rolled suspiciously at this, but she said nothing.

"I am," said Vonnie, made more stubborn by the unspoken protest. "And I'll have Dr. O'Neill try him for allergies!"

"Leeches won't do nothin' but weaken him," the other woman said uncertainly.

"Allergies mean things that he can't eat and that hurt him," Vonnie said lifelessly.

"If he can't eat thim," Mrs. Crowley observed rationally, "how can they hur'rt him?"

"They scratch his arm and put them in," Vonnie explained.

At this Mrs. Crowley looked frankly outraged.

"He'd never l'ave thim do it," she protested. "I know thim Considine boys! They'd sphring at annyone——"

"But it's a part of a treatment," Vonnie urged as the older woman stopped short, staring at her for an explanation.

"Then lucky thim if Pether didn't start a threatment in retur'rn," Mrs. Crowley said roundly.

"They might tell him at least what's the matter with him," Vonnie persisted, discouraged but patient.

To this her hostess made no immediate answer. She carried her string beans into the great gaunt kitchen closet and covered the battered old saucepan that contained them. When she came out she bore a dark bent roasting pan blackened by twenty years' hard service and holding the remains of not one but two cold legs of lamb. These she proceeded to reduce to stewing proportions, cutting the meat into trim chunks, scraping up every vestige of gravy, cracking the bones into short pieces with a potato masher. Vonnie looked on, her expression desolate, but for a while the other woman did not meet her eye.

Then she looked up with her faded Irish eyes keen and her mouth firm in what might have been half a smile and half a frown.

"Why, you know what's the matther wit' Pether, Vonnie ger'rl," she said.

"I don't!" Vonnie said quickly. "I wish to goodness I did!"

"He's worrit," Mrs. Crowley submitted.

"Well, then, he has no business to bring office worries into his own house!" Vonnie countered sharply.

"So ye moved all the furniture about on him to make the place look like he'd never seen it before?" the older woman mused.

Vonnie made no reply.

"Yure poor mother there," Mrs. Crowley went on, "an' the children breakin' pencils an' climbin' up an' down on the chair'rs. An' whin that didn't wor'rk ye all got up an' follered him—ah, dear'r!"

"She told me to!" Vonnie burst out in self-defense.

"Miss Leonard did. Lisa Lotta Leonard. An' that was her way of makin' a tired man feel good?"

"It was a joke," Vonnie said, coloring uncomfortably.

"Men don't see jokes very good whin they come home after wor'rk," Mrs. Crowley said thoughtfully.

"So it seems!" Vonnie agreed dryly with the air of one who scores at last.

"What's worryin' him?" the other woman demanded suddenly.

"Oh, Andy Buckley!" Vonnie answered carelessly. "There isn't a man in the office who doesn't hate him. And for some reason he seems to hate Peter. For one thing, Andy's brother Steve was head of the old foundry when they moved him down and moved Peter up. But, as I tell Peter, Andy's boss of the office——"

"But Pether isn't in the office?"

"Oh yes, he is. He was transferred by Mr. O'Grady. And Buckley hates O'Grady, and anyone O'Grady puts in. Yes, Peter's been in the office since November."

"What doin'?"

"Routing freight. Finding out the best ways to send shipments to—oh, Buffalo or San Diego or anywhere."

"Can Pete do that?"

"Oh yes. O'Grady's delighted with Pete. But Andy Buckley makes everything as hard as he can. Won't let Pete answer the telephone or make any little trip to see the railroad men instead of phoning. Things like that."

"Why don't Pete tell Andy he's goin' back to the old foundry?"

"Because it was a promotion, moving him to the routing desk," Vonnie answered readily.

"Betther money, didn't ye tell me?"

"Oh yes, a good raise. And with two girls to educate, and music lessons, and the new stove not paid for, and Peter talking about turning the car in——" Vonnie left the sentence unfinished except for an eloquent shrug.

"Where's Pether sleepin' now?" was the older woman's next query.

"At home," Vonnie answered, surprised.

"In what room?"

"In the—well, the other room, with Jerry," Vonnie explained. "I have to have Mama, and someone always has to be with Jerry. If she gets a cold she has to have medicine in the night."

"So Pether sleeps in the little room an' gives her her medicine? Walks the floor afther dinner," Mrs. Crowley said musingly. "An' has Buckley over him all day."

"It's not my fault," Vonnie began warmly, in a silence that had become uncomfortable.

"How long since Pether has slep' where he belonged?" demanded the older woman suddenly. Vonnie's face grew scarlet.

"Where d'you mean?"

"Wit' yure ar'rm about him, Von, an' his head on yure shoulder?"

"Really!" Vonnie stammered, rising. Her glasses fell loose and jerked on their little gold chain.

"Wit' his head on yure shoulder," repeated Mrs. Crowley in the absent accents of some old seer or prophet, but with her narrowed gaze fixed upon her guest. "An' wit' you talkin' to him, tellin' him that music lessons an' livin' in Marleborough Mansions Cour'rt didn't matther, but that the love an' the sharin' of troubles by a man an' his wife was all that mat- thered! That you cud live annywhere an' on annything, just so long as he loved you an' thrusted you—— Sit down, Veronica. Yu're in no hurry! Sit down there, an' listen to me, becuz I have somethin' to say to you!"

Peter Considine had promised his own mother in words, and his own conscience without words, that on his way home at night, to bridge the interval between Buckley's tyranny at the office and the disturbed arrival at home, he would stop in at church rather than at Clancy's saloon at the close of day. Coming out of the church into winter darkness at half past five on a certain winter evening, he saw Joe Byrnes and Jim Casey leaving Clancy's, and he knew that the immediate temptation was over. If the boys were through at Clancy's he had no especial reason for going in; he had never been in the habit of drinking before dinner and he did not miss it.

He walked along the street between Joe and Jim, feeling somewhat lonely and tired. Joe was a widower, going home to a mother and a young daughter who could not spoil him hard enough. Jim was boarding at the Crowleys' while his wife and son were visiting in Illinois. God knew there'd be fun and warmth and good food and excitement enough in *that* house to make a man forget a hundred Andy Buckleys!

The entrance to Marleborough Mansions Court was less imposing than its name. But rents here were somewhat higher than in the blocks of tenements near by, tenants quieter, and the general atmosphere recognized as refined. Crude electric bulbs dangled over many dinner tables in the neighborhood; in the Marleborough wives went in somewhat for pale green candles in glass candlesticks. Several of the drawing rooms boasted vene- tian blinds; the somewhat battered, carefully numbered garage doors that were aligned under the first-floor windows indicated that the residents of the Court had risen from the lower strata of working people and were culturally and financially on the upgrade.

When Vonnie several years earlier had suggested to Peter that they move into the newly built Marleborough apartments, Peter had laughed in a startled fashion as at a daring joke. But it had been no joke to Von- nie; she had been only one of several hundred wives who had argued con- vincingly that, what with hall and sidewalk service and window cleaning and steam heat, they would actually save by the change. Peter had agreed and had never regretted it; it helped his self-esteem to live in such a place.

He did not think of it as outside his reach even now, when bills were slowly but steadily accumulating, when matters at the office were in so uncomfortable a state, when money was worth so much less than it had been. He rather took Vonnie's often-expressed view that he and she were as well entitled as their neighbors to the good things of life, and that if a man were not making sufficient money he must find means to make more. That, Vonnie sometimes reminded him bracingly, was the American story!

But even this consideration did not lighten his step or his eye as he came wearily into his home. There was, however, a slight and involuntary and entirely unconscious brightening of his whole aspect as he perceived the parlor to be unoccupied. His children were helping their mother with dinner preparations in the kitchen; Vonnie's mother was nowhere in sight.

"Grandma feeling badly?" he said, coming in.

"She's staying with Lizzie."

"With your sister? I thought Lizzie said time and time again she couldn't have your mother?"

"Lizzie was saying yesterday," Vonnie began, firmly dishing up hot cutlets, "that she didn't know when she could pay you back that hundred and seventeen dollars she borrowed when Maurice was sick. But he's working now, and they're doing well, and I told her she could take Mama for a month. We moved her this afternoon. Mama doesn't know or care where she is, and we've had her seven years. If Maurice doesn't like it they can put Mama with the Sisters. After all, his father gave them the property for the new convent, and they're always saying they'd take her. While Mama knew us all, and used to cry if we left her, it was different, but now—— Marie, take the potatoes. I can manage this, Peter, if you'll bring the tea."

"Well, that means a rest for you!" Peter said, pleased and relieved to an extent that his loyalty would not let him show. He sat down at table; mutton cutlets and baked sweet potatoes and tapioca pudding were favorites with him, and their appearance all together made him wonder if the occasion were a birthday, an anniversary? No, nothing of that kind.

The children did not come into the parlor after dinner; it seemed that Vonnie had decided they could well do their homework in the dinette. They settled down there in orderly fashion and he and his wife had the best room to themselves. That was oddly restful too. He turned the radio dials.

But as the hearty dinner and his own fatigue and confusion of mind began to have an effect on him the familiar worries gained on him too. And presently, without knowing that he was doing it, he sprang to his feet in the old way and began his restless habitual pacing of the floor. And at the signal Vonnie appeared in the room with her big coat on, a scarf snug over her head.

"Get your coat on, Peter; let's walk around the block."

"I'm pretty tired for the movies, dear——" he began. But she interrupted him.

"No movies! Just some fresh air for us both. You've been shut up in the office and I've been home most of the day."

In the dark cold street she took his arm.

[453]

"Now let's walk fast and breathe deep. To the reservoir and back?" And then, when they had crossed several streets and he had laughed out once involuntarily at the undignified skip of a pompous old man before a honking car, she asked suddenly: "Pete, what's the real trouble? Buckley?"

"Oh, nothing, I suppose," he said. "Anyway, I feel now as if some of it had blown away. It's Buckley—and bills. We're a little behind, and it kind of gripes me. And then the boys and Mr. Garvey want me back at the old foundry, and Andy keeps sneering at me as if I didn't belong in the office. But that means less money—with the girls growing up——"

They reached the reservoir and turned back for the brisk walk home. When they came into the parlor the opened windows had given the air a change, and Peter settled down with newspaper and radio like a completely contented man.

"Make me do that again some night, Von," he said gratefully. "Just telling you things makes me feel I can best 'em."

Vonnie went into the kitchen; he heard plates clicking; she always set the breakfast table before she went to bed. His daughters came tiptoeing in to kiss him good night; the apartment was quiet. Peter dozed in his chair, started up to find the clock on the stroke of ten, and Vonnie quietly going about straightening things, laying out kitchen-dried coats and rubbers for the morning, sharpening pencils.

"I put the girls in Mama's room; they're tickled to death," she said casually. "You're back in our room."

Peter looked up, his mouth half opened for an exclamation that he did not voice. Vonnie was in the familiar gray-and-blue striped wrapper that he had seen many times, but she looked different somehow. She was not wearing her glasses, for one thing, which made her face look younger, and her soft dark hair, with just a few silver threads in it here and there, lay in a loose curly braid over one shoulder.

"O.K.," Peter said. Vonnie said nothing more; she fussed about for a little while and then went away.

But much later, when everything was dark, and the snow-wrapped world outside very still, and when his head was where it belonged on her shoulder, and they were talking together, she said:

"What I mean is—what I'm getting at is, that you're not to worry, Peter. It seems to me that the cruelest thing a human being can do to another is to let him worry. I've not seen this Casey place at Cow Hill Lizzie was talking about—I know it's in pretty bad shape. But good heavens, you used to be able to paint——"

"I worked in Pop's carpenter shop for seven years," Peter put in, his voice a little hoarse and trembling with eagerness.

"And we could buy it for less than we pay here for rent. Both lots. Mr. Garvey'd back you. He's the one told Maurice and Lizzie that you or someone ought to buy it."

"He would. But there's the girls' school, dear," Peter said, on a sobering second thought.

"They'd not be going to that school. I was thinking," Vonnie said, stirring comfortably, without disturbing the head that rested on her shoulder, or the hand that gripped hers, "that I'd open a little private school, Peter. I'm qualified, dear knows, and Cow Hill isn't far from the new machine shops. There'll be lots of officers' wives looking for little places out there, and glad to send their girls to a cheap school. And you'll be nearer the foundry than you are now. You walk into the office tomorrow morning and tell Andy Buckley where he gets off, and then you go back to the foundry! Ah, now listen," protested Vonnie, as her hand touched his cheek, "you don't have to be a big baby about it!"

Peter gulped, was silent awhile. Then he said:

"Won't you miss all your friends in town, Von? Tom Crowley was telling me today that you went in to see his mother and Ellen yesterday and that they were awfully pleased."

"I'll get in to see them, now and then," Vonnie said.

"Mrs. Crowley may be kinder old-fashioned, but she's a grand woman," Peter mused aloud.

"Amen," said Veronica Considine. But she said it only in her soul.

The Inimitable

A PLAY IN THREE ACTS

THE INIMITABLE

ACT ONE

THE INIMITABLE

THE PLAYERS

Charles Dickens
Kate, his wife
Dickens' children:

Charley, aged 21
Mamie,   ”   20
Katy,   ”   19
Walter, ”   17, in India
Francis, ”   14
Alfred, ”   13
Sidney, ”   11
Henry,   ”   9
Edward, ”   6

Georgie, Kate's sister
Mrs. Hogarth, Kate's mother
Walter Landor
Mark Lemon
John Forster
Ellen
Arthur Smith, Dickens' manager
Wilkie Collins
Mollie, head maid
Mrs. Mouseworthy, cook
Nancy ⎫ maids
Phoebe ⎭

The scene is unchanged throughout. It is the sitting room of Dickens'
home in London, Devonshire Terrace. The year, 1858, at the time immediately preceding Dickens' separation from his wife, and before the
removal to Gad's Hill, where he subsequently lived until his death.

THE PERSONS

Charles Dickens: Nervous, eager, amusing, self-pleased, whiskered like the pictures.

Kate: Plump, sleepy, good-natured, a little self-pitying, lazy.

Georgie: Pretty, capable, middle thirties, youngish for her age, happy, and liking her job.

Mamie and Katy: These girls at 19 and 20 are homely, undersized. They seem more like 15 and 13. They wear plain sober-colored dresses, moderate crinolines, and their hair netted in dull lumps on their necks. They herd together, nervous and giggling, adolescence personified.

Charley: Is gawky at 21, throaty, beginnings of sideburns, neck cloth, trousers strapped into boots, attempted air of elegance.

Francis to Edward: Small boys in long trousers and short armpit jackets, long unruly hair. Edward wears curls and a round baby collar of embroidery.

Mrs. Hogarth: Is an elderly woman, peaceful looking, dowdy in spreading taffeta skirts trimmed with bands of plush. She wears a bonnet, tied under her chin. She talks steadily, but quietly without spinstery stress or hurry, her words streaming along almost absently.

Mollie: Is stout, red-faced, truculent.

Nancy and Phoebe: Are slatternly, hair twisted into walnuts on their necks, Nancy's head bound up, both wear aprons. They have a continual air of being driven and overworked and in terror of scoldings.

Ellen: Extremely pretty, about 22, beautifully bonneted and feathered; small parasol, full hoop skirts.

The other male characters wear clothes of the time; needn't be differentiated.

ACT ONE

SCENE: The Dickens' sitting room. This is a comfortable, informal room, with worn furniture, pictures, and many books. At the right a fireplace, with a doorway behind it leading to the dining room. Center rear a stairway flanked by windows with looped lace curtains; under the stairway a coat closet. At the left a square piano that ordinarily wears a purple flannel scalloped cover; music books are piled up, and a curve of curtained windows. Back of these a door into the lobby and the street door. The lighting arrangements are several lamps, and beside the fireplace are two jointed gas brackets. Antimacassars, vases, statues, amateur portraits. Several child-sized chairs.

Discovered are Kate Dickens and her mother, Mrs. Hogarth. They have been having tea, and a disordered tea tray is in sight. Also the used cups and saucers of several other tea drinkers. Children have built a railway of chairs, draped with the piano cover; a house of books has been erected close to the front of the stage. The whole room is disorderly. Both women are rocking comfortably. The curtains are not drawn, and twilight is at the windows.

TIME: 4:30 on a winter afternoon.

Mrs. Hogarth

I suppose Mr. Dickens lets you know whether or not he is coming to dinner? My husband—your father, Kate, has his faults—no man more, but that is not one of them.

[463]

Kate

Charles is very good about that, Ma. *That* isn't the trouble. He always lets Georgie know his plans.

Mrs. Hogarth

Well, when I asked you if he was expected, you sighed. I know a sigh when I hear one, Kate, and that's what you did. Your mother may not be brilliant, but she has a heart. That, nobody has ever denied. And I see what I see.

Kate

I don't know why I sighed, Ma, or if I did.

Mrs. Hogarth

(*Quietly singsong, no stress or hurry*)
I may be a person of discernment, Kate, I may not be. That is not for me to say.

Kate

(*Rousing*)
I am sure you are, Ma.

Mrs. Hogarth

I hope you are sure, Kate. My children always seem to be rather in doubt about it. But then you are too mild, Kate. You don't put your foot down, Kate. It is a great distress to me, for my own nature is a decided one. On one occasion—I was only seventeen; in fact, it was my birthday, or perhaps it was your brother's birthday when we were all at Vauxhall—but what nonsense, for I was not married at the time, and the absurdity of any man buying a ridiculous amount of little ginger buns and attempting—— Sadler, that was his name—Shelter, Sanford—at all events, his crying out "Who is she? Why don't I know her?" was most embarrassing—I've told you that man's name, Kate, now what was it? You're woolgathering again.

Kate

You were saying that I was too mild, Ma.

Mrs. Hogarth

And so you are. For of course I instantly rejected any such advances, and your grandfather was amazed that a girl of seventeen—— I was pretty I suppose, at least they said so, and what with a new mantle and bonnet—— But it won't answer, Kate, she will never be well settled in life if this goes on.

Kate

Who won't, Ma? What won't?

Mrs. Hogarth

Well, I really am amazed, after I have just told you—— Saunders, that was his name, and they moved into our block afterward and lived in that house that always smelled of slippery elm—excellent in the nursery, for raw their poor little throats will get, but if it is not selfish in you, Kate, it certainly is in Mr. Dickens, and that I must and will say.

Kate

(*Yawning, indifferent*)
Charles isn't more selfish than most men.

Mrs. Hogarth

Charles is a man, my dear, and when you say that you say a great deal, and whether it is good or bad is the question, but impudence from that big rawboned woman from Cornwall about the girls' white petticoats in the wash and burning a whole batch of crumpets, no, *that*, poor Georgie should not be forced to take, nor the leak in the front entry forcing us to walk through coal dust at the side door with the boys—who will be boys and subdue their spirits you cannot unless sick like poor Julia's unfortunate child—so Bridget O'Connor in his poor little face——

Kate

Bridget O'Connor? You mean the Bridget O'Connor who never would get the biscuits brown, Ma, but what has that to do with the leak in the glass at the side door?

Mrs. Hogarth

Why, nothing. How absurd you are! Julia's child was as pale as your handkerchief, and your children—or perhaps Charles, when the biscuits were pale, naturally called them Bridget O'Connors—but that has nothing to do with Georgie's prospects, Kate, and it seems to me rather unsisterly—yes, it does, devoted as you are, to allow your thoughts to wander about so when I am talking seriously to you. What chance has Georgie now?

Kate

Georgie hasn't fallen in love, has she, Ma?

Mrs. Hogarth

Ah, now you rouse up, and no wonder, for I'm quite aware that you'd put the whole family right into the river rather than have Georgie cut her finger! Well, now, how do you like it?

[465]

Kate

Georgie? But who?

Mrs. Hogarth

Who? Nobody. And not likely to be anybody while Georgie continues to sacrifice her life to you and Mr. Dickens, for sacrifice it is, Kate. A mother's life is one continual sacrifice——

Kate

Mother, Georgie hasn't any children. I've had all the children in this house. (*Pause.*) Ten of them.

Mrs. Hogarth

Are you accusing me of saying that your sister, one of the most beautiful natures God ever put on this earth, is a mother?

Kate

Ma, for heaven's sake, don't be idiotic.

Mrs. Hogarth

I am idiotic. I will say no more.

Kate

Georgie. I don't believe it. What man?

Mrs. Hogarth

If you are determined to misunderstand me, I am helpless. I am saying that there is no man, that I wish there was a man, that it is high time there was a man, that Georgie is throwing away the best years of her life here!

Kate

(*Half to herself, struck*)
She meets as many men here as she would anywhere.

Mrs. Hogarth

Married men.

Kate

Not all. And certainly she is happy here. Why, she went to visit Annie five days ago, and the good-by kisses from the children, and Georgie almost in tears! Georgie wouldn't live anywhere else.

That's as may be. But your Mamie is twenty now, and Katy nineteen, and they are perfectly capable of taking over! I was nineteen when I was married, and when your brother was born the doctor—dear old doctor—like a father to me—can't remember the name—Dodder, Fodder, Fumble, I am surprised that *you* can't remember the name, Kate, for two years later he brought you into the world—— What did you say?

Kate

(*Not listening*)
Ma, I'd cry my eyes out if Georgie got married. But she hasn't had a disappointment?

Mrs. Hogarth

How do we know? It may have been a disappointment, you know, that took my poor little Mary. And she lived with you, too, Kate.

Kate

Mary! Mary was seventeen, poor darling love.

Mrs. Hogarth

It may have been a secret affair.

Kate

It wasn't; beside, that has nothing to do with Georgie. Mary is dead.

Mrs. Hogarth

I hope I don't have to be reminded that your sister is dead. Really, Kate, I may be only your mother, but I am capable of remembering the loss of my own child.

Kate

No danger of our forgetting Mary.

Mrs. Hogarth

Like myself, Mr. Dickens never will recover from that blow.

Kate

How Charles loved her!

Mrs. Hogarth

I wonder that you can be so pleased about it.

[467]

Kate

Charles's loving Mary? Why, Mary was the darling of both our hearts. You know how hard and sad Charles's childhood was—— poor little shabby, hungry, grubby love.

Mrs. Hogarth

Still he didn't marry Mary.

Kate

Ma! She was a child when we were married. And things with us became practical so soon. It was money worry, and his father needing help, and his mother and the children, and our own babies coming along so fast. I was either expecting or nursing a baby for ten years. (*Musing.*)

Mrs. Hogarth.

I know that, Kate. That is woman's lot. Ha. A few moments' pleasure for the man, and one more ball and chain for the woman, as my poor mother used to say. She gets heavy, she gets homely, she faces her hour of terror and agony and danger—I was three days having you and unconscious all the last day and the next four, and they fed me through a tube, so that when you show complete indifference to what I am talking about——

Kate

(*Not listening, thinking aloud*)
When Mary came to live with us I really think it brought Charles something that he had missed in his life—fun, you know, and laughing, and games. He'd take her off in the morning, and send the market boys back with baskets from the market—they had great jokes together.

Mrs. Hogarth

Ha. It seems to me that in your case I might not be so good-natured. But you always were soft, Kate. No backbone.

Kate

I couldn't be jealous of a girl of seventeen.

Mrs. Hogarth

Georgie is—*not* seventeen. When does she get home, by the way?

Kate

Georgie? Today. She's been gone five days now and I simply can't wait to have her back. This house isn't the same without her. The children are perfectly unmanageable, the maids fight with themselves and with the boy, and Cook comes in every hour of the day with complaints. The fish hasn't come, the laundry roof leaks, the hot-water tank isn't working—— (*Amiable laugh.*) I believe this house could get along without me or without Charles, but not without Georgie!

Mrs. Hogarth

So after all I've said you think it's perfectly right to keep your sister here as a sort of servant.

Kate

(*Laughing*)
Ask Georgie! As I tell you she shed tears when she went away on Sunday, and she said she'd get back this afternoon if she possibly could. And I know she will.

Mrs. Hogarth

And does Mr. Dickens take *her* off marketing, too?

Kate

No, that was only Mary, poor little love. Anyway that was years ago, Ma, when I was tied down with the babies, and we were poor—and young. But now, with three maids and a cook, and a boy, and Charles writing his books, it's different. We entertain everyone. Georgie has no time to go out with Charles or anyone else.

Mrs. Hogarth

Exactly. Georgie's chances of settling aren't good, Kate, you see that.

Kate

I tell you she meets lots of men here, Ma. More than I did at home.

Mrs. Hogarth

She don't seem to attract any special one.

Kate

(*Comfortably confidential*)
To tell you the truth, Ma, Georgie and I are so close that we don't need anyone else. From morning until night I'm in here with the younger children, and Georgie coming and going, talking to Mollie and Nancy, giving orders to Cook, sending the boy off with Charles's boots. Then when the children are off to school and Nurse takes the little ones, Georgie and I walk around the square, or we bring out our water colors, and the day just rushes by. And often in the evening she'll say "Let's play our four-hands, Kate," or "Let's sing our duets," or she'll write a letter to someone and read it to me, or we play dumb crambo or backgammon; often we're up

[469]

when Charles comes in and he makes us a punch and we all talk. Now we've been rehearsing the children in the Christmas play, and we get laughing so—what was it made us laugh so, that last night she was here——?

Mrs. Hogarth

Well, I wish she'd get here now. She was to hold the cab for me.

Kate

(*Not stirring*)
We ought to get this room into some sort of shape.

Mrs. Hogarth

When's Mr. Dickens get back?

Kate

Any time now. I had a letter—from Manchester, I think it was, and it said the end of the week.

Mrs. Hogarth

Let's hope he doesn't come before Georgie gets here, and doesn't bring half a dozen of his precious friends with him——

(*There is a noisy interruption of children from the next room; a rabble of small boys in high-waisted trousers, tight jackets, and white collars. All shouting and rushing to the door, screaming "Aunt Georgie! There's the cab. It's Aunt Georgie!" Confusion. They escort Georgie in.*)

Georgie

Oh, it's so good to get home! (*Kissing and hugging.*)

Mrs. Hogarth

Did you hold the cab? For if you didn't it's sixpence—thrown away——

Georgie

(*Undoing scarf, shawl, mittens, hat*)
I kept him, Ma. Good-by, Ma. Good heavens, what a room, and Charles getting here any minute! Boys, all of you, into the schoolroom! Good-by, Ma dear. You'll be in tomorrow? Kate, dear love, I'm back! Everyone back into the schoolroom, and send Nancy or Nurse here this minute——

(*Both daughters go to door. Room empties. Maids come in. Georgie chattering to Kate, who goes back to her chair.*)

Georgie

Yes, this time it's Cousin Annie, my dear. Having another! And the baby not walking. "Well," I said, "Kate's got the laugh on you this time." Girls, look at this room—— (*She has thrown aside her wraps.*) Yes, take the tray out. Did the sole come? Does Cook know there may be men for dinner? Take those upstairs, Phoebe—— How clumsy you are, child, you never learn, and come straight back and get these chairs straightened out— they were playing railway, were they? Railway, railway, that's all the children think of now. I wish to goodness the wretched shrieking things never had been invented! Tell Cook mutton broth with a chop in it, to start with, and get the cheese up, here's the key. (*Recklessly massing cups on a great tray.*) What were you girls doing? Did you expect to leave the tea things in here all night? Look sharp there, Nancy, and stop snorting. Yo*u're* not a steam engine! Yes, we'll have the lights. (*Girls draw shades.*) Kate, for heaven's sake, tell me every single thing that's happened, and did you miss me, love? That's better, Nancy. All right, girls. Ask Cook to come up. Now, Kate (*taking a hassock at her knee and taking possession of both hands*), how has it been? How have they behaved? And, my love, I had an offer! Ridiculous man, seven children all ages—but a good living, and some four hundred pounds a year. But can you see me in a country parsonage, Kate, with a baby every year? Annie's house is sweet, and they were all angels to me, but this is where I belong!

Kate

(*Fondly*)
Ma's been telling me I impose on you, Georgie.

Georgie

How like Ma. Poor Ma. Why, Kate, she knows that I'm perfectly wretched when I'm away from you. No sketching, no four-hands and backgammon and talk! You broke my heart when I was only a little girl, and you married Charles.

Kate

(*Playfully*)
You've forgiven him? Charles can do no wrong.

Georgie

What—what do you mean? I—I don't idealize him.

Kate

Oh, of course you don't. But we both feel that even if everything he does is done noisier and harder——

[471]

Georgie

(*Laughing*)
—and better——

Kate

And better than anyone else, of course, still, we understand him, don't we? You really love him, don't you, Georgie?

Georgie

Why I—yes, of course, he's always been like a real brother to me. I—I—you don't mean——

Kate

I mean that as long as you're happy, Georgie, and you and I can have such wonderful times together, fifty temperamental geniuses like Charles shan't separate us! You'll not leave me for anyone, will you, Georgie?

Georgie

Never. I'll always play fair with you. Now tell me, is dinner ordered, for I have every reason to believe that Charles is bringing some men—Collins, I think, and Smith and Forster.

Kate

I haven't the slightest idea, love—but here's Cook.

Georgie

Good afternoon, Mrs. Mouseworthy. You got the barrel of apples I sent up on Wednesday? Good. And the sole came? Mr. Dickens is bringing some friends, so the boys will have their dinner in your dining room. We'll start with mutton broth with the kidneys in it, then the fish, and you'd better have a good side dish with that. Grilled oysters, or cutlets, perhaps? Then the joint and plenty of potatoes and the chicken pasty; and spinach with the cold ham. You've made the tarts?

Cook

I have, mum. But them apples is nothing but worms, and your thumbs sliding into them in a way Mrs. Fallow, that was here to finish the ironing, said made her stomach go up in waves like she was at sea.

Georgie

The new apples!

Cook

No, mum. But I thought we should use up the old.

Quite right, Cook. What else was it?

Cook

(*Stolidly*)
Them fowls, mum, for the children's dinner. They smelled kind of strong and when I opened them they whistled.

Georgie

Did you cook them?

Cook

I boiled them, miss, and poured off the liquor for the dog's mess, and they smell good now.

Georgie

I think that's all right, then. If the children don't like them, give them boiled bread and milk, and the jam. And have lemons and hot water for punch up here at ten o'clock.

Cook

(*Curtsying*)
Yes'm. (*Going.*)

Georgie

And can't Nancy take that rag off her head?

Cook

Mollie spoke to her and she says it's swelled up like a potato if you'll excuse me, and the strength of the weakness that comes over——

Georgie

All right, Cook. That's enough.

Kate

(*Nibbling a cooky, dreaming*)
You're home, Georgie.

Georgie

And so glad to get back! Everything else seems like a dream—so dull after this house.

Kate

Is it raining?

Georgie

Stormy. More like snow. It's glorious out.

Kate

I meant to get out this morning. But I felt as if one of my headaches was coming on, and didn't dare.

Georgie

November. Remember how every one of the children used to get colds this time of year?

Kate

And Nana with her onion syrup.

Georgie

And a baby coming. Well, we haven't got *that* this winter, at any rate.

Kate

Well, naturally not. And that's what makes me—— Well, no matter!

Georgie

Kate, you don't think you're started again!

Kate

(*Sharply*)

I know very well I'm not. There are things I can't very well explain to a sister of mine who isn't married, but what with Charles saying he can't sleep any longer in his own bed that we've slept—— However, I don't know how we got on to this. I don't know what I'm talking about! I suppose it's that wall that got me started. I suppose your husband could build a wall between your rooms and not mean that he didn't love you any more. I might have ten more children, as far as that goes! (*Vexed and a little confused.*)

Georgie

As Ma would say, God forbid!

Kate

Georgie, do you know what starts a baby?

Georgie

No, I don't, and I don't want to know. You know how Ma always is about such things.

Kate

Well, anyway, when a man who's been married twenty-two years has carpenters come into the house and wall up a door between his wife's room and the study where he's been sleeping lately——

Georgie

Kate, I felt badly when he asked Mollie and me to see that that was done, but what else could I do?

Kate

Oh, nothing. What did he say?

Georgie

Just that he wanted that partition put in, between the two rooms, and all his things moved into the study. What did he say to you?

Kate

That he would sleep better there.

Georgie

Well, maybe he has been restless. He's doing too much.

Kate

The girls asked me about it. Asked me if their pa didn't love me any more.

Georgie

That's what comes of their reading novels. You don't believe that.

Kate

That he no longer loves me? No, I don't think that.

Georgie

He has been sleeping badly, he's always restless.

Kate

No, it doesn't mean—what in a different man it might. He is still so kind to me, Georgie, still so generous. He spoke last week of our going on a trip together.

Georgie

I know he did.

Kate

So I try to tell myself that it means nothing. Just a whim.

Georgie

You said the girls had noticed it. But they've said nothing to me. Perhaps girls of their ages don't attempt to understand.

Kate

Charles must run the risk of their criticizing his treatment of their mother.

Georgie

My dear Kate, they will.

Kate

My dear Georgie, they won't. One word from him, one laugh, and anything he does will seem admirable. You know him.

Georgie

(*Rueful laugh*)
I know him! Hark a moment. Was that a cab? Ah, here he is! I thought he would come tonight.

(*The girls and small boys stream across the room, this time shouting "Papa!" Confusion in the passage outside the door, left, and Dickens comes in, muffled, shawled, hatted, sprinkled with snow. Shouting and laughing.*)

Dickens

(*Above babel*)
Well, here we are—home again, eh? It seems years! Ah, you're snug in here—it's blizzard weather without! Mamie—Katy. Hello, who are these ruffians—— I don't know this one— (*to small boy*) don't know you at all, sir, face very familiar—but bad memory. Bufferwhistle—that's an odd name—(*arms full of boys*) Nehemiah Bufferwhistle, good name. Strong Anglo-Saxon flavor. Here's another. I confess I don't like your looks, my good fellow. You're called the Ocean Specter, eh? Here's a suspicious character, if ever there was one! Thank you, Mollie.

(*In the confusion of welcome, Mollie has come in and taken Dickens' coat and wraps; Georgie returns to herd the older children away, and Nancy, slatternly, breathless, with her head tied up in a towel, takes two or three small ones upstairs.*)

All home, are we? Good. Ah, Kate. All well? Good. And there's Georgie. How is my little housekeeper? (*He has dropped into a fireside chair, warming his hands, happy and genial.*) Dinner on the fire, Georgie?

Georgie

Cook said she had a feeling in her bones that you would be back for dinner. So she went ahead with the joint and the beef and kidney pie. (*In an aside, businesslike.*) I'd bespoken a sole at Murray's, and there's the big cheese. Oh yes, and she had cutlets cooking when I went down. You've asked some men here?

Dickens

Good. Kate, you look hearty.

Kate

You wrote that they liked your readings, Charles.

Dickens

(*Exchanges a swift amused glance with Georgie*)
They did.

Georgie

Oh, Charles, tell us more than that! They were packed?

Dickens

Packed! By God, Georgie, they were packed out into the street. The applause breaking out as I read—the women fainting——

Kate

(*Mildly disapproving, amused*)
Why on earth should they faint!

Dickens

I myself in tears—when I come to his death, girls, I feel the water in my eyes.

Kate

But you've read it so many times——

Georgie

It's because you feel it that they feel it.

Dickens

When Paul dies, I lose my child again—my little innocent, friendly Dora—so light when I picked her up that night, before I went away—— (*He is moved; covers his eyes with his hand.*)

[477]

(*Vaguely, amiably hurt*)
But the story of a child in a book, Charles, surely isn't anything like the loss of our Dora.

Dickens

(*Paying no attention*)
The laughter, turning so suddenly quiet, and then feeling my own voice break—and hearing the first sob, and the second sob. And afterward (*talking to himself*) the moment of complete silence, a hush over the whole house—— As God is my judge I would rather have that moment—I would rather stand there, sweating and panting and shaken—and wait through that hush—— And then the hands, and the shouts! But you've heard it, Kate.

Kate

(*Rising, sighs*)
Oh yes. Well, I must change. You'll be up?

Dickens

(*Quietly*)
Yes. Presently.

Kate

(*Drowsily, moving toward stairway*)
I miss the old blue curtains.

Dickens

(*Under almost violent restraint*)
Yes, by all means. What happened to them?

Georgie

Boys, and ink, and moths, and everything. You like these?

Dickens

Nicely. Nicely. (*Puts his head in his hands and groans.*)

Georgie

Kate's like that. But believe me—believe me, Charles, she cares for your success as much as I do!

Dickens

"As much as I do!" Why, your liking it is the criterion, then?

I didn't mean quite that. But, oh, it must be so glorious! To know that you can stir them so—to see them waiting—crowded in——

Dickens

Georgie, it is stupendous. There has never been anything like it. And to know that nobody else can do it, that it's the Inimitable himself who must walk across that stage, must take his bow. Georgie, it's to drink intoxication from the most brimming cup that ever was held to a man's lips!

Georgie

(*In chair opposite his*)
Don't I know. Haven't you spellbound us all, Forster and Collins and Landor—all of us, with the simplest charade?

Dickens

Smith was with me, of course, and a fellow named Bede, and Macready and Collins came down to Wolverhampton Sunday night. To see those fellows in tears, laughing while they wiped them away—but in tears—and to get through the crowd afterward, hoarse voices on all sides, hands gripping mine, men holding up their children to see! And then afterward, at the inn, a snug fire in the little parlor and the red curtains drawn, and a bowl of punch at the fire—— Ah, those are the hours!

Georgie

You've earned them. Carrying the load you have, all these years. This house full of noisy children—your own family making one demand after another.

Dickens

(*Musing on*)
And in that circle, 'round the inn fire, a dozen of the most brilliant men of England! Thackeray, perhaps, Macaulay, Collins, Macdonald, Macready. Georgie, sometimes then I think of my childhood, when these hands—that weave all these dreams!—were set to washing bottles, pasting labels on blacking tins, and my little old self slipping in and out of the Marshalsea Prison as if its unwholesome vapors had taken the form of a sickly, shabby boy, to whom gates and walls were no barrier! By God, they might have spared me the debtors' prison!

Georgie

Life has been good to you since. And who knows, you needed that acid, Charles, to give you your knowledge of men, and men's hearts.

Dickens

That is a gentle loving thing to say, worthy of Dame Durden.

Georgie

Dame Durden indeed, you would have thought so if you could have seen this room an hour ago, when I got home!

Dickens

A mess, eh?

Georgie

They'd had tea, all over the room, and built trains with the chairs and piano cover and pillows.

Dickens

Trains! They've come to stay, Georgie. It's good-by to the grand old stage coaches. Yes, the boys run over Kate roughshod, of course. What should we do without you, Georgie? When the domestic sea gets rough, you are there to shorten sail and throw out the kedge anchor.

Georgie

Why not? I love it. I confess I love ordering the maids about, Charles, and Kate hates it. After all, this has been my home almost since I left school. And Kate's been as much mother as sister to me.

Dickens

As she was to little Mary.

Georgie

You never forget Mary.

Dickens

(*Touches heart*)
Not until all's still and cold here.

Georgie

You had more of her than I ever did. I was so young when she came to live with you and Kate.

Dickens

Your mother's was a houseful of pretty girls—pretty girl children, when I met your sister Kate.

Georgie

Be fair to Kate. She's given so much of her life to the children, her thoughts are always with them.

Dickens

(*After thoughtful glance and pause*)
So you visited Annie?

Georgie

With Leonard penniless, as usual, and her house full of children.

Dickens

How many little pledges of affection now?

Georgie

Five. And another at Easter.

Dickens

Good God. It was yesterday that we were at her wedding.

Georgie

It's six years. (*Demurely.*) And Leonard's brother did me a great honor.

Dickens

The Reverend? Whose wife died and left a pack of children?

Georgie

The Reverend Howard. He's got a living in Cornwall now.

Dickens

The deuce he has! The deuce he did!

Georgie

On his knees, on a nice clean handkerchief.

Dickens

I like his insolence! Does he think we'd give you up?

Georgie

That seemed to be the idea. I declined.

Dickens

You respectfully declined. You a clergyman's wife. I can see the vicarage,

[481]

smothered in earwiggy ivy, with little Georgie wiping porridge from small ecclesiastical faces. Clergymen have full quivers, Georgie.

Georgie

His quiver's full now! Well, those little arrows must be launched by some-one else.

Dickens

Good girl. Kate can't do without you. The whole house goes topsy-turvy.

Georgie

And I can't do without Kate. There never were such sisters, nor such loving children. There never was a house like this, with the books and the plays and the people who come and go. Why, when you were a little grubby boy, forgotten and neglected by those who should have cared for you, who would have dreamed this for you? Fame, wealth——

Dickens

A little Dame Durden in my house to spoil me.

Georgie

And love. The whole world loves you! Sometimes, when I realize (*faltering*) how good you are to me—you and Kate—and how privileged millions of persons would think I am—it makes my heart tremble, Charles.

Dickens

As even the Reverend Howard never stirred it, eh? Why, my dear girl— my dearer than sister, did the wretched fellow move you so?

(*Georgie has turned away her face, and is in tears.*)

Georgie

It is nothing. Nothing. Just a moment's weakness.

Dickens

But even a moment's weakness in one we love is important.

Georgie

I beg you—it will pass—it is gone.

Dickens

And you turn me your good happy face again.

(*They smile steadily at each other; then Dickens looks back at the fire. Pause. Georgie wipes her eyes, blows her nose, laughs shakily.*)

I could not be the student of human hearts that I am, Georgie, and find myself so fortunate in interpreting them, if I did not know that during the past few months something is troubling my sister. You can't tell me what it is?

Georgie

You would be the first to know. But it is nothing.

Dickens

(*Stretched back in chair, hands in pockets*)
You've given your heart away too quickly, eh?

Georgie

No, not like that. Not—quickly. It's—it's all—it's different. It's not what you think.

Dickens

Someone at Annie's? May I guess who?

Georgie

(*Suffocating*)
No. You don't know him.

Dickens

By God, I'll make it my business to know him. What? The treasure of Georgie's heart going begging, and the ruffian at large? I'll hale him here, crop and heels, and have it out with him. (*Lazily, humorously*) I'll run the fellow through.

Georgie

Please—Kate mustn't guess—nobody must. It—it isn't true, anyway. I never realized——

Dickens

Of course you didn't. What pearl, lying down under the deep waves, ever knew its own value. You thought you only liked him, eh?

Georgie

(*Whisper*)
Yes.

Dickens

And then the big waves; rearing their great heads, roaring at you; plunging

[483]

over you with a great smothering wash of emerald—and you said, "This is not what I expected! This is pain. This is fright. This can't be love!"

Georgie

Oh yes, Charles.

Dickens

Well, now you must let me—and Kate of course—take over. We'll run this paragon to earth; we'll spit him like a woodcock, we'll serve him up with onions and potatoes boiled in their jackets.

Georgie

(*Amused, maternal, but tremulous*)
You take it for granted he is a paragon and can be caught. But I'm far from admitting there is such a creature.

Dickens

I think you don't have to tell me, my dear girl. I have been seeing it—I have been sure of some change in you, without realizing what it must mean.

Georgie

Then if I have a secret I must watch it better.

Dickens

We admit the secret? There's a point gained.

Georgie

A woman would be wretched without a secret.

Dickens

By Jove, you may be right. But if there is anything a brother can do, my dear, he claims his right to do it.

Georgie

(*Agitated again*)
If there were ever anything—to whom could I turn so quickly as to you and Kate? But there is nothing.

Dickens

And I am to know no more?

Georgie

I think not, Charles.

Dickens

It is not our selfishness in keeping you here, Georgie?

Georgie

No, no, not that at all. Where else could I be so happy? I am quite happy. If I had a dream, it was only a dream. It is gone.

Dickens

You see him no longer?

Georgie

No.

Dickens

But this is no new thing, Georgie. This did not arise from any five-day visit to Annie. It was before that.

Georgie

Oh yes, before that.

Dickens

And I haven't seen it, months before that, haven't suspected it?

Georgie

It is not a new thing. It is not a hopeful thing. It is nothing with which I cannot deal—and have dealt. I am happier, as it is, than I could be under any other circumstances.

Dickens

Then I can only thank the gods that the time has not come when I must give you my blessing.

Georgie

Not yet.

Dickens

I can only fear that he is a married man, Georgie?

Georgie

(*Desperate*)
If I ask you, I know that you will not press me, my dear brother.

Dickens

You have only to ask. I will say no more. (*Pause.*) But—— There is another thing of which I must speak to you. Have you noticed any resentment in Kate? About that change of rooms?

Georgie

In Kate? What sort of a resentment?

Dickens

(*Restless*)
I don't know. Maybe it is in me. Maybe I want something—— (*Pause.*)

Georgie

Something you have not, Charles? Ah, what could that be? Your houseful of children, your work, your success with the magazine, your friends. Can you not see that this only means that you are working too hard? We all see that. Forster and Macready, all of us.

Dickens

(*Rumpling hair*)
Yes, perhaps I am.

Georgie

The readings are too much; they exhaust you. They mean trips, rehearsals, meeting strange people all the time. No man could stand that with everything else you do. The trial from Pickwick—that's funny—and Mrs. Gamp, and *Boots at the Holly-Tree Inn*—those are great fun. But Nell—and that dreadful Sikes and Nancy—they kill you.

Dickens

They are the very breath of my life. They are too much. I know it. I feel it. But I can't give them up.

Georgie

Charles, it isn't what they do to the audience, the women screaming and fainting. It's what they do to you!

Dickens

(*Dreamy*)
A great fellow met me in the lobby, sobbing. "Sir," he said, "every man must treat women more tenderly for the sake of that poor unfortunate girl!" I was shaken myself, I wrung his hand.

Georgie

Exactly. But it's that emotional strain that I hate—that Kate and I hate.

Dickens

I could follow such a man to his poor squalid home, I could clasp his wife's hand as if it were that of the finest lady of the land. By all that makes life and friendship and brotherhood holy I could make such a man my friend—

Georgie

Exactly. But that's just what you can't afford to do. No money is worth it. Let us plan a visit to France, or to Italy again. Kate loved that, and all the children did, too.

Dickens

My dear Georgie, that is out of the question. Financially it would ruin me.

Georgie

But, Charles, we did all sorts of things when you were just beginning, before the magazine, before the readings! How did we do it then?

Dickens

My dear girl, I haven't the faintest shred of an idea. I only know that at the present moment every sixpence upon which I can lay my hands is pledged to get a boy off to some promising situation in China, or get a boy back again, or pay off a bunch of press workers or meet some little sneak of a forgotten bill looking up at me from a heap on my desk.

Georgie

It seems to me we did less worrying when we were much poorer.

Dickens

You are absolutely right.

Georgie

But how do you explain it?

Dickens

I don't. I only know that it means "Keep going. Don't weaken. Keep the office running full tilt, keep the weekly installment of the novel a little ahead of the printer, and get away for the readings in between times!"

Georgie

Doesn't it help to have Kate go with you for those reading engagements?

(*Dickens does not answer. He is stretched in his chair, hands in trouser pockets, eyes closed. A maid comes in and puts coal on the*

[487]

fire; two small boys come halfway downstairs in nightgowns, look over, go up again. Mamie and Katy in dressing gowns, come running down, hair in curl papers.)

Katy

Is Papa asleep?

Dickens

Sound.

Mamie

You're home again! You don't know how we need you.

Georgie

Ah, we waked him.

Dickens

No. Come here and toast your toes. (*Kisses them.*)

Mamie

We're sitting up for dinner, we're going up to dress in a minute.

Dickens

Great occasion. Beer and skittles, eh?

Katy

Rather. There's mutton broth with chops in it, and a roast saddle and cabinet pudding and sole with oyster sauce—and baked sweet potatoes——

Mamie

And cutlets, and didn't they look good!

Dickens

Look here, some men are coming in for supper and I am supposed to introduce my daughters in their nightgowns?

Katy

We'll run like rabbits.

Mamie

They won't come. It's snowing.

Katy

This is so comfortable!

Believe me, posting down here from Wolverhampton, I thought of this old room, and this big chair, and the firelight on all your faces. Snow or no snow, there's nothing like a room such as this, at the end of a journey. High up on the coach the wind hardens your face, the lights shine out from inn bars, and you huddle in your greatcoat and think that the children are all at home, waiting, and that Mollie is drawing the shades, and Aunt Georgie has got all the materials of a hot dinner ready.

Katy

Aunt Georgie's been crying.

Dickens

(*Glancing aside at her as she stands by the mantel looking down*)
Eh? We can't have that.

Georgie

Smoke in my eyes, Katy.

Dickens

Aunt Georgie looks out for all of us; we can't let anything make her cry.

Georgie

You all spoil me.

Katy

P'pa, when you wrote *Bleak House*, was Dame Durden, Aunt Georgie?

Dickens

Some of her was, perhaps.

Mamie

And some was Ma.

Dickens

Maybe.

Georgie

Does it anger you, Charles, to have us trying to identify the people in the stories?

Dickens

Not here at home. It maddens me when every casual person I meet does it.

[489]

Mamie

Asking if this one is Quilp and that one is Micawber.

Dickens

And the Pickwicks! Everybody knows a Pickwick.

Georgie

What's your mother doing, Katy?

Katy

Fixing her hair, when we came by.

Georgie

I wonder if I could help her.

Dickens

We'll all go up in a minute. Wait.

Mamie

Did you tell Papa about the boys and me in a play?

Georgie

Oh no. They're preparing a surprise for you, Charles.

Katy

They've been rehearsing all week.

Dickens

Good. May we have it for the company tonight?

Georgie

Yes. Right here. They've got their properties stowed away behind the piano.

Mamie

But we want you to see it first and make suggestions.

Dickens

Why, this is capital! Was this their own idea?

Georgie

Entirely.

Oh no, Aunt Georgie. Don't you remember you said we must have a surprise for Papa?

Georgie

So I did. But the selection was their own idea.

Dickens

Ah-h-h, I'm home again! This is my world, these are my people.

Georgie

Here they come.

(Frank and Alfred come downstairs and, facing the group at the fireside, make a deep bow. Dickens and girls applaud. Frank is fattened out, with gaiters and top hat, as Pickwick, and Alfred dressed as Sam Weller. Pickwick Papers, I. Chapter 10. Dickens squares his chair about, rubbing hands in anticipation. Georgie produces a prompt book. Mamie, as the maid, has run up to the stair landing and calls down from it.)

Maid

Sam!

Sam

(Polishing boots)
Hallo!

Maid

Number twenty-two wants his boots.

Sam

(Drawling)
Ask number twenty-two if he wants 'em now, or would he rather wait until he gets 'em?

Maid

Come, don't be a fool, Sam, the gentleman wants his boots directly.

Sam

Well, you'd be a nice young woman for a musical party, wouldn't you? Look at these here boots, eleven pairs of boots, and one shoe as belongs to number six, with the wooden leg. Who's number twenty-two, that's to put all the others out? No, no; regular rotation, as Jack Ketch the hangman said, when he tied the men up.

Pickwick

(*Coming in*)
Morning, Sam. Pretty busy, eh?

Sam

Oh, werry well, sir. We shan't be bankrupts, and we shan't make our fortunes. We eats our biled mutton without capers, and don't care about the horse-radish if we can get beef.

Pickwick

Sam, you're something of a wag.

Sam

My eldest brother was troubled with that complaint, sir. Maybe it's catching. I used to sleep with him.

Pickwick

This is a curious old inn of yours.

Sam

If we'd know you wos comin', sir, we'd a had it made over.

Pickwick

I am looking for a friend. Can you give me an idea of who is in the inn? A—a lady may be with him.

Sam

(*Musing*)
A wooden leg in number six, a pair of Hessians in thirteen, two pairs of halves in the commercial, there's these here painted tops in the snuggery behind the bar, and—stop a bit, there's a pair of Wellingtons a good deal worn—yes, and a pair of lady's shoes, in number five.

Pickwick

What sort of shoes, what maker's name?

Sam

Brown, Muggleton. And the Wellingtons has gone to Doctor's Commons for a license.

Pickwick

By heavens, I have found them! A license?

Sam

And a license tout at Paul's Churchyard got hold of him, sir.

Pickwick

A license tout!

Sam

Coves in white aprons, touches their hats when you walk in. "License, sir?"

Pickwick

What do they do, in heaven's name?

Sam

Do! They do *you*, sir. And that ain't the verst of it. They put things into old gen'lemen's heads as they never would dream of. My father, sir, wos a coachman. A widower he was, and uncommon fat, and his missus had left him four hundred pound. Down he goes to see the lawyer and draw the money—werry smart, white hat, nosegay in his buttonhole, green shawl, top boots. Goes through archway, tout comes up, touches hat. "License, sir?" "I'm too old for it, dash it, and too fat," says my father, never having given it a thought. "Not a bit, sir," says the tout, "we married a bigger man last Monday, you're a babby to him!" So my father follers him in and gets his affidavit, and when the feller says, "What's the lady's name?" he says, "Blessed if I know. Can't I put that in afterward?" But they says no, and he thought up a name, Susan Clarke, Marquis of Grandby, Dorking. "She'll have me, if I ask, I dessay," my father says. "I never said nothing to her, but she'll have me." Well, sir, she did have him, and she's got him now, and that's all I'll ever see of the four hundred pound.

Pickwick

There are other ways of improving your situation, Sam, and that's another reason why I stepped down to speak to you.

Sam

That's the p'int, sir. Out with it, as the father said to the child who swallowed a farden.

Pickwick

I want to know, in the first place, if you are satisfied to go on as you are, as boots at the inn?

[493]

Afore I answers that question, let me ask, are you ready to purwide me with a better?

Pickwick

Ah. I have half made up my mind to employ you myself.

Sam

(*Shrewd look*)
Have you, now?

Pickwick

Thinking of it.

Sam

Wages?

Pickwick

Twelve pounds a year.

Sam

Clothes?

Pickwick

Two suits.

Sam

Work?

Pickwick

To attend upon me, to travel about with me and my friends, to make yourself useful in a hundred ways.

Sam

Take the bill down, the premises is let. I'm engaged to a single gen'leman, and the terms is agreed upon.

Pickwick

You accept, then?

Sam

Cert'n'y. If the clothes fits me half as well as the place, they'll do.

You can get a character, of course?

Ask the landlady at the White Hart.

And you can come this evening?

I'll get into the clothes this minute, if you've them about you.

(*Shaking hands and laughing heartily*)
No, no, no. No necessity for that, but I'll look for you tonight, and I'll treat you fairly, Sam, and I know you will me.

Amen to that, sir! I'll be there.

(*Boys face audience and bow. Dickens laughs and applauds.*)

Bravo. Hands under the coattails, Frank, and balancing back and forth on your toes, see? Oh, we must have this later, eh? Can you fix that up, Georgie?

Surely. We're all actors now.

(*The children gather properties and disappear.*)

Aunt Georgie doesn't quite approve, eh?

Aunt Georgie worries.

About me. Why, I've never been in better trim!

You've always been restless, Charles. But now it seems like something devouring you. The books aren't enough. They are the talk of all England, but that's not enough.

Dickens

(*In chair again, half desperate, half whimsical*)
Not enough. Good God, so much more than I ever dreamed.

Georgie

Then you tell Kate and me that you think a magazine will distract you. Well, you have it.

Dickens

I have it.

Georgie

And that's not enough.

Dickens

No, that's not enough.

Georgie

Then it's the Pyrenees. You want to get up into the snows, far above the world, and be shut in there, out of touch with us all, leaving Kate and the children, and Forster and Smith, leaving the magazine—leaving everything.

Dickens

Snows. Cold, clear, blue. It might be wonderful.

Georgie

But what are you running away from?

Dickens

Oh, God knows. Even my good little sister and housekeeper doesn't know?

Georgie

If I could only help.

Dickens

(*Catching at her hand, as she stoops to throw a paper on the fire*)
You don't know how you help. And someday you're going to let me help you. You'll tell me the whole story someday, eh?

(*Faintly*)
Someday. (*Goes out.*)

Dickens

(*Dreams on for a moment, then his face sobers, and he begins to pace to and fro*)
Little Georgie, too? Lucky fellow, whoever he is. I'll get Kate to get it out of her. Sly little minx that she is, not a word about it. Well, I'll have to get upstairs and change. Georgie, eh? (*Quotes.*) "It is not a new thing. It is not a hopeful thing. I can deal with it—I have dealt with it. It is not a new thing." Good God! (*Sits down.*) Good God. Georgie. But of course. But of course. No, it could hardly be that. Always here, always so good and so busy. Ha. Here's a complication. How to handle this now? Not a word to her, not a word to Kate. I must know nothing, suspect nothing. If anything could make me love the dear girl more than I do it would be this—her poor pitiful little secret. Truly, my dear girl, I would have spared you this. But no change of expression from me, no hint in my look or manner will ever embarrass you. I may be the most conceited coxcomb —but I believe I have it. Ha. To think this out now——

Kate

(*Descending stairs*)
Charles, really—with gentlemen coming for dinner. Aren't you going to change?

Dickens

I am on my way. You look your best, Kate.

Kate

I am aware that I am a stone wall.

Dickens

My unfortunate expression. Cannot that be forgotten?

Kate

I think very few wives would forget being called a stone wall.

Dickens

My very dear girl, what I said was that often of late there appears to be a stone wall between us. It was not always there.

[497]

Kate

When a woman has given a man ten children, it's hard to understand why she should be accused of living on the other side of a stone wall.

Dickens

You have an undeniable argument there, my dear.

Kate

But as Ma says, if the man had to have every other child——

Dickens

Yes, I know your mother's idea on that point—— (*Suddenly earnest.*) Kate, what would you think—— (*Stops.*)

Kate

Think of what?

Dickens

No matter. (*Halfway upstairs, hesitant.*) I was just thinking—wondering —wondering how it would be, since I cannot get away——

Kate

(*In chair by fire*)
Away for what?

Dickens

Nothing. Did you see the children's Pickwick and Sam?

Kate

Did Georgie rehearse them just now? Yes, I've been helping them rehearse.

Dickens

Deuced good, too.

Kate

I'll be glad if I ever get used to these new curtains. There's the bell. Here they are!

(*Dickens goes on upstairs, as a maid comes through the room. She disappears, left, and an immediate uproar of voices bursts in the hall. Five men come in unwinding scarves, throwing off coats and shawls, giving maid hats. Kate rises to greet them; maid takes wraps.*)

Georgie comes running downstairs, jumble of greetings as they warm hands at the fire. Forster. Collins. Smith. Lemon. Landor.)

Men

Miss Georgie, your servant. Mrs. Dickens. Gad, this is a bad night! Snowing. Dickens here? He came on ahead of us! Ah, that heat is good. Good to be indoors.

Georgie

And the readings were a success?

Forster

Never anything like it.

Collins

Never saw anything like it. He was tremendous.

Georgie

He's doing too much—he's tired. But he said it had been good.

Forster

Good!

Kate

Tickets sold well?

Forster

Sellout, everywhere. Crowds turned away. I tell you there has never been anything like this—never. I can see him again and again, Miss Georgie, and yet I feel the salt water in my eyes every time.

Georgie

I know how it is! I know how it is when he does the simplest reading. Ah, here is Charles!

(*They break into applause as Dickens comes downstairs. One man, Landor, goes to stairway and, meeting Dickens, who stands above him on lower step, bursts out incoherently, taking both his hands.*)

Landor

No, Dickens—no—my dear fellow—my dear fellow—I couldn't catch you after the reading—I must say it—my heart has been bursting with it ever since last night—that the child should die—the little innocent boy, never knowing his mother, with the angelic sister holding his hand—— By God,

[499]

Dickens, I have felt actual deaths less, I have felt my own personal griefs less! My dear fellow, congratulations—

Others

So say we all of us.

Dickens

It's for Smith here to say whether it was a success or not.

Kate

(*Half amused, half shocked*)
Charles, you sound so mercenary!

Smith

Nothing to worry about there, Mrs. Dickens.

Dickens

No, we were stupendous and we outdid Cicero, Diogenes, and Mrs. Bracegirdle! So how about some dinner? Everything ready (*to Georgie*), my dear girl? (*She gives him a quick look*)

Forster

(*Detaining him as the others stream out*)
Just a word with you, Dickens.

Dickens

Yours to command, sir.

Forster

Smith tells me this trip will net you more than a thousand pounds.

Dickens

By gad, I have use for them.

Forster

Dickens, should you get into this thing?

Dickens

You just answered that, my dear Forster.

Forster

I answered it in the negative, then.

A thousand pounds; there's your answer.

Forster

With *Household Words*—with the Christmas story coming on, with your new novel—is this sane? Is this wise?

Dickens

The strain will be nothing to me. Smith will make this possible, Forster. When I get to a town, as you know, I'll have only to go to my hotel, my rooms will be ready, my fire lighted, and afterward a hot little supper set out and waiting.

Forster

And the crowds in the street, and the cheering under your window, those won't tire you?

Dickens

Those are the very wine of life. No (*face darkening*), I told you what tires me.

Forster

I hope devoutly you have changed your mind.

Dickens

(*Irritable*)
I can hardly change my mind unless I have already made it up. Forster, no man alive knows less of my mind than I!

Forster

I thank God if you have not made it up. Think of Kate.

Dickens

(*Walking about, Forster seated, looking at him with troubled expression*)
I am different from other men. The flow of images here (*touches head*), the pressure of constantly keeping these book men and women of mine in order, the pressure of praise—you saw Landor a moment ago—I must not be regarded as other men. I am talking like a fool, Forster, a conceited fool—but—but I am not as other men. I am hungry—I am never filled!

Forster

That gives me a right to ask if there may be another woman?

[501]

Dickens

(*Hesitant half a second*)

No. If there is she is out of my reach—she has no idea—— No, there is no other woman.

Forster

Then for God's sake, man, why not go on? Feeling less for Kate than you did—yes. But many a marriage has that situation to meet.

Dickens

This is not many a marriage. This is my marriage, with all its extraordinary changes and contrasts. The early years, Forster, the first contracts, the first trip abroad. The Italian winters—the constant coming of children. Kate's sinking—sinking into comfort and indifference——

Forster

Never that. Only consider the difference in your natures, and accept it, and handle it.

Dickens

Only the difference in our natures. Ha.

Forster

Think of the talk. Think of your friends.

Dickens

A week's talk. Then the Dickens' children go to school—the boys go to India and China—the little ones are tutored. Then Mrs. Dickens lives where she likes, Brighton, Paris, Florence. Then Dickens works away in utter peace—as much peace, to be sure, as the racket a houseful of children provide—but I like that——

Forster

Dickens, this is all wrong. What does Kate do that disturbs that peace?

Dickens

What does one sharp cinder do to your eye, my dear fellow.

Forster

But, good God, according to that rule what home can endure?

Dickens

And according to that saying of yours, what have we men and women come to!

Take time. Consider it. Get away.

Dickens

I am the last man alive who can get away. You know my program, my obligations. I need your help; I'll need everyone's help. I'm not happy, Forster. I have to work my way out, somewhere. With all I have—so many thousand times more than the desolate child I was ever could have dreamed!—I must have happiness, too.

Forster

Georgie to go on here, I suppose?

Dickens

Certainly Georgie to go on here. Georgie is the heart of the house—children, servants, tradespeople, we all depend on her.

Forster

Charles, my dear fellow, is this fair to Georgie?

Dickens

(*Pause*)
It shall be fair to Georgie.

Forster

Does Kate know anything of this?

Dickens

Not yet.

Forster

She will take it hard. It's a hard thing to explain, hard to defend.

Dickens

I will not defend it. I need not defend it.

Forster

This is just one of your restless, nervous times. You must fight it. You must not do anything that you cannot undo.

Dickens

Forster, I have never in my life been so sure of anything as I am of this.

[503]

Forster

And your public will accept this?

Dickens

The public will continue to be absorbed in its own affairs.

Forster

My dear fellow, have you thought that everyone who knows you will know that there is no shred of reflection against her?

Dickens

Good God, do you suppose me for one moment implying that there is?

Forster

Of course not. Of course not. But the whole thing is fantastic. The whole thing is much better put aside, forgotten for a while.

Dickens

Ha. (*Walking.*)

Forster

Or go away for a while yourself, Dickens. Why not slip off to Paris, loaf along to Italy—Venice, Florence, eh? Don't move too fast. Get through these present engagements, and then we'll talk of it again.

Dickens

We are now talking of it again.

Forster

I hate to see you do this. Once again, what about Miss Georgie?

Dickens

Well, what about Miss Georgie? Why harp on Georgie? Georgie doesn't come into this.

Forster

It must be obvious to you that her name will come into the talk about it, too.

Dickens

Not by anyone who has the faintest knowledge of the circumstance or the faintest respect for the family. Why can't you see it as it is?

[504]

I do see it. Why, there is hardly a marriage that wouldn't be the happier for a break now and then. Many a man has wanted to run away from a crowded nursery—changes of servants—that sort of thing. We all feel it. But why not leave Georgie and Kate here with the children, why not keep the surface smooth and wait until you sail into pleasanter waters? Just a suggestion, my dear boy—merely the way the thing looks to me.

Dickens

I am not a boy now, Forster. I am a man, burdened more heavily than the ordinary run of men, perhaps, perhaps not as fitted as most of them to meet these—these slings and arrows of outrageous fortune. My home I must have, my children I must have, and if I feel that my engagements— my productivity is jeopardized by any personality—however blameless— however once beloved—— (*He puts his head in his hands.*)

Forster

May we leave this now—speak of it later?

Dickens

Yes, yes. By all means. By all means. Let's dine. There's a capital sole, Georgie tells me, and a saddle of mutton.

Forster

You might sign this—any time.

Dickens

I'll sign it now—contract, eh? I've read it.

(*He walks to the desk, Forster turns to the dining-room door as Georgie comes in.*)

Georgie

Dinner, you two. We're all eating.

Forster

And I'm famished.   (*Goes out.*)

Dickens

Georgie. (*Not turning from desk.*)

Georgie

Charles.

Dickens

(*Sanding document*)

Just a moment.

Georgie

(*Hurriedly, agitated*)

I wanted to see you a moment, too. I wanted to ask you never to give Kate a hint of anything I might have said today—not that anything was definite, but she would tell Ma, and Ma would worry—so—you won't, will you?

Dickens

But you told me nothing.

Georgie

I know. I know. But you said that you had noticed a change in me—and I don't want Ma—or Kate—— I shall be going away for a while—presently——

Dickens

What could I tell anyone? What do I know?

Georgie

Then you won't—because it is nothing——

Dickens

I wonder if it would help you to know that I think I know what it is—what is wrong, what worries you.

Georgie

(*Walking over to look out of the window, Dickens in his chair*)

You—couldn't possibly know.

Dickens

Why could I not possibly know?

Georgie

Because—because if I have been foolish enough to give away my heart—it doesn't mean that I could ever dream that there could be happiness of that sort for me! It would not be in reference to—to anyone that you know —to any circumstance—however unexpected now—— (*She flounders to silence. Dickens sits looking at her.*)

Dickens

Don't be frightened. There's nothing to be afraid of. After all, the situation is one that concerns no one but yourself.

Georgie

Oh yes. No one but myself.

Dickens

So there is no reason why it should be discussed at all.

Georgie

No.

Dickens

No one—no kind heart is to be hurt by it.

Georgie

Oh, never, Charles, never. It would break my heart.

Dickens

Nor any life upset in its usual course?

Georgie

Not if it killed me, keeping it in my own breast.

Dickens

It couldn't have a safer haven, Georgie.

Georgie

And we won't think of it any more. Except that I think I must go away—for a while——

Dickens

Go away? Why?

Georgie

I am tired. I am not sleeping well. It would not be for long.

Dickens

I think I wouldn't plan that, Georgie.

Georgie

(A *little wildly*)
I have no plan. I only feel that I would be happier away.

Dickens

Supposing—supposing we look at it this way, Georgie. Let us suppose a lovely and devoted—well, member of a family——

Georgie

(*Sobs*)

Whose one hope has always been only—only to make that family happier.

Dickens

Whose one unselfish thought is to smooth the way for every member of that family. Let us suppose she lives in a sister's house.

Georgie

(*Almost inaudible*)

In her sister's house.

Dickens

And let us suppose her an angel in that house.

Georgie

A pretty poor angel! (*Shaky laugh.*)

Dickens

If a child is ill, if a servant gives notice, if a joint doesn't come from the pastry cooks, this little sister's hand is there, soothing and straightening and solving. There is no person in the house, from the youngest child to the oldest guest, who does not feel her influence—for good, for harmony, every day.

Georgie

It is an influence very much overestimated.

Dickens

I don't think so. Well, let us suppose that this sister's husband has won to eminence of some sort, is followed, admired, spoiled by his public. He doesn't always like it, like the strain and the crowds, he likes to get home to his own fireside, and find peace there, and the welcome of children, and the lamps lighted, and his dinner smoking hot on the table.

Georgie

And he earns that—surely, with all he does, he deserves that.

Dickens

Perhaps he doesn't. But we'll suppose that he does. Perhaps he doesn't, perhaps he is an ordinary enough fellow, but we'll suppose that he does. At all events he needs that home of his, he needs that welcome at night. He would miss it.

[508]

Georgie

But whatever this sister—this housekeeper and manager of his decided to do wouldn't he still have that?

Dickens

Its very flavor would be gone—oh, not only for him, but for them all. For her sister, who depends on her——

Georgie

(*Automatically*)
Who depends on her.

Dickens

So—would it be so hard for her to go on, quietly, knowing herself so loved, knowing herself so needed, knowing that she could not be more respected if she were the Queen herself—would that be more than she could do?

Georgie

(*Desperate*)
It would be the one place she would want to be.

Dickens

Then why leave it? Sensibly now, should the fact that her secret is suspected make it harder for her?

Georgie

No. Easier. Easier.

Dickens

Easier. Bravo. For believe me, Georgie, if this—this lovely girl were that man's own sister, he could not feel a deeper responsibility for her happiness, a deeper admiration. He could not determine more seriously—yes, reverently, that she should feel his respect and his protection about her.

Georgie

He—he would not despise her?

Dickens

Despise her? No, if by chance he had suspected her secret, he would only honor her the more; he would feel that the confidence between them was a bond that made their relationship only the more secure—a relationship of brother and sister, Georgie.

Georgie

She would believe that, Charles. She would—she would need to know that.

Dickens

And on her side, it would mean safety for her—and someday it might mean happiness, to know that the first pure love of her heart—I know that heart! —is placed so safely. And believe me, when the time comes for this—this adopted brother of hers to turn her over to some fortunate man, it will be with the knowledge that her secret has robbed no one, has hurt no one, and that no man—no, not even that happy husband, will rejoice in her happiness as does that same brother.

Georgie

There will never be such a man. But you help me, Charles, you make it all so plain. I can go on, now, seeing my way clear ahead.

Dickens

Straight ahead now. Steady, eh? No more tears.

Georgie

No. No more tears. And Kate needn't know.

Dickens

There is nothing for her to know.

Georgie

Nothing. Except that—(*a little tearful*) that I love all of you more than ever.

Dickens

That's the dear, dear girl.

Georgie

(*Broken*)
Thank you, Charles. (*Exit.*)

Dickens

I'm the one to say thanks. You go on in, I'll sign this for Forster. (*Signs.*) *Walks about.*) Georgie. I might have seen it at any time. I suppose I did see it, but I didn't think she knew her own heart. But no, she did surprise me just now! Well, it mustn't make any difference. Kate needn't suspect it—it might make a difference in her going away. (*Restless, working up to frenzy.*) She must go away. Her going away doesn't mean that I lose all

sense of what's decent and right. It only means that I've one less worry—
one less pressure. Poor Georgie. She said "you make it all so plain!" As if
I could ever make anything plain, to myself or anyone else! The girls grown
up—to be married someday soon, I suppose. Some young fool—Collins'
brother, is after Katy now. Ha. And boys to get placed and then get un-
placed—and the magazine, and the Ormond Street Hospital for the children—I said I'd talk for that—and the Christmas story, good God how it all
piles up! And the wretchedness, the wretchedness—here. (*Arm on mantelpiece, head on arm.*) To know I've no right to her, no right to touch her
hand, and she wouldn't let me! How to get the good ground under my feet
again in the old way, to feel the glory of writing, the books coming right,
to feel my brain singing again——

Edward

(*Comes shyly in from the dining room, goes over to slip his hand in
his father's. Dickens starts, looks down, laughs.*)

Dickens

Supper of course! Mutton soup with the chops in it, eh? In we go.

(*Shout from dining room as they go in.*)

CURTAIN

THE INIMITABLE
ACT TWO

ACT TWO

SCENE: Same room.
TIME: Morning, a week later.

*(Kate and her mother. They are working at a heap of clothes that lie
on the floor and in baskets, between their chairs.)*

Mrs. Hogarth

This dress has been turned twice, Kate, and I think you might give it to
the poor. I'll cut the buttons off, they're good. I don't know but what I'll
rip off this binding, too. Georgie was saying she needed some for her
brigadier. Lizzie has braid on hers, so of course Georgie has to have some,
too. Though how she could marry a man on three hundred pounds a year,
to say nothing of his hangdog look—whatever that means, for I never heard
of a dog hanging anyone or anyone hanging a dog as far as that goes—
but three rooms over a mews, that's what Fanny Lipett said, if I understood her—but you may be sure it means something bad, for we all give
the dumb brutes the worst of it. Except Dora Norman—I told you that,
or I told Georgie—buying a blanket for her dog in Bond Street and her
little girls in dresses so long-waisted they sit down above their belts, and
yet her father could buy the Sir Joshua that your father said was no more a
Sir Joshua than the cat, supposing anyone knows what a thing like that is
worth which I frankly say I don't. I wish you could remember the name,
Kate, but you never listen to me any more.

Kate

Wasn't that Mrs. Norman, Ma?

Mrs. Hogarth

Truly, my love, you will have to keep your thoughts a little better collected. Whoever spoke of poor Dora Norman, except to say that she was

[515]

buying her dog a blanket—you don't think I was asking the dog's name? Why on earth should I care what she calls the poor animal? They're all Spotty or Snuffy or Flash—except Lydia Park's dog, or rather her husband's that had the silver pipe in his throat, who named the dog Lady Blessington—— How on earth they ever keep such a thing clean I'm sure I don't know—— He said he did it just for the pleasure of saying, "My dear, I think Lady Blessington wants to go out," which is merely childish, and that he was! So what do you really think, Kate?

Kate

Think about what, Ma?

Mrs. Hogarth

You are very trying, love. You really are. When my one thought is your welfare. However, if you wish to change the subject by all means do so. But that will merely encourage a husband, yours or any other woman's, in feeling that he is free to indulge in any sort of erratic behavior.

Kate

You mean Charles's saying he wishes to have a room of his own for a while? That's what we were talking about.

Mrs. Hogarth

For a while? Well, pray keep me informed. I was not aware that this was a passing whim.

Kate

It may be or it may not be. You know Charles. He never was like other husbands.

Mrs. Hogarth

When it comes to freakishness and perversity and selfishness, he is exactly like all of them.

Kate

No, Ma. A writer is different. He is under much more of a nervous strain.

Mrs. Hogarth

Nervous strain fiddlesticks. I'd nervous strain him.

Kate

If you were writing day and night, Ma, you'd know what I mean. Georgie keeps his pens trimmed for him, and you should see how he goes through them.

[516]

Mrs. Hogarth

I may be logical, Kate, and I may not. My dear P'pa always said that I was. He was probably mistaken, although a brilliant man of whom the doctor said, when he expired, that his brain should have been preserved, but as he was drowned at sea that was not to be thought of—a mind like a steel trap was his expression for me, prejudiced, I grant you, paternally biased, certainly. But I cannot for the life of me see what Georgie's trimming his pens has to do with the fact that Mr. Dickens has left your room. Pray be so extremely good as to enlighten me.

Kate

He explained that he is nervous—working too hard.

Mrs. Hogarth

Without mentioning any subject, Kate, that no woman ever allows to enter her thoughts much less her speech, I should say that the comfort of his wife's company—you understand perfectly that I am alluding to his room, to his—shall I say, embraces—

Kate

Ma, for heaven's sake!

Mrs. Hogarth

I am silent. But if a man is so tired that he does not look for comfort there, believe me, he looks elsewhere.

Kate

I have not the slightest suspicion of that.

Mrs. Hogarth

When a man asks his housekeeper to have a wall built between his room and his wife's room——

Kate

Please let's not go over all that again.

Mrs. Hogarth

Very well, Kate. But with all your father's peculiarities, and of course his father, and your grandfather too, were both considered decidedly erratic men, he never so much as suggested that he should sleep anywhere else but in his own bed. Why, when you children were growing up he was right there in the same bed beside me to get up in the night if one of you was croupy or crying in the night. Miles upon miles has that poor man walked, objecting only once when the man who laid the carpet overlooked quite a few tacks——

Kate

Yes, it was like that with us, too. But our children have outgrown the croupy years.

Mrs. Hogarth

I know that quite well, Kate, as who should know better than the children's grandmother, a fact that a good many people seem to have forgotten, but even when your children were born—and it seems to me very sad to hold children responsible for this sort of thing, which I am sure you never would do, Kate, if you were not so terribly distressed and disturbed by walling up a door—for when every one of your children was born I would be the last to say that your husband did not continue to sleep in his own bed with you, with the child in a bassinet beside you, and poor old Fanning as the monthly until she died, which (*musing*) was of course after Alfred—was it Alfred?—on a bed by the fire, for summer or winter she would have a fire for the infant's gruel—so why pretend it is nothing?

Kate

If you mean Charles, Ma, I am not saying it is nothing. I simply say that that is the way he wants it to be, and that is the way it is.

Mrs. Hogarth

I would like to know exactly what reasons he gave for it. When Mollie explained it to me this morning—I happened to go upstairs with the drawers I have made for the boys, I noticed the door blocked up and asked Mollie what that meant.

Kate

It means just what it is. That Charles wants to sleep in the old study for a while.

Mrs. Hogarth

With no explanation? You didn't quarrel?

Kate

Of course we didn't quarrel. Everything's just as before.

Mrs. Hogarth

Except that your husband's left you.

Kate

Left me? No! The theatricals and dinners and all the rest of it will go on here just as usual. Probably this sort of thing happens in a great many families with no fuss at all.

Mrs. Hogarth

I well remember Lizzie and Ronnie Cheeseman living in different rooms, but that was because he had scarlet and the doctor thought it was better for her to move into the spare room until he felt better—that was when she was in a delicate situation of course, with that child who squinted and was sent home from school because the teacher thought he was mocking her—— I suppose she squinted, too—I mean that was later, for he wasn't born when Ronnie had—— Or was it scarlet, I think it was Lizzie who had it whatever it was. Her father had cataracts, Lizzie's did, I mean. It was the first time I'd ever heard the word except for the waterfalls, but as far as that goes, what more beautiful example of married life need we look for than the Queen and the Prince, so how can you take the opposite view?

Kate

Did I, Ma?

Mrs. Hogarth

Did you what, Kate?

Kate

Take the opposite view. What opposite view?

Mrs. Hogarth

Sometimes I think you are very strange, Kate. You seem to talk purposely to confuse me. It's very distracting. I was merely saying that everyone knows that the Queen would no more think of spending the night——

Kate

I think perhaps if you stop worrying about it, Ma, we'll all feel better. Charles and I never have had a serious disagreement, and we are quite capable of managing this matter ourselves.

Mrs. Hogarth

(Rising)
Thanking you for the suggestion, Kate, that I had better mind my own business, which I have always striven to do from my very childhood, and thanking you for a delightful lunch——

Kate

Oh, now, Ma, for pity's sake, sit down, and don't act as if your under-petticoat was a backboard.

[519]

Mrs. Hogarth

Kate!

Kate

Well, I know. But it does get me exasperated to have you harping on Charles. He's a genius, and he's odd, and that's all there is to it.

(*Georgie has come in, with parcels. She sinks wearily into a chair. She speaks with half-amused impatience.*)

Georgie

Is Ma asking you to consider Charles as if he was like anyone else? Ah, don't, Ma. We get so tired in this house—there's so much confusion, so many rehearsals and costumes and cabs at the door, and Charles going to be here for dinner and not going to be here, and bills, and Cook getting mad because we never give the soup a chance to jelly and Mamie crying because she's never been to a kettledrum—— Well, perhaps I'm tired.

Kate

Oh, Georgie, I'm so sorry.

Georgie

I'll be all right with a cup of tea. The minute I get where you are, Kate, everything seems to smooth out. Don't worry about me. I'm where I want to be and doing what I want to do.

Mrs. Hogarth

Sacrificing your life and losing any chance for a suitable match—ha. (*Falls forbiddingly silent.*)

Georgie

I've had several suitable chances, Ma.

Mrs. Hogarth

Nobody ever believes a girl when she says that. Ha.

Georgie

I don't care what anyone believes.

Mrs. Hogarth

No, Georgie, nobody ever believes anything but that a girl will snap at any good chance, rather than live with her family, being treated like a sort of servant in the house.

Georgie

(Exchanging a long-suffering glance with Kate)
Children had their tea?

Kate

Mamie had charge of it, in the old schoolroom. Katy's gone across the square to see Sybil.

Georgie

Ma, you'll stay for tea?

Mrs. Hogarth

I'm so vexed at Kate, Georgie. I've been telling her so.

Georgie

What has Kate done?

Mrs. Hogarth

Why, this business of a man's building a wall between his room and his wife's.

Georgie

Oh, that doesn't mean anything. What can Kate do, anyway?

Mrs. Hogarth

I'd chop it down.

Kate

Oh, Ma, if you'd only concentrate on what concerns you. I'm sure I'd pay no attention at all if you and Pa decided to build a few walls.

Mrs. Hogarth

I would be pleased if my children did pay more attention to the affairs of their father and myself, but I never have asked it and I do not expect it; why should we intrude our dull existence upon members of our family who have risen to heights of fame and wealth running to three house-maids, a cook and a boy, to say nothing of wine put down to the tune of forty pounds a quarter, with the heeltaps never accounted for, and prob-ably sold for a good price, either by that boy who looks exactly like that Willie Curran that you children named the biscuits for, when Cook didn't brown them enough and a silly name it was—because it was Lennie who was the pale one, Willie was the one that sewing woman that I had, whose husband was the man they thought robbed the fish stall, and it turned

[521]

out to be that poor little woman in the red cape—certainly a man's cape and probably her sister's husband's who was in the mutiny—you remember, Kate? Certainly you do, Georgie.

Georgie

Certainly, Ma.

Kate

I know, Ma.

Mrs. Hogarth

Well, then, what's so extraordinary about it?

Georgie

Nothing, really.

Mrs. Hogarth

(*Triumphant*)
So you see!

Kate

How about tea, Georgie?

(*Georgie gets up and rings.*)

Mrs. Hogarth

As for applying significance to circumstances and things that are entirely unimportant, that is something entirely out of my nature. If Mr. Dickens chose to build an Indian wigwam on the top of his house and leave it in a balloon every morning, it would never occur to me to comment upon it, I am sure. Although the crowd of people out here in Devonshire Terrace staring up at the windows would certainly cause remark, because whenever somebody tried to turn the grays they would be in danger of being knocked down—— You laugh, Georgie, but it would make Kate and Mr. Dickens extremely unpopular, and it would result in you and Kate not using the carriage, which is the last thing you'd enjoy with the Prendergasts getting a new phaeton only last week—— (*Stops as maid enters.*)

Georgie

Tea, please, Nancy. Ma, you'll stay?

Mrs. Hogarth

No, I'm going to sit with dear Aunt Jane, right around the corner. All alone, and she has them send up crumpets and teacakes and almost always a great big seed cake from the kitchen, with that poor red-faced maid of hers buttering toast at the fire—how she does it, who eats up what's left, that's what I ask her? The girls in the kitchen do, that's who eats it up—four pounds a year, their beer, two dresses at Christmas—what are they coming to and finishing off all that cake every day. Georgie, you watch these girls here, don't you?

Georgie

I really do, Ma.

Mrs. Hogarth

(*Putting on coat*)

Well, Kate, if I've helped you at all with your problem, I'm sure I'm glad; I've had to be rather frank, but when it's for the good of any one of my children you'll not find me flinching or keeping anything back. If you'll think of what I've said—I have no objection to your discussing it with Georgie—I think you'll find Mother was right. The family, your nine children, this handsome home, and Mr. Dickens' success all indicate to anyone who has given this sort of thing the least thought, that guiding and directing you from your very babyhood has been someone with—yes, someone well versed in worldly lore——

(*Goes out, escorted to the door by Georgie. Tea arrives.*)

Georgie

Ah, this is wonderful, Kate. Nobody can deny we love Ma—at least I suppose we do—but isn't it restful to be just by ourselves?

Kate

That's it, Georgie. As long as things go on well here, and the children are well, and the servants behaving themselves, why, what Charles does is—well, just what Charles does.

Georgie

He's done queer things before.

Kate

And he's gotten so lately that he doesn't really want to see many people. He doesn't go to dinners as he did, he's just in one of those times—— Georgie, should I give this old coat of Walter's to the poor?

Georgie

I should think so. The lining's practically worn out. Wait and I'll cut the buttons off it.

Kate

I had Mamie and Katy ripping lace and trimmings off old dresses for the poor, just before you came in.

Georgie

This ought to go to the poor, too. (*Holds up garment actually in large holes*)

Kate

I suppose so. This is an awful winter for the poor. When I see those barefooted little boys sweeping the crossings, I wonder how their parents can let them go out at all in this weather.

Georgie

Is it his newest book?

Kate

Is what his newest book?

Georgie

Whatever's making Charles so nervous and keeping him so busy?

Kate

Forster says it's the kind of nervous tiredness that resting wouldn't help. That sounds like nonsense, to me. See if you can match this yarn, Georgie. It's for Mamie's fascinator.

Georgie

All we can do is go along as if nothing was unusual and let time take care of things.

Kate

You *are* a comfort, Georgie.

Georgie

I am, aren't I, Kate? (*Troubled*)

Kate

More than you'll ever know.

Georgie

Then I know everything will come out all right.

Kate

There's one thing I want to ask you.

Georgie

This is the mate to that stocking, isn't it?

Kate

Yes. One faded more than the other. This is what I want to ask you.

Georgie

Yes?

Kate

Tell me honestly. You aren't giving up anything, Georgie, you aren't holding off any eligible man just because we need you here?

Georgie

(*Pause*)
What eligible man?

Kate

Why, I don't know. I know that you've never given me a hint of it. But sometimes, when I see you so serious over your work, or notice that you look pale for a few days, I wonder if you have some secret attachment—

Georgie

(*Very busy, but laughing lightly*)
To whom, Kate?

Kate

Perhaps to some man Charles and I don't know.

Georgie

No, I have no secret attachment.

Kate

(*Giving up*)
Well, certainly it isn't an open one.

Georgie

You—and Charles—know every man I know, Kate.

[525]

Yes, and I've thought of every one a hundred times, and there isn't one that's worthy of you.

Georgie

I assure you, Kate, that if I ever want to run away with this legendary gentleman, you will be the first to hear of it.

Kate

When I will immediately scratch his eyes out. Nobody in the world is good enough for my Georgie. Georgie, do you think this could be turned and washed and combined with the red plush and made into a sack for mornings?

(*Dickens comes in, hair somewhat mussed, velvet morning coat, tired and quiet. He nods in turn to each. Georgie pours him a cup of tea.*)

Georgie

This may not be very hot.

Dickens

It's all right.

(*Gulps it. Georgie sits down again. Silence.*)

Kate

(*In a low tone*)
That stain's not going to show, is it, Georgie?

Georgie

Never in the world. (*Murmuring.*)

Kate

Should it be faced?

Georgie

I would. And I think I'll ask Mollie to mend this fire.

(*Dickens has stretched himself full-length in his chair, eyes shut, hands thrust into his trouser pockets. Georgie goes out, Mollie comes in and kneels, fixing the fire. Mollie goes out. Silence. Kate matches darning wools.*)

Dickens

Kate.

Kate

I thought you were asleep.

Dickens

No. I tried lying down upstairs. No sleep.

Kate

(*Pointedly, mildly malicious*)
Perhaps you belong back in your own room.

Dickens

(*Pause*)
No, it's not that.

Kate

Well, when things quiet down you'll be all right again.

Dickens

When what things quiet down?

Kate

Oh, getting these lectures organized, and your newest book, and the Christmas story, and everything.

Dickens

I wish things disturbed me as little as they do you, Kate.

Kate

I don't allow them to.

Dickens

Harder than it sounds, my dear.

Kate

I wish you had a—well, say a brother, Charles, who meant to you what Georgie means to me.

Dickens

(*Sardonic, thinking of his worthless relatives*)
My brother. Ha.

[527]

Through these years when the children were coming, and when they were babies, to have someone to talk to, and laugh with, and plan with——

Dickens

She's a wonderful girl, Georgie.

Kate

I don't think you begin to know how wonderful.

Dickens

I have a pretty fair idea, after what she's been to you and the children all these years.

Kate

Have you thought any more of what I suspected, I mean that she's been impressed by someone—that she's thinking of someone?

Dickens

Georgie isn't a young girl any more, Kate.

Kate

I know. But she'll always seem young to me.

Dickens

I suppose so. But our own girls are in the market now.

Kate

Oh no, I hate to think that. I'd hate to be a grandmother.

Dickens

(Struck)

That just doesn't seem possible. A grandfather! Why, I've hardly begun to live. (Musing.) I wonder if life's like that; by the time you begin living you find you're beginning dying.

Kate

What a horrible way to put it. Don't talk so.

Dickens

In a way, it brings me to speak of something else, Kate. I've been thinking of this for some time. I've been wondering how you'd like to go away for a while?

Kate

(Looks up from work)
Go away?

Dickens

Yes. To—well, to Brighton. To—Paris, maybe.

Kate

Charles, what a ridiculous time to think of leaving everything! The children's schools, Mamie and Katy hoping to go about a good deal—after all, both girls are out in society now—and Eddy's throat so delicate——

Dickens

Why, I'll be here, and Georgie can handle everything.

Kate

You'll be here?

Dickens

I have to, my dear. Couldn't possibly get away now.

Kate

I don't think I understand you.

Dickens

I'm asking you to understand. I'm asking you to leave home for a while.

Kate

Why should I?

Dickens

Because—frankly—I believe it would be wise.

Kate

Wise!

Dickens

I believe it would be.

Kate

What would be wise about my taking a trip now? I'm not tired.

Dickens

I'm trying to tell you. I want you—I ask you—to consider going to—well, Brighton.

Kate

Alone!

Dickens

Unless you want to upset things here by taking Charley, or either of the girls. And that, I think, would be a mistake.

Kate

But what—why—why?

Dickens

Well, don't take that amazed tone, my dear. It isn't unheard of.

Kate

I think it is unheard of. I'm to move out because you are restless. Charles, it doesn't sound sensible!

Dickens

It may not be sensible. But it's the way I want it to be.

Kate

But—but—what's gone wrong? What have I done?

Dickens

That is exactly the question I dreaded. You have done nothing.

Kate

You are the one who told us the other night that you would like to go up into Switzerland and write all winter without seeing a soul.

Dickens

And so I would. But it's impossible now for me to think of leaving.

Kate

You mean that my being here makes you nervous?

Dickens

I do mean that. If I could go away, I would. Not that I want to go away. I want my children, I want my home, my friends in for suppers after the play. I've no relief now, Kate, but in action, to do everything I can, to keep going. I dare not go away. The silence of the Alps might kill me, might drive me out of my mind. (*Head grasped in hands.*)

Kate

Charles, this will not last.

Dickens

(*He rises, agitated. Desperately*)
It will not last if you will agree with me that our marriage, from the beginning, was a mistake. That we are better apart.

Kate

A mistake! A mistake! Why, whose marriage isn't, Charles? After so many years, the cares and worries of so many children—and especially with your work so pressing—so anxious——

Dickens

Exactly. I've tried to tell you this before, Kate. I am not like other men. Nature made me as I am, my life confirmed what I am. Poverty, a child's shame, struggle, responsibility, these made me. And I must be alone.

Kate

Hardly alone, in this house.

Dickens

You force me to say it. I want that sort of solitude.

Kate

Without your wife.

Dickens

That is solitude, no matter how big the household.

Kate

And what of *my* solitude?

Dickens

It isn't as serious a tragedy as ill-assorted companionship.

[531]

Kate

Is that the way you have come to see it?

Dickens

Yes, God help me.

Kate

And I've done nothing?

Dickens

You are always amiable, you are always compliant. But I want to be alone.

Kate

Then be alone. Go away. You have gone to Paris, to Italy, before this.

Dickens

I cannot go now. Oh, God knows I am not enjoying this!

Kate

Then—ah, be sensible. Why talk of it at all?

Dickens

Too late for that. Too late to go back. The children are older now—life has changed since you and I were the only ones to consider.

Kate

I can't tell how I will feel about this in the morning, Charles. But I can say that if I feel as I do now, I refuse to be sent away like an unsatisfactory servant.

Dickens

God knows it isn't like that. (*Coaxing.*) Kate, I've been uneasy and unhappy for months. You have been, too. I make you so. I see it. The children see it.

Kate

(*Proudly*)
The children see nothing. That's merely your idea.

Dickens

Why pull against the grain for the rest of our lives? Believe me, if you could meet my wishes in this I would do everything I could to see that you were comfortable, that you would want for nothing.

Kate

You would expect it to be permanent?

Dickens

Yes.

Kate

But suppose I don't want to do this—to make this change at all!

Dickens

I hope to make you see it as the wisest thing to do.

Kate

Brighton? Why Brighton?

Dickens

Canterbury, Folkestone, anywhere you liked.

Kate

Are you aware of how very strange this will sound?

Dickens

I am aware that I have not the slightest interest in anyone's reaction to it.

Kate

And you've been feeling this way for some time?

Dickens

For some time I have been aware of an unhappy sense of something lacking—something lost. For a long time I have been cut to the heart thinking what a pity it is—for your sake!—that I ever fell in your way. God knows you would have been a thousand times happier with another man.

Kate

(*Huffy*)
If I did go away, it would be only until you came to your senses.

Dickens

I can't deceive you—I cannot let you deceive yourself with any such dream, Kate.

Kate

You can't mean—forever!

[533]

Dickens

I am very sure I do. I have seen this coming steadily toward us since the very days when Mamie was born.

Kate

Why, but what a wayward—what an inexcusable feeling—what a ridiculous plan this is! No, I won't have anything to do with it.

Dickens

If you wanted five hundred—six hundred a year——

Kate

I wish you wouldn't talk that way.

Dickens

But we *must* discuss it.

Kate

I don't see why.

Dickens

Nothing in our two lives is as important.

Kate

Charles, you have been doing a great deal in these last years to show me how completely tired—how bored you have been with everything here at home. These reading engagements, the trips anywhere and everywhere—the plays. It all shows that this restlessness of yours has become an actual disease.

Dickens

And you are the one person who can cure me. All this that you describe is the result of—of unsettledness here. (*Touching his heart.*) I ask you, I humbly ask you to do what you can to cure it.

Kate

(*Maternal*)
My going away won't cure anything.

Dickens

You'll drive me to something—something mad.

Kate

I'll do anything in reason, Charles, you know it. But I cannot see any reason for a sensational change like this, with all the gossip it would mean, and I think when you give it serious consideration you'll agree with me.

Dickens

Serious consideration! Good God, you haven't grasped the situation at all. I've told you the one thing that will restore me to peace of mind. And you say that because of the silly gossip of a lot of women for whom you care nothing you won't agree to it.

Kate

Have you ever heard of any other mother walking away from her home and her children? I don't know how such an idea ever got into your head.

Dickens

It got into my head because it is the one possible solution. I don't know why—I don't defend myself—but I know that it is this way. I belong to the public, Kate—God knows I'm not boasting—but my life is not my own. The restlessness, the feeling you call wayward, is part—I suppose it is part! —of the tenure which one has on an imaginative life.

Kate

We loved each other once. We married for love.

Dickens

We did. And I agree that there are incidents—conditions—in the married life of many a man, far less bearable than mine. I am sensible of the wonderful exercise—to call it that—that I have of life, Kate—its highest sensations—and I have honestly and truly felt that this—this young, unthinking marriage of ours was the drawback unavoidable to such a career —expected, not to be complained of. I know your side of the story. There is plenty of fault on my side, I dare say. But admitting causes doesn't cure them, Kate.

Kate

(*Sharply*)
And finding the wrong cure doesn't cure them, either.

Dickens

But cutting straight to the root of the matter does. A little courage now, and we may find ourselves free for long, happy years, you developing a new life, I satisfied in the old one. Kate, I'll be the one blamed. I accept it. "Thence comes it that my name receives a brand, And almost thence my nature is subdued

[535]

To what it works in, like the dyer's hand;
Pity me then and wish I were renewed."

Kate

Yes, I know. That's Shakespeare. You read that to all of us at supper the other night.

Dickens

But haven't you any pity, Kate?

Kate

Of course I have, as any wife would have for any husband. But pity's one thing, and moving out of your home is another.

Dickens

Well! We waste words—— Hark.

(*A maid streaks across to the door, tying on her apron, and bolting a piece of bread and butter. Mrs. Hogarth and Georgie come in by street-door hall. Mamie and Katy peer over the upstairs rail and come down. Kate discovered crying.*)

Mamie

Ma, what's the matter?

Katy

Why are you crying, Ma?

Georgie

Kate!

(*Kate droops against Georgie, as Georgie kneels beside her.*)

Kate

Oh, Ma! Oh, Georgie!

Mrs. Hogarth

What has Mr. Dickens taken it into his head to do now?

(*Dickens has flung himself into his chair, hands in pockets, and defiant eyes on the group.*)

Mamie

Pa's going away again!

He wants *me* to go away.

(*Faint*)
Oh no.

Me, to leave my home and children and live at Dover or Brighton!

(*General amazement. Dickens defiant, silent.*)

Why, love? Why should you?

All of us?

No, we're to be separated, forever!

Why, we simply won't!

I may be growing feeble in my intellect, I daresay there are those within a hundred miles of this room who would say I am. I have not done too badly in raising my family and making friends, and even in the darkest periods of my life when my own mother developed a habit of trying to abduct the family possessions from the various rooms and claim that all the maids robbed her——

Ma, in heaven's name, don't meander, but let's try to understand why Kate should go away.

You'll never understand, because there's no reason.

(*Loyal*)
There *can't* be any reason.

My love. (*Rests face wearily against Mamie*)

Katy

(*At sea*)
But you *did* like Brighton, Ma.

Mrs. Hogarth

Perhaps somebody will explain why Kate and the girls are in such a state? Genius is genius, as we all know, and if a great many critics do not consider such lugubrious works as *Nicholas Nickleby* and *Pickwick Papers* to be genius, why, as we are all aware, several others do. But that genius should be an excuse for any such high jinks as this, doesn't excuse making heroes of criminals like Fagin and delving into the very slums of London which we know are there, and it's a pity, but God's will is God's will and what good it does——

Katy

(*To Kate*)
Ma, for how long?

Mamie

But you don't have to go if you don't *want* to?

Georgie

Now let's talk reasonably. It'll all come out right. Charles wouldn't ask you to do anything that made you unhappy.

Kate

(*Lugubrious*)
I don't know what I have done to deserve this.

Mrs. Hogarth

You have done nothing, my child. True, many a man does not feel that seven sons and two daughters make for a completely restful home, but if you will excuse me, Kate, your husband was partially responsible for the situation——

Kate

(*Wearily*)
Ma. The girls.

Mrs. Hogarth

I presume the girls know that their brothers have a father.

Kate

There is a great deal into which it isn't necessary to go now.

Mrs. Hogarth

No, the mischief's done. But after all this, to calmly——

Georgie

(*Gently*)
I am sure Charles is anything but calm about such a tremendous change, Ma. I am sure he has everyone's good at heart.

Dickens

(*Bitterly*)
Thank you, Georgie.

Mamie

Did you think Ma was tired, Pa? Is that it?

Katy

But we still go to the rout at Lady Blessinglores, don't we?

Georgie

(*Hushing her*)
Yes, yes, yes. Of course you'll go.

Kate

I suppose it is all right to mention these matters now, Charles. If everyone is to know. If it's to be a seven-day scandal.

Mrs. Hogarth

A seven-*year* scandal! Consider your position. Consider Mr. Dickens' prominence!

Kate

Ask *him* to consider it.

Dickens

I didn't know he was to be consulted.

Georgie

But of course we want you to tell us what the idea is.

[539]

Dickens

The idea might conceivably have been a matter between my wife and me.

Mrs. Hogarth

A fine chance you'd have to keep it between you and Kate, Mr. Dickens, with every newspaper in London talking about it.

Dickens

It is none of the newspapers' business.

Georgie

(Still trying to keep it playful)
They might make it their business. But that isn't the important thing. The important thing is, what is the object of this plan?

Dickens

I have not the slightest objection to placing the matter before those nearest and dearest to me. You would have to know sooner or later. I have asked your sister—your mother—to move to comfortable and spacious lodgings, which will be provided for her in any place she selects——

Kate

Never to see her children.

Dickens

To see her children, of course. But the children would remain here with me—— Charley, come in.

(Charles comes in; looks bewilderedly from one to the other.)

Charley

What's up? Where lies the wind?

Kate

(Grasping him as he kneels)
Oh, Charley, don't you desert me, too!

Charley

Don't worry, Ma. What's the rumpus?

Dickens

(Walking up and down)
Sit down, Charley. We may as well have this out. I've asked your mother to leave us for a while, to establish herself comfortably wherever she

chooses, to accept a fine income, and leave this house and all the bills and leaks and accidents and children's shoes to me. I accept full responsibility. I free your mother from all the burdens she has been carrying for so many years. I've my own reasons for asking this. If she has failed me in small things—never intentionally, I know that, Kate!—why, I have failed her a hundred times more seriously in great things. This is our own affair. This is part of our own knowledge of our souls and hearts. There is no longer compatibility there. (*Perfect silence. They all look at him.*) Kate is unhappy; I am unhappy. Our effect on each other is to neutralize whatever is useful and satisfying.

Charley

(*After a silence*)
Ma doesn't want to go?

Kate

(*Feebly*)
I want to do what's right.

Charley

I go with you, Ma.

(*Kate embraces him*)

Dickens

Certainly you may go with your mother, if you like. It might be an excellent idea. (*Mamie and Katy scared, quietly crying.*) It seems to me we'd all show better sense if we didn't treat this as a calamity. It's a perfectly simple decision, made by a man and woman who are free to determine their own course. If you say that it's unusual, I can only say that it ought not be. Such adjustments—such rearrangements—ought to be everyday affairs.

Mrs. Hogarth

Well, may I be laid in my grave before——

Kate

Well, now you've all heard it, and you may as well hear my side of it. I do not intend to leave my home. I will appeal to every friend we have. I will speak to our clergyman who, whatever you may say, Charles, and we all know what you think of the clergy, is a fine, good, helpful man.

Mrs. Hogarth

Supports his blind mother and three aunts, and has been engaged to Rose Livingston for eleven years, if you call that good!

Kate

Saintly.

Dickens

By all means ask his advice. Ask him to step in here and carry the expenses of this family and a few other families——

Mrs. Hogarth

It isn't Kate's fault if your family is dependent, Mr. Dickens.

Georgie

Ma.

Mrs. Hogarth

Georgie, I will speak.

Dickens

Is it believable—is it believable that a man should be submitted to this sort of thing, merely because he chooses, in the privacy of his own home, to make this arrangement—or any arrangement—with his wife.

Mrs. Hogarth

Your circumstances make everything you do a public affair, Mr. Dickens. From the beginning, as everyone here present knows, I was against Kate's marrying a hack writer—everyone here, I mean of course except the children, who were not born yet, for there has never been the breath of suspicion of *that* kind against Kate, nor any of my daughters. Careful supervision, with a healthful amount of recreation interspersed with normal household duties, and association with the opposite sex only on general terms——

Dickens

Well, do we understand each other now?

Kate

Too well.

(*Maid crosses the room to answer door.*)

Mamie

(*Hysterical*)
Ma, we will always love you and Pa, too!

Katy

Because he doesn't *mean* to be nasty to you, Ma.

Georgie

Both of you—that's it, go along now, all this will be settled without your bothering your little heads.

Dickens

(*Aside*)
Thanks, Georgie—— Whew!

(*Exit girls.*)

Maid

Mr. Forster.

Forster

Hello, everyone. Mrs. Hogarth. Miss Georgie.

Dickens

Forster.

Forster

Had to tell you. The new story is going like wildfire.

Dickens

Good.

Forster

Something up? I say, I'll cut along—see you sometime later.

Dickens

Sit down. You know about this. I was talking things over with my wife and Georgie. It seems that there must be considerable conversation and some publicity to our private arrangements.

Forster

(*In troubled silence*)
I was afraid—— Yes, my dear old fellow, of course. You don't need me. I'll—terribly sorry——

Kate

(*Stony*)
Mr. Forster, you've known everything that concerns us for many years now. It's only right that you should know this. Charles proposes to send me away.

[543]

Georgie

Ah, Kate! (*Pitifully.*)

Forster

He—— Ah. Yes, he said something to me. A change, a rest, eh? Wonderful time of year to—take a little holiday. Nerves get jangled—same way in our house——

Kate

So a mother is supposed to leave her home and children——

Forster

Oh, I wouldn't look at it that way, Mrs. Dickens.

Kate

I don't know what other way there is. Charley says he is going with his mother. The others I am to see whenever they choose to come! You know, Mr. Forster, how often that would be! Little boys like that!

Georgie

(*Low voice*)
You know it wouldn't be that way, Kate.

Mrs. Hogarth

It seems to me positively indecent that this should be openly discussed, when we are all aware that this is just one more exhibition of Mr. Dickens' temper, and probably tomorrow he will be giving one of his wild parties to fifty or sixty of his bosom friends and entirely forget the whole thing. If my opinion is of any value, which of course I know and have always known, Kate and Georgie, that it is not, I would say that if Mr. Forster will excuse himself now and feel free at any time to pay us a visit at a more fortunate moment, we can go over this whole affair from the beginning——

Dickens

(*Low*)
Don't move, Forster. I need you.

Mrs. Hogarth

—hearing my daughter Kate's side of it as well as Mr. Dickens'——

(*Jumping up*)
Oh, good God, we've been over this fifty times!

Forster

This is distressing the ladies, Dickens. I propose——

Dickens

I propose no longer to listen to my wife's mother, who through the mere circumstance of having brought a few unhappy and ill-balanced females into the world——

Mrs. Hogarth

Kate, am I to endure this?

Kate

(*Weary*)
Ma, for heaven's sake——

Georgie

Please, Ma, we'll get nowhere this way.

Forster

Everyone, now. There's no sense in working up our feelings this way. Mrs. Hogarth——

Mrs. Hogarth

Oh no, I'm going. I bid you all a very good day. Georgie, perhaps you'll be so very kind as to see your mother to the door. Charley, will you run to the corner and get me a cab. Mr. Forster, good morning. (*To Dickens*) To you, sir, I have nothing to say. Kate, I pity you with all my heart. No man with feelings stronger than those of a brute would make such a proposition to a fine, pure woman who ten separate times has faced the primal curse and prolonged agony of childbirth—— Thank you, Georgie. My cab?

(*Exit, preceded by young Charley, accompanied by Georgie.*)

Forster

I can only say that I am heartily sorry about all this, Dickens—and Mrs. Dickens. Now, old chap, you've not been walking as you did, and I propose that you and I put ten good miles between now and dinner. Get your coat, and we'll brush off some of these cobwebs.

Dickens

Any objection, Kate?

Kate

(Roused from apathy)
No. None at all. Why should I object?

Dickens

And think it over. Think it over, Kate. You have it in your power to make me very grateful and very happy.

(Kate rises silently and goes out left. Forster watches her, troubled. Dickens has gotten his topcoat. Georgie comes in and nods significantly to Forster, meaning "Give me a moment with Dickens." Forster intercepts young Charles and takes him to the door.)

Forster

Just a moment, Charley. There was a question about that curtain call——

Charley

(Youthfully resentful)
I don't suppose we'll have the play now—— *(Exit.)*

Georgie

Charles, Charles, was this necessary?

Dickens

What do you think?

Georgie

I think no. No. You've hurt her.

Dickens

Georgie, I hurt her a thousand times a day, right here, in her own home. Isn't one clear cut of the surgeon's knife better in the end?

Georgie

She'll not consent, Charles.

Dickens

I think she will. You have an unlimited influence over Kate.

[546]

Georgie

But to use it that way——?

Dickens

(*Urgently, at her shoulder*)
This will change nothing, Georgie. Kate will still be Kate, and much freer than she is now. I will still have my little housekeeper, my daughters will have their loved companion, why should any of that be upset?

Georgie

But, Charles, it seems so sad.

Dickens

The sad thing is to endure conditions when they have become outworn and galling. You know, Georgie, that my heart long ago left Kate, and I think you suspect where it is.

Georgie

I don't want to.

Dickens

Let all this confusion die down, Georgie; keep the girls to their regular occupations and amusements. Give us a little time and you'll see how different the whole thing looks.

Georgie

In urging it, in agreeing to it, one can't help feeling so—so horribly guilty.

Dickens

Guilty? You! Why, my dear girl, if any one of us has clean hands, if any one of us has shown nothing but love and loyalty, you are that person. Only trust me. Georgie, you are not afraid of me?

Georgie

(*Agitated*)
I know I never need be. I believe that with all my heart.

Dickens

You may. In your position here as housekeeper and companion to my girls you will deserve—and you will have—the deepest gratitude and respect of my heart. There could be no such change without your help.

Georgie

That's what makes me feel that I don't know what to do. I don't know what's right.

[547]

Dickens

Talk with Kate, consider it from every angle, and I will not be afraid of the outcome.

Forster

(*At the door*)
Dickens! Come on, man. We'll just catch the storm.

Dickens

Is there a storm blowing up?

Forster

You should see the smoke from the chimney pots. Yes, we'll be drenched, and that's what this fellow likes.

Georgie

(*Significantly*)
Charles, you are heading straight into the storm.

Dickens

Heading straight into the storm!

(*Exit Forster and Dickens.*)

Charley

(*Coming in*)
What's all this mean, Aunt Georgie?

Georgie

Nothing. There'll be no change. You heard your mother.

Charley

I heard my father, too.

Georgie

(*Busily straightening music on the piano*)
You know, Charley, there must be much more of this sort of thing than we realize. We've always been particularly united, but other families go through regular scenes; I'm sure they do.

Charley

I know. But when the governor gets a maggot on the brain he goes crazy.

[548]

Georgie

You must remember, Charley, that when your father and mother married he had no such prospects as this. None of us dreamed of fame and wealth and success like this. Your mother couldn't have expected that he would leave them all behind. Why, you see how many of your father's friends are trying to write. How they rejoice over telling just one story, one poor play. While all he has to do is wave his wand, and the thousands fall down and adore him.

Charley

Oh, damn it all!

Georgie

Think of all your mother's had, Charley, while other women are scrimping along in poor rooms, never sure of the next shilling. You've traveled, you've had servants to care for you, horses to ride, dinners and theatricals right in this house. And your father loves you—loves every one of you. He doesn't want to part with one of you. Mustn't you expect a little eccentricity, a little oddness, to make up for that?

Charley

Why should I? Why can't he be like other people?

Georgie

I don't know. How should I, I'm only an ordinary woman. But doesn't it make you a little sorry for him, Charley, struggling somehow to get free of his own fretted spirit—reaching for one thing after another? Plays, managing the magazine, editing, trips abroad, readings—and frantic because something—something still escapes him?

Charley

(*Gruffly*)
Sure, I'm sorry for him if he feels that way.

(*He has been sitting in a chair almost square on to the audience, and Georgie has perched on one arm of it and laid her arm about his shoulder. Lights are fading outside the window, and Kate has come quietly down and taken a neighboring chair.*)

Kate

Oh, Georgie, you're so right. I don't see how you can be so patient with him, I can't. But it's all true.

Georgie

(*As she and Charley start in surprise*)

It's all wrong, Kate, all of it. But we have to see if we can work right out of it somehow.

Kate

A talk like that leaves me so tired that I don't feel equal to fighting.

Charley

What do you think Ma ought to do, Aunt Georgie?

Georgie

(*Bravely. Making herself say it*)
Face him down, and wait.

Kate

That's so easy to say, Georgie. But when you're married to a man it's different.

Georgie

Don't you give in.

Charley

Yep. You're in the right, Ma, and you stick it out.

Kate

I'd rather go to Brighton—I'd rather go to China, than be unwelcome in my own house.

Georgie

Kate, don't talk that way, don't feel that way. Give it time.

Kate

You love me more than anyone else in the world. You tell me what to do.

Georgie

Oh, Kate, you make me cry.

Kate

I'd never see you, Georgie.

Georgie

Kate! I'd go down there, and you'd come here. Oh, I'm not saying it's the thing to do, but only that I'd always see you.

Kate

Georgie, you'd stay here? If I knew you were here——

[550]

Georgie

Why, I suppose— I don't know, I've never thought. If you and Charles wanted me to.

Kate

This doesn't make you angry at him, you don't despise him? Georgie, if you resented this, and he knew it, the whole family would be miserable.

Georgie

No. I wouldn't. No. Not despise him.

Charley

I'd not stay here. I'd go with Ma.

Kate

You like Brighton, dear. When summer comes there's the boating and swimming. We could walk, evenings, on the pier.

Charley

How about old Larky selling winkles?

Kate

(*Feebly brightening*)
And the man with the monkey.

Charley

Aunt Georgie, Ma could come up here whenever she wanted, couldn't she?

Georgie

Oh, good heavens, Charley, don't talk as if it was all settled, or my head will split. I don't know what to say!

Kate

My head, too. Charley, will you go and see if Mollie has given the boys their dinner.

Georgie

I'm sure she did. It was all arranged.

Charley

You and me, hey, Ma? Swelling it along the pier.

[551]

Kate

(*Forlorn laugh*)
Maybe, Charley.

Charley

(*From door, left*)
Music and lanterns. We'll invite you down there some Saturday night,
Aunt Georgie. Moonlight, hey? (*Exit.*)

Kate

(*Half rueful, half amused*)
Oh, you go on!

Georgie

Your champion, Kate. Did you see the way he ruffled up the moment he
understood what was going on.

Kate

The girls didn't.

Georgie

They were taken too completely by surprise, Kate.

Kate

You can't blame them.

Georgie

Hadn't you any hint of it?

Kate

None. Had you?

Georgie

Not the least.

Kate

Well, now, Georgie, we're alone together. We've settled things ever
since we were little girls. What do you make of it? Has Charles lost his
mind?

Georgie

(*Slowly*)
No-o. But it would be a terrible thing for us all if he did, of course—if he
was so crossed and angered——

Kate

You don't mean you think there's any danger?

Georgie

No. No, I don't. But he's so tense—he's so desperately in earnest.

Kate

What do you suppose put this into his head?

Georgie

Nobody. You could see how Forster felt.

Kate

Everyone will hate him for this.

Georgie

He evidently doesn't think so.

Kate

He feels sure that everyone is going right on thinking he is perfect!

Georgie

I don't know. I think if anything could stop him it would be that he might be criticized. You saw that he gave Charley a pretty sharp look, when Charley said he was going with you.

Kate

The girls didn't say anything.

Georgie

They're probably crying their eyes out.

Kate

What's the sense—what's the purpose of making everyone so unhappy! We were going on so nicely. Why can't he act like other people!

(*Short silence.*)

Georgie

Come on down, girls.

(*Mamie and Katy come down and cross to their mother's chair, looking at her anxiously. Go on their knees beside her chair.*)

Mamie

You all right, Ma?

Katy

We got to crying, and Aunt Georgie sent us upstairs.

Mamie

Are you and Charley really going to Brighton, Ma?

Katy

Lucky Charley!

Mamie

And you'll walk on the boardwalk and have rooms at Mrs. Stodgers'. Oo-oo, I wish I could go!

Kate

You'll come down and see Mama.

Mamie

And swim, and take walks.

Georgie

Kate, with six hundred a year you won't have to stay at Mrs. Stodgers'. You could have your own place and find a couple of good little maids.

Kate

(*Awakening*)
One of those little white places, on the cliff?

Georgie

Well, why not? Remember he said twelve pounds a year, all furnished and everything.

Kate

Then if I didn't want dinner at home, or the maids were out, we could walk down to the inn.

Georgie

It mightn't be so bad, Kate. But no—you're not to go!

[554]

Kate

Well, I may not. I'm certainly going to talk to Charles again.

Georgie

(*Laughs nervously*)
It would serve him right to have you go and enjoy it.

Kate

Ah, I don't see myself *enjoying* it.

Georgie

Of course not, you poor love.

Kate

And at the same time, I have been suffering a lot with Ma's headaches, you know.

Georgie

And you always feel well at the shore.

Kate

That's what I was thinking, Georgie.

Georgie

It'd be a wonderful rest, Kate.

Kate

But when he wants me back he needn't think he can whistle me back.

Georgie

(*Noncommittal*)
No.

Kate

I wouldn't be surprised when it comes right down to it if he didn't want me to go.

Georgie

Hm. You never can tell.

Kate

So that it would be just paying him out right to pack up and walk off.

Georgie

To take him at his word.

Kate

Exactly.

Mamie

(*Who with Katy has been listening intently*)
Oh, Ma, one of those little white houses on the cliff!

Kate

(*Virtuous*)
Well, it would never have entered my head to leave your father, but it is he himself suggests it.

Katy

Aunt Georgie'll take care of us here, won't you, Aunt Georgie?

Georgie

If your Ma asks me to.

Kate

Oh, Georgie, you said you would!

Georgie

But I'm still so turned around by the whole thing!

Mamie

Maybe the next time Pa comes in he'll have forgotten all about it. You know how he is.

Kate

I'll remind him! He can't blow hot and blow cold that way.

Mamie

But if he said he didn't mean it and takes it all back, like he always does——?

Kate

No, this time I think I'll give him a lesson. Even if I don't stay long I believe I'll go.

Katy

You never stay mad at Pa.

Kate

I'm not mad. He's asked me to do something and I'm going to do it. Georgie, if any of the boys ever was sick, you'd let me know.

Georgie

Oh, Kate, of course. I'd write—every week—but I'm still so confused by the whole idea——

Kate

If Charles is so anxious to take over the entire expense of the children—why, for heaven's sake, let him have it!

Georgie

But don't go in that spirit, Kate. Wait, and consider.

Kate

Oh, he's done the considering.

Mamie

We'll always stand by you, Ma!

Kate

As if I didn't know that, my loves. But now you must help me do this my way, and show Pa exactly how much trouble this silly notion of his is going to make for all of us.

Mamie

You can't call Brighton trouble, and one of those darling houses up on the cliff!

Kate

No, but he's not to think I like going. I'm never going to admit to him that it's anything but a sacrifice.

Georgie

(*Halfheartedly*)
If you take it this way he may give up the whole idea.

Kate

(*Grimly*)
It takes two to give up a plan.

Georgie

I declare it has come up so suddenly that it makes me quite lightheaded.

[557]

Kate

Evidently Forster knew of it.

Mamie

And what does Mr. Forster think, Ma?

Kate

Of course he thinks it's preposterous.

Mamie

He's probably talking Pa out of it.

Kate

No, nobody can do that. Here's your father now.

(*Dickens comes in, drags off topcoat, goes to hang it under stairs.*)

Dickens

(*Feeling for their mood*)
Well, hello, everybody. Forster's no walker. Turns his ankle before we're a dozen squares away. (*Flings himself into chair.*) What about dinner, Georgie?

Georgie

Soon now.

Kate

I've been telling the girls about my going away, Charles.

Dickens

(*His eyes move instantly about the circle*)
Ha.

Mamie

(*Defiant*)
We think she'll love it, Pa.

Katy

And Charley will too. I wish it was us!

Dickens

(*Mildly*)
I wouldn't ask it if I didn't believe she would like it.

Kate

I'm not at all sure of that. I may as well say at once that I am doing this because on consideration it seems to me a wise thing to do.

Dickens

(*Glance at Georgie*)
I am glad to hear you say so.

Kate

Georgie, I wish you would inform Charles that I am not saying this for his benefit.

Mamie

Ma, Pa doesn't mean to make you mad.

Dickens

I stay here. I carry the load. I work—God knows, and you know, how steadily I work. I ask you to do something perfectly simple that puts no burden on you. But, by God, if you feel that you are being martyred —and it's a position for which your mother's daughters have had a good example—why, for God's sake——

Georgie

(*Low*)
Charles, don't be violent. Please.

Dickens

(*Blandly*)
I say then that by all means please yourself. I have used up all my ammunition, and I'm tired. By all means stay right where you are, and when I break down and can't write another line—and am shut up in Bedlam— and I've felt myself close to it for more than a few years now—then perhaps you and your mother can work out something else.

Kate

Please leave Ma out of this. And I did not say that I was not going. I merely said that I am not doing it to please you.

Mamie

Ma's going to take one of those cliff cottages at Brighton, Pa. 'Member? That you come down the long stairs to get to the pier from?

(*Dickens looks from one face to another, alert and freshly hopeful*)

Georgie

We've just been talking of some of the details, Charles. With six hundred pounds, Kate wouldn't have to live at Mrs. Stodgers'.

Kate

(*To Georgie and girls, hurt and proud*)
I would want my own parlor, and my own maid. After all—one has one's friends——

Dickens

(*Mollified and trying to mollify them*)
I suppose you could manage on six hundred? But, good God, if you want more——

Kate

(*To Georgie*)
Clara Smoker keeps a lovely place down there, and she doesn't have a cent over three.

Dickens

(*To Georgie*)
Kate knows that if ever she needed more she need only ask for it.

Kate

(*Stiffly, not to him*)
If that time comes it will be plenty of time to arrange it.

Dickens

Exactly, if that times comes.

Mamie

And we may go see Ma?

Katy

In the holidays, Pa.

Dickens

I'm to be the villain of the piece, I suppose, and tell you that you are not to see your mother. Bah! How women love to dramatize things.

Georgie

Come now, Charles, don't you think Kate is being very generous about this? I'm sure you do.

Kate

It's of no consequence, Georgie, I'm sure.

Dickens

(*Looking significantly at Georgie*)
I do appreciate that. So, girls, you think I'm ill-treating your mother?

Katy

Oh no, Papa. It'll be lovely down by the sea this time of year.

Mamie

We're wishing we could go!

Dickens

Well, that's more like it. Come, let's all be cheerful. I came in a few minutes ago tired and discouraged, and to find you all talking this over so reasonably cheers me up mightily.

Kate

I am going upstairs. Come, girls.

(*Kate and girls go upstairs.*)

Dickens

Georgie.

Georgie

Yes, Charles?

Dickens

How did you do that?

Georgie

(*At mantel, looking uncomfortably down at him*)
What?

Dickens

How did you ever persuade her?

Georgie

But I didn't. She did it all herself.

[561]

Dickens

No. Kate wouldn't. She was hurt and furious and determined. Now I find her quiet and manageable. You did it.

Georgie

Not consciously, not on purpose. I feel too badly, I feel too guilty, for that.

Dickens

Guilty?

Georgie

Oh yes, horribly guilty. There's no use fooling myself. Her being gone—clears the air. She no longer knows exactly what goes on.

Dickens

(*Attentive*)
Clears the air.

Georgie

I don't think I mean that, either. But I've thought, of late—I've wondered if Kate noticed anything—suspected anything.

Dickens

And you don't think she did?

Georgie

I know she didn't. But that doesn't make me feel any better. I feel—horrible.

Dickens

Oh, good God, so do I.

Georgie

And when the girls and Charley were talking Brighton, and her having a nice little place there, I didn't—truly, I didn't—say one word to influence her.

Dickens

Of course you didn't. I know Kate. You had only to dissuade her.

Georgie

It was Charley and then the girls who got talking, and she began to brighten up.

[562]

They may have. But of course you took the dubious side. It was your good quiet matter-of-fact way of refusing to consider it, Georgie, that brought it all down into focus.

Georgie

I don't think she'll change now. I think she'll go.

Dickens

(*Upward glance*)
You do think so.

Georgie

Now I think she will. I wouldn't have thought so an hour or two ago.

Dickens

My dear girl, I won't try to express what I feel in gratitude to you for this.

Georgie

Ah, I wish you wouldn't. I didn't do anything. It just—came about that way.

Dickens

Come. You don't mean Kate came to this conclusion herself?

Georgie

No-o. Not exactly. We were talking, and the girls came in.

Dickens

Exactly. And you steered them all your way.

Georgie

(*Slowly, thinking it out*)
Charles, this isn't my way. The way things have been, the way we've all been living—that's my way.

Dickens

That's my way. That's the way that means peace, for me, and for you, and freedom for my own thoughts. My dear girl, this half hour has shown me a door opening—a garden beyond—a brightness beyond—that my heart hasn't known these many years.

Georgie

Kate would be the first to want that for you.

Dickens

And now she makes it possible.

Georgie

You don't think she'll regret it someday, she'll be lonely? She and I have always been so happy——

Dickens

You'll not lose Kate. And can't you imagine yourself as even happier than ever, managing this household of boys, being a mother to my girls.

Georgie

(*Humbly*)

I'll try to keep everyone happy.

Dickens

You will, my dear.

Georgie

And the children will see no difference.

Dickens

No. We must let them see no difference.

Georgie

If this is wrong, how can Kate ever forgive me?

Dickens

If this is wrong, how will you ever forgive me, Georgie?

Georgie

It will not be wrong. Not between you and me. We'll—we'll keep it right.

Dickens

I think you are not afraid of that. You are not afraid of me. Not after all these years when you have known what you meant to me and mine and my house?

Georgie

I might be afraid of myself, Charles.

Dickens

(*Who has left his chair and come to put one arm about her*)

[564]

You will have a protector in me, an ally, someone always ready to help you handle this difficult situation.

Georgie

I know that.

Dickens

And the miracle is that you understand, Georgie, understand what has been disturbing—distracting—maddening me during these last months. It's a feeling that is stronger than I—oh, a thousand times stronger than I, as strong as love—tearing me in two opposite directions, making everything unreal here, and doubly unreal before the eyes of the world—

Georgie

But taking from Kate something that was hers.

Dickens

Something that for a long time has not been hers! No, I abandon hypocrisy now, I can breathe freely now. You and I can't look ahead, dear girl, but we can work our problems out as they arise.

Georgie

Never to do anything that will make Kate feel that we love her less?

Dickens

It will be no harder now than it has been, it will be easier.

Georgie

Oh, I do believe that!

Dickens

Trust me, Georgie.

Georgie

(*Rueful*)
Now I must. There will be no one else—— Someone coming——

Dickens

It's Forster, back for dinner. I'll let him in. Tell Mollie.

(*Georgie goes out; Dickens opens door, left. Forster comes in.*)

Forster

(*Glancing about*)

Settle it with the women?

                              Dickens

She is going to give me my way, old fellow.

                              Forster

     (Shocked)
No!

                              Dickens

Georgie worked it by some hocus-pocus. God knows how they influence
each other, sisters were never nearer together. She has Kate now thinking
of a little place in Brighton, with a garden—and the big feller, Charley,
with her most of the time.

                              Forster

     (Musing)
I should have thought Georgie to be hardest against it.

                              Dickens

Not when I ask it. The Inimitable, my dear fellow. The Inimitable can
do no wrong. Ask anyone in this great city of London. Come, let's have
dinner.

                              Forster

There's just one person I wish could think he might.

                              Dickens

Might what?

                              Forster

Believe he might do wrong.

                              Dickens

Who's that?

                              Forster

The Inimitable himself.

     (Dickens laughs in a rather hushed shocked way as they go off, right.
     Kate comes slowly downstairs, looks wearily about the sitting room,
     lays her hand on the piano, moves slowly to the window and stands
     looking out, a figure of desolation, as the curtain falls.)

                    CURTAIN

                     [566]

THE INIMITABLE

ACT THREE

ACT THREE

SCENE: Same. Dickens' sitting room.
TIME: Summer.

(*Windows open, pampas plumes in the fireplace. Georgie, Mamie, Katy, Forster, one or two boys, others, grouped left, listening to Dickens who is seated at a little table, right.*)

Dickens

(*Manuscript in hand*)
This is the new revision for my next reading. Anyone can make suggestions. This is just a rehearsal, to see how you think it'll go. Interruptions in order, eh? Georgie, worried about something?

Georgie

No. Nothing.

Dickens

I'm starting, this time, with Paul at school, hem! A homesick, tired little boy, whom they all know now is dying. And especially does his proud heartbroken father know it. (*Reads*)
" 'You'll soon be grown up now,' said Mr. Dombey.
" 'Oh, very soon,' Paul replied, and once more the old, old look passed over his features like a strange light. Florence ran back to throw her arms about his neck; hers was the last face in the doorway; turned toward him with a smile of encouragement, the brighter for the smile through which it beamed.
"It made his childish bosom heave and swell when it was gone, and sent the globes and books, blind Homer and Minerva, swimming round the room. But they stopped, all of a sudden, and he heard the loud clock in the hall still inquiring gravely; how-is-my-little-friend?
"He might have answered 'weary, weary, very sad!' as with an aching

[569]

void in his heart he sat alone, with all outside so cold and bare and strange, as if he had taken life unfurnished, and the upholsterer were never coming.

"But Florence was coming to the school party; this was his great hope. Florence would see that the boys had grown fond of him; that he had become a little favorite among them, and that would make her happy.

"And as the end of school drew near, fifty times a day his noiseless little feet went up the stairs to his own room, as he gathered every book and scrap and trifle that belonged to him, and put them all together for taking home!

"At his bedroom window he would stand lost in crowds of thoughts that came on, one upon another, one upon another, like rolling waves. Where those wild birds lived that were always hovering out at sea in troubled weather, where the clouds rose and first began, whence the wind issued in its rushing flight, and where it stopped.

"In these days before the holidays, Paul was a privileged pupil such as had never been seen in that house before. His liberty lasted from hour to hour and day to day, and little Dombey was caressed by everyone. When the great day of the party came and Paul was dressed—which was very soon done, for he felt unwell and drowsy, and was not able to stand about it long—he was tenderly taken down to the drawing room. And presently when Florence came in, looking so beautiful in her simple ball gown, with her fresh flowers in her hand, and knelt down on the rug to kiss him, he could hardly make up his mind to let her go again, or take away her bright and loving eyes from his face.

" 'But what is the matter, Floy?' Paul asked, almost sure he saw a tear there.

" 'Nothing, darling, nothing,' Florence returned. And the dancing and the lights and flowers went on.

"There was much soon afterwards, next day, and after that, which Paul could only recollect confusedly. But he could remember when they took him home, and he was carried up the well-remembered stairs, and laid him down in his own old bed. But there was something else, and recent, too, that perplexed him.

" 'Floy, was that Papa in the hall, when they brought me from the coach?'

" 'Yes, dear.'

" 'He didn't cry, and go into his room, Floy, when he saw me coming in?'

"Florence shook her head, and pressed her lips against his cheek.

" 'I'm very glad he didn't cry,' said little Paul. 'I thought he did. Don't tell him that I asked.'

"He did not rise again from his bed. He lay there listening to the noises of the street, and watching the sunbeams that struck into his room through the rustling blinds, and quivered on the opposite wall like golden water. And at night he thought of the long streets dotted with lamps, and how the peaceful stars were shining overhead, and he would lie and watch the many-colored ring about the candle, and wait patiently for day.

"The people around him changed unaccountably, except Florence. Florence never changed. Old Mrs. Pipkin dozing in an easy chair often changed to Miss Tox. Paul was quite content to shut his eyes again and see what change came next. But one figure, with its head upon its hand, returned so often, and remained so long, and sat so still, never speaking, that Paul began to wonder languidly if it were real. Only once it lifted up its head, and rose, and coming to the bedside said, 'My own boy. Don't you know me?' But before he could reach out with both his hands to take this face between them and draw it to him, it was gone. The figure turned quickly from the little bed and went out at the door.

" 'Floy,' he asked in one of the long quiet days, 'did I ever see Mamma?'

" 'No, darling. Why?'

" 'But I did see a kind face, looking at me when I was a baby, Floy?'

" 'Your old nurse's, Paul. And she is here.'

" 'Then will she lay me down, Floy. And will you come close to me and let me see you.'

"Sister and brother wound their arms about each other, and the golden light came streaming in, and fell upon them, locked together.

" 'How fast the river runs, between the green banks and the rushes, Floy. But it's very near the sea. I hear the waves! They always said something to me—something. The motion of the boat upon the waves is lulling me to rest, Floy. It is out at sea, and gliding on—and there's a shore before me. But who is standing on the bank, Floy?

" 'Ah, Floy, Mamma is like you. I know her by the face. But tell them that the picture on the stairs is not divine enough. The light upon, about her head is shining on me as I go!' "

(Silence. Then, sniffs, throat clearing, broken laughter. Confusion. Pa, it's wonderful— Oh, Charles, how you read that. Bravo, Pa, you've got it now—Dickens, etc., etc.)

That ought to go. *(Shaken, wipes face.)*

Katy

Go! You'll have the ladies swooning again, Pa.

Dickens

Oh, the reading's a failure if a dozen of the dear creatures aren't carried out to have their staylaces cut.

Forster

Gad, I feel that every time, as if a child of mine had died!

[571]

Georgie

Oh, so do I.

Mamie

(*Weepily*)
It reminds me of darling little Dora that died.

Katy

Pa, is that the one that makes them cry most?

Dickens

Well—and Little Nell.

Forster

Whew! That's terrific. Well, come on, old fellow, we were going to walk a couple of miles before tea.

Dickens

I'm with you. I was working all morning and I'm seedy.

Georgie

Pretty hot to walk.

Dickens

Oh, there's something about this dry, gusty, summer London that has its fascination, too. But we'll soon be out of it at Gad's Hill.

Mamie

And won't we love it.

(*They scatter, girls going off right, Dickens and Forster by street hallway, left. Georgie, left alone, goes to stairway, runs up a few steps and is met by Kate coming down.*)

Kate

(*Coldly*)
Thank you very much for letting me know that Edward was ill.

Georgie

Kate, I said I always would. But he's all right now.

Kate

Yes, he seems quite well.

[572]

That was a close shave. I didn't know Charles was coming back; you might have run into him.

I heard him reading. Those readings are going well?

Oh, tremendously. They tire him terribly. He puts himself into them so. Kate, you're not angry at me?

Angry? No. Why should I be?

(*Stir, left, at the doorway*)

It's Ma.

Ma's coming for me, by the way.

Oh, Kate, that's dangerous. Charles would be very angry.

It's too bad to make the infallible Charles angry.

(*Coaxing*)
No, it isn't that. But Charles said the arrangement was that you were not to come here.

I made no such arrangement, I made no promises at all. I was put out of my own house and I went.

And you have a perfect right here. But—just to save trouble, Ma oughtn't to come here. Charles knows perfectly well that Ma is furious at him.

Kate

Ma has good reason.

Georgie

You didn't think so when you went away, Kate. You know you didn't. It's Ma and Pa and the family talking it all over, and telling you that you ought to resent it, that makes you mad.

Kate

Mad? What an idea! I'm not mad.

Georgie

(Sadly)
You're changed.

Kate

(Airily)
Oh, why should just being separated from my seven sons and two daughters and sent away from home as if one was an idiot or a murderess make one change?

Georgie

You didn't feel that way at first. You make me feel that you hate me, Kate.

Kate

Not at all. I don't hate you, and I don't like you. I just don't think about you at all.

Georgie

You must. You know you do.

Kate

I don't see any sense in discussing it. If you don't mind, I'll sit here until Ma arrives.

Georgie

Kate, don't be hard.

Kate

Not be hard on the person who has taken my place with my husband and with my children. Really, Georgie, you make one laugh!

Georgie

(*Warming*)
Then I wonder that you would deign to come here and see the children
when they're sick.

Kate

I refuse to answer that.

Georgie

Kate, please try to understand my side of it.

Kate

Yours and Charles's side of it. I don't know how I could have been so
blind!

Georgie

Kate! You know—you know that's not fair!

Kate

(*Calm, quiet*)
I don't know a woman—and there are many of our old friends down at
Brighton—who doesn't regard me as an absolute fool not to have seen it all
along. But I've always thought that the devotion between us too—
(*Breaks.*)

Georgie

Oh, Kate, it shouldn't come out this way! Not after all we've been to
each other. We're sisters!

Kate

(*Head haughtily turned away*)
Not any more.

Georgie

Kate, think of the fun we've had together, the mornings we've walked
and sketched and played duets together. Think of the days the boys were
born, when I've been in your room when even Charles couldn't stand it,
holding your hand, and so glad when the baby was safely there!

Kate

There's no use talking like that. Do you suppose I don't think of all that?

Georgie

(*Stormily*)
You act as if it meant nothing to you!

Kate

Tell me something. Tell me the truth. I always was a good sister to you,
I may not see you again for a long time. Do you love Charles?

Georgie

(*Evasively*)
Well, haven't I always?

Kate

You know what I mean.

Georgie

Not—not any different from always. *Please*, Kate—

Kate

(*Pauses, watching her*)
That means you love him; *my* husband?

Georgie

But not the way you think. Not the way that changes anything, or ever
will.

Kate

Ha.

Georgie

No, Kate, you're wrong.

Kate

All right, I'm wrong.

Georgie

Charles has never said one word to me—ask anyone, ask anyone in this
house, ask the girls.

Kate

Ask my daughters!

[576]

I couldn't help feeling–I know how hard he is sometimes–I know how silly it sounds to you–but it's not a new thing, Kate. I've always–and Mary, too, poor little Mary, she was in love with him, and you know it, and you said so.

Kate

Mary was seventeen. But I don't care to talk about it, Georgie. It's too–utterly–disgusting.

Georgie

But that's just it! Things are just as they were, Kate. If you hadn't been talking to Ma, and listening to other people talk–– Oh, Kate, we used to love each other so! We used to be so happy!

Kate

(To Mollie, who comes in left)
Was that the bell, Mollie?

Mollie

Yes, Mrs. Dickens.

(Awkward silence, Kate and Georgie look away, look toward each other, look away again–as Mrs. Hogarth comes in.)

Kate

Hello, Ma.

Mrs. Hogarth

(Majestically, to Kate)
Are you ready, love?

Kate

All ready, Ma.

Mrs. Hogarth

How is the child?

Kate

Quite all right again. Delighted with the red fish you sent.

Mrs. Hogarth

I'm holding the cab. Good-by, Georgina.

Georgie

Ma, how is Pa?

Mrs. Hogarth

Very well. You have your reticule, Kate? Your pelisse?

Georgie

Ma, please sit down, please talk to me a little, you don't know how quiet it is here now, how few people I have to talk to.
(*Almost crying.*)

Mrs. Hogarth

Georgina, I have nothing to say to you. Nothing whatsoever. You have chosen your path and while a Lady Hamilton may associate with kings and queens in Italy—not at all the home life of our beloved Queen and the dear Prince—but still I have no doubt with crowns and carpets rolled out for them, to say nothing of being painted by Sir Joshua who was, I daresay, and a good many other people might think pretty free in his manner with her himself, at least all that lying down on couches and striking attitudes but nevertheless a national hero and a man whose courage never has been in question. So let us not be absurd enough to argue about *that*.

Georgie

(*Turning a good-humored, indulgent smile toward Kate, as being used to Mrs. Hogarth's vagaries, meets a stony evasion of glance. Sobers.*)
I wish you'd stay awhile.

Mrs. Hogarth

Good-by, my dear. (*Aloof.*) We'll not trouble you again.

Georgie

The boys all understand—they'll not say anything, if you want to wait and see them.

(*Kate troubled, but does not speak.*)

Mrs. Hogarth

No, thank you. We're holding a cab. Come, Kate.

(*Georgie stands stunned as they go off left, slam of street door is heard. Mamie comes in, right.*)

[578]

Mamie

Did Pa see her?

Georgie

No. He's never suspected.

Mamie

Well, they don't come very often.

Georgie

No. (*Pause.*) Where are you going, Mamie?

Mamie

Mrs. Stanfield is picking me up for tonight, and tomorrow I'm driving down with them to be with Ma again.

Georgie

What's Katy doing?

Mamie

Oh, she's always at the Collinses now.

Georgie

I suppose so.

Mamie

This is when you and Ma used to be mending, and laughing, and talking about everybody, isn't it?

Georgie

Yes. Or we might walk with you children about the square, if Nurse was busy. I remember four or five of you, in little new red coats—

Mamie

(*Not listening*)
There's the carriage. Good-by! I wish you were down at Brighton with us, it's lovely now. Boating, and bath machines and lovely moonlight. Good-by!

Georgie

Good-by.

(Mamie runs off, laughing excitedly. Four young boys race across stage, paying no attention to Georgie, one shouts "Pa's here! He's in the dining room." Mollie comes in, her approach and voice startling Georgie from painful musing.)

Mollie

Excuse me, Miss Georgie, but Cook says she don't like the smell of the joint.

Georgie

I'll be out directly.

Mollie

You feel real lonely, don't you, Miss Georgie, now that Mrs. Dickens and Miss Mamie are away. They don't stay very long, do they? I guess that's because they don't want to run into the Master.

Georgie

Yes. Yes. It is quiet—terribly quiet. I ought to have plenty to keep me busy—mending and working as my sister and I used to do. *(Half to herself. Then rousing.)* All right, Mollie. If he's sent us high meat again this is the end. Tell Cook I'm coming and I'll attend to it.

(As Mollie goes out, and she moves a chair or two into position, Dickens comes in with a glass in his hand.)

Dickens

Ah, Georgie. I stopped in the dining room. Been here alone all afternoon?

Georgie

All alone.

Dickens

Little Edward better? *(Takes chair.)*

Georgie

Oh yes, it was just too much candy at the party.

Dickens

It'll be good to get out of the city, eh? You seem a little droopy. Sticky summer weather.

[580]

Perhaps I'm tired, a little.

Dickens

I can't have little Dame Durden laid up. (*Quotes.*) "They said there could be no east wind where Somebody was; they said that wherever Dame Durden went there was sunshine and summer air."

Georgie

(*Moved, turning away her head*)
Charles, somehow, in these days I seem to be neither one thing nor another.

Dickens

You mean as regards you, and me, and Kate? But how could it be different, Georgie?

Georgie

Oh, it couldn't. I know that.

Dickens

Georgie, the love that came into your heart you didn't invite there. And the love that came into mine, God knows, was like the bursting of a river dam.

Georgie

You, too?

Dickens

Ah, you know it. You've seen it. You've seen me holding myself in check until I feared that all the world would see in me a sort of madness. For of course it is madness——

Georgie

Charles, it must be only happiness. Without robbing Kate, without hurting her, it must be only happiness.

Dickens

Ah, Georgie, that's so like you! To think of sparing her. Yes, and the girls—the children—they must be spared, too.

Georgie

It must make no difference here.

Dickens

It shall make no difference here. You and I will see to that. Georgie, do you know what I did a few days ago?

Georgie

(*Trembling, averted eyes*)
What did you do?

Dickens

I walked past a row of little houses in Ampthill Square. Unpretentious, simple houses, with picket fences, and casement windows opening into gardens. And I thought (*thinking aloud, not looking at her*) that if ever a man were to find the true, simple woman he loved, and might dare hope that he would win her in honor to his arms, how his very soul must burst with ecstasy when he took her to that little house, and closed the door upon the world outside, and caught her to his heart. To be free, Georgie! And the miracle of love, and of that moment when a man and woman know they love!

Georgie

Love—love has to have its way, Charles. (*Hesitating.*) It must be free.

Dickens

You feel it, too! And to know that you understand! Now, whatever comes, we can go on steadily, knowing that we see by the same light.

Georgie

The children—the girls—mustn't know anything.

Dickens

Not until I can go to them, free, with the woman I love on my arm.

Georgie

You can trust me never to betray, by the slightest word, that this—thing has come to us.

Dickens

I trust you with every fiber of my being. Your influence with the children, your understanding of my problem—which is yours too, of course—will keep all serene here.

Georgie

(*At window, speaking over her shoulder*)
And I am so glad—I am so grateful to you that you have told me. Of

[582]

course I knew—I hoped that you would not always be alone. But it lifts my heart to have you say it, and I can wait now for time to make all the rest clear.

Dickens

(*Favorite attitude, stretched in chair, hands in pockets*)
Good God, Georgie, if Kate had something of your understanding, your generosity——

Georgie

(*Ruefully*)
Kate is in every way finer than I am.

Dickens

But not as loving. Kate never, even if your positions had been reversed, could have spoken as you have today.

Georgie

It is all like a dream. (*Coming back.*)

Dickens

(*On his feet, both her hands taken and held against his breast*)
You don't despise me for loving where I have no right? For wanting my children, and the world, someday to recognize that love?

Georgie

(*Whispers*)
How could I, of all women, blame you?

Dickens

My little Dame Durden! And for the present we go on here as if nothing had occurred?

Georgie

Everything here will be as it always has been. And you don't despise me for seeing our side of it as well as Kate's?

Dickens

Respect you the less! Georgie, under everything else I feel for you, there has always been the deepest admiration and respect. Only now it is deepened, a thousand times deepened, and in this new happiness of mine I almost feel that I could be content with nothing more!

[583]

Georgie

(Whimsical)
Without even a little cottage in Ampthill Square, with the windows opened on the garden!

Dickens

And the river path right there, where a man and woman might walk, on a late summer afternoon, after tea.

Georgie

How do people stand so much bliss!

Dickens

I ask myself that, seriously.

(Interruption; the maid Phoebe comes in. They spring apart.)

Phoebe

Miss Georgie, the barrel of oysters has come, but Sim isn't here, and Cook can't open it, and the men are here for the leak and Master Henry has been real sick in the kitchen buttery, and he wants to see his mother too, and Mollie thinks he's got what Master Edward did and he wants you to put a cold rag on his head.

Georgie

(Fondly)
My dear little boys!

Dickens

How they victimize you!

Phoebe

(Accompanying Georgie off right)
What he threw up was winkles, and them winkles lay on their stomachs like they was cast-iron bolts——

Dickens

(Left alone, paces the floor smiling, lost in thought, hands in trouser pockets. Stands at window, starts suddenly, and disappears to street entry. Comes back with Ellen. All rapture and excitement)

My dear, dear reckless girl, what brings you here!

[584]

Ellen

(Saucy and breathless)
Oh, isn't this fun!

Dickens

(Overcome)
Ellen, Ellen, Ellen! You wonder——

Ellen

I'm being terrible. M'ma left me to wait in the carriage while she went to pay a call, and I had him drive me here!

Dickens

My dear—I'm knocked silly—I can't believe that you're here—actually here—in my house. Oh, this is—this is too wonderful——

Ellen

(Coquettish)
Is this the room where you write the big books!

(She walks about, inspecting, Dickens watches her incredulously.)

Dickens

(Awakening)
Is—is what?

Ellen

Is this where you write?

Dickens

(Laughing joyously and nervously)
No, this isn't where I write.

Ellen

Oh, you couldn't. *(Coquettish.)* Everything would have to be still—still—still!

Dickens

(Competely besotted)
I'm so completely the slave of the speaker that I can't hear what she says!

Ellen

I don't believe it!

[585]

Dickens

(Seriously)
You must believe it, dear girl.

Ellen

If I were here I could help keep people out of your room, couldn't I?

Dickens

Would you do that for me?

Ellen

I'd be wonderful. You—keep—out—of—his—room!

Dickens

Ah, you're delicious. So you'd protect me?

Ellen

Fe-ro-cious-ly. I'd do more than that—for my friend.

Dickens

How much would you do for him?

Ellen

(Pettish, retreating)
Everyone does things for friends.

Dickens

But I'm not content to be just a friend, Ellen. I've told you that!

Ellen

No, you mustn't touch me. Remember what M'ma said. Can't you like me without always wanting me to say how much I like you?

Dickens

(Reduced to idiocy)
I don't like you. Like—what a word! I only think you the most fascinating, the most enchanting—ah, there aren't any words for you, Ellen!

Ellen

I'll tell you what I *do* love.

Dickens

You're not going to make me the happiest man alive by saying it's me?

[586]

Ha-ha! No. This. (*Holding out arm.*)

Dickens

Ah, the bracelet came? And how much less lovely than the arm.

Ellen

(*Real feeling for the first time*)
It's beautiful.

Dickens

And did you have my letter with it?

Ellen

Oh yes.

Dickens

And what's your answer?

Ellen

Answer?

Dickens

Ah, Ellen, how can you play with me so? What pleasure do you get hurting me?

Ellen

Oh, about the house?

Dickens

About the little house in Ampthill Square. Didn't that mean anything to you?

Ellen

(*Twisting bracelet*)
Of course it did.

Dickens

Then why can't you tell me just once—why can't you say "I trust you, Charles." Just once, "I love you."

Ellen

Oh, because——

Dickens

Because you don't love me, is that it?

Ellen

I don't know.

Dickens

You loved another man once, you said so.

Ellen

Oh, my father's friend, when I was just a little girl, that doesn't count.

Dickens

Just tell me that *I* count.

Ellen

You've been kinder to me than anyone else ever was. This divine bracelet, and the wine and the birds always being sent M'ma, and the horrid coal bill that that horrid man came about.

Dickens

My dear, that's nothing. Those aren't the things that matter. What matters is that someday you put your arms about me and say "Charles, I am yours." Do you see yourself doing that someday?

Ellen

I don't know. But I think—maybe!

Dickens

You can't know how you torture me. Ellen, do you know that when I give my readings hundreds of women crowd about just to touch my hand —just to look at me!

Ellen

Of course I do. But that wouldn't make a person like a person.

Dickens

Then I'm going to ask you—is there anyone else?

Ellen

Anyone else—who——?

Dickens

Who attracts you now. Ellen, I must know. I must know! Is there someone else who makes you hold back, who makes you feel that you can't give yourself to me?

Ellen

I wish you wouldn't be so silly.

Dickens

Silly! (*To himself.*) Good God, talk of silliness between a man my age and a child of yours. It's folly. Who would believe it?

Ellen

Believe that you were a fool to like me?

Dickens

No, no, a thousand times no!

Ellen

Because of *course* I like you. (*Studies bracelet.*) Sophy had one like it, but just the turquoise, not the garnets.

Dickens

And the note? The note that came with the bracelet. I want my answer.

Ellen

Yes. And it came on the prettiest blue velvet cushion. Ma thought it was beautiful.

Dickens

The bracelet did, yes. But the note. You'll let me look at the little house—our little house?

Ellen

(*Primly*)
Ma will. Ma said she wanted it rented in her name. That is, *if* we move.

Dickens

And will you come and look at it with me?

Ellen

I don't know.

[589]

Dickens

Ah, Ellen, you have to know. You're not a child now: you're a woman. Can't you give me a woman's answer?

Ellen

I can't see that I would gain much by it.

Dickens

By letting yourself love me?

Ellen

My mother says she will always expect you to behave like a gentleman.

Dickens

My God, you are maddening! Ellen, can't you be a little kind to me? Can't you have a little pity? Does all I am, all I have given the world, mean nothing to you? I love you so much. If you knew how you make me suffer, you'd be sorry for me.

Ellen

(*Pouting*)
I am sure I never tried to make anyone unhappy.

Dickens

No, I don't blame you. I don't blame you. I only wish to God I never had seen you!

Ellen

First you give me lovely presents like my bracelet and paying that bad coal man, and then you tell me I am cruel! And last Sunday you made me cry, and M'ma said I never need see you again if I didn't want to.

Dickens

(*Under violent restraint*)
No, no. You are quite right. I'll not be unhappy, dear. I'll be the way we were when we first knew each other. The day we walked together and saw the river, and all the daffodils, and you picked me blue violets. Ellen, I never have been so happy as that day. I'll not reproach you again, and you'll be as kind to me as you can, and we'll be happy.

Ellen

(*As he kneels beside her*)
I like you when you're like this. Remember the little old woman at the inn, and the chicken pasty?

Dickens

We'll have another pasty, and more daffodils.

Ellen

And you won't be mad if I tell you that sometimes I liked other men? I mean like that Henry Codman that you hate.

Dickens

No. Because you didn't. And don't speak of him. You don't know your own mind. You didn't like him.

Ellen

Not as much as I like you.

Dickens

Not at all. I'm not in the least jealous, because I know him. Ha. Callow, like a calf. A drooling great booby who belongs on a farm somewhere. A hunking, blundering—

Ellen

(*Tossing her head*)
Whatever he is, he's a friend of mine.

Dickens

(*Angry*)
If I could, I would forbid you ever to speak to him again.

Ellen

But you can't.

Dickens

Ellen, that's childish. That's unworthy of you.

Ellen

Excuse me, I think I know what's worthy of me and what's not worthy of me.

Dickens

You'll pay for the way you treat me. You'll suffer as I suffer someday.

Ellen

No, I won't. For I won't speak to you again. And now I think I'll go back to M'ma. She must have made her call by this time, and she'll be wild. (*As she rises, shows bracelet.*) Isn't it pretty?

Dickens

(*Desperate*)

There's a brooch and a ring that match it, you know.

Ellen

(*Afire*)

Oh, Charley, you wouldn't! Oh, you mustn't spend money on me that way!

Dickens

(*Swinging both her hands*)

If I had a little woman with me, to be sure that I picked up the right ones.

Ellen

This afternoon, when M'ma thinks I'm rehearsing?

Dickens

I meet you at the Bond Street shop, at two, say?

Ellen

Oh, Charley, I love you!

Dickens

My little love!

Ellen

You mustn't! Suppose one of your daughters came in, or Miss Georgie! Does Miss Georgie know—about me?

Dickens

She's been suspecting something for a long time. Yes, I told her today.

Ellen

Was she surprised?

Dickens

She was wonderful. You'll like her.

Ellen

I'll hate her. Is she in love with you?

[592]

Dickens

You don't think every woman is in love with me. It wouldn't be quite fair to answer that, would it?

Ellen

You've answered it. Oh, poor Miss Georgie! To live here and take care of a lot of grubby little boys, and have me take you away from her!

Dickens

(Hoarse, as he embraces her)
Are you going to take me away from her? Are you really going to make me the proudest of men? Ellen, the reverence—the honor that my heart will pay you, when once you trust yourself to me—when you are mine——

Ellen

(Daintily pulling free)
Now you're talking like a book again! Tell me, do Mamie and Katy know?

Dickens

No. They're little girls. They're—well, yes, they're growing up. Katy has even set up a beau—Collins' brother. But they—I don't think of them as understanding me at all.

Ellen

They understood you enough to stay here when their mother left. They know their chances of a good settlement are better here.

Dickens

Mamie sees her mother, I believe. I don't ask. Don't fret your little head about it.

Ellen

Are Mamie and Katy pretty?

Dickens

Good God, no. All elbows and pimples. Nice girls, though.

Ellen

They wouldn't let a married man fall in love with *them.*

Dickens

It isn't a likely occurrence. It worries you to have me give you the ring, the brooch?

(*Alarmed*)
Oh no, no. Not that! But men *do* get divorces, don't they?

Dickens

Not men in my position. Smith—Forster—all against it. It would cut the sales in half—cut the ground from under the Inimitable. No more money for rings and brooches then, eh?

Ellen

(*Laughing lovingly into his face*)
We can't have that!

Dickens

You wouldn't have come today if you didn't love me.

Ellen

M'ma will be all upset again if I don't run. Oh-h-h——

(*Georgie comes downstairs, stands amazed.*)

Dickens

Ah, here she is. My good Dame Durden. Come down, Georgie.

Ellen

Are you Dame Durden? I loved her, in the book.

Dickens

Georgie, this is the young lady I told you about. Ellen, this is our indispensable Aunt Georgie.

Ellen

I feel as if I knew you, Miss Georgie.

Georgie

How—how do you do?

Ellen

I suppose Mr. Dickens has told you how kind he has been to M'ma and me? He's found my mother a dear little house so that we'll be nearer my work.

[594]

Georgie

In Ampthill Square? Yes, he told me.

Ellen

I've not seen it yet. (*Arch look at Dickens.*) But if I didn't have a shopping engagement, I might go look at it this afternoon. Don't you forget our shopping engagement, sir! I'm running. No, you mayn't see me to the carriage. M'ma's probably raging, but you may take me to the door and see me safe across the square. Good-by, Miss Georgie. Charles is never tired sounding your praises! Shall we have tea together someday and talk about this bad man!

Georgie

Thank you. Good-by.

> (*Dickens goes out with Ellen. Georgie stands perfectly still, staring before her, both hands over her heart. Dickens comes back.*)

Dickens

Isn't that a lovely girl? I've never known such a heart—such complete unconsciousness of how wonderful she is. Has no idea of it! Georgie, you like her?

Georgie

She's very pretty. (*Sits down suddenly.*)

Dickens

That's more than surface beauty—it goes deep down into her soul. She knows I care for her, Georgie, but she's like a frightened bird. I scare her with my vehemence, and she flutters away, and then I have it all to do again. You like her?

Georgie

She's very pretty.

Dickens

When you know her, you'll feel as I do. It's so long—it's so many years since I've thought of this sort of happiness for myself, that I'm clumsy—my touch is too rough. But I know where that loving little heart is going to flutter someday. You say she's lovely—yes, she is. Lovely in body and soul, soul and body. And my dear girl—my dear Dame Durden, that you understand, that you could sympathize with me as you did—ah, you don't know how my heart sang, this afternoon, when you told me that you knew, and that you would be the last person in the world to blame me!

[595]

Georgie

(*Lifeless, hopeless*)
I suppose I should think of Kate.

Dickens

The less we go back to the past, my dear girl, the easier it will be for all of us. The girls will meet Ellen of course, in time. By the way, from now on, I will be away several nights a week—well, you can cover that with some explanation. They need never know any details—I must protect Ellen as well as Mamie and Katy from gossip. I leave that to you.

Georgie

(*Looking at him steadily*)
I see.

Dickens

(*Fatuously*)
Strike a wrong note now—the mother's a handful, too—I have to go slowly. Mustn't scare her off. She's a child, you saw that. Head over heels in love and doesn't know what's the matter with her. Head over heels in love and hasn't the faintest idea—— Oh, by the way, Georgie (*sudden change of tone*) what did that girl say? That Henry wanted to see his mother too? What does that mean? Kate wasn't here today?

Georgie

Kate heard that Edward was ill.

Dickens

And she came in? When?

Georgie

She was upstairs while you were reading.

Dickens

Now, my dear girl, didn't we have a complete understanding about that?

Georgie

(*Gruffly*)
I suppose we did.

Dickens

I told Kate she was never to come here.

[596]

Georgie

The child was sick.

Dickens

(*After a pause, during which he watches her closely*)
Georgie, are you unhappy? This new thing doesn't shock you?

Georgie

No. I don't—I don't feel well. I'm not myself. My head—my head aches.

Dickens

You and I have got to face it. For good or ill, we have to make this arrangement work, now. There mustn't be any more talk, any more changes. Whatever the situation is, I want you to ask yourself; wouldn't I rather be here, Charles's trusted housekeeper, the guardian of his home and his children, than anywhere else?

Georgie

Oh yes. I couldn't live anywhere else.

Dickens

Of course you couldn't. You and I must pull together, and we can't have the children's lives upset, the success of the whole thing jeopardized. There'll be no talk, Georgie, nothing sensational, and after a while Ellen will be here now and then—— I want my children to love her—is there anything so formidable in that prospect?

Georgie

No.

Dickens

I want to know what you honestly think of Ellen.

Georgie

She's very pretty.

Dickens

But it was the mind—the mind that first drew me to her. That's a very brilliant girl. Ha. And another time if Kate comes I think Mollie might tell her that the boys are out. We can't have that sort of thing. Kate mustn't come here. Ellen might run into her.

We won't. Ma came to get Kate——

Dickens

Your mother! Good God!

Georgie

And they feel that I have deserted them now; they certainly won't come again.

Dickens

Blame you, eh?

Georgie

Yes. Ma says I broke up Kate's home.

Dickens

What ridiculous nonsense. *You!* But one might have expected that of your mother. But it doesn't matter, does it?

Georgie

No. Nothing matters.

Dickens

I'll go up and change. (*Mounts stairs, humming.*)

Nancy

(*Coming in*)

Miss Georgie, I don't know what's got into the boys. Master Edward has got out of his bed and him and the others is surging and leapin' from bed to bed without a blanket or a sheet on them. Cook says to say the barrels of sugar has come, and where to put them she don't know, as there's some left in the old barrels, and after the way rats has got into the buttery she wouldn't put nothing eatable in there unless it was to get it strewed all over with rat dirt——

Georgie

Oh, Nancy, hush. Tell Cook to settle it any way she likes, and if Sim doesn't turn up by dinnertime she'll have to send to the fish stall and have a man come in and open the oysters. (*Crash from upstairs.*) Send Mollie up there, will you? I'm tired of trying to keep those boys quiet! (*Exit Nancy.*) I'm tired. (*She wanders to the window, looks out. Wanders back, picks up a sketch from a portfolio on the piano and studies it.*)

London Bridge, oh, we had fun sketching London Bridge that morning. We had tea and crumpets at a stall, and an old woman followed Kate and said she looked like her daughter that was dead. (*Puts down sketch and goes to piano; turns music pages, lightly touches a treble phrase from "Poet and Peasant." Hums it. Then drops on piano stool and puts her head down on rack.*) Oh, Kate, Kate, Kate!

CURTAIN

My California

Between the magnificent purples and granites of the High Sierras and the sapphire rollers of the blue, blue Pacific, my state lies stretched out dreaming in the eternal sunshine, humming with bees, washed by waves of fruit blossoms, breathing the deep sweet breath of a million wild flowers into the crystal cleanness of the salty Western air.

No one of us knows how to hymn California, how to express—or to begin to express, what she means to her own people. Her bigness silences us; her infinite variety baffles us; her romance is the secret romance of our own innermost souls,—we cannot vaunt it in the market place. When we answer, "Oh, from California," it is with quiet, but fathomless assurance. "Belittle that, if you dare!" says something within us with the simple words. And to do the generous aliens from forty-seven other states justice, they rarely do belittle the Golden State; the trailing fringes of her garments have touched their own imaginations, too. "Ah, that's where I'm going some day!" they say, with infinite tact. Perhaps they have learned that no other answer registers on the infatuated ears of the native-born.

When I hear the word "California" in some unexpected place or connection, a long line of images begins to move through my mind and my soul and my heart and my memory. Some of them are honestly mine—some are second-hand; passed down to me from the grandmother who crossed the plains from "St. Joe" in a covered wagon nearly eighty-five years ago, and settled down on a farm in that fertile valley where the Yuba and the Plumas rivers run together to encircle Marysville. Placerville was "Hangtown" then, and what is now the very center of Sacramento was Sutter's Fort. And there were Spanish ranchers left, and widespreading Spanish ranches, with chapels and bells, tiled roofs and pigeons, grazing sheep and galloping horses. Through my grandmother's eyes I used to see the old days, when the mail stages thundered through the villages, thick with dust, and the Chinese camped under the great fig trees at the turn of the river. Chinese, Mexicans, prospectors, adventurers, curly-headed little Lotta Crabtree and her traveling show, the hoop-skirted, ringleted women who flounced downtown on the wooden sidewalks to catch a glimpse of her,—a listening child knew them all.

It was all free, simple, exciting,—one wonders what the railroads presently brought that was as valuable as what they destroyed: the old days when Benicia and San José and Sacramento were the centers for so rich a stream of frontier life, and Los Angeles was yet unborn, and San Francisco merely the uncivilized port of Yerba Buena.

My grandfather, evidently in the spirit of prophecy, wrote an article, in about the year 1855, to prove that there was no real geological reason why wheat and fruit might not be grown on the sheep ranges of the new territory. It was all untried, promising, there was no telling what might be done agriculturally in this place where, miraculously, there were no snow and no thunderstorms, no long hard winter and burning summer, no factories, newspapers, cities, nothing established, nothing known.

There was a man in old California who lived about a day's ride north of San Bernardino, about a day's ride south of Benicia, then the capital. His were broad acres, with running rivers, fruit, great forests, cattle ranges, sheep, pigs, chickens, horses. He kept open house.

Just that. Not to selected friends, or recommended strangers, but to everyone. If cowboys came that way, they found bunkhouses and beds, long tables spread royally under the pepper trees, company, singing, rest for themselves and their "cayuses." If more distinguished guests arrived: delicate women in crinolines, small grit-faced children, an old Mammy, an old "spring wagon" powdered gray, these were offered big dim sweet bedrooms in the "long adobe," cool water, fine wines, delicious fare, and they were entreated to stay just as long as their plans would permit. Sometimes the host had a hundred travelers under his roof, sometimes only a dozen,— always there were fresh figs, and trout, newly killed lamb and quail and turkeys, great cuts of fresh bread, honey, preserves, corn on the cob.

For a whole generation he was host to the state,—priests, gentlefolk, miners, adventurers, ranchers; and to this day they point out the scene of his lordly hospitalities.

That is only one detail of many. Things were done magnificently in California then, and to some extent she retains even today her half-frontier, half-Castilian attitude; is still the shy yet friendly senorita, with poppies in her dark hair, whose full lace skirts are always ready to sweep the ground in a great courtesy of welcome.

You can find all the forty-eight states of the union in California by traveling from the Oregon line down to the Mexican border, and even a dash of old England and more than a hint of Switzerland, too. She strives to meet all tastes, and when the shivering East gets off the train in

Pasadena or San Diego down south, it can look off toward the whiteness of the snow-topped mountains, even while gathering delicious great sweet spicy oranges and spicier waxen orange blossoms from the same tree, in the hot valley sunshine below.

We say we have only two kinds of weather: perfect and most unusual. Down toward Hollywood we have everything and more than ever takes a cold city dweller to Miami and Palm Beach in February, and up toward Piedmont we have everything and more than ever drives a sweltering Easterner out of a summer city. In Santa Monica, for instance, about twenty minutes away from Hollywood, there are miles of boardwalk, and on the eve of last Thanksgiving Day there were thousands of bathers idling in the warm soft waters of the really Pacific Ocean. On the other hand, about the time that Philadelphians and Bostonians are beginning to get the first furnace-breath of July, and the city streets catch the cruel heat and send it back in sickening waves from the high buildings, we put on big topcoats in San Francisco and look from restaurant windows at sidewalks shrouded with heavy fogs.

You can see cotton fields in California, and bananas, and dates. Moving northward up the state's magnificent thousand miles are such oddities as bamboo plantations, rice, tobacco, citron orchards, an ostrich farm, a lion farm. The great central valleys are carpeted close with fruit trees; the world knows Imperial Valley prunes, Contra Costa peaches, Santa Clara cherries. The coast is strewn with delicious little villages, where summer homes push boldly out from under oaks to touch the very rocks of the shore that shows alternately great crescents of white beach and rocky cliffs running out to long headlands, and crescents of beach again. Never were there so many rose-smothered little homes along one shore before; Spanish houses with patios, trim New England's green and white, plain brown shingles, French plaster and green shutters,—everyone builds exactly what he likes, and the gardens reconcile all sorts and types of architecture into one harmonious whole.

One has to live in other climates for a while to grasp fully what one's seniors, grandparents and their congeners, meant by their wild enthusiasm on the score of climate. One has to remember that these pioneers came from the East coast states, and many of them from the North coast states. It was like a miracle to them that there could be a beautiful and fertile country into whose unvarying sunshine children might be turned to riot free three hundred and twenty-five days a year.

Even today the management of small children—and these pioneer women had droves of them!—is difficult in the Eastern states. What problems nurseries presented, say in the state of New Hampshire, and say in the year 1833, the maternal imagination staggers to contemplate today. No electric lights, no hot water except from the kettle, no cooking heat except through the difficult way of coal and kindling and ashes, no canned foods or bottled milk, no furnace warmth,—small wonder that the primitive graveyards of old New England record youthful tragedy upon youthful tragedy: "third wife of the above," "beloved infant daughters—beloved infant sons of the above." The cruel conditions of their lives mowed down the soft and tender, the delicate and young, like April's wild flowers; they struggled with washing, soap-making, pig-pickling, yeast, ashes, cold, damp, baby illnesses, for a while, and then succumbed. There was no merciful chloroform to carry them through the hour of ordeal; no quiet efficient nurse with a hot-water bag and a cup of chicken broth. They fought on starkly, unassisted, until the day when the cold bedroom walls and the winter odors of grease and cinders, loom and candle moulds, faded from their tired eyes.

To such women the westering adventure must have presented hours of absolute ecstasy. To be out on the open sun-washed prairie, with the oxen plodding along across the wild grass, and the wagon tilting and creaking gently, and the children growing browner and taller and wilder every day; to have every meal a picnic under the enormous blue canvas of the sky, to find the cold streams, and watch the camp-fire smoke going straight up against the back-drop of solemn mountains,—what hosannahs the heart of many a demurely bonneted woman must have sung as the road unfolded and the setting sun came nearer!

To be sure this trip was dangerous,—they never could forget that for long. It was the three-year-old son of a kinswoman of mine who wandered away from the wagons, one summer noon, and could not be found again. The mother began the search; she had a child of six, was close to a third confinement; time was precious. In her old age, not so long ago, she told me once of that search,—through the prairie grass, along the shallow little stream. They asked her finally how long they should hunt; there was every reason to move: Indians were trailing them; they could see the enemy fires at night. And half a day's forced march ahead was a larger caravan, that meant safety for them all,—the anxious men, the quiet, dutiful women, the children, the unborn.

She told them to search until sundown, and at sundown they had not found the child. Desperately she still hunted, but when the oxen were yoked she climbed to her familiar place on the front seat, picked up the reins. She told me mildly that even after that "she kep' a-lookin' for a spell." But she saw only the waving grasses, and the groups of yellowed cottonwoods, and the faint trail westward—westward. Of the three-year-old they never had any further news.

But what a day it must have been for each of these gallant bands in turn, when the last great mountain had been scaled, and the road turned downward, downward, to California and the sea. What a night when, dusty and weary, and so much older, with their quilted frocks and hoods shabby, and their children awkward in clothes much too small,—what a night when they saw the lights of Fort Sutter, and heard the voices, and could begin to murmur at last about "settling," "locating!"

And then commenced the talk of climate that never will be wholly stilled, even when artificial heat and ice and light and electric stoves and modern hospitals have all exerted their leveling sway. Even then there will always be the mother of small babies rejoicing because she can turn them into a grassy dooryard for hours of hot sunlight in June, in October, in January, in March. They can wade on Christmas Day, swim on Washington's Birthday,—no bundling into "woolies" and fumbling with gaiters for them; nor any airing of blankets, clearing away of winter mud, no "spring house-cleaning" in California! We used to hear this phrase with great amusement when I was small. Why *should* houses be specially cleaned and aired at any special season? We speculated about snow and thunderstorms; it must be "funny" to run home from school over snow!

My own first look at snow did not come until I was a woman grown and married and visiting a certain editor's delightful storybook family in Goshen, New York. The smallest daughter of a delicious row of small girls watched my excitement in a real New England snowstorm with eager sympathy and amaze. We went from window to window, and I marveled at it. "Look, Elizabeth, 'way up the street there on the church and the courthouse, and 'way down there on the barns,—so much of it—such tons of it!"

Elizabeth presently stole away for an aside to her mother. "Has that lady been shut up all this time, Mother?"

It is memorable, a first snow. But perhaps not more thrilling than those first winters must have been to the women who had burned all their bridges behind them and migrated to the West. Breathing that valley air that is scented with eucalyptus and redwood balm, and that blows over acres of spicy tarweed and wild mustard and yarrow,—waiting for the blizzard—the storm—the biting, ominous, hovering iron cold that never came, must have been a second adventure almost as thrilling as the first.

Every town, from Eureka down to Calixeco, has its pages of strange history: hangings, murders, stage robberies, fires, earthquakes, floods. But far from blushing over these records of her wild youth, California cherishes them; Fort Gunnybags, and the old headquarters of the Vigilantes, the haunts of "King of William," are just as sacred to her as are her souvenirs of Bret Harte and Charles Warren Stoddard, Robert Louis Stevenson and Mark Twain. They all helped to build her story, as did the padres and the Indians, and the Spanish ranchers whose crumbling adobe haciendas are still landmarks, up and down the state.

As for the Missions, what visitor has not deluged the homestayers with postcards of them, on candy boxes, fruit boxes, slabs of white orangewood? Their bland plain outlines, their bastion-thick adobe walls and cloisters shaded by bell towers and gnarled pines, are a part of America's wealth; the twisting old dirt road that Padre Junipero Serra followed so painfully on muleback, a hundred years ago, runs straight now for a thousand miles, and is named for the Missions: "El Camino Real de la Santa Cruz,"—

the royal highway of the Holy Cross. Piety trails up and down the state; the towns are dedicated to the good saints: Luke, Barbara, Anthony, Clara. We have Sacramento and Santa Fe and Trinidad and Purisima, and enthusiastic newcomers, entering into the spirit of the thing, have been known to go so far as to speak feelingly of Santa Los Gatos and Mount San Diabolo.

Holding tight to her none-too-edifying past, California breaks, every year, into a very glory of fiesta. Up and down the state goes the wave of carnivals, community celebrations, pageants, rose festivals, flower fêtes. Punctually, annually, the streets of every city, village, and town are threaded by mummers; great floats studded with flowers, ropes of roses, canopies of satiny poppies, turning wheels of pale pink hydrangea, bursting spikes of delphinium and phlox. Whole communities appear in hoopskirts, beards, sombreros and chaps, poke bonnets and pantalettes, and the shops sell bandanas and braided quirts, and there are bullfights and horse races, and dancing in the streets, with the moon and a hundred banjos for local color. Spanish is good English in California even today; a donkey is a burro, a farm is a rancho, we buy fifty vara lots, and revel in a diet enriched by tamales and enchiladas. And on such occasions as the Los Gatos Pageant, and the Salinas Rodeo, everyone goes Spanish for a few exciting hours.

Rodeo means "round-up," and round-up is cowboy for checking up the year's run of cattle from the ranges. Naturally there are always confusion, danger, showing-off, at a rodeo, and naturally the public gathers on the long hot bleachers to see what the boys are up to. They see the vaqueros ride in on their magnificent horses, the boys themselves very brown and clean and young in purple shirts and flaming bandanas. They see the calves and the big heavy bulls waiting in their pens; the band plays and the flags blow in the sunshine; somebody exhibits a famous claybank pacer, or a "high-school horse" whose rider hangs on upside down at a gallop by only one spurred heel.

Then suddenly—pandemonium. Bulls are charging dummies, men are standing on their heads in the dust while the great furious bodies lurch by; blinded unbroken horses are being saddled by cowboys who must dance continually out of the way of the plunging heels; riders are flung to the track as the races come around the curve, and an odd bull or two, plunging madly at the stands themselves, scatter spectators and guards indiscriminately with the effect of a sea bursting over a rock. The laughter, the screams, the gasps of a rodeo culminate always with what is modestly announced as the "wild horse race," when perhaps forty unbroken hill ponies are saddled on the track immediately in front of the grand stand and ridden once about the course. At this point every woman spectator is screaming, praying aloud, shrieking directions to the already distracted cowboys, covering her eyes, attempting to climb down and help. The horses roll, plunge, bite, kick, and squeal without cessation; men are flung down like chaff before a reaper, dragged helter-skelter through the boiling confusion, stepped upon, charged. Outraged, the horses start backward, forward, sideways; they are with difficulty restrained from jumping into the bandstand or the boxes. A boy sits on a blinded head, fanning it with his hat; horse and head are freed suddenly, with a desperate plunge, and the boy finds himself jumping the paddock fence at the south end of the course, hanging like a scarf to his mount's wet neck, hitting the ground occasionally with a sprawling foot or a clutching hand. That young horses can act like starfish, eels, firecrackers, and volcanoes is a truth reserved for those who follow like guiding stars those roadway signs that announce, all through the summer months, that fifty miles south—fifty miles north, there will presently be a rodeo.

Other states have to put in a proviso—"in case of rain"—when they plan these open-air things: tennis and golf tournaments, garden parties and orchard weddings, parades and pageants and rodeos and picnics. California doesn't; sometimes there is one good rain in between May first and the end of November; sometimes there isn't. All the days of the long summers are hot and sweet and clear, and all the nights are cold, and good for wood fires and deep sleep. The hills turn as brown as panthers, somewhere in June, and most of the watercourses go dry, but there are drenching dews to keep the gardens green, and the whir of water sprinklers is never still. Hence the younger generation can move its beds out onto porches—lawns—roofs, somewhere around Easter, and never come indoors at all until winter, if it likes. Californians eat out of doors habitually; even the smallest and most modest homes boast squares of lawn, or the shade of one great tree, or the Spanish balcony where a table may be set.

One of my favorite sights in the world begins in June and ends in October; I mean the hegira of the campers to the Big Basin, twenty miles up our road. Their shabby little cars begin to wind up hill under the redwoods at about cherryblossom time, and never stop until the season is open for turkeys with chestnut stuffing. They go by our gates: dusty car, Dad driving, Mother with the baby on the front seat, Grandma and Bobby in the back, with Sandy the dog, and Minny the cat; with a box of groceries and a paper bag of corn; with blankets and tin cups and a coffee pot; with a chair and a broom tied on somewhere for good measure.

Over to the great clean magnificent woods they go, to unpack and settle wherever they like; on the stream, or up the hill, but always under the piny majesty and sweetness of the giant sequoias. They find a tent platform up, felled leveled logs for seats, and a brick grill; they gather their own fuel, and their enchanted holiday begins. No rent to pay: California is their hostess, and every night she entertains them, if they choose. All about a mammoth camp fire the tipped scooped logs make comfortable seats; there is a community "sing," or dramatics, or the radio, or a program of good records; or there is a dance. Year after year they come, and the youngsters get to know each other, and something even Russia might envy is achieved; something near an ideal of individual development along community lines.

There are other state reservation camping grounds for these insatiably camp-minded Westerners, and in almost every spare-room closet a few odd treasures in the shape of red shirts, jeans, boots, fishing tackle and ponchos and sleeping bags are stored against the day when the red gods make their medicine again. Then the old car makes the first stage of the trip, and borrowed horses the next day's riding, and the next, and then the initiate perhaps finds himself in that same complete solitude the first settlers knew: up in the high crystal-clear airs of the Sierras, following a trail marked by only three or four little rocks piled on another rock surface as Nature never could pile them. Just that—among the pines and junipers and the ages-old tumble of boulders—three or four tiny rocks piled into a "monument," and that means the trail, and that is all he has to identify it. His horse walks slowly along the shelf of narrow path above the foaming river, or picks his way through the trackless meadows; he rides for days, weeks, if he likes, and sees no other human being nor any sign of one. Late in the afternoon he may plunge into a lake so clear that he may look down and see the trout flitting against the white rock bottom forty feet below; he may presently broil some of these same trout over his pine-scented fire, and watch the blue smoke go up straight into the mingled sunset and moonrise of the star-pricked sky.

Up in the High Sierras, comfortable in leather coat and jeans, living on oatmeal and bacon and trout and venison, it is hard to believe that sophisticated Los Angeles, with its incomparable out-of-door concerts, its Paris and New York shops, its bored young movie beauties trailing their sables and chinchilla, its great arenas that welcomed the Olympic games one year,—it is hard to believe that Los Angeles lies only a few hundred miles to the southwest, and that San Francisco,—the most romantic port in the world, the hilliest, foggiest, sunniest, most fascinating city of them all, with the ships along its waterfront, and the gulls lording it over the very whiteness, the Grecian beauty of the Civic Centre itself—it is hard to believe that San Francisco lies only a few hundred miles to the west and north. The loneliness, the silences, the peace of the great mountains seem another world from—well, say Stanford University and the other big state universities with their great auditoriums, their arcades and libraries and tree-shaded walks, or from Chinatown, bustling, chattering, crowded; its gay bazaars and dark alleys, its strange markets and filigree upper balconies packed with the sights and sounds and smells of the oldest civilization of all.

The Chinese children trot off every morning from their lairs to American schools, and make speeches about George Washington, and often shame the native-born; the girls stump along in high heels just about as healthful and comfortable as the bound embroidered tiny shoes that crippled and tortured their grandmothers' feet; they cut their thick black hair short and frizz it into ringlets. But old China is there just the same, in the dim shops with their fretted teakwood grills and their odors of tea and opium, and in the theater where interminable plays go on, night after night, and the plump, pale-skinned merchants watch them stoically, chewing sunflower seeds the while.

The property man, a harassed coolie in his shirt-sleeves or his Canton coat of blue silk, wanders at large through the play, changing cushions, lighting lights, unseen by either audience or actors, even though he actually gets in the Princess's way when she would commit suicide, or drops exhausted upon the chair the hero was about to occupy. And perhaps a delicious child or two, shaven-headed, awkward in wadded minute garments, will come to stand peeping at the scene, and presently make his way to the very center of it, and sit there, unreproved and watching, and waiting for mother or father to finish his part. All the while the strange Chinese music whines and bangs, and the house lights are bright, and the crunching of sunflower seeds continues uninterruptedly.

In a Chinese theater you pay a minimum price when the play begins at six, less at seven, and so on, like the Mock Turtle's lessons that "lessened from day to day"; an hour before the midnight closing the entrance fee is only a few cents, and then the place is always packed. The actor is expert in symbolism: a short feathered and tasseled whip means that he is on horseback; to display the sole of his foot as he turns away means he is off on a journey; and if he is killed, after dying with a horrid realism that makes one feel faint, immediately he gets up, placidly strolls off the stage, perhaps stopping to light a cigarette or speak to the property man as he goes. The property man, yawning, then comes out with a doll dressed like the murdered actor, and flings it down where his body might be lying. If he were beheaded,—and these men play such a part with a gusto that makes one see the clean-severed flesh, the rush of blood, the whitening face,—then the doll that replaces him has a neat little detached head, with a red line about the neck.

All these things,—the cities with their opera houses and their beautiful women, the movie world with its luxury and its cardboard crowns, the seals barking on Seal Rock, valleys where grapes ripen and figs fall black and heavy, lakes where trout shoot through shallows, marshes where the ducks fly; muttering, vari-colored strange-scented Chinatown, and the Rose Bowl at Pasadena, and the rodeos up and down the highways, the mellowed old Missions with their bells and their shadowy cloisters, wheat waving in the hot sunshine for hundreds of acres, and oranges in dark polished leaves with the water of the irrigating ditches shining beneath them,—all these are a part of my own state.

Her gallantry is a part of her; that gallantry with which she awakened on an April morning not much more than a quarter of a century ago and found herself the object of the whole world's horrified pity and concern. She did not pity herself; there was wild laughter on the morning of the earthquake, there was that scrambling and planning, that snatching of gipsy meals and spreading of gipsy beds that in our hearts we all welcome as a delicious break in the monotony of living. Depression! We didn't know the word then, nor the feeling either, although homes were gone and jobs were gone and some of the old ways were gone forever. Nobody's money was any good, shops were wet ruins smelling of ashes, nobody could get at his securities, or indeed knew whether they still existed, buried under fallen walls and smoking pyres. And for a little while life was simple, communal, right; women were serving meals all day long in the long sunshiny eating sheds, anyone who was hungry could eat. Men were busy raking, leveling, assorting scrambled possessions, building the green two-room cabins that filled our parks for actual years after the earthquake. The memories of those days have no horror and no sting; all that was transmuted into high adventure and the thrill of complete, dramatic, exciting change, by a people only a little removed from the pioneer generation that had done it all before them.

"Scraping bats" was the job then, and anyone who wanted a few dollars could earn them by spending an hour or two scraping and piling the still-warm fallen bricks. These were banked into great stacks, and presently the roasted earth was flattened again, and the bricks began to go up into great buildings once more, and California did a little scrubbing here and a little sweeping there, and smoothed everything down with sprinklings of oil,—and behold!—was ready for the most successful of all the International Expositions—the tremendous Panama-Pacific Fair in 1915, and for the long string of golf and tennis, football and baseball tournaments that followed it. Her earthquake, in short, was only a sort of glorified picnic,—her days, come what may, have a way of turning themselves into one long fiesta.

Sophisticated she never can be, despite the vice-regal estates of the Pasadena millionaires, the yachts in Pebble Beach harbor, the modernity and luxury of the movie world. She still retains some flavor of her old wild grace; the glory of the past is with her. Still the mountains shut her away from all the rest of the world; and when the gulls cry over the foggy sand-hills, and the dancing waves all down her thousand miles of ocean shore are breaking white on the sand, it is easy to remember the fierce, splendid, praying, fighting, fast-riding days of her youth, cowled padres, haciendas shadowed in still midsummer heat by fig trees and eucalyptus, dusty hooped wagons rumbling in on rough meadow trails, and bonneted, weary, brave women lifting children down, to run on the poppied grass, and shout at the high blue skies, and breathe in that combination of elixir and champagne, south wind and peach blossoms, that is the air of California.

My San Francisco

We who were born in San Francisco, back in the dim primeval era known to the rising generation as "before the big fire," have a calm, deep-rooted conviction that there is no other city in the world comparable to it. Our position is that of the Virginia gentleman of long ago who warned his son: "Never ask a man from what state he comes. If he's a Virginian, you'll know it. If he isn't, you'll shame him."

Perhaps it is a common human experience to go all through childhood in a state of complete admiration of one's native town. No doubt of my own city's supremacy ever crossed my own mind in the first years I remember. San Francisco was mine, my own people had builded it, had shared the fierce, simple, thrilling days of the gold rush with adventurers and horse thieves, Spanish rancheros and tonsured Franciscan priests; had watched the prairie schooners coming in over the sierras with "Hangtown or Bust" lettered on their dirty canvas tops, and with wistful women and children looking down from the high, hooded front seats. They had seen the merchant steamers reaching at last the Golden Gate, and had heard the boys in the unpaved, wooden-sidewalked streets shouting the news that a ship was in, and that silks and muslins, china and tinware, knives and ink and artificial flowers, rum and tobacco and ginger and rope and nails would presently be on sale.

And they had joined the crowds hurrying down to the piers—those long, shabby wooden piers that my childhood remembers—the crowds of horse thieves and camp women, Spanish rancheros, Chinese mine laborers and laundrymen. And gentry, of course,—ladies in hoops and scoop bonnets and shawls, leaning in delicate elegance upon the arm of the man of the house, who wore a bell silk hat and a skirted coat, and pointed with his careless cane at such merchandise as he fancied for his womenkind.

Wooden sidewalks: how the words say old San Francisco! Even in 1888, when I wrote my first date with a hollowed piece of chalk that, screwed down on its open end, formed the eights with dazzling accuracy—even in 1888 there were wooden sidewalks in all the quieter, residential neighborhoods, and all the short streets ended in hills, and most of them were sand hills. Looking down from the fenced back garden that was our playground, we small children, like all San Francisco's children then, commanded all the Bay and the long sharp fringe of masts along the docks. Ships came into our harbor then that will sail the seas no more; three-masters and four-masters with all sails set, moving majestically through the shining Gate, anchoring against the blue waters off Alcatraz or Goat Island. Every morning the fishing fleet returned from the Pacific just as we were half-heartedly dressing, at our eastern nursery windows, and while we fumbled laboriously for buttons or struggled into starched Holland aprons, the brown sails flitted like water bugs along the ferry front, and the strengthening sun flashed silver on the glittering haul that weighed down the boats.

In those days ours was a cosmopolitan world. We thought all children knew the bewildering range of personalities and nationalities that we knew; we could not have imagined an existence devoid of this rich background of colors, accents, entangled languages. It was natural to hear Spanish, Mexican, Chinese chattered all about us; all house servants were foreign born, and certain sections of the straggling, hilly, open city were given over entirely to the different races.

There were Spanish Town and Mexican Town and Chinatown, and Tuckertown and North Beach and the Mission, and they were all part of San Francisco, all built on the site of the old Franciscan fathers' little Castilian settlement of Yerba Buena.

There were French families, too, fine quiet folk who lived a life apart in brick-walled gardens and dim old three-story mansions: "Jean" and "Louis," thin-legged little boys in tight jerseys, and "Marie" and "Clotilde," thin-legged little girls with straight black manes falling down their backs, almost to their knees. How or why so many émigrées had reached this farthest-flung frontier no one ever explained—to me, at least; but there they were, behind their dreary eucalyptus and cypress trees, living in the dignified and elegant fashion of the old châteaux of their native land.

There was a French church on the steep slope of Bush Street above Chinatown, and there was a Spanish church on another sharp hill in the Latin Quarter: the Church of Nuestra Señora de Guadalupe. The latter was a favorite with children because it was so entertaining; fat dark babies circulated the aisles through all religious ceremonies, tying handkerchiefs to pew ropes, draping rosaries about their small ears, and whispering "Sí, madre!" in the silences, and the señoras wept audibly into their mantillas during the Long Gospel in Lent. But most interesting was the statue of Our Lady, dressed as we felt entirely fitting, in beautiful watered black brocade, with fine lace frills at her wrists, and a real lace handkerchief in her ringed hand. The Spanish used to throw small sweet candies after a bride in those days—indeed, I believe they do still; I have known it to be done at a brilliant Portuguese wedding in Rio—and there is a faded, shameful memory in my heart of certain American children in long-ago San Francisco who once sank so low as to conceal themselves behind the old leather, nail-studded doors of the church foyer, where they gathered up handfuls of the tiny little colored sweets, and probably gathered up plenty of dirt, mud, dust and germs with them, for their contraband feast.

Those were unsanitary days everywhere, and especially in San Francisco, the pioneer port of the great Orient. Malaria and mosquitoes flourished everywhere, sand hills swarmed with fleas, flies drifted through unscreened windows and were affectionately apostrophized. "Baby bye," said the old song placidly, "here's a fly, let us watch him, you and I."

The children we knew sometimes boasted queer diseases—hip disease and fits and convulsions—and one bustled and crimped friend of my mother elegantly explained that "all her children were bilious babies." The eleven young and charming sons and daughters of a Spanish family, right on our corner, were resignedly succumbing to consumption one after another all through the first years I remember, and small pox was an everyday affair.

Epidemics of the last-named often swept over our cheerful little days; faces we loved were scarred deep by it; our nurses, our friends the policemen, the cable-car conductors, the salesmen in bakeries and groceries, all wore the brand of the little pocks.

Well, that was long ago. That was old San Francisco, the gay, young, wind-swept, fog-shrouded city scattered about on seven times seven sand hills; a city ringed with dunes and with steep cobbled streets going down to wooden piers, and masts and hulls, and the blue waters of the bay. That was the San Francisco of Nob Hill and Seal Rocks; the San Francisco of the "Monkey House," where men went to drink beer in grape arbors on Sundays, and monkeys, scores of them, climbed and swung and chattered overhead. But the real fascination here was neither the monkeys nor the beer, but the famous spider webs and their horrible tenants. The webs hung softly, fold on filthy swinging fold, two feet—three feet below the hidden ceiling of the saloon, and great fat spiders rushed and sidled darkly in their shadows.

In that old San Francisco, as today, there were found the most delicious sour, crusty, webby French bread in the world—not even in Paris do they have such bread—and the most exquisite hand laundries. Nowhere in the world is fine linen so sympathetically treated, restored to such unimaginable crispness, freshness, daintiness, as in San Francisco.

All up the steep hills below Chinatown were restaurants in the old days. Some were in balconied French houses with Nottingham lace curtains in the windows that came down to the floor, and heavy glass carafes on the coarse white tablecloths. Some were in dark downtown lairs, betrayed only by a wilted orange or two in the street window. All were alike in the plainness of their service and the glory of their food. There has never been such food in the world: such cold shrimps and crabs just fresh from the Bay; such soups, served magnificently from enormous tureens that were passed many times; such delicate salads of wilted silky lettuce faintly redolent of chives and garlic; such bread, such coffee, such chicken *à la famille*. And the bill ran to thirty-five cents a head!

The grace, the charm, the flavor of those long-ago meals! At the really French restaurants decorum prevailed. The mirrors, with their soapy scrolls, reflected many a decorous family group: Papa bearded and patriarchal, and even the breast-baby on Mamma's lap getting a sip of red wine. But at Coppa's, at Solari's, at the Trovatore, and at Sanguinetti's, young Bohemian San Francisco wittled free, and struggling artists arose between courses to embellish the walls with dancing Pierrettes and demons.

Stevenson, Bret Harte, Mark Twain were but memories then; they had loved our city, and left their mark upon her, and gone their way. But George Sterling, Gelett Burgess, Will and Wallace Irwin, and a hundred other newspaper men who were to make their names famous one day, were all a part of it, and the days of high revelry among the cabins and shanties of Telegraph Hill are wonderful to remember.

It is all wonderful to remember: the peppers and eucalyptus trees in the old gardens, the sand blowing over the wooden sidewalks in hot spring gales, the city where Santa Claus sweltered in sunshine, and the flags hung wet and still on a foggy Fourth of July.

And wonderful to remember is the April morning when we awakened in a hazy, exquisite dawn to feel our familiar world rocking, to hear it creaking and groaning, to see it go to pieces before our eyes.

We knew all about earthquakes: the story of 'Sixty-eight was a favorite and familiar one. Had not my great-aunt Sarah Alden slumbered ever since that event with her famous "paddysoy" laid on a chair beside her bed, awaiting the *next* earthquake? The paddysoy—could it once have been a *"padua soie"*?—was a wrapper in whose deep pockets were secured money, valuable papers, a New Testament, handkerchiefs, slippers, stockings, soap, pen, photographs, and any other small articles indispensable to the happiness of Aunt Sarah.

And on the eighteenth of April, 1906, Aunt Sarah, in extreme old age, was justified in her precautions, and while we all fled in ecstatic disarray into the shaken streets, she stepped forth in complete possession of her valuables and her dignity.

At twenty minutes past five, with the sun just up, and the birds singing, down came the chimneys, down crashed china obscurely in dark kitchens, out went lights, and the world had gone mad. How I wish that to every life there might come, if once only, such days of change and freedom, so deep and intoxicating a draught of realities, after all the artificialities of civilization and society. Just to eat, to be alive, to work and sleep and eat again, was to live on life's most satisfying terms.

Everyone talking together, disheveled, excited, running to see what was happening elsewhere, running back, endlessly diverted, satiated for once with excitement. Authority was in the saddle by six. "You keep out of that house, lady, and keep them children out!" said the voice behind the Star. Delight of delights, nobody could make beds or dust on that enchanted morning!

Elderly ladies saw fit to faint, for there were a dozen lesser shocks to keep them uneasy, and thus improved the occasion in their own way. But Youth led forbidden forays into the forbidden kitchens, came forth to cook at curbstones, realized at last its rebel dream of the tiresome old office burning down! The triumph of extricating one's curbstone kitchen from complete chaos, of bringing forth the laundry stove upon which to cook, and the parlor blinds to form a shelter, the thrill of standing in line for hot, badly baked bread, and signing for tomatoes or pounds of butter, as in a real siege—these things survive in our memories as the very cream of living!

We had no news of the outside world: our wires were down, and anyway, we were making all the history there was. No news of our own catastrophe, but could we not walk to the corner to look down upon it, smoldering and crashing in the jaws of a fire twenty blocks square, the shaken buildings and the empty window frames falling into its roar and smoke as it reached them, line by line?

Our parks were great refugee camps; our only newspaper a sheet printed across the bay and containing nothing but personals. The Smith family was with Grandma in Oakland. The Brown family, tent 343, Presidio, couldn't find their smallest boy. The Robinsons were all together except Mary; would Mary come to Uncle Frank's? Pleading, agonized, insistent, page after page of the desperate messages were scattered abroad, and as families sat on their steps, eating their canned meat and spongy bread, other families trailed by, thirsty, weary, homeless, hungry; and bread and water and the news were shared.

"If you're the Kings of Howard Street, they've got your little boy safe: it says so in the paper. If your name is Roberts, maybe it's your little girl that was found?"

These were days of high emotion, of change, of bewildered partings and ecstatic reunion; presently everyone could get food, and nobody had a job, and to certain young hearts wearied with routine and responsibilities these conditions spell complete satisfaction with life.

San Francisco has had her great Exposition since then. Rebuilt in enthusiasm and courage and love, again her great buildings shadow decorous downtown streets; again flowers bank Lotta's Fountain, and green lace balconies, blooming dimly with gilded fretwork and great paper lanterns, hang above the crowded, narrow, odorous, enchanted streets of China-town. Again soft summer fogs wreath the French bakeries, the *blan-chisseries de fin*, the steep cobbled streets where grass spurts between the stones, and the long line of the piers. Again the tourist learns to his eternal surprise that July and August call for overcoats in the old city of Spanish Saint Francis.

San Francisco had her Exposition and the same grace and eagerness that she brings to her simplest hospitality were evident throughout every detail of that colossal entertainment. Two hundred thousand visitors streamed through the gates of the Panama-Pacific Industrial Exposition on an April day in 1915. Handing up their tickets at gates? Oh, not at all: that is not my city's way.

No, the first day's ticket was represented by a ribbon badge. And the hundreds, thousands, scores of thousands of wearers of the ribbons streamed joyously down wide Van Ness Avenue and took possession of the great Fair with a royal rush. No one questioned them; no one stopped them; there were no delays. Some cities would have protested that they could not trust their people to that extent: San Francisco could.

For months the oriental beauty of the Fair lay between the shining hills of the city and the blue waters of the Bay. It was a world of creamy sur-faces, and castles on which blue and umber shadows lay, the Exposition City; its walls were pierced with tiny Turkish balconies and screens, its courtyards spurted with fountains and were laid with a succession of blaz-ing flowers; some of its trees, transplanted with infinite wisdom and care, rose a hundred feet in blue air.

Not a great country's industrial exhibition: it was more like a glimpse of some dreamy Eastern palace in Peking or Lucknow; it was Bagdad. The people loved it with a deep personal love; they lived in their new world of jewels and perfumes and blossoms and strange lights. And when the Fair—the only one that ever paid fully for itself and left a balance—when the Fair was over, they left it as they had entered it, *en masse*, sorrow-fully, slowly, with the enchanted lights dying away behind them, and the music of the fountains stilled, with puzzled gulls walking undisturbed in the streets that had held high carnival. And as they went a solitary bugle, from some high tower, sounded taps in the warm November moonlight.

All that was characteristic of San Francisco. She manages, mysteriously, through all the years, to preserve the romantic, the dramatic attitude of her younger days. She is still as surprising, as fascinating, as original as ever she was in the first days of all, when a hundred ships, deserted by gold-mad sailors, rotted in her harbor, and bells rang in the old Mission of Our Lady of Sorrows out on Dolores Street.

Coming home from other cities and other parts, one crosses the Bay to reach San Francisco and sees first the gray silhouette of her hills, shingled with roofs and roofs and roofs; the royal fringe of masts and spars along her waterfronts; the gray fog circling and fuming softly over it all, and the gulls flying and crying. The little boats, plying to and fro, sound their hoarse, sweet notes of warning, and perhaps the noon whistles and the Angelus bells take up the sound in a long chord that to some hearts says, "Welcome home!"

Each to his own city. But do you love them as we do, I wonder, you whose cities are not steep and narrow streeted, scented with the spices of the Orient and the good tarry smell of ships and fishing, lulled by the deep rushing of ocean surges on a long beach, and the lapping of bay water against piers?

Beauty in Letters

"Let thanks be to Allah," says some character in a Kipling story, when old friends gather after long changes and separations in wartime, "that He has not terminated all the Delights!"

No, nor will He, while the miracle of beauty lives on and on, caged for us, captured for us, between the covers of beloved books.

Yesterday and today treat us cruelly, and we fear tomorrow. Life, although it takes us many years and many tears to discover it, life is only another name for death; they cannot exist independently. The child just born is already beginning the dull process of dying. Youth dies, physical perfection and beauty die, friendships die, love vanishes, vanity is mortally hit, pride goes down in the dust. The years bring us surprises increasingly painful; we marvel innocently at life's swiftness, its shortness, its unimportance, at our own ineffectual groping.

School-day agonies and fears, the teacher that laughed at us, the lost circus tickets,—are gone like a dream. The mating years are dim in the past, with the dance that was a failure, the invitation that did not come, the week-end that was one long triumph of fun and popularity. All gone. . . .

And gone the speculations and doubts of early marriage, not all good, not all bad; the first year, the first five, the first ten are over and done with. The endless months of waiting for the baby, the croupy nights, the threat of a neighboring lawsuit, the worry about the lost trunk and the mislaid deed, these have flown by like the slits in a zoetrope. Gray hair is no longer a joke, to be merrily explained away as premature, as characteristic in the family. Wrinkles, this time, are not going to disappear after a little rest and restored weight.

All this hurts and puzzles us extremely. If we are really to be so soon done for, we wonder what we were begun for, anyway. If stupid mistakes, made in ignorant youth, are to grow to great vines, and strangle us in middle life, then the game is not quite fair, we don't know the rules, we refuse to play with anything like the old enthusiasm.

Our mood becomes quieter, soberer, a little watchful, a little affronted. It is all too short, this delusion called living, too jumbled, too hurried. What we have won, putting youth and hope and courage and labor generously into the scales—what we have won wasn't worth winning. The real things have somehow escaped our eager fingers.

Baffled, we withdraw with dignity into the world of the mind. What success and money and fame refuse us, we can always find in those shady forests rich with sun and moon tracery, filled with exquisite images, threaded with the moving figures of the great who have preceded us, who have stepped in between the covers of books.

For if, at the end of the saddest, the most disappointing and hurtful day, each one of us may come to a quiet room somewhere, and that room his own, if there is a light burning above white pillows, and a pile of books waiting under the light, then indeed we may still praise Allah, that He has not terminated all the Delights.

Even in a day reasonably full of service and occupation, friendship, movement through the busy streets, breakfast, lunch, dinner, telephone, a day full of everyday fatigues and interests, there is no moment comparable to this one, that finds the harassed spirit in blessed solitude, the tired body resting, the gypsy mind off to palms and lazy surf in Tahiti, or cresting the rough salty waves of some northern sea.

Beauty,—healing, miraculous, inexhaustible,—lives on in books, even when beauty elsewhere is dead. The clearing-house of the brain, the wings of the spirit, books lift us away from the petty, crowded day's smallness and entanglement. Trifles no longer concern us,—with Plague stalking in London Town, or Caponsacchi and Pompilia leaving Rome in sunset light. We must accompany our friends through greater crises than our lives will ever know, and when we leave them our own sense of balance and proportion is once more restored.

The actual Bay of Naples may lose something of its charm for the arriving traveler; he has trunks, checks, and hotel reservations on his mind, at best. At worst he adds to these anxieties a natural concern for his missing overcoat,—could he have left it at the Palermo hotel?—a faint consciousness that too much auction bridge has brought back the eye-strain, and a humiliated conviction that he has overtipped those stewards again. Perhaps the sky is clouding over ominously, perhaps Vesuvius is not acting in a way to please a hurried visitor; the volcano was infinitely more thrilling last week, and may be even better yet next month. Perhaps some member of the party has enthusiastically allied us with those awful Scotts, from Detroit, for the Pompeiian expedition tomorrow.

Even Barbadoes harbor—Barbadoes, on a still, silky-blue June morning!—may be completely spoiled by a murmuring steamer-acquaintance at one's ear. The woman who was heard saying loudly, in a pianissimo passage, at the opera, "We fry ours in lard!" is a traveler, too, as well as a music-lover. The golf fiend travels, the divorced woman with a grievance travels, the woman who collected funds for the new community club building travels.

But none of these, on a winter evening at home, can penetrate into the pages of De Quincey and Boswell; their voices cannot break the exquisite solitude in which Shelley heard a skylark, or a melon-flower took one rugged old poet's heart back to spring in England.

Books better than reality?—Yes, I think so. In some cases they are, anyway. Perhaps certain tourists in London love it more than we love it who found London years ago, in the pages of Thackeray and Fielding and the Kingsleys and Sterne. Perhaps they get from the modern, electric-lighted, much-motored London of today, with its chocolate signs and its movies, its clean pavements and twinkling teashop windows, more than we got from the London of books. But I doubt it. Ours was the truer, the realer London, who read about it when we were young, years and years and years ago, and who threaded its dark and dirty streets hand in hand with the magicians who wrote the books we loved.

We knew the mysterious Thames as they can never know it who look down upon it from the safe warm dining rooms of the Cecil or the Savoy; we saw it grim and menacing, the sinister lights of coffee houses and pubs shedding an eerie glow upon it, strange characters oaring to and fro upon its tides; we spoke of the Strand and the Marshalsea and Limehouse as familiarly as their inhabitants ever did.

To be lying, at fifteen, in a field of California oats and poppies, and at the same time to be fingering frugal pennies for the purchase of fried fish at a smoky stall in the Old Roman Road, or to be bumping in a tumbril through the streets of eighteenth-century Paris, is to be part of a magic that the most fortunate tourist in the world can never know.

The lover of books is a miner, searching for gold all his life long. He finds his nuggets, his heart leaps in his breast; he cannot believe in his good fortune. Traversing a slow page, to come upon a lode of the pure shining metal is to exult inwardly for greedy hours. It belongs to no one else; it is not interchangeable.

"Ha!" says the reader involuntarily, as one struck. A casual bystander may ask what stirs him.

"Nothing. Only this is—some of this is good," he mumbles grudgingly. He is immersed again.

But to find beauty in great books is an art. It must be cultivated, like all the arts. Every second-hand bookstore contains a million raptures. But only one out of every five hundred persons ever thinks of going into a second-hand bookshop, and only one out of every score of those knows what he wants, and how to find it.

The violinist, the astronomer, the doctor are resigned to days, months, years of patient study, to endless effort and experiment. They know that they must dig deep into the hard, resisting earth before the crystal waters of any art will begin to flow. They must suspect, surmise, hypothecate. What part of their work these laborers can do easily, in the beginning, they soon learn to despise, they cast it aside. For years they must do what they do not like, must persist in what is difficult and thankless.

We all see that, for them. But what we do not see is that book-reading is a fine art, too, perhaps the highest and finest of them all; we do not arrive at its perfection overnight. Thoreau's *Walden*, Emerson's *Essays* we know must be good, because they are being eternally republished in the little leather classics; and then there are always the *Iliad*, and *Paradise Lost*, and Dante, books we have always meant to read.

But *Murder in a Nunnery*—incidentally, one of the best of its type—is certain to be easier reading. People are talking about it, too, and who ever hears any talk nowadays about Homer or Milton?

And after the *Murder in a Nunnery* there is always the cross-word puzzle in the evening paper, or a not-too-imbecile movie around the corner.

Thus we stroll comfortably through the shallows under which lies the lode of pure gold.

Gold it is. To buy a neat new book, *Excerpts from Shakespeare*, is sacrilege, and whoso does it is repaid by nothing but boredom.

But to read steadily through the Tragedies and come legitimately upon —well, say that matchless page in which fatuous old Pandarus stands with Cressida watching the return of the Roman warriors, is to taste Delight indeed. Henry Percy provokingly baiting his pompous uncle, or the exquisite Cleopatra turning valet when Anthony arms for the wars, these are more alive at this moment than many of the living folk with whom we have talked in the course of the day. Your true Shakespeare lover cannot read certain of these pages continuously. He must shut the book now and then, and stare into space a moment, recovering his breath.

And like the aviator, he must have his hundred hours of daring the blue before he feels his wings secure beneath and about him.

One must know all of Emily Dickinson, to begin to glimpse the faint little vanishing drift of woodsmoke that really was Emily Dickinson. The shyness of her, the boldness of her, the flaming joy and agony of her love, the cloistered years when bashful glasses of her currant jelly, each with its diamond verse, were all that even her closest and dearest knew of her, these are not to be captured by any casual eye.

"Parting is all we know of Heaven, and all we need of Hell," says this most authentic of all our poets' voices. And of great grief she gives us a matchless line: "some losses are so great, we measure them by gain!"

Ringleted, hoop-skirted little New England spinster, "disappointed in love," who else ever captured for us, as you have done, the heart-breaking beauty of the reluctant northern seasons, matching some other mystical seasons in your own being?

Who else ever longed "for a bee's experience of clovers and of noon," or set November in eight lines? These lines:

> "*The sky is low, the clouds are mean,*
> *A traveling flake of snow*
> *Across a barn or through a rut*
> *Debates if it will go.*
> *A narrow wind complains all day*
> *How someone treated him;*
> *Nature, like us, is sometimes caught*
> *Without her diadem.*"

In response to a letter praising her work,—work which only once or twice in her lifetime she permitted other eyes than her own to see—Emily Dickinson ends a breathless answer with a spontaneous burst of verse.

> "*. . . as if I asked the Orient*
> *Had it for me a morn?*
> *And it should ope its purple gates*
> *And shatter me with dawn!*"

she writes, shattering us completely with her own more subtle dawn.

And all this—this "music that is too grievous of the height for safe and low delight," brings us to the almost unbearable climax, the last flying message of all, when her bewildered child-heart had somehow stumbled through all the green, still Junes, and all the snowy Novembers, to the end, and when she penciled to two girl nieces who loved her only the two words: "Called back!"

One closes the book, and goes out into the bright commonplace daylight dazed and hurt. Emily Dickinson is dead.

Equally, it is necessary, it is imperative, to read every word of Strachey's *Queen Victoria* to get the value, to appreciate the sheer beauty and daring and imagination of that final passage that paints the failing old monarch who is about to close her eyes on England, remembering—remembering the days of her power and glory. Remembering her great ministers, and her widowhood, and going back beyond that to Albert's nearness and dearness, Albert's help close beside her when the world was rocked with battles, with international problems. And beyond that again to youth— the first adored baby—"this first wonderful year of my reign," and a royal girlhood at Canterbury, and poor Uncle Willie's failing health—and so to the Archbishop, upon his knees in the cool summer morning, and the sheltered, German-governessed childhood, "and some friendly flounces of sprigged muslin, and the trees and grass at Kensington."

These discoveries, these joys, naturally, are not for the skimmer. What is Steerforth to him, or he to Steerforth? He has not followed David through that lonely cheated childhood into his first rush of hero-worshipping friendship. He has not flushed, as David must have flushed, with shame and pleasure, under Steerforth's negligent, "Why, you are a very Daisy!" His eyes are dry, when David says good-by to his sleeping friend, in one of those passages that will save Dickens for us when Thackeray and Scott are forgotten.

"*Never again, oh, Steerforth, Steerforth, to touch that passive hand in love and friendship,—never, never more!*"

How many thousand pages of Dickens, you lovers of the greatest English novelist of them all, how many thousand pages had we read, slowly, savoringly, before we came to the tea party on Rumpty's perch, with Rumpty himself running eagerly for another pint of milk, another threepenny loaf, and with lovely, gracious, whimsical, maddening Bella making love to her wistful little drudge of a father, on an office window seat? How long were we faithful to Dickens before Tulkinghorn came down to Sir Leicester's seat in Lincolnshire and trapped Lady Deadlock in her own past?

"Of remorse, of explanation," says Lady Deadlock, beautiful, stricken, cold, in her exquisite robes, in the exquisite moonlight, "I say nothing to you. If I were not dumb, you must be deaf to any such words from me!"

When Dick Swiveller begins to reward the Marchioness's ridiculous devotion with his careless love, when Sydney Carton plays a certain game of cards, when little Paul—so small and weak and uninterested at the school party!—goes down to the healing seashore with Florence—ah, what heart-stopping, what heart-filling moments a reader knows! What oases in the long, dry search across the sands.

It was not for the skimmer that William Stirling wrote his all too-scanty pages, that Tomlinson conquered sea and jungle as Balboa never conquered them, that Stevenson fared forth on donkey back.

The skimmer laughs at Mark Twain. Mark Twain was the great humorist, one must laugh at him. That is enough for the skimmer.

But the children of the Kingdom of Books know that sweeter than any laughter it is to find, among the highways and byways of Clemens's more than two hundred tales, those things that do not make for laughter, those direct and poignantly touching passages that reach the source of tears instead. They are everywhere. They are in *Tom Sawyer* and in *Huckleberry Finn*, sudden flashes of surpassing sorrowful beauty and truth, sudden revelations of something deeper than mirth.

For sure and heart-breaking beauty, read into their own particular tale, I know nothing more telling in all Mark Twain's work than a sentence or two in an insignificant story supposedly funny; the name is something like "Every Man His Own Courier," and the tone, at the beginning, anyway, hilarious. But presently Mark gets into deep water, loses tickets, mislays umbrella, forgets time-table, returns to the trusting women at the hotel confessedly inefficient.

And it is then that he defines for us, in a few simple, infinitely pathetic words, that weakness that we all feel for the praise of those we love, our confusion and shame, our shallow, pitiful bravado when we fail them. Nobody else who ever lived could have written those phrases—not as he wrote them. And reading that story, one muses, "Fun may have made him popular. But the heart that dictated that passage made him great."

To the reader who "can't get into" the Russian novels, and who "read a part of" this or that by Tolstoi, how could one possibly describe the thrill with which one shares a certain hot summer morning with a puzzled, gentle, rural landowner, following the plow over the rich earthy furrows, listening to the peasants' talk, and finally stooping to drink from a dipper "filled with clear warm spring water, in which bits of grass and leaves were floating"? Detached, this means nothing. But discovered inadvertently, as the simple hero discovered it, when his troubled heart was so much in need of nature's healing, it makes one once more a child, one with the beauty and bigness of a summer field.

There is a talk, in Anna's bedroom at night, in that same story, between the beautiful Madame Karénina and her drab little sister-in-law, that is like the turning of a searchlight upon the hearts not only of those two women but of all women. Yet it is an insignificant talk, during which the older, plainer woman is miserably conscious of her own virtuous nightgown, high and tucked and practical and coarse, and of Anna's thrillingly fragile finery. One wants to tear the pages to minute pieces and put them under the microscope, determined to drag from them the secret of their power.

How many written words did the old Russian master destroy before he wrote that scene to his liking? How many seas did Balboa sail? "What of the way to the end?" asks Robert Browning. We neither know nor care, as long as it is ours to share the treasure they found at the foot of the rainbow.

And speaking of Browning, the lover of beautiful words who is not at home in the "wonder and the wild desire" of him knoweth not bad from good. To quote the words "a ring without a posy, and that ring mine?" is to quote nothing. But to find them, written into the text through which that great broken heart was struggling somehow to recapture its "lyric love," its "half-angel and half-bird," is to share with him something of the agony and the ecstasy that found in the end perhaps the most exquisite "posy" of all that ever went into any fortunate woman's love-ring.

"A ring without a posy, and that ring mine?"

If Browning had never written "One Word More," the world of words in matchless combination would have been the poorer. Greater than any of Elizabeth Barrett Browning's poetry is the poetry she inspired in him.

To her, as his "moon of poets," he points out that Raphael, "Raphael of the dear Madonnas," wrote one sonnet, to the woman he loved, and that when Dante loved he changed his art, too, for the beloved woman, and painted her a picture.

"You and I," says Browning to his wife—

> *"You and I would rather see that angel,*
> *Painted with the tenderness of Dante,*
> *Would we not?—than read a fresh Inferno."*

Simple, simple words, as simple as Ruth in tears amid the alien corn, as simple as Louise Imogen Guiney's shower-stricken earth, and earth-colored streams. But for all their artless simplicity we cannot analyze or fathom them.

—And they are such legions! They are hiding everywhere, beautiful, unforgettable phrases, pages of exquisite description in Stevenson and Morris, pages in Conrad and Henley. There is the hot, shining summer sunset in *Adam Bede*, when Hetty lingers with Adam among the currant bushes, and supper is waiting in the cool, deep-silled kitchen of the Poyser farm, there are all the prim New England ways of Sarah Orne Jewett, with the sea shining at the end of every crooked little hollyhock-lined, maple-shaded street. There are a thousand lines of incomparable clarity in any one of a dozen of Hudson's books—notably in a child's memories of Argentina, of the pampas country, the book he called *Far Away and Long Ago*; there are sunsets in Hardy's books, and sunrises, there is a stark, pure loveliness about Mrs. Gaskell's *Life of Charlotte Brontë* that makes even a dour Scotch parsonage and a family of unbalanced and badly nourished spinsters seem enchanting.

But how choose scores, among so many hundreds, and how express, in any case, the debt we owe them, and the mystery of their straining—their great need to say what they said just as they said it?

Kipling expresses it, expresses the unattainable ideal of them all, little and big, when he says, of the Perfect Vision,

> *"Thy face is far from this our war,*
> *Our call and counter-cry,*
> *I shall not find Thee quick and kind,*
> *Nor know Thee till I die.*
> *Enough for me in dreams to see*
> *And touch Thy garment's hem;*
> *Thy feet have trod so near to God*
> *I may not follow them."*

And as we rise to the heights, in all humility we learn this. We may not follow. The path leads straight away from this little world,—up, up to the stars.

"'Tis to have drunk too well the drink that is divine," says Francis

Thompson, complaining, in words that are themselves immortal in beauty, of the "mystic wall of strange felicity, the incredible excess of unsensed sweet."

" 'Tis to have drunk too well the drink that is divine, maketh the kind earth waste, and life intolerable."

Our own American poet, Edna St. Vincent Millay, says it not less well, in half-a-dozen wonderful lines about early spring in New England.

"I had forgotten how the frogs would sound
After a year of silence, or I think
I would not thus have ventured forth alone
At dusk, upon this unfrequented road.
I am beset by Beauty. Who will stand
Between me and the crying of the frogs . . . ?"

To anyone who has ever walked a twilight road, in that chill sweet hush that comes over the world in April, before even the willows are green, but after the brooks start rushing, there is something higher than mortal glory in such words, the written page holds more of young spring than even the fields and meadows do. Who will stand between us and this devastating pen, indeed?

Greatest of all, simplest of all, come with splitting light and force the phrases of the Carpenter. Caught by the ears of peasants, filtered through their slow pens, we still must shade our eyes away from them, even after two thousand years:

"Consider the lilies of the field, how they grow: they labor not, neither do they spin. . . ."

"He that is without sin among you, let him first cast a stone. . . ."

"Blessed are they that mourn, for they shall be comforted. . . ."

"I will arise, and will go to my father, and say unto him: Father, I have sinned against heaven, and before thee: I am not worthy to be called thy son."

What would our life, our civilization, be without these words, and words like these? It would be the life and civilization of animals in a jungle, or cows grazing endlessly in a field. Animals never cry, or laugh, or dream of anything but clover tops and tree shade. Animals never joke; theirs is but a brief knowledge of grief. The cat that loses her kittens, the cow that loses her calf—these cry for a few hours, and eat, and forget.

They feel no kinship with Tennyson, watching the gray seas break on an English coast, or with the father of "W.V.," who made a radiant little daughter's short life only a little less exquisite than her death. Without David's grief for his "little lad," and the thousand songs and sonnets that it has inspired, we should have lost one of our permanent heritages.

Our lives are quick with more and more intensified emotions. We do more than our forbears did, see more, feel more. Above all, we love more; the harsh father, the cruel stepmother and uncles, the scornful and jealous sisters of the fairy tales and the old novels are vanishing from our midst. Even to the criminal, even to the nameless, superfluous baby of the slums, our concern, our affection goes out, in a way that was never dreamed in Dante's or in Shakespeare's day, or even in Dickens's time.

And in our quickened lives we need more and more the guidance and sustenance of inspired words. They show us how to live.

As for dying—who could die unchanged and untouched, who could die afraid, if in a rambling lifetime of reading he had chanced upon "Ben Ezra" or "Prospice," if he had found those pages in Jowett that tell how Socrates died? The fear of death fades—it dies away—under the contemplation of that death that was life itself, and those strange, living words, "Into Thy hands, O Father, I commend my spirit."

A life-term in any prison—the prison of illness, or poverty, or humdrum petty routine—holds no terrors, holds rather a promise, for the lover of true books. He knows that Keats and Shelley, Newman and Dryden and Emerson and Thoreau and Browne and a thousand others have yielded unto him only a tithe of their sweetness; from one stout volume of Whitman or Wordsworth he will gather enough honey to make bearable even the hardest sentence, for his sixty or seventy years—even the dullest.

Life without books would be, to him, the only real prison. Books are the stairs by which his years and his soul must mount,—from *Nick Carter* and *Little Women* to Dickens and Tennyson,—on through the biographies, the histories, the essays. And so to poetry, and so to mysticism, and so up —up—up from the shadow of living into the light.